"POSITIVELY CHILLING"
—*USA Today*

FALSE MEMORY

Dean Koontz stuns readers with a deeply sinister tale of a true-life psychological condition shockingly close to home: autophobia—fear of oneself.

Martie Rhodes is a young wife and successful video-game designer. Then one morning she experiences a sudden and inexplicable fear, a fleeting but disquieting terror of . . . her own shadow. Later she realizes that she is terrified to look in the mirror and confront the reflection of her own face. As these traumatic episodes build, the lives of Martie and her husband, Dustin, change drastically. Desperate to discover the reasons for his wife's sudden descent into mental chaos, Dusty takes Martie to the renowned therapist who has been treating her best friend, and begins a frantic search for clues. As he comes closer to the shocking truth, Dusty finds himself afflicted with a condition even more fearsome than Martie's. No fan of Dean Koontz or of classic psychological suspense will want to miss this extraordinary novel of the human mind's capacity to torment—and destroy—itself.

"Spooky . . . haunting . . .
I'D ADVISE NOT STARTING THIS COMPULSIVE PAGE-TURNER IN BED."
—*The Philadelphia Inquirer*

"Viscerally exciting . . . amazing fertility of prose . . . one deliciously malevolent villain and pacing that starts at a gallop and only gets faster . . . an expertly crafted, ornate suspenser with an affecting love story. Koontz fans will love it."
—*Publishers Weekly*

CRITICAL ACCLAIM FOR *FALSE MEMORY*

"A masterful thriller. With all its twists and reversals—and a psychopathic villain second only to Hannibal Lecter—*Memory* is not easily forgotten."
—*People*

"[A book] that makes us want a reassuring hug from Mommy. Koontz seems to know us, our deepest foibles and fears. Chilling, can't-take-your-eyes-off-the-page horrors [and] some sly humor."
—*USA Today*

"AN EDGE OF YOUR SEAT PSYCHOLOGICAL THRILLER, a six-hundred-plus-page gorilla of a book that will not let you down once you pick it up."
—AOL

"Dean Koontz unfolds this bizarre story with his typical patience and authority. . . . With its echoes of *The Manchurian Candidate* and *The Matrix*, *False Memory* delivers a ROUSING TALE."
—*Chicago Tribune*

"PAGE BY PAGE THE TERROR MOUNTS. THIS IS COMPELLING STORYTELLING that will leave you feeling like a limp dishrag. . . . The action begins and never slows down. The villain is one of the most heinous that Koontz has ever dreamed up."
—San Francisco *Examiner*

"A FIRST-RATE PSYCHOLOGICAL THRILLER . . . Koontz possesses the extraordinary ability to create stunning plausibility from the improbable. The plot twists, turns, and surprises. Once engaged in this sometimes self-spoofing yarn, the reader finds it hard to put down."
—Minneapolis *Star Tribune*

"After three dozen novels and more than 200 million copies sold, Dean Koontz can still reach out and pull the reader into terror. . . . KOONTZ VIVIDLY CAPTURES THE HORRORS OF DISABLING PHOBIAS AND THE MIND OF A MADMAN."
—*San Antonio Express-News*

"KOONTZ HAS DONE WHAT HE DOES SO WELL: create smart and likeable characters, subject their virtues to extreme pressure, maintain suspense on two narrative lines at once, and conjure creepiness out of a place whose palm trees and pastels and security gates have been designed precisely to keep the dark side of life at bay. . . . EXCITING."

—*Los Angeles Times*

"KOONTZ WIDENS HIS CANVAS DRAMATICALLY . . . [he] deftly sidesteps clichés of expression while applying an air pump to the suspense." —*Kirkus Reviews*

"*False Memory* once again features THE MASTER OF THE PSYCHOLOGICAL DRAMA in peak form."

—Larry King, *USA Today*

"A tale that is REMARKABLY ENGAGING." —*Booklist*

"The vilest villain Koontz has created . . . the characters are rich, and the main story is compelling." —*Library Journal*

"Koontz's plots and characters are always compelling, absorbing, and beautifully drawn with a deep respect for the redemptive power of love." —*Orange Coast*

"A GRIPPING STUDY IN PSYCHOLOGICAL TERROR that should leave you riveted to your psychiatrist's couch."

—*The Medina Gazette*

"A solid story, painstakingly plotted, expertly staged, and satisfactorily resolved . . . A MASTER OF THE [SUSPENSE] GENRE." —*Richmond Times-Dispatch*

"He gave me not only goose bumps but a sleepless night or two. Koontz is a master at creating believable characters and realistic dialogue. . . . He has few peers when it comes to snappy one-liners and irreverent humor. If you're in search of a good time and a good scare, crack open this book, pull up the covers, and prepare to shiver."

—*Pittsburgh Post-Gazette*

"One of Dean Koontz's most ambitious works . . . The tireless author generates unceasing suspense and frequent terror. The last one hundred pages yield one surprise after another. But Koontz also makes room for explorations of old family tensions and for a tender love story . . . and a rich appreciation of the canine kingdom . . . A THRILLER TO REMEMBER." —*The Sunday News Journal*

"The best dog writer since Jack London . . . GRIPPING . . . A REAL PAGE-TURNER . . . I COULDN'T PUT IT DOWN." —*Rocky Mountain News*

"[*False Memory*] TAKES FEAR TO THE MAXIMUM: autophobia, fear of oneself. Koontz knows how to turn the screws, and dealing with internal terrors, really takes the reader for a ride." —*The Globe and Mail*

"A RIVETING TALE." —*The Tampa Tribune and Times*

"*False Memory* is A PSYCHOLOGICAL THRILLER OF THE FIRST ORDER." —*Delaware Wave*

"Dean Koontz draws the reader into A SPELLBINDING RIDE OF TERROR, weaving his characters into A GRIPPING PSYCHOLOGICAL THRILLER. The major players jump out of the pages. A brilliantly executed plot."

—Newcastle *Journal*

"A knockout tale . . . which will make even the most rational reader shudder." —*The Evening Telegraph*

"His writing has a certain brilliance. [His books] pull you in and push you forward. Koontz plants an experience and images in your mind that will never leave you."

—*Oklahoma Gazette*

"A THRILLING RIDE. Koontz never skimps on action or characterization, and humorous touches are injected in just the right places." —*The MetroWest Daily News*

"Koontz takes [his] premise and runs with it brilliantly. The narrative picks up steam, hurtling with roller-coaster intensity toward a nail-biting climax."

—*The Windsor Star*

"Koontz offers a cast of characters so intimately portrayed you are immediately drawn into their world. A tale not only of gripping fear but also of the power of love and friendship."

—*Tulsa World*

"Dean Koontz's INTENSE psychological thriller should be scary enough to keep you looking over your shoulder for weeks. BRILLIANT moments filled with tense suspense lead up to [an] exhilarating conclusion." —*Lansing State Journal*

"Koontz not only creates a terrifying situation, but always knows so much about his subject, it's like reading a well-written encyclopedia on it. . . . The story spans just a few days of time, but seems as intensely interminable to the reader as it must to the characters. . . . Koontz manages to make the psychological damage much more fearsome than the physical." —*Colorado Springs Gazette-Telegraph*

"One of the best thriller-suspense novelists of recent years has written an unusual and compelling novel in which his characters and their plight grab you from page one and keep you till the last moment. . . . By the end of the book you discover that you've laughed a bit, cried a lot, been absolutely horrified and ultimately found yourself cheering."

—*Sullivan County Democrat*

"This level of torment could only be exacted by one author—Dean Koontz. . . . *False Memory* is not a book for the phobically faint of heart. . . . The author has the power to scare the daylights out of us. *False Memory* is no exception."

—*Ottawa Citizen*

BY DEAN KOONTZ

Ashley Bell • *The City* • *Innocence* • *77 Shadow Street*
What the Night Knows • *Breathless* • *Relentless*
Your Heart Belongs to Me • *The Darkest Evening of the Year*
The Good Guy • *The Husband* • *Velocity* • *Life Expectancy*
The Taking • *The Face* • *By the Light of the Moon*
One Door Away From Heaven • *From the Corner of His Eye*
False Memory • *Seize the Night* • *Fear Nothing*
Mr. Murder • *Dragon Tears* • *Hideaway* • *Cold Fire*
The Bad Place • *Midnight* • *Lightning* • *Watchers*
Strangers • *Twilight Eyes* • *Darkfall* • *Phantoms*
Whispers • *The Mask* • *The Vision* • *The Face of Fear*
Night Chills • *Shattered* • *The Voice of the Night*
The Servants of Twilight • *The House of Thunder*
The Key to Midnight • *The Eyes of Darkness*
Shadowfires • *Winter Moon* • *The Door to December*
Dark Rivers of the Heart • *Icebound* • *Strange Highways*
Intensity • *Sole Survivor* • *Ticktock*
The Funhouse • *Demon Seed*

JANE HAWK

The Silent Corner • *The Whispering Room*
The Crooked Staircase • *The Forbidden Door* • *The Night Window*

ODD THOMAS

Odd Thomas • *Forever Odd* • *Brother Odd* • *Odd Hours*
Odd Interlude • *Odd Apocalypse* • *Deeply Odd* • *Saint Odd*

FRANKENSTEIN

Prodigal Son • *City of Night* • *Dead and Alive*
Lost Souls • *The Dead Town*

A Big Little Life: A Memoir of a Joyful Dog Named Trixie

DEAN KOONTZ

FALSE MEMORY

A Novel

BANTAM BOOKS
NEW YORK

False Memory is a work of fiction.
Names, characters, places, and incidents are
the products of the author's imagination or are
use fictitiously. Any resemblance to actual events, locales,
or persons, living or dead, is entirely coincidental.

2023 Bantam Books Mass Market Edition

Published in the United States by Bantam Books,
an imprint of Random House, a division of
Penguin Random House LLC, New York.

BANTAM BOOKS is a registered trademark and
the B colophon is a trademark of
Penguin Random House LLC.

Originally published in hardcover in the United States
by Bantam Books, an imprint of Random House,
a division of Penguin Random House LLC, in 1999.

ISBN 978-0-345-53329-6
Ebook ISBN 978-0-307-41412-0

Cover art: Franco Accornero

Printed in the United States of America

randomhousebooks.com

12 14 16 18 20 21 19 17 15 13

Bantam Books mass market edition: September 2023

This book is dedicated to
Tim Hely Hutchinson.
Your faith in my work,
a long time ago
—and now for many years—
gave me heart
when I most needed it.
And to
Jane Morpeth.
Ours is the longest
editorial relationship
of my career,
which is a testament to
your exceptional patience,
kindness, and tolerance for fools!

AUTOPHOBIA is a real personality disorder. The term is used to describe three different conditions: (1) fear of being alone; (2) fear of being egotistical; (3) fear of oneself. The third is the rarest of these conditions.

This phantasm
of falling petals vanishes into
moon and flowers . . .

—OKYO

Whiskers of the cat,
webbed toes on my swimming dog:
God is in details.

—THE BOOK OF COUNTED SORROWS

In the real world
as in dreams,
nothing is quite
what it seems.

—THE BOOK OF COUNTED SORROWS

Life is an unrelenting comedy.
Therein lies the tragedy of it.

—MARTIN STILLWATER

FALSE MEMORY

1

On that Tuesday in January, when her life changed forever, Martine Rhodes woke with a headache, developed a sour stomach after washing down two aspirin with grapefruit juice, guaranteed herself an epic bad-hair day by mistakenly using Dustin's shampoo instead of her own, broke a fingernail, burnt her toast, discovered ants swarming through the cabinet under the kitchen sink, eradicated the pests by firing a spray can of insecticide as ferociously as Sigourney Weaver wielded a flamethrower in one of those old extraterrestrial-bug movies, cleaned up the resultant carnage with paper towels, hummed Bach's *Requiem* as she solemnly consigned the tiny bodies to the trash can, and took a telephone call from her mother, Sabrina, who still prayed for the collapse of Martie's marriage three years after the wedding. Throughout, she remained upbeat—even enthusiastic—about the day ahead, because from her late father, Robert "Smilin' Bob" Woodhouse, she had inherited an optimistic nature, formidable coping skills, and a deep love of life in addition to blue eyes, ink-black hair, and ugly toes.

Thanks, Daddy.

After convincing her ever hopeful mother that the Rhodes marriage remained happy, Martie slipped into a leather jacket and took her golden retriever, Valet, on his morning walk. Step by step, her headache faded.

Along the whetstone of clear eastern sky, the sun sharpened scalpels of light. Out of the west, however, a cool onshore breeze pushed malignant masses of dark clouds.

The dog regarded the heavens with concern, sniffed the air warily, and pricked his pendant ears at the hiss-clatter of palm fronds stirred by the wind. Clearly, Valet knew a storm was coming.

He was a gentle, playful dog. Loud noises frightened him, however, as though he had been a soldier in a former life and was haunted by memories of battlefields blasted by cannon fire.

Fortunately for him, rotten weather in southern California was seldom accompanied by thunder. Usually, rain fell unannounced, hissing on the streets, whispering through the foliage, and these were sounds that even Valet found soothing.

Most mornings, Martie walked the dog for an hour, along the narrow tree-lined streets of Corona Del Mar, but she had a special obligation every Tuesday and Thursday that limited their excursion to fifteen minutes on those days. Valet seemed to have a calendar in his furry head, because on their Tuesday and Thursday expeditions, he never dawdled, finishing his toilet close to home.

This morning, only one block from their house, on the grassy sward between the sidewalk and the curb, the pooch looked around shyly, discreetly lifted his right leg, and as usual made water as though embarrassed by the lack of privacy.

Less than a block farther, he was preparing to conclude the second half of his morning business when a passing garbage truck backfired, startling him. He huddled behind a queen palm, peering cautiously around one side of the tree bole and then around the other, convinced that the terrifying vehicle would reappear.

"No problem," Martie assured him. "The big bad truck is gone. Everything's fine. This is now a safe-to-poop zone."

Valet was unconvinced. He remained wary.

Martie was blessed with Smilin' Bob's patience, too, especially when dealing with Valet, whom she loved almost as much as she might have loved a child if she'd had one. He was sweet-tempered and beautiful: light gold, with gold-and-white feathering on his legs, soft snow-white flags on his butt, and a lush tail.

Of course, when the dog was in a doing-business squat, like now, Martie never looked at him, because he was as self-conscious as a nun in a topless bar. While waiting, she softly sang Jim Croce's "Time in a Bottle," which always relaxed him.

As she began the second verse, a sudden chill climbed the ladder of her spine, causing her to fall silent. She was not a woman given to premonitions, but as the icy quiver ascended to the back of her neck, she was overcome by a sense of impending danger.

Turning, she half expected to see an approaching assailant or a hurtling car. Instead, she was alone on this quiet residential street.

Nothing rushed toward her with lethal purpose. The only moving things were those harried by the wind. Trees and shrubs shivered. A few crisp brown leaves skittered along the pavement. Garlands of tinsel and Christmas lights, from the recent holiday, rustled and rattled under the eaves of a nearby house.

Still uneasy, but feeling foolish, Martie let out the breath that she'd been holding. When the exhalation whistled between her teeth, she realized that her jaws were clenched.

She was probably still spooked from the dream that awakened her after midnight, the same one she'd had on a few other recent nights. The man made of dead, rotting leaves, a nightmare figure. Whirling, raging.

Then her gaze dropped to her elongated shadow, which

stretched across the close-cropped grass, draped the curb, and folded onto the cracked concrete pavement. Inexplicably, her uneasiness swelled into alarm.

She took one step backward, then a second, and of course her shadow moved with her. Only as she retreated a third step did she realize that this very silhouette was what frightened her.

Ridiculous. More absurd than her dream. Yet something in her shadow was not right: a jagged distortion, a menacing quality.

Her heart knocked as hard as a fist on a door.

In the severe angle of the morning sun, the houses and trees cast distorted images, too, but she saw nothing fearsome in their stretched and buckled shadows—only in her own.

She recognized the absurdity of her fear, but this awareness did not diminish her anxiety. Terror courted her, and she stood hand in hand with panic.

The shadow seemed to throb with the thick slow beat of its own heart. Staring at it, she was overcome with dread.

Martie closed her eyes and tried to get control of herself.

For a moment, she felt so light that the wind seemed strong enough to sweep her up and carry her inland with the relentlessly advancing clouds, toward the steadily shrinking band of cold blue sky. As she drew a series of deep breaths, however, weight gradually returned to her.

When she dared to look again at her shadow, she no longer sensed anything unusual about it. She let out a sigh of relief.

Her heart continued to pound, powered not by irrational terror anymore, but by an understandable concern as to the cause of this peculiar episode. She'd never previously experienced such a thing.

Head cocked quizzically, Valet was staring at her.

She had dropped his leash.

Her hands were damp with sweat. She blotted her palms on her blue jeans.

When she realized that the dog had finished his toilet, Martie slipped her right hand into a plastic pet-cleanup bag, using it as a glove. Being a good neighbor, she neatly collected Valet's gift, turned the bright blue bag inside out, twisted it shut, and tied a double knot in the neck.

The retriever watched her sheepishly.

"If you ever doubt my love, baby boy," Martie said, "remember I do this every day."

Valet looked grateful. Or perhaps only relieved.

Performance of this familiar, humble task restored her mental balance. The little blue bag and its warm contents anchored her to reality. The weird incident remained troubling, intriguing, but it no longer frightened her.

2

Skeet sat high on the roof, silhouetted against the somber sky, hallucinating and suicidal. Three fat crows circled twenty feet over his head, as if they sensed carrion in the making.

Down here at ground level, Motherwell stood in the driveway, big hands fisted on his hips. Though he faced away from the street, his fury was evident in his posture. He was in a head-cracking mood.

Dusty parked his van at the curb, behind a patrol car emblazoned with the name of the private-security company that served this pricey, gated residential community. A tall guy in a uniform was standing beside the car, managing to appear simultaneously authoritative and superfluous.

The three-story house, atop which Skeet Caulfield contemplated his fragile mortality, was a ten-thousand-square-foot, four-million-dollar atrocity. Several Mediterranean styles—Spanish modern, classic Tuscan, Greek Revival, and early Taco Bell—had been slammed together by an architect who had either a lousy education or a great sense of humor. What appeared to be acres of steeply pitched, barrel-tile roofs hipped into one another with chaotic exuberance, punctuated by too many chimneys badly disguised as bell towers with cupolas, and poor Skeet was perched on the highest ridge line, next to the most imposingly ugly of these belfries.

Perhaps because he was unsure of his role in this situation and needed something to do, the security guard said, "Can I help you, sir?"

"I'm the painting contractor," Dusty replied.

The sun-weathered guard was either suspicious of Dusty or squint-eyed by nature, with so many lines folded into his face that he looked like a piece of origami. "The painting contractor, huh?" he said skeptically.

Dusty was wearing white cotton pants, a white pullover, a white denim jacket, and a white cap with RHODES' PAINTING printed in blue script above the visor, which should have lent some credibility to his claim. He considered asking the leery guard if the neighborhood was besieged by professional burglars disguised as housepainters, plumbers, and chimney sweeps, but instead he simply said, "I'm Dustin Rhodes," and pointed to the lettering on his cap. "That man up there is one of my crew."

"Crew?" The security man scowled. "Is that what you call it?"

Maybe he was being sarcastic or maybe he was just not good at conversation.

"Most painting contractors call it a crew, yeah," Dusty said, staring up at Skeet, who waved. "We used to call ours a strike force, but that scared off some homeowners, sounded too aggressive, so now we just call it a crew, like everyone else."

"Huh," the guard said. His squint tightened. He might have been trying to figure out what Dusty was talking about, or he might have been deciding whether or not to punch him in the mouth.

"Don't worry, we'll get Skeet down," Dusty assured him.

"Who?"

"The jumper," Dusty elucidated, heading along the driveway toward Motherwell.

"You think I should maybe call the fire department?" the guard asked, following him.

"Nah. He won't torch himself before he jumps."

"This is a nice neighborhood."

"Nice? Hell, it's perfect."

"A suicide is going to upset our residents."

"We'll scoop up the guts, bag the remains, hose away the blood, and they'll never know it happened."

Dusty was relieved and surprised that no neighbors had gathered to watch the drama. At this early hour, maybe they were still eating caviar muffins and drinking champagne and orange juice out of gold goblets. Fortunately, Dusty's clients—the Sorensons—on whose roof Skeet was schmoozing with Death, were vacationing in London.

Dusty said, "Morning, Ned."

"Bastard," Motherwell replied.

"Me?"

"Him," Motherwell said, pointing to Skeet on the roof.

At six feet five and 260 pounds, Ned Motherwell was half a foot taller and nearly one hundred pounds heavier than Dusty. His arms could not have been more muscular if they had been the transplanted legs of Clydesdale horses. He was wearing a short-sleeve T-shirt but no jacket, in spite of the cool wind; weather never seemed to bother Motherwell any more than it might trouble a granite statue of Paul Bunyan.

Tapping the phone clipped to his belt, Motherwell said, "Damn, boss, I called you like yesterday. Where you been?"

"You called me ten minutes ago, and where I've been is running traffic lights and mowing down schoolkids in crosswalks."

"There's a twenty-five-mile-an-hour speed limit inside this community," the security guard advised solemnly.

Glowering up at Skeet Caulfield, Motherwell shook his fist. "Man, I'd like to hammer that punk."

"He's a confused kid," Dusty said.

"He's a drug-sucking jerk," Motherwell disagreed.

"He's been clean lately."

"He's a sewer."

"You've got such a big heart, Ned."

"What's important is I've got a brain, and I'm not going to screw it up with drugs, and I don't want to be around people who self-destruct, like him."

Ned, the crew foreman, was a Straight Edger. This unlikely but still-growing movement among people in their teens and twenties—more men than women—required adherents to forgo drugs, excess alcohol, and casual sex. They were into head-banging rock-'n'-roll, slam-dancing, self-restraint, and self-respect. One element or another of the establishment might have embraced them as an inspiring cultural trend—if Straight Edgers had not loathed the system and despised both major political parties. Occasionally, at a club or concert, when they discovered a doper among them, they beat the crap out of him and didn't bother to call it tough love, which was also a practice likely to keep them out of the political mainstream.

Dusty liked both Motherwell and Skeet, although for different reasons. Motherwell was smart, funny, and reliable—if judgmental. Skeet was gentle and sweet—although probably doomed to a life of joyless self-indulgence, days without purpose, and nights filled with loneliness.

Motherwell was by far the better employee of the two. If Dusty had operated strictly by the textbook rules of intelligent business management, he would have cut Skeet from the crew a long time ago.

Life would be easy if common sense ruled; but sometimes the easy way doesn't feel like the right way.

"We're probably going to get rained out," Dusty said. "So why'd you send him up on the roof in the first place?"

"I didn't. I told 'im to sand the window casings and the trim on the ground floor. Next thing I know, he's up there, saying he's going to take a header into the driveway."

"I'll get him."

"I tried. Closer I came to him, the more hysterical he got."

"He's probably scared of you," Dusty said.

"He damn well better be. If *I* kill him, it'll be more painful than if he splits his skull on the concrete."

The guard flipped open his cell phone. "Maybe I'd better call the police."

"*No!*" Realizing that his voice had been too sharp, Dusty took a deep breath and more calmly said, "Neighborhood like this, people don't want a fuss made when it can be avoided."

If the cops came, they might get Skeet down safely, but then they would commit him to a psychiatric ward, where he'd be held for at least three days. Probably longer. The last thing Skeet needed was to fall into the hands of one of those head doctors who were unreservedly enthusiastic about dipping into the psychoactive pharmacopoeia to ladle up a fruit punch of behavior-modification drugs that, while imposing a short-term placidity, would ultimately leave him with more short-circuiting synapses than he had now.

"Neighborhoods like this," Dusty said, "don't want spectacles."

Surveying the immense houses along the street, the regal palms and stately ficuses, the well-tended lawns and flower beds, the guard said, "I'll give you ten minutes."

Motherwell raised his right fist and shook it at Skeet.

Under the circling halo of crows, Skeet waved.

The security guard said, "Anyway, he doesn't look suicidal."

"The little geek says he's happy because an angel of

death is sitting beside him," Motherwell explained, "and the angel has shown him what it's like on the other side, and what it's like, he says, is really awesomely cool."

"I'll go talk to him," Dusty said.

Motherwell scowled. "Talk, hell. Give him a push."

3

As the heavy sky, swollen with unspent rain, sagged toward the earth and as the wind rose, Martie and the dog returned home at a trot. She repeatedly glanced down at her pacing shadow, but then the storm clouds overwhelmed the sun, and her dark companion vanished as if it had seeped into the earth, returning to some netherworld.

She surveyed nearby houses as she passed them, wondering if anyone had been at a window to see her peculiar behavior, hoping that she hadn't actually looked as odd as she'd felt.

In this picturesque neighborhood, the homes were generally old and small, though many were lovingly detailed, possessing more charm and character than half the *people* of Martie's acquaintance. Spanish architecture dominated, but here were also Cotswold cottages, French *chaumières*, German Häuschens, and Art Deco bungalows. The eclectic mix was pleasing, woven together by a green embroidery of laurels, palms, fragrant eucalyptuses, ferns, and cascading bougainvillea.

Martie, Dusty, and Valet lived in a perfectly scaled, two-story, miniature Victorian with gingerbread millwork. Dusty had painted the structure in the colorful yet sophisticated tradition of Victorian houses on certain streets in San Francisco: pale yellow background; blue, gray, and green ornamentation; with a judicious use of pink in a single detail along the cornice and on the window pediments.

Martie loved their home and thought it was a fine testament to Dusty's talent and craftsmanship.

Her mother, however, upon first seeing the paint job, had declared, "It looks as if clowns live here."

As Martie opened the wooden gate at the north side of the house and followed Valet along the narrow brick walkway to the backyard, she wondered if her unreasonable fear somehow had its origins in the depressing telephone call from her mother. After all, the greatest source of stress in her life was Sabrina's refusal to accept Dusty. These were the two people whom Martie loved most in all the world, and she longed for peace between them.

Dusty wasn't part of the problem. Sabrina was the only combatant in this sad war. Frustratingly, Dusty's refusal to engage in battle seemed only to harden her hostility.

Stopping at the trash enclosure near the back of the house, Martie removed the lid from one of the cans and deposited the blue plastic bag full of Valet's finest.

Perhaps her sudden inexplicable anxiety had been spawned by her mother's whining about Dusty's supposed paucity of ambition and about his lack of what Sabrina deemed an adequate education. Martie was afraid that her mother's venom would eventually poison her marriage. Against her will, she might start to see Dusty through her mother's mercilessly critical eyes. Or maybe Dusty would begin to resent Martie for the low esteem in which Sabrina held him.

In fact, Dusty was the wisest man Martie had ever known. The engine between his ears was even more finely tuned than her father's had been, and Smilin' Bob had been immeasurably smarter than his nickname implied. As for ambition . . . Well, she would rather have a kind husband than an ambitious one, and you'd find more kindness in Dusty than you'd find greed in Vegas.

Besides, Martie's own career didn't fulfill the expectations her mother had for her. After earning a bachelor's degree—

majoring in business, minoring in marketing—followed by an M.B.A., she had detoured from the road that might have taken her to high-corporate-executive glory. Instead, she became a freelance video-game designer. She'd sold a few minor hits entirely of her own creation, and on a for-hire basis she had designed scenarios, characters, and fantasy worlds based on concepts by others. She earned good money, if not yet great, and she suspected that being a woman in a male-dominated field would ultimately be an enormous advantage, as her point of view was fresh. She liked her work, and recently she'd signed a contract to create an entirely new game based on J.R.R. Tolkien's *The Lord of the Rings* trilogy, which might produce enough royalties to impress Scrooge McDuck. Nevertheless, her mother dismissively described her work as "carnival stuff," apparently because Sabrina associated video games with arcades, arcades with amusement parks, and amusement parks with carnivals. Martie supposed she was lucky that her mother hadn't gone one step further and described her as a sideshow freak.

As Valet accompanied her up the back steps and across the porch, Martie said, "Maybe a psychoanalyst would say, just for a minute back there, my shadow was a symbol of my mother, her negativity—"

Valet grinned up at her and wagged his plumed tail.

"—and maybe my little anxiety attack expressed an unconscious concern that Mom is . . . well, that she's going to be able to mess with my head eventually, pollute me with her toxic attitude."

Martie fished a set of keys from a jacket pocket and unlocked the door.

"My God, I sound like a college sophomore halfway through Basic Psych."

She often talked to the dog. The dog listened but never replied, and his silence was one of the pillars of their wonderful relationship.

"Most likely," she said, as she followed Valet into the

kitchen, "there was no psychological symbolism, and I'm just going totally nutball crazy."

Valet chuffed as though agreeing with the diagnosis of madness, and then he enthusiastically lapped water from his bowl.

Five mornings a week, following a long walk, either she or Dusty spent half an hour grooming the dog on the back porch, combing and brushing. On Tuesdays and Thursdays, grooming followed the afternoon stroll. Their house was pretty much free of dog hair, and she intended to keep it that way.

"You are obliged," she reminded Valet, "not to shed until further notice. And remember—just because we're not here to catch you in the act, doesn't mean suddenly you have furniture privileges and unlimited access to the refrigerator."

He rolled his eyes at her as if to say he was offended by her lack of trust. Then he continued drinking.

In the half bath adjacent to the kitchen, Martie switched on the light. She intended to check her makeup and brush her windblown hair.

As she stepped to the sink, sudden fright cinched her chest again, and her heart felt as though it were painfully compressed. She wasn't seized by the certainty that some mortal danger loomed behind her, as before. Instead, she was afraid to look in the mirror.

Abruptly weak, she bent forward, hunching her shoulders, feeling as if a great weight of stones had been stacked on her back. Gripping the pedestal sink with both hands, she gazed down at the empty bowl. She was so bowed by irrational fear that she was physically unable to look up.

A loose black hair, one of her own, lay on the curve of white porcelain, one end curling under the open brass drain plug, and even this filament seemed ominous. Not daring to raise her eyes, she fumbled for a faucet, turned on the hot water, and washed the hair away.

Letting the water run, she inhaled the rising steam, but it did not dispel the chill that had returned to her. Gradually the edges of the sink became warmer in her white-knuckled grip, though her hands remained cold.

The mirror waited. Martie could no longer think of it as a mere inanimate object, as a harmless sheet of glass with silvered backing. It *waited.*

Or, rather, something within the mirror waited to make eye contact with her. An entity. A presence.

Without lifting her head, she glanced to her right and saw Valet standing in the doorway. Ordinarily, the dog's puzzled expression would have made her laugh; now, laughter would require a conscious effort, and it wouldn't sound like laughter when it grated from her.

Although she was afraid of the mirror, she was also—and more intensely—frightened of her own bizarre behavior, of her utterly uncharacteristic loss of control.

The steam condensed on her face. It felt thick in her throat, suffocating. And the rushing, gurgling water began to sound like malevolent voices, wicked chuckling.

Martie shut off the faucet. In the comparative quiet, her breathing was alarmingly rapid and ragged with an unmistakable note of desperation.

Earlier, in the street, deep breathing had cleared her head, flushing away the fear, and her distorted shadow had then ceased to be threatening. This time, however, each inhalation seemed to fuel her terror, as oxygen feeds a fire.

She would have fled the room, but all her strength had drained out of her. Her legs were rubbery, and she worried that she would fall and strike her head against something. She needed the sink for support.

She tried to reason with herself, hoping to make her way back to stability with simple steps of logic. The mirror couldn't harm her. It was *not* a presence. Just a thing. An inanimate object. Mere glass, for God's sake.

Nothing she would see in it could be a threat to her. It

was not a window at which some madman might be standing, peering in with a lunatic grin, eyes burning with homicidal intent, as in some cheesy screamfest movie. The mirror could not possibly reveal anything but a reflection of the half bath—and of Martie herself.

Logic wasn't working. In a dark territory of her mind that she'd never traveled before, she found a twisted landscape of superstition.

She became convinced that an entity in the mirror was gaining substance and power *because* of her efforts to reason herself out of this terror, and she shut her eyes lest she glimpse that hostile spirit even peripherally. Every child knows that the boogeyman under the bed grows stronger and more murderous with each denial of its existence, that the best thing to do is not to think of the hungry beast down there with the dust bunnies under the box springs, with the blood of other children on its fetid breath. *Just don't think of it at all*, with its mad-yellow eyes and thorny black tongue. *Don't think of it*, whereupon it will fade entirely away, and blessed sleep will come at last, followed by morning, and you will wake in your cozy bed, snug under warm blankets, instead of inside some demon's stomach.

Valet brushed against Martie, and she almost screamed.

When she opened her eyes, she saw the dog peering up with one of those simultaneously imploring and concerned expressions that golden retrievers have polished to near perfection.

Although she was leaning into the pedestal sink, certain that she couldn't stand without its support, she let go of it with one hand. Trembling, she reached down to touch Valet.

As if the dog were a lightning rod, contact with him seemed to ground Martie, and like a crackling current of electricity, a portion of the paralyzing anxiety flowed out of her. High terror subsided to mere fear.

Although affectionate and sweet-tempered and beautiful, Valet was a timid creature. If nothing in this small room had frightened him, then no danger existed here. He licked her hand.

Taking courage from the dog, Martie finally raised her head. Slowly. Shaking with dire expectations.

The mirror revealed no monstrous countenance, no otherworldly landscape, no ghost: only her own face, drained of color, and the familiar half bath behind her.

When she looked into the reflection of her blue eyes, her heart raced anew, for in a fundamental sense, she had become a stranger to herself. This shaky woman who was spooked by her own shadow, who was stricken by panic at the prospect of confronting a mirror . . . this was not Martine Rhodes, Smilin' Bob's daughter, who had always gripped the reins of life and ridden with enthusiasm and poise.

"What's happening to me?" she asked the woman in the mirror, but her reflection couldn't explain, and neither could the dog.

The phone rang. She went into the kitchen to answer it.

Valet followed. He stared at her, puzzled, tail wagging at first, then not wagging.

"Sorry, wrong number," she said eventually, and she hung up. She noticed the dog's peculiar attitude. "What's wrong with you?"

Valet stared at her, hackles slightly raised.

"I swear, it wasn't the girl poodle next door, calling for you."

When she returned to the half bath, to the mirror, she still did not like what she saw, but now she knew what to do about it.

4

Dusty walked under the softly rustling fronds of a wind-stirred phoenix palm and along the side of the house. Here he found Foster "Fig" Newton, the third member of the crew.

Hooked to Fig's belt was a radio—his ever-present electronic IV bottle. A pair of headphones dripped talk radio into his ears.

He didn't listen to programs concerned with political issues or with the problems of modern life. Any hour, day or night, Fig knew where on the dial to tune in a show dealing with UFOs, alien abductions, telephone messages from the dead, fourth-dimensional beings, and Big Foot.

"Hey, Fig."

"Hey."

Fig was diligently sanding a window casing. His callused fingers were white with powdered paint.

"You know about Skeet?" Dusty asked as he followed the slate walkway past Fig.

Nodding, Fig said, "Roof."

"Pretending he's gonna jump."

"Probably will."

Dusty stopped and turned, surprised. "You really think so?"

Newton was usually so taciturn that Dusty didn't expect more than a shrug of the shoulders by way of reply. Instead Fig said, "Skeet doesn't believe in anything."

"Anything what?" Dusty asked.

"Anything period."

"He isn't a bad kid, really."

Fig's reply was, for him, the equivalent of an after-dinner speech: "Problem is, he isn't much of anything."

Foster Newton's pie-round face, plum of a chin, full mouth, cherry-red nose with cherry-round tip, and flushed cheeks ought to have made him look like a debauched hedonist; however, he was saved from caricature by clear gray eyes which, magnified by his thick eyeglasses, were full of sorrow. This was not a conditional sorrow, related to Skeet's suicidal impulse, but a perpetual sorrow with which Fig appeared to regard everyone and everything.

"Hollow," Fig added.

"Skeet?"

"Empty."

"He'll find himself."

"He stopped looking."

"That's pessimistic," Dusty said, reduced to Fig's terse conversational style.

"Realistic."

Fig cocked his head, attention drawn to a discussion on the radio, which Dusty could hear only as a faint tinny whisper that escaped one of the headphones. Fig stood with his sanding block poised over the window casing, eyes flooding with an even deeper sorrow that apparently arose from the weirdness to which he was listening, as motionless as if he had been struck by the paralytic beam from an extraterrestrial's ray gun.

Worried by Fig's glum prediction, Dusty hurried to the long aluminum extension ladder that Skeet had climbed earlier. Briefly, he considered moving it to the front of the house. Skeet might become alarmed by a more direct approach, however, and leap before he could be talked down. The rungs rattled under Dusty's feet as he rapidly ascended.

When he swung off the top of the ladder, Dusty was at the back of the house. Skeet Caulfield was at the front, out of sight beyond a steep slope of orange clay tiles that rose like the scaly flank of a sleeping dragon.

This house was on a hill, and a couple miles to the west, beyond the crowded flats of Newport Beach and its sheltered harbor, lay the Pacific. The usual blueness of the water had settled like a sediment to the ocean floor, and the choppy waves were many shades of gray, mottled with black: a reflection of the forbidding heavens. At the horizon, sea and sky appeared to curve together in a colossal dark wave which, if real, would have rushed ashore with enough force to sweep past the Rocky Mountains more than six hundred miles to the east.

Behind the house, forty feet below Dusty, were slate-paved patios that posed a more immediate danger than the sea and the oncoming storm. He could more easily envision himself splattered across that slate than he could conjure, in his mind's eye, an image of the Rockies awash.

Turning his back to the ocean and to the perilous drop, leaning from the waist, with his arms slightly spread and thrust forward to serve as counterweights to the dangerous backward pull of gravity, Dusty clambered upward. The onshore flow was still just a strong breeze, not yet grown into a full-fledged wind; nevertheless, he was grateful to have it at his back, sticking him to the roof instead of lifting him away from it. At the summit of the long incline, he straddled the ridge line and looked toward the front of the house, past additional slopes of the complex roof.

Skeet was perched on another ridge parallel to this one, beside a double-stack chimney disguised as a squat bell tower. The stucco tower was surmounted by Palladian arches, the faux-limestone columns of which supported a copper-clad Spanish-colonial cupola, and atop the cupola was a shortened but ornate Gothic spire that was no more out of place in this screwball design than would have been a giant neon sign for Budweiser.

With his back toward Dusty, knees drawn up, Skeet gazed at the three crows circling above him. His arms were raised to them in an embracive gesture, inviting the birds to settle upon his head and shoulders, as though he were not a housepainter but Saint Francis of Assisi in communion with his feathered friends.

Still straddling the ridge, waddling like a penguin, Dusty moved north until he came to the point at which a lower roof, running west to east, slid under the eaves of the roof that he was traversing. He abandoned the peak and descended the rounded tiles, leaning backward because gravity now inexorably pulled him forward. Crouching, he hesitated near the brink, but then jumped across the rain gutter and dropped three feet onto the lower surface, landing with one rubber-soled shoe planted on each slope.

Because his weight wasn't evenly distributed, Dusty tipped to the right. He struggled to regain his balance but realized that he wasn't going to be able to keep his footing. Before he tilted too far and tumbled to his death, he threw himself forward and crashed facedown on the ridge-line tiles, right leg and arm pressing hard against the south slope, left leg and arm clamped to the north slope, holding on as though he were a panicked rodeo cowboy riding a furious bull.

He lay there for a while, contemplating the mottled orange-brown finish and the patina of dead lichen on the roofing tiles. He was reminded of the art of Jackson Pollock, though this was more subtle, more fraught with meaning, and more appealing to the eye.

When the rain came, the film of dead lichen would quickly turn slimy, and the kiln-fired tiles would become treacherously slippery. He had to reach Skeet and get off the house before the storm broke.

Eventually he crawled forward to a smaller bell tower.

This one lacked a cupola. The surmounting dome was a miniature version of those on mosques, clad in ceramic tiles that depicted the Islamic pattern called the Tree of Paradise. The owners of the house weren't Muslims, so they apparently included this exotic detail because they found it visually appealing—even though, up here, the only people who could get close enough to the dome to admire it were roofers, housepainters, and chimney sweeps.

Leaning against the six-foot tower, Dusty pulled himself to his feet. Shifting his hands from one vent slot to another, under the rim of the dome, he edged around the structure to the next length of open roof.

Once more straddling the ridge, crouching, he hurried forward toward another damn false bell tower with another Tree of Paradise dome. He felt like Quasimodo, the high-living hunchback of Notre Dame: perhaps not nearly as ugly as that poor wretch but also not a fraction as nimble.

He edged around the next tower and continued to the end of the east-west span, which slid under the eaves of the north-south roof that capped the front wing of the residence. Skeet had left a short aluminum ladder as a ramp from the lower ridge line to the slope of the higher roof, and Dusty ascended it, rising from all fours to an apelike crouch as he moved off the ladder onto one more incline.

When at last Dusty reached the final peak, Skeet was neither surprised to see him nor alarmed. "Morning, Dusty."

"Hi, kid."

Dusty was twenty-nine, only five years older than the younger man; nonetheless, he thought of Skeet as a child.

"Mind if I sit down?" Dusty asked.

With a smile, Skeet said, "I'd sure like your company."

Dusty sat beside him, butt on the ridge line, knees drawn up, shoes planted solidly on the barrel tiles.

Far to the east, past wind-shivered treetops and more roofs, beyond freeways and housing tracts, beyond the San

Joaquin Hills, the Santa Ana Mountains rose brown and sere, here at the beginning of the rainy season; around their aged crowns, the clouds wound like dirty turbans.

On the driveway below, Motherwell had spread a big tarp, but he himself was nowhere to be seen.

The security guard scowled up at them, and then he consulted his wristwatch. He had given Dusty ten minutes to get Skeet down.

"Sorry about this," Skeet said. His voice was eerily calm.

"Sorry about what?"

"Jumping on the job."

"You *could* have made it a leisure-time activity," Dusty agreed.

"Yeah, but I wanted to jump where I'm happy, not where I'm unhappy, and I'm happiest on the job."

"Well, I do try to create a pleasant work environment."

Skeet laughed softly and wiped his runny nose on the back of his sleeve.

Though always slender, Skeet had once been wiry and tough; now he was far too thin, even gaunt, yet he was soft-looking, as if the weight he had lost consisted entirely of bone mass and muscle. He was pale, too, although he often worked in the sun; a ghostly pallor shone through his vague tan, which was more gray than brown. In cheap black-canvas-and-white-rubber sneakers, red socks, white pants, and a tattered pale-yellow sweater with frayed cuffs that draped loosely around his bony wrists, he looked like a boy, a lost child who had been wandering in the desert without food or water.

Wiping his nose on the sleeve of his sweater again, Skeet said, "Must be getting a cold."

"Or maybe the runny nose is just a side effect."

Usually, Skeet's eyes were honey-brown, intensely luminous, but now they were so watery that a portion of the color seemed to have washed out, leaving him with a dim and yellowish gaze. "You think I've failed you, huh?"

"No."

"Yes, you do. And that's all right. Hey, I'm okay with that."

"You can't fail me," Dusty assured him.

"Well, I did. We both knew I would."

"You can only fail yourself."

"Relax, bro." Skeet patted Dusty's knee reassuringly and smiled. "I don't blame you for expecting too much of me, and I don't blame myself for being a screwup. I'm past all that."

Forty feet below, Motherwell came out of the house, single-handedly carrying the mattress from a double bed.

The vacationing owners had left keys with Dusty, because some interior walls in high-traffic areas had also needed to be painted. That part of the job was finished.

Motherwell dropped the mattress on the previously positioned tarpaulin, glanced up at Dusty and Skeet, and then went back into the house.

Even from a height of forty feet, Dusty could see that the security guard didn't approve of Motherwell raiding the residence to put together this makeshift fall-break.

"What did you take?" Dusty asked.

Skeet shrugged and turned his face up toward the circling crows, regarding them with such an inane smile and with such reverence that you would have thought he was a total naturehead who had begun the day with a glass of fresh-squeezed organic orange juice, a sugarless bran muffin, a tofu omelet, and a nine-mile hike.

"You must remember what you took," Dusty pressed.

"A cocktail," Skeet said. "Pills and powders."

"Uppers, downers?"

"Probably both. More. But I don't feel bad." He looked away from the birds and put his right hand on Dusty's shoulder. "I don't feel like crap anymore. I'm at peace, Dusty."

"I'd still like to know what you took."

"Why? It could be the tastiest recipe ever, and you'd never use it." Skeet smiled and pinched Dusty's cheek affectionately. "Not you. You're not like me."

Motherwell came out of the house with a second mattress from another double bed. He placed it beside the first.

"That's silly," Skeet said, pointing down the steep slope to the mattresses. "I'll just jump to one side or the other."

"Listen, you're not going to take a header into the Sorensons' driveway," Dusty said firmly.

"They won't care. They're in Paris."

"London."

"Whatever."

"And they will care. They'll be pissed."

Blinking his bleary eyes, Skeet said, "What—are they really uptight or something?"

Motherwell was arguing with the guard. Dusty could hear their voices but not what they were saying.

Skeet still had his hand on Dusty's shoulder. "You're cold."

"No," Dusty said. "I'm okay."

"You're shaking."

"Not cold. Just scared."

"You?" Disbelief brought Skeet's blurry eyes into focus. "Scared? Of what?"

"Heights."

Motherwell and the security guard headed into the house. From up here, it appeared as though Motherwell had an arm around the guy's back, as if maybe he was lifting him half off his feet and hurrying him along.

"Heights?" Skeet gaped at him. "Whenever there's anything on a roof to be painted, you always want to do it yourself."

"With my stomach in knots the whole time."

"Get serious. You're not afraid of anything."

"Yes, I am."

"Not you."

"Me."

"*Not you!*" Skeet insisted with sudden anger.

"Even me."

Distressed, having undergone a radical mood swing in an instant, Skeet snatched his hand off Dusty's shoulder. He hugged himself and began to rock slowly back and forth on the narrow seat provided by the single-width cap of ridgeline tiles. His voice was wrenched with anguish, as though Dusty had not merely acknowledged a fear of heights but had announced that he was riddled with terminal cancer: "Not you, not you, not you, not you . . ."

In this condition, Skeet might respond well to several sweet spoonfuls of sympathy; however, if he decided that he was being coddled, he could become sullen, unreachable, even hostile, which was annoying in ordinary circumstances, but which could be dangerous forty feet above the ground. Generally he responded better to tough love, humor, and cold truth.

Into Skeet's *not you* chant, Dusty said, "You're such a feeb."

"*You're* the feeb."

"Wrong. You're the feeb."

"You are so completely the feeb," Skeet said.

Dusty shook his head. "No, I'm the psychological progeriac."

"The what?"

"*Psychological*, meaning 'of, pertaining to, or affecting the mind.' *Progeriac*, meaning 'someone afflicted with progeria,' which is a 'congenital abnormality characterized by premature and rapid aging, in which the sufferer, in childhood, appears to be an old person.' "

Skeet bobbed his head. "Hey, yeah, I saw a story about that on *60 Minutes*."

"So a psychological progeriac is someone who is *mentally* old even as a kid. Psychological progeriac. My dad used to call me that. Sometimes he shortened it to the initials—PP. He'd say, 'How's my little pee-pee today?' or 'If you don't want to see me drink another Scotch, you little pee-pee, why don't you just hike your ass out to the tree house in the backyard and play with matches for a while.' "

Casting anguish and anger aside as abruptly as he had embraced them, Skeet said sympathetically, "Wow. So it wasn't like a term of endearment, huh?"

"No. Not like *feeb*."

Frowning, Skeet said, "Which one was your dad?"

"Dr. Trevor Penn Rhodes, professor of literature, specialist in deconstructionist theory."

"Oh, yeah. Dr. Decon."

Gazing at the Santa Ana Mountains, Dusty paraphrased Dr. Decon: "Language can't describe reality. Literature has no stable reference, no real meaning. Each reader's interpretation is equally valid, more important than the author's intention. In fact, nothing in life has meaning. Reality is subjective. Values and truth are subjective. Life itself is a kind of illusion. Blah, blah, blah, let's have another Scotch."

The distant mountains sure looked real. The roof under his butt felt real, too, and if he fell headfirst onto the driveway, he would either be killed or crippled for life, which wouldn't prove a thing to the intractable Dr. Decon, but which was enough reality for Dusty.

"Is he why you're afraid of heights," Skeet asked, "because of something he did?"

"Who—Dr. Decon? Nah. Heights just bother me, that's all."

Sweetly earnest in his concern, Skeet said, "You could find out why. Talk to a psychiatrist."

"I think I'll just go home and talk to my dog."

"I've had a lot of therapy."

"And it's done wonders for you, hasn't it?"

Skeet laughed so hard that snot ran out of his nose. "Sorry."

Dusty withdrew a Kleenex from a pocket and offered it.

As Skeet blew his nose, he said, "Well, me . . . now I'm a different story. Longer than I can remember, I've been afraid of *everything*."

"I know."

"Getting up, going to bed, and everything between. But I'm not afraid now." He finished with the Kleenex and held it out to Dusty.

"Keep it," Dusty said.

"Thanks. Hey, you know why I'm not afraid anymore?"

"Because you're shitfaced?"

Skeet laughed shakily and nodded. "But also because I've seen the Other Side."

"The other side of what?"

"Capital *O*, capital *S*. I had a visitation from an angel of death, and he showed me what's waiting for us."

"You're an atheist," Dusty reminded him.

"Not anymore. I'm past all that. Which should make you happy, huh, bro?"

"How easy for you. Pop a pill, find God."

Skeet's grin emphasized the skull beneath the skin, which was frighteningly close to the surface in his gaunt countenance. "Cool, huh? Anyway, the angel instructed me to jump, so I'm jumping."

Abruptly the wind rose, skirling across the roof, chillier than before, bringing with it the briny scent of the distant sea—and then briefly, like an augury, came the rotten stink of decomposing seaweed.

Standing up and negotiating a steeply pitched roof in this blustery air was a challenge that Dusty did not want to face, so he prayed that the wind would diminish soon.

Taking a risk, assuming that Skeet's suicidal impulse actually arose, as he insisted, from his newfound fearlessness, and hoping that a good dose of terror would make the kid want to cling to life again, Dusty said, "We're only forty feet off the ground, and from the edge of the roof to the pavement, it's probably only thirty or thirty-two. Jumping would be a classic feeb decision, because what you're going to do is maybe end up not dead but paralyzed for life, hooked up to machines for the next forty years, helpless."

"No, I'll die," Skeet said almost perkily.

"You can't be sure."

"Don't get an attitude with me, Dusty."

"I'm not getting an attitude."

"Just denying you have an attitude *is* an attitude."

"Then I've got an attitude."

"See."

Dusty took a deep breath to steady his nerves. "This is so lame. Let's get down from here. I'll drive you over to the Four Seasons Hotel in Fashion Island. We can go all the way up to the roof, fourteen, fifteen floors, whatever it is, and you can jump from there, so you'll be sure it'll work."

"You wouldn't really."

"Sure. If you're going to do this, then do it right. Don't screw this up, too."

"Dusty, I'm smacked, but I'm not stupid."

Motherwell and the security guard came out of the house with a king-size mattress.

As they struggled with that ungainly object, they had a Laurel and Hardy quality that *was* amusing, but Skeet's laugh sounded utterly humorless to Dusty.

Down in the driveway, the two men dropped their burden squarely atop the pair of smaller mattresses that were already on the tarp.

Motherwell looked up at Dusty and raised his arms, hands spread, as if to say, *What're you waiting for?*

One of the circling crows went military and conducted a bombing run with an accuracy that would have been the envy of any high-tech air force in the world. A messy white blob splattered across Skeet's left shoe.

Skeet peered up at the incontinent crow and then down at his soiled sneaker. His mood swung so fast and hard that it seemed his head ought to have spun around from the force of the change. His eerie smile crumbled like earth into a sinkhole, and his face collapsed in despair. In a wretched voice, he said, "This is my life," and he reached down to poke one finger into the mess on his shoe. "My life."

"Don't be ridiculous," Dusty said. "You're not well enough educated to think in metaphors."

This time, he couldn't make Skeet laugh.

"I'm so tired," Skeet said, rubbing bird crap between his thumb and forefinger. "Time to go to bed."

He didn't mean *bed* when he said *bed.* He didn't mean he was going to take a nap on the pile of mattresses, either. He meant that he was going to settle in for the big sleep, under a blanket of dirt, and dream with the worms.

Skeet got to his feet on the peak of the roof. Although he was hardly more than a wisp, he stood at his full height and didn't seem unduly bothered by the hooting wind.

When Dusty rose into a cautious crouch, however, the onshore flow hit him with gale force, rocking him forward, off the heels of his shoes, and he teetered for a moment before he settled into a position that gave him a lower center of gravity.

Either this was a deconstructionist's ideal wind—the effect of which would be different according to each person's interpretation of it, a mere breeze to me, a typhoon to thee—or Dusty's fear of heights caused him to have an exaggerated perception of every gust. Since he'd long ago rejected his old man's screwy philosophies, he figured that if Skeet could stand erect with no risk of being spun away like a Frisbee, then so could he.

Raising his voice, Skeet said, "This is for the best, Dusty."

"Like you would know what's for the best."

"Don't try to stop me."

"Well, see, I've got to try."

"I can't be talked down."

"I've become aware of that."

They faced each other, as though they were two athletes about to engage in a strange new sport on a slanted court: Skeet standing tall, like a basketball player waiting for the opening toss-up, Dusty crouched like an underweight sumo wrestler looking for leverage.

"I don't want to get you hurt," Skeet said.

"I don't want to get me hurt, either."

If Skeet was determined to jump off the Sorensons' house, he couldn't be prevented from doing so. The steep pitch of the roof, the rounded surfaces of the barrel tiles, the wind, and the law of gravity were on his side. All that Dusty could hope to do was to make sure the poor son of a bitch went off the edge at exactly the right place and onto the mattresses.

"You're my friend, Dusty. My only real friend."

"Thanks for the vote of confidence, kid."

"Which makes you my best friend."

"By default," Dusty agreed.

"A guy's best friend shouldn't get in the way of his glory."

"Glory?"

"What I've seen it's like on the Other Side. The glory."

The only way to be sure that Skeet went off the roof precisely above the fall-break was to grab him at the right instant and hurl him to the ideal point along the brink. Which meant going down the roof and over the edge with him.

The wind tossed and whipped Skeet's long blond hair, which was the last attractive physical quality that he had left. Once, he'd been a good-looking boy, a girl magnet. Now his body was wasted; his face was gray and haggard; and his eyes were as burnt out as the bottom of a crack pipe. His thick, slightly curly, golden hair was so out of sync with the rest of his appearance that it seemed to be a wig.

Except for his hair, Skeet stood motionless. In spite of being more stoned than a witch in Salem, he was alert and wary, deciding how best to break away from Dusty and execute a clean running dive headfirst into the cobblestones below.

Hoping to distract the kid or at least to buy a little time, Dusty said, "Something I've always wondered. . . . What does the angel of death look like?"

"Why?"

"You saw him, right?"

Frowning, Skeet said, "Yeah, well, he looked okay."

A hard gust of wind tore off Dusty's white cap and spun it to Oz, but he didn't take his attention off Skeet. "Did he look like Brad Pitt?"

"Why would he look like Brad Pitt?" Skeet asked, and his eyes slid sideways and back to Dusty again, as he glanced surreptitiously toward the brink.

"Brad Pitt played him in that movie, *Meet Joe Black.*"

"Didn't see it."

With growing desperation, Dusty said, "Did he look like Jack Benny?"

"What're you talking about?"

"Jack Benny played him once in a really old movie. Remember? We watched it together."

"I don't remember much. You're the one with the photographic memory."

"Eidetic. Not photographic. Eidetic and audile memory."

"See? I can't even remember what it's called. You remember what you had for dinner five years ago. I don't remember yesterday."

"It's just a trick thing, eidetic memory. Useless, anyway."

The first fat drops of rain spattered across the top of the house.

Dusty didn't have to look down to see the dead lichen being transformed into a thin film of slime, because he could *smell* it, a subtle but singular musty odor, and he could smell the wet clay tiles, too.

A daunting image flickered through his mind: *He and Skeet were sliding off the roof, then tumbling wildly, Skeet landing on the mattresses without sustaining a single cut or bruise, but Dusty overshooting and fracturing his spine on the cobblestones.*

"Billy Crystal," Skeet said.

"What—you mean Death? The angel of death looked like Billy Crystal?"

"Something wrong with that?"

"For God's sake, Skeet, you can't trust some wise-ass, maudlin, shtick-spouting Billy Crystal angel of death!"

"I liked him," Skeet said, and he ran for the edge.

5

As though the great guns of battleships were providing cover fire for invading troops, hard hollow explosions echoed along the southfacing beaches. Enormous waves slammed onto the shore, and bullets of water, skimmed off the breakers by a growing wind, rattled inland through the low dunes and sparse stalks of grass.

Martie Rhodes hurried along the Balboa Peninsula boardwalk, which was a wide concrete promenade with ocean-facing houses on one side and deep beaches on the other. She hoped the rain would hold off for half an hour.

Susan Jagger's narrow, three-story house was sandwiched between similar structures. The weather-silvered, cedar-shingle siding and the white shutters vaguely suggested a house on Cape Cod, although the pinched lot did not allow for a full expression of that style of architecture.

The house, like its neighbors, had no front yard, no raised porch, only a shallow patio with a few potted plants. This one was paved with bricks and set behind a white picket fence. The gate in the fence was unlocked, and the hinges creaked.

Susan had once lived on the first and second floors with her husband, Eric, who had used the third floor—complete with its own bath and kitchen—as a home office. They were currently separated. Eric had moved out a year ago, and Susan had moved up, renting the lower two floors to a quiet retired couple whose only vice seemed to be two martinis each before dinner, and whose only pets were four parakeets.

A steep exterior set of stairs led along the side of the house to the third story. As Martie climbed to the small covered landing, shrieking seagulls wheeled in from the Pacific and passed overhead, crossing the peninsula, flying toward the harbor, where they would ride out the storm in sheltered roosts.

Martie knocked, but then unlocked the door without waiting for a response. Susan was usually hesitant to welcome a visitor, reluctant to be confronted with a glimpse of the outside world; so Martie had been given a key almost a year previously.

Steeling herself for the ordeal ahead, she stepped into the kitchen, which was revealed by a single light over the sink. The blinds were tightly shut, and lush swags of shadows hung like deep-purple bunting.

The room was not redolent of spices or lingering cooking odors. Instead, the air was laced with the faint but astringent scents of disinfectant, scouring powder, and floor wax.

"It's me," Martie called, but Susan didn't answer.

The only illumination in the dining room came from behind the doors of a small breakfront, in which antique majolica china gleamed on glass shelves. Here, the air smelled of furniture polish.

If all the lights had been ablaze, the apartment would have proved to be spotless, cleaner than a surgery. Susan Jagger had a lot of time to fill.

Judging by the mélange of odors in the living room, the carpet had been shampooed recently, the furniture polished, the upholstery dry-cleaned in place, and fresh citrus-scented potpourri had been placed in two small, ventilated, red-ceramic jars on the end tables.

The expansive windows, which framed an exhilarating ocean view, were covered by pleated shades. The shades were for the most part concealed by heavy drapes.

Until four months ago, Susan had been able at least to look out at the world with wistful longing, even though for sixteen months she had been terrified of venturing into it and had left her home only with someone upon whom she could lean for emotional support. Now merely the sight of a vast open space, with no walls or sheltering roof, could trigger a phobic reaction.

All the lamps glowed, and the spacious living room was brightly lighted. Yet because of the shrouded windows and the unnatural hush, the atmosphere felt funereal.

Shoulders slumped, head hung, Susan waited in an armchair. In a black skirt and black sweater, she had the wardrobe and the posture of a mourner. Judging by her appearance, the paperback book in her hands should have been the Bible, but it was a mystery novel.

"Did the butler do it?" Martie asked, sitting on the edge of the sofa.

Without looking up, Susan said, "No. The nun."

"Poison?"

Still focused on the paperback, Susan said, "Two with an ax. One with a hammer. One with a wire garrote. One with an acetylene torch. And two with a nail gun."

"Wow, a nun who's a serial killer."

"You can hide a lot of weapons under a habit."

"Mystery novels have changed since we read them in junior high."

"Not always for the better," Susan said, closing the book.

They had been best friends since they were ten: eighteen years of sharing more than mystery novels—hopes, fears, happiness, sorrow, laughter, tears, gossip, adolescent enthusiasms, hard-won insights. During the past sixteen months, since the inexplicable onset of Susan's agoraphobia, they had shared more pain than pleasure.

"I should have called you," Susan said. "I'm sorry, but I can't go to the session today."

This was ritual, and Martie played her part: "Of course, you can, Susan. And you will."

Putting the paperback aside, shaking her head, Susan said, "No, I'll call Dr. Ahriman and tell him I'm just too ill. I'm coming down with a cold, maybe the flu."

"You don't sound congested."

Susan grimaced. "It's more a stomach flu."

"Where's your thermometer? We'd better take your temperature."

"Oh, Martie, just look at me. I look like hell. Pasty-faced and red-eyed and my hair like straw. I can't go out like this."

"Get real, Sooz. You look like you always look."

"I'm a mess."

"Julia Roberts, Sandra Bullock, Cameron Diaz—they'd all kill to look as good as you, even when you're sick as a dog and projectile vomiting, which you aren't."

"I'm a freak."

"Oh, yeah, right, you're the Elephant Woman. We'll have to put a sack over your head and warn away small children."

If beauty had been a burden, Susan would have been crushed flat. Ash-blond, green-eyed, petite, with exquisitely sculptured features, with skin as flawless as that of a peach on a tree in Eden, she had turned more heads than a coven of chiropractors.

"I'm bursting out of this skirt. I'm gross."

"A virtual blimp," Martie said sarcastically. "A dirigible. A giant balloon of a woman."

Although Susan's self-imprisonment allowed her no exercise except housecleaning and long walks on a treadmill in the bedroom, she remained svelte.

"I've gained more than a pound," Susan insisted.

"My God, it's a liposuction emergency," Martie said, bolting up from the sofa. "I'll get your raincoat. We can call the plastic surgeon from the car, tell him to get an industrial-size sump pump to suck out all the fat."

In the short hall that led to the bedroom, the coat closet featured a pair of sliding, mirrored doors. As Martie approached it, she tensed and hesitated, concerned that she would be overcome by the same irrational fear that had seized her earlier.

She had to keep a grip on herself. Susan needed her. If she leaped into looniness again, her anxiety would feed Susan's fear, and perhaps vice versa.

When she confronted the full-length mirror, nothing in it made her heart race. She forced a smile, but it looked strained. She met her eyes in the reflection, and then quickly looked away, sliding one of the doors aside.

As she slipped the raincoat off the hanger, Martie considered, for the first time, that her recent peculiar bouts of fear might be related to the time that she'd spent with Susan during the past year. Maybe you should expect to absorb a little overspill of anxiety if you hung out a lot with a woman suffering from an extreme phobia.

A faint heat of shame flushed Martie's face. Even to consider such a possibility seemed superstitious, uncharitable, and unfair to poor Susan. Phobic disorders and panic attacks weren't contagious.

Turning away from the closet door and then reaching back to slide it shut, she wondered what term psychologists used to describe a fear of one's shadow. A disabling fear of open spaces, which afflicted Susan, was called agoraphobia. But shadows? Mirrors?

Martie stepped out of the hall and into the living room before she realized that she had reached behind her back to pull shut the sliding door in order to avoid glancing in the mirror again. Startled that she had acted with such unconscious aversion, she considered returning to the closet and confronting the mirror.

From the armchair, Susan was watching her.

The mirror could wait.

Holding the raincoat open, Martie approached her friend. "Get up, get in this, and get moving."

Susan gripped the arms of the chair, miserable at the prospect of leaving her sanctuary. "I can't."

"If you don't cancel a session forty-eight hours ahead, you have to pay for it."

"I can afford to."

"No, you can't. You don't have any income."

The only psychological malady that could have destroyed Susan's career as a real-estate agent more effectively than agoraphobia was uncontrollable pyromania. She had felt reasonably safe inside any property while showing it to a client, but such paralyzing terror had overcome her while she was traveling between houses that she hadn't been able to drive.

"I have the rent," Susan said, referring to the monthly check from the parakeet-infatuated retirees downstairs.

"Which doesn't quite cover the mortgage, taxes, utilities, and maintenance on the property."

"I have a lot of equity in the house."

Which might eventually be the only thing between you and total destitution, if you don't beat this damn phobia, Martie thought, but she could not bring herself to speak those words, even if that dire prospect might motivate Susan to get out of the armchair.

Raising her delicate chin in an unconvincing expression of brave defiance, Susan said, "Besides, Eric sends me a check."

"Not much. Hardly more than pocket change. And if the swine divorces you, maybe there won't be anything more at all from him, considering you came into this marriage with more assets than he did, and there aren't any kids."

"Eric's not a swine."

"Pardon me for not being blunt enough. He's a pig."

"Be nice, Martie."

"I gotta be me. He's a skunk."

Susan was determined to avoid self-pity and tears, which was highly admirable, but she was equally determined not to admit to her anger, which was less so. "He just was so upset seeing me . . . this way. He couldn't take it anymore."

"Oh, the poor sensitive darling," Martie said. "And I guess he was just too distressed to remember the part of the marriage vows that goes 'in sickness and in health.' "

Martie's anger at Eric was genuine, although she made an effort to stoke it like a fire and keep it ever alive. He had always been quiet, self-effacing, and sweet—and in spite of his abandonment of his wife, he remained hard to hate. Martie loved Susan too much *not* to despise Eric, however, and she believed that Susan needed anger to motivate her in her struggle against agoraphobia.

"Eric would be here if I had cancer or something," Susan said. "I'm not just sick, Martie. I'm crazy, is what I am."

"You aren't crazy," Martie insisted. "Phobias and anxiety attacks aren't the same as madness."

"I feel mad. I feel stark raving."

"He didn't last four months after this started. He's a swine, a skunk, a weasel, and worse."

This grim part of each visit—which Martie thought of as the *extraction phase*—was stressful for Susan, but it was downright grueling for Martie. To get her resistant friend out of the house, she had to be firm and relentless; and although this was a firmness informed by much love and compassion, she felt as though she were hectoring Susan. It wasn't within Martie's character to be a bully, even in a good cause, and by the end of this brutal four- or five-hour ordeal, she would return home to Corona Del Mar in a state of physical and emotional exhaustion.

"Sooz, you're beautiful, kind, special, and smart enough to whip this thing." Martie shook the raincoat. "Now get your ass out of that chair."

"Why can't Dr. Ahriman come to me for these sessions?"

"Leaving this house twice a week is part of the therapy. You know the theory—immersion in the very thing you're frightened of. A sort of inoculation."

"It isn't working."

"Come on."

"I'm getting worse."

"Up, up."

"It's so cruel," Susan protested. Letting go of the arms of the chair, she fisted her hands on her thighs. "So damn cruel."

"Whiner."

She glared at Martie. "Sometimes you can be such a mean bitch."

"Yeah, that's me. If Joan Crawford were alive, I'd challenge her to a wire coat-hanger fight, and I'd *lacerate* her."

Laughing, then shaking her head, Susan rose from the armchair. "I can't believe I said that. I'm sorry, Martie. I don't know what I'd do without you."

Holding the raincoat as Susan slipped her arms into it, Martie said, "You be good, girlfriend, and on the way back from the doctor, we'll get some great Chinese takeout. We'll open a couple bottles of Tsingtao, and we'll play some killer two-hand pinochle over lunch, fifty cents a point."

"You already owe me over six hundred thousand bucks."

"So break my legs. Gambling debts aren't legally collectible."

After Susan switched off all but one of the lamps, she retrieved her purse from the coffee table and led Martie through the apartment.

As she was crossing the kitchen behind Susan, Martie found her attention drawn to a wicked-looking item that lay on a cutting board near the sink. It was a mezzaluna knife, a classic Italian kitchen tool: The curved stainless-steel blade was shaped like a half-moon, with a handle at each end, so it could be rocked rapidly back and forth to dice and slice.

Like an electric current, scintillant light seemed to sizzle along the cutting edge.

Martie could not look away from it. She didn't realize how completely the mezzaluna had mesmerized her—until she heard Susan ask, "What's wrong?"

Her throat was tight, and her tongue felt swollen. With audible thickness, she asked a question to which she already knew the answer: "What's that?"

"Haven't you ever used one? It's great. You can dice an onion in a flash."

The sight of the knife didn't fill Martie with terror, as had her shadow and the bathroom mirror. It did, however, make her uneasy, although she couldn't explain her queer reaction to it.

"Martie? Are you okay?"

"Yeah, sure, let's go."

Susan twisted the knob but hesitated to open the kitchen door.

Martie put her hand over her friend's, and together they pulled the door inward, admitting cold gray light and a sharp-toothed wind.

Susan's face drained of color at the prospect of entering the roofless world beyond her threshold.

"We've done this a hundred times before," Martie assured her.

Susan clutched the doorjamb. "I can't go out there."

"You will," Martie insisted.

Susan attempted to return to the kitchen, but Martie blocked her. "Let me in, this is too hard, it's *agony*."

"It's agony for me, too," Martie said.

"Bullshit." Desperation clawed some of the beauty out of Susan's face, and a feral terror darkened the green of her jungle eyes. "You're getting off on this, you love it, you're crazy."

"No, I'm mean." Martie gripped the doorjamb with both hands, holding her ground. "I'm the mean bitch. *You're* the crazy bitch."

Suddenly Susan stopped pushing at Martie and clutched at her instead, seeking support. "Damn, I want that Chinese takeout."

Martie envied Dusty, whose biggest worry of the morning would be whether the rain would hold off long enough for his crew to get some work done.

Fat drops of rain—at first in fitful bursts but soon more insistently—began to rattle on the roof that covered the landing.

Finally, they stepped across the threshold, outside. Martie pulled the door shut and locked it.

The extraction phase was behind them. Worse lay ahead, however, and Martie was unable to see most of it coming.

6

Skeet ran exuberantly down the steeply pitched roof, toward the brink, angling for a point of departure that would ensure he landed on skull-cracking pavement rather than on mattresses, bounding along the convex orange-brown tiles as though he were a kid racing across a cobbled street to an ice-cream vendor, and Dusty ran grimly after him.

To those watching from below, it must have appeared that the two men were equally deranged, fulfilling a suicide pact.

More than halfway down the slope, Dusty caught up with Skeet, grabbed him, wrenched him off his intended trajectory, and stumbled diagonally across the incline with him. Some clay tiles cracked underfoot, dislodging small chunks of roofer's mortar, which rattled toward the rain gutter. Remaining upright on this rolling debris was no less difficult than walking on marbles, with the added challenges of the rain and the slimy lichen and Skeet's energetic and gleeful resistance, which he waged with flailing arms and spiking elbows and disturbing childlike giggles. Skeet's invisible dance partner, Death, seemed to give him supernatural grace and balance, but then Dusty fell and took Skeet down with him, and entwined they rolled the last ten feet, perhaps toward the mattresses or perhaps not—Dusty had lost his bearings—and across the copper gutter, which twanged like a plucked bass string.

Airborne, plummeting, letting go of Skeet, Dusty

thought of Martie: the clean smell of her silky black hair, the mischievous curve of her smile, the honesty of her eyes.

Thirty-two feet wasn't far, merely three stories, but far enough to split open the most stubborn head, far enough to crack a spine as easily as one might snap a pretzel stick, so when Dusty fell flat on his back on the piled mattresses, he thanked God as he bounced. Then he realized that in free fall, when each lightning-quick thought could have been his last, his mind had been filled with Martie, and that God had occurred to him after the fact.

The Sorensons had purchased first-rate mattresses. The impact didn't even knock the wind out of Dusty.

Skeet, too, had crashed into the safety zone. Now he lay as he had landed, face planted in the satin-weave ticking, arms over his head, motionless, as though he had been so fragile that even a fall into layers of cotton batting, foam rubber, and airy eiderdown had shattered his eggshell bones.

As the top mattress quickly became sodden with rain, Dusty got onto his hands and knees. He rolled the kid faceup.

Skeet's left cheek was abraded, and a small cut bisected the shallow cleft in his chin. Both injuries had probably occurred as he had rolled across the roof tiles; neither produced much blood.

"Where am I?" Skeet asked.

"Not where you wanted to be."

The kid's bronze eyes had a dark patina of anguish that hadn't been evident during the manic minutes on the roof. "Heaven?"

"I'll make it seem like Hell, you smacked-out creep," Motherwell said, looming over them, grabbing Skeet by his sweater and hauling him to his feet. If the sky had been split by lightning and shaken by thunder, Motherwell could have passed for Thor, Scandinavian god of the storm. "You're off my crew, you're finished, you hopeless screwup!"

"Easy, easy," Dusty said, scrambling to his feet and off the mattress.

Still holding Skeet a foot off the ground, Motherwell rounded on Dusty. "I mean it, boss. Either he's gone, he's history, or I can't work with you anymore."

"Okay, all right. Just put him down, Ned."

Instead of releasing Skeet, Motherwell shook him and shouted in his face, spraying enough foamy spittle to flock him like a Christmas tree: "By the time we buy new mattresses, three *expensive* mattresses, there goes most of the profit. Do you have any clue, you shithead?"

Dangling from Motherwell's hands, offering no resistance, Skeet said, "I didn't ask you to put down the mattresses."

"I wasn't trying to save *you*, asshole."

"You're always calling me names," Skeet said. "I never call you names."

"You're a walking pus bag." Straight Edgers, like Motherwell, denied themselves many things, but never anger. Dusty admired their efforts to lead a clean life in the dirty world they had inherited, and he understood their anger even as he sometimes wearied of it.

"Man, I *like* you," Skeet told Motherwell. "I wish you could like me."

"You're a pimple on the ass of humanity," Motherwell thundered, casting Skeet aside as if tossing a bag of garbage.

Skeet almost slammed into Foster Newton, who was passing by. Fig halted as the kid collapsed in a heap on the driveway, glanced at Dusty, said, "See you in the morning if it doesn't rain," stepped over Skeet, and proceeded to his car at the curb, still listening to talk radio through his headphones, as though he'd seen people jumping off roofs every day of his working life.

"What a mess," Ned Motherwell said, frowning at the drenched mattresses.

"I've got to check him into rehab," Dusty told Motherwell, as he helped Skeet to his feet.

"I'll take care of this mess," Motherwell assured him. "Just get that cankerous little weasel-dick out of my sight."

All along the rainwashed circular driveway to the street, Skeet leaned on Dusty. His previous frenetic energy, whether it had come from drugs or from the prospect of successful self-destruction, was gone, and he was limp with weariness, almost asleep on his feet.

The security guard fell in beside them as they neared Dusty's white Ford van. "I'll have to file a report about this."

"Yeah? With whom?"

"The executive board of the homeowners' association. With a copy to the property-management company."

"They won't kneecap me with a shotgun, will they?" Dusty asked as he propped Skeet against the van.

"Nah, they never take my recommendation," the guard said, and Dusty was forced to reevaluate him.

Rising out of his stupor, Skeet warned, "They'll want your soul, Dusty. I know these bastards."

From behind a veil of water that drizzled off the visor of his uniform cap, the security guard said, "They might put you on a list of undesirable contractors they'd rather not have in the community. But probably all that'll happen is they'll want you never to bring this guy inside the gates again. What's his full name, anyway?"

Opening the passenger door of the van, Dusty said, "Bruce Wayne."

"I thought it was Skeet something."

Helping Skeet into the van, Dusty said, "That's just his nickname." Which was truthful yet deceptive.

"I'll need to see his ID."

"I'll bring it later," Dusty said, slamming the door. "Right now I've got to get him to a doctor."

"He hurt?" the guard asked, following Dusty around the van to the driver's side.

"He's a wreck," Dusty said as he got in behind the wheel and pulled the door shut.

The guard rapped on the window.

Starting the engine with one hand, winding down the window with the other, Dusty said, "Yeah?"

"You can't go back to *strike force*, but *crew* isn't the right word, either. Better call them your *circus* or maybe *hullabaloo*."

"You're all right," Dusty said. "I like you."

The guard smiled and tipped his sopping hat.

Dusty rolled up the window, switched on the wipers, and drove away from the Sorensons' house.

1

Descending the exterior stairs from her third-floor apartment, Susan Jagger stayed close to the house, sliding her right hand along the shingle siding, as though constantly needing to reassure herself that shelter was close by, fiercely clutching Martie's arm with her left hand. She kept her head down, focusing intently on her feet, taking each ten-inch-high step as cautiously as a rock climber might have negotiated a towering face of sheer granite.

Because of Susan's raincoat hood and because she was shorter than Martie, her face was concealed, but from rainless days, Martie knew how Susan must look. Shock-white skin. Jaw set, mouth grim. Her green eyes would be haunted, as though she'd glimpsed a ghost; however, the only ghost in this matter was her once vital spirit, which had been killed by agoraphobia.

"What's wrong with the air?" Susan asked shakily.

"Nothing."

"Hard to breathe," Susan complained. "Thick. Smells funny."

"Just humidity. The smell is me. New perfume."

"You? Perfume?"

"I've got my girlish moments."

"We're so exposed," Susan said fearfully.

"It's not a long way to the car."

"Anything could happen out here."

"Nothing will happen."

"There's nowhere to hide."

"There's nothing to hide from."

Fifteen-hundred-year-old religious litanies were no less rigidly structured than these twice-a-week conversations on the way to and from therapy sessions.

As they reached the bottom of the steps, the rain fell harder than before, rattling through the leaves of the potted plants on the patio, clicking against the bricks.

Susan was reluctant to let go of the corner of the house.

Martie put an arm around her. "Lean on me if you want."

Susan leaned. "Everything's so strange out here, not like it used to be."

"Nothing's changed. It's just the storm."

"It's a new world," Susan disagreed. "And not a good one."

Huddling together, with Martie bending to match Susan's stoop, they progressed through this new world, now in a rush as Susan was drawn forward by the prospect of the comparatively enclosed space of the car, but now haltingly as Susan was weighed down and nearly crushed by the infinite emptiness overhead. Whipped by wind and lashed by rain, shielded by their hoods and their billowing coats, they might have been two frightened holy sisters, in full habit, desperately seeking sanctuary in the early moments of Armageddon.

Evidently Martie was affected either by the turbulence of the incoming storm or by her troubled friend, because as they proceeded fitfully along the promenade toward the side street where she had parked her car, she became increasingly aware of a strangeness in the day that was easy to perceive but difficult to define. On the concrete promenade, puddles like black mirrors swarmed with images so shattered by falling rain that their true appearance could not be discerned, yet they disquieted Martie. Thrashing palm trees clawed the air with fronds that had darkened from green to green-black, producing a thrum-hiss-rattle that resonated with a primitive and reckless passion deep inside her. On their right, the sand was smooth and pale, like the skin of some vast sleeping beast, and on their left, each house appeared to be filled with a storm of its own, as colorless images of roiling clouds and wind-tossed trees churned across the large ocean-view windows.

Martie was unsettled by all these odd impressions of unnatural menace in the surrounding landscape, but she was more disturbed by a new strangeness within herself, which the storm seemed to conjure. Her heart quickened with an irrational desire to surrender to the sorcerous energy of this wild weather. Suddenly she was afraid of some dark potential she couldn't define: afraid of losing control of herself, blacking out, and later coming to her senses, thereupon discovering she had done something terrible . . . something unspeakable.

Until this morning, such bizarre thoughts had never occurred to her. Now they came in abundance.

She remembered the unusually sour grapefruit juice that she'd drunk at breakfast, and she wondered if it had been tainted. She didn't have a sick stomach; but maybe she was suffering from a strain of food poisoning that caused mental rather than physical symptoms.

That was *another* bizarre thought. Tainted juice was no more likely an explanation than the possibility that the CIA was beaming messages into her brain via a microwave transmitter. If she continued down this twisty road of illogic, she'd soon be fashioning elaborate aluminum-foil hats to guard against long-distance brainwashing.

By the time they descended the short flight of concrete steps from the beach promenade to the narrow street where the car was parked, Martie was drawing as much emotional support from Susan as she was giving, although she hoped Susan didn't sense as much.

Martie opened the curbside door, helped Susan into the red Saturn, and then went around and got in the driver's seat.

Rain drummed on the roof, a cold and hollow sound that brought hoofbeats to mind, as though the Four Horsemen of the Apocalypse—Pestilence, War, Famine, and Death—were approaching at full gallop along the nearby beach.

Martie pulled back her hood. She fished in one coat pocket and then in the other until she found her keys.

In the passenger seat, Susan remained hooded, head bowed, hands fisted against her cheeks, eyes squeezed shut, and face pinched, as if the Saturn were in one of those hydraulic car crushers, about to be squashed into a three-foot cube.

Martie's attention fixed on the car key, which was the same one she had always used, yet suddenly the point seemed wickedly sharp, as never before. The serrations resembled those on a bread knife, which then reminded her of the mezzaluna in Susan's kitchen.

This simple key was a potential weapon. Crazily, Martie's mind clotted with images of the bloody damage a car key could inflict.

"What's wrong?" Susan asked, though she had not opened her eyes.

Thrusting the key into the ignition, struggling to conceal her inner turmoil, Martie said, "Couldn't find my key. It's okay. I've got it now."

The engine caught, roared. When Martie locked herself into her safety harness, her hands were shaking so badly that the hard plastic clasp and the metal tongue on the belt chattered together like a pair of windup, novelty-store teeth before she finally engaged the latch.

"What if something happens to me out here and I can't get home again?" Susan worried.

"I'll take care of you," Martie promised, although in light of her own peculiar state of mind, the promise might prove empty.

"But what if something happens to *you?*"

"Nothing is going to happen to me," Martie vowed as she switched on the windshield wipers.

"Something can happen to anybody. Look at what happened to me."

Martie pulled away from the curb, drove to the end of the short street, and turned left onto Balboa Boulevard. "Hold tight. You'll be in the doctor's office soon."

"Not if we're in an accident," Susan fretted.

"I'm a good driver."

"The car might break down."

"The car's fine."

"It's raining hard. If the streets flood—"

"Or maybe we'll be abducted by big slimy Martians," Martie said. "Be taken up to the mother ship, forced to breed with hideous squidlike creatures."

"The streets *do* flood here on the peninsula," Susan said defensively.

"This time of year, Big Foot hides out around the pier, bites the heads off the unwary. We better hope we don't have a breakdown in that area."

"You're vicious," Susan complained.

"I'm mean as hell," Martie confirmed.

"Cruel. You are. I mean it."

"I'm loathsome."

"Take me home."

"No."

"I hate you."

"I love you anyway," Martie said.

"Oh, shit," Susan said miserably. "I love you, too."

"Hang in there."

"This is so hard."

"I know, honey."

"What if we run out of fuel?"

"The tank's full."

"I can't breathe out here. I can't *breathe.*"

"Sooz, you're breathing."

"But the air's like a . . . sludge. And I'm having chest pains. My heart."

"What *I've* got is a pain in the ass," Martie said. "Guess its name."

"You're a mean bitch."

"That's old news."

"I hate you."

"I love you," Martie said patiently.

Susan began to cry. She buried her face in her hands. "I can't go on like this."

"It's not much farther."

"I hate myself."

Martie frowned. "Don't say that. Don't ever."

"I hate what I've become. This frightened, quivering *thing* I've become."

Martie's eyes clouded with tears of pity. She blinked furiously to clear her vision.

From off the cold Pacific, waves of black clouds washed across the sky, as though the tide of night were turning and would drown this bleak new day. Virtually all the oncoming traffic, northbound on Pacific Coast Highway, approached behind headlights that silvered the wet blacktop.

Martie's perception of unnatural menace had passed. The rainy day no longer seemed in the least strange. In fact, the world was so achingly beautiful, so *right* in every detail, that although she was no longer afraid of anything in it, she was terribly afraid of losing it.

Despairing, Susan said, "Martie, can you remember me . . . the way I used to be?"

"Yes. Vividly."

"I can't. Some days I can't remember me any other way but how I am now. I'm scared, Martie. Not just of going outside, out of the house. I'm scared of . . . all the years ahead."

"We'll get through this together," Martie assured her, "and there'll be a lot of good years."

Massive phoenix palms lined the entrance road to Fashion Island, Newport Beach's premier shopping and business center. In the wind, the trees, like agitated lions preparing to roar, shook their great green manes.

Dr. Mark Ahriman's suite of offices was on the fourteenth floor of one of the tall buildings that surrounded the sprawling, low-rise shopping plaza. Getting Susan from the parking lot to the lobby and then across what seemed like acres of polished granite into an elevator was not as arduous a trek as Frodo's journey from the peaceful Shire to the land called Mordor, there to destroy the Great Ring of Power—but Martie was nonetheless relieved when the doors slid shut and the cab purred upward.

"Almost safe," Susan murmured, gaze fixed on the indicator board inset in the transom above the doors, watching the light move from number to number, toward 14, where sanctuary waited.

Though entirely enclosed and alone with Martie, Susan never felt secure in the elevator. Consequently, Martie kept one arm around her, aware that from Susan's troubled point of view, the fourteenth-floor elevator alcove and the corridors beyond it—even the psychiatrist's waiting room—were also hostile territories harboring uncountable threats. Every public space, regardless of how small and sheltered, was an *open* space in the sense that anyone could enter at any time. She felt safe only in two places: in her home on the peninsula—and in Dr. Ahriman's private office, where even the dramatic panoramic view of the coastline did not alarm her.

"Almost safe," Susan repeated as the elevator doors slid open at the fourteenth floor.

Curiously, Martie thought of Frodo again, from *The*

Lord of the Rings. Frodo in the tunnel that was a secret entrance to the evil land of Mordor. Frodo confronting the guardian of the tunnel, the spiderlike monster Shelob. Frodo stung by the beast, apparently dead, but actually paralyzed and set aside to be devoured later.

"Let's go, let's go," Susan whispered urgently. For the first time since leaving her apartment, she was eager to proceed.

Inexplicably, Martie wanted to pull her friend back into the elevator, descend to the lobby, and return to the car.

Once more she sensed a disquieting strangeness in the mundane scene around her, as if this were not the ordinary elevator alcove that it appeared to be, but was in fact the tunnel where Frodo and his companion Sam Gamgee had confronted the great pulsing, many-eyed spider.

Responding to a sound behind her, she turned with dread, half expecting to see Shelob looming. The elevator door was rolling shut. Nothing more than that.

In her imagination, a membrane between dimensions had ruptured, and the world of Tolkien was seeping inexorably into Newport Beach. Maybe she had been working too long and too hard on the video-game adaptation. In her obsession with doing honor to *The Lord of the Rings*, and in her mental exhaustion, was she confusing reality and fantasy?

No. Not that. The truth was something less fantastic but equally strange.

Then Martie caught a glimpse of herself in the glass panel that covered a wall niche containing an emergency fire hose. Immediately, she turned away, rattled by the razor-sharp anxiety in her face. Her features appeared jagged, with deep slashes for laugh lines, a mouth like a scar; her eyes were wounds. This unflattering expression was not what made her look away. Something else. Worse. Something to which she couldn't quite put a name.

What's happening to me?

"Let's go," Susan said more insistently than before. "Martie, what's wrong? *Let's go.*"

Reluctantly, Martie accompanied Susan out of the alcove. They turned left into the corridor.

Susan took heart from her mantra—"almost safe, almost safe"—but Martie found no comfort in it.

8

As the wind stripped wet leaves off trees and as cataracts gushed along gutters toward half-clogged street drains, Dusty drove down through the Newport hills.

"I'm soaked. I'm cold," Skeet complained.

"Me too. Fortunately, we're high-order primates with lots of gadgets." Dusty switched on the heater.

"I screwed up," Skeet mumbled.

"Who, you?"

"I always screw up."

"Everybody's good at something."

"Are you angry with me?"

"Right now I'm sick to death of you," Dusty said honestly.

"Do you hate me?"

"No."

Skeet sighed and slid down farther in his seat. In his boneless slump, as a faint steam rose off his clothes, he looked less like a man than like a pile of damp laundry. His chafed and swollen eyelids drooped shut. His mouth sagged open. He appeared to be asleep.

The sky pressed down, as gray-black as wet ashes and char. The rain wasn't the usual glittering silver, but dark and dirty, as if nature were a scrubwoman wringing out a filthy mop.

Dusty drove east and south, out of Newport Beach, into the city of Irvine. He hoped that the New Life Clinic, a drug-and-alcohol-rehabilitation facility, would have an open bed.

Skeet had been in rehab twice before, once at New Life six months ago. He came out clean, sincerely intending to stay that way. After each course of therapy, however, he gradually slid backward.

Until now he'd never gotten low enough to try suicide. Perhaps, from this new depth, he'd realize that he was facing his last chance.

Without lifting his chin from his chest, Skeet said, "Sorry . . . back there on the roof. Sorry I forgot which one was your dad. Dr. Decon. It's just that I'm so wrecked."

"That's okay. I've been trying to forget him most of my life."

"You remember *my* dad, I'll bet."

"Dr. Holden Caulfield, professor of literature."

"He's a real bastard," Skeet said.

"They all are. She's attracted to bastards."

Skeet slowly raised his head, as though it were a massive weight elevated by a complex system of powerful hydraulic lifts. "Holden Caulfield's not even his real name."

Dusty braked at a red traffic signal and regarded Skeet with skepticism. The name, identical to that of the protagonist in *The Catcher in the Rye*, seemed too pat to have been an invention.

"He changed it legally when he was twenty-one," Skeet said. "Sam Farner was his born name."

"Is this stoned talk or true talk?"

"True," Skeet said. "Old Sam's dad was a career military man. Colonel Thomas Jackson Farner. His mom, Luanne, she taught nursery school. Old Sam had a falling-out with them—*after* the colonel and Luanne finished putting him through college and after old Sam got a scholarship toward his master's degree. Otherwise, he might've waited to have his falling-out, until his folks ponied up more tuition."

Dusty knew Skeet's father—the false Holden

Caulfield—and knew him far too well, because the pretentious bastard was his stepfather. Trevor Penn Rhodes, Dusty's father, was the second of their mother's four husbands, and Holden Sam Caulfield Farner was her third. From before Dusty's fourth birthday until past his fourteenth, this self-styled blue blood had ruled their family with a lofty sense of divine right, and with enough authoritarian zeal and sociopathic ferocity to earn praise from Hannibal Lecter. "He said his mother had been a professor at Princeton, his father at Rutgers. All those stories . . ."

"Not biography," Skeet insisted. "Just his cooked-up résumé."

"Their tragic death in Chile? . . ."

"Another lie." In Skeet's bloodshot eyes was a fierce light that might have been vengeance. For a moment, the kid appeared not sad at all, not drawn and gaunt and ruined, but full of a wild and barely contained glee.

Dusty said, "He had such a tremendous disagreement with Colonel Farner that he wanted to change his name?"

"I guess he liked *The Catcher in the Rye.*"

Dusty was amazed. "Maybe he liked it, but did he understand it?" Which was a dumb question. Skeet's father was as shallow as a petri dish, culturing one short-lived enthusiasm after another, most of them as destructive as salmonella. "Who would want to *be* Holden Caulfield?"

"Sam Farner, my good old dad. And I'll bet it hasn't hurt the bastard's career at the university. In his line of work, that name makes him memorable."

A horn sounded behind them. The traffic signal had changed from red to green.

Resuming the drive to New Life, Dusty said, "Where did you learn all this?"

"To begin with—on the Internet." Skeet sat up straighter, and with his bony hands, he smoothed his damp hair back from his face. "First, I checked out the faculty emeritus at Rutgers, on their website. Everyone who'd ever taught there. Same at Princeton. No one with his parents' names had been professors at either place. His *invented* parents, I mean."

With an unmistakable note of pride in his voice, Skeet recounted the tortuous route he'd followed in his search for the simple truth about his father. The investigation had required concerted effort and considerable creative thought, not to mention sober logic.

Dusty marveled that this fragile kid, ravaged by life as well as by his own addictions and compulsions, had been able to focus sharply enough and long enough to get the job done.

"My old man's old man, Colonel Farner—he's long dead," Skeet said. "But Luanne, his mother, she's alive. She's seventy-eight, lives out in Cascade, Colorado."

"Your grandmother," Dusty said.

"Didn't know she existed till three weeks ago. Talked to her on the phone twice. She seems real sweet, Dusty. Broke her heart when her only kid cut them out of his life."

"Why did he?"

"Political convictions. Don't ask me what that means."

"He changes convictions with his designer socks," Dusty said. "It must have been something else."

"Not according to Luanne."

Pride of accomplishment, which had given Skeet the strength to sit up straighter and lift his chin off his chest, was no longer sufficient to sustain him. Gradually he slid down and retreated turtlelike into the steam, the wet smell, and the soggy folds of his loose rain-soaked clothes.

"You can't afford all this again," Skeet said as Dusty drove into the New Life Clinic parking lot.

"Don't worry about it. I have two major jobs lined up. Besides, Martie's designing all kinds of hideous deaths for Orcs and assorted monsters, and there's serious bucks in that."

"I don't know if I can go through the program again."

"You can. You jumped off a roof this morning. Hell, getting through rehab should be a piece of cake."

The private clinic was in a building styled like the corporate headquarters for a prosperous chain of Mexican fast-food restaurants: a two-story hacienda with arched loggias on the first floor, covered balconies on the second, too precisely prettified with royal-purple bougainvillea, which had been meticulously handwoven around columns and across archways. Perfection had been sought so aggressively that the result was a Disneyesque artificiality, as if everything from the grass to the roof were stamped out of plastic. Here, even the dirty rain had a tinsel glimmer.

Dusty parked at the curb near the entrance, in the zone reserved for patient admissions. He switched off the wipers, but didn't kill the engine. "Have you told him what you've learned?"

"You mean good old Dad?" Skeet closed his eyes, shook his head. "No. It's enough I know it myself."

In truth, Skeet was afraid of Professor Caulfield, née Farner, no less now than when he'd been a boy—and perhaps with good reason.

"Cascade, Colorado," Skeet said, pronouncing it as if it were a magical place, home to wizards and gryphons and unicorns.

"You want to go there, see your grandma?"

"Too far. Too hard," Skeet said. "I can't drive anymore."

Because of numerous moving violations, he had lost his driver's license. He rode to work each day with Fig Newton.

"Listen," Dusty said, "you get through the program, and I'll take you out there to Cascade to meet your grandma."

Skeet opened his eyes. "Oh, man, that's risky."

"Hey, I'm not that bad a driver."

"I mean, people let you down. Except you and Martie. And Dominique. She never let me down."

Dominique was their half sister, born to their mother's

first husband. She'd been a Down's baby and had died in infancy. Neither of them had ever known her, though sometimes Skeet visited her grave. *The one who escaped,* he called her.

"People always let you down," he said, "and it's not smart to expect too much."

"You said she sounded sweet on the phone. And evidently your dad despises her, which is a good sign. Damn good. Besides, if she turns out to be the grandmother from Hell, I'll be there with you, and I'll break her legs."

Skeet smiled. He stared wistfully through the rain-washed windshield, not at the immediate landscape but perhaps at an ideal portrait of Cascade, Colorado, which he'd already painted in his mind. "She said she loved me. Hasn't met me, but said it anyway."

"You're her grandson," Dusty said, switching off the engine.

Skeet's eyes appeared to be not just swollen and bloodshot but *sore,* as if he'd seen too many painful things. But in the ice-pale, sunken wreckage of his gaunt face, his smile was warm. "You're not just a half brother. You're a brother and a half."

Dusty cupped a hand against the back of Skeet's head and pulled him close, until their foreheads touched. They sat for a while, brow to brow, neither of them saying anything.

Then they got out of the van, into the cold rain.

9

Dr. Mark Ahriman's waiting room featured two pairs of Ruhlman-style lacquered lacewood chairs with black leather seats. The floor was black granite, as were the two end tables, each of which held fanned copies of *Architectural Digest* and *Vanity Fair.* The color of the walls matched the honey tone of the lacewood.

Two Art Deco paintings, nighttime cityscapes reminiscent of some early work by Georgia O'Keeffe, were the only art.

The high-style decor was also surprisingly serene. As always, Susan was visibly relieved the moment she crossed the threshold from the fourteenth-floor corridor. For the first time since leaving her apartment, she didn't need to lean on Martie. Her posture improved. She raised her head, pushed back the raincoat hood, and took long breaths, as if she'd broken through the surface of a cold, deep pond.

Curiously, Martie, too, felt a measure of relief. Her floating anxiety, which didn't seem to be anchored to any particular source, abated somewhat as she closed the waiting-room door behind them.

The doctor's secretary, Jennifer, could be seen through the receptionist's window. Sitting at a desk, talking on the phone, she waved.

An inner door opened soundlessly. As if telepathically informed of his patient's arrival, Dr. Ahriman entered from the equally well-furnished chamber in which he conducted therapy sessions. Impeccably dressed in a dark gray Vestimenta suit, as stylish as his offices, he moved with the easy grace characteristic of professional athletes.

He was forty-something, tall, well-tanned, with salt-and-pepper hair, as handsome as the photographs on the dust jackets of his best-selling books about psychology. Though his hazel eyes were unusually direct, his stare wasn't invasive or challenging, not clinical—but warm and reassuring. Dr. Ahriman looked nothing like Martie's father; however, he shared Smilin' Bob's affability, genuine interest in people, and relaxed self-confidence. To her, he had a fatherly air.

Rather than reinforce Susan's agoraphobia by solicitously asking how she had handled the trip from her apartment, he spoke eloquently about the beauty of the storm, as though the soggy morning were as luminous as a painting by Renoir. As he described the pleasures of a walk in the rain, the chill and the damp sounded as soul-soothing as a sunny day at the beach.

By the time Susan stripped out of her raincoat and handed it to Martie, she was smiling. All the anxiety was gone from her face, if not entirely from her eyes. As she left the waiting room for Dr. Ahriman's inner office, she no longer moved like an old woman, but like a young girl, apparently unintimidated by the expansive view of the coastline that awaited her from his fourteenth-floor windows.

As always, Martie was impressed by the instant soothing effect that the doctor had on Susan, and she almost decided against sharing her concern with him. But then, before he followed Susan into the office, Martie asked if she might have a word with him.

To Susan, he said, "I'll be right with you," and then shut his office door.

Moving to the center of the waiting room with Ahriman, keeping her voice low, Martie said, "I'm worried about her, Doctor."

His smile was as comforting as hot tea, sugared shortbread, and a fireside armchair. "She's doing well, Mrs. Rhodes. I couldn't be more pleased."

"Isn't there medication you could give her? I was reading that anxiety medication—"

"In her case, anxiety medication would be a very grave mistake. Drugs aren't always the answer, Mrs. Rhodes. Believe me, if they would help her, I'd write the prescription in a minute."

"But she's been like this for sixteen months."

He cocked his head and regarded her almost as if he suspected that she was teasing him. "Have you really seen no change in her, especially over the last few months?"

"Oh, yes. Plenty. And it seems to me . . . Well, I'm no doctor, no therapist, but lately Susan seems to be worse. A lot worse."

"You're right. She's getting worse, but that's not a bad sign."

Baffled, Martie said, "It's not?"

Sensing the depth of Martie's distress, perhaps intuitively aware that her anxiety arose not entirely from her concern about her friend, Dr. Ahriman guided her to a chair. He settled into the seat beside her.

"Agoraphobia," he explained, "is almost always a sudden-onset condition, rarely gradual. The intensity of the fear is as severe during the first panic attack as during the hundredth. So when there's a change in the intensity, it often indicates the patient is on the edge of a breakthrough."

"Even if the fear gets worse?"

"Especially when it gets worse." Ahriman hesitated. "I'm sure you realize I can't violate Susan's privacy by discussing the details of her specific case. But in general the agoraphobic often uses his or her fear as a refuge from the world, as a way to escape engagement with other people or to avoid dealing with particularly traumatic personal experiences. There's a perverse comfort in the isolation—"

"But Susan hates being so fearful, trapped in that apartment."

He nodded. "Her despair is deep and genuine. However, her need for isolation is even greater than her anguish over the limitations imposed by her phobia."

Martie *had* noticed that sometimes Susan seemed to cling to her apartment because she was happy there more than because she was too frightened of the world beyond.

"If the patient begins to understand *why* she's embracing her loneliness," Ahriman continued, "if at last she starts to identify the *real* trauma she's trying not to face, then sometimes, in denial, she will cling to the agoraphobia more fiercely. An intensification of symptoms usually means she's making a last-ditch defense against the truth. When that defense fails, she'll finally face the thing she *really* fears—not open spaces, but something more personal and immediate."

The doctor's explanation made sense to Martie, yet she couldn't easily accept the idea that an ever steeper decline would inevitably lead to a cure. Last year, her father's battle with cancer progressed along a relentless downward spiral, and at the bottom there had been no joyful breakthrough, only death. Of course a psychological illness could not be compared to a physical disease. Nevertheless . . .

"Did I set your mind at rest, Mrs. Rhodes?" A twinkle of humor enlivened his eyes. "Or do you think I'm full of psychobabble?"

His charm won her over. The impressive array of diplomas in his office, his reputation as the finest specialist in phobic therapy in California and perhaps in the nation, and his keen mind were no more important to building patient trust than was his bedside manner.

Martie smiled and shook her head. "No. The only babble is coming from me. I guess . . . I feel like I've failed her somehow."

"No, no, no." He placed a hand reassuringly on her shoulder. "Mrs. Rhodes, I can't stress strongly enough how important you are to Susan's recovery. Your commitment to her means more than anything I can do. You must always feel comfortable about expressing your worries to me. Your concern for her is the rock on which she stands."

Martie's voice thickened. "We've been friends since we were kids, most of our lives. I love her so much. I couldn't love her more if she were my sister."

"That's what I mean. Love can accomplish more than therapy, Mrs. Rhodes. Not every patient has someone like you. Susan is so very lucky in that regard."

Martie's vision blurred. "She seems so lost," she said softly.

His hand tightened slightly on her shoulder. "She's finding her way. Believe me, she is."

She did believe him. Indeed, he had comforted her so much that she almost mentioned her own peculiar rushes of anxiety this morning: her shadow, the mirror, the mezzaluna, the point and the serrated edge of the car key. . . .

In the inner office, Susan was waiting for her session. This time was hers, not Martie's.

"Is there something else?" Dr. Ahriman asked.

"No. I'm all right now," she said, getting to her feet. "Thank you. Thank you so much, Doctor."

"Have faith, Mrs. Rhodes."

"I do."

Smiling, he gave her a thumbs-up sign, went into his office, and closed the door.

Martie followed a narrow hallway between the doctor's private office and a large file room, to a second waiting area. This was smaller than—but similar to—the first.

Here, a back door led into Dr. Ahriman's office, and another door opened onto the fourteenth-floor corridor. This double-waiting-room arrangement ensured that arriving patients and their companions, if any, wouldn't encounter departing patients, thus guaranteeing everyone's privacy.

Martie hung Susan's raincoat and her own on a pair of wall hooks beside the exit door.

She had brought a paperback book, a thriller, to pass the time, but she couldn't focus on the story. None of the creepy things happening in the novel was as disquieting as the real events of this morning.

Soon Jennifer, the doctor's secretary, brought a mug of coffee—black, without sugar, as Martie liked it—and a chocolate biscotto. "I didn't ask if you'd rather have a soft drink. I just assumed, on a day like this, coffee was the thing."

"Perfect. Thank you, Jenny."

When Martie first accompanied Susan here, she had been surprised by this simple courtesy; although having no previous experience with psychiatrists' offices, she was sure that such thoughtful treatment was not common to the profession, and she was still charmed by it.

The coffee was rich but not bitter. The biscotto was excellent; she would have to ask Jennifer where to buy them.

Funny, how one good cookie could calm the mind and even elevate a troubled soul.

After a while, she was able to concentrate on the book. The writing was good. The plot was entertaining. The characters were colorful. She enjoyed it.

The second waiting room was a fine place to read. Hushed. No windows. No annoying background music. No distractions.

In the story, there was a doctor who loved haiku, a concise form of Japanese poetry. Tall, handsome, blessed with a mellifluous voice, he recited a haiku while he stood at a huge window, watching a storm:

"Pine wind blowing hard,
quick rain, torn windpaper
talking to itself."

Martie thought the poem was lovely. And those succinct lines perfectly conveyed the mood of this January rain as it swept along the coast, beyond the window. Lovely—both the view of the storm and the words.

Yet the haiku also disturbed her. It was haunting. An ominous intent lurked beneath the beautiful images. A sudden disquiet came over her, a sense that nothing was what it seemed to be.

What's happening to me?

She felt disoriented. She was standing, though she had no memory of having risen from her chair. And for God's sake, what was she doing *here*?

"What's happening to me?" she asked aloud this time.

Then she closed her eyes, because she must relax. She must relax. Relax. Have faith.

Gradually she recovered her composure.

She decided to pass the time with a book. Books were good therapy. You could lose yourself in a book, forget your troubles, your fear.

This particular book was especially good escape reading. A real thriller. The writing was good. The plot was entertaining. The characters were colorful. She enjoyed it.

10

The one available room at New Life was on the second floor, with a view of the well-landscaped grounds. Queen palms and ferns thrashed in the wind, and beds of blood-red cyclamens throbbed.

Rain clicked against the window so hard that it sounded like sleet, though Dusty could see no beads of ice sliding down the glass.

His clothes only slightly damp now, Skeet sat in a blue tweed armchair. He paged desultorily through an ancient issue of *Time*.

This was a private rather than semiprivate room. A single bed with yellow-and-green-checked spread. One blond, wood-grain Formica nightstand, a small matching dresser. Off-white walls, burnt-orange drapes, bile-green carpet. When they went to Hell, sinful interior designers were assigned to quarters like this for eternity.

The attached bath featured a shower stall as cramped as a phone booth. A red label—TEMPERED GLASS—was fixed to a corner of the mirror above the sink: If broken, it would not produce the sharp shards required to slash one's wrists.

Although the room was humble, it was costly, because the care given by the staff at New Life was of a far higher quality than their furniture. Skeet's health insurance didn't include I-was-stupid-and-self-destructive-and-now-I-need-to-have-a-full-brain-flush coverage, so Dusty had already written a check for four weeks of room and board, and he had signed a commitment to pay for the services of therapists, physicians, counselors, and nurses as needed.

As this was Skeet's third course of rehabilitation—and his second at New Life—Dusty was beginning to think that to have any hope of success, what he needed were not psychologists, physicians, and therapists—but a wizard, a warlock, a witch, and a wishing well.

Skeet was likely to be at New Life for a minimum of three weeks. Perhaps six. Because of his suicide attempt, a series of nurses would be with him around the clock for at least three days.

Even with painting contracts lined up and with Martie's deal to design a new *Lord of the Rings* game, they were not going to be able to afford a long Hawaiian vacation this year. Instead, they could put a few tiki lanterns in the backyard, wear aloha shirts, crank up a Don Ho CD, and have a canned-ham luau. That would be fun, too. Any time spent with Martie was fun, whether the backdrop was Waimea Bay or the painted board fence at the end of their flower garden.

As Dusty sat on the edge of the bed, Skeet dropped the issue of *Time* that he'd been reading. "This magazine sucks since they stopped running nudes." When Dusty didn't respond, Skeet said, "Hey, that was just a joke, bro, not the drugs talking. I'm not particularly high anymore."

"You were funnier when you were."

"Yeah. But after the flight goes down, it's hard to be funny in the wreckage." His voice wobbled like a spinning top losing momentum.

The rataplan of rain on the roof was usually soothing. Now it was depressing, a chilling reminder of all the dreams and drug-soaked years washed down the drain.

Skeet pressed pale, wrinkled fingertips to his eyelids. "Saw my eyes in the bathroom mirror. Like someone hocked wads of phlegm in a couple dirty ashtrays. Man, that's how they feel, too."

"Anything particular you'd like besides your gear? Some new magazines, books, a radio?"

"Nah. For a few days, I'll be sleeping a lot." He stared at his fingertips, as if he thought part of his eye might have stuck to them. "I appreciate this, Dusty. I'm not worth it, but I do appreciate it. And I'll pay you back somehow."

"Forget it."

"No. I want to." He slowly melted down into the chair, as though he were a wax candle in the shape of a man. "It's important to me. Maybe I'll win the lottery or something big. You know? It could happen."

"It could," Dusty agreed, because although he didn't believe in the lottery, he did believe in miracles.

The first-shift nurse arrived, a young Asian American named Tom Wong, whose air of relaxed competence and boyish smile gave Dusty confidence that he was putting his brother in good hands.

The name on the patient-ID sheet was Holden Caulfield Jr., but when Tom read it aloud, Skeet was roused from his lethargy. "*Skeet!*" he said ferociously, sitting up straighter in his chair, clenching his fists. "That's my name. Skeet and nothing but Skeet. Don't you ever call me Holden. Don't you *ever*. How can I be Holden *junior* when my phony shit of a father isn't even Holden *senior*? Who I should be is Sam Farner Jr. Don't you call me that, either! You call me anything but Skeet, then I'll strip naked, set my hair on fire, and throw myself through that freaking window. Okay? You understand? Is that what you want, me taking a flaming-naked suicide leap into that pretty little garden of yours?"

Smiling, shaking his head, Tom Wong said, "Not on my shift, Skeet. The flaming hair would be an amazing sight, but I sure don't want to see you naked."

Dusty smiled with relief. Tom had struck the perfect note.

Slumping in the armchair again, Skeet said, "You're all right, Mr. Wong."

"Please call me Tom."

Skeet shook his head. "I'm a bad case of arrested development, stuck in early adolescence, more screwed-up-twisted-up-tangled-up than a couple earthworms makin' babies. What I need here aren't a bunch of new friends, Mr. Wong. What I need here, you see, are some authority figures, people who can show me the way, 'cause I really can't go on like this and I really do want to find the way, I really do. Okay?"

"Okay," said Tom Wong.

"I'll be back with your clothes and stuff," Dusty said.

When Skeet tried to get to his feet, he didn't have sufficient strength to push himself up from the chair.

Dusty bent down and kissed him on the cheek. "Love you, bro."

"Truth is," Skeet said, "I'll never pay you back."

"Sure you will. The lottery, remember?"

"I'm not lucky."

"Then I'll buy the ticket for you," Dusty said.

"Hey, would you? You're lucky. Always were. Hell, you found Martie. You walk around in luck up to your ears."

"You have some pay coming. I'll buy you two tickets a week."

"That would be cool." Skeet closed his eyes. His voice settled into a murmur. "That would be . . . cool." He was asleep.

"Poor kid," Tom Wong said.

Dusty nodded.

From Skeet's room, Dusty went directly to the second-floor care station, where he spoke to the head nurse, Colleen O'Brien: a stout, freckled woman with white hair and kind eyes, who could have played the mother superior in every convent in every Catholic-themed movie ever produced. She claimed to be aware of the treatment limitation special to Skeet's case, but Dusty went through it with her anyway.

"No drugs. No tranquilizers, no sedatives. No antidepressants. He's been on one damn drug or another since he was five, sometimes two or three at once. He had a learning disability, and they called it a behavior disorder, and his old man had him on a series of drugs for that. When one drug had side effects, then there were drugs to counter the side effects, and when *those* produced side effects, there were more drugs to counter the new side effects. He grew up in a chemical stew, and I *know* that's what screwed him up. He's so used to popping a pill or taking an injection that he can't figure how to live straight and clean."

"Dr. Donklin agrees," she said, producing Skeet's file. "He's got a zero-medication advisory in place."

"Skeet's metabolism is so out of whack, his nervous system so shot, you can't always be sure what reaction he'll have even to some usually harmless patent medicine."

"He won't even get Tylenol."

Listening to himself, Dusty could hear that in his concern for Skeet, he was babbling. "He nearly killed himself once with caffeine tablets, they were such a habit. Developed caffeine psychosis, had some amazingly weird hallucinations, went into convulsions. Now he's incredibly sensitized to it, allergic. You give him coffee, a Coke, he could go into anaphylactic shock."

"Son," she said, "that's here in the file, too. Believe me, we're going to take good care of him." To Dusty's surprise, Colleen O'Brien made the sign of the cross and then winked at him. "No harm is going to come to your little brother on my watch."

If she *had* been a mother superior in a movie, you would have had full confidence that she was speaking both for herself and for God.

"Thank you, Mrs. O'Brien," he said softly. "Thank you very, very much."

Outside again, in his van, he did not at once switch on the engine. He was trembling too badly to drive.

The shakes were in part a delayed reaction to the fall off the Sorensons' roof. Anger shook him, too. Anger at poor screwed-up Skeet and the endless burden he imposed. And the anger made Dusty tremble with shame, because he loved Skeet, as well, and felt responsible for him, but was powerless to help him. Being powerless was the worst of it.

He folded his arms across the steering wheel, put his forehead on his arms, and did something that he had rarely permitted himself to do in his twenty-nine years. He cried.

11

After the session with Dr. Ahriman, Susan Jagger appeared to be restored to her former self, the woman she had been prior to the agoraphobia. As she slipped into her raincoat, she declared that she was famished. With considerable humor and flair, she rated the three Chinese restaurants that Martie suggested for takeout. "I don't have a problem with MSG or too many hot red peppers in the Szechuan beef, but I'm afraid I must rule out choice number three based on the possibility of getting an unwanted cockroach garnish." Nothing in her face or in her manner marked her as a woman in the nearly paralytic grip of a severe phobia.

As Martie opened the door to the fourteenth-floor corridor, Susan said, "You forgot your book."

The paperback was on the small table beside the chair in which Martie had been sitting. She crossed the room, but she hesitated before picking up the book.

"What's wrong?" Susan asked.

"Huh? Oh, nothing. Seem to have lost my bookmark." Martie slipped the paperback into her raincoat pocket.

All the way along the corridor, Susan remained in good spirits, but as the elevator descended, her demeanor began to change. When they reached the lobby, she was whey-faced, and a tremor in her voice quickly curdled the note of good humor into sour anxiety. She hunched her shoulders, hung her head, and bent forward as though she could already feel the cold, wet lash of the storm outside.

Susan exited the elevator on her own, but four or five steps into the lobby, she had to grip Martie's arm for support. As they approached the lobby doors, her fear reduced her nearly to paralysis and to abject humiliation.

The return trip to the car was grueling. By the time they reached the Saturn, Martie's right shoulder and that entire side of her neck ached, because Susan had clutched so tenaciously and had clung so helplessly to her arm.

Susan huddled in the passenger's seat, hugging herself, rocking as if racked by stomach pain, head bent to avoid a glimpse of the wide world beyond the windows. "I felt so good upstairs," she said miserably, "with Dr. Ahriman, through the whole session, so good. I felt *normal*. I was sure I would be better coming out, at least a little better, but I'm worse than when I went in."

"You're not worse, honey," Martie said, starting the engine. "Believe me, you were a pain in the ass on the way in, too."

"Well, I *feel* worse. I feel like something's coming down on top of us, out of the sky, and I'm going to be crushed by it."

"It's just the rain," Martie said, because the rain drumming on the car was cacophonous.

"Not the rain. Something worse. Some tremendous weight. Just hanging over us. Oh, God, I *hate* this."

"We'll get a bottle of Tsingtao into you."

"That's not going to help."

"Two bottles."

"I need a keg."

"Two kegs. We'll get sloppy together."

Without raising her head, Susan said, "You're a good friend, Martie."

"Let's see if you still think so when we're both committed to some alcohol-rehab hospital."

12

From New Life, in the grip of something close to grief, Dusty went home to change out of his damp work clothes into dry civvies. At the connecting door between the garage and the kitchen, Valet greeted him with doggy enthusiasm, tail wagging so hard that his whole butt swayed. The very sight of the retriever began to bring Dusty out of his internal darkness.

He squatted and gave the dog a nose-to-nose greeting, gently scratching behind the velvety ears, slowly down the crest of the neck to the withers, under the chin, along the dewlaps, and into the thick winter fur on the chest.

He and Valet enjoyed the moment equally. Petting, scratching, and cuddling a dog could be as soothing to the mind and heart as deep meditation—and almost as good for the soul as prayer.

When Dusty plugged in the coffeemaker and began to spoon some good Colombian blend into the filter, Valet rolled onto his back, with all four legs in the air, seeking a belly rub.

"You're a love hog," Dusty said.

Valet's tail swished back and forth across the tile floor.

"I need my fur fix," Dusty admitted, "but right now I need my coffee more. No offense."

His heart seemed to be pumping Freon instead of blood. A chill had settled deep in his flesh and bones; even deeper. Turned up full blast, the van heater hadn't been able to warm him. He was counting on the coffee.

When Valet realized that he wasn't going to receive a belly rub, he got to his feet and padded across the kitchen to the half bath. The door was ajar, and the dog stood with his snout poked through the six-inch gap, sniffing the darkness beyond.

"You've got a perfectly fine water dish there in the corner," Dusty said. "Why do you want to drink out of a toilet?"

Valet glanced back at him, but then returned his attention to the dark bathroom.

As fresh-brewed coffee began to drip into the glass pot, the kitchen filled with a delicious aroma.

Dusty went upstairs and changed into jeans, a white shirt, and a navy-blue wool sweater.

Usually, when only the two of them were in the house, the dog followed him around, hoping for a cuddle, a treat, a play session, or merely a word of praise. This time, Valet remained downstairs.

When Dusty returned to the kitchen, the retriever was still at the door to the half bath. He came to his master's side, watched as Dusty filled a cup with the steaming java, then returned to the bathroom door.

The coffee was strong, rich, and plenty hot, but what warmth it provided was superficial. The ice in Dusty's bones didn't begin to thaw.

In fact, as he leaned against the counter and watched Valet sniffing at the gap between the bathroom door and the jamb, he was overcome by a new and separate coldness. "Something wrong in there, fluffy butt?"

Valet looked at him and whined.

Dusty poured a second cup of coffee, but before sampling it, he went to the bathroom, nudged Valet aside, pushed the door inward, and switched on the light.

A few soiled Kleenex had been emptied out of the brass waste can, into the sink. The can itself lay on its side atop the closed lid of the toilet seat.

Someone apparently had used the waste can to smash the mirror on the medicine cabinet. Jagged shards like solidified lightning blazed across the bathroom floor.

13

When Martie went into the restaurant to get the takeout—moo goo gai pan, Szechuan beef, snow peas and broccoli, rice, and a cold six-pack of Tsingtao—she left Susan in the car, with the engine running and the radio tuned to a station playing classic rock. She had placed the order from her cell phone, en route, and it was ready when she arrived. In respect of the rain, the cardboard containers of food and the beer were packed in two plastic bags.

Even before Martie stepped out of the restaurant, just a few minutes later, the car-radio volume had been cranked so high that she could hear Gary U.S. Bonds belting "School Is Out," saxophones wailing.

She winced when she got into the car. The woofer diaphragms were vibrating so violently in the radio speakers that several loose coins in a change tray jingled against one another.

Left alone in a car, even though she was technically not in an open space, and though she kept her head down and her eyes away from the windows, Susan could often be overwhelmed by an awareness of the vast world beyond. Sometimes loud music helped by distracting her, diminishing her ability to obsess on her fear.

The severity of her attack could be measured by how loud she needed the music to be if it were to help her. This had been a grim seizure: The radio couldn't be turned any louder.

Martie drastically reduced the volume. The driving rhythms and booming melody of "School Is Out" had completely masked the sounds of the storm. Now the drumbeat, maracas rattle, and cymbal hiss of the downpour washed over them again.

Shuddering, breathing raggedly, Susan didn't look up or speak.

Martie said nothing. Sometimes Susan had to be coached, cajoled, counseled, and occasionally even bullied out of her terror. At other times, like this, the best way to help her climb down from the top of the panic ladder was to make no reference to her condition; talking about it propelled her toward an even higher anxiety.

After she had driven a couple of blocks, Martie said, "I got some chopsticks."

"I prefer a fork, thanks."

"Chinese food doesn't taste fully Chinese when you use a fork."

"And cow milk doesn't taste fully like milk unless you squirt it directly into your mouth from the teat."

"You're probably right," Martie said.

"So I'll settle for a reasonable approximation of the authentic taste. I don't mind being a philistine as long as I'm a philistine with a fork."

By the time they parked near her house on Balboa Peninsula, Susan was sufficiently in control of herself to make the trek from the car to her third-floor apartment. Nevertheless, she leaned on Martie all the way, and the journey was grindingly difficult.

Safe in her apartment, with all the blinds and drapes tightly shut, Susan was again able to stand fully erect, with her shoulders drawn back and her head held up. Her face was not wrenched anymore. Although her green eyes remained haunted, they were no longer wild with terror.

"I'll zap the takeout containers in the microwave," Susan said, "if you'll set the table."

In the dining room, as Martie was putting a fork beside Susan's plate, her hand began to shake uncontrollably. The stainless-steel tines rattled against the china.

She dropped the fork on the place mat and stared at it with a queer dread that rapidly escalated into a repulsion so severe that she backed away from the table. The tines were wickedly pointed. She had never before realized how dangerous a simple fork might be in the wrong hands. You could tear out an eye with it. Gouge a face. Shove it into someone's neck and snare the carotid artery as though you were twisting a strand of spaghetti. You could—

Overcome by a desperate need to keep her hands busy, *safely* busy, she opened one of the drawers in the breakfront, located a sixty-four-card pinochle deck used for playing a two-hand game, and took it out of the box. Standing at the dining table, as far from the fork as she could get, she shuffled the deck. At first she repeatedly fumbled, spilling cards across the table, but then her coordination improved.

She couldn't shuffle the cards forever.

Stay busy. Safely busy. Until this strange mood passed.

Trying to conceal her agitation, she went into the kitchen, where Susan was waiting for the microwave timer to buzz. Martie took two bottles of Tsingtao from the refrigerator.

The complex fragrances of Chinese food filled the room.

"Do you think I'm getting the authentic smell of the cuisine when I'm dressed like this?" Susan asked.

"What?"

"Or to *really* smell it, maybe I should put on a cheongsam."

"Ho, ho," Martie said, because she was too rattled to think of a witty reply.

She almost put the two bottles of beer on the cutting board by the sink, to open them, but the mezzaluna was still there, its wicked crescent edge gleaming. Her heart hammered almost painfully hard at the sight of the knife.

Instead, she set the beers on the small kitchen table. She got two glasses from a cabinet and put them beside the beers.

Stay busy.

She searched through a drawer full of small utensils until she found a bottle opener. She plucked it from among the other items, and returned to the table.

The opener was rounded on one end, for bottles. The other end was pointed and hooked, for cans.

By the time she reached the kitchen table, the pointed end of the opener appeared to be as murderous an instrument as the fork, as the mezzaluna. She quickly put it beside the Tsingtaos before it dropped out of her trembling hand or she threw it down in horror.

"Will you open the beers?" she asked on her way out of the kitchen, leaving before Susan could see her troubled face. "I've got to use the john."

Crossing the dining room, she avoided looking at the table, on which the fork lay, tines up.

In the hallway leading off the living room, she averted her eyes from the mirrored sliding doors on the closet.

The bathroom. Another mirror.

She almost backed out into the hall. She could think of nowhere else to go to collect her wits in private, however, and she didn't want Susan to see her in this condition.

Summoning the courage to confront the mirror, she found nothing to fear. The anxiety in her face and eyes was distressing, although not as evident as she had thought it must be.

Martie quickly closed the door, lowered the lid on the toilet, and sat down. Only when her breath burst from her in a raw gasp did she realize that she'd been holding it for a long time.

14

Upon discovering the shattered mirror in the half bath off the kitchen, Dusty first thought that a vandal or a burglar was in the house.

Valet's demeanor didn't support that suspicion. His hackles weren't raised. Indeed, the dog had been in a playful mood when Dusty first came home.

On the other hand, Valet was a love sponge, not a serious watchdog. If he had taken a liking to an intruder—as he did to ninety percent of the people he met—he would have followed the guy around, licking his larcenous hands as the family treasures were loaded into gunnysacks.

With the dog trailing after him this time, Dusty searched the house room by room, closet by closet, first the lower floor and then the upper. He found no one, no further vandalism, and nothing missing.

Dusty instructed the obedient Valet to wait in a far corner of the kitchen, to prevent him from getting slivers of glass in his paws. Then he cleaned up the mess in the half bath.

Maybe Martie would be able to explain the mirror when Dusty saw her later. It must have been an accident of some kind, which had happened just before she'd needed to leave for Susan's place. Either that, or an angry ghost had moved in with them.

They would have a lot to talk about over dinner: Skeet's

would-be suicide plunge, another expedition with Susan, poltergeists . . .

Doing deep-breathing exercises in Susan's bathroom, Martie decided that the problem was stress. Most likely that was the explanation for all this. She had so much on her mind, so many responsibilities.

Designing a new game based on *The Lord of the Rings* was the most important and difficult job she'd ever undertaken. And it came with a series of looming deadlines that put a lot of pressure on her, perhaps more pressure than she had realized until now.

Her mother, Sabrina, and the endless antagonism toward Dusty: That stress had been with her a long time, too.

And last year, she'd had to watch her beloved father succumb to cancer. The last three months of his life had been a relentless, gruesome decline, which he had endured with his customary good humor, refusing to acknowledge any of the pains or the indignities of his condition. His soft laughter and his charm had, in those final days, failed to buoy her as they usually did; instead, his ready smile had pierced her heart each time she saw it, and though from those wounds she had lost no blood, a little of her lifelong optimism had bled away and had not yet been entirely replenished.

Susan, of course, was a source of more than a little stress. Love was a sacred garment, woven of a fabric so thin that it could not be seen, yet so strong that even mighty death could not tear it, a garment that could not be frayed by use, that brought warmth into what would otherwise be an intolerably cold world—but at times love could also be as heavy as chain mail. Bearing the burden of love, on those occasions when it was a solemn weight, made it more precious when, in better times, it caught the wind in sleeves like wings—and lifted you.

In spite of the stress of these twice-weekly outings, she could no more walk away from Susan Jagger than she could have turned her back on her dying father, on her difficult mother, or on Dusty.

She would go out to the dining room, eat Chinese food, drink a bottle of beer, play pinochle, and pretend that she was not full of strange forebodings.

When she got home, she'd call Dr. Closterman, her internist, and make an appointment for a physical examination, just in case her self-diagnosis of stress was incorrect. She felt physically fit, but so had Smilin' Bob just before the sudden onset of a curious little pain that had signaled terminal illness.

Crazy as it sounded, she was still suspicious of that unusually sour grapefruit juice. She'd been drinking it most mornings lately, instead of orange juice, because of the lower calorie count. Maybe that explained the dream about the Leaf Man, too: the raging figure formed of dead, rotting leaves. Perhaps she would give a sample of the juice to Dr. Closterman to have it tested.

Finally she washed her hands and confronted the mirror again. She thought that she appeared passably sane. Regardless of how she looked, however, she still *felt* like a hopeless nutcase.

After Dusty finished sweeping up the broken mirror, he gave Valet a special treat for being a good boy and staying out of the way: a few pieces of roasted chicken breast left over from dinner the previous night. The retriever took each bit of meat from his master's hand with a delicacy almost equal to that of a hummingbird sipping sugar water from a garden feeder, and when it was all gone, he gazed up at Dusty with an adoration that could not have been much less than the love with which the angels regard God.

"And you are an angel, all right," Dusty said, as he gently scratched under Valet's chin. "A furry angel. And with ears that big, you don't need wings."

He decided to take the dog with him to Skeet's apartment and then to New Life. Although no intruder was in the house, Dusty didn't feel comfortable leaving the pooch here alone, until he knew what had happened to the mirror.

"Man, if I'm this overprotective with you," he said to Valet, "can you imagine how impossible I'm going to be with kids?"

The dog grinned as though he liked the idea of kids. And as if he understood that he was to ride shotgun on this trip, he went to the connecting door between the kitchen and the garage, where he stood patiently fanning the air with his plumed tail.

As Dusty was pulling on a hooded nylon jacket, the telephone rang. He answered it.

When he hung up, he said, "Trying to sell me a subscription to the L.A. *Times*," as though the dog needed to know who had called.

Valet was no longer standing at the door to the garage. He was lying in front of it, half settled into a nap, as though Dusty had been on the phone ten minutes rather than thirty seconds.

Frowning, Dusty said, "You had a shot of chicken protein, golden one. Let's see some vigor."

With a long-suffering sigh, Valet stood.

In the garage, as he buckled the collar around the dog's neck and snapped a leash to it, Dusty said, "Last thing I need is a daily newspaper. Do you know what newspapers are full of, golden one?"

Valet looked clueless.

"They are full of the stuff newsmakers do. And do you know who the newsmakers are? Politicians and media types and big-university intellectuals, people who think too much of themselves and think too much in general. People like Dr.

Trevor Penn Rhodes, my old man. And people like Dr. Holden Caulfield, Skeet's old man."

The dog sneezed.

"Exactly," Dusty said.

He didn't expect Valet to ride in the back of the van, among the painting tools and supplies. Instead, the mutt jumped onto the front seat; he enjoyed gazing out the windshield when he traveled. Dusty buckled the safety harness around the retriever, and received a face-lick of thanks before closing the passenger door.

Behind the wheel, as he started the engine and backed out of the garage into the rain, he said, "Newsmakers screw up the world while trying to save it. You know what all their deep thinking amounts to, golden one? It amounts to the same thing we scoop up in those little blue bags when we follow you around."

The dog grinned at him.

Pressing the remote control to close the garage door, Dusty wondered why he hadn't said all this to the telephone salesperson who had been pushing the newspaper. Those incessant calls from the *Times* subscription hawkers were one of the few serious drawbacks to living in southern California, on a par with earthquakes, wildfires, and mudslides. If he'd delivered this same rant to the woman—or had it been a man?—pitching the *Times*, maybe his name would finally have been removed from their solicitation list.

As he backed out of the driveway into the street, Dusty had the peculiar realization that he couldn't recall whether the *Times* representative on the phone had been a man or a woman. No reason why he should remember, really, since he had listened only to enough of the spiel to realize what it was, whereupon he had hung up.

Usually, he ended a *Times* call by making a proposition, to have fun with the salesperson. *Okay, I'll subscribe if you'll take barter. I'll paint one of your offices, you give me three years of the* Times. *Or, yeah, I'll take a* lifetime *subscription if your paper promises never again to refer to a mere sports star as a* hero.

He hadn't made them a proposition this time. On the other hand, he couldn't remember what he *had* said, even if it was as simple as *no thanks* or *stop bothering me.*

Odd. His mind was blank.

Evidently, he was even more preoccupied with—and disturbed by—the business with Skeet this morning than he had realized.

15

The Chinese takeout was no doubt as delicious as Susan said it was, but although Martie, too, exclaimed over it, she actually found the food flavorless. The Tsingtao tasted bitter today.

Neither the food nor the beer was at fault. Martie's free-floating anxiety, although ebbing at the moment, robbed her of the ability to take pleasure in anything.

She ate with chopsticks, and at first she thought that merely watching Susan use a fork would induce another panic attack. But the sight of the wicked tines didn't alarm her, after all, as it had earlier. She had no fear of the fork, per se; she was afraid, instead, of what damage could be done with the fork *if it were in her own hand.* In Susan's possession, the utensil seemed harmless.

The apprehension that she, Martie herself, harbored the dark potential for some unspeakable act of violence was so disturbing that she refused to dwell on it. This was the most irrational of fears, for she was certain in mind and heart and soul that she had no capacity for savagery. And yet she had not trusted herself with the bottle opener. . . .

Considering how edgy she was—and how hard she was trying not to reveal that edginess to Susan—she should have been an even bigger loser at pinochle than usual. Instead, the cards favored her, and she played with masterful skill, taking full advantage of each piece of good luck, perhaps because the game helped to distract her from morbid considerations.

"You're a champ today," Susan said.

"I'm wearing my lucky socks."

"Already your debt is down from six hundred thousand to five hundred and ninety-eight thousand."

"Great. Now maybe Dusty will be able to sleep at night."

"How is Dusty?"

"Even sweeter than Valet."

"You get a man who's more lovable than a golden retriever." Susan sighed. "And I marry a selfish pig."

"Earlier, you were defending Eric."

"He's a swine."

"That's my line."

"And I thank you for it."

Outside, a wolfish wind growled, scratched on the windows, and raised mournful howls to the eaves.

Martie said, "Why the change of heart?"

"The root of my agoraphobia might lie in problems between Eric and me, going back a couple years, things I've been in denial about."

"Is that what Dr. Ahriman says?"

"He doesn't really direct me toward ideas like that. He just makes it possible for me to . . . figure it out."

Martie played a queen of clubs. "You never mentioned problems between you and Eric. Not until he wasn't able to handle . . . this."

"But I guess we had them."

Martie frowned. "You *guess*?"

"Well, there's no guessing. We had a problem."

"Pinochle," Martie said, taking the last trick. "What problem?"

"A woman."

Martie was stunned. Real sisters could be no closer than she and Susan. Although they both had too much self-respect to share intimate details of their sex lives, they never kept big secrets from each other, yet she'd never before heard of this woman.

"The creep was cheating on you?" Martie asked.

"A discovery like that, all of a sudden, it makes you feel so vulnerable," Susan said, but without the emotion the words implied, as though quoting a psychology textbook. "And that's what agoraphobia is about—an overwhelming, crippling feeling of vulnerability."

"You never even hinted at this."

Susan shrugged. "Maybe I was too ashamed."

"Ashamed? What would *you* have to be ashamed about?"

"Oh, I don't know. . . ." She looked puzzled and finally said, "Why *would* I feel ashamed?"

To Martie it appeared, amazingly, as though Susan were thinking this through for the first time, right here, right now.

"Well . . . I guess maybe because . . . because I wasn't enough for him, not good enough in bed for him."

Martie gaped at her. "Who am I talking to? You're gorgeous, Sooz, you're erotic, you have a healthy sex drive—"

"Or maybe I wasn't there for him emotionally, wasn't supportive enough?"

Pushing the cards aside without totaling the points, Martie said, "I don't believe what I'm hearing."

"I'm not perfect, Martie. Far from it." A sorrow, quiet but as heavy and gray as lead, pressed her voice thin. She lowered her eyes, as though embarrassed. "I failed him somehow."

Her contrition seemed profoundly inappropriate, and her words angered Martie. "You give him everything—your body, your mind, your heart, your life—and you give it in that totally over-the-top, all-or-nothing, passionate Susan Jagger trademark style. Then he cheats on you, and you blame *yourself*?"

Frowning, turning an empty beer bottle around and around in her slender hands, gazing at it as though it were a talisman that might, with sufficient handling, magically provide full understanding, Susan said, "Maybe you've just put your finger on it, Martie. Maybe the trademark Susan Jagger style just . . . smothered him."

"Smothered him? Give me a break."

"No, maybe it did. Maybe—"

"What's with all these maybes?" Martie asked. "Why are you inventing a series of excuses for the pig? What was *his* excuse?"

Hard shatters of rain made tuneless music against the windowpanes, and from a distance came the ominous, rhythmic booming of storm waves hammering the shore.

"What was *his* excuse?" Martie pressed.

Susan turned the beer bottle more slowly than before, and now slower still, and when at last she stopped turning it altogether, she was frowning in evident confusion.

Martie said, "Susan? What was his excuse?"

Putting the bottle aside, gazing at her hands as she folded them on the table, Susan said, "His excuse? Well . . . I don't know."

"We're all the way down the rabbit hole and at the tea party," Martie declared, exasperated. "What do you *mean* you don't know? Honey, you catch him having an affair, and you don't want to know *why*?"

Susan shifted uneasily in her chair. "We didn't talk about it much."

"Are you serious? That isn't you, girlfriend. You're no milquetoast."

Susan spoke more slowly than usual, with a thickness of tone like that in the voice of a freshly roused sleeper who was not yet fully awake: "Well, we talked about it a little, you know, and this could be the cause of my agoraphobia, but we didn't talk the dirty details."

This conversation had grown so deeply strange that

Martie sensed a hidden and perilous truth in it, an elusive insight that would suddenly explain all of this troubled woman's problems, if only she could grasp it.

Susan's statements were simultaneously outrageous and vague. Disturbingly vague.

"What was this woman's name?" Martie asked.

"I don't know."

"Good God. Eric didn't tell you?"

Finally Susan raised her head. Her eyes were unfocused, as though she were staring at someone other than Martie, in another place and time. "Eric?"

Susan had spoken the name with such puzzlement that Martie turned in her chair to survey the room behind her, expecting to find that Eric had silently entered. He wasn't there.

"Yeah, Sooz, remember old Eric? Hubby. Adulterer. Swine."

"I didn't . . ."

"What?"

Now Susan's voice faded to a whisper, and her face was eerily devoid of expression, as inanimate as the face of a doll. "I didn't learn about this from Eric."

"Then who told you?"

No reply.

The wind dropped, not shrieking anymore. But its cold whispering and sly cooing knotted the nerves more effectively than had its voice at full bleat.

"Sooz? Who told you Eric was screwing around?"

Susan's flawless skin was no longer the color of peaches and cream, but as pale and translucent as skimmed milk. A single drop of perspiration appeared at her hairline.

Reaching across the table, Martie held one hand in front of her friend's face.

Susan apparently didn't see it. She stared *through* the hand.

"Who?" Martie gently insisted.

Suddenly, numerous beads of sweat were strung across Susan's brow. Her hands had been folded on the table, but now they were fiercely clenched, the skin stretched tight and white across the knuckles, the fingernails of her right hand digging hard into the flesh of her left.

Ghost spiders crawled along the back of Martie's neck and crept down the staircase of her spine.

"Who told you Eric was screwing around?"

Still staring at some specter, Susan tried to speak but could not get a word out. Her mouth turned soft, trembled, as though she were about to break into tears.

Susan seemed to have been silenced by a phantom hand. The sense of another presence in the room was so powerful that Martie wanted to turn again and look behind her; but no one would be there.

Her hand was still raised in front of Susan. She snapped her fingers.

Susan twitched, blinked. She looked at the cards that Martie had pushed aside, and incredibly she smiled. "Whipped my ass good. You want another beer?"

Her demeanor had changed in an instant.

Martie said, "You didn't answer my question."

"What question?"

"Who told you Eric was screwing around?"

"Oh, Martie, this is too boring."

"I don't find it boring. You—"

"I won't talk about this," Susan said with airy dismissiveness, rather than with anger or embarrassment, either of which would have seemed more appropriate. She waved one hand as if she were chasing off a bothersome fly. "I'm sorry I brought it up."

"Good grief, Sooz, you can't drop a bombshell like that and then just—"

"I'm in a good mood. I don't want to spoil it. Let's talk Martha Stewart crap or gossip, or something frivolous." She sprang up from her chair almost girlishly. On the way into the kitchen, she said, "What was your decision on that beer?"

This was one of those days when being sober didn't have a lot of appeal, but Martie declined a second Tsingtao anyway.

In the kitchen, Susan began singing "New Attitude," Patti LaBelle's classic tune. Her voice was good, and she sang with buoyant conviction, especially when the lyrics claimed *I'm in control, my worries are few.*

Even if Martie had known nothing about Susan Jagger, she was sure that nevertheless she would have detected a note of falseness in this apparently cheerful singing. When she thought of how Susan had looked only minutes ago—in that trancelike state, unable to speak, skin as pale as a death mask, brow beaded with sweat, eyes focused on a distant time or place, hands clawing at each other—this abrupt transition from catatonia to exuberance was eerie.

In the kitchen, Susan sang, " 'Feelin' good from my head to my shoes.' "

Maybe the shoes part. Not the head.

16

Dusty never failed to be surprised by Skeet's apartment. The three small rooms and bath were almost obsessively well ordered and scrupulously clean. Skeet was such a shambling wreck, physically and psychologically, that Dusty always expected to find this place in chaos.

While his master packed two bags with clothes and toiletries, Valet toured the rooms, sniffing the floors and furniture, enjoying the pungent aromas of waxes and polishes and cleaning fluids that were different from the brands used in the Rhodeses' home.

Finished with the packing, Dusty checked the contents of the refrigerator, which appeared to have been stocked by a terminal anorexic. The only quart of milk was already three days past the freshness date stamped on the carton, and he poured it down the drain. He fed a half loaf of white bread to the garbage disposal, and followed it with the hideously mottled contents of an open package of bologna that looked as if it would soon grow hair and growl. Beer, soft drinks, and condiments accounted for everything else in the fridge; and all of it would still be fresh when Skeet came home.

On the counter next to the kitchen phone, Dusty found the only disorder in the apartment: a messy scattering of loose pages from a notepad. As he gathered them, he saw that the same name had been written on each piece of paper, sometimes only once, but more often three or four times.

On fourteen sheets of paper, one—and only one—name appeared thirty-nine times: *Dr. Yen Lo.* None of the fourteen pages featured a phone number or any additional message.

The handwriting was recognizably Skeet's. On a few pages, the script was fluid and neat. On others, it appeared as if Skeet's hand had been a little unsteady; furthermore, he had borne down hard with the pen, impressing the seven letters deep into the paper. Curiously, on fully half the pages, *Dr. Yen Lo* was inscribed with such apparent emotion—and perhaps struggle—that some letters were virtually slashed onto the paper, gouging it.

A cheap ballpoint pen also lay on the counter. The transparent plastic casing had snapped in two. The flexible ink cartridge, which had popped out of the broken pen, was bent in the middle.

Frowning, Dusty swept the counter with his hand, gathering the pieces of the pen into a small pile.

He spent only a minute sorting the fourteen sheets from the notepad, putting the neatest sample of writing on top, the messiest on the bottom, ordering the other twelve in the most obvious fashion. There was an unmistakable progression in the deterioration of the handwriting. On the bottom page, the name appeared only once and was incomplete—*Dr. Ye*—probably because the pen had broken at the start of the *n*.

The obvious deduction was that Skeet had become increasingly angry or distressed until finally he exerted such ferocious pressure on the pen that it snapped.

Distress, not anger.

Skeet didn't have a problem with anger. Quite the opposite.

He was gentle by nature, and his temperament had been further cooked to the consistency of sweet pudding by the pharmacopoeia of behavior-modification drugs to which a fearsome series of clinical psychologists with aggressive-treatment philosophies had subjected him, with the enthusiastic encouragement of Skeet's dear old dad, Dr. Holden Caulfield, alias Sam Farner. The kid's sense of self was so faded by years of relentless chemical bleaching that it could not hold red anger in its fibers; the meanest offense, which would enrage the average man, drew from Skeet nothing more than a shrug and a fragile smile of resignation. The bitterness he felt toward his father, which was the closest to anger that he would ever come, had sustained him through his search for the truth of the professor's origins, but it hadn't been potent enough or enduring enough to give him the strength to confront the phony bastard with his discoveries.

Dusty carefully folded the fourteen pages from the notepad, slipped them into a pocket of his jeans, and scooped the fragments of the pen off the counter. The ballpoint was inexpensive but not poorly made. The one-piece transparent plastic casing was rigid and strong. The pressure required to snap it like a dry twig would have been tremendous.

Skeet was incapable of the necessary rage, and it was difficult to imagine what could have caused him such extreme distress that he would have pressed down on the ballpoint with the requisite ferocity.

After a hesitation, Dusty threw the broken pen in the trash.

Valet stuck his snout in the waste can, sniffing to determine if the discarded item might be edible.

Dusty opened a drawer and withdrew a telephone directory, the Yellow Pages. He looked under PHYSICIANS for Dr. Yen Lo, but no such entry existed.

He tried PSYCHIATRISTS. Then PSYCHOLOGISTS. Then finally THERAPISTS. No luck.

17

While Susan put the pinochle deck and score pad away, Martie rinsed the lunch plates and the takeout cartons, trying not to look at the mezzaluna on the nearby cutting board.

Susan brought her fork into the kitchen. "You forgot this."

Because Martie was already drying her hands, Susan washed the fork and put it away.

While Susan drank a second beer, Martie sat with her in the living room. Susan's idea of background music was Glenn Gould on piano, playing Bach's *Goldberg Variations.*

As a young girl, Susan had dreamed of being a musician with a major symphony orchestra. She was a fine violinist; not world-class, not so great that she could be the featured performer on a concert tour, but fine enough to ensure that her more modest dream could have become a reality. Somehow, she had settled for real-estate sales instead.

Even until late in her final year of high school, Martie had wanted to be a veterinarian. Now she designed video games.

Life offers infinite possible roads. Sometimes your head chooses the route, sometimes your heart. And sometimes, for better or worse, neither head nor heart can resist the stubborn pull of fate.

From time to time, Gould's exquisite sprays of silvery notes reminded Martie that although the wind had diminished, cold rain was still falling outside, beyond the heavily draped windows. The apartment was so cloistered and cozy that she was tempted to succumb to the dangerously comforting notion that no world existed beyond these protective walls.

She and Susan talked about the old days, old friends. They devoted not a word to the future.

Susan wasn't a serious drinker. Two beers were, to her, a binge. Usually, she got neither giddy nor mean with drink, but pleasantly sentimental. This time, she became steadily quieter and solemn.

Soon, Martie was doing most of the talking. To her own ear, she sounded increasingly inane, so at last she stopped babbling.

Their friendship was deep enough to make them comfortable with silence. This silence, however, had a weird and edgy quality, perhaps because Martie was surreptitiously watching her friend for signs of the trancelike condition that had previously overtaken her.

She couldn't bear to listen to the *Goldberg Variations* yet again, because suddenly the music's piercing beauty was depressing. Strangely, for her, it had come to signify loss, loneliness, and quiet desperation. The apartment quickly became stifling rather than cozy, claustrophobic rather than comforting.

When Susan used the remote control to replay the same CD, Martie consulted her watch and recited a series of nonexistent errands to which she must attend before five o'clock.

In the kitchen, after Martie slipped into her raincoat, she and Susan embraced, as they always did on parting. This time the hug was more fierce than usual, as though both of them were trying to convey a great many important and deeply felt things that neither was able to express in words.

As Martie turned the knob, Susan stepped behind the door, where she would be shielded from a glimpse of the fearsome world outside. With a note of anguish, as if suddenly deciding to reveal a troubling secret that she had been keeping with difficulty, she said, "He's coming here at night, when I'm asleep."

Martie had opened the door two inches. She closed it but left her hand on the knob. "Say what? Who's coming here while you're asleep?"

The green of Susan's eyes seemed to be an icier shade than before, the color having been intensified and clarified by some new fear. "I mean, I think he is." Susan lowered her gaze to the floor. Color had risen in her pale cheeks. "I don't have proof it's him, but who else could it be but Eric?"

Turning away from the door, Martie said, "Eric comes here at night while you're asleep?"

"He says he doesn't, but I think he's lying."

"He has a key?"

"I didn't give him one."

"And you've changed the locks."

"Yeah. But somehow he gets in."

"Windows?"

"In the morning . . . when I realize he's been here, I check all the windows, but they're always locked."

"How do you know he's been here? I mean, what's he do?"

Instead of answering, Susan said, "He comes . . . sneaking around . . . sneaking, slinking like some mongrel dog." She shuddered.

Martie was no great fan of Eric's, but she had difficulty picturing him slinking up the stairs at night and slithering into the apartment as if through a keyhole. For one thing, he didn't have sufficient imagination to figure out an undetectable way to slip in here; he was an investment adviser with a head full of numbers and data, but with no sense of mystery. Besides, he knew Susan kept a handgun in her nightstand, and he was highly aversive to risk; he was the least likely of men to take a chance at being shot as a burglar, even if he might harbor a twisted desire to torment his wife.

"Do you find things disturbed in the morning—or what?"

Susan didn't reply.

"You never heard him in the apartment? You never woke up when he's been here?"

"No."

"So in the morning there are . . . clues?"

"Clues," Susan agreed, but offered no specifics.

"Like things out of order? The smell of his cologne? Stuff like that?"

Still staring at the floor, Susan nodded.

"But exactly what?" Martie persisted.

No answer.

"Hey, Sooz, could you look at me?"

When Susan raised her face, she was blushing brightly, not as if with mere embarrassment, but as if with shame.

"Sooz, what aren't you telling me?"

"Nothing. I'm just . . . being paranoid, I guess."

"There *is* something you're not saying. Why bring it up at all, and then hold out on me?"

Susan hugged herself and shivered. "I thought I was ready to talk about this, but I'm not. I've still got to . . . work some things out in my head."

"Eric sneaking in here at night—that's a weird damn thing. It's creepy. What would he be doing—watching you sleep?"

"Later, Martie. I've got to think this through a little more, work up the courage. I'll call you later."

"Now."

"You've got all those errands."

"They're not important."

Susan frowned. "They sounded like they were pretty important a minute ago."

Martie wasn't capable of hurting Susan's feelings by admitting that she had invented the errands as an excuse to get out of this dreary, suffocating place, into fresh air and the invigorating chill of cold rain. "If you don't call me later and tell me all of it, every last detail, then I'll drive back here tonight and sit on your chest and read you pages and pages of the latest book of literary criticism by Dusty's old man. It's *The Meaning of Meaninglessness: Chaos as Structure*, and halfway through *any* paragraph, you'll swear that fire ants are crawling across the surface of your brain. Or what about *Dare to Be Your Own Best Friend*? That's his stepfather's latest. Listen to that one on audiotape, and it'll make you want to cut off your ears. They're a family of writing fools, and I *could* inflict them on you."

Smiling thinly, Susan said, "I'm suitably terrified. I'll call you for sure."

"Guaranteed?"

"My solemn oath."

Martie grasped the knob again, but she didn't open the door. "Are you safe here, Sooz?"

"Of course," Susan said, but Martie thought she saw a flicker of uncertainty in those haunted green eyes.

"But if he's sneaking—"

"Eric's still my husband," Susan said.

"Watch the news. Some husbands do terrible things."

"You know Eric. Maybe he's a pig—"

"He *is* a pig," Martie insisted.

"—but he's not dangerous."

"He's a wimp."

"Exactly."

Martie hesitated but then finally cracked open the door. "We'll be finished with dinner by eight o'clock, maybe sooner. In bed by eleven, as usual. I'll be waiting for your call."

"Thanks, Martie."

"De nada."

"Give Dusty a kiss for me."

"It'll be a dry peck on the cheek. All the good wet stuff comes strictly from me."

Martie pulled her hood over her head, stepped out onto the landing, and drew the door shut behind her.

The air had grown still, as though the wind had been pressed out of the day by this enormous weight of falling rain, which came down like cataracts of iron pellets.

She waited until she heard Susan engage the dead bolt, a solid Schlage lock that would hold against serious assault. Then she quickly descended the long, steep flight of stairs.

At the bottom, she stopped, turned, and peered up toward the landing and the apartment door.

Susan Jagger seemed like a beautiful princess in a fairy tale, imprisoned in a tower, besieged by trolls and malevolent spirits, with no brave prince to save her.

As the gray day reverberated with the ceaseless booming of big storm waves on the nearby shore, Martie hurried along the beach promenade to the nearest street, where gutters overflowed and dirty water churned around the tires of her red Saturn.

She hoped Dusty had taken advantage of the bad weather to be domestic and to make his incomparable meatballs and spicy tomato sauce. Nothing would be more reassuring than stepping into the house and seeing him in a cooking apron, a glass of red wine near at hand. The air would be full of delicious aromas. Good retro pop music—maybe Dean Martin—on the stereo. Dusty's smile, his embrace, his kiss. After this bizarre day, she needed all the cozy reassurances of home and hearth and husband.

As Martie started the car, a sickening vision blazed through her mind, burning away all hope that the day might yet bring her a small measure of peace and reassurance. This was more real than an ordinary mental picture, so detailed and intense that it seemed as if it were happening right here, right now. She was convinced that she was flashing forward to a terrible incident that *would* happen, receiving a glimpse of an inevitable moment in the future, toward which she was plunging as surely as if she'd thrown herself off a cliff. When she thrust the key into the ignition, her mind filled with an image of an eye pierced by the wicked point of the key, gouged by the serrated edge, which sank into the brain behind the eye. Even as she jammed the key into the car ignition, she twisted it, and simultaneously the key in her vivid premonition also twisted in the eye.

Without any conscious awareness of having opened the door, Martie found herself out of the car, leaning against the side of it, bringing up her lunch onto the rainwashed street.

She stood there for a long while, head bent.

Her raincoat hood had slipped back. Soon her hair was soaked.

When she was sure that she was fully purged, she reached into the car, plucked tissues from a box of Kleenex, and wiped her lips.

She always kept a small bottle of water in the car. Now she used it to rinse out her mouth.

Though still a little queasy, she got into the Saturn and pulled the door shut.

The engine was idling. She wouldn't have to touch the key again until she was parked in her garage in Corona Del Mar.

Wet, cold, miserable, frightened, confused, she wanted more than anything to be safe at home, to be dry and warm and among familiar things.

She was shaking too much to drive. She waited almost fifteen minutes before she finally released the hand brake and put the car in gear.

Although she desperately wanted to go home, she was

afraid of what might happen when she got there. No. She was being dishonest with herself. She wasn't afraid of what would *happen.* She was afraid of *what she might do.*

The eye that she had seen in her premonition—if, indeed, that's what it had been—was not merely any eye. It had been a distinctive shade of gray-blue, lustrous and beautiful. Just like Dusty's eyes.

18

At New Life Clinic, the positive psychological influences provided by animals were thought to be useful in certain cases, and Valet was welcome. Dusty parked near the portico, and by the time they got into the building, they were only slightly damp, which was a disappointment to the dog. Valet was a retriever, after all, with webbed feet, a love of water, and enough aquatic talent to qualify him for the Olympic synchronized-swimming team.

In his second-floor quarters, Skeet was fast asleep atop the covers, fully clothed, shoes off.

The bleak winter afternoon pressed its fading face to the window, and shadows gathered in the room. The only other light issued from a small battery-powered reading lamp clipped to the book that Tom Wong, the male nurse, was reading.

After scratching Valet behind the ears, Tom took advantage of their visit to go on a break.

Dusty quietly unpacked both suitcases, stowed the contents in dresser drawers, and took up the vigil in the armchair. Valet settled at his feet.

Two hours of daylight remained, but the shadows in the corners spun expanding webs until Dusty switched on the pharmacy lamp beside the chair.

Although Skeet was curled in the fetal position, he looked not like a child, but like a desiccated corpse, so gaunt and thin that his clothes appeared to be draped over a fleshless skeleton.

Going home, Martie drove with extreme care not only because of the bad weather but also because of her condition. The prospect of a sudden-onset anxiety attack at sixty miles an hour was daunting. Fortunately, no freeways connected the Balboa Peninsula with Corona Del Mar; the entire trip was on surface streets, and she remained behind the slowest-moving vehicles.

On Pacific Coast Highway, before she was even halfway home, traffic came to a complete stop. Forty or fifty cars ahead, the revolving red and blue emergency beacons of ambulances and police cars marked the site of an accident.

Caught in the jam-up, she used her cell phone to call Dr. Closterman, her internist, hoping to get an appointment the next day, in the morning if possible. "It's something of an emergency. I mean, I'm not in pain or anything, but I'd rather see him about this as soon as possible."

"What're your symptoms?" the receptionist asked.

Martie hesitated. "This is pretty personal. I'd rather talk about it only with Dr. Closterman."

"He's gone for the day, but we could squeeze you in the schedule about eight-thirty in the morning."

"Thank you. I'll be there," Martie said, and she terminated the call.

A thin shroud of gray fog billowed in from the harbor, and needles of rain stitched it around the body of the dying day.

From the direction of the accident, an ambulance approached along the oncoming lanes, which contained little traffic.

Neither the siren nor the emergency beacons were in operation. Evidently the patient was beyond all medical help, not actually a patient anymore, but a package bound for a mortuary.

Solemnly, Martie watched the vehicle pass in the rain, and then turned her gaze to the side mirror, where the taillights dwindled in the mist. She had no way of knowing for sure that the ambulance was indeed now a morgue wagon; nevertheless, she was convinced that it held a corpse. She felt Death passing by.

As he watched over Skeet while waiting for Tom Wong to return, the last thing Dusty wanted to think about was the past, yet his mind drifted back to the childhood he'd shared with Skeet, to Skeet's imperial father—and, worse, to the man who had followed that bastard as head of the household. Husband number four. Dr. Derek Lampton, neo-Freudian psychologist, psychiatrist, lecturer, and author.

Their mother, Claudette, had a fondness for intellectuals—especially for those who were also megalomaniacs.

Skeet's father, the false Holden, had lasted until Skeet was nine years old and Dusty was fourteen. The two of them celebrated his departure by staying up all night, watching scary movies, eating bales of potato chips and buckets of Baskin-Robbins chocolate-peanut-butter ice cream, which had been verboten under the strict low-fat, no-salt, no-sugar, no-additives, no-fun Nazi diet enforced for all kids—though not adults—during his dictatorship. In the morning, half nauseated from their gluttony, grainy-eyed with exhaustion, but giddy with their newfound freedom, they managed to stay awake a few extra hours in order to search the neighborhood until they accumulated two pounds of dog droppings, which they hermetically boxed and posted to the deposed despot's new digs.

Although the package was sent anonymously, with a false return address, they figured that the professor might deduce the identities of the senders, because after enough double martinis, he sometimes bemoaned his son's learning disability by claiming that a reeking pile of manure had greater potential for academic accomplishment than did Skeet: *You are about as erudite as excrement, boy, no more scholarly than a stool sample, as cultured as crap, less comprehending than cow chips, as perceptive as poop.* By sending him the box of dog waste, they were challenging him to put his lofty educational theories to work and transform the dog droppings into a better student than Skeet.

Days after the counterfeit Caulfield's butt was kicked out into the rye field, Dr. Lampton took up residence. Because all the adults were excruciatingly civilized and eager to facilitate one another's quests for personal fulfillment, Claudette announced to her children that a quick and uncontested divorce would be followed immediately by a new marriage.

Dusty and Skeet ceased all celebration. Within twenty-four hours, they knew that soon the day would come when they would be nostalgic for the golden age during which they had been marked by the ruling thumb of the humbug Holden, because Dr. Derek Lampton would no doubt brand them with his traditional ID number: 666.

Now Skeet brought Dusty back from the past: "You look like you just ate a worm. What're you thinking about?"

He was still in the fetal position on the bed, but his rheumy eyes were open.

"Lizard Lampton," Dusty said.

"Oh, man, you think too much about him, and I'll be trying to talk *you* down from a roof." Skeet swung his legs off the bed and sat up.

Valet went to Skeet and licked his trembling hands.

"How're you feeling?" Dusty asked.

"Postsuicidal."

"Post is good." Dusty withdrew two lottery tickets from his shirt pocket and offered them to Skeet. "As promised.

Picked these up at the convenience store near here, where they sold the big winning ticket last November. That thirty-million-dollar jackpot."

"Keep them away from me. My touch'll suck the luck right out of 'em."

Dusty went to the nightstand, opened the drawer, and withdrew the Bible. He paged through it, scanning the verses, and then read a line from Jeremiah: " 'Blessed is the man who trusts in God.' How's that?"

"Well, I've learned not to trust in methamphetamines."

"That's progress," Dusty said. He tucked the pair of tickets into the Bible, at the page from which he'd read, closed the book, and returned it to the drawer.

Skeet got up from the bed and tottered toward the bathroom. "Gotta pee."

"Gotta watch."

Turning on the bathroom light, Skeet said, "Don't worry, bro. Nothing in here I could kill myself with."

"You might try to flush yourself down the john," Dusty said, stepping into the open doorway.

"Or make a hangman's noose out of toilet paper."

"See, you're too clever. You require diligent security."

The toilet had a sealed tank and a button-flush mechanism: no parts that could be easily disassembled to locate a metal edge sharp enough to slash a wrist.

A minute later, as Skeet was washing his hands, Dusty withdrew the folded pages of the notepad from his pocket and read aloud Skeet's handwritten message: "Dr. Yen Lo."

The bar of soap slipped out of Skeet's grip, into the sink. He didn't try to pick it up. He leaned against the sink, his hands under the spout, water sluicing the lather off his fingers.

He had said something as he dropped the soap, but his words had not been clear over the sound of the running water.

Dusty cocked his head. "What'd you say?"

Raising his voice slightly, Skeet repeated: "I'm listening."

Puzzled by that response, Dusty asked, "Who's Dr. Yen Lo?"

Skeet didn't reply.

His back was to Dusty. Because his head was bowed, his face couldn't be seen in the mirror. He seemed to be staring at his hands, which he still held under the running water, although every trace of soap had been rinsed from them.

"Hey, kid?"

Silence.

Dusty moved into the cramped bathroom, beside his brother.

Skeet stared down at his hands, eyes shining as if with wonder, mouth open in what appeared to be awe, as though the answer to the mystery of existence was in his grasp.

Soap-scented clouds of steam had begun to rise out of the sink. The running water was fiercely hot. Skeet's hands, usually so pale, were an angry red.

"Good God." Dusty quickly turned off the water. The metal faucet was almost too hot to touch.

Evidently feeling no pain, Skeet kept his half-scalded hands under the spout.

Dusty turned on the cold water, and his brother submitted to this new torrent without any change of expression. He had exhibited no discomfort whatsoever from the hot water and now appeared to take no relief from the cold.

In the open doorway, Valet whimpered. Head raised, ears pricked, he backed a few steps into the bedroom. He knew that something was profoundly wrong.

Dusty took his brother by one arm. Hands held in front of him, gaze still fixed on them, Skeet allowed himself to be led out of the bathroom. He sat on the edge of the bed, hands in his lap, studying them as if reading his fate in the lines of his palms.

"Don't move," Dusty said, and then he hurried out of the room, in search of Tom Wong.

19

When Martie drove into the garage, she was disappointed to see that Dusty's van wasn't there. Because his work would have been rained out, she had hoped to find him at home.

In the kitchen, a ceramic-tomato magnet held a brief note to the refrigerator door: *Oh, Beautiful One. I'll be home by 5:00. We'll go out for dinner. Love you even more than I love tacos. Dusty.*

She used the half bath—and not until she was washing her hands did she realize the mirror was missing from the door of the medicine cabinet. All that remained was a tiny splinter of silvered glass wedged in the lower right-hand corner of the metal frame.

Evidently, Dusty had accidentally broken it. Except for the one small sliver stuck in the frame, he'd done a thorough job of cleaning up the debris.

If broken mirrors meant bad luck, this was the worst of all possible days to shatter one.

Although she had no lunch left to lose, she still felt queasy. She filled a glass with ice and ginger ale. Something cold and sweet usually settled her stomach.

Wherever he had gone, Dusty must have taken Valet with him. In reality, their house was small and cozy, but at the moment it seemed big and cold—and lonely.

Martie sat at the breakfast table by the rainwashed window to sip the ginger ale, trying to decide if she preferred to go out this evening or stay home. Over dinner—assuming she could eat—she intended to share the unsettling events of the day with Dusty, and she worried about being overheard by a waitress or by other diners. Besides, she didn't want to be out in public if she suffered another episode.

On the other hand, if they stayed home, she didn't trust herself to cook dinner. . . .

She raised her eyes from the ginger ale to the rack of knives on the wall near the sink.

The ice cubes rattled against the drinking glass clutched in her right hand.

The shiny stainless-steel blades of the cutlery appeared to be radiant, as though they were not merely reflecting light but also generating it.

Letting go of the glass, blotting her hand on her jeans, Martie looked away from the knife rack. But at once her eyes were drawn to it again.

She knew that she was not capable of doing violence to others, except to protect herself, those she loved, and the innocent. She doubted that she was capable of harming herself, either.

Nevertheless, the sight of the knives so agitated her that she couldn't remain seated. She rose, stood in indecision, went into the dining room and then into the living room, moving about restlessly, with no purpose except to put some distance between herself and the knife rack.

After rearranging bibelots that didn't need to be rearranged, adjusting a lampshade that was not crooked, and smoothing pillows that were not rumpled, Martie went into the foyer and opened the front door. She stepped across the threshold, onto the porch.

Her heart knocked so hard she shook from its blows. Each pulse pushed such a tide through her arteries that her vision throbbed with the heavy surge of blood.

She went to the head of the porch steps. Her legs were weak and shaky. She put one hand against a porch post.

To get farther from the knife rack, she'd have to walk

out into the storm, which had diminished from a downpour to a heavy drizzle. Wherever she went, however, in any corner of the world, in good and bad weather, in sunshine and in darkness, she would encounter pointed things, sharp things, jagged things, instruments and utensils and tools that could be used for wicked purposes.

She had to steady her nerves, slow her racing mind, push out these strange thoughts. Calm down.

God help me.

She tried taking slow, deep breaths. Instead, her breathing became more rapid, ragged.

When she closed her eyes, seeking inner peace, she found only turmoil, a vertiginous darkness.

She wasn't going to be able to regain control of herself until she found the courage to return to the kitchen and confront the thing that had triggered this anxiety attack. The knives. She had to deal with the knives, and quickly, before this steadily growing anxiety swelled into outright panic.

The knives.

Reluctantly, she turned away from the porch steps. She went to the open front door.

Beyond the threshold, the foyer was a forbidding space. This was her much-loved little home, a place where she'd been happier than ever before in her life, yet now it was almost as unfamiliar to her as a stranger's house.

The knives.

She went inside, hesitated, and closed the door behind her.

20

Although Skeet's hands were badly irritated, they were not as raw-looking as they had been a few minutes ago, and they were not scalded. Tom Wong treated them with a cortisone cream.

Because of Skeet's eerie detachment and his continued failure to respond to questions, Tom drew a blood sample for drug testing. Upon checking into New Life, Skeet had submitted to a strip search for controlled substances, and none had been found either in his clothing or secreted in any body cavities.

"It could be a delayed secondary reaction to whatever he pumped into himself this morning," Tom suggested as he left with the blood sample.

During the past few years, through the worst of his periodic phases of addiction, Skeet had exhibited more peculiar behavior than Donald Duck on PCP, but Dusty had never before seen anything like this semi-catatonic glaze.

Valet enjoyed no furniture privileges at home, but he seemed to be so troubled by Skeet's condition that he forgot the rules and curled up on the armchair.

Fully understanding the retriever's distress, Dusty left Valet undisturbed. He sat on the edge of the bed, beside his brother.

Skeet lay flat on his back now, head propped on a stack of three pillows. He stared at the ceiling. In the light of the nightstand lamp, his face was as placid as that of a meditating yogi.

Remembering the apparent urgency and emotion with which the name had been scrawled on the notepad, Dusty murmured, "Dr. Yen Lo."

Although still in a state of disengagement from the world around him, Skeet spoke for the first time since Dusty had initially mentioned that name when they had been in the adjacent bathroom. "I'm listening," he said, which was precisely what he had said before.

"Listening to what?"

"Listening to what?"

"What're you doing?"

"What am I doing?" Skeet asked.

"I asked what you were listening to."

"You."

"Yeah. Okay, so tell me who's Dr. Yen Lo."

"You."

"Me? I'm your brother. Remember?"

"Is that what you want me to say?"

Frowning, Dusty said, "Well, it's the truth, isn't it?"

Although his face remained slack, expressionless, Skeet said, "Is it the truth? I'm confused."

"Join the club."

"What club do you want me to join?" Skeet asked with apparent seriousness.

"Skeet?"

"Hmmm?"

Dusty hesitated, wondering just how detached from reality the kid might be. "Do you know where you are?"

"Where am I?"

"So you don't know?"

"Do I?"

"Can't you look around?"

"Can I?"

"Is this an Abbott and Costello routine?"

"Is it?"

Frustrated, Dusty said, "Look around."

Immediately, Skeet raised his head off the pillows and surveyed the room.

"I'm sure you know where you are," Dusty said.

"New Life Clinic."

Skeet lowered his head onto the pillows once more. His eyes were again directed at the ceiling, and after a moment, they did something odd.

Not quite certain what he had seen, Dusty leaned closer to his brother, to look more directly at his face.

In the slant of the lamplight, Skeet's right eye was golden, and his left was a darker honey-brown, which gave him an unsettling aspect, as if two personalities were staring out of the same skull.

This trick of light was not, however, the thing that had caught Dusty's attention. He waited for almost a minute before he saw it again: Skeet's eyes jiggled rapidly back and forth for a few seconds, then settled once more into a steady stare.

"Yes, New Life Clinic," Dusty belatedly confirmed. "And you know why you're here."

"Flush the poisons out of the system."

"That's right. But have you taken something since you checked in, did you sneak drugs in here somehow?"

Skeet sighed. "What do you want me to say?"

The kid's eyes jiggled. Dusty mentally counted off seconds. Five. Then Skeet blinked, and his gaze steadied.

"What do you want me to say?" he repeated.

"Just tell the truth," Dusty encouraged. "Tell me if you snuck drugs in here."

"No."

"Then what's wrong with you?"

"What do you want to be wrong with me?"

"Damn it, Skeet!"

The faintest frown creased the kid's forehead. "This isn't the way it's supposed to be."

"The way *what* is supposed to be?"

"This." Tension lines tweaked the corners of Skeet's mouth. "You aren't following the rules."

"What rules?"

Skeet's slack hands curled and tightened into half-formed fists.

His eyes jiggled again, side to side, this time while also rolling back in his head. Seven seconds.

REM. Rapid eye movement. According to psychologists, such movements of the closed eyes indicated that a sleeper was dreaming.

Skeet's eyes weren't closed, and though he was in some peculiar state, he wasn't asleep.

Dusty said, "Help me, Skeet. I'm not on the same page. What rules are we talking about? Tell me how the rules work."

Skeet didn't at once reply. Gradually the frown lines in his brow melted away. His skin became smooth and as pellucid as clarified butter, until it appeared as though the white of bone shone through. His stare remained fixed on the ceiling.

His eyes jiggled, and when the REM ceased, he spoke at last in a voice untouched by tension but also less flat than before. A whisper: "Clear cascades."

For all the sense they made, those two words might have been chosen at random, like two lettered Ping-Pong balls expelled from a bingo hopper.

"Clear cascades," Dusty said. When his brother didn't respond, he pressed: "I need more help, kid."

"Into the waves scatter," Skeet whispered.

Dusty turned his head toward a noise behind him.

Valet had gotten down from the armchair. The dog padded out of the room, into the hallway, where he turned and stood with his ears pricked, tail tucked, staring warily in at them from the threshold, as though he had been spooked.

Into the waves scatter.

More bingo balls.

A small snowflake moth, with delicate patterns of piercing along the edges of its fragile white wings, had landed on Skeet's upturned right hand. As the moth crawled across his palm, his fingers didn't twitch; there was no indication that he could feel the insect. His lips were parted, jaw slack. His breathing was so shallow that his chest didn't rise and fall. His eyes jiggled again; but when that quiet seizure ended, Skeet could have passed for a dead man.

"Clear cascades," Dusty said. "Into the waves scatter. Does this mean anything, kid?"

"Does it? You asked me to tell you how the rules work."

"Those are the rules?" Dusty asked.

Skeet's eyes twitched for a few seconds. Then: "You know the rules."

"Pretend I don't."

"Those are two of them."

"Two of the rules."

"Yes."

"Not quite as straightforward as the rules of poker."

Skeet said nothing.

Though it all sounded like sheer gibberish, the ramblings of a drug-soaked mind, Dusty had the uncanny conviction that this strange conversation had real—if hidden—meaning and that it was leading toward a disturbing revelation.

Watching his brother closely, he said, "Tell me how many rules there are."

"You know," Skeet said.

"Pretend I don't."

"Three."

"What's the third rule?"

"What's the third rule? Blue pine needles."

Clear cascades. Into the waves scatter. Blue pine needles.

Valet, who rarely barked, who growled more rarely still, now stood at the open door, peering in from the hallway, and issued a low, menacing grumble. His hackles were raised as dramatically as those of a cartoon dog encountering a cartoon ghost. Although Dusty couldn't identify, with certainty, the cause of Valet's displeasure, it seemed to be poor Skeet.

After brooding for a minute or so, Dusty said, "Explain these rules to me, Skeet. Tell me what they mean."

"I am the waves."

"Okay," Dusty said, although this made less sense to him than if, in the tradition of the Beatles' psychedelic-era lyrics, Skeet had claimed, *I am the walrus.*

"You're the clear cascades," Skeet continued.

"Of course," Dusty said, merely to encourage him.

"And the needles are missions."

"Missions."

"Yes."

"All this makes sense to you?"

"Does it?"

"Apparently it does."

"Yes."

"It doesn't make sense to me."

Skeet was silent.

"Who is Dr. Yen Lo?" Dusty asked.

"Who is Dr. Yen Lo?" A pause. "You."

"I thought I was the clear cascades."

"They're one and the same."

"But I'm not Yen Lo."

Frown lines reappeared in Skeet's forehead. His hands, which had fallen slack, once more curled slowly into half-formed fists. The delicate snowflake moth flew out from among the pale clutching fingers.

After watching another REM seizure, Dusty said, "Skeet, are you awake?"

After a hesitation, the kid replied, "I don't know."

"You don't know if you're awake. So . . . you must be asleep."

"No."

"If you're not asleep and you're not sure if you're awake—then what are you?"

"What am I?"

"That was my question."

"I'm listening."

"There you go again."

"Where?"

"Where what?"

"Where should I go?" Skeet asked.

Dusty had lost the gut feeling that this conversation was full of profound if mysterious meaning and that they were approaching a revelation that would suddenly make sense of it all. Though unique and extremely peculiar, it now seemed as irrational and depressing as numerous other discussions they'd had when Skeet had been brain-bruised from a self-inflicted drug bludgeoning.

"Where should I go?" Skeet inquired again.

"Ah, give me a break and go to sleep," Dusty said irritably.

Obediently, Skeet closed his eyes. Peace descended upon his face, and his half-clenched hands relaxed. Immediately, his breathing settled into a shallow, slow, easy rhythm. He snored softly.

"What the hell happened here?" Dusty wondered aloud. He cupped his right hand around the back of his neck, to warm and smooth away a sudden stippling of goose-flesh. His hand had gone cold, however, and it pressed the chill deeper, into his spine.

With hackles no longer raised, sniffing quizzically, peering into shadowy corners and under the bed, as if in search of someone or something, Valet returned from the hall. Whatever spooked him had now departed.

Apparently, Skeet had gone to sleep because he had been told to do so. But surely it wasn't possible to fall asleep on command, in an instant.

"Skeet?"

Dusty put a hand on his brother's shoulder and shook him gently, then less gently.

Skeet didn't respond. He continued to snore softly. His eyelids twitched as his eyes jiggled beneath them. REM. He was without a doubt in a dream state this time.

Lifting Skeet's right hand, Dusty pressed two fingers against the radial artery in his brother's wrist. The kid's pulse was strong and regular but slow. Dusty timed it. Forty-eight beats per minute. That rate seemed worrisomely slow, even for a sleeper.

Skeet was in a dream state, all right. *Deep* in a dream state.

21

The stainless-steel rack of knives hung from two hooks on the wall, like the totem of some devil-worshiping clan that used its kitchen for more sinister work than cooking dinner.

Without touching the knives, Martie unhooked the rack. She slid it onto a shelf in a lower cupboard and quickly closed the door.

Not good enough. Out of sight was not out of mind. The knives remained readily accessible. She must make them harder to reach.

In the garage, she found an empty cardboard box and a roll of strapping tape, and she returned to the kitchen.

When she squatted before the cabinet in which she had stowed the knives, Martie wasn't immediately able to open the door. In fact, she was afraid even to touch it, as though this were not an ordinary cabinet but a satanic reliquary in which reposed a paring from one of Beelzebub's cloven hooves. She had to work up the courage to retrieve the cutlery, and when at last she cautiously withdrew it from the shelf, her hands shook so badly that the blades rattled in the slots of the rack.

She dropped the knives into the box and folded shut the flaps of cardboard. She began to use strapping tape to seal the box—but then realized she would need to cut the tape.

When she opened a drawer and reached for a pair of scissors, she wasn't able to pick them up. They would make a lethal weapon. She had seen uncountable movies in which a killer had used a pair of scissors instead of a butcher knife.

So many soft, vulnerable spots on the human body. The groin. The stomach. Between the ribs and straight into the heart. The throat. The side of the neck.

Like an official serial-killer deck of cards—ALL OF JACK THE RIPPER'S MURDERS DEPICTED IN GRAPHIC DETAIL! EVERY JOKER FEATURES A DIFFERENT FULL-COLOR ILLUSTRATION OF JEFFREY DAHMER'S REFRIGERATED HEAD COLLECTION!—grotesque and bloody pictures shuffled through Martie's mind.

Slamming shut the drawer, turning her back to it, she struggled to suppress the brutal images that some demented part of her psyche dealt out with savage glee.

She was alone in the house. She could harm no one with the scissors. Except, of course, herself.

Since reacting so bizarrely to the mezzaluna in Susan's kitchen and to the car key a few minutes thereafter, Martie had sensed that she was possessed of—or by—a strange and inexplicable new potential for violence, and she'd been afraid of what injury she might inflict on some innocent person during a spell of transient madness. Now, for the first time, she suspected that in a fit of irrationality, she might be capable of harming herself.

She stared down at the box in which she'd deposited the rack of knives. If she carried it out to the garage, put it in a corner, and piled other stuff on top of it, the box could still be retrieved in a minute. The single strip of tape—and the big roll dangling at the end of it—could be easily ripped away, the lid flaps torn open, and the knives recovered.

Although the butcher knife—all the knives—remained in the box, she could feel the weight of that weapon as if she were holding it now in her right hand: thumb pressed flat against the cold blade, fingers clenched around the wooden handle, forefinger jammed against the guard, little finger tight against the neb. This was the grip she might use if she were to strike with the knife from a low angle, swing it up, hard and fast, and drive it deep, to disembowel some unsuspecting victim.

Her right hand began to shake, and then her arm, and finally her entire body. Her hand flew open, as though she were trying to fling aside the imaginary knife; crazily, she half expected to hear the steel blade ring against the tile floor.

No, dear God, she wasn't capable of committing such atrocities with one of these knives. She wasn't capable of suicide, either, or of disfiguring herself.

Get a grip.

Yet she couldn't stop thinking about shiny blades and sharp edges, slashing and gouging. She strove to put away that mental Jack the Ripper deck, but a rapid-fire game of solitaire brought a series of horrific scenes in front of her mind's eye, one card sliding-spinning over another, *flick-flick-flick*, until a spasm of vertigo spiraled down from her head, through her chest, into the pit of her stomach.

She didn't remember dropping to her knees in front of the box. She didn't recall grabbing the roll of strapping tape, either, but suddenly she found herself turning the box over and over, frantically pulling the tape securely around it, again and again, first around the long circumference several times, then around the short, then diagonally.

She was frightened by the frenzy with which she addressed the task. She tried to pull her hands back, turn away from the box, but she couldn't stop herself.

Working so fast and so intensely that she broke into a thin greasy sweat, breathing hard, whimpering with anxiety, Martie wound the entire economy-size roll around the carton in one continuous loop to avoid using the scissors. She *encased* it in the tape as thoroughly as ancient Egypt's royal embalmers had wrapped their dead pharaohs in tannin-soaked cotton shrouds.

When she came to the end of the roll, she wasn't satisfied, because she still knew where the knives could be found. Granted: They were no longer easy to reach. She would have to carve through the many layers of strapping tape to open the box and get at the cutlery, but she would never dare allow herself to pick up a razor blade or scissors, with which to perform the task, so she should have felt relieved. The box, however, wasn't a bank vault; it was nothing but cardboard, and she wasn't safe—no one was safe—as long as she knew exactly where the knives could be found and as long as there was the slightest chance that she could get at them.

A murky red mist of fear churned across the sea of her soul, a cold boiling fog arising from the darkest heart of her, spreading through her mind, clouding her thoughts, increasing her confusion, and with greater confusion came greater terror.

She carried the box of knives out of the house, onto the back porch, intending to bury it in the yard. Which meant digging a hole. Which meant using a shovel or a pick. But those implements were more than mere tools: They were also potential weapons. She could not trust herself with a shovel or a pick.

She dropped the package. The knives clattered together inside the box, a muffled but nonetheless gruesome sound.

Get rid of the knives altogether. Throw them away. That was the only solution.

Tomorrow was trash-pickup day. If she put the knives out with the trash, they would be hauled to the dump in the morning.

She didn't know where the dump was located. Had no idea. Far out to the east somewhere, a remote landfill. Maybe even in another county. She'd never be able to find the knives again once they were taken to the dump. After the trash collectors visited, she would be safe.

With her heart rattling its cage of ribs, she snatched up the hated package and descended the porch steps.

Tom Wong timed Skeet's pulse, listened to his heart, and took his blood pressure. The cold stethoscope diaphragm against the kid's bare chest and the tightness of the pressure cuff around his right arm failed to elicit even a slight response from him. Not a twitch, blink, shiver, sigh, grunt, or grumble. He lay as limp and pale as a peeled, cooked zucchini.

"His pulse was forty-eight when I took it," Dusty said, watching from the foot of the bed.

"Forty-six now."

"Isn't that dangerous?"

"Not necessarily. There's no sign of distress."

According to his chart, Skeet's average normal pulse, when he was clean and sober and awake, was sixty-six. Ten or twelve points lower when sleeping.

"Sometimes you see sleeping pulse rates as low as forty," Tom said, "although it's rare." He peeled back Skeet's eyelids, one at a time, and examined his eyes with an ophthalmoscope. "Pupils are the same size, but it could still be apoplexy."

"Brain hemorrhage?"

"Or an embolism. Even if it's not apoplectic, it could be another type of coma. Diabetic. Uremic."

"He's not diabetic."

"I better get the doctor," Tom said as he left the room.

The rain had stopped, but the oval leaves of the Indian laurels wept as if with green-eyed grief.

Carrying the package of knives, Martie hurried to the east side of the house. She wrenched open the gate of the trash-can enclosure.

An observant part of her, a *sane* part of her imprisoned by her fear, was grimly aware that her posture and her movements were like those of a marionette: head thrust forward on a stiff neck, shoulders drawn up sharply, seemingly all elbows and knees, rushing forward in herky-jerky urgency.

If she were a marionette, then the puppeteer was Johnny Panic. In college, some of her friends had been devoted to the brilliant poetry of Sylvia Plath; and though Martie had found Plath's work too nihilistic and too depressive to be appealing, she had remembered one painful observation by the poet—a convincing explanation of what motivated some people to be cruel to one another and to make so many self-destructive choices. *From where I sit,* Plath wrote, *I figure the world is run by one thing and this one thing only. Panic with a dog-face, devil-face, hag-face, whore-face, panic in capital letters with no face at all—it's the same Johnny Panic, awake or asleep.*

For all her twenty-eight years, Martie's world had been largely free of panic, rich instead with a serene sense of belonging, peace, purpose, and connection with creation, because her dad had brought her up to believe that every life had meaning. Smilin' Bob said that if you were always guided by courage, honor, self-respect, honesty, and compassion, and if you kept your mind and your heart open to the lessons that this world teaches you, then you would eventually understand the meaning of your existence, perhaps even in this world, but certainly in the next. Such a philosophy virtually guaranteed a brighter life, less shadowed by fear than the lives of those who were convinced of meaninglessness. Yet here, at last, inexplicably, Johnny Panic came into Martie's life, too, somehow snared her in his controlling strings, and was now jerking her through this demented performance.

In the trash enclosure alongside the house, Martie removed the clamp-on lid from the third of three hard-plastic cans, the only one that was empty. She dropped the tape-encased box of knives into the can, jammed the lid on, and fumbled the steel-wire clamp into place.

She should have felt relieved.

Instead, her anxiety grew.

Fundamentally, nothing had changed. She knew where the knives were. She could retrieve them if she was determined. They would not be beyond her reach until the trash collector tossed them into his truck and drove away with them in the morning.

Worse, these knives weren't the only instruments with which she could give expression to the new violent thoughts that terrified her. Her brightly painted house, with its charming gingerbread millwork, might appear to be a place of peace, but it was in fact a well-equipped abattoir, an armory bulging with weapons; if you had a mind for mayhem, many apparently innocent items could be used as blades or bludgeons.

Frustrated, Martie clasped her hands to her temples as though she could physically suppress the riot of frightful thoughts that churned and shrieked through the dark, twisted streets of her mind. Her head throbbed against her palms and fingers; her skull suddenly seemed elastic. The harder she pressed, the greater her inner tumult became.

Action. Smilin' Bob always said that action was the answer to most problems. Fear, despair, depression, and even a lot of anger result from a sense that we're powerless, helpless. Taking action to resolve our problems is healthy, but we must apply some intelligence and a moral perspective if we have any hope of doing the right and most effective thing.

Martie didn't have a clue as to whether she was doing either the right thing or the most effective thing when she pulled the big, wheeled trash can out of the enclosure and hurriedly rolled it along the walkway toward the back of the house. Applying intelligence and sound moral principles required a calm mind, but she was swept up in a mental tempest, and those inner storm winds were gaining power by the second.

Here, now, Martie knew not what she ought to do, only what she *must* do. She couldn't wait for the serenity required to logically assess her options; she must act, do something, do anything, because when she remained still, even for a moment, a hard gale of spinning-tumbling dark thoughts battered her more fiercely than when she kept moving. If she dared to sit or even to pause for a few deep breaths, she would be torn asunder, scattered, blown away; however, if she kept moving, maybe she would do more things wrong than not, maybe she would take one stupid action after another, but there was always the chance, no matter how slim, that by sheer instinct she would do something right and thereby earn some relief, at least a small measure of peace.

Besides, on a gut level, where thought and reflection were not valued, where only feelings mattered, she knew that somehow she must alleviate her anxiety and regain control of herself before nightfall. The primitive in each of us climbs closer to the surface during the night, for the moon sings to it, and the cold void between the stars speaks its language. To that savage self, evil can look lovely in too little light. With darkness, a panic attack might degenerate into something worse, even into gibbering madness.

Although the rain had stopped, an ocean of black thunderheads remained overhead, from horizon to horizon, and a premature twilight drowned the day.

True twilight wasn't far off, either. When it arrived, the cloud-throttled sky would seem as black as night.

Already, fat night crawlers squirmed out of the lawn, onto the walkway. Snails had come forth, too, oozing silvery trails behind them.

A fecund odor arose from the wet grass, from the mulch

and the rotting leaves in the flower beds, from the darkly glistening shrubbery, and from the dripping trees.

In the gloaming, Martie was uneasily aware of the fertile life to which the sun was forbidding but to which the night offered hospitality. She was aware, too, that an awful centipedal part of herself shared an enthusiasm for the night with all the wriggling-creeping-crawling-slithering life that came out of hiding between dusk and dawn. The squirming she felt within herself was not just fear; it was a dreadful hunger, a need, an urge that she dared not contemplate.

Keep moving, keep moving, keep moving, and make a safe house, make a refuge in which nothing remains that might be dangerous in violent hands.

New Life was staffed primarily by nurses and therapists, but a medical doctor was on site from six o'clock in the morning until eight o'clock at night. The current shift was covered by Dr. Henry Donklin, whom Dusty had first met during Skeet's previous course of treatment at the clinic.

With curly white hair, with baby-pink skin remarkably smooth and supple for his age, Dr. Donklin had the cherubic good looks of a successful televangelist, although he was without the concomitant oiliness that suggested an easy slide into damnation for many of those electronic preachers.

After closing his private practice, Dr. Donklin had discovered that retirement was hardly more appealing than death. He had taken this position at New Life because the work was worthwhile even if not challenging and, in his words, "saves me from the stifling purgatory of endless golf and the living hell of shuffleboard."

Donklin gripped Skeet's left hand, and even in his sleep, the kid weakly returned the squeeze. The physician successfully repeated the test with Skeet's right hand.

"No obvious signs of paralysis, no stertorous breathing," Donklin said, "no puffing of the cheeks on expiration."

"Pupils are equally dilated," Tom Wong noted.

After checking the eyes himself, Donklin continued his brisk examination. "Skin isn't clammy, normal surface temperature. I'd be surprised if this is apoplectic coma. Not hemorrhage, embolism, or thrombosis. But we'll revisit that possibility and transfer him to a hospital if we can't identify the problem quickly."

Dusty allowed himself a measure of optimism.

Valet stood in a corner, head raised, intently watching the proceedings—perhaps alert for a return or reoccurrence of whatever had raised his hackles and had driven him from the room a short while ago.

At the doctor's direction, Tom prepared to catheterize Skeet and obtain a urine sample.

After leaning close to his unconscious patient, Donklin said, "He doesn't have sweet breath, but we'll want to check the urine for albumin and sugar."

"He's not diabetic," Dusty said.

"Doesn't look like uremic coma, either," the physician observed. "He'd have a hard, fast pulse. Elevated blood pressure. None of the symptoms here."

"Could he be just sleeping?" Dusty asked.

"Sleep this deep," Henry Donklin said, "you need a wicked witch casting a spell or maybe a bite from Snow White's apple."

"The thing is—I got a little frustrated with him, the way he was behaving, and I told him to just go to sleep, said it sort of sharply, and the moment I said it, he zonked out."

Donklin's expression was so dry that his face looked as if it needed to be dusted. "Are you telling me you're a witch?"

"Still a housepainter."

Because he didn't believe that apoplexy was involved, Donklin risked the application of a restorative; however, a whiff of ammonium carbonate—smelling salts—failed to revive Skeet.

"If he's just sleeping," the physician said, "then he must be a descendant of Rip Van Winkle."

Because the trash container held only the box of cutlery and because its wheels were large, Martie was able to drag it up the short flight of stairs onto the back porch with little difficulty. From inside the well-taped box, through the walls of the can, came the angry music of knives ringing against one another.

She had intended to roll the container inside. Now she realized that she would be bringing the knives into the house again.

Hands locked on the handle of the trash can, she was frozen by indecision.

Ridding her home of all potential weapons must be priority one. Before full darkness descended. Before she surrendered more control of herself to the primitive within.

Into her stillness came a greater storm of fear, rattling all the doors and windows of her soul.

Move, move, move.

She left the back door standing open and parked the wheeled trash can on the porch, at the threshold, where it was near enough to be convenient. She removed the lid and put it aside on the porch floor.

In the kitchen once more, she pulled open a cabinet drawer and scanned the gleaming contents: flatware. Salad forks. Dinner forks. Dinner knives. Butter knives. Also ten steak knives with wooden handles.

She didn't touch the dangerous items. Instead, she carefully removed the safer pieces—tablespoons, teaspoons, coffee spoons—and placed them on the counter. Then she removed the drawer from the cabinet, carried it to the open door, and upended it.

Along with a set of plastic drawer dividers, a steely cascade of forks and knives clinked and jingled into the trash can. The marrow in Martie's bones rang in sympathy with the icy sound.

She put the drawer on the kitchen floor, in a corner, out of her way. She didn't have time to return the salvaged spoons to it and slide it back into the cabinet.

The false twilight was bleeding into true twilight. Through the open door, she could hear the first rough songs of the little winter toads that ventured forth only at night.

Another drawer. Miscellaneous culinary tools and gadgets. A bottle opener. A potato peeler. A lemon-peel shaver. A wicked-looking spikelike meat thermometer. A small meat-tenderizing hammer. A corkscrew. Miniature yellow-plastic ears of corn with two sharp pins protruding from one end, which could be jammed into a cob to make fresh corn easier to eat.

She was astonished by the number and variety of common household items that could also serve as weapons. On his way to an inquisition, any torturer would feel well prepared if his kit contained nothing more than the items now before Martie's eyes.

The drawer also contained large plastic clips for bags of potato chips, measuring spoons, measuring cups, a melon scoop, a few rubber spatulas, wire whisks, and other items that didn't look as if they would be lethal even in the possession of the cleverest of homicidal sociopaths.

Hesitantly, she reached into the drawer, intending to sort the dangerous items from the harmless things, but at once she snatched her hand back. She wasn't willing to trust herself with the task.

"This is crazy, this is totally nuts," she said, and her voice was so torqued by fear and by despair that she barely recognized it as her own.

She dumped the entire collection of gadgets into the

trash can. She put the second empty drawer atop the first, in the corner.

Dusty, where the hell are you? I need you. I need you. Come home, please, come home.

Because she had to keep moving to avoid being paralyzed by fear, she found the courage to open a third drawer. Several big serving forks. Meat forks. An electric carving knife.

Outside, the shrill singing of toads in the wet twilight.

22

Martie Rhodes, struggling to stave off total panic, pushed by obsession, pulled by compulsion, moved through a kitchen that now seemed no less filled with mortal threats than a battlefield torn by clashing armies.

She found a rolling pin in a drawer near the ovens. You could bash in someone's face with a rolling pin, smash his nose, split his lips, club and club and club him until you fractured his skull, until you left him on the floor, gazing sightlessly at you, with starburst hemorrhages in both his eyes. . . .

Although no potential victim was present, and although she knew she was incapable of bludgeoning anyone, Martie nonetheless had to talk herself into plucking the rolling pin from the drawer. "Get it, come on, for God's sake, get it, get it out of here, get rid of it."

Halfway to the trash can, she dropped the pin. It made a hard, sickening sound when it struck the floor.

She couldn't immediately summon the nerve to pick up the pin again. She kicked it, and it rolled all the way to the threshold of the open door.

With the rain, the last of the wind had drained out of the day, but the twilight exhaled a cold draft across the porch and through the kitchen door. Hoping the chilly air would clear her head, she took deep breaths, shuddering with each.

She gazed down at the rolling pin, which lay at her feet.

All she had to do was snatch up the damn thing and drop it into the can beyond the threshold. It wouldn't be in her hand more than a second or two.

Alone, she couldn't harm anyone. And even if she was seized by a self-destructive impulse, a rolling pin wasn't the ideal weapon with which to commit hara-kiri, although it was better than a rubber spatula.

With that little joke, she humiliated herself into plucking the rolling pin off the floor and dropping it in the can.

When she searched the next drawer, she found an array of tools and devices that for the most part didn't alarm her. A flour sifter. An egg timer. A garlic press. A basting brush. A colander. A juice strainer. A lettuce dryer.

Mortar and pestle. No good. The mortar was about the size of a baseball, carved out of a chunk of solid granite. You could brain someone with it. Step up behind him and swing it down hard, in a savage arc, cave in his skull.

The mortar had to go, right away, now, before Dusty came home or before some unwary neighbor rang the doorbell.

The pestle seemed harmless, but the two items composed a set, so she took both to the trash can. The granite mortar was cold in her cupped hand. Even after she threw it away, the memory of its coolness and satisfying heft tantalized her, and she knew that she had been right to dispose of it.

As she was pulling open another drawer, the telephone rang. She answered it hopefully: "Dusty?"

"It's me," Susan Jagger said.

"Oh." Her heart withered with disappointment. She tried not to let her distress color her voice. "Hey, what's up?"

"Are you all right, Martie?"

"Yeah, sure."

"You sound funny."

"I'm okay."

"You sound out of breath."

"I was just doing some heavy lifting."

"Something *is* wrong."

"Nothing is wrong. Don't grind me, Sooz. I've got a mother for that. What's up?"

Martie wanted to get off the phone. She had so much to do. So many kitchen drawers and cupboards had not yet been searched. And dangerous items, potential weapons, were in other rooms, as well. Instruments of death were scattered throughout the house, and she needed to find them all, dispose of every last one.

"This is a little embarrassing," Susan said.

"What is?"

"I'm not paranoid, Martie."

"I know you're not."

"He *does* come here sometimes, you know, sometimes at night when I'm sleeping."

"Eric."

"It must be him. All right, I know, he doesn't have a key, and the doors and windows are all locked, there's no way in, but it's got to be him."

Martie opened one of the drawers near the telephone. Among other things, it contained the pair of scissors that she had not been able to touch earlier, when she had wanted to cut the strapping tape.

Susan said, "You asked me how I know when he's been here, were things out of order, the smell of his cologne on the air, anything like that."

The handles of the scissors were coated in black rubber to provide a sure grip.

"But it's a lot worse than cologne, Martie, it's creepy . . . and embarrassing."

The steel blades were as polished as mirrors on the outside, with a dull brushed finish on the inner cutting surfaces.

"Martie?"

"Yeah, I heard." She was pressing the phone so tightly to her head that her ear hurt. "So tell me the creepy thing."

"How I know he's been here, he leaves his . . . his stuff."

One of the blades was straight and sharp. The other had teeth. Both were wickedly pointed.

Martie struggled to keep track of the conversation, because her mind's eye was suddenly filled with bright flashing images of the scissors in motion, slashing and stabbing, gouging and tearing. "His stuff?"

"You know."

"No."

"His stuff."

"What stuff?"

Engraved in one blade, just above the screwhead pivot, was the word *Klick*, which was probably the name of the manufacturer, although it resonated in a strange way with Martie, as if it were a magical word with secret power, mysterious and full of grave meaning.

Susan said, "His stuff, his . . . spunk."

For a moment, Martie couldn't make sense of the word *spunk*, simply couldn't connect with it, couldn't process it, as though it were a nonsense word invented by someone talking in tongues. Her mind was so preoccupied with the sight of the scissors lying in the drawer that she couldn't concentrate on Susan.

"Martie?"

"Spunk," Martie said, closing her eyes, striving to push all thoughts of the scissors out of her mind, trying to focus on the conversation with Susan.

"Semen," Susan clarified.

"His stuff."

"Yes."

"That's how you know he's been there?"

"It's impossible but it happens."

"Semen."

"Yes."

Klick.

The sound of snipping scissors: *klick-klick.* But Martie wasn't touching the scissors. Although her eyes were closed, she knew the shears were still in the drawer, because there was nowhere else they possibly could be. *Klick-klick.*

"I'm scared, Martie."

Me too. Dear God, me too.

Martie's left hand was clenched around the phone, and her right hand hung at her side, empty. The scissors couldn't operate under their own power, and yet: *klick-klick.*

"I'm scared," Susan repeated.

If Martie hadn't been shaken by fear and struggling determinedly to conceal her anxiety from Susan, if she'd been able to concentrate better, perhaps she wouldn't have found Susan's claim to be bizarre. In her current condition, however, each turn of the conversation led her deeper into confusion. "You said he . . . leaves it? Where?"

"Well . . . in me, you know."

To prove to herself that her right hand was empty, that the scissors weren't in it, Martie brought it to her chest, pressed it over her pounding heart. *Klick-klick.*

"In you," Martie said. She was aware that Susan was making truly astonishing statements with shocking implications and terrible potential consequences, but she wasn't able to bring her mind to bear exclusively on her friend, not with that infernal *klick-klick, klick-klick, klick-klick.*

"I sleep in panties and a T-shirt," Susan said.

"Me too," Martie said inanely.

"Sometimes I wake up, and in my panties there's this . . . this warm stickiness, you know."

Klick-klick. The sound must be imaginary. Martie wanted to open her eyes just to confirm that the scissors were, indeed, in the drawer, but she would be entirely lost if she looked at them again, so she kept her eyes shut.

Susan said, "But I don't understand how. It's nuts, you know? I mean . . . *how?*"

"You wake up?"

"And I have to change underwear."

"You're sure that's what it is? The stuff."

"It's disgusting. I feel dirty, used. Sometimes I have to shower, I just *have* to."

Klick-klick. Martie's heart was racing already, and she sensed that the sight of the gleaming blades would plunge her into a full-fledged panic attack far worse than anything that she had experienced previously. *Klick-klick-klick.*

"But, Sooz, good God, you mean he makes love to you—"

"There's no love involved."

"—he *does* you—"

"Rapes me. He's still my husband, we're just separated, I know, but it's rape."

"—but you don't wake up during it?"

"You've got to believe me."

"All right, of course, honey, I believe you. But—"

"Maybe I'm drugged somehow."

"When would Eric be able to slip the drugs to you?"

"I don't know. All right, yeah, it's crazy. Totally whacked, paranoid. But it's *happening.*"

Klick-klick.

Without opening her eyes, Martie pushed the drawer shut.

"When you wake up," she said shakily, "you've got your underwear on again."

"Yes."

Opening her eyes, staring at her right hand, which was knotted around the drawer pull, Martie said, "So he comes in, undresses you, rapes you. And then before he goes, he puts your T-shirt and panties on you again. Why?"

"So maybe I won't realize he's been here."

"But there's his stuff."

"Nothing else has that same smell."

"Sooz—"

"I know, I know, but I'm agoraphobic, not totally psychotic. Remember? That's what you told me earlier. And listen, there's more."

From inside the closed drawer came a muffled *klick-klick.*

"Sometimes," Susan continued, "I'm sore."

"Sore?"

"Down there," Susan said softly, discreetly. The depth of her anxiety and humiliation was more clearly revealed by this modesty than it had been by anything she'd previously said. "He's not . . . gentle."

Inside the drawer, blade pivoting against blade: *klick-klick, klick-klick.*

Susan was whispering now, and she sounded farther away, too, as though a great tide had lifted her beachfront house and carried it out to sea, as if she were steadily drifting toward a far and dark horizon. "Sometimes my breasts are sore, too, and once there were bruises on them . . . bruises the size of fingertips, where he'd squeezed too hard."

"And Eric denies all this?"

"He denies being here. I haven't . . . I haven't discussed the explicit details with him."

"What do you mean?"

"I haven't accused him."

Martie's right hand remained on the drawer, pushing against it as though something inside might force its way out. She applied herself with such intensity that the muscles in her forearm began to ache.

Klick-klick.

"Sooz, for God's sake, you think maybe he's drugging you and screwing you in your sleep, but you haven't confronted him about it?"

"I can't. I shouldn't. It's forbidden."

"Forbidden?"

"Well, you know, not right, not something I can do."

"No, I don't know. What an odd word—*forbidden*. By whom?"

"I didn't mean forbidden. I don't know why I said that. I just meant . . . well, I'm not sure what I meant. I'm so confused."

Although she was distracted by her own anxiety, Martie sensed something profound in Susan's word choice, and she wouldn't drop the issue. "Forbidden by whom?"

"I've had the locks changed three times," Susan said, instead of answering the question. Her voice rose from a whisper, sharpened by a brittle note of nascent hysteria that she was struggling mightily to repress. "Always a different company. Eric can't know someone at *every* locksmith, can he? And I didn't tell you this before, because maybe it makes me sound loopy, but I've dusted the windowsills with talcum powder, so if he *did* come through a locked window somehow, there'd be evidence of it, there'd be handprints in the powder, some mark of disturbance, but the talcum is always perfect in the morning. And I've wedged a kitchen chair under the doorknob, too, so even if the bastard has a key, he can't open the door, and the next morning the chair is always there, where I put it, yet I've got his *stuff* in me, in my panties, and I'm sore, and I know I've been used, brutally, I *know* it, and I shower and shower, hotter and hotter water, so hot it hurts sometimes, but I can't get clean. I never feel really clean anymore. Oh, God, sometimes I think what I need are exorcists—you know?—some priests to come here and pray over me, priests who really believe in the devil if there are any like that today, holy water and crucifixes, incense, because this is something that defies all logic, this is utterly supernatural, that's what it is, *supernatural*. And now you're thinking I'm a fully rounded nutball, but I'm really not, Martie, I'm not. I'm messed up, no question about that, okay, but this is apart from the agoraphobia, this is really happening, and I can't go on like this, waking up and finding . . . It's creepy, disgusting. It's destroying me, but I don't know what the hell to do. I feel helpless, Martie, I feel so vulnerable."

Klick-klick.

Martie's right arm ached from the wrist to the shoulder now, as she pressed on the drawer with all her weight, all her strength. Her jaw was clenched. Her teeth ground together.

Bright needles drew hot threads of pain up through her neck, and the pain sewed a little reason into her confusion-torn thoughts. In truth, she wasn't concerned that something would escape from the drawer. The scissors weren't magically animated like the brooms that plagued the beleaguered sorcerer's apprentice in Disney's *Fantasia.* The crisp dry sound—*klick-klick*—was in her mind. She was not actually afraid of the scissors or of the rolling pin, not afraid of the knives, the forks, the corkscrew, the corncob skewers, the meat thermometer. For hours now, she had known the true object of her terror, and she had fleetingly considered it several times during this strange day, but until now she had not faced it directly and without equivocation. The sole menace before which she cowered was Martine Eugenia Rhodes: She feared herself, not knives, not the hammers, not the scissors, but *herself.* She was forcing the drawer shut with unwavering determination because she was convinced that otherwise she would yank it open, would seize the shears—and, in the absence of any other victim, would rip brutally at herself with the pointed blades.

"Are you there, Martie?"

Klick-klick.

"Martie, what am I going to do?"

Martie's voice trembled with compassion, with anguish for her friend, but also with fear for herself and fear *of* herself. "Sooz, this is spooky shit, this is weirder than hoodoo." A cold brine of sweat drenched her as thoroughly as if she had just stepped out of the sea. *Klick-klick.* Her arm, shoulder, and neck ached so intensely that tears flooded her eyes. "Listen, I've got to wrap my brain around this a little while before I can advise you what to do, before I can figure out how I can help."

"It's all true."

"I know it's true, Sooz."

She was frantic to be off the telephone. She must get away from the drawer, get away from the scissors that waited in it, because she couldn't escape from the violent potential within herself.

"It's happening," Susan insisted.

"I know it is. You've convinced me. That's why I've got to mull it over. Because it's so strange. We've got to be careful, be sure we do the right thing."

"I'm afraid. I'm so alone here."

"You aren't alone," Martie promised, her voice beginning to break apart, not just quaverous anymore, but quaking and cracking. "I won't let you be alone. I'll call you back."

"Martie—"

"I'll think about this, think it through—"

"—if anything happens—"

"—figure out what's best—"

"—if anything happens to me—"

"—and I'll call you back—"

"—Martie—"

"—call you back soon."

She racked the wall phone, although at first she couldn't release it. Her grip was locked around the handset. When finally she was able to let go, her hand remained cupped, holding fast to a phantom phone.

Releasing the drawer, Martie winced as cramps spasmed through her right hand. Like a clay mold, the soft interdigital pads at the base of her fingers had taken a clear impression of the drawer handle, and the metacarpals ached as if the red groove in her flesh were reflected in the bone beneath.

She backed away from the drawer until she bumped against the refrigerator. Inside the fridge, bottles rattled softly against one another.

One of them was a half-empty bottle of Chardonnay, left over from dinner the previous night. A wine bottle is thick, especially at the bottom, which features a sediment-collecting, concave punt. Solid. Blunt. Effective. She could swing it like a club, crack someone's skull with it.

A *broken* wine bottle could be a particularly devastating weapon. Hold it by the neck, jagged points thrust forward. Rake it down some unsuspecting person's face, jam it into his throat.

Slamming doors could have been no louder than the crash of her heart resonating through her body.

23

"Urine doesn't lie," said Dr. Donklin.

From his sentinel post near the door, Valet raised his head and twitched his ears as if in agreement.

Skeet, who was now hooked to an electrocardiograph, remained in a sleep so deep that it appeared to be cryogenic suspension.

Dusty watched the tracery of green light spiking across the readout-window on the heart monitor. His brother's pulse was slow but steady, no arrhythmia.

New Life Clinic was neither a hospital nor a diagnostic lab. Nevertheless, because of the self-destructiveness and cleverness of its patients, it had the sophisticated equipment required to provide rapid analysis of bodily fluids for the presence of drugs.

Earlier, Skeet's initial blood samples, taken upon admission, had revealed the recipe for the chemical cocktail with which he had started his day: methamphetamine, cocaine, DMT. Meth and coke were stimulants. Dimethyltryptamine—DMT—was a synthetic hallucinogen, similar to psilocybin, which itself was an alkaloid crystal derived from the mushroom *Psilocybe mexicana*. This constituted a breakfast with a lot more punch than oatmeal and orange juice.

Analysis of the latest blood sample, drawn while Skeet lay in a comalike slumber, had not yet been completed; however, the urine sample, acquired by catheter, indicated that no new drugs had been introduced into his system and, moreover, that his body had largely metabolized the methamphetamine, cocaine, and DMT. For the time being, at least, he would be seeing no more of the angel of death who had induced him to leap off the Sorensons' roof.

"We'll get the same data from the second blood samples," Donklin predicted. "Because it's true, urine *doesn't* lie. Or in laymen's terms . . . there's truth in a tinkle. Pee-pee can't prevaricate."

Dusty wondered if the physician's bedside manner had been so irreverent when he'd had his own practice or if irreverence had come upon him after retirement, when he'd taken this for-hire position at New Life. In either case, it was refreshing.

The urine sample had also been analyzed for urethral casts, albumin, and sugar. The results failed to support a diagnosis of either diabetic or uremic coma.

"If the new blood workup doesn't tell us anything," Dr. Donklin said, "we'll probably want to transfer him to a hospital."

Inside the refrigerator, against which Martie leaned, the clink of glass against glass gradually subsided.

The pain in her cramped hands wrung tears from her. With the sleeves of her blouse, she blotted her eyes, but her vision remained blurred.

Her hands were hooked, as if she were clawing at an adversary—or at a crumbling ledge. Seen through a salty veil, they might have been the menacing hands of a demon in a dream.

With the image of a jaggedly broken wine bottle still vivid in her mind's eye, she remained so frightened of her potential for violence, of her unconscious intentions, that she was paralyzed.

Action. Her father's admonition. Hope lies in action. But she didn't have the clarity of mind to consider, analyze, and then judiciously choose the right and most effective action.

She acted anyway, because if she didn't do *something*, she would lie on the floor, curl into a ball like a pill bug, and remain there until Dusty came home. By the time he arrived, she might have turned in upon herself so tightly that she'd never be able to uncurl.

So, now, with pale resolve, push away from the refrigerator. Cross the kitchen. To the cabinet from which she'd retreated only moments ago.

Fingers hooking around the handle. *Klick-klick.* Pulling open the drawer. The gleaming scissors.

Martie almost faltered. Almost lost her shaky conviction when she saw the shiny blades.

Action. All the way out of the cabinet with the damn drawer. All the way out. Heavier than she expected.

Or perhaps the drawer wasn't in fact as heavy as it seemed, was heavy only because, for Martie, the scissors possessed more than mere physical weight. Psychological weight, moral weight, the weight of malevolent purpose residing within the steel.

Now to the open back door. The trash can.

She tipped the drawer away from herself, intending to let the contents spill into the can. The sliding scissors rattled against other objects, and the sound so alarmed Martie that she dropped the drawer itself into the trash, along with everything it contained.

When Tom Wong brought the results of the latest blood-sample analysis to Skeet's room, Dr. Donklin's prediction was fulfilled. The mystery of Skeet's condition remained unsolved.

The kid hadn't ingested drugs of any kind within the past few hours. Residual traces of this morning's indulgence were barely detectable.

His white-blood-cell count, which was normal, and his lack of fever didn't support the theory that he might be afflicted by an acute meningeal infection. Or any infection whatsoever.

If the problem were food poisoning, specifically botulism, the coma would have been preceded by vomiting and stomach pain, and most likely by diarrhea, as well. Skeet hadn't suffered from any of those complaints.

Although clear symptoms of apoplexy were not apparent, the grave possibilities of cerebral hemorrhage, embolism, and thrombosis must be reconsidered.

"This isn't a rehab case, anymore," Dr. Donklin decided. "Where do you prefer we transfer him?"

Dusty said, "Hoag Hospital, if they have an open bed."

"Something's happening here," Tom Wong noted, drawing their attention to the electrocardiograph.

Because the annoying audio module on the EKG was switched off, neither Dusty nor Donklin had noticed that Skeet's pulse rate had increased. The tracery of green light and the digital readout indicated that it was up from a low of forty-six beats per minute to fifty-four.

Suddenly yawning, stretching, Skeet opened his eyes.

His heart rate, now up to sixty beats per minute, was still rising.

Skeet blinked at Tom Wong, at Dr. Donklin, and at Dusty. "Hey, we havin' a party or something?"

The open bottle of Chardonnay, two bottles of Chablis that were unopened: into the trash can.

In the laundry room, hideous weapons. A bottle of blinding, suffocating ammonia. Bleach. A lye-based drain cleaner. All of it into the trash.

She remembered the matches. In a kitchen cabinet. In a tall tin container that had once held biscotti. Several books of paper matches. Boxes of short wooden matches. A bundle of matches with ten-inch sticks, used to light the floating wicks in long-necked glass oil lamps.

If a person were capable of raking a broken wine bottle across an innocent victim's face, if a person were dangerous enough to have no compunction about plunging a car key into a loved one's eye, then setting fire to him—or to an entire house—would pose no significant moral hurdle.

Martie dropped the unopened container of matches into the trash can, and the contents made a raspy sound like a rattlesnake issuing a warning.

A quick trip to the living room. So much to do, so much to do. The gas fireplace featured a set of realistic-looking ceramic logs. A battery-fired butane match lay on the hearth.

Returning to the open kitchen door, dropping the butane match into the trash can on the back porch, Martie was troubled by the possibility that she had turned on the gas in the fireplace. She had no reason to turn it on, and she had no memory of having done so, but she didn't trust herself.

Didn't *dare* trust herself.

With the valve cranked wide open, a mortal flood of natural gas would escape in a minute or two. Any spark might set off an explosion powerful enough to destroy the house.

To the living room again. Like a frantic character in a video game. Ricocheting from peril to peril.

No rotten-egg odor.

No hiss of escaping gas.

The geared shank of the valve protruded from the wall beside the hearth. A key chuck was required to turn it, and the brass key lay on the mantel.

Relieved, Martie left the room. By the time she

returned to the kitchen, however, she was once more concerned that in the grip of a fugue, she had keyed on the gas *after* satisfying herself that it was off.

This was ridiculous. She couldn't spend the rest of her life bouncing in and out of the living room, ceaselessly checking on the fireplace. She didn't suffer from fugues, amnesiac phases, didn't commit acts of sabotage while blacked out.

For reasons she could not grasp, Martie thought of the second waiting room at Dr. Ahriman's offices, where she had read part of a novel during Susan's therapy session. A fine place to read. No windows. No annoying background music. No distractions.

A windowless room. And yet hadn't she stood at an enormous window, watching the gray rain sweep along the coast?

No, that had been a scene in the paperback novel.

"It's a real thriller," she said aloud, though she was alone. "The writing's good. The plot is entertaining. The characters are colorful. I'm enjoying it."

Now, here in the disordered kitchen, she remained troubled by a perception of time lost. She sensed an ominous gap in her day, during which something terrible had happened.

Consulting her wristwatch, she was surprised to see that the hour had grown so late—5:12 P.M. The day had dissolved and washed away with the rain.

She didn't know when she had first gone into the living room to inspect the fireplace. Perhaps a minute ago. Perhaps two or four or ten minutes ago.

Early-winter night breathed at the open door to the back porch. She couldn't recall if darkness had pressed against the living-room windows when she had been in there. If a gap existed in her day, it *must* have been in that room, at the fireplace.

Martie raced toward the front of the house, and the territory through which she passed was familiar yet different from what it had been this morning. No space was quite rectangular or precisely square anymore; each was fluid—now almost triangular, now hexagonal, and now curved, or otherwise curiously proportioned. Ceilings that had been flat appeared to be subtly pitched. She could have sworn that the floor canted under her, as if it were the deck of a tacking ship. The powerful anxiety that warped her mental processes also at times seemed to bend the physical world into strange shapes, although she knew that this surreal plasticity was imaginary.

In the living room: no hiss of escaping gas. No odor.

The key lay on the mantel. She didn't touch it. Gaze fixed on that shiny brass item, Martie retreated from the fireplace, carefully backing between the armchairs and the sofa, out of the room.

When she reached the hall, she glanced at her watch. Five-thirteen. One minute had passed. No lost time. No fugue.

In the kitchen, shaking uncontrollably, she consulted her watch again. Still—5:13. She was all right. She hadn't blacked out. She couldn't have returned to the living room in a fugue and switched on the gas. One number changed before her eyes—5:14.

In his note, Dusty had promised to be home by five o'clock. He was overdue. Dusty was usually prompt. He kept his promises.

"God, please," she said, shocked by the pathetic tone of her voice, by the wretched tremor that distorted her words, "bring him home. God, please, please, help me, please bring him home *now.*"

When Dusty returned, he would drive his van into the garage, park it beside her Saturn.

No good. The garage was a dangerous place. Uncounted sharp tools were stored out there, deadly machinery, poisonous substances, flammable fluids.

She would stay in the kitchen, wait for him here. Nothing would happen to him in the garage if she weren't out there when he arrived. Sharp tools, poisons, flammables—they were not dangerous. Martie herself was the real danger, the only threat.

From the garage, he would come directly into the kitchen. She must be sure that she had stripped from this room everything that might serve as a weapon.

Yet to continue this purge of the sharp and the blunt and the toxic was sheer madness. She would never harm Dusty. She loved him more than she loved life. She would die for him, as she knew he would die for her. You didn't kill someone whom you loved that much.

Nevertheless, these irrational fears infected her, swarmed in her blood, bred in her bones, crawled in bacterial plenitude through her mind, and she was growing sicker by the second.

24

Skeet was sitting in bed, propped against pillows, pallid and sunken-eyed, his lips more gray than pink, and yet he had a tattered and tragic dignity, as though he were not merely one of the legion of lost souls who wandered through the ruins of this crumbling culture, but was instead a consumptive poet, living during a distant past more innocent than this new century, perhaps taking the tuberculosis cure in a private sanatorium, struggling not against his own compulsions, not against a hundred years of cold philosophies that denied purpose and meaning to life, but against nothing more than stubborn bacteria. A footed bed tray bridged his lap.

Standing at the window, Dusty might have been gazing at the night sky, reading his fate in the patterns of the lingering storm clouds. The prows and keels of the eastward-tacking thunderheads appeared to be filigreed with gold leaf, for they were uplighted by the luminous suburban sea above which they sailed.

In truth, the night transformed the glass into a black mirror, allowing Dusty to study Skeet's colorless reflection in the pane. He expected to see his brother do something strange and revealing that he would not have done if he'd known he was being observed.

This was a curiously paranoid expectation, but it clung like a prickly bur, and Dusty could not shake it off. This odd day had brought him deep into a forest of suspicion that was formless and without object, though nonetheless disturbing.

Skeet was enjoying an early dinner: tomato-basil soup seasoned with chips of Parmesan, followed by rosemary-garlic chicken with roasted potatoes and asparagus. The meals at New Life were superior to ordinary hospital fare—though solid food came precut into bite-size pieces, because Skeet was on a suicide watch.

Sitting erect on the armchair, Valet watched Skeet with the interest of a born gourmand. He was a good dog, however, and though his dinner was overdue, he didn't beg.

Around a mouthful of chicken, Skeet said, "Haven't eaten like this in weeks. I guess nothing gives you an appetite like jumping off a roof."

The kid was so thin that he appeared to have taken bulimia lessons from a supermodel. Considering how shrunken his stomach must be, it was difficult to believe that he had the capacity to pack away as much as he had already eaten.

Still pretending to be seeking portents in the clouds, Dusty said, "You seemed to fall asleep just because I told you to."

"Yeah? Well, it's a new leaf, bro. From now on I do everything you want."

"Fat chance."

"You'll see."

Dusty slipped his right hand into a pocket of his jeans and felt the folded pages from the notepad that he had found in Skeet's kitchen. He considered asking about Dr. Yen Lo again, but intuition told him that this name, when spoken, might precipitate a second catatonic withdrawal followed by another frustrating, inscrutable dialogue similar to the one in which they had engaged earlier.

Instead, Dusty said, "Clear cascades."

As revealed by his ghostly reflection in the window, Skeet did not even lift his gaze from his dinner. "What?"

"Into the waves scatter."

Now Skeet looked up, but he said nothing.

"Blue pine needles," Dusty said.

"Blue?"

Turning from the window, Dusty said, "Does that mean anything to you?"

"Pine needles are green."

"Some are blue-green, I guess."

Having cleaned his dinner plate, Skeet slid it aside in favor of a dessert cup containing fresh strawberries in clotted cream and brown sugar. "I think I've heard it somewhere."

"I'm sure you have. Because I heard it from you."

"From me?" Skeet seemed genuinely surprised. "When?"

"Earlier. When you were . . . out of it."

After savoring a cream-slathered berry, Skeet said, "That's weird. I'd hate to think the literary thing is in my genes."

"Is it a riddle?" Dusty asked.

"Riddle? No. It's a poem."

"You write poetry?" Dusty asked with undisguised disbelief, aware of how assiduously Skeet avoided every aspect of the world that his father, the literature professor, inhabited.

"Not mine," Skeet said, as like a little boy he licked cream from his dessert spoon. "I don't know the poet's name. Ancient Japanese. Haiku. I must have read it somewhere, and it just stuck."

"Haiku," Dusty said, trying and failing to find useful meaning in this new information.

Using his spoon as if it were a symphony conductor's baton, Skeet emphasized the meter as he recited the poem:

"Clear cascades
into the waves scatter
blue pine needles."

Given structure and meter, the nine words no longer sounded like gibberish.

Dusty was reminded of an optical illusion that he had seen once in a magazine, many years ago. It was a pencil drawing of serried ranks of trees, pines and firs and spruces and alders, towering and dense and regimented, which had been titled *Forest.* The accompanying text claimed that this woodland concealed a more complex scene that could be perceived if you put aside your expectations, if you could make yourself forget the word *forest,* and if you could peer through the surface image to another panorama far different from the sylvan scene. Some people required as little as a few minutes to comprehend the second picture, while others struggled more than an hour before achieving a revelation. After only ten minutes, frustrated, Dusty had pushed aside the magazine—and then from the corner of his eye had glimpsed the hidden city. When again he stared directly at the drawing, he saw a vast Gothic metropolis, where granite buildings crowded one another; shadowy woodland paths between tree trunks had metamorphosed into narrow streets buried deep in a gloom cast by man-made cliffs of stone rising cold and gray against a bleak sky.

Similarly, new meaning arose from these nine words the moment that Dusty heard them read as haiku. The poet's intent was evident: The "clear cascades" were gusts of wind stripping pine needles off trees and casting them into the sea. It was a pure, evocative, and poignant observation of nature, which on analysis would surely prove to have numerous metaphorical meanings pertinent to the human condition.

The poet's intent, however, was not the sole meaning to be found in those three brief lines. There was another interpretation that had profound importance to Skeet when he was in his peculiar trance, but he now appeared to have forgotten all that. Previously, he'd called each line a *rule,* although he hadn't been coherent in his attempt to explain what conduct, procedure, sport, or game these cryptic rules governed.

Dusty considered sitting on the edge of his brother's bed and questioning him further. He was inhibited by the concern that under pressure Skeet might retreat into a semi-catatonic state and might not easily wake the next time.

Besides, together they had been through a difficult day. Skeet, in spite of his nap and fortifying dinner, must be nearly as weary as Dusty, who felt clipped, ripped, and whipped.

Shovel.

Pick.

Hatchet.

Hammers, screwdrivers, saws, drills, pliers, wrenches, long steel nails by the fistful.

Although the kitchen was not yet entirely a safe place, and though other rooms of the house must be inspected and secured, as well, Martie couldn't stop thinking about the garage, mentally cataloging the numerous instruments of torture and death that it contained.

At last, she was no longer able to maintain her resolve to stay out of the garage and to avoid the risk of being among its sharp temptations when Dusty eventually arrived. She opened the connecting door from the kitchen, fumbled for the light switch, and turned on the overhead fluorescent panels.

As Martie stepped across the threshold, her attention was first drawn to the Peg-Board on which were racked a collection of gardening tools that she had forgotten. Trowels. One pair of snips. A hand spade. Spring-action clippers with Teflon-coated blades. A battery-powered hedge trimmer.

A pruning hook.

Noisily, Skeet scraped the last traces of clotted cream and brown sugar from the dessert cup.

As though summoned by the clatter of spoon against china, a new private nurse arrived for the night shift: Jasmine Hernandez, petite, pretty, in her early thirties—with eyes the purple-black shade of plum skins, mysterious yet clear. Her white uniform was as bright and crisp as her professionalism, although red sneakers with green laces suggested—correctly, as it turned out—a playful streak.

"Hey, you're just a little bit of a thing," Skeet told her. He winked at Dusty. "If I want to kill myself, Jasmine, I don't see you being able to stop me."

As she removed the dinner tray from the bed and set it on the dresser, the nurse said, "Listen, my little *chupaflor*, if the only way to keep you from hurting yourself is to break every bone in your body, then put you in a cast from the neck down, I can handle that."

"Holy shit," Skeet exclaimed, "where'd you go to nursing school—Transylvania?"

"Tougher than that. I was taught by nuns, the Sisters of Mercy. And I'm warning you, *chupaflor*—no bad language on my shift."

"Sorry," Skeet said, genuinely chagrined, though still in a mood to tease. "What happens when I have to go pee-pee?"

Scratching Valet's ears, Jasmine assured Skeet, "You don't have anything I haven't seen before, though I'm sure I've seen larger."

Dusty smiled at Skeet. "From now on, it would be wise to say nothing but *Yes, ma'am.*"

"What is *chupaflor*?" Skeet asked. "You're not trying to slip some bad language by me, are you?"

"*Chupaflor* means 'hummingbird,'" Jasmine Hernandez

explained as she stuck a digital thermometer in Skeet's mouth.

In a thermometer-punctuated mumble, Skeet said, "You're calling me *hummingbird*?"

"*Chupaflor,*" she confirmed. Skeet was no longer hooked to the electrocardiograph, so she lifted his bony wrist to time his pulse.

A new uneasiness slid into Dusty, as cold as a shiv between the ribs, though he couldn't identify the cause. Not wholly new, in fact. It was the free-floating suspicion that earlier had motivated him to watch Skeet's reflection in the night-mirrored window. Something was *wrong* here, but not necessarily with Skeet. His suspicion refocused on the place, the clinic.

"Hummingbirds are cute," Skeet told Jasmine Hernandez.

"Keep the thermometer under your tongue," she admonished.

Mumbling again, he pressed: "Do you think I'm cute?"

"You're a nice-looking boy," she said, as though she could see Skeet as he had once been—healthy, fresh-faced, and clear-eyed.

"Hummingbirds are charming. They're free spirits."

With her attention on her wristwatch, counting Skeet's pulse, the nurse said, "Yes, exactly, the *chupaflor* is a cute, charming, free, insignificant little bird."

Skeet glanced at his brother and rolled his eyes.

If something were wrong about this moment, this place, these people, Dusty was unable to pinpoint the falsity. The bastard son of Sherlock Holmes, born of Miss Jane Marple, would be hard-pressed to find good reason for the suspicion that sawed at Dusty's nerves. His edginess probably arose from weariness and from his worry about Skeet; until he was rested, he couldn't trust his intuition.

In response to his brother's rolling eyes, Dusty said, "I

warned you. Two words. *Yes, ma'am.* You can't go wrong with *Yes, ma'am.*"

As Jasmine let go of Skeet's wrist, the digital thermometer beeped, and she took it out of his mouth.

Moving to the bed, Dusty said, "Gotta split, kid. Promised Martie we'd go out to dinner, and I'm late."

"Always keep your promises to Martie. She's special."

"Didn't I marry her?"

"I hope she doesn't hate me," Skeet said.

"Hey, don't be stupid."

Unspent tears shimmered in Skeet's eyes. "I love her, Dusty, you know? Martie's always been so good to me."

"She loves you, too, kid."

"That's a pretty small club—People Who Love Skeet. But People Who Love Martie—now, that's bigger than the Rotary and the Kiwanis and the Optimist clubs all rolled into one."

Dusty could think of no comforting reply, because Skeet's observation was undeniably true.

The kid wasn't speaking from self-pity, however. "Man, that's a load I wouldn't want to carry. You know? People love you, they have expectations, and then you have responsibilities. The more people who love you—well, it goes round and round, it never stops."

"Love is hard, huh?"

Skeet nodded. "Love *is* hard. Go, go take Martie out for a nice dinner, a glass of wine, tell her how beautiful she is."

"I'll see you tomorrow," Dusty promised, picking up Valet's leash and clipping it to the dog's collar.

"You'll find me right here," Skeet said. "I'll be the one in a body cast from the neck down."

As Dusty led Valet out of the room, Jasmine approached the bed with a sphygmomanometer. "I need your blood pressure, *chupaflor.*"

Skeet said, "Yes, ma'am."

That skewering sense of wrongness again. Ignore it. Weariness. Imagination. It could be cured with a glass of wine and the sight of Martie's face.

All the way along the hall to the elevator, Valet's claws ticked softly on the vinyl-tile flooring.

Nurses and nurses' assistants smiled at the retriever. "Hi, puppy." "What a handsome fella." "You're a cutie, aren't you?"

Dusty and Valet shared the elevator with a male orderly who knew just the spot on the ears that, when gently rubbed, caused the dog's eyes to take on a dreamy cast. "Had a golden myself. A sweet girl named Sassy. She got cancer, had to put her to sleep about a month ago." His voice caught briefly on the word *sleep*. "Couldn't get her to go for a Frisbee, but she'd chase tennis balls all day."

"Him, too," Dusty said. "He won't drop the first ball when you throw a second, brings them both back, looking like the world's worst case of mumps. You going to get a new puppy?"

"Not for a while," said the orderly, which meant not until the loss of Sassy hurt a little less than it hurt now.

On the ground floor, in the recreation room adjacent to the lobby, a dozen patients, at tables in groups of four, were playing cards. Their conversation and easy laughter, the click of shuffling decks, and the mellow strains of an old Glenn Miller swing tune on the radio contributed to such a cozy mood that you might have thought this was a gathering of friends at a country club, a church hall, or a private home, instead of a physically shaky and psychologically desperate collection of middle-class and upper-middle-class crack smokers, snow blowers, crank freaks, cross-top poppers, acidheads, cactus eaters, and shit spikers with Swiss-cheese veins.

At a desk next to the front door, a guard was posted to ensure that upon the premature departure of a headstrong patient, family members and officers of the court would be phoned depending upon the notification requirements of each case.

During the current shift, the security station was manned by a fiftyish man dressed in khakis, a light-blue shirt, a red tie, and a navy-blue blazer. His name tag identified him as WALLY CLARK, and he was reading a romance novel. Pudgy, dimpled, well-scrubbed, smelling faintly of a spice-scented aftershave, with the kind blue eyes of a sincere pastor and a smile just sweet enough—but not too sweet—to replace the vermouth in a not-too-dry martini, Wally was every Hollywood casting director's ideal choice for the star's favorite uncle, mentor, dedicated teacher, beloved father, or guardian angel.

"I was here the last time your brother stayed with us," Wally Clark said, leaning forward in his chair to pet Valet. "I didn't expect he'd be back. Wish he wasn't. He's a good-hearted boy."

"Thank you."

"Used to come down here to play some backgammon with me. Don't you worry, Mr. Rhodes. Your brother, deep inside, he's got the right stuff. He'll fly straight out of here this time, and stay straight."

Outside, the night was cool and damp, although not unpleasant. The woolen clouds unraveled, revealing a silver moon skating serenely across the lake of the sky, before quickly knitting up again.

Shallow puddles remained in the parking lot, and Valet weaved to the limits of his leash to prance through each of them.

When Dusty reached the van, he looked back at the hacienda-style clinic. With queen palms whispering lullabies in the sleepy breeze, with bougainvillea entwining the columns of the loggias and draping like bedclothes in graceful swags across the arches, this might have been the home of Morpheus, the Greek god of dreams.

Yet Dusty was unable to peel off a clinging suspicion that there was another, darker reality beneath the picturesque surface: a place of ceaseless activity, of secret scurrying and scheming, a nest, a hive, in which a nightmare colony labored to some hideous purpose.

Tom Wong, Dr. Donklin, Jasmine Hernandez, Wally Clark, and all the staff at New Life appeared to be smart, professional, dedicated, and compassionate. Nothing in their behavior or demeanor gave Dusty the slightest reason to question their motives.

Perhaps what bothered him was that they were all too perfect to be real. If one New Life employee had been slow on the uptake or sloppy, rude or disorganized, Dusty might have been free of this peculiar new distrust of the clinic.

Of course, the unusual competence, commitment, and friendliness of the staff meant only that New Life was well managed. Evidently, the head of personnel had a gift for hiring and nurturing first-rate employees. The happy consequences should have inspired gratitude in Dusty, not a paranoid perception of conspiracy.

Yet something felt *wrong*. He worried that Skeet was not safe here. The longer he stared at the clinic, the stronger his suspicion grew. Frustratingly, the reason for it continued to elude him.

The spring-action clippers with the long blades and the battery-powered hedge trimmer were so wicked-looking that Martie was not satisfied merely to throw them away. She would not feel safe until they were reduced to useless scrap.

Larger garden tools were stored neatly in a tall cabinet. Rake, leaf rake, shovel, hoe. Sledgehammer.

She put the hedge trimmer on the concrete floor, where Dusty would park his van when he came home, and she swung the sledge at it. Under the impact of the large blunt hammerhead, the trimmer shrieked as though it were a living thing, but Martie judged the damage to be insufficient. She hefted the hammer and swung it again, then a third time, a fourth.

Pieces of plastic from the shattered handle, a couple screws, and other debris rattled off nearby cabinets, pinged off the Saturn. With each loud blow, the garage windows vibrated in their frames and chips of concrete exploded out of the floor.

All this shrapnel peppered Martie's face. She recognized the danger to her eyes, but she didn't dare pause to search for safety goggles. Much work remained to be done, and at any moment, the big garage door might rumble upward, announcing Dusty's arrival.

She threw the hedge clippers on the floor. She pounded them ferociously, until the spring popped out and the handles came apart.

Then a spading fork. Pounding and pounding it until the wooden handle was smashed into splinters. Until the tines were bent and squashed together in a useless tangle.

The sledgehammer was a three-pound rather than a five-pound model. Nevertheless, strength and balance were required to wield it with the desired devastating effect. Sweating, gasping for breath, mouth dry, throat hot, Martie repeatedly swung the hammer high and drove it down smoothly, with calculated rhythm.

She would suffer in the morning; every muscle in her shoulders and arms would ache, but right now the sledge felt so glorious in her hands that she didn't care about the pain to come. A sweet current of power flowed through her, a gratifying sense of being in control for the first time all day. Each solid thud of the hammerhead thrilled her; the hard reverberation of the impact, traveling up the long handle, into her hands, along her arms, into her shoulders and neck, was deeply satisfying, almost erotic. She sucked air with each upswing, grunted when she drove the hammer down, issued a wordless little cry of pleasure each time that something bent or cracked under the pummeling weight—

—until abruptly she heard herself and realized that she sounded more animal than human.

Panting, still gripping the hammer in both hands, Martie turned from the ruined tools and caught sight of her reflection in a side window of the Saturn. Her shoulders were hunched, head thrust forward and cocked at a weird angle, like that of a condemned murderess who had been reprieved but deformed when a hangman's noose had snapped. Her dark hair was tangled and bristling as though she'd received an electric shock. Dementia carved her face into that of a hag, and a wild thing glared from behind her eyes.

Crazily, she recalled an illustration in a storybook she'd treasured as a child: an evil troll under an old stone bridge, bent over a glowing forge, working with hammer and tongs to make chains and shackles for his victims.

What would she have done to Dusty if he had arrived at the very moment when her frenzied hammering had been at a peak—or, for that matter, if he arrived now?

With a shudder of revulsion, she dropped the hammer.

25

Having expected to be away from home past feeding time, Dusty had brought Valet's dinner in a Ziploc bag: two cups of dry lamb-and-rice kibble. He poured it into a plastic bowl and put the bowl on the pavement beside the van.

"Sorry about the lousy ambience," he apologized.

If the clinic parking lot had been a lush meadow or a penthouse, Valet would have approached his dinner with no greater pleasure than he showed now. Like all of his kind, he had no pretensions.

Dogs possessed so many admirable qualities, in fact, that Dusty sometimes wondered if God had created this world expressly for them above all other creatures. Human beings might have been put here as an afterthought, to ensure that dogs would have companions to prepare their meals, to groom them, to tell them they were cute, and to rub their bellies.

While Valet made quick work of the kibble, Dusty fished his cell phone from under the driver's seat and called home. On the third ring, the answering machine responded.

Assuming that Martie was screening calls, he said, "Scarlett, it's me. Rhett. Just calling to say I *do* give a damn, after all."

She didn't pick up.

"Martie, are you there?" He waited. Then, stretching the message to give her time to get to the study—and the answering machine—from anywhere in the house, he said:

"Sorry I'm running late. Hell of a day. I'll be there in half an hour, we'll go out for dinner. Somewhere we can't afford. I'm sick of always being so damn responsible. Choose something extravagant. Maybe even a place where the food comes on real plates instead of in Styrofoam containers. We'll take a bank loan if we have to."

Either she hadn't heard the phone or she wasn't home.

Valet had finished his kibble. He used his tongue to imitate an airplane propeller, making 360-degree sweeps of his chops and muzzle, collecting crumbs.

When traveling with the dog, Dusty carried bottled water. He poured a few ounces into the blue dish.

After Valet finished drinking, they walked the dimly lighted lawns that embraced three sides of New Life Clinic. This stroll was ostensibly for the purpose of giving the dog a chance to do his postdinner dump, but it also provided Dusty with an opportunity to examine more closely the rambling structure.

Even if the clinic were less legitimate than it appeared to be, Dusty had no idea where he should look for clues to its true nature. There would be no hidden door to the vast subterranean headquarters of a flamboyant James Bond-style villain. Nor could he expect to discover the soulless personal servant of Count Dracula clandestinely transferring the undead nobleman's coffin from a horse-drawn lorry into the basement of the building. This was southern California in the dazzling new millennium, and it was, therefore, full of far stranger creatures than Goldfinger and vampires—though currently none appeared to be lurking in this neighborhood.

Dusty's suspicion was difficult to sustain in the face of the unrelenting ordinariness of the clinic grounds. The grass was well manicured, the earth still slightly squishy from the recent rain. The shrubs were neatly trimmed. The night shadows were only shadows.

Although Valet was easily spooked, he was so comfortable here that he completed his toilet without any nervous hesitation—and did it in the amber glow of a landscape lamp, which allowed his master to pick up easily after him.

The fully loaded, conspicuous blue bag gave Dusty an excuse to explore the alleyway behind the clinic, where no grass bordered the pavement. As he located a small trash Dumpster and deposited the bag, he surveyed this more humble aspect of the building: delivery and service entrances, utilities boxes, a second small Dumpster.

Neither he nor his four-legged Dr. Watson discovered anything amiss in the backstreet—although beside the second Dumpster, the dog found a grease-stained Big Mac container that he would have enjoyed sniffing and licking for six or seven hours.

Retreating from the alley, passing once more across the lawn along the south side of the clinic, Dusty glanced up at Skeet's room—and saw a man standing at the window. Backlit by a single well-shaded lamp, he was a featureless silhouette.

Though the angle was deceiving, the guy seemed too tall and too broad-shouldered to be Skeet or Dr. Donklin. Tom Wong was gone for the night, but he, too, was a different physical type from this man.

Dusty could discern nothing of the stranger's face, not even the vague glint of his eyes. Nevertheless, he was sure the man was watching him.

As though he were in a staring contest with a ghost, Dusty gazed up at the window until, with the ectoplasmic fluidity of a haunting spirit, the dark form turned away from the glass and drifted out of sight.

Dusty considered hurrying to his brother's room to learn the identity of the watcher. Almost certainly, however, the man would prove to be a staff member. Or another patient, visiting Skeet.

On the other hand, if this nagging suspicion were merited, rather than being mere paranoia, if the man at the window were up to no good, he would not hang around now that Dusty had seen him. No doubt he was already gone.

Common sense argued against suspicion. Skeet had no money, no prospects, no power. There was nothing to be gotten from him that would motivate anyone to engineer an elaborate conspiracy.

Besides, an enemy—in the unlikely event that gentle Skeet had one—would realize the futility of engaging in elaborate schemes to torment and destroy the kid. Left to his own devices, Skeet would torture himself more ruthlessly than could the most cruel dungeon master, and he would diligently pursue his own destruction.

Maybe this wasn't even Skeet's room. Dusty had been sure it was the kid's window when he first looked up. But . . . perhaps Skeet's window was to the left of this one.

Dusty sighed. The ever sympathetic Valet sighed as well.

"Your old man's losin' it," Dusty said.

He was eager to go home to Martie, to walk out of the insanity of this day and return to reality.

Lizzie Borden took an ax and gave her husband forty whacks.

That bastardized line of verse swung back and forth through Martie's mind, repeatedly cleaving her train of thought, so she had to struggle to remain focused.

The workbench in the garage featured a vise. After bracing the ax with a block, Martie cranked the jaws shut until they tightened on the handle.

She was able to pick up a pistol-grip hacksaw only with great effort. It was a dangerous instrument, but less fearsome than the ax, which *must* be destroyed. Later, she'd wreck the hacksaw, too.

Using the saw, she attacked the wooden handle at the

neck. The cast-steel head would still be deadly once it had been severed, but the ax, intact, was far more lethal than either of its parts.

Lizzie Borden took an ax and gave her husband forty whacks.

The hacksaw blade torqued, bound in the ax handle, stuttered loose, torqued again, and made a sloppy kerf in the hard wood. She threw it on the floor.

In the tool collection were two carpenter's saws. One was a ripsaw, for cutting with the grain of the wood, the other a crosscut saw, but Martie didn't know which was which. Hesitantly, she tried one, then the other, and both frustrated her.

When the job was neatly done, she gave him another forty-one.

Among the power tools was a handheld reciprocating saw with a blade so fierce that she required all the courage she could muster to plug it in, pick it up, and switch it on. Initially the teeth stuttered with little effect across the oak, and the saw vibrated violently, but when Martie bore down, the blade buzzed through the wood, and the severed ax head, with handle stump, fell onto the workbench.

She switched off the saw and set it aside. Opened the jaws of the vice. Freed the ax handle. Threw it on the floor.

Next, she decapitated the sledgehammer.

Then the shovel. Longer handle. Cumbersome. Getting it into the vise was more difficult than dealing with the ax or sledgehammer. The reciprocating saw tore through it, and the shovel blade clattered onto the workbench.

She sawed through the hoe.

The rake.

What else?

A crowbar. A pointed pry blade at one end, leveraging hook at the other. All steel. Couldn't be sawn.

Use it to smash the reciprocating saw. Steel ringing off steel, off concrete, the garage reverberating like a great bell.

When she had disabled the saw, she still held the crowbar. It was as dangerous as the sledgehammer, which had driven her to use the saws in the first place.

She had come full circle. She hadn't accomplished anything. In fact, the crowbar was more effective than the sledgehammer, because it was easier to wield.

There was no hope. No way to make the house safe, not even one room within the house, not as little as one corner within one room. It couldn't be done as long as she remained in residence. She, not any inanimate object, was the source of these vicious thoughts, the sole threat.

She should have clamped the reciprocating saw in the jaws of the vise, switched it on, and cut off her own hands.

Now she held the crowbar in the same grip with which she had held the hammer. Through her mind spiraled bloody thoughts that terrified her.

The garage-door motor kicked in. The door clattered upward, and she turned to face it.

Tires, headlights, the windshield, Dusty in the driver's seat of the van, Valet beside him. Normal life on wheels, motoring into Martie's personal Twilight Zone. This was a collision of universes that she had been fearing since the portentous mental image of a key-skewered eye—Dusty's eye—had caused her heart to plummet like an express elevator and her lunch to rise like a counterweight.

"Stay away from me!" she cried. "For God's sake, stay away! There's something wrong with me."

Almost as effectively as a mirror, Dusty's expression revealed to Martie how bizarre—how crazed—she looked.

"Oh, God."

She dropped the crowbar, but the head of the ax and the head of the sledgehammer were within reach on the workbench. She could easily snatch them up, pitch them at the windshield.

The key. The eye. Thrust and twist.

Suddenly Martie realized that she had not thrown away

the car key. How could she have failed to dispose of it immediately upon getting home, before dealing with the knives, the rolling pin, the garden tools, and everything else? If in fact the vision she had experienced was a premonition, if this hideous act of violence was inevitable, the car key was the *first* thing she should have mangled and then buried at the bottom of the trash can.

Enter Dusty, and therefore on to the next level of the game, where the humble key of Level 1 now becomes a powerful and magical object, equivalent to the One Ring, the Master of all the Rings of Power, which must be conveyed back to Mordor and destroyed in the Fire from which it came, must be melted down before it can be used for evil purpose. But this was no game. These horrors were real. The blood, when it came, would be thick, warm, and wet, rather than a two-dimensional arrangement of red pixels.

Martie turned away from the van and hurried into the house.

The car key wasn't hanging on the Peg-Board, where it should have been.

The sweating glass of unfinished ginger ale and a cork coaster were the only things on the kitchen table.

Draped over a chair: her raincoat. Two deep pockets. A few Kleenex in one. The paperback book in the other.

No key.

In the garage, Dusty was calling her. He must be out of the van, picking his way through the debris that she had left on the floor. Each repetition of her name was louder than the previous one, closer.

Out of the kitchen, into the hall, past the dining room, living room, into the foyer, Martie fled toward the front door, with the sole intention of putting distance between herself and Dusty. She was unable to think ahead to the consequence of this mad flight, to where she would ultimately go, to what she would do. Nothing mattered except getting far enough away from her husband to ensure that she couldn't harm him.

The foyer carpet, small and Persian, slid on the polished-oak tongue and groove, and for a moment she was floor-surfing. Then she wiped out and went down hard on her right side.

When her elbow rapped the oak, wasps of pain took flight along the nerves of her forearm, swarming in her hand. More pain buzzed along her ribs, stung through her hip joint.

The most shocking pain was the least acute: a quick jabbing in her right thigh, sharp but short-lived pressure. She had been poked by something in the right-hand pocket of her jeans, and she knew at once what it was.

The car key.

Here was incontestable proof that she couldn't trust herself. On some level, she must have known the key was in her pocket, when she had checked the Peg-Board, when she had scanned the table, when she had frantically searched her raincoat. She'd deceived herself, and there was no reason to have done so unless she intended to use the key to blind, to kill. Within her was some Other Martine, the deranged personality she feared, a creature who was capable of any atrocity and who intended to fulfill the hateful premonition: *the key, the eye, thrust and twist.*

Martie scrambled up from the foyer floor and to the windowed front door.

At the same instant, Valet leaped against the outside of the door, paws planted at the base of the leaded-glass pane, ears pricked and tongue lolling. The many squares, rectangles, and circles of beveled glass, punctuated by jewel-like prisms and round glass beads, transformed his furry face into a cubist portrait that looked both amusing and demonic.

Martie reeled back from the door, not because Valet

frightened her, but because she was afraid of harming him. If she were truly capable of hurting Dusty, then the poor trusting dog was not safe, either.

In the kitchen, Dusty called, "Martie?"

She didn't answer.

"Martie, where are you? What's wrong?"

Up the stairs. Quickly, silently, two steps at a time, half limping because pain lingered in her hip. Clutching at the railing with her left hand. Digging in a pocket with her right.

She reached the top with the key buried in her fist, just the silvery tip poking out from her tightly clenched fingers. Little dagger.

Maybe she could toss it out a window. Into the night. Throw it into thick shrubbery or over the fence into the neighbor's yard, where she couldn't easily retrieve it.

In the shadowy upstairs hall, which was lit only by the foyer light rising through the stairwell, she stood in indecision, because not all the windows were operable. Some were fixed panes. Of those that could be opened, many were sure to be swollen after a long day of rain, and they wouldn't slide easily.

The eye. The key. Thrust and twist.

Time was running out. Dusty would find her at any moment.

She didn't dare delay, couldn't risk trying a window that more likely than not would be stuck, and have Dusty come upon her while she still held the key. At the sight of him, she might snap, might commit one of the unthinkable atrocities with which her mind had been preoccupied throughout the afternoon. Okay, then the master bathroom. Flush the damn thing down the toilet.

Crazy.

Just do it. Move, move, do it, crazy or not.

On the front porch, muzzle to the jeweled window, the usually quiet Valet began barking.

Martie dashed into the master bedroom, switched on the overhead light. She started toward the bathroom—but halted when her gaze, as swift and sharp as a guillotine, fell on Dusty's nightstand.

In her frenzied attempt to make the house safe, she had thrown out gadgets as innocuous as potato peelers and corn-cob holders, yet she had not given a thought to the most dangerous item in the house, a weapon that was nothing *but* a weapon, that did not double as a rolling pin or a cheese grater: a .45 semiautomatic, which Dusty had purchased for self-defense.

This was one more example of clever self-deception. The Other Martie—the violent personality buried within her for so long, but now disinterred—had misdirected her, encouraged her hysteria, kept her distracted until the penultimate moment, when she was least able to think clearly or act rationally, when Dusty was near and drawing nearer, and *now* she was permitted—oh, encouraged—to remember the pistol.

Downstairs in the foyer, Dusty spoke to the retriever through the window in the front door—"Settle! Valet, settle!"—and the dog stopped barking.

When Dusty had first purchased the pistol, he had insisted that Martie take firearms training with him. They had gone to a shooting range ten or twelve times. She didn't like guns, didn't want this one, even though she understood the wisdom of being able to defend herself in a world where progress and savagery grew at the same pace. She had become surprisingly competent with the weapon, a thoroughly customized stainless-steel version of the Colt Commander.

Down in the foyer, Dusty said, "Good dog," rewarding Valet's obedience with praise. "Very good dog."

Martie wanted desperately to dispose of the Colt. Dusty wasn't safe with the gun in the house. No one in the neighborhood was safe if she could get her hands on a pistol.

She went to the nightstand.

For God's sake, leave it in the drawer.

She opened the drawer.

"Martie, honey, where are you, what's wrong?" He was on the stairs, ascending.

"Go away," she said. Although she tried to shout, the words came out in a thin croak, because her throat was tight with fear and because she was out of breath—but perhaps also because the murderess within her didn't really want him to leave.

In the drawer, between a box of tissues and a remote control for the television, the pistol gleamed dully, fate embodied in a chunk of beautifully machined steel, her dark destiny.

Like a deathwatch beetle, its mandibles *tick-tick-tick*ing as it quarried tunnels deep within a mass of wood, the Other Martie squirmed in Martie's flesh, bored through her bones, and chewed at the fibers of her soul.

She picked up the Colt. With its single-action let-off, highly controllable recoil, 4.5-pound trigger pull, and virtually unjammable seven-round magazine, this was an ideal close-up, personal-defense piece.

Until she stepped on it while turning away from the nightstand, Martie didn't realize that she had dropped the car key.

26

Falling off a roof, Dusty had not been this scared, because now he was frightened for Martie, not for himself.

Her face, before she dropped the crowbar and ran away, had been as stark as the face of an actor in a Kabuki drama. White-greasepaint skin, pale and smooth. Eyes darkly outlined, not with mascara but with anguish. Red slash of a mouth.

Stay away from me! For God's sake, stay away! There's something wrong with me.

Even above the engine noise, he'd heard her warning, the terror scraping her voice raw.

Debris in the garage. A mess in the kitchen. Trash can on the back porch, at the open door, stuffed full of everything but trash. He couldn't extract meaning from any of it.

The downstairs was cold because the kitchen door wasn't closed. He found it too easy to imagine that part of the chill resulted from the presence of an icy spirit that had come through another door, one not visible, from a place infinitely stranger than the back porch.

The silver candlesticks on the dining-room table appeared to be as translucent as they were reflective, as though carved from ice.

The living room was filled with the wintry glitter of glass bibelots, brass fireplace tools, porcelain lamps. The grandfather clock had frozen time at 11:00.

On their honeymoon, they had found the clock in an

antique shop and acquired it for a reasonable price. They weren't interested in its value as a timepiece, and they didn't intend to have it repaired. Its hands were stopped at the hour of their wedding, which seemed like a good omen.

After silencing Valet, Dusty decided to leave the dog on the front porch for now, and he quickly climbed the stairs. Although he ascended into increasingly warmer air, he brought with him the chill that had pierced him at the sight of Martie's tortured face.

He found her in the master bedroom. She was standing beside the bed, with the .45 pistol.

She had ejected the magazine. Muttering frantically to herself, she was prying the bullets out of it. Jacketed hollowpoints.

When she extracted a round, she threw it across the room. The cartridge snapped against a mirror without cracking it, rattled onto the top of the vanity, and came to rest among the decorative combs and hairbrushes.

Dusty couldn't at first understand what she was saying, but then he recognized it: ". . . full of grace, the Lord is with thee; blessed art thou among women . . ."

In a whispery voice, pitched high with anxiety, a voice almost like that of a frightened child, Martie was reciting the Hail Mary, fingering another round out of the magazine, as if the bullets were rosary beads and she were paying penance with prayer.

Watching Martie from the doorway, Dusty felt his heart swell with fear for her, swell and swell impossibly, until the pressure made his chest ache.

She flung another bullet, which cracked off the dresser—and then saw him in the doorway. Already sufficiently white-faced for a Kabuki stage, she grew even paler.

"Martie—"

"No!" she gasped, as he stepped off the threshold.

She dropped the pistol and kicked it across the carpet so

hard that it traveled the length of the room and clattered noisily against a closet door.

"It's only me, Martie."

"Get out of here, go, go, go."

"Why are you afraid of me?"

"I'm afraid of *me*!" Her fingers, sharp and white, plucked at the pistol magazine with carrion-crow tenacity, extracting one more cartridge. "For God's sake, *run*!"

"Martie, what—"

"Don't get close to me, don't, don't trust me," she said, her voice as thin, shaky, and urgent as that of a high-wire walker losing balance. "I'm all screwed up, totally screwed."

"Honey, listen, I'm not going anywhere until I know what's happened here, what's wrong," Dusty said as he took another step toward her.

With a despairing wail, she threw the bullet and the half-empty magazine in different directions, neither at Dusty, and then ran to the bathroom.

He pursued her.

"Please," Martie pleaded, determinedly trying to close the bathroom door in his face.

Only a minute ago, Dusty would not have been able to imagine any circumstances in which he would have used force against Martie; now his stomach fluttered queasily as he resisted her. Inserting one knee between the door and the jamb, he tried to shoulder into the room.

She abruptly stopped resisting and backed away.

The door banged open so hard that Dusty winced as he stumbled across the threshold.

Martie retreated until she bumped against the entrance to the shower stall.

Catching the bathroom door as it rebounded from the rubber stop, Dusty kept his attention on Martie. He fumbled for the wall switch and clicked on the fluorescent panel in the soffit above the twin sinks.

Hard light ricocheted off mirrors, porcelain, white-and-green ceramic tile. Off nickel-plated fixtures as shiny as surgical steel.

Martie stood with her back to the glass-enclosed shower. Eyes shut. Face pinched. Hands fisted against her temples.

Her lips moved rapidly but produced not a sound, as if she had been stricken mute by terror.

Dusty suspected that she was praying again.

He took three steps, touched her arm.

As dire blue and full of trouble as a hurricane sea, her eyes snapped open. "*Get away!*"

Rocked by her vehemence, he relented.

The seal on the shower door popped with a *twonk*, and she eased backward over the raised sill, into the stall. "You don't know what I'll do, my God, you can't imagine, you can't *conceive* how vicious, how cruel."

Before she could pull the shower door shut, he intervened and held it open. "Martie, I'm not afraid of you."

"You should be, you've *got* to be."

Bewildered, he said, "Tell me what's wrong."

The radiant patterns of striations in her blue eyes resembled cracks in thick glass, her black pupils like bullet holes at the center.

Explosive shatters of words broke from her: "There's more to me than you see, another me down inside somewhere, full of hate, ready to hurt, cut, smash, or if maybe there's no Other and there's just me alone, then I'm not the person I always thought I was, I'm something twisted and horrible, horrible."

In his worst dreams and in the most desperate moments of his waking life, Dusty had never been this profoundly frightened, and in his private image of himself as a man, he had not allowed for the possibility that he could be so utterly humbled by fear as he was now.

He sensed that Martie, as he had always known her, was

slipping away from him, inexplicably but inexorably being sucked down into a psychological vortex stranger than any black hole at the far end of the universe, and that even if some aspect of her remained when the vortex closed, she would be as enigmatic as an alien life-form.

Although, until this moment, Dusty had never realized the depth of his capacity for terror, he had always understood how bleak this world would be if Martie were not in it. The prospect of life without her, joyless and lonely, was the source of the fear that racked him now.

Martie backed away from the glass door, until she wedged herself into a corner of the shower, shoulders cramped forward, arms crossed over her breasts, hands fisted in her armpits. All her bones seemed to be surfacing—knees, hips, elbows, shoulder blades, skull—as if her skeleton might secede from its union with her flesh.

When Dusty stepped into the shower, Martie said, "Don't, oh, please, please, don't," her voice resonating hollowly along the tile walls.

"I can help you."

Weeping, face wrenched, mouth soft and trembling, she said, "Baby, no. Stay back."

"Whatever this is about, I can help you."

When Dusty reached for her, Martie slid down the wall and sat on the floor, because she could not back away from him any farther.

He dropped to his knees.

As he put a hand on her shoulder, she convulsed in panic around a word: *"Key!"*

"What?"

"Key, the key!" She extracted her fists from under her clamping arms and raised them to her face. Her clenched fingers sprang open, revealing an empty right hand, then an empty left, and Martie looked amazed, as if a magician had caused a coin or a wadded silk scarf to vanish from her grasp without her sensing a thing. "No, I had it, still have it, the car key, somewhere!" Frantically she patted the pockets of her jeans.

He recalled seeing the car key on the floor near the nightstand. "You dropped it in the bedroom."

She regarded him with disbelief, but then appeared to remember. "I'm sorry. What I would've done. Thrust, twist. Oh, Jesus, God." She shuddered. Shame welled in her eyes and washed across her face, imparting faint color to her unnaturally chalky skin.

When Dusty tried to put his arms around her, Martie resisted, urgently warning him not to trust her, to shield his eyes, because even if she didn't possess the car key, she had acrylic fingernails sharp enough to gouge his eyes, and then suddenly she attempted to tear off those nails, clawing at her hands, acrylic scraping against acrylic with the insectile *click-click-click* of beetles swarming over one another. At last Dusty stopped *trying* to put his arms around her and just, damn it, *put* them around her, overwhelmed her, forced his loving embrace upon her, drew her fiercely against him, as though his body were a lightning rod with which he could ground her to reality. She went stiff, retreating into an emotional carapace, and though she was already physically drawn in upon herself, she curled tighter now, so it seemed the tremendous power of her fear would press her ever inward, condensing her, until she became as solid as stone, as hard as diamond, until she imploded into a black hole of her own making and vanished into the parallel universe where she'd briefly imagined that the car key had gone when it had been in neither of her fists. Undeterred, Dusty held her, rocked slowly back and forth with her on the floor of the shower, telling her that he loved her, that he cherished her, that she was not an evil Orc but a good Hobbit, telling her that her Hobbitness could be proved by taking one look at the curious, unfeminine, but charming toes that she had inherited from Smilin' Bob, telling her anything he could think to tell her that might make her smile. Whether she smiled or not, he didn't know, for her head was tucked down, face hidden. In time, however, she ceased resistance. After a while longer, her body unclenched, and she returned his embrace, tentatively at first, but then less tentatively, until by degrees she opened entirely and clung to him as he clung to her, with a desperate love, with an acute awareness that their lives had changed forever, and with an unnerving sense that they now existed under the shadow of a great looming unknown.

27

After watching the evening news, Susan Jagger went through the apartment, synchronizing all the clocks with her digital wristwatch. She performed this task every Tuesday evening at the same hour.

In the kitchen, clocks were built into the oven and microwave, and another hung on the wall. A stylish, battery-operated Art Deco clock stood on the fireplace mantel in the living room, and on the nightstand beside her bed was a clock radio.

On average, none of these timepieces lost or gained more than a minute during the week, but Susan took pleasure in keeping them running tick for tick.

Through sixteen months of near isolation and chronic anxiety, she had relied on ritual to save her sanity.

For every household chore, she established elaborate procedures to which she adhered as rigorously as an engineer would follow the operational manual in a nuclear power plant where imprecision might mean meltdown. Waxing floors or polishing furniture became a lengthy enterprise that filled otherwise empty hours. Performing any task to high standards, while conforming to codified housekeeping rules, gave her a sense of control that was comforting even though she recognized that it was fundamentally an illusion.

After the clocks were synchronized, Susan went into the

kitchen to prepare dinner. A tomato-and-endive salad. Chicken marsala.

Cooking was her favorite work of the day. She followed recipes with scientific exactitude, measuring and combining ingredients as carefully as a bombmaker handling explosive, unstable chemicals. Culinary rituals and religious rituals, like no others, could calm the heart and quiet the mind, perhaps because the former fed the body and the latter fed the soul.

This evening, however, she wasn't able to concentrate on dicing, grating, measuring, stirring. Her attention repeatedly strayed to the silent telephone. She was eager to hear from Martie, now that she'd at last found the courage to mention the mysterious night visitor.

Before recent events, she'd thought she could reveal anything to Martie with complete comfort, without feeling self-conscious. For six months, however, she'd been unable to speak of the sexual assaults committed against her while she slept.

Shame silenced her, but shame inhibited her less than did the concern that she'd be thought delusional. She herself found it hard to believe that she could have been stripped out of her sleepwear, raped, and re-dressed on numerous occasions without being awakened.

Eric was no sorcerer with the ability to steal in and out of the apartment—and in and out of Susan herself—utterly undetected.

Although Eric might be as weak and morally confused as Martie said, Susan was reluctant to consider that he might hate her enough to do these things to her, and hatred was undeniably at the heart of this abuse. They had loved each other, and their separation had been marked by regret, not by anger.

If he wanted her, even without the obligation to stand by her in time of need, she might welcome him. There was no reason, then, why he should scheme so elaborately to take her against her will.

Yet . . . if not Eric, who?

Having shared this house with her and having used this top floor as his home office, Eric might know a way to circumvent the doors and windows—as unlikely as that seemed. No one else was sufficiently familiar with the place to come and go undetected.

Her hand trembled, and salt spilled from the measuring spoon.

Turning from the dinner preparations, she blotted her suddenly damp palms on a dish towel.

At the apartment door, she checked the dead bolts. Both were engaged. The security chain was in place.

She leaned with her back against the door.

I am not delusional.

On the phone, Martie had seemed to believe her.

Convincing others, however, might not be easy.

Evidence supporting her contention of rape was inconclusive. Sometimes she experienced vaginal tenderness, but not always. Bruises the size of a man's fingertips occasionally appeared on her thighs and breasts, but she couldn't prove they were the work of a rapist or that she hadn't sustained them during ordinary physical activity.

Immediately on waking, she always knew when the phantom intruder had visited her during the night, even if she wasn't sore or bruised, even before she grew aware of the deposit he left in her, because she felt violated, unclean.

Feelings, however, were not proof.

The semen was the only evidence that she had been with a man, but it did not absolutely confirm rape.

Besides, presenting her stained panties to the authorities—or, worse yet, submitting to a vaginal swab in a hospital emergency room—would involve more embarrassment than she'd be able to endure in her current condition.

Indeed, her condition, the agoraphobia, was the primary reason she had been reluctant to confide in Martie, let alone in the police or other strangers. Although enlightened people knew that an extreme phobia wasn't a form of madness, they could not help but regard it as *odd.* And when she claimed that she was being sexually violated in her sleep, by a ghostly assailant whom she'd never seen, by a man who could enter through bolted doors . . . Well, even her lifelong best friend might wonder if the agoraphobia, while not itself a form of madness, was a precursor to genuine mental illness.

Now, after checking the dead bolts yet again, Susan impatiently reached for the telephone. She couldn't wait a minute longer for Martie's considered response. She needed to be reassured that her best friend, if no one else, believed in the phantom rapist.

Susan keyed the first four digits of Martie's number—but hung up. Patience. If she appeared fragile or too needy, she might seem less believable.

Returning to the marsala sauce, she realized she was too nervous to be lulled by culinary rituals. She wasn't hungry, either.

She opened a bottle of Merlot, poured a glassful, and sat at the kitchen table. Lately, she was drinking more than usual.

After sipping the Merlot, she held the glass up to the light. The dark ruby liquid was clear, apparently uncontaminated.

For a while, she had been convinced that someone was drugging her. That possibility was still troubling but not as likely as it had once seemed.

Rohypnol—which the news media had dubbed the date-rape drug—might explain how she was able to remain unconscious, or at least oblivious, even during rough intercourse. Mix Rohypnol into a woman's drink, and she appears to be in an advanced stage of inebriation: disoriented, pliant—defenseless. The drugged state ultimately gives way to genuine sleep, and upon waking, she has little or no memory of what took place during the night.

In the morning, however, after her mysterious visitor ravaged her, Susan never experienced any symptoms of Rohypnol hangover. No queasy stomach, no dry mouth, no blurring of vision, no throbbing headache, no lingering disorientation. Routinely, she woke clear-headed, even refreshed, though feeling violated.

Nevertheless, she had repeatedly changed grocers. Sometimes Susan relied on Martie to do her shopping, but for the most part she ordered groceries and other supplies from smaller family-owned markets that offered home delivery. Few provided that extra service these days, even for a charge. Although Susan had tried all of them, paranoically certain that someone was lacing her food with drugs, changing vendors didn't bring an end to the post-midnight assaults.

In desperation, she had sought answers in the supernatural. The mobile library brought her lurid books about ghosts, vampires, demons, exorcism, black magic, and abductions by extraterrestrials.

The delivering librarian, to his credit, never once commented upon—or even raised an eyebrow at—Susan's insatiable appetite for this peculiar subject matter. Anyway, it was no doubt healthier than an interest in contemporary politics or celebrity gossip.

Susan had been particularly fascinated by the legend of the incubus. This evil spirit visited women in their sleep and had sex with them while they dreamed.

Fascination had never become conviction. She hadn't descended so far into superstition that she had slept with copies of the Bible at all four corners of her bed or while wearing a necklace of garlic.

Ultimately, she ceased researching the supernatural, because as she delved into those irrational realms, her agoraphobia intensified. By sitting down to a banquet of unreason, she seemed to be feeding the sick part of her psyche in which her inexplicable fear thrived.

Her glass of Merlot was half empty. She refilled it.

Carrying the wine with her, Susan set out on a circuit of the apartment, to ascertain that all possible entrances were secured.

Both windows in the dining room faced the residence next door, which crowded close to Susan's house. They were locked.

In the living room, she switched off the lamps. She sat in an armchair, sipping Merlot, while her eyes adjusted to the darkness.

Although her phobia had progressed until she had difficulty looking at the daylight world even through windows, she could still tolerate the night view when the sky was overcast, when no deep sea of stars awaited her contemplation. In weather like this, she never failed to test herself, for she worried that if she didn't exercise her weak muscle of courage, it would atrophy altogether.

When her night vision improved and the Merlot lubricated the little engine of fortitude in her heart, she went to the middle pane of the three big ocean-facing windows. After a brief hesitation and a deep breath, she raised the pleated shade.

Immediately in front of the house, the paved promenade lay under the false frost of widely separated streetlamps. Though the hour was not yet late, the promenade was nearly deserted in the January chill. A young couple skated by on Rollerblades. A cat scurried from one drift of shadows to another.

Thin tendrils of mist wound between the few palm trees and the streetlamps. In the still air, the fronds hung motionless, so the creeping mist seemed to be alive, advancing with silent menace.

Susan couldn't see much of the night-cloaked beach. She could not see the Pacific at all: A bank of dense fog had advanced as far as the shore, where it could be glimpsed only intermittently—high, gray, like a towering tsunami flash-frozen an instant before it would have smashed across the coast. The lazy mist writhed off the face of the fog bank, as cold steam rises off a block of dry ice.

With the stars lost above the low clouds, with darkness and fog partitioning the world into small spaces, Susan should have been able to stand at the window for hours, insulated from her fear, but her heart began to race. Agoraphobia was not the cause of her sudden apprehension; rather, she was overcome by a sense of being watched.

Since the night assaults had begun, she was increasingly plagued by this new anxiety. Scopophobia: fear of being watched.

Surely, however, this wasn't just another phobia, not just an unreasonable fear, but an entirely rational one. If her phantom rapist was real, he must at times keep her home under surveillance, to be sure that he'd find her alone when he paid a visit.

Nevertheless, she was concerned about acquiring new layers of fear atop her agoraphobia, until eventually she would be bound up like an Egyptian mummy, wrapped by smothering shrouds of anxiety, paralyzed and effectively embalmed alive.

The promenade was deserted. The palm boles weren't wide enough to conceal anyone.

He's out there.

For three nights in a row, Susan hadn't been assaulted. This all too human incubus was due. He exhibited a pattern of need, more regular than—but as reliable as—the pull of the moon on the blood tides of a werewolf.

Often she had tried to stay awake on the nights she expected him. When she succeeded, exhausted and grainy-eyed by dawn, he never showed. Usually, if her willpower failed her and she dozed off, he paid a visit. Once, she fell asleep fully dressed, in an armchair, and she woke fully dressed, but in bed, with the faint scent of his sweat clinging to her and with his hateful, sticky issue clotted in her panties. He seemed to know, by some sixth sense, when she was sleeping and most vulnerable.

He's out there.

On the generally flat beach, a few low dunes rose at the outer limit of visibility, curving smoothly away into darkness and mist. An observer might be watching from behind one of them, although he would have to be lying prone in the sand to remain hidden.

She felt his gaze upon her. Or thought she felt it.

Susan quickly lowered the pleated shade, covering the window.

Furious with herself for being so shamefully timid, shaking more with anger and frustration than with fear, sick of being a helpless victim, after having been anything *but* a victim for most of her life, she wished fervently that she could overcome her agoraphobia and go outside, storm across the beach, kick through the sand to the crest of each dune, and either confront her tormentor or prove to herself that he was not out there. But she didn't have the courage to stalk the stalker, wasn't able to do anything but hide and wait.

She couldn't even hope for deliverance, because her hope, which had long sustained her, had recently shrunk until, if given physical substance, it would not be visible through either a magnifying glass or the most powerful microscope.

Magnifying glass.

As she dropped the cord of the window shade, Susan picked up a new idea, turned it around in her mind, and liked the shape of it. Housebound by agoraphobia, she couldn't stalk her stalker, but maybe she could watch him while he watched her.

In the bedroom closet, above the hanging clothes, on

the top shelf, was a vinyl carrying case containing a pair of high-power binoculars. In better days, when she had not been unnerved by the very sight of the sunlit world in all its vastness, she had enjoyed watching sailboat regattas staged along the coast and larger ships bound for South America or San Francisco.

With a two-step folding stool borrowed from the kitchen, she hurried to the bedroom. The binoculars were where she expected to find them.

Stored on the same shelf, among other stuff, was an item that she had forgotten. A video camera.

The camcorder had been one of Eric's short-lived enthusiasms. Long before he moved out, he had lost interest in taping and editing home movies.

An electrifying possibility short-circuited Susan's plan to survey the dunes for a concealed observer.

Leaving the binoculars untouched, she lifted down the hard-plastic case containing the video camera and associated gear. She opened it on the bed.

In addition to the camcorder, the case contained a spare battery pack, two blank tapes, and an instruction book.

She had never used the camera. Eric had done all the taping. Now she read the instruction book with keen interest.

As usual when pursuing a new hobby, Eric had not been satisfied with ordinary tools. He insisted on owning the best, state-of-the-art equipment, cutting-edge gadgetry. This handheld video camera was compact but nevertheless provided the finest available lenses, near flawless image and sound recording, and whisper-quiet operation that would not register through the microphone.

Instead of accepting only twenty- or thirty-minute tapes, it could accommodate a two-hour cassette. It also featured an extended-recording mode, using fewer inches of tape per minute, which allowed three hours of recording on a two-hour tape, though the resultant image was said to be ten percent less clear than that produced at standard speed.

The camcorder was so energy efficient and the rechargeable battery pack was so powerful that two to three hours of operation could be expected, depending on how much you used the image monitor and the various other power-draining features.

According to the built-in gauge, the installed battery pack was dead. Susan tested the spare pack, which held a partial charge.

Not certain that the dead pack could be revived, she used the charging cord to plug the livelier battery into a bathroom outlet, to bring it up to full readiness.

The glass of Merlot was on an end table in the living room. She raised it as if making a silent toast, and this time she drank not for solace but in celebration.

For the first time in months, she genuinely felt that she was in control of her life. While she knew that she was taking just a single small step to resolve only one of the many grievous problems that plagued her, knew that she was far from truly being in control, Susan didn't temper her excitement. At least she was doing *something*, at long last, and she desperately needed to be lifted by this rush of optimism.

In the kitchen, as she cleaned up the preparations for chicken marsala and took a pepperoni pizza from the freezer, she wondered why she hadn't thought of the camcorder weeks or months ago. Indeed, she began to realize that she had been surprisingly passive, considering the horror and abuse she'd endured.

Oh, she had sought therapy. Twice a week for almost sixteen months now. That was no small accomplishment, the struggle to and from each session, the perseverance in the face of limited results, but submitting to therapy was the very least she could have done when her life was falling apart. And the key word was *submitting*, because she'd deferred to Ahriman's therapeutic strategies and advice with uncharacteristic docility, considering that in the past she had dealt with physicians as skeptically as she did with high-pressure car salesmen, double-checking them through her own research and by seeking second opinions.

Popping the pizza into the microwave, Susan was happy to be relieved of the necessity to cook a complicated dinner, and she understood, almost with the power of an epiphany, that she'd held fast to her sanity through ritual *at the expense of action.* Ritual anesthetized, made the misery of her condition bearable, but it did not bring her closer to a resolution of her troubles; it didn't heal.

She filled her wineglass. Wine didn't heal, either, and she needed to be careful not to get bagged and then screw up the work ahead of her, but she was so excited, so adrenaline-stoked, that she could probably finish the whole bottle and, with her metabolism in high gear, burn it off by bedtime.

As Susan paced the kitchen, waiting for the pizza to be ready, her bafflement at her long passivity grew into amazement. Looking over the past year with new detachment, she could almost believe she'd been living under a warlock's evil spell that had clouded her thinking, sapped her willpower, and shackled her soul with dark magic.

Well, the spell was broken. The old Susan Jagger was back—clearheaded, energized, and ready to *use* her anger to change her life.

He was out there. Maybe he was even watching from the dunes this very minute. Maybe he would skate past her house on Rollerblades now and then, or jog past, or ride past on a bike, to all appearances only one more California fun freak or exercise fanatic. But he was out there, for sure.

The creep hadn't visited her for three successive nights, but he followed a pattern of need that all but assured he would come to her before dawn. Even if she could not fend off sleep, even if she was somehow drugged and unaware of what he was doing to her, she would know all about him in the morning, because with a little luck, the hidden camcorder would capture him in the act.

If the tape revealed Eric, she would kick his sorry ass until her shoe would need to be surgically removed from his cheeks. And then get him out of her life forever.

If she caught a stranger, which seemed highly unlikely, she would have proof for the police. As deeply mortifying as it would be to surrender a tape of her own rape into evidence, she would do what she must.

Returning to the table for her glass of wine, she wondered what if . . . what if . . .

What if upon waking she felt used and sore, felt the insidious warmth of semen, and yet the tape showed her alone in bed, tossing either in ecstasy or in terror, like a madwoman in a fit? As though her visitor were an entity—call him Incubus—who cast no reflection in mirrors and left no image on videotape.

Nonsense.

The truth was out there, but it wasn't supernatural.

She raised the glass of Merlot for a sip—and took half of it in one thick swallow.

28

Like a shrine to Martha Stewart, goddess of the modern American home. Two floor lamps with fringed silk shades. Two big armchairs with footstools, facing each other across a tea table. Needlepoint pillows on the chairs. The living-room fireplace to one side.

This was Martie's favorite spot in the house. Many nights during the past three years, she and Dusty had sat here with books, quietly reading, each lost in a separate fiction, yet as intimate as if they had been holding hands and gazing into each other's eyes.

Now her legs were drawn up on the chair, and she was turned slightly to her left, sans book. She sat quite still, in a languid attitude, which must have looked like the posture of serenity, when in fact she was not so much serene as emotionally exhausted.

In the other chair, Dusty tried to settle back in an assumption of calm consideration and analysis, but he slid repeatedly to the edge of his seat.

Occasionally halted by embarrassment, more often silenced because she couldn't help pausing to marvel at the weird details of her own demented behavior, Martie recounted her ordeal in short installments, resuming her story when Dusty gently encouraged her with questions.

The very sight of Dusty calmed her and gave her hope, but Martie sometimes could not meet his eyes. She gazed into the cold fireplace as if hypnotic flames licked the ceramic logs.

Surprisingly, the decorative set of brass fireplace tools didn't alarm her. A small shovel. Pointed tongs. A poker. Only a short while ago, the sight of the poker alone would have plucked arpeggios of terror from her harp-string nerves.

Embers of anxiety remained aglow in her, but right now she was more afraid of another crippling panic attack than of her potential to do violence.

Although she recounted the attack in all its gaudy detail, she couldn't convey how it *felt*. Indeed, she had difficulty remembering the full intensity of her terror, which seemed to have happened to another Martie Rhodes, to a troubled persona that had briefly risen from the muck of her psyche and had now submerged again.

From time to time, Dusty noisily rattled the ice in his Scotch to get her attention. When she looked at him, he raised his drink, reminding her to sample her serving. She'd been reluctant to accept the Scotch, fearful of losing control of herself again. Ounce by ounce, however, Johnny Walker Red Label was proving to be effective therapy.

Good Valet lay by her chair, rising now and then to rest his chin on her bent legs, submitting to a smoothing hand on his head, commiseration in his soulful eyes.

Twice she gave the dog small cubes of ice from her drink. He crunched them with a strangely solemn pleasure.

When Martie finished her account, Dusty said, "What now?"

"Dr. Closterman, in the morning. I made an appointment today, coming back from Susan's, even before things got really bad for me."

"I'll go with you."

"I want a full physical. Complete blood workup. A brain scan, in case maybe there's a tumor."

"There's no tumor," Dusty said with a conviction based solely on hope. "There's nothing serious wrong with you."

"There's something."

"No." The thought of her being ill, perhaps terminal, caused Dusty such dread that he could not conceal it.

Martie treasured every line of anguish in his face, because more than all the love talk in the world, it revealed how much he cherished her.

"I'd accept a brain tumor," she said.

"Accept?"

"If the alternative is mental illness. They can cut out the tumor, and there's a chance of being what you were."

"It's not that, either," he said, and the lines in his face grew deeper. "It's not mental."

"It's something," she insisted.

Sitting in bed, Susan ate pepperoni pizza and drank Merlot. This was the most delicious dinner she had ever known.

She was sufficiently perceptive and self-aware to realize that the ingredients of the simple meal had little or nothing to do with its special succulence and flavor. Sausage, cheese, and well-browned crust were not as tasty as the prospect of justice.

Freed from her peculiar spell of timidness and helplessness, she was in fact less hungry for justice than for a thick cold slice of vengeance. She had no illusions about her primitive capacity to take delight in retribution. After all, her teeth, like those of every human being, included four canines and four incisors, the better to rip and tear.

Remembering how she'd defended Eric to Martie, Susan bit off a mouthful of pizza and chewed it with fierce pleasure.

If she had developed agoraphobia as an insulating response to the pain of Eric's adultery, then perhaps he deserved some payback for that. But if he were her phantom visitor, mercilessly screwing with her mind and her body, he was a far different man from the one she'd thought he'd been when she married him. Not a man at all, in fact, but a creature, a hateful thing. A serpent. With evidence, she would use the law to chop him, as a woodsman might use an ax on a rattlesnake.

As she ate, Susan studied the bedroom, seeking the best place in which to secrete the camcorder.

Martie sat at the kitchen table, watching as Dusty cleaned up the mess that she had made.

When he dragged the trash can off the porch, into the kitchen, the contents rattled and chimed like the tools in a knacker's bag.

Martie held her second glass of Scotch with both hands as she raised it to her lips.

After closing the door, Dusty loaded the knives, forks, and other eating utensils into the dishwasher.

The sight of the sharp blades and pointed tines, the clink and steely scrape of them against one another, did not alarm Martie. Her throat thickened, however, and the warm Scotch trickled slowly down, as though melting through a clog in her esophagus.

Dusty returned the Chardonnay and Chablis to the refrigerator. Those bottles would still make effective bludgeons, lacerating scalp and cracking skull bone, but Martie's mind was no longer acrawl with the temptation to heft them, swing them.

After he slid the emptied drawers into the cabinets and put away those items that didn't need to be washed, Dusty said, "The stuff in the garage can wait till morning."

She nodded but said nothing, in part because she didn't trust herself to speak. Here at the scene of her bizarre seizure, memories of madness floated upon the air, like poisonous spores, and she half expected to be recontaminated by them, whereupon she might open her mouth only to hear herself spouting lunacies.

When Dusty suggested dinner, Martie pleaded no appetite, but he insisted she must eat.

In the refrigerator was a casserole with enough leftover lasagna for two. Dusty heated it in the microwave.

He cleaned and sliced some fresh mushrooms.

The knife looked harmless in his hands.

As Dusty sautéed the mushrooms with butter and diced onion, then stirred them into a pot with a package of sugar snap peas, Valet sat in front of the microwave, dreamy-eyed, deeply inhaling the aroma of cooking lasagna.

In light of what Martie had done here a short time ago, this cozy domesticity struck her as surreal. Like wandering across vast burning fields of sulfur and coming upon a doughnut shop in Hell.

When Dusty served dinner, Martie wondered if earlier she might have poisoned the leftover lasagna.

She couldn't recall committing such treachery. But she still suspected that she suffered fugues: spasms of time during which she functioned as if conscious, though nothing stuck in her memory.

Certain that Dusty would eat the lasagna just to prove his trust in her, Martie restrained herself and didn't caution him. To guard against the dismal prospect of surviving dinner alone, she overcame her lack of appetite to eat most of what he had put on her plate.

She refused a fork, however, and ate with a spoon.

A Biedermeier pedestal stood in one corner of Susan Jagger's bedroom. Atop the pedestal was a bronze bowl containing a miniature ming tree, which received no sunshine from the perpetually covered windows but flourished because a small plant light stood behind it.

At the base of the ming tree was lush ivy with small star-shaped leaves, which covered the potting soil and trailed over the curves of bronze. After calculating the best angle of view between bowl and bed, she placed the camcorder in the container and artfully arranged the trailers of ivy to conceal it.

She switched off the plant light, leaving on a nightstand lamp. The room couldn't be dark if she were to get anything useful on tape.

To explain the lamp, she would appear to have fallen asleep while reading. Only a half-finished glass of wine on the nightstand and an open book, precisely tumbled among the bedclothes, would be necessary to create that impression.

She circled the room, studying the bronze bowl. The camcorder was well hidden.

From one acute angle, an amber reflection of the lamp glowed like animal eyeshine in the dark lens, as though a cyclopean lizard were peering from the loops of ivy. This telltale was so small that it wouldn't draw the attention of either incubus or mere mortal.

Susan returned to the camcorder, slipped one finger into the ivy, searched briefly, and pressed a button.

She retreated two steps. Stood very still. Head cocked, breath held. Listening.

Though the heat was off and no furnace fan was churning, though no wind whispered in the eaves or at the windows, though the silence in the bedroom was as complete as one could hope for in this age of omnipresent mechanisms, Susan couldn't hear the hum of the camcorder motor. Indeed, the equipment fulfilled the manufacturer's guarantee of whisper-quiet operation, and the faint sibilant sigh of turning tape reels was completely muffled by the shrouding ivy.

Aware that quirks of architecture could cause sound to

travel in unexpected arcs, amplifying it at the end of its bounce, she moved around the room. Five times she paused to listen, but she could hear nothing suspicious.

Satisfied, Susan returned to the pedestal and extracted the camcorder from the ivy. She reviewed the recording on the camera's built-in monitor.

The entire bed was visible in the frame. The entrance to the room was captured at the extreme left side of the image.

She watched herself move in and out of the shot. In and out again. Pausing to listen for the softly whirring motor.

She was surprised that she appeared so young and attractive.

These days, she didn't see herself this clearly when she looked in mirrors. In mirrors, she perceived less of a physical reflection than a psychological one: a Susan Jagger aged by chronic anxiety, features softened and blurred by sixteen months of reclusion, gray with boredom and gaunt with worry.

This woman on the tape was slim, pretty. More important, she was full of purpose. This was a woman with hope—and a future.

Pleased, Susan replayed the recording. And here she came once more, out of the camcorder's iron-oxide memory, moving purposefully around the bedroom, in and out of frame, pausing to listen: a woman with a plan.

Even a spoon could be a weapon if she reversed her grip on it, held it by the bowl, and stabbed with the handle. Although not as sharp as a knife, it could be used to gouge, to blind.

Fits of tremors came and went, causing the spoon to oscillate between Martie's fingers. Twice it rattled against her plate, as though she were calling for attention before raising a toast.

She was tempted to put the spoon out of reach and eat with her hands. For fear of appearing even crazier in Dusty's eyes than she did already, she persevered with the flatware.

Dinner conversation was awkward. Even after the detailed account she had given in the living room, he had many questions regarding the panic attack. She grew increasingly reluctant to talk about it.

For one thing, the subject depressed her. Recalling her queer behavior, she felt helpless, as though she had been cast back to the powerless and dependent condition of early childhood.

In addition, she was troubled by an irrational but nonetheless firm conviction that talking about the panic attack would induce another one. She felt as if she were sitting on a trapdoor, and the longer she talked, the more likely she was to speak the trigger word that would release the hinges and drop her into an abyss below.

She asked about his day, and he recited a list of business errands that he usually attended to when the weather didn't favor housepainting.

Although Dusty never lied, Martie sensed that he wasn't giving her the full story. Of course, in her current condition, she was too paranoid to trust her feelings.

Pushing aside his plate, he said, "You keep avoiding my eyes."

She didn't deny it. "I *hate* for you to see me like this."

"Like what?"

"Weak."

"You aren't weak."

"This lasagna has more spine than I do."

"It's two days old. For lasagna . . . hell, that's eighty-five in human years."

"I feel eighty-five."

He said, "Well, I'm here to testify, you look way better than that damn lasagna."

"Gee, mister, you sure can charm a girl."

"You know what they say about housepainters."

"What do they say?"

"We know how to roll it on thick."

She met his eyes.

He smiled and said, "It's going to be all right, Martie."

"Not unless your jokes get better."

"Weak, my ass."

Walking the battlements of her four-room fortress, Susan Jagger satisfied herself that all the windows were locked.

The only apartment door opening to the outside world was in the kitchen. It was protected by two dead bolts and a security chain.

Finished checking the locks, she tipped a kitchen chair onto its back legs and wedged it under the doorknob. Even if Eric somehow had obtained a key, the chair would prevent the door from being opened.

Of course, she had tried the chair trick before. It hadn't foiled the intruder.

After hiding the camcorder and testing the view angle, she had removed the battery pack to plug it into a bathroom outlet once more. Now it was fully charged.

She inserted the battery and hid the camcorder in the ivy under the potted ming tree. She would switch it on just before she got into bed, and then would have three hours of tape—in extended mode—on which to catch Eric in the act.

All the synchronized clocks agreed on the hour: 9:40 P.M. Martie had promised to call before eleven o'clock.

Susan remained eager to hear what analysis and advice her friend might offer, but she wasn't going to tell Martie about the camcorder. Because maybe her phone was tapped. Maybe Eric was listening.

Oh, how lovely it was here on the dance floor

at the Paranoia Cotillion, gliding around and around in the fearsome embrace of a malevolent stranger, while the orchestra played a threnody and she grimly worked up the courage to look into the face of the dancer whose lead she followed.

29

Two glasses of Scotch, a brick of lasagna, and the events of this terrible day left Martie half numb with exhaustion. As Dusty cleaned up the dinner dishes, she sat at the table, watching him from under heavy eyelids.

She had expected to lie awake until dawn, racked by anxiety, dreading the future. But now her mind rebelled at assuming an even heavier burden of worry; it was shutting down for the night.

A new fear of sleepwalking was the only thing preventing her from nodding off here at the kitchen table. Somnambulism had never previously afflicted her, but then she had never suffered a panic attack until this morning, either, and now all things were possible.

If she walked in her sleep, perhaps that Other Martie would control her body. Slipping out of bed, leaving Dusty to dream on, the Other might descend barefoot through the house, as comfortable as the blind in darkness, to extract a clean knife from the utensils basket in the dishwasher.

Dusty took her hand and led her through the downstairs, turning off lights as they went. Valet padded after them, his eyes red and shining in the gloom.

Having brought Martie's raincoat from the kitchen, Dusty paused to hang it in the foyer closet.

Sensing a weight in one of the coat pockets, he fished out the paperback book. "Are you still reading this?" he asked.

"It's a real thriller."

"But you've been taking it to Susan's sessions forever."

"Not all that long." She yawned. "The writing's good."

"A real thriller—but you can't get through it in six months?"

"It hasn't been six months, has it? No. Can't be. The plot is entertaining. The characters are colorful. I'm enjoying it."

He was frowning at her. "What's wrong with you?"

"Plenty. But, right now, mostly I'm just so damn tired."

Handing the book to her, he said, "Well, if you have trouble going to sleep, obviously a page of this is better than Nembutal."

To sleep: perchance to walk, to knife, to burn.

Valet preceded them up the stairs.

As Martie ascended with one hand on the banister and Dusty's supportive arm around her waist, she took some comfort from the realization that the dog might wake her if she went sleepwalking. Good Valet would lick her bare feet, slap his handsome tail against her legs as she went down the stairs, and certainly bark at her if she withdrew a butcher knife from the dishwasher without using it to carve a snack for him from the brisket in the refrigerator.

Susan dressed for bed in simple white cotton panties—no embroidery or lace, no adornment of any kind—and a white T-shirt.

Prior to the past few months, she had favored colorful lingerie with frills. She had enjoyed feeling sexy. No more.

She understood the psychology behind her change in sleepwear. Sexiness was now linked in her mind to rape. Appliquéd lace, fimbria, furbelow, plicated selvage, bargello stitchery, point de gaze, and the like might offer encouragement to her mysterious postmidnight visitor; he might interpret frills as an invitation to further abuse.

For a while she had gone to bed in men's pajamas, loose and ugly, and then in baggy exercise cottons. The creep hadn't been turned off by either.

In fact, after undressing her and brutally using her, he took the time to re-dress her with attention to detail that was obvious mockery. If she had buttoned every button on her pajama top before going to bed, he buttoned each; but if she had left one unbuttoned, the same remained unbuttoned when she woke. He retied the waistband drawstring in precisely the bow knot that she had used.

These days, simple white cotton. An assertion of her innocence. A refusal to be degraded or soiled, regardless of what he did to her.

Dusty was worried about Martie's sudden torpor. She pleaded bone-deep weariness, but judging by her demeanor, she was succumbing less to exhaustion than to profound depression.

She moved sluggishly, not with the loose-limbed awkwardness of exhaustion, but with the grim and determined plodding of one who labored under a crushing burden. Her face was tight, pinched at the corners of the mouth and eyes, rather than slack with fatigue.

Martie was only a half step down the ladder from fanaticism when it came to dental hygiene, but this evening she didn't want to bother brushing her teeth. In three years of marriage, this was a first.

On every night in Dusty's memory, Martie washed her face and applied a moisturizing lotion. Brushed her hair. Not this time.

Forgoing her nightly rituals, she went to bed fully dressed.

When Dusty realized she was not going to take off her clothes, he untied her laces and removed her shoes. Her socks. Skinned off her jeans. She didn't resist, but she didn't cooperate, either.

Getting Martie out of her blouse was too difficult, especially as she lay on her side, knees drawn up, arms crossed on her breasts. Leaving her partially dressed, Dusty pulled the covers over her shoulders, smoothed her hair back from her face, kissed her brow.

Her eyelids drooped, but in her eyes was something more stark and sharp-edged than weariness.

"Don't leave me," she said thickly.

"I won't."

"Don't trust me."

"But I do."

"Don't sleep."

"Martie—"

"Promise me. Don't sleep."

"All right."

"Promise."

"I promise."

"Because I might kill you in your sleep," she said, and closed her eyes, which seemed to change from cornflower-blue to cyanine and then to purple madder just as her eyelids slipped shut.

He stood watching her, frightened not by her warning, not for himself, but for her.

She mumbled, "Susan."

"What about her?"

"Just remembered. Didn't tell you about Susan. Strange stuff. Supposed to call her."

"You can call her in the morning."

"What sort of friend am I?" she muttered.

"She'll understand. Just rest now. Just rest."

In seconds, Martie appeared to be asleep, lips parted, breathing through her mouth. The pinched lines of anxiety were gone from the corners of her eyes.

Twenty minutes later, Dusty was sitting up in bed, combing back through the tangled story that Martie had told him, trying to pull the burs out and smooth it into a fully intelligible narrative, when the telephone rang. In the interest of uninterrupted sleep, they kept the ringer switched off in the bedroom, and what he heard now was the phone in Martie's office down the hall; the answering machine picked up after the second ring.

He assumed Susan was calling, though it might have been Skeet or one of the staff at New Life. Ordinarily, he would have gone to Martie's office to monitor the incoming message, but he didn't want her to wake up while he was out of the room and discover that he had broken his promise to remain with her. Skeet was safe in good hands, and whatever "strange stuff" was going on with Susan, it couldn't be any stranger or more important than what had transpired right here this evening. It could wait until morning.

Dusty turned his attention once more to what Martie had told him of her day. As he worried at each bizarre event and quirky detail, he was overcome by the peculiar conviction that what had happened to his wife was somehow associated with what happened to his brother. He sensed parallel oddities in both events, though the precise nature of the connections eluded him. Undeniably, this was the strangest day of his life, and instinct told him that Skeet and Martie had not unraveled simultaneously by mere coincidence.

In one corner of the room, Valet was curled on his bed, a large skeepskin-covered pillow, but he remained awake. He lay with his chin propped on one paw, intently watching his mistress sleeping in the golden lamplight.

Because Martie had never failed to keep a commitment and thus had banked a lot of moral capital, Susan didn't feel aggrieved when the promised phone call failed to come in by eleven o'clock; however, she was uneasy. She placed her own call, got an answering machine, and grew worried.

No doubt Martie had been rocked and mystified by Susan's claim of a phantom rapist to whom locked doors were no impediment. She'd asked to be given some time to think. But Martie wasn't prone either to waffle or to be unnecessarily diplomatic. By now she would have arrived at some considered advice—or would have called to say she needed more convincing if she were to believe this tall, tall story.

"It's me," Susan told the answering machine. "What's wrong? You okay? You think I'm nuts? It's all right if you do. Call me."

She waited a few seconds, then hung up.

Most likely, Martie would not have suggested a course of action with more potential for success than the camcorder sting, so Susan went forward with her preparations.

She placed a half-full glass of wine on the nightstand, not to be drunk, but as a prop.

She settled into bed with a book, sitting up against a pile of pillows. She was too nervous to read.

For a while she watched an old movie on TV, *Dark Passage*, but she couldn't concentrate on the story. Her mind wandered down darker and more frightening alleyways than any that Bogart and Bacall had ever traveled.

Although Susan was preternaturally alert, she recalled other nights when apparent insomnia had abruptly given way to unnaturally deep sleep—and to victimization. If she was secretly being drugged, she couldn't predict when the chemicals might kick in, and she did not want to wake up to discover that she had been violated *and* that she had failed to activate the camcorder.

At midnight, she went to the Biedermeier pedestal, slipped one finger into the ivy under the little ming tree, started the videotape rolling, and returned to bed. If she was still awake at one o'clock, she would rewind the cassette and start recording from the beginning, and again at two and three o'clock, so in the event that she slept, there would be less of a chance that the tape would run out before the creep entered the room.

She switched off the television, the better to support the fell-asleep-while-reading scenario, but also because it might mask sounds arising elsewhere in the apartment.

After less than a minute of silence, as she was about to pick up the book, the telephone rang. Assuming that Martie was calling, Susan answered. "Hello?"

"This is Ben Marco."

As though Ben Marco were a magic mason whose very voice could conjure stone and mortar, sudden walls of granite seemed to enclose Susan's heart, confining it, pressing upon auricles and ventricles. Even as her heart rapped frantically against its prison, her mind opened as if it were a house from which the roof had been torn away by a cyclone; suddenly as wispy as dust and cobwebs, her thoughts dispersed on an updraft, and into her head, from the black infinity above, sifted a whispering darkness, an irresistible Presence that glided, as invisible and cold as a haunting spirit, first through the attic of her mind and then down, down into deeper regions.

"I'm listening," Susan told Ben Marco.

At once her racing heart began to settle, and in her blood, the insectile twitching of fear subsided.

And now the rules.

He said, "The winter storm—"

"The storm is you," she replied.

"—hid in the bamboo grove—"

"The grove is me."

"—and quieted away."

"In the quiet, I will learn what is wanted," Susan said.

The winter storm
hid in the bamboo grove
and quieted away.

Beautiful, really.

With the litany of the rules completed, Susan Jagger was awash in a sea of quiet: the apartment profoundly silent around her, all hushed within her, as soundless as the lifeless void must have been only an instant before Creation, when God had not yet said, *Let there be light.*

When the winter storm spoke again, his soft deep voice seemed not to come from the telephone but from within Susan. "Tell me where you are."

"In bed."

"I believe you're alone. Tell me if I'm correct."

"You are."

"Let me in."

"Yes."

"Quickly."

Susan put down the phone, got out of bed, and hurried through the dark apartment.

In spite of her quickened pace, her heartbeat continued to grow slower: strong, steady, calm.

In the kitchen, the only light was green and pale, issuing from the numerals on the digital clocks in the microwave and in the oven. The inky shadows didn't hinder her. For too many months, this small apartment had been her world; and she was as intimately familiar with it as if she'd been raised here blind since birth.

A chair was wedged firmly under the doorknob. She removed it and slid it aside, and the wooden legs squeaked faintly on the tile floor.

The slide bolt at the end of the brass security chain rasped out of the slot in the latch plate. When she let go, the links rattled against the door casing.

She disengaged the first dead bolt. The second.

She opened the door.

A storm he was, and wintry, too, waiting on the landing at the head of the stairs, quiet now but filled with the rage of hurricanes, a fury usually well hidden from the world but always churning in him, revealed in his most private moments, and as he crossed the threshold into the kitchen, forcing her backward, shoving the door shut behind him, he clamped one strong hand around her slender throat.

30

The left and right common carotid arteries, providing the principal blood supply to the neck and head, arise directly from the aorta, which itself arises from the upper surface of the left ventricle. Having so recently departed the heart, the blood surging through both vessels is particularly rich in oxygen and is driven with force.

Hand cupped around the front of Susan's throat, fingers spread along the left side of her neck, the pad of his thumb pressed just under her jawbone and over her right carotid, Dr. Mark Ahriman held her thus for perhaps a minute, enjoying the strong, steady throb of her pulse. She was so wonderfully full of life.

If he'd wanted to strangle her to death, he could have done so without fear of resistance. In this altered state of consciousness, she would stand, docile and unprotesting, while he choked the life out of her. She would ease to her knees when she could no longer stand, and then fold quietly into a graceful mound on the floor as her heart stuttered to a stop, apologizing with her eyes for being unable to die on her feet and, therefore, requiring him to kneel with her as he finished the job.

In fact, while dying, Susan Jagger would favor Dr. Ahriman with whatever attitude and expression he requested. Childlike adoration. Erotic rapture. Impotent rage or even lamblike meekness with a glaze of bafflement, if either of those responses amused him.

He had no intention of killing her. Not here, not now—though soon.

When the time inevitably came, he wouldn't act directly to snuff Susan, because he had great respect for the scientific-investigation division of virtually any contemporary American police agency. When wet work was required, he always used intermediaries to deliver the death blow, sparing himself the risk of suspicion.

Besides, his purest bliss came from clever manipulation, not directly from mutilation and murder. Pulling the trigger, shoving in the knife, twisting the wire garrote—none of that would thrill him as keenly as using someone to commit atrocities on his behalf.

Power is a sharper thrill than violence.

More precisely, his greatest delight arose not from the end effect of using power but from the *process* of using it. Manipulation. *Control.* The act of exerting absolute control, pulling strings and watching people perform as commanded, was so profoundly gratifying to the doctor that in his finest moments of puppeteering, plangent peals of pleasure shook through him like great gongs of sound shivering the cast bronze of massive cathedral bells.

Susan's throat beneath his hand reminded him of a long-ago thrill, of another slender and graceful throat that had been torn by a pike, and with this memory came a tintinnabulation through the bone bells of his spine.

In Scottsdale, Arizona, stands a Palladian mansion in which a willowy young heiress named Minette Luckland pounds her mother's skull to mush with a hammer and shortly thereafter shoots her father in the back of the head while he is eating a slice of crumb cake and watching a rerun of Seinfeld. *Subsequently, she leaps from a second-floor gallery, free-falling eighteen feet, impaling herself on a spear held by a statue of Diana, goddess of the moon and the hunt, which stands on a fluted plinth in the center of the entry rotunda. The suicide note, indisputably written in Minette's own neat hand, claims that she has been sexually abused since childhood by both parents—an outrageous slander that Dr. Ahriman had suggested to her. Around Diana's bronze feet: spatters of blood like red plum-flower petals on white marble floor.*

Now, standing half naked in the shadowy kitchen, green eyes reflecting the faint green light of the digital clock in the nearby oven, Susan Jagger was even lovelier than the late Minette. Although her face and form were the stuff of an erotomaniac's sweat-drenched dreams, Ahriman was less excited by her looks than by the knowledge that in her lithe limbs and supple body was a lethal potential as great as that unleashed in Scottsdale so many years ago.

Her right carotid artery throbbed against the doctor's thumb, her pulse slow and thick. Fifty-six beats per minute.

She was not afraid. She was calmly awaiting use, as though she were an unthinking tool—or, more accurately, a toy.

By using the trigger name *Ben Marco* and then by reciting the conditioning haiku, Ahriman had transferred her into an altered state of consciousness. A layman might have used the term *hypnotic trance*, which to a certain extent it was. A clinical psychologist would have diagnosed it as a fugue, which was closer to the truth.

Neither term was adequately defining.

Once Ahriman recited the haiku, Susan's personality was more deeply and firmly repressed than if she were hypnotized. In this peculiar condition, she was no longer Susan Jagger in any meaningful sense, but a nonentity, a meat machine whose mind was a blank hard-drive waiting for whatever software Ahriman chose to install.

If she had been in a classic fugue state, which is a serious personality disassociation, she would have appeared to function almost normally, with a few eccentric behaviors but with far less detachment than she now exhibited.

"Susan," he said, "do you know who I am?"

"Do I?" she asked, her voice fragile and distant.

In this state, she was incapable of answering any question, because she was waiting to be told what he wanted of her, what act she must commit, and even how she must feel about it.

"Am I your psychiatrist, Susan?"

In the gloom, he could almost see the puzzlement on her face. "Are you?"

Until she was released from this state, she would respond only to commands.

He said, "Tell me your name."

Receiving this direct instruction, she was free to provide whatever knowledge she possessed. "Susan Jagger."

"Tell me who I am."

"Dr. Ahriman."

"Am I your psychiatrist?"

"Are you?"

"Tell me my profession."

"You're a psychiatrist."

This more-than-trance-not-quite-fugue state had not been easily engineered. Much hard work and professional dedication had been required to remake her into this pliant plaything.

Eighteen months ago, before he had been her psychiatrist, on three separate carefully orchestrated occasions, without Susan's knowledge, Ahriman had administered to her a potent brew of drugs: Rohypnol, phencyclidine, Valium, and one marvelous cerebrotropic substance not listed in any published pharmacopoeia. The recipe was his own, and he personally compounded each dose from the stock in his private and quite illegal pharmacy, because the ingredients must be precisely balanced if the desired effect were to be achieved.

The drugs themselves had not reduced Susan to her current obedient condition, but each dose had rendered her semiconscious, unaware of her situation, and supremely malleable. While she had been in this twilight sleep,

Ahriman had been able to bypass her conscious mind, where volitional thinking occurred, and speak to her deep subconscious, where conditioned reflexes were established and where he met no resistance.

What he had done to her during those three long sessions would tempt tabloid newspapers and writers of spy novels to use the word *brainwashing*, but it was nothing as twentieth-century as that. He had not torn down the structure of her mind, with the intention of rebuilding it in a new architecture. That approach—once favored by the Soviet, the Chinese, and the North Korean governments, among others—was too ambitious, demanding months of around-the-clock access to the subject in a dreary prison environment, with lots of tedious psychological torture, not to mention a tolerance for the wretch's annoying screams and cowardly pleading. Dr. Ahriman's IQ was high, but his boredom threshold was low. Besides, the rate of success using traditional brainwashing techniques was uninspiring and the degree of control seldom total.

Rather, the doctor had gone down into Susan's subconscious, into the cellar, and he had added a new chamber—call it a secret chapel—of which her conscious mind remained unaware. There, he conditioned her to worship one god to the exclusion of all others, and that god was Mark Ahriman himself. He was a stern deity, pre-Christian in his denial of free will, intolerant of the slightest disobedience, merciless with transgressors.

Thereafter, he had never again drugged her. There was no need to do so anymore. In those three sessions, he had established the control devices—the Marco name, the haiku—that instantly repressed her personality and took her to the same deep realms of her psyche to which the chemicals had taken her.

In the final drug session, he also implanted her agoraphobia. He thought it was an interesting malady, ensuring satisfying drama and many colorful effects as she gradually cracked apart and finally came to ruin. The whole point, after all, was entertainment.

Now, with his hand still upon Susan's throat, he said, "I don't think I'll be myself this time. Something kinky tonight. Do you know who I am, Susan?"

"Who are you?"

"I'm your father," Ahriman said.

She did not reply.

He said, "Tell me who I am."

"You're my father."

"Call me Daddy," he instructed.

Her voice remained distant, devoid of emotion, because he had not yet told her how she was required to feel about this scenario. "Yes, Daddy."

Her carotid pulse, under his right thumb, remained slow.

"Tell me the color of my hair, Susan."

Although the kitchen was too dark for her to determine his hair color, she said, "Blond."

Ahriman's hair was salt-and-pepper, but Susan's father was indeed a blond.

"Tell me the color of my eyes."

"Green like mine."

Ahriman's eyes were hazel.

With his right hand still pressed to Susan's throat, the doctor leaned down and kissed her almost chastely.

Her mouth was slack. She was not an active participant in the kiss; in fact, she was so passive that she might as well have been catatonic if not comatose.

Biting gently at her lips, then forcing his tongue between them, he kissed her as no father should ever kiss a daughter, and although her mouth remained slack and her carotid pulse did not accelerate, he sensed her breath catch in her throat.

"How do you feel about this, Susan?"

"How do you want me to feel?"

Smoothing her hair with one hand, he said, "Deeply ashamed, humiliated. Full of terrible sorrow . . . and a little resentful at being used like this by your own father. Dirty, debased. And yet obedient, ready to do what you're told . . . because you're also aroused against your will. You have a sick, hungry need that you want to deny but can't."

Again he kissed her, and this time she tried to close her mouth to him; she relented, however, and her mouth softened, opened. She put her hands against his chest, to fend him off, but her resistance was weak, childlike.

Under his thumb, the pulse in her right carotid artery raced like that of a hare in the shadow of a hound.

"Daddy, no."

The reflection of green light in Susan's green eyes glistered with a new watery depth.

Those shimmering fathoms produced a subtle fragrance, faintly bitter, briny, and this familiar scent caused the doctor to swell with fierce desire.

He lowered his right hand from her throat to her waist, holding her close.

"Please," she whispered, managing to make that one word both a protest and a nervous invitation.

Ahriman breathed deeply, then lowered his mouth to her face. The reliability of a predator's sense of smell was confirmed: Her cheeks were wet and salty.

"Lovely."

With a series of quick little kisses, he moistened his lips on her damp skin, and then explored his flavored lips with the tip of his tongue.

Both hands around her waist now, he lifted her and carried her backward, until he was pressing her between his body and the refrigerator.

"Please" again, and then once more "please," the dear girl so conflicted that eagerness and dread spiced her voice in equal measure.

Susan's weeping was accompanied by neither whimper nor sob, and the doctor savored these silent streams, seeking to slake the thirst that he could never satisfy. He licked a salty pearl from the corner of her mouth, licked another from the flared rim of a nostril, and then suckled on the droplets beaded across her eyelashes, relishing the flavor as though this would be his sole sustenance for the day.

Letting go of her waist, stepping back from her, he said, "Go to your bedroom, Susan."

Sinuous shadow, she moved like hot tears, clear and bitter.

The doctor followed, admiring her graceful walk, to her bed in Hell.

31

Valet dozed, twitching and snuffling in the company of phantom rabbits, but Martie lay in stone-still silence, as though she were a death sculpture upon a catafalque.

Her sleep seemed deeper than possible in the turbulent wake of the day's events, and it was reminiscent of Skeet's plumbless slumber in his room at New Life.

Sitting up in bed, barefoot, in jeans and a T-shirt, Dusty once more sorted through the fourteen pages that had come from the notepad in Skeet's kitchen, brooding on the name *Dr. Yen Lo* in all thirty-nine renditions.

That name, when spoken, had seemed to traumatize Skeet, causing him to lapse into a twilight consciousness in which he answered every question with a question of his own. Open eyes jiggling as in REM sleep, he responded directly—if often cryptically—only to questions that were framed as statements or commands. When Dusty's frustration had led him to say *Ah, give me a break and go to sleep,* Skeet dropped into an abyss as abruptly as a narcoleptic responding instantaneously to the flipping of an electrochemical switch in the brain.

Of the many curious aspects of Skeet's behavior, one currently interested Dusty more than any other: the kid's failure to remember anything that had happened between the moment when he had heard the name *Dr. Yen Lo* and, minutes later, when he had obeyed Dusty's unthinking demand that he go to sleep. Selective amnesia might be blamed. But it was more as though Skeet had conducted the conversation with Dusty while in a blackout.

Martie had spoken of her suspicion that she was "missing time" from her day, though she could not identify precisely when any gap or gaps had occurred. Fearful that she had opened the gas valve in the fireplace without lighting the ceramic logs, she had repeatedly returned to the living room with an urgent conviction that a furious explosion was imminent. Although the valve had always been tightly closed, she continued to be troubled by a perception that her memory had been nibbled like a holey woolen scarf beset by moths.

Dusty had witnessed his brother's blackout. And he sensed truth in Martie's fear of having fallen into a fugue.

Perhaps a link.

This had been an extraordinary day. The two people dearest to Dusty's heart had suffered quite different but equally dramatic episodes of aberrant behavior. The odds of such serious—even if temporary—psychological collapse striking twice, this close, were surely a great deal smaller than the one-in-eighteen-million chance of winning the state lottery.

He supposed that the average citizen of our brave new millennium would think this was a grim coincidence. At most they would consider it an example of the curious patterns that the grinding machinery of the universe sometimes randomly produces as a useless by-product of its mindless laboring.

To Dusty, however, who perceived mysterious design in everything from the color of daffodils to Valet's pure joy in pursuit of a ball, there was no such thing as coincidence. The link was tantalizing—though difficult to fathom. And frightening.

He put the pages of Skeet's notepad on his nightstand and picked up a notepad of his own. On the top page, he had printed the lines of the haiku that his brother had referred to as *the rules.*

Clear cascades
into the waves scatter
blue pine needles.

Skeet was the waves. According to him, the blue pine needles were missions. The clear cascades were Dusty or Yen Lo, or perhaps anyone who invoked the haiku in Skeet's presence.

At first everything that Skeet said seemed to be gibberish, but the longer Dusty puzzled over it, the more he sensed structure and purpose waiting to be discerned. For some reason, he began to perceive the haiku as a sort of mechanism, a simple device with a powerful effect, the verbal equivalent of a compressor-driven paint sprayer or a nail gun.

Give a nail gun to a carpenter from the preindustrial age, and although he might intuit that it was a tool, he would be unlikely to understand its purpose—until he accidentally fired a nail through his foot. The possibility of unintentionally causing psychological harm to his brother motivated Dusty to contemplate the haiku at length, until he understood the use of this tool, before deciding whether to explore further its effect on Skeet.

Missions.

To grasp the purpose of the haiku, he had to understand, at the very least, what Skeet had meant by *missions.*

Dusty was certain he precisely remembered the haiku and the kid's odd interpretation, because he was blessed with a photographic and audio-retentive memory of such high reliability that he cruised through high school and one year of college with a perfect 4.0 grade average, before deciding that he could experience life more fully as a housepainter than as an academic.

Missions.

Dusty considered synonyms. *Task. Work. Chore. Job. Calling. Vocation. Career. Church.*

None of them furthered his understanding.

From the big sheepskin pillow in the corner, Valet whimpered anxiously, as though the rabbits in his dreams had grown fangs and were now doing the dog's work while he played rabbit in the chase.

Martie was too zonked to be roused by the dog's thin squeals.

Sometimes, however, Valet's nightmares escalated until he woke with a terrified bark.

"Easy boy. Easy boy," Dusty whispered.

Even in dreams, the retriever seemed to hear his master's voice, and his whimpering subsided.

"Easy. Good boy. Good Valet."

Although the dog didn't wake, his feathery plumed tail swished across the sheepskin a few times before curling close around him once more.

Martie and the dog slept on peacefully, but suddenly Dusty sat up from the pillows piled against the headboard, the very thought of sleep banished by a rattling insight. Mulling over the haiku, he'd been fully awake, but by comparison to this wide-eyed state, he might as well have been drowsing. He was now hyperalert, as cold as if he had ice water for spinal fluid.

He had been reminded of another moment with the dog, earlier in the day.

Valet stands in the kitchen, at the connecting door to the garage, ready to ride shotgun on the trip to Skeet's apartment, patiently fanning the air with his plumed tail while Dusty pulls on a hooded nylon jacket.

The phone rings. Someone peddling subscriptions to the Los Angeles Times.

When Dusty racks the wall phone after only a few seconds, he turns toward the door to the garage and discovers that Valet is no longer standing, but lying on his side at the threshold, as though ten minutes have passed, as if he has been napping.

"You had a shot of chicken protein, golden one. Let's see some vigor."

With a long-suffering sigh, Valet gets to his feet.

Dusty was able to move through the scene in his mind's eye as though it were three-dimensional, studying the golden retriever with acute attention to detail. Indeed, he could see the moment more clearly now than he'd seen it then: In retrospect the dog obviously, inarguably *had* been napping.

Even with his eidetic and audile memory, he could not recall whether the *Times* salesperson had been a man or woman. He had no memory of what he had said on the phone or of what had been said to him, just a vague impression that he had been the target of a phone-sales campaign.

At the time, he had attributed his uncharacteristic memory lapse to stress. Taking a header off a roof, watching your brother suffer a breakdown before your eyes: This stuff was bound to mess with your mind.

If he had been on the phone five or ten minutes instead of a few seconds, however, he couldn't possibly have been speaking with anyone in the *Times* subscription-sales operation. What the hell would they have talked about for so long? Typefaces? The cost of newsprint? Johannes Gutenberg—What a cool guy!—and the invention of movable type? The tremendous effectiveness of the *Times* as a puppy-training aid in Valet's early days, its singular convenience, its remarkable absorbency, its admirable service as an environment-friendly and fully biodegradable poop wrap?

During the minutes that Valet had settled down to nap at the connecting door to the garage, Dusty either had been on the phone with someone other than a *Times* salesperson or had been on the phone only a few seconds and had been engaged in some other task the rest of the time.

A task that he could not remember.

Missing time.

Impossible. Not me, too.

Ants with urgent purpose, busy bustling multitudes, seemed to be swarming up his legs, down his arms, across his back, and although he knew that no ants had invaded the bed, that what he felt was the nerve endings in his skin responding to the sudden dimpling from a case of universal gooseflesh, he brushed at his arms and at the back of his neck, as if to cast off an army of six-legged soldiers.

Unable to sit still, he got quietly to his feet, but he couldn't stand still, either, and so he paced, but here and there the floor squeaked under the carpet, and he could not pace quietly, so he eased into bed again and sat motionless, after all. His skin was cool and antless now. But things were crawling along the surface convolutions of his brain: a new and unwelcome sense of vulnerability, an *X Files* perception that unknown presences, strange and hostile, had entered his life.

32

Tear-damp flush of face, white cotton so sweetly curved, bare knees together. Susan was sitting on the edge of the bed, waiting.

Ahriman sat across the room from her, in an armchair upholstered with peach-colored moiré silk. He was in no hurry to have her.

Even as a young boy, he had understood that the cheapest toy was fundamentally like one of his father's expensive antique automobiles. As much pleasure could be taken from the leisurely study of it—from the appreciation of its lines and fine details—as from its use. In fact, to truly possess a plaything, to be a worthy master of it, one must understand the art of its form, not merely the thrill of its function.

The art of Susan Jagger's form was twofold: physical, of course, and psychological. Her face and body were exceptionally beautiful. But there was beauty in her mind, too—in her personality and in her intellect.

As a toy, she also had a twofold function, and the first was sexual. Tonight and for a few more nights, Ahriman would use her savagely and at length.

Her second function was to suffer and die well. As a plaything, she had already given him considerable delight with her courageous if hopeless battle to overcome agoraphobia, her anguish and despair as rich as marzipan. Her brave determination to keep her sense of humor and to win back her life was pathetic and therefore delectable. Soon he would enhance and complicate her phobia, sending her into a swift and irreversible decline, and then he would enjoy the final—and sharpest—thrill that she was capable of providing.

Now she sat tearful and timid, conflicted by the prospect of imagined incest, repulsed and yet full of a sick sweet yearning, as programmed. Trembling.

From time to time, her eyes jiggled, the telltale REM that marked the deepest state of personality submersion. It distracted the doctor and compromised her beauty.

Susan already knew the roles they were playing tonight, knew what was expected of her in this erotic scenario, so Ahriman brought her closer to the surface, though nowhere near to full consciousness. Just far enough to put an end to the spasms of rapid eye movement.

"Susan, I want you to move out of the chapel now," he said, referring to that imaginary place in her deepest subconscious where he had taken her for instruction. "Come out and move up the stairs, but not too far, one flight, where a little more light filters down. There, right there."

Her eyes were like clear ponds made murky by the reflections of gray clouds on their surfaces, suddenly touched by a few faint beams of sunshine, and now revealing greater depths.

"What you're wearing still appeals to me," he said. "White cotton. The simplicity." Several visits ago, he had instructed her to dress for bed in this fashion until he suggested something different; the look excited him. "The innocence. Purity. Like a child, yet so incredibly ripe."

The roses in her cheeks blossomed brighter, and she lowered her eyes demurely. Tears of shame, like beads of dew, quivered on the petals of the blush.

She actually saw her father when she dared to look at the doctor. Such was the power of suggestion when Ahriman spoke to her one-on-one in the deep sanctity of that mind chapel.

When they were finished playing tonight, he would instruct her to forget all that had happened from the moment he phoned until he left her apartment. She would recall neither his visit nor this fantasy of incest.

If he chose to do so, however, Ahriman could concoct for Susan a detailed history of sexual abuse at the hands of her father. Many hours would be required to weave that lurid narrative through the tapestry of her real memories, but thereafter he could instruct her to believe in her lifelong victimization and gradually to "recover" those repressed traumas during her therapy sessions.

If her belief drove her to report her father to the police, and if they asked her to submit to a lie-detector test, she would respond to each question with unwavering conviction and precisely the correct shadings of emotion. Her respiration, blood pressure, pulse, and her galvanic skin response would convince any polygraph examiner that she was telling the truth, because she would be convinced that her vile accusations were indeed factual in every detail.

Ahriman had no intention of toying with her in that fashion. He had enjoyed that game with other subjects; but it bored him now.

"Look at me, Susan."

She raised her head. Her eyes met his, and the doctor recalled a bit of verse by e. e. cummings: *In your eyes there lives / a green egyptian noise.*

"Next time," he said, "I'll bring my camcorder, and we'll make another videotape. Do you remember the first one I shot of you?"

Susan shook her head.

"That's because I've forbidden you to remember. You so debased yourself that any memory of it might have left you suicidal. I wasn't ready for you to be suicidal yet."

Her gaze slid away from him. She stared at the miniature ming tree in the pot atop the Biedermeier pedestal.

He said, "One more tape to remember you by. Next time. I've been giving my imagination a workout. You'll be a very dirty girl next time, Susie. It'll make the first tape look like Disney."

Keeping a video record of his most outrageous puppetry was not wise. He stored this incriminating evidence—currently totaling 121 tapes—in a locked and well-hidden vault, although if the wrong people suspected its existence, they would tear his house apart board by board, stone by stone, until they found his archives.

He took the risk because he was at heart a sentimentalist, with a nostalgic yearning for days past, old friends, discarded toys.

Life is a train ride, and at the many stations along the route, people important to us debark, never to get aboard again, until by the end of our journey, we sit in a passenger car where most of the seats are empty. This truth saddens the doctor no less than it does other men and women who are given to reflection—although his sorrow is undeniably of a quality different from theirs.

"Look at me, Susan."

She continued to stare at the potted plant on the pedestal.

"Don't be willful. Look at your father *now.*"

Her tearful gaze flowed away from the lacy ming tree, and upon it she floated a plea to be allowed at least some small measure of dignity, which Dr. Ahriman noted, enjoyed, and disregarded.

Undoubtedly, one evening long after Susan Jagger is dead, the nostalgic doctor will think fondly of her, and will be overcome by a wistful desire to hear her musical voice again, to see her lovely face, to relive the many good times they had together. This is his weakness.

He will indulge himself, on that evening, by resorting to his video archives. He'll be warmed and gladdened to see Susan engaged in acts so sordid, so squalid, that they transform her almost as dramatically as a lycanthrope is transformed in the fullness of the moon. In these wallows of obscenity, her radiant beauty dims sufficiently to allow the doctor to see clearly the essential animal that lives within her, the preevolutionary beast, groveling and yet cunning, fearful and yet fearsome, darkling in her heart.

Besides, even if he did not get so much pleasure from reviewing these home movies, he would maintain his videotape archives, because he is by nature an indefatigable collector. Room after room in his rambling house is dedicated to displays of the toys that he has so tirelessly acquired over the years: armies of toy soldiers; charming hand-painted, cast-iron cars; coin-operated mechanical banks; plastic playsets with thousands of miniature figures, from Roman gladiators to astronauts.

"Get up, girl."

She rose from the bed.

"Turn."

Slowly she turned, slowly for his examination.

"Oh, yes," he said, "I want more of you on tape for posterity. And perhaps a little blood next time, a minor bit of self-mutilation. In fact, bodily fluids in general could be the theme. Very messy, very degenerate. That should be fun. I'm sure that you agree."

Again, she favored the ming tree over his eyes, but this was a passive disobedience, for she looked at him again when commanded to do so.

"If you think that will be fun, tell me so," he insisted.

"Yes, Daddy. Fun."

He instructed her to get on her knees, and she settled to the floor.

"Crawl to me, Susan."

Like a gear-driven figure on a mechanical bank, as

though she had a coin gripped in her teeth and were following a rigorous track toward a deposit slot, she approached the armchair, face painted with realistic tears, a superb example of her kind, an acquisition that would delight any collector.

33

The Moment When Dusty Had Noticed the Napping Dog had been scissored from the earlier Moment When the Kitchen Phone Had Rung, and no matter how many times he replayed the scene in his mind, he could not tie together those severed threads of his day. One moment the dog stood, tail wagging, and the next moment the dog was waking from a short sleep. Missing minutes. Spent talking to whom? Doing what?

He was replaying the episode yet again, concentrating on the dark hole between when he'd picked up the phone and when he'd put it down, striving to bridge the memory gap, when beside him on the bed, Martie began to groan in her sleep.

"Easy. It's okay. Easy now," he whispered, lightly placing a hand on her shoulder, trying to gentle her out of the nightmare and into untroubled sleep again, much as he had done for Valet earlier.

She would not be gentled. As her groans became whimpers, she shuddered, kicking feebly at the entangling sheets, and as whimpers skirled into shrill cries, she thrashed, abruptly sat up, flung off the bedclothes, and shot to her feet, no longer squealing in terror, but choking, gagging thickly, on the queasy verge of regurgitation, vigorously scrubbing at her mouth with both hands, as though repulsed by something on the menu in a dream feast.

Up and moving almost as explosively as Martie, Dusty started around the bed, aware of Valet alert beyond her.

She swung toward him: "*Stay away from me!*"

Such emotion rushed through her voice that Dusty halted, and the dog began to shake, the hair standing straight up along the length of his withers.

Still wiping at her mouth, Martie looked at her hands, as if she expected to see them gloved in fresh blood—and perhaps not her own. "Oh, God, oh, my God."

Dusty moved toward her, and again she ordered him to stay away, no less fiercely than before. "You can't trust me, you can't get near me, don't think you can."

"It was only a nightmare."

"*This* is the nightmare."

"Martie—"

Convulsively, she bent forward, gagging on the memory of the dream, then letting out a miserable groan of disgust and anguish.

Despite her warning, Dusty went to her, and when he touched her, she recoiled violently, shoving him away. "Don't *trust* me! Don't, for Christ's sake, don't."

Rather than step around him, she scrambled monkey-like across the disheveled bed, bounded off the other side, and hurried into the adjoining bathroom.

A short sharp bleat escaped the dog, a plucked-wire sound that twanged through Dusty and struck in him a fear that he had not known before.

Seeing her like this a second time was more terrifying than the first episode. Once could be an aberration. Twice was a pattern. In patterns could be seen the future.

He went after Martie and found her at the bathroom sink. The cold water gushed into the basin. The door of the medicine cabinet, which had been open, was swinging shut of its own accord.

"It must've been worse than usual this time," he said.

"What?"

"The nightmare."

"It wasn't the same one, nothing as pleasant as the Leaf Man," she said, but clearly she had no intention of elaborating.

She popped the cap off a bottle of an effective nonprescription sleeping aid that they rarely used. A slurry of blue caplets spilled into her cupped left hand.

At first, Dusty thought she was intending to overdose, which was ridiculous, because even a full bottle probably wouldn't kill her—and, anyway, she must know that he would knock them out of her hand before she could swallow so many.

But then she let most of the pills rattle back into the bottle. Three were left on her palm.

"Two's the maximum dosage," he said.

"I don't give a rat's ass about the maximum dosage. I want to be out cold. I've got to sleep, got to rest, but I'm *not* going to go through another dream like that, not another one like that."

Her black hair was damp with sweat and tangled like the crowning snakes of whatever Gorgon she had encountered in her dream. The pills were to vanquish monsters.

Water slopped into the drinking glass, and she chased the three caplets with a long swallow.

At her side, Dusty didn't interfere. Three pills didn't warrant paramedics and a stomach pump, and if she was a little groggy in the morning, she might be somewhat less anxious, as well.

He saw no point in suggesting that deeper slumber might not be as dreamless as she expected. Even if she slept in the scaly arms of nightmares, she would be more rested in the morning than if she didn't sleep at all.

As she lowered the glass from her lips, Martie caught

sight of herself in the mirror. Her reflection strummed a shiver from her, which the cold water had been unable to induce.

As winter freezes the blueness out of a pond, so fear had frozen much of the color out of Martie. Face as pale as ice. Lips less pink than they were mallow-purple, with dry peels of zinc-gray skin that had been rubbed loose by her scrubbing hands.

"Oh, God, look what I am," she said, "look what I *am*."

Dusty knew that she was not referring to her damp and tangled hair or to her blanched features, but to something hateful that she imagined she saw in the depths of her blue eyes.

Splashing out the last of its contents, the glass arced back in her hand, but Dusty seized it before she could throw it at the mirror, tore it from her clutching fingers as water spattered on the tile floor.

At his touch, she erupted away from him with such alarm that she crashed into the bathroom wall hard enough to rattle the shower door in its frame.

"Don't get near me! For God's sake, don't you realize what I could do, all the things I could *do?*"

Half-nauseated by worry, he said, "Martie, I'm not afraid of you."

"How far is it from a kiss to a bite?" she asked, her voice hoarse and ragged with dread.

"What?"

"Not far from a kiss to a bite, your tongue in my mouth."

"Martie, please—"

"A kiss to a bite. So easy to tear off your lips. How do you know I couldn't? How do you know I wouldn't?"

If she hadn't already reached a full-blown panic attack, she was running downhill toward one, and Dusty didn't know how to stop her, or even how to slow her.

"Look at my hands," she demanded. "These fingernails.

Acrylic nails. Why do you think I couldn't blind you with them? You think I couldn't gouge out your eyes?"

"Martie. This isn't—"

"There's something in me I never saw before, something that scares the shit out of me, and it could do something terrible, it really could, it could make me blind you. For your own good, you better see it, too, and you better be afraid of it."

Tidal emotion swept through Dusty, terrible pity and fierce love, crosscurrents and rips.

He reached for Martie, and she squeezed past him, out of the bathroom. She slammed the door between them.

When he followed her into the bedroom, he found her at his open closet. She was riffling through his shirts, rattling the hangers on the metal pole, searching for something.

The tie rack. Most of the rack pegs were empty. He owned only four neckties.

She pulled a plain black tie and a red-and-blue striped number from the closet and held them out to Dusty. "Tie me."

"What? No. Good God, Martie."

"I mean it."

"So do I. No."

"Ankles together, wrists together," she said urgently.

"No."

Valet was sitting up in his bed, twitchy eyebrows punctuating a series of worried expressions as his attention bounced from Martie to Dusty to Martie.

She said, "So if I go psycho, total blood nuts, during the night—"

Dusty tried to be firm but calm, hoping that his example would settle her. "Please, stop it."

"—total blood nuts, then I'll have to get loose before I can screw up anybody. And when I'm trying to get loose, that'll wake you if you've fallen asleep."

"I'm not afraid of you."

His feigned calm didn't infect her, and in fact words gushed out of her in an ever more feverish stream: "All right, okay, maybe you're not afraid, even if you should be, maybe you're not, *but I am.* I *am* afraid of me, Dusty, afraid of what the hell I might do to you or to somebody else when I'm having a fit, some crazy seizure, afraid of what I might do to *myself.* I don't know what's happening here, to me, it's weirder than *The Exorcist* even if I'm not levitating and my head isn't spinning around. If I managed to get my hands on a knife at the wrong time, or your pistol, when I'm in this crazy mood, then I'd use it on myself, I know I would. I feel this sick desire in here"—she rapped her stomach with a fist—"this evil, this worm of a thing curled inside me, whispering to me about knives and guns and hammers."

Dusty shook his head.

Martie sat on the bed and began cinching her ankles together with one of the neckties, but after a moment she stopped, frustrated. "Damn it, I don't know knots the way you do. You've got to help me with this."

"One of those pills usually does the job. You took three. You don't need to be tied."

"I'm not going to trust pills, not pills alone, no way. Either you help me with this, or I'll puke up the pills, stick a finger down my throat and puke 'em right now."

Reason wasn't going to sway her. She was as high on fear as Skeet on his drug cocktail, and hardly more rational than the kid had been on the Sorensons' roof.

Sitting in an ineffective tangle of ties, sweating, shaking, she began to cry. "Please, baby, please. Please help me. I've got to sleep, I'm so tired, I need some rest, or I'm going to go bugshit. I need some *peace,* and I'm not going to have any peace if you don't help me. Help me. Please."

Tears moved him as fury couldn't.

When he went to her, she lay back on the bed and covered her face with her hands, as though ashamed of the helplessness to which fear had reduced her.

Dusty trembled as he bound her ankles together.

"Tighter," she said through her mask of hands.

Although he obliged, he didn't draw the knots as tight as she would have preferred. The thought of hurting her, even inadvertently, was more than he could bear.

She held her clasped hands toward him.

Using the black necktie, Dusty hitched wrist to wrist tightly enough to secure her until morning, but he was careful not to cut off her circulation.

As he bound her, she lay with her eyes shut, head turned to one side and away from him, perhaps because she was mortified by the disabling intensity of her fear, perhaps because she was embarrassed by her disheveled appearance. Perhaps. But Dusty suspected that she was trying to hide her face largely because she equated tears with weakness.

The daughter of Smilin' Bob Woodhouse—who had been a genuine war hero, as well as a hero of another kind more than once in the years following the war—was determined to live up to the legacy of honor and courage she had inherited. Of course, life as a young wife and a video-game designer in a balmy California coastal town didn't provide her with frequent opportunities for heroics. This was a good thing, not a reason to move to a perpetual cauldron of violence like the Balkans or Rwanda, or the set of the *Jerry Springer Show*. But living in peace and plenty, she could honor her father's memory only through the small heroics of daily life: by doing her job well and paying her way in the world, by commitment to her marriage in good times and in bad, by giving all possible support to her friends, by having true compassion for life's walking wounded, like Skeet, while living with honesty and truthfulness and enough self-respect to avoid becoming one of them. These small heroics, never acknowledged with awards and stirring marches, are the fuel and the lubrication that keep the machine of civilization humming, and in a world rife with temptations to be self-indulgent, self-centered, and self-satisfied, there are surprisingly more small heroes than might be expected. When you stood in the shadow of great heroics, however, as Martie did, then merely living a decent life—lifting others by your example and by your acts of kindness—might make you feel inadequate; and maybe tears, even in moments of extreme tribulation, might seem to be a betrayal of your father's legacy.

All this Dusty understood, but he could say none of it to Martie now, or perhaps ever, because to speak of it would be to say that he recognized her deepest vulnerabilities, which would imply a pity that robbed her of some measure of dignity, as pity always does. She knew what he knew, and she knew that he knew it; but love grows deeper and stronger when we have both the wisdom to say what must be said *and* the wisdom to know what never needs to be put into words.

So Dusty knotted the black tie with formal, solemn silence.

When Martie was securely tied, she turned onto her side, closed eyes still damming a lake of tears, and as she turned, Valet padded to the bed, craned his neck, and licked her face.

The sob that she had been repressing broke from her now, but it was only half a sob, because it was also half a laugh, and then another followed that was more laugh than sob. "My furry-faced baby boy. You knew your poor mama needed a kiss, didn't you, sweet thing?"

"Or is it the lingering aroma of my truly fine lasagna on your breath?" Dusty wondered, hoping to provide a little oxygen to make this welcome, bright moment burn a little longer.

"Lasagna or pure doggy love," Martie said, "doesn't matter to me. I know my baby boy loves me."

"So does your big boy," Dusty said.

At last she turned her head to look at him. "That's what kept me sane today. I need what we've got."

He sat on the edge of the bed and held her bound hands.

After a while her eyes fell shut under a weight of weariness and patent medicine.

Dusty glanced at the nightstand clock, which reminded him about the issue of missing time. "Dr. Yen Lo."

Without opening her eyes, Martie said thickly, "Who?"

"Dr. Yen Lo. You've never heard of him?"

"No."

"Clear cascades."

"Huh?"

"Into the waves scatter."

Martie opened her eyes. They were dreamy, gradually darkening with clouds of sleep. "Either you're making no sense, or this stuff is kicking in."

"Blue pine needles," he finished, although he no longer thought that any of this might resonate with her as it had with Skeet.

"Pretty," she mumbled, and she closed her eyes again.

Valet had settled on the floor near the bed instead of returning to his sheepskin pillow. He wasn't dozing. From time to time he raised his head to look up at his sleeping mistress or to survey the shadows in farther corners of the room. He lifted his pendant ears as much as they would lift, as if listening to faint but suspicious sounds. His damp black nostrils flared and quivered as he tried to identify the plaited odors on the air, and he growled softly. Gentle Valet seemed to be trying to remake himself into a guard dog, though he remained puzzled as to what, exactly, he was guarding against.

Watching Martie sleep, her skin still ashen and her lips as unnaturally dark as a fresh purple bruise, Dusty became strangely convinced that his wife's descent into long-term mental instability wasn't the greatest threat, as he had thought. Instinctively, he sensed that death stalked her, not madness, and that she was already half in the grave.

He was, in fact, overcome by a preternatural sense that the instrument of her death was here in the bedroom this very minute, and with prickles of superstition stippling the nape of his neck, he rose slowly from the edge of the bed and looked up with dread, half expecting to see an apparition floating near the ceiling: something like a swirl of black robes, a hooded form, a grinning skeletal face.

Although nothing but smoothly troweled plaster hung overhead, Valet let out another low, protracted growl. He had gotten to his feet beside the bed.

Martie slept undisturbed, but Dusty lowered his attention from the ceiling to the retriever.

Valet's nostrils flared as he drew a deep questing breath, and as if thus inflated, his golden hackles rose, bristled. Black lips skinned back, baring formidable teeth. The retriever seemed to see the deadly presence that Dusty could only sense.

The dog's guardian stare was fixed sharply on Dusty himself.

"Valet?"

Even in spite of the dog's thick winter coat, Dusty could see the muscles tighten in his shoulders and thighs. Valet assumed an aggressive stance totally out of character for him.

"What's wrong, fella? It's only me. Just me."

The low growl faded. The dog was silent but tense, alert.

Dusty took a step toward him.

The growl again.

"Just me," Dusty repeated.

The dog seemed unconvinced.

34

When at last the doctor was finished with her, Susan Jagger lay on her back, thighs pressed together demurely, as if in denial of how widely they had been spread. Her arms were crossed modestly over her breasts.

She was still crying, but not silently as before. For his own pleasure, Ahriman had allowed her some vocalization of her anguish and shame.

Buttoning his shirt, he closed his eyes to hear broken bird sounds. Her feather-soft sobs: lonely pigeons in rafters, misery of windblown gulls.

When he first moved her to the bed, he had used the techniques of hypnotic-regression therapy to return her to the age of twelve, to a time when she was untouched, innocent, a rosebud without thorns. Her voice acquired a tender tone, higher pitched; her phrasing was that of a precocious child. Her brow had actually become smoother, her mouth softer, as if time had indeed run backward. Her eyes did not become a brighter green, but they grew clearer, as though sixteen years of hard experience had been filtered from them.

Then, behind the mask of her father, he had deflowered her. She was at first allowed to resist feebly, then more actively, initially frightened and confused in her rediscovered sexual innocence. Bitter resistance was soon sweetened with tremulous hunger. At the doctor's suggestion, Susan was seized by quickening animal need; she rocked her hips and rose to him.

Throughout what followed, Ahriman shaped her psychological state with murmured suggestions, and always, always, her thrilling girlish cries of pleasure were tempered by fear, shame, sorrow. To him, her tears were a more essential lubricant than the erotic oils that her body secreted to facilitate his entry. Even in ecstasy, tears.

Now, as he finished dressing, Ahriman studied her flawless face.

Moonlight on water, eyes brimming ponds of spring rain—dark fish in the mind.

No. No good. He wasn't able to compose a haiku to describe her bleak expression as she stared at the ceiling. His talent for writing poetry was but a fraction as great as his ability to appreciate it.

The doctor had no illusions about his gifts. Although by all measures of intelligence, he was a high-range genius, he nevertheless was a player, not a creator. He had a talent for games, for using toys in new and imaginative ways, but he was no artist.

Likewise, although he had been interested in the sciences since childhood, he didn't possess the temperament to be a scientist: the patience, the acceptance of repeated failures in a quest for ultimate success, the preference for knowledge over sensation. The respect given to most scientists was a prize the young Ahriman coveted, and the authority and quiet superiority with which they often conducted themselves—high priests in this culture that worshiped change and progress—were attitudes that came naturally to Ahriman. The gray, joyless atmosphere of laboratories had no appeal for him, however, nor did the tedium of serious research.

When he was thirteen, a child prodigy already in his first year of college, he realized that psychology offered him an ideal career. Those who claimed to understand the secrets of the mind were regarded with respect bordering on reverence, much as priests must have been in prior centuries, when belief in the soul was as widespread as the current belief in the id and the ego. Upon a psychologist's claim of authority, laymen at once accorded it to him.

Most people regarded psychology as a science. Some called it a *soft science*, but those making such a distinction grew fewer by the year.

In the hard sciences—like physics and chemistry—a hypothesis was proposed to guide inquiry into a group of phenomena. Thereafter, if a large enough body of research by many scientists supported the propositions of that hypothesis, it might become a general theory. In time, if a theory proved universally effective in thousands of experiments, it might become a law.

Some psychologists strove to hold their field to this standard of proof. Ahriman pitied them. They operated under the illusion that their authority and their power were linked to the discovery of timeless truths, when in reality, truth was an annoying constraint on authority and power.

Psychology, in Ahriman's view, was an appealing field because you needed only to compile a series of subjective observations, find the proper prism through which to view a set of statistics, and then you could leap over the hypothesis and the theory, declaring the discovery of a law of human behavior.

Science was tedium, work. To young Ahriman, psychology clearly was *play*, and people were the toys.

He always pretended to share his colleagues' outrage when their work was denigrated as soft science, but in fact he thought of it as *liquid* science, even gaseous, which was the very quality that he cherished about it. The power of the scientist, who must work with hard facts, was limited by those facts; but within psychology was the power of superstition, which could shape the world more completely than electricity, antibiotics, and hydrogen bombs.

Having entered college at thirteen, he acquired his doctorate of psychology by his seventeenth birthday. Because a psychiatrist is even more widely admired and highly esteemed than a psychologist, and because the greater authority of the title would facilitate the games that he wished to play, Ahriman added a medical degree and other necessary credentials to his résumé.

Considering that medical school requires so much real science, he thought that it would be tedious, but on the contrary, it proved to be great fun. After all, a good medical education involved much blood and viscera; he had numerous opportunities to witness suffering and grievous pain, and wherever suffering and pain flourished, there was no shortage of tears.

When he was a little boy, he was as filled with wonder at the sight of tears as other children were affected by rainbows, starry skies, and fireflies. Upon achieving puberty, he discovered that the mere sight of tears, more than hard-core pornography, enflamed his libido.

He himself had never cried.

Now fully dressed, the doctor stood at the foot of Susan's bed and studied her tear-stained face. Desolate pools, her eyes. Her spirit floated in them, almost drowned. The objective of his game was to finish the drowning. Not this night. But soon.

"Tell me your age," he said.

"Twelve," she replied in the voice of a schoolgirl.

"You will now come forward in time, Susan. You are thirteen . . . fourteen . . . fifteen . . . sixteen. Tell me your age."

"Sixteen."

"You are now seventeen . . . eighteen. . . ."

He brought her all the way forward to the present, to the hour and minute on the bedside clock, and then he instructed her to get dressed.

Her nightclothes were scattered on the floor. She retrieved them with the slow, deliberate movements of anyone in a trance.

Sitting on the edge of the bed, as she drew the white cotton panties up her slender legs, Susan suddenly bent forward as though she'd taken a blow in the solar plexus, breath exploding from her. She inhaled with a shudder, and then spat in disgust and horror, saliva glistening like snail trails on her thighs, and spat again, as though she were desperate to rid herself of an intolerable taste. Spitting led to gagging, and between these wretched sounds were two words that she wrenched from herself at great cost—*"Daddy, why, Daddy, why?"*—because although she no longer believed that she was twelve years old, she remained convinced that her beloved father had brutally raped her.

To the doctor, this final unexpected spasm of grief and shame was lagniappe, a little dinner mint of suffering, a chocolate truffle after cognac. He stood before her, breathing deeply of the faint but astringent, briny fragrance arising from her cascade of tears.

When he placed a hand paternally upon her head, Susan flinched from his touch, and *Daddy, why?* deteriorated into a soft and wordless wail. This muffled ululation reminded him of the eerie puling of distant coyotes in a warm desert night even farther in the past than Minette Luckland impaled on the spear of Diana out there in Scottsdale, Arizona.

Just beyond the glow of Santa Fe, New Mexico, lies a horse ranch: a fine adobe house, stables, riding rings, fenced meadows mottled with sweet bunchgrass, all surrounded by chaparral in which rabbits tremble by the thousands and coyotes hunt at night in packs. One summer evening two decades before anyone has yet begun to ponder the approaching dawn of a new millennium, the rancher's lovely wife, Fiona Pastore, answers the phone and listens to three lines of haiku, a poem by Buson. She knows the doctor socially—and also because her ten-year-old son, Dion, is his patient, whom he has been endeavoring to cure of a severe stutter. On a score of occasions, Fiona has engaged in sex with the doctor, often of such depravity that she has suffered bouts of depression afterward, even though all memory of their trysts has been scrubbed from her mind. She poses no danger to the doctor, but he is finished with her physically and is ready now to proceed to the final phase of their relationship.

Remotely activated by haiku, Fiona receives her fatal instructions without protest, proceeds directly to her husband's study, and writes a brief but poignant suicide note accusing her innocent spouse of an imaginative list of atrocities. Note finished, she unlocks a gun cabinet in the same room and removes a six-shot .45 Colt built on a Seville frame, which is a lot of gun for a woman only five feet four, 110 pounds, but she can handle it. She is a girl of the Southwest, born and raised; she has shot at game and targets for more than half her thirty years. She loads the piece with 325-grain, .44 Keith bullets and proceeds to her son's bedroom.

Dion's window is open for ventilation, screened against desert insects, and when Fiona switches on a lamp, the doctor is afforded the equivalent of a fifty-yard-line view. Ordinarily, he is unable to be present during these episodes of ultimate control, because he does not wish to risk incriminating himself—although he has friends in places high enough to all but ensure his exoneration. This time, however, circumstances are ideal for his attendance, and he is unable to resist. The ranch, although not isolated, is reasonably remote. The ranch manager and his wife, both employees of the Pastores, are on vacation, visiting family in Pecos, Texas, during the lively annual cantaloupe festival, and the other three ranch hands do not live on site. Ahriman placed his call to Fiona from a car phone, only a quarter of a mile from the house, whereafter he traveled on foot to Dion's window, arriving only a minute before the woman entered the bedroom and clicked on the lamp.

The sleeping boy never wakes, which is a disappointment to the doctor, who almost speaks through the fine-mesh screen, like a priest assigning penance in a confessional, to instruct Fiona to rouse her son. He hesitates, and she does not, dispatching the dreaming child with two rounds. The husband, Bernardo, arrives at a run, shouting in alarm, and his wife squeezes off another pair of shots. He is lean and tan, one of those weather-beaten Westerners whose sun-cured skin and heat-tempered bones give them an air of imperviousness, but instead of bouncing off his hide, of course, the bullets punch him with terrible force. He staggers, slams into a tall chest of drawers, and hangs desperately on to it, his shattered jaw askew. Bernardo's lamp-black eyes reveal that surprise has hit him harder than either of the .44 slugs. His stare grows wider when, through the window screen, he sees the visiting doctor. Black under lampblack, a lightless eternity, in his startled eyes. A tooth or bit of bone falls from his crumbling jaw: He sags and follows that white morsel to the floor.

Ahriman finds the show to be even more entertaining than he had anticipated, and if he has ever doubted the wisdom of his career choice, he knows that he will never do so again. Because certain hungers are not easily sated, he wants to amplify these thrills, crank up the volume, so to speak, by bringing Fiona at least part of the way out of her more-than-trance-not-quite-fugue state into a higher level of consciousness. Currently her personality is so firmly repressed that she is not emotionally aware of what she has done and has, therefore, no visible reaction to the carnage. If she could be released from control just enough to understand, to feel—then her agony would bring a singular storm of tears, a tide on which the doctor could sail to places he has never been before.

Ahriman hesitates, but for good reason. Released from bondage enough to realize the enormity of her crimes, the woman might behave unpredictably, might slip her fetters altogether and resist being hobbled again. He is sure that in the worst case, he will be able to reestablish control using vocal commands within a minute, but only seconds are required for her to turn toward the open window and fire one round point-blank. Potential injuries can be incurred in any game or playground sport: skinned knees, abraded knuckles, contusions, the occasional minor cut, now and then a perfectly good tooth knocked loose in a tumble. As far as the doctor is concerned, however, the mere possibility of taking a bullet in the face is enough to drain all the fun out of this frolic. He does not speak, leaving the woman to finish this Grand Guignol puppet show in a state of benightedness.

Standing over her dead family, Fiona Pastore calmly puts the barrel of the Colt in her mouth and, regrettably tearless, destroys herself. She falls so softly, but the hard clatter of steel coldly resonates: The gun in her hand, snagged on her trigger finger, raps the pine bed rail.

With the toy broken and the thrill of its function no longer to be enjoyed, the doctor stands at the window for a while, studying the art of her form for the last time. This is not as pleasurable as it once was, what with the back of her head gone, but the exit wound is turned away from him, and the distortion of her facial bone structure is surprisingly slight.

The unearthly cries of coyotes have shivered the air since the doctor first arrived at the ranch house, but until now they have been hunting through the chaparral a couple miles to the east. A change of pitch, a new excitement in their puling, alerts the doctor to the fact that they are drawing nearer. If the scent of blood travels well and quickly on the desert air, these prairie wolves may soon gather beneath the screened window to bay for the dead.

Throughout Indian folklore, the trickiest creature of all is named Coyote, and Ahriman sees no amusement value in matching wits with a pack of them. He walks quickly but does not run toward his Jaguar, which is parked a quarter mile to the north.

The night bouquet features the silicate scent of sand, the oily musk of mesquite, and a faint iron smell the source of which he can't identify.

As the doctor reaches the car, the coyotes fall silent, having caught a whiff of some new spoor that makes them cautious, and no doubt the cause of their caution is Ahriman himself. In the sudden hush, a sound above makes him look up.

Rare albino bats, calligraphy on the sky, sealed by the full moon. High looping white wings, faint buzz of fleeing insects: The killing is quiet.

The doctor watches, rapt. The world is one great playing

field, the sport is killing, and the sole objective is to stay in the game.

Carrying moonlight on their pale wings, the freak bats recede, vanishing into the night, and as Ahriman opens the car door, coyotes begin to wail again. They are close enough to include him in the chorus if he wished to raise his voice.

By the time he pulls shut the door and starts the engine, six coyotes—eight, ten—appear out of the brush and gather on the graveled lane in front of the car, their eyes fiery with reflections of the headlights. As Ahriman drives forward, loose stones crunching together under the tires, the pack divides and moves ahead along both shoulders of the narrow lane, as though they are the outrunners of a Praetorian guard, escorting the Jaguar. A hundred yards later, when the car turns west, where the high city rises in the distance, the slouching beasts break away from it and continue toward the ranch house, still in the game, as is the doctor.

As is the doctor.

Although Susan Jagger's soft quaverous cries of grief and shame were a tonic, and though the memories of the Pastore family that her tortured voice had resurrected were refreshing, Dr. Ahriman was not a young man now, as he'd been in his New Mexico days, and he needed to get at least a few hours of sound sleep. The day ahead would require vigor and an especially clear mind, because Martine and Dustin Rhodes would become far bigger players in this complex game than they had been thus far. Consequently, he ordered Susan to overcome her emotions and finish getting dressed.

When she was in her panties and T-shirt once more, he said, "Get to your feet."

She rose.

"You are a vision, daughter. I wish I could've gotten you on video tonight instead of next time. Those sweet tears. *Why, Daddy? Why?* That was particularly poignant. I won't ever forget that. You've given me another albino-bats moment."

Her attention had shifted from him.

He followed her gaze to the ming tree in the bronze pot atop the Biedermeier pedestal.

"Horticulture," he said approvingly, "is a therapeutic pastime for an agoraphobic. Ornamental plants allow you to remain in touch with the natural world beyond these walls. But when I'm talking to you, I expect your attention to remain on me."

She looked at him again. She was no longer weeping. The last of her tears were drying on her face.

An oddness about her, subtle and indefinable, nagged at the doctor. The levelness of her stare. The way her lips were pressed together, mouth pinched at the corners. Here was a tension unrelated to her humiliation and shame.

"Spider mites," he said.

He thought he saw worry crawling through her eyes.

"They're hell on a ming tree, spider mites."

Unmistakably, what spun across her face was a web of worry, but surely not about the health of her houseplants.

Sensing trouble, Ahriman made an effort to clear the postcoital haze from his mind and concentrate on Susan. "What are you worried about?"

"What am I worried about?" she asked.

He rephrased the question as a command: "Tell me what you're worried about."

When she hesitated, he repeated the command, and she said, "The video."

35

Valet's hackles smoothed. He stopped growling. He became his familiar, tail-wagging, affectionate self, insisted upon a cuddle, and then returned to his bed, where he dozed off as though he had never been bothered.

Bound hand and foot at her insistence, even more profoundly subdued by three sleeping pills, Martie was unnervingly still and silent. A few times, Dusty raised his head from the pillow and leaned close to her, worried until he heard her faint respiration.

Although he expected to lie awake all night, and therefore left his nightstand lamp aglow, eventually he slept.

A dream stirred his sleep, blending dread and absurdity into a strange narrative that was disturbing yet nonsensical.

He is lying in bed, atop the covers, fully dressed except for his shoes. Valet is not present. Across the room, Martie sits in the lotus position on the dog's big sheepskin pillow, utterly still, eyes closed, fingers laced in her lap, as though lost in meditation.

He and Martie are alone in the room, and yet he is talking to someone else. He can feel his lips and tongue moving, and although he can hear his own voice reverberating—deep, hollow, fuzzy—in the bones of his skull, he cannot quite make out a single word of what he is saying. The pauses in his speech indicate that he is engaged in a conversation, not a monologue, but he can hear no other voice, not a murmur, not a whisper.

Beyond the window, the night is slashed by lightning, but no thunder protests the wound, and no rain drizzles on the roof. The only sound arises when a large bird flies past the window, so close that one of its wings brushes the glass, and it squawks. Although the creature appears and vanishes in an instant, Dusty somehow knows that it is a heron, and the cry it makes seems to travel in a circle through the night, fading and then growing louder, again faint but then near once more.

He becomes aware of an intravenous needle in his left arm. A plastic tube loops from the needle to a clear plastic bag, which is plump with glucose and dangling from a pharmacy-style floor lamp that serves as a makeshift IV rack.

Again the storm flashes and the huge heron passes the window in the pulsing glare, its shriek traveling into the darkness behind the lightning.

The right sleeve of Dusty's shirt is rolled higher than the left, because his blood pressure is being taken; the pressure cuff of a sphygmomanometer wraps his upper arm. Black rubber tubing extends from the cuff to the inflation bulb, which floats in midair like an object in zero gravity. Strangely, as if in the grip of an unseen hand, the bulb is being rhythmically compressed and released, while the pressure cuff tightens on his arm. If a third person is in the room, this nameless visitor must have mastered the magic of invisibility.

When lightning flares again, it is borne and comes to ground in the bedroom, not in the night beyond the window. Many-legged, nimble, slowed from the speed of light to the speed of a cat, the bolt hisses out of the ceiling as it usually sizzles from a cloud, springs to a metal picture frame, from there to the television, and finally to the floor lamp that serves as an IV rack, spitting sparks as it gnashes its bright teeth against the brass.

Immediately behind the leaping lightning swoops the big heron, having entered the bedroom through a closed window or a solid wall, its swordlike bill cracking wide as it shrieks. It's huge, at least three feet, head to foot: prehistoric-looking, with its pterodactyl glare. Shadows of wings wash the walls, fluttering feathery forms in the flickering light.

Leading its shadow, the bird darts toward Dusty, and he

knows it will stand upon his chest and pluck out his eyes. His arms feel as if they are strapped to the bed, although the right is restrained only by the pressure cuff and the left is weighed down by nothing but the bracing board that prevents him from bending his elbow while the needle is in the vein. Nevertheless, he lies immobile, defenseless, as the bird shrieks toward him.

When lightning arcs from television to floor lamp, the clear-plastic glucose bag glows like the gauzy sac in a pressurized gas lantern, and a hot rain of brassy sparks—which ought to set the bedclothes afire but does not—showers upon Dusty. The shadow of the descending heron shatters into as many black fragments as there are sparks, and when the clouds of bright and dark mites swarm dazzlingly together, Dusty closes his eyes in terror and confusion.

He is assured, perhaps by the invisible visitor, that he need not be afraid, but when he opens his eyes, he sees a fearsome thing hanging over him. The bird has been impossibly condensed, crushed-twisted-squeezed, until it now fits inside the bulging glucose bag. In spite of this compression, the heron remains recognizable—though it resembles a bird painted by some half-baked Picasso wanna-be with a taste for the macabre. Worse, it is somehow still alive and shrieking, although its shrill cries are muted by the clear walls of its plastic prison. It tries to squirm inside the bag, tries to break free with sharp beak and talons, cannot, and rolls one bleak black eye, glaring down at Dusty with demonic intensity.

He feels trapped, too, lying here helpless under the pendant bird: he with the weakness of one crucified, it with the dark energy of an ornament fashioned for a satanist's mock Christmas tree. Then the heron dissolves into a bloody brown slush, and the clear fluid in the intravenous line begins to cloud as the substance of the bird seeps out of the bag and downward, downward. Watching this filthy murk contaminate the tube inch by inch, Dusty screams, but he makes no sound. Paralyzed, drawing great draughts of air but as silently as one struggling to breathe in a vacuum, he tries to lift his right hand and tear out the IV, tries to cast himself off the bed, annot, and he rolls his eyes, straining to see the last inch of the ube as the toxin reaches the needle.

A terrible flash of inner heat, as though lightning arcs hrough his veins and arteries, is followed by a shriek when the ird enters his blood. He feels it surging up his median basilic vein, hrough biceps and into torso, and almost at once an intolerable luttering arises within his heart, the busy twitching-pecking-luffing of something making a nest.

Still in the lotus position on Valet's sheepskin pillow, Martie pens her eyes. They are not blue, as before, but as black as her air. No whites at all: Each socket is filled with a single, smooth, vet, convex blackness. Avian eyes are generally round, and these re almond-shaped like those of a human being, but they are the yes of the heron nonetheless.

"Welcome," she says.

Dusty snapped awake, so clearheaded the instant he pened his eyes that he didn't cry out or sit up in bed to orint himself. He lay very still, on his back, staring at the eiling.

His nightstand lamp was aglow, as he had left it. The loor lamp was beside the reading chair, where it belonged; t had not been pressed into service as an IV stand.

His heart didn't flutter. It pounded. As far as he could ell, his heart was still his private domain, where nothing oosted except his own hopes, anxieties, loves, and prejulices.

Valet snored softly.

Beside Dusty, Martie enjoyed the deep slumber of a ood woman—albeit goodness was in this case assisted by hree doses of sleep-inducing antihistamines.

While the dream remained fresh, he walked around it in is mind, considering it from a variety of perspectives. He ried to apply the lesson he had long ago learned from the encil drawing of a forest primeval that morphed into an mage of a Gothic metropolis when it was approached without preconceptions.

Ordinarily, he didn't analyze his dreams.

Freud, however, had been convinced that fishy expressions of the subconscious could be seined from dreams to provide a banquet for a psychoanalyst. Dr. Derek Lampton, Dusty's stepfather, fourth of Claudette's four husbands, also cast his lines into that same sea and regularly reeled in strange, squishy hypotheses that he force-fed to his patients without regard for the possibility that they might be poisonous.

Because Freud and Lizard Lampton had faith in dreams, Dusty had never taken them seriously. Now he was loath to admit there might be meaning in this one, and yet he sensed a morsel of truth in it. Finding one scrap of clear fact in that heap of trash, however, was going to be a Herculean task.

If his exceptional eidetic and audile memory preserved all the details of dreams as well as it stored away real experiences, then at least he could be sure that if he sorted through the refuse of this nightmare carefully enough, he would eventually find any shiny truth that might await discovery, like a piece of heirloom silverware accidentally thrown out with the dinner garbage.

36

"The video," Susan repeated, in response to Ahriman's inquiry, and once more she looked away from him, toward the ming tree.

Surprised, the doctor smiled. "You're still such a modest girl, considering the things you've done. Relax, dear. I've made only one tape of you—a ninety-minute astonishment, I will admit—and there'll be just one more, next time we meet. Nobody but me gets to see my little home movies. They will never be broadcast on CNN or NBC, I assure you. Although the Nielson ratings would be through the roof, don't you think?"

Susan continued to stare at the potted ming tree, but now the doctor understood why she was able to look away from him even though he had commanded her to stand eye to eye. Shame was a powerful force, from which she drew the strength for this one small rebellion. We all commit acts that shame us, and with varying degrees of difficulty, we reach accommodation with ourselves, forming pearls of guilt around each offending bit of moral grit. Guilt, unlike shame, can be nearly as soothing as virtue, because the jagged edges of the thing that it encapsulates can no longer be felt, and the guilt itself becomes the object of our interest. Susan could have made a necklace from all the moments of shame to which Ahriman had subjected her, but because she was aware of the videotape record, she was not able to form her little pearls of guilt and thus smooth the shame away.

The doctor commanded her to look at him, and after a hesitation, she once more shifted her attention from the ming tree to his eyes.

He instructed her to descend the steps of her subconscious, until she returned to the mind chapel, from which he had previously allowed her to ascend a short distance in order to enhance their play session.

When she was once more in that deep redoubt, her eyes jiggled briefly. Her personality had been filtered from her and set aside, as a chef would strain the solids out of beef broth to make bouillon, and now her mind was a pellucid liquid, waiting to be flavored according to Ahriman's recipe.

He said, "You will forget your father was here tonight. Memories of his face where you should have seen mine, memories of his voice when you should have heard mine, are now dust, and less than dust, all blown away. I am your doctor, not your father. Tell me who I am, Susan."

Her whispery voice seemed to echo from a subterranean room: "Dr. Ahriman."

"As always, of course, you will have absolutely no accessible memory of what happened between us, absolutely no accessible memory of my presence here tonight."

In spite of his best efforts, somewhere memory survived, perhaps in an unknowable realm *below* the subconscious. Otherwise, she would not suffer shame at all, because no recollection of these depravities or those of other nights would remain. Her lingering shame was, in the doctor's view, proof of a sub-subconscious—a level even beneath the id—where experience left an indelible mark. This deepest of all memory was, Ahriman believed, virtually inaccessible and of no danger to him; he needed only to wipe clean the slates of her conscious and subconscious to be safe.

Some would have wondered if this sub-subconscious might be the soul. The doctor was not one of them.

"If nevertheless you have any reason to feel that you have been sexually assaulted, any soreness or other clue, you will suspect no one other than your estranged husband, Eric. Tell me now whether or not you fully understand what I've just said."

A spasm of REM accompanied her reply, as if the specified memories were being shaken out of her through her oscillating eyes: "I understand."

"But you are strictly forbidden from confronting Eric with your suspicions."

"Forbidden. I understand."

"Good."

Ahriman yawned. Regardless of how much fun a play session had been, it was ultimately diminished by the need to clean up at the end, to put away the toys and straighten the room. Although he understood why neatness and order were absolute necessities, he begrudged the time spent on this put-away period as much now as he had when he was a boy.

"Please lead me to the kitchen," he requested, yawning around his words.

Still graceful in spite of the crude use to which she had been put, Susan moved through the dark apartment with the fluid suppleness of a pale koi swimming in a midnight pond.

In the kitchen, as thirsty as any player would be after a long and demanding game, Ahriman said, "Tell me what beer you have?"

"Tsingtao."

"Open one for me."

She got a bottle from the refrigerator, fumbled in a drawer in the dark until she found an opener, and popped the cap off the beer.

While in this apartment, the doctor took care to touch as seldom as possible those surfaces on which fingerprints could be left.

He hadn't yet decided if eventually Susan would self-destruct when he was finished with her. If he concluded that suicide would be sufficiently entertaining, then her long and depressing struggle to overcome agoraphobia would provide a convincing motive, and her handwritten farewell note would close the case without a rigorous investigation. More likely, she would be used in the bigger game with Martie and Dusty, culminating in mass murder in Malibu.

Other options included arranging to have Susan murdered by her estranged husband or even by her best friend. If Eric snuffed her, a homicide investigation would ensue—even if he phoned the cops from the scene, confessed, blew his own brains out, and fell dead beside his wife, with all the forensic evidence supporting the conclusion that an ugly domestic altercation was to blame. Then the Scientific Investigation Division would move in, with their pocket protectors and bad haircuts, seeking fingerprints with powders, iodines, silver nitrate solutions, ninhydrin solutions, cyanoacrylate fumes, even with methanol solution of rhodamine 6G and an argo ion laser. If Ahriman had inadvertently left a single print where these tedious but meticulous scientific types thought to look for it, his life would be changed, and not for the better.

His well-placed friends could ensure that he was not easily brought to trial. Evidence would disappear or be altered. Police detectives and prosecutors in the district attorney's office would repeatedly screw up, and those obstructionists who tried to conduct a credible investigation would have their lives complicated and even ruined by all manner of troubles and tragedies that would appear to have nothing whatsoever to do with Dr. Ahriman.

His friends would not be able to prevent him from falling under suspicion, however, or be able to protect him from sensationalistic speculations in the media. He would become a celebrity of sorts. That was not acceptable. Fame would cramp his style.

When he accepted the bottle of Tsingtao from Susan, he thanked her, and she said, "You're welcome."

Regardless of the circumstances, the doctor believed that good manners should be observed. Civilization is the greatest game of all, a wonderfully elaborate communal tournament in which one must play well in order to have the license to pursue secret pleasures; mastering its rules—manners, etiquette—is essential to successful gamesmanship.

Politely, Susan followed him to the door, where he paused to communicate his final instructions for the night. "Assure me that you're listening, Susan."

"I'm listening."

"Be calm."

"I'm calm."

"Be obedient."

"Yes."

"The winter storm—"

"The storm is you," she replied.

"—hid in the bamboo grove—"

"The grove is me."

"—and quieted away."

"In the quiet, I will learn what is wanted," Susan said.

"After I leave, you will close the kitchen door, engage all the locks, and wedge the chair under the knob, just as it was. You will return to bed, lie down, switch off the lamp, and close your eyes. Then, in your mind, you will leave the chapel where you are now. When you close the chapel door behind you, all recollection of what has happened from the moment you picked up the telephone and heard my voice until you wake in bed will have been erased—every sound, every image, every detail, every nuance will vanish from your memory, never to be recovered. Then, counting to ten, you will ascend the stairs, and when you reach ten, you will regain full consciousness. When you open your eyes, you will believe you have awakened from a refreshing sleep. If you understand all that I've said, please tell me so."

"I understand."

"Good night, Susan."

"Good night," she said, opening the door for him.

He stepped out onto the landing and whispered, "Thank you."

"You're welcome."

She softly closed the door.

Like an invading armada that meant to steal all memory of the world from those sleeping in their cozy homes, galleons of heavy fog sailed in from the sea, plundering all color first, then detail, depth, and shape.

From the other side of the door came the sound of the security chain sliding into the latch-plate slot.

The first dead bolt snapped shut, followed a moment later by the second.

Smiling, nodding with satisfaction, the doctor drank a little beer and stared at the steps in front of him, waiting. Glistening dewdrops, cold on the gray rubber treads: tears on a dead face.

The backrail of the maple chair rapped once against the other side of the door as Susan wedged it under the knob.

Now she would be padding barefoot back to bed.

Without need of the handrail, as nimble as a boy, Dr. Ahriman went down the steep stairs, turning up the collar of his coat as he descended.

The bricks on the front patio were wet and as dark as blood. As far as he could discern in the fog, the boardwalk beyond the patio appeared to be deserted.

The gate in the white picket fence squeaked. In this earthbound cloud bank, the sound was muffled, too slight even to prick the ears of a cat on guard for mice.

Departing, the doctor averted his face from the house. He had been equally discreet upon arrival.

No lights had shone at the windows earlier. None were visible now. The retirees renting the lower two floors were no doubt snug under their blankets, as oblivious as their parakeets dozing in covered cages.

Nevertheless, Ahriman took sensible precautions. He was the lord of memory, but not everyone was susceptible to his mind-clouding power.

Its voice muted by the dense mist, the lazy surf crumbling to shore was less a sound than a vibration, less heard than felt as a tingle in the chilly air.

Palm trees hung limp. Condensation dripped from the points of every blade of every frond, like clear venom from the tongues of serpents.

He paused to look up at the fog-veiled crowns of the palms, suddenly uneasy for reasons he could not identify. After a moment, puzzled, he took another swallow of beer and continued along the boardwalk.

His Mercedes was two blocks away. He encountered no one en route.

Parked under a huge, dripping Indian laurel, the black sedan plinked, tinked, and tatted like an out-of-tune xylophone.

In the car, as he was about to start the engine, Ahriman paused again, still uneasy, brought closer to the source of his uneasiness by the tuneless music of water droplets snapping steel. Finishing the beer, he stared out at the massive overhanging canopy of the laurel, as if revelation awaited him in the complex patterns of those branches.

When revelation didn't come, he started the car and drove west on Balboa Boulevard, toward the head of the peninsula.

At three o'clock in the morning, traffic was light. He saw only three moving vehicles in the first two miles, their headlights ringed by fuzzy aureoles in the fog. One was a police car, heading down the peninsula, in no hurry.

Across the bridge to Pacific Coast Highway, glancing at the westernmost channel of the huge harbor to his right, where yachts loomed like ghost ships at docks and moorings in the mist, and then south along the coast, all the way into Corona Del Mar, he puzzled over the cause of his uneasiness, until he came to a stop at a red traffic light and found his attention drawn to a large California pepper tree, lacy and elegant, rising out of low cascades of red bougainvillea. He thought of the potted ming tree with the sprays of ivy at its base.

The ming tree. The ivy.

The traffic light changed to green.

So green, her eyes riveted on the ming tree.

The doctor's mind raced, but he kept his foot hard on the brake pedal.

Only when the light turned yellow did he finally drive through the deserted intersection. He pulled to the curb in the next block, stopped, but didn't switch off the engine.

An expert on the nature of memory, he now applied his knowledge to a meticulous search of his own recollections of events in Susan Jagger's bedroom.

37

Nine.

Waking in darkness, Susan Jagger thought she heard someone speak that number. Then she surprised herself by saying, "Ten."

Tense, listening for movement, she wondered if she had spoken both numbers or whether her *ten* had been a reply.

A minute passed, another, with no sound but her low breathing, and then, when she held her breath, no sound at all. She was alone.

According to the glowing numbers on the digital clock, it was shortly after three in the morning. Apparently she had been asleep more than two hours.

Finally she sat up in bed and switched on the lamp.

The half-finished glass of wine. The book tumbled among the rumpled bedclothes. The blind-covered windows, the furniture—all as it should be. The ming tree.

She raised her hands to her face and smelled them. She sniffed her right forearm, as well, and then her left.

His scent. Unmistakable. Partly sweat, partly the lingering fragrance of his preferred soap. Perhaps he used a scented hand lotion, as well.

If she could trust her memory, this was not how Eric smelled. Yet she remained convinced that he, and no other, was her too-real incubus.

Even without the residual scent, she would have known

that he had paid her a visit while she slept. A soreness here, a tenderness there. The faint ammonia odor of his semen.

When she threw back the covers and got out of bed, she felt his viscid essence continuing to seep from her, and she shuddered.

At the Biedermeier pedestal, she parted the concealing runners of ivy to reveal the camcorder under the ming tree. At most, the cassette could contain a few remaining feet of unused tape, but the camera was still recording.

She switched it off and extracted it from the pot.

Her curiosity and eagerness for justice were suddenly outweighed by her disgust. She put the camcorder on the nightstand and hurried into the bathroom.

Often, upon awakening to the discovery that she had been used, Susan's disgust settled into nausea, and she purged herself, as if by emptying her stomach she could turn back the clock to just prior to dinner and, therefore, to a time hours before she had been violated. Now, however, the nausea passed when she reached the bathroom.

She wanted to take a long and extremely hot shower with lots of fragrant soap and shampoo, scrubbing herself vigorously with a loofah sponge. She was tempted, in fact, to shower first and watch the video later, because she felt dirtier than ever before, intolerably filthy, as though she were smeared with a vile grime she couldn't see, acrawl with hordes of microscopic parasites.

The videotape first. The truth. Then the cleansing.

Although she was able to delay her shower, repulsion drove her to strip out of her clothes and wash her privates. She scrubbed her face, too, and then her hands, and she gargled with a mint-flavored mouthwash.

She tossed the T-shirt into the clothes hamper. The panties, with his odious ooze, she placed atop the closed lid of the hamper, because she didn't intend to launder them.

If she had captured the intruder on videotape, she probably had all the evidence she needed to file rape charges. Preserving a semen sample for DNA testing was nonetheless wise.

Her condition and demeanor on the tape would no doubt convince the authorities that she had been drugged—not a willing participant, but a victim. Yet when she called the police, she would ask them to take a blood sample from her as soon as possible, while traces of the drug remained in her system.

Once she knew the camcorder had worked, that the image was good, and that she had irrefutable proof against Eric, she would be tempted to phone him before ringing the cops. Not to accuse him. To ask *why*. Why this viciousness? Why this secretive scheming? Why would he jeopardize her life and sanity with some devil's brew of narcotics? Why such hatred?

She wouldn't make that call, however, because alerting him might be dangerous. It was forbidden.

Forbidden. What an odd thought.

She realized that she had used the same word with Martie. Maybe it was the right word, because what Eric had done to her was worse than abuse, seemed to be beyond mere unlawful behavior, felt almost like an act of sacrilege. Marriage vows are sacred, after all, or ought to be; therefore, these assaults were arguably profane, forbidden.

In the bedroom again, she dressed in a clean T-shirt and fresh panties. The thought of being naked while watching the hateful video was intolerable.

She sat on the edge of the bed and picked up the camera from the nightstand. She rewound the cassette.

The preview window on the camcorder provided a three-inch-square image. She saw herself returning to the bed after starting the tape, which she'd done a few minutes past midnight.

The single bedside lamp provided adequate—though

not ideal—light for videotaping. Consequently, the clarity of the image on the small preview window was not good.

She ejected the cassette from the camcorder, put it in the VCR, and turned on the television. Holding the remote control in both hands, she sat on the foot of the bed and watched with fascination and apprehension.

She saw herself as she had been at midnight, returning to the bed after resetting the tape in the camcorder, saw herself get into bed and switch off the TV.

For a moment, she sits in bed, listening intently to the silent apartment. Then as she reaches for the book, the telephone rings.

Susan frowned. She had no recollection of having received a phone call.

She picks up the handset. "Hello?"

At best the videotape could provide her with only one side of the telephone conversation. Her distance from the camcorder ensured that some of her words were fuzzy, but what she heard made even less sense than she had expected.

Hurrying, she hangs up the phone, gets out of bed, and leaves the room.

From the moment she had taken the call, there had been subtle changes in her face and body language that she perceived but could not easily define. Subtle as those changes were, however, as she watched herself leaving this bedroom, she seemed to be watching a stranger.

She waited half a minute, and then fast-forwarded through the tape until she saw movement.

Shadowy forms in the hallway beyond the open bedroom door. Then she herself, returning. Behind her, a man moves out of the dark hall, across the threshold. Dr. Ahriman.

Astonishment left Susan breathless. Stiller than stone, colder, too, she was suddenly deaf to the audio portion of the tape, deaf to her own heartbeat, as well. She sat like a marble maiden sculpted for the focal point of a boxwood-hedge parterre in a formal garden, and here misplaced.

After a moment, astonishment spawned disbelief, and

she inhaled sharply. She pressed the *pause* button on the remote control.

In the frozen image, she sat on the edge of the bed, rather as she was sitting now. Ahriman stood over her.

She pressed *rewind*, reversing herself and the doctor out of the room. Then she touched *play* and watched the shadows in the hallway resolve into people once more, half convinced that this time Eric would follow her across the threshold. Because Dr. Ahriman—his being here was impossible. He was ethical. Widely admired. So professional. Compassionate. Concerned. Simply impossible: here, like this. She would have been no more disbelieving if she had seen her own father on the tape, and less shocked if what followed her into the room had been a demonic incubus with horns sprouting from its forehead, eyes as yellow and radiant as those of a cat. Tall, self-assured, and hornless, here came Ahriman once more, puncturing disbelief.

Handsome as ever, handsome in an actorly way, the doctor's face was the stage for an expression she had never before seen on it. Not entirely raw lust, as might have been expected, although lust was a component. Not a mask of madness, though his chiseled features were ever so slightly misaligned, as if they were being distorted by some inner pressure that had only just begun to build. Studying his face, Susan at last recognized the attitude: smugness.

This wasn't the prim-mouth, pinched-eye, cocked-head smugness of a moralizing preacher or of a temperance-sotted prude announcing his disdain for all those who drank, who smoked, and who ate a high-cholesterol diet. Here, instead, was the smirking superiority of an adolescent. Once he passed through the bedroom doorway, Ahriman had the lazy posture, the loose-limbed movements, and the cockiness of a schoolboy who believed that all adults were morons—and a shiny, hot-eyed stare of squirmy pubescent need.

This criminal and the psychiatrist whose office she

attended twice each week were physically identical. The difference between them was entirely one of attitude. And yet the difference was so alarming that her heart rapped hard and fast.

Her disbelief gave way to anger and to a sense of betrayal so intense that she spat out a series of expletives, in a bitter voice unlike her own, as if she suffered from Tourette's syndrome.

On the tape, the doctor moved out of frame to the armchair.

He orders her to crawl to him, and crawl she does.

Watching this record of her humiliation was almost more than Susan could bear, but she did not press *stop*, because watching fed her anger, and that was good right now. Anger gave her strength, empowered her after sixteen months of feeling powerless.

She fast-forwarded until she and the doctor returned to the frame. They were naked now.

Grim-faced, using the fast-forward button several times, she watched a series of depravities interspersed with periods of ordinary sex that seemed, by comparison, as innocent as teenagers necking.

How he could effect this control of her, how he could erase such shocking events from her mind—these mysteries seemed as deep as the origins of the universe and the meaning of life. She was overcome by a feeling of unreality, as though nothing in the world was what it appeared to be, all of it just an elaborate stage setting and the people merely players.

This trash on the TV was real, however, as real as the stains in the underwear that she had left on the hamper lid in the bathroom.

Leaving the tape running, she turned away from the television and went to the phone. She keyed in two digits—9, 1—but not the second 1.

If she called the police, she would have to open the door

to let them into the apartment. They might want her to go with them somewhere, to make a full statement, or to a hospital emergency room to be examined for indications of rape that later would be useful evidence in court.

Although strong with anger, she was not nearly strong enough to overcome her agoraphobia. The mere thought of going outside was enough to bring the familiar panic back into her heart.

She *would* do what was necessary, go where they wanted, as often as they wanted. She would do anything she was required to do if it would put the sick son of a bitch Ahriman behind bars for a long, long time.

The prospect of going outside with strangers, however, was too distressing to contemplate, even if those strangers were policemen. She needed the support of a friend, someone she trusted with her life, because going outside felt as close to death as anything but dying itself.

She called Martie and got the answering machine. She knew their phone didn't ring through to their bedroom at night, but one of them might be awakened by the ringing down the hall, might go to Martie's office out of curiosity, to see who was phoning at this ungodly hour.

After the beep, Susan said, "Martie, it's me. Martie, are you there?" She paused. "Listen, if you're there, for God's sake, pick up." Nothing. "It isn't Eric, Martie. It's Ahriman. It's *Ahriman.* I've got the bastard on videotape. The *bastard*—after the good deal he got on his house. Martie, please, please, call me. I need help."

Suddenly sick to her stomach again, she hung up.

Sitting on the edge of the bed, Susan clenched her teeth and put one cold hand on the nape of her neck, the other on her abdomen. The spasm of nausea passed.

She glanced at the television—and looked at once away.

Staring at the phone, willing it to ring, she said, "Martie, please. Call me. Now, now."

The half glass of wine had been sitting untouched for hours. She drained it.

She pulled open the top drawer in her nightstand and withdrew the pistol that she kept for protection.

As far as she knew, Ahriman never visited her twice in one night. As far as she knew.

She suddenly realized the absurdity of something she had said to Martie's answering machine: *The* bastard—*after the good deal he got on his house.* She had sold Mark Ahriman his current residence eighteen months ago, two months before the onset of her agoraphobia. She represented the seller, and the doctor walked in during an open house, and he asked her to represent him as well. She'd done a damn good job looking after the interests of buyer and seller, but it was admittedly a stretch to expect that if her client was a seriously demented sociopathic rapist, he would cut her a little slack because she had been an ethical Realtor.

She started to laugh, choked on the laugh, sought refuge in the wine, realized none was left, and put down the empty glass in favor of the handgun. "Martie, please. Call, call."

The telephone rang.

She set the gun aside and snatched up the phone.

"Yeah," she said.

Before she could say more, a man said, "Ben Marco."

"I'm listening."

38

Having rebuilt the dream in his memory, Dusty walked through it as though touring a museum, leisurely contemplating each Gothic image. Heron at the window, heron in the room. Silent strikes of lambent lightning in a thunderless, rainless storm. Brass tree with glucose fruit. Martie meditating.

Studying the nightmare, Dusty was increasingly convinced that a monstrous truth was concealed in it, like a scorpion waiting in the smallest container in a stack of Chinese boxes. This particular stack contained a lot of boxes, however, many of them tricky to open, and the truth remained hidden, poised to sting.

Eventually, frustrated, he got out of bed and went to the bathroom. Martie was sleeping so soundly, was cuffed and hobbled so securely by Dusty's neckties, that she was unlikely either to wake up or to leave the room while he was away from her side.

A few minutes later, as he was washing his hands at the bathroom sink, Dusty was visited by a revelation. It was not a sudden insight into the meaning of the dream, but an answer to a question over which he'd been puzzling earlier, before Martie had awakened and demanded to be tied hand and foot.

Missions.

Skeet's haiku.

Clear cascades. Into the waves scatter. Blue pine needles.

The pine needles were missions, Skeet had said.

Trying to make sense of this, Dusty had made a mental list of synonyms for *mission*, but nothing he'd come up with had furthered his understanding. *Task. Work. Chore. Job. Calling. Vocation. Career. Church.*

Now, as he held his hands under the hot water, rinsing the soap from them, another series of words poured into his mind. *Errand. Charge. Assignment. Instructions.*

Dusty stood at this sink almost as Skeet had stood with his hands under the near-scalding water in the bathroom at New Life, brooding about the word *instructions.*

The fine hairs on the back of his neck suddenly felt as stiff as tightly stretched piano wires, and a reverberant chill like a silent glissando shivered down the keys of his spine.

The name *Dr. Yen Lo*, when spoken to Skeet, had elicited a formal reply: *I'm listening.* Thereafter, he'd answered questions only with questions.

Skeet, do you know where you are?

Where am I?

So you don't know?

Do I?

Can't you look around?

Can I?

Is this an Abbott and Costello routine?

Is it?

Skeet had answered questions only with questions of his own, as if seeking to be told what he should think or do, but he had responded to statements as though they were commands, and to actual commands as though they came directly from the lips of God. When, in frustration, Dusty had said, *Ah, give me a break and go to sleep*, his brother had fallen instantly unconscious.

Skeet had referred to the haiku as "the rules," and Dusty later had thought of the poem as a mechanism of some kind, a simple device with a powerful effect, the verbal equivalent of a nail gun, though he had not been quite sure what he meant by that.

Now, as he continued to explore the ramifications of the word *instructions*, he realized that the haiku might better be defined not as a mechanism, not as a device, but as a computer operating system, the software that allows the instructions to be received, understood, and followed.

And what the hell was the logical deduction to be drawn from the haiku-as-software hypothesis? That Skeet was . . . programmed?

As Dusty shut off the water, he thought he heard the faint ringing of a phone.

Dripping hands raised as though he were a surgeon fresh from a scrub sink, he stepped out of the bathroom, into the bedroom, and listened. The house was silent.

If a call had come in, it would have been picked up after the second ring by the answering machine in Martie's office.

Most likely, he had imagined the ringing. No one ever called them at this hour. Nevertheless, he ought to check it out before he returned to bed.

In the bathroom once more, drying his hands on a towel, he turned the word *programmed* over and over in his mind, considering all the ramifications of it.

Staring into the mirror, Dusty saw not his reflection but a replay of the strange events in Skeet's room at New Life Clinic.

Then his memory wound time backward to the previous morning, to the roof of the Sorensons' house.

Skeet claimed to have seen the Other Side. An angel of death had shown him what waited beyond this world, and the kid had liked what he'd seen. Then the angel had instructed him to jump. Skeet's very word: *Instructed.*

That icy glissando again, along Dusty's spine. Another

of the Chinese boxes had been opened, though yet another box lay inside it. Each box smaller than the last. Perhaps not many layers of the puzzle were left to be resolved. He could almost hear the scorpion scuttle: the sound of a nasty truth waiting to sting when the last lid was lifted.

39

The soft *shush* of surf, conspiratorial fog cover his return.

Dew on the gray steps. Snail on the second wet tread. Crushed hard underfoot.

Ascending, the doctor whispered into his cell phone: "The winter storm—"

Susan Jagger said, "The storm is you."

"—hid in the bamboo grove—"

"The grove is me."

"—and quieted away."

"In the quiet, I will learn what is wanted."

Arriving at the landing outside her door, he said, "Let me in."

"Yes."

"Quickly," he said, and then terminated the call and pocketed the phone.

He glanced worriedly toward the deserted boardwalk.

Hanging in the fog, cascades of dead-still palm fronds, like cold dark fireworks.

With a rattle and scrape, the bracing chair was removed from under the doorknob in the kitchen. The first dead bolt. The second. The clatter of the security chain being disengaged.

When Susan greeted him demurely, without a word but with an obedient half bow, as though she were a geisha, Ahriman stepped inside. He waited while she closed the door again and engaged one of the locks, and then he instructed her to lead him to her bedroom.

Across the kitchen, through the dining room and living room, along the short hall to the bedroom, he said, "I think you've been a bad girl, Susan. I don't know how you could scheme against me, why it would even occur to you to do such a thing, but I'm pretty sure that's what you've done."

Earlier, every time she had looked away from him, she had turned her eyes toward the potted ming tree. And each time, before her gaze was drawn to that bit of greenery, Ahriman had first made reference either to the videotape he'd shot of her or to the tape he intended to shoot on his next visit. When she appeared to be tense and racked by worry, he directed her to reveal the source of her anxiety, and when she said simply, *The video*, he made the obvious assumption. Obvious and perhaps wrong. His suspicion had been aroused, almost too late, by the fact that she *always* looked toward the ming tree: not at the floor, as might be expected when bowed by shame, and not at the bed where so much of her humiliation had occurred, but always at the ming tree.

Now, following her into the bedroom, he said, "I want to see what's in that pot, under the ivy."

Dutifully, she led him toward the Biedermeier pedestal, but the doctor stopped short when he saw what was playing on the TV.

"I'll be damned," he said.

He would have been damned, in fact, if he had not recognized the cause of his suspicion, if he had finally driven home and gone to bed without returning here.

"Come to me," he said.

As Susan approached, the doctor made fists of his hands. He wanted to punch her pretty face.

Girls. They were all alike.

As a boy, he'd seen no use for them, had wanted nothing to do with them. Girls had made him sick with all their coy manipulations. The best thing about them was that he could make them cry without much effort—all those beautiful, salty tears—but then they always ran to their mothers or fathers to tattle. He was good at defending himself against their hysterical accusations; adults tended to find him charming and convincing. He had soon realized, however, that he must learn discretion and not let his thirst for tears control him the way that a taste for cocaine controlled more than a few people in the Hollywood crowd with which his father worked.

Eventually, victimized by his hormones, he discovered that he needed girls for more than their tears. He learned, too, how easily a handsome lad like him could play games that put girls' hearts in his hands, allowing him to wring more tears from them through calculated romance and betrayal than, as a younger boy, he had ever gotten from them by pinching, poking, boxing ears, and pushing them into mud puddles.

Decades of torturing them emotionally had not, however, made them any more appealing to him than they had been when he was just a preschooler dropping caterpillars down their blouses. Girls still annoyed more than charmed him, left him feeling vaguely ill after he had indulged with them, and the fact that he was also fascinated by them only made him resent them more. Worse, sex was never enough for them; they wanted you to father their children. The marrow crawled in his bones at the thought of being anyone's father. He had once nearly fallen into that trap, but fate had favored his escape. You couldn't trust children. They were inside your defenses, and when you least expected it, they could kill you and steal your wealth. The doctor knew all about such treachery. And if you fathered a daughter, the mother and child would surely conspire against you at every turn. In the doctor's view, all other men belonged to a breed different from—and far inferior to—his own, but girls were another species entirely, not merely another breed; girls were alien and ultimately unknowable.

When Susan stopped before him, the doctor raised one fist.

She appeared free of fear. Her personality was now so deeply repressed that she was unable to exhibit emotion until instructed to do so.

"I should beat your face in."

Although he heard the boyish petulance in his voice, he wasn't embarrassed by it. The doctor was sufficiently self-aware to realize that during these games of control, he was undergoing personality regression, descending the ladder of years. This descent was not mortifying or troubling in the least; indeed, it was essential if he were to enjoy the moment in its fullness. As an adult of broad experience, he was jaded; but as a boy, he still had a delightfully raw sense of wonder, was still thrilled by every nuance of the imaginative abuse of power.

"I should just beat your stupid face so hard you'll be ugly forever."

Deep under his spell, Susan remained serene. A spasm of REM seized her for a few seconds, but it was unrelated to his threat.

Discretion and restraint were now essential. Ahriman dared not strike her. Her death, if properly staged, was unlikely to generate a homicide investigation. Bruised and battered, however, she would not be a credible suicide.

"I don't like you anymore, Susie. I don't like you at all."

She was silent, because she hadn't been instructed to reply.

"I assume that you haven't yet called the police. Tell me if that's correct."

"That's correct."

"Have you spoken to anyone about that videotape on the TV?"

"Have I?"

Cautioning himself that her response was not defiant, that this was only how she was programmed to reply to questions when she was far down in the mind chapel, the doctor lowered his fist and slowly unclenched it. "Tell me, yes or no, if you have spoken to anyone about that videotape on the TV."

"No."

Relieved, he took her by the arm and led her to the bed. "Sit down, girl."

She sat on the edge of the bed, knees pressed together, hands folded in her lap.

For a few minutes the doctor quizzed her, phrasing his questions as statements and commands, until he understood why she had set the trap with the camcorder. She had been after evidence against Eric, not against her psychiatrist.

Although her memory was erased after each of their assignations, Susan was certain to suspect that she had been sexually used, and if the doctor did not choose to sponge up and take with him every drop of sweat and passion that he produced, Susan was also certain to find evidence to support her suspicion. Ahriman chose not to be obsessive about postcoital cleanup, because that would diminish the thrill of power and compromise the pleasing illusion that his awesome control was absolute. There would be little fun in either a food fight or bloody murder if, afterward, one were required to wash the walls and mop the floor.

He was an adventurer, after all, not a housekeeper.

He had numerous techniques with which to mitigate or misdirect Susan's suspicion. For one thing, he could have suggested to her that upon waking she would simply ignore all signs of physical abuse, be unaware of even the most obvious evidence of intercourse.

In a more playful mood, the doctor could have implanted in her the conviction that she was being visited by a yellow-eyed spawn of the brimstone pit determined to breed with her and bring forth the Antichrist. By seeding dream-like memories of an evil night-lover with a coarse leathery body, sulfurous breath, and a forked black tongue, he literally could have made her life a living Hell.

Ahriman had played that tune with others, strumming the harp of superstition, inducing severe cases of demonophobia—the fear of demons and devils—that had shattered his patients' lives. He had found such sport highly entertaining, but only for a while. This phobia could be more poisonous than others, often advancing swiftly to a complete mental decline and outright insanity. In the long run, therefore, Ahriman found it to be less than fully satisfying, because the tears of the mad, who were detached from their suffering, were not as invigorating as the tears of the sane, who still believed that they had a hope of recovery.

From his many other options, the doctor had chosen to direct Susan's suspicion toward her estranged husband. This current game, for which he'd mentally composed a particularly bloody and intricate scenario, was meant to end in a storm of violence that would make nationwide news. The precise details of the final inning were constantly being revised in the doctor's mind, although Eric might be either a significant perpetrator or a victim.

By encouraging Susan to focus her suspicion on Eric and then forbidding her to confront him, Ahriman had crafted a clockspring of psychological tension. Week by week, the spring wound tighter, until Susan could barely contain the tremendous emotional energy coiled in it. Consequently, desperate to relieve that tension, she had sought proof of her estranged husband's guilt, sufficient evidence to make it possible for her to go directly to the police and avoid the forbidden confrontation with Eric himself.

Ordinarily, this situation would not have arisen, because the doctor never toyed with anyone as long as he had played with Susan Jagger. He had begun to drug and condition her a year and a half ago, for God's sake, and she had been his patient for sixteen months. Usually he grew bored in six months, sometimes in as few as two or three. Then either he cured the patient, stripping away the phobia or the obsession that he'd implanted in the first place, thereby adding to his singular reputation as a therapist—or he devised a death colorful enough to be satisfying to a gamesman of his experience. Bewitched by Susan's exceptional beauty, he had dallied far too long, allowing her stress to build, until she was driven to this act of entrapment.

Girls. They were always trouble, sooner or later.

Rising from the edge of the bed, Ahriman ordered Susan to stand, as well, and she obeyed.

"You've really messed up my game," he said, impatient with her now. "I'll have to figure out a whole new ending."

He could question her to discover when the camcorder scheme had first occurred to her, and could then follow through from that moment to the present, excising all related memories; in the end, however, she might be aware of odd gaps in her day. He could relatively easily erase a whole block of time from a subject's memory and then fill the gap with false recollections that, though painted with a broad brush, were convincing in spite of their lack of detail. Comparatively, it was quite difficult to finesse out a single narrative thread from the broader weave of memory—like trying to strip out the fine veins of fat from a well-marbled filet mignon, while leaving the cut of meat intact. He could rectify the situation and remove from Susan's mind all knowledge that he was her tormentor, but he didn't have enough time, energy, or patience to do so.

"Susan, tell me where you keep the nearest pen and notepaper."

"Beside the bed."

"Get them, please."

When he followed her around the bed, he saw the pistol on the nightstand.

She appeared to have no interest in the gun. She opened

the nightstand drawer and withdrew a ballpoint pen and a lined notepad the size of a stenographer's tablet. At the top of each page in the pad was her photograph, plus the logo and phone numbers of the real-estate company for which she had worked before agoraphobia had ended her career.

"Put the gun away, please," he directed, with no fear whatsoever that she would use the weapon on him.

She placed the pistol in the nightstand and closed the drawer. Turning to Ahriman, she held out the pen and the notepad.

He said, "Bring them with you."

"Where?"

"Follow me."

The doctor led her to the dining room. There, he instructed her to switch on the chandelier and sit at the table.

40

Still staring into the bathroom mirror, reviewing yet again his rooftop conversation with Skeet, trying to marshal details that would lend credibility to his incredible theory that his brother had been programmed, Dusty realized that he was finished with sleep for the night. Mosquito swarms of questions buzzed through his mind, their bites more ruinous of sleep than pots of black coffee boiled to the thickness of molasses.

Who would have programmed Skeet? When? How? Where? For what possible purpose? And why Skeet, of all people: self-admitted feeb, druggie, sweet loser that he was?

The whole thing smelled-smacked-reeked of paranoia. Perhaps this crazy-ass theory would make sense in the world of paranormal talk radio, in which Fig Newton lived while painting houses—and in fact during most of his waking hours—in that unreal but widely cherished America where scheming extraterrestrials were busily crossbreeding with hapless human females, where transdimensional beings were reputed to be responsible for both global warming and outrageous credit-card interest rates, where the President of the United States had been secretly replaced by a look-alike android assembled in Bill Gates's basement, where Elvis was alive and living on an elaborate space station built and operated by Walt Disney, whose brain had been transplanted into a host body that we now know as the rap star and movie titan, Will Smith. But the idea of a programmed Skeet didn't make sense *here,* not here in the real world, where Elvis was thoroughly dead, where Disney was dead, too, and where the closest things to horny extraterrestrials were the aging cast of *Star Trek* on Viagra.

Dusty would have laughed off his harebrained theory . . . assuming that Skeet had not said he'd been *instructed* to take a header from the Sorensons' roof, assuming the kid hadn't dropped into that eerie trance at New Life Clinic, assuming all of them—Skeet, Martie, and Dusty himself—had not been missing bits of time from their day, and assuming their lives hadn't abruptly fallen apart with such uncanny simultaneity and with the cataclysmic weirdness of a two-part *X Files* episode. If laughs were dollars, if chuckles were quarters, and if smiles were pennies, Dusty would at the moment be flat broke.

Are you lonesome tonight, Elvis, up there in orbit?

Certain that insomnia would be his companion until dawn, he decided to shave and shower while Martie was still deep in a drugged sleep. When she woke, if she was once more gripped by that grotesque fear of herself, she wouldn't want him to let her out of his sight, for fear she would somehow wrench loose of her restraints and creep up on him with homicidal intent.

A few minutes later, smooth-cheeked, Dusty switched off his electric razor—and heard muffled cries of distress coming from the bedroom.

When he reached Martie's side, he found her whimpering in her sleep, dreaming again. She strained at her bonds and murmured, "No, no, no, no."

Stirred from dog fantasies no doubt full of tennis balls and bowls of kibble, Valet raised his head to crack a wide and toothy yawn worthy of a crocodile, but he did not growl.

Martie rolled her head back and forth on her pillow, grimacing and softly groaning, like a feverish malaria patient wandering the land of delirium.

Dusty blotted her damp brow with a few Kleenex,

smoothed her hair away from her face, and held her stylishly shackled hands until she quieted.

In which nightmare was she snared? The one that had plagued her on several other occasions over the past half year, involving the hulking figure composed of dead leaves? Or the new spook show from which she awakened earlier, choking and gagging and scrubbing at her mouth with both hands?

As Martie settled into silent sleep once more, Dusty wondered if her recurring dream of the Leaf Man might be as meaningful as his encounter with the lightning-chased heron had seemed to him.

She had described the nightmare to him months ago, the second or third time that she had suffered through it. Now he brought it forth from his vaultlike memory and examined it as he watched over her.

Though at first consideration, their dreams appeared to be utterly different from each other, analysis revealed disturbing similarities.

Increasingly mystified rather than enlightened, Dusty pondered the points of intersection, nightmare to nightmare.

He wondered if Skeet had been dreaming recently.

Still lying on his sheepskin pillow, Valet blew air out of his nostrils, one of those forceful but entirely voluntary quasi-sneezes with which he cleared his nose when preparing to seek the scent of rabbits on a morning walk. This time, with no rabbits in the house, it seemed to be a skeptical judgment of his master's sudden new obsession with dreams.

"There's something to it," Dusty muttered.

Valet blew air again.

41

Restlessly circling the room, Ahriman composed a wonderfully poignant farewell to life, which Susan took down in her graceful handwriting. He knew exactly what to put in and what to leave out in order to convince even the most skeptical police detective that the note was authentic.

Handwriting analysis would, of course, leave little or no room for doubt, but the doctor was meticulous.

Composition under these circumstances was not easy. His mouth was sour with the lingering aftertaste of Tsingtao. Weary to the bone, eyes hot and grainy, mind fuzzy from lack of sleep, he mentally polished every sentence before dictating it.

He was distracted by Susan, as well. Perhaps because he would never possess her again, she seemed more beautiful to him than at any previous moment of their relationship.

Banners of gold hair. Egyptian-green firework eyes. Sad, this broken toy.

No. That was a lousy haiku. Embarrassing. It had seventeen syllables, all right, and the ideal five-seven-five pattern, but not much else.

He could occasionally compose a reasonably good verse about a snail on a stair tread, crushed hard underfoot, and stuff like that, but when it came to writing lines to capture the look, the mood, the essence of a girl, any girl, then he floundered.

Some truth in his lousy haiku: She *was* broken, this once-fine toy. Although she still looked great, she was badly damaged, and he couldn't simply fix her with a little glue, as he might have repaired a plastic figurine from a classic Marx playset like Roy Rogers Rodeo Ranch or Tom Corbett Space Academy.

Girls. They always let you down when you're counting on them.

Filled with a strange mix of sentimental yearning and sullen resentment, Ahriman finished composing the suicide note. He stood over Susan to watch as she signed her name at the bottom.

Her long-fingered hands. The gracefully looping pen. Last words without tears.

Shit.

Leaving the notepad on the table for now, the doctor led Susan into the kitchen. At his request she produced a spare apartment key from the built-in secretaire where she sat to compose shopping lists and plan menus. He already had a key, but he hadn't brought it with him. He pocketed this one, and they returned to the bedroom.

The videotape was still playing. At his direction, she used the remote to stop it; then she ejected it from the VCR and put it on the nightstand beside the empty wineglass.

"Tell me where you usually store the camcorder."

Her eyes jiggled. Then her gaze steadied. "In a box on the top shelf of that closet," she said, pointing.

"Please pack it up and put it away."

She had to bring a two-step folding stool from the kitchen to complete the task.

Next, he instructed her to use a hand towel from the bathroom to wipe down the nightstands, the headboard of the bed, and anything else he might have touched while in the bedroom. He monitored her to ensure that she did a thorough job.

Because he was careful to avoid touching most surfaces in the apartment, Ahriman had little concern that his prints would be found anywhere but in Susan's two most private chambers. When she finished in the bedroom, he stood in the doorway of the bathroom for about ten minutes, watching as she polished tile, glass, brass, and porcelain.

Task completed, she folded the hand towel into perfectly aligned thirds and draped it on a brushed-brass bar beside another hand towel that was folded and hung in precisely the same manner. The doctor valued neatness.

When he saw the folded white cotton panties on the hamper lid, he had almost instructed her to toss them in with the other laundry, but instinct had led him to question her about them. When he learned that they had been set aside to provide a DNA sample to the police, he was shocked.

Girls. Devious. Cunning. More than once, when the doctor was a boy, girls had taunted him into pushing them down a flight of porch steps or shoving them into a thorny rosebush, whereupon they had always run to the nearest adults, claiming that the assault had been unprovoked, that it had been pure meanness. Here, now, these decades later, more treachery.

He could have instructed her to wash the panties in the sink, but he decided that prudence required him to take them when he left, remove them from the apartment altogether.

The doctor wasn't an expert on the latest forensic techniques of practical homicide investigation, but he was reasonably sure that latent fingerprints on human skin lasted only a few hours or less. They could be lifted with the use of lasers and other sophisticated equipment, but he knew simpler procedures might also be effective. Kromekote cards or unexposed Polaroid film, pressed firmly to the skin, will transfer the incriminating print; when the card or film is dusted with black powder, a mirror image of the latent print appears and must then be reversed through photography. Magnetic powder applied with a Magna Brush directly to the skin is acceptable in a pinch, and the iodine-silver transfer method is an alternative if a fuming gun and silver sheets are close at hand.

He didn't expect Susan's body to be found for five or six hours, perhaps much longer. By then, the early stages of decomposition would have eradicated all the latent prints on her skin.

Nevertheless, he had touched virtually every plane and curve of her body—and often. To be a winner at these games, one had to play with energetic enthusiasm but also with a detailed knowledge of the rules and with a talent for strategy.

He suggested that Susan draw a hot bath. Then step by step he walked her through the remaining minutes of her life.

While the tub was filling, she got a safety razor from one of the vanity drawers. She had used it to shave her legs; but now it would serve a more serious purpose.

She twisted open the razor and extracted the single-edge blade. She put the blade on the flat rim of the bathtub.

She undressed for the bath. Naked, she didn't look broken, and Ahriman wished he could keep her.

Waiting for further instruction, Susan stood beside the bathtub, watching the water gush out of the faucet.

Studying her reflection in the mirror, Ahriman took pride in her tranquility. Intellectually, she was aware that she would soon be dead, but because of the excellent work he'd done with her, she lacked the capacity for genuine and spontaneous emotional response while in this state of total personality submersion.

The doctor regretted that the time inevitably came when each of his acquisitions must be discarded and allowed to go the way of all flesh.

He wished he could preserve each of them in perfect condition and set aside a few rooms of his house to a display of them, just as he currently dedicated space to his Corgi model cars, die-cast banks, playsets, and other enthusiasms. What a delight it would be to walk among them at will, these women and men who had been both his cat's-paws and his companions over the years. With his own engraving kit, he could lovingly prepare brass plaques featuring their names, vital statistics, and dates of acquisition—just as he did for items in his other collections. His videotapes were splendid mementos, but they were all motion in two dimensions, providing none of the depth or the satisfying tactility that physically preserved playthings could offer.

The problem was rot. The doctor was a perfectionist who would not add an item to one of his collections unless it was in mint or near-mint condition. Not for him the merely excellent or very good example. Because no known form of preservation, from mummification to state-of-the-art embalming, could meet his high standards, he would of necessity continue to rely on his videotapes when overcome by a nostalgic and sentimental mood.

Now, he sent Susan to the dining room to retrieve the notepad on which she had written her farewell to life. She returned with it and placed it on the freshly polished tile top of the vanity, next to the sink, where it would be found simultaneously with her cadaver.

The bath was ready. She turned off both faucets.

She added scented salts to the water.

The doctor was surprised, because he had not instructed her to spice the bath. Evidently, she always did so before stepping into the tub, and this act was essentially a conditioned reflex that required no volitional thinking. Interesting.

Writhing vines of steam, rising from the water, now bloomed with the faint fragrance of roses.

Sitting on the closed lid of the toilet, careful not to touch anything with his hands, Ahriman instructed Susan to enter the bath, to sit, and to bathe herself with special thoroughness. There was no longer any danger that a laser, Kromekote card, Magna Brush, or fuming gun could turn up incriminating fingerprints on her skin. He was counting on the action of her bath to flush out and disperse all of his semen, as well.

No doubt, in the bedroom and elsewhere in the apartment, he had left behind hairs and fibers from his clothing that could be gathered in a police-lab vacuum. Without good fingerprints, however, or other direct evidence that could put him on a list of suspects, they would not be able to trace these scraps of evidence back to him.

Besides, because he had taken such pains to present the police with a convincing tableau and a solid motivation for suicide, they were not likely to pursue even a cursory homicide investigation.

He would have liked to watch Susan bathe a while longer, for she was an enchanting sight; however, he was weary, sleepy. Furthermore, he wanted to leave the apartment well before dawn, when there was only a small chance of encountering witnesses.

"Susan, please pick up the razor blade."

For a moment, the steel blade stuck to the wet rim of the tub. Then she got it between the thumb and forefinger of her right hand.

The doctor preferred flamboyant destruction. Easily bored, he saw no thrill in a poisoned cup of tea, in a simple hangman's noose—or, in this case, in the severance of a radial artery or two. The real fun was in shotguns, large-caliber handguns, axes, chain saws, and explosives.

Her pistol had interested him. But a gunshot would wake the retirees downstairs, even if they had gone to bed martini-sotted, as usual.

Disappointed but determined not to surrender to his taste for the theatrical, Ahriman told Susan how to grip the blade, precisely where to cut on her left wrist, and how hard to press. Before the mortal slice, she scored her flesh lightly, and then lightly again, producing the hesitation marks that the police were accustomed to seeing in more than half of such suicides. Then, with no expression on her face and with only pure green beauty in her eyes, she made a third cut, much deeper than the first two.

Because some tendon damage was unavoidably sustained in addition to the severing of the radial artery, she couldn't hold the blade as firmly in her left hand as she had held it in her right. The wound in her right wrist was comparatively shallow and bled less heartily than the wound in her left; but that, too, would be consistent with police expectations.

She dropped the blade. Lowered her arms into the water.

"Thank you," he said.

"You're welcome."

The doctor waited with her for the end. He could have walked out, confident that in this obedient state, even unchaperoned, she would sit calmly in the tub until she died. Already in this game, however, fate had thrown him a couple of change-up pitches, and he was going to remain alert for another.

Far less steam arose from the water now, and attar of roses was not the only scent it carried anymore.

Yearning for greater drama, Ahriman considered bringing Susan out of the mind chapel and up a flight or two of stairs, nearer to full consciousness, where she could better appreciate her plight. Although he could control her at higher levels of awareness, there was a slim but real chance that an involuntary cry of terror or despair would escape her, just loud enough to wake pensioners and parakeets downstairs.

He waited.

The bathwater grew darker as it cooled, though the color that Susan lent to it was hot.

She sat in silence, no more touched by emotion than the tub that contained her, and the doctor was, therefore, shocked to see a single tear track down her face.

He leaned forward, disbelieving, certain that it must be mere water or perspiration.

When the drop had descended the length of her face, another—larger than the first, enormous—welled from the same eye, and there could be no question that this was the genuine article.

Here was more entertainment than he had expected. Fascinated, he monitored the descent of the tear over the elegant swell of her high cheekbone, into the pocket of her cheek, to the corner of her ripe mouth, and then toward the line of her jaw, where it arrived diminished but large enough to quiver like a pendulous jewel.

This second tear was not followed by a third. The dry lips of Death had kissed away the excess moisture in her eyes.

When Susan's mouth sagged open, as though with awe, the second—and last—tear trembled and fell from her delicate jaw into the bathwater, with the faintest detectable *plink* like a note struck from the highest octave on a piano keyboard rooms and rooms away.

Green eyes growing gray. Rosy skin borrows color . . . from the razor blade.

He rather liked that one.

Leaving the lights on, of course, Ahriman picked up her soiled underwear from the hamper lid and stepped out of the bathroom, into the bedroom, where he retrieved the videotape.

In the living room, he paused to enjoy the subtle scent of citrus potpourri seeping from the ceramic jars. He had always meant to ask Susan where she'd purchased this particular melange, so that he could acquire some for his own home. Too late.

At the kitchen door, fingers safely wrapped in Kleenex, he twisted the thumbturn on the only lock that she had engaged following his arrival. Outside, after quietly pulling the door shut, he used the spare key from the secretaire to engage both dead bolts.

He could do nothing about the security chain. This one detail should not make the authorities unduly suspicious.

The night and the fog, his conspirators, still waited for him, and the surf had grown louder since last he'd heard it, masking what little noise his shoes made on the rubber treads of the stairs.

Again, he reached his Mercedes without encountering anyone, and on the pleasant drive home, he found the streets only slightly busier than they had been forty-five minutes earlier.

His hilltop house stood on two acres in a gated community: a sprawling, futuristic, artful stack of square and rectangular forms, some in polished poured-in-place concrete and others clad in black granite, with floating decks, deep cantilevered roofs, bronze doors, and floor-to-ceiling windows so massive that birds were knocked unconscious against them not just one at a time but in flocks.

The place had been built by a young entrepreneur who had been made improbably rich from the IPO of his Internet retailing company. By the time it was completed, he had become enamored of Southwest architecture and had begun building a forty-thousand-square-foot faux adobe pile in the pueblo style, somewhere in Arizona. He'd offered this residence for sale without moving into it.

The doctor parked in the eighteen-car subterranean garage and took the elevator up to the ground floor.

The rooms and hallways were of grand proportions, with polished black granite floors. The antique Persian rugs—in lustrous shades of teal, peach, jade, ruby—were exquisitely patinaed by lifetimes of wear; they seemed to float upon the black granite as if they were magic carpets in flight, the blackness beneath them not stone, but the deep abyss of night.

In corridors and major chambers, lights came on to preset scenes as he entered, triggered by motion sensors managed by thousand-year universal clocks. In smaller rooms, lamps answered to vocal commands.

The young internet billionaire had computerized all the house systems in obsessive detail. When he had seen *2001: A Space Odyssey*, no doubt he had been under the impression that Hal was the hero.

In his lacewood-paneled study, the doctor phoned his office and left a voice-mail message for his secretary, asking her to cancel and reschedule his ten- and eleven-o'clock appointments to next week. He would be in after lunch.

There were no patient sessions filled on the second half of his Wednesday calendar. He had left his afternoon open for Dustin and Martine Rhodes, who would call in the morning, desperate for help.

Eighteen months ago, the doctor had realized that Martie could be one of his key toy soldiers in a marvelous game more elaborate than any he had played heretofore. Eight months ago, he served his witches' brew of drugs to her in coffee, with a chocolate biscotto on the side, and programmed her during three of Susan's office visits, as Susan herself had long previously come under his thrall.

Since then, Martie had awaited use, unaware that she'd been added to Ahriman's collection.

Tuesday morning, eighteen hours ago, when Martie

came to the office with Susan, the doctor at last put her into play, escorting her down into her mind chapel, where he implanted the suggestion that she could not trust herself, that she was a grave danger to herself and others, a monster capable of extreme violence and unspeakable atrocities.

After he wound her up and sent her off with Susan Jagger, she must have had an interesting day. He looked forward to hearing the gaudy details.

He had not yet used Martie sexually. Although she was not as beautiful as Susan, she was quite attractive, and he looked forward to seeing just how completely and deliciously sordid she could be if she really tried. She was not yet in sufficient misery to have much erotic appeal for him.

Soon.

Now, he was in a dangerous mood—and knew it. The personality regression he underwent during intense play sessions didn't reverse instantly upon conclusion of the games. Like a deep-sea diver rising through the fathoms at a measured pace to avoid the bends, Ahriman ascended toward full adulthood in decompressive stages. He was not entirely man or boy at the moment, but in emotional metamorphosis.

At the corner bar in his study, he poured a bottle of Coke—the classic formula—into a cut-crystal Tom Collins glass, added a thick squirt of cherry syrup and ice, stirring the concoction with a long-handled sterling-silver spoon. He tasted it and smiled. Better than Tsingtao.

Exhausted yet restless, he walked the house for a while, after instructing the computer to precede him neither with blazes of light nor with softly luminous preset scenes. He wanted darkness in those spaces that had a view, and a single lamp dimmed so far as to be nearly extinguished in those chambers that did not benefit from the nighttime panorama of Orange County.

On the vast flatlands below these hills, although most of the county's multitudes were still asleep, millions of lights glimmered even at this hour. View windows admitted just enough ambient light for the doctor to make his way with catlike surety, and he found the golden glow appealing.

Standing at a huge sheet of glass in the dark, basking in the incoming radiance, gazing at this urban sprawl that lay before him like the biggest playset in the world, he knew how God would feel, looking down on Creation, if there had been a god. The doctor was a player, not a believer.

Sipping cherry Coke, he roamed room to room, along passageways and galleries. The huge house was a labyrinth in more ways than one, but eventually he returned to the living room.

Here, more than eighteen months ago, he acquired Susan. On the day that escrow closed, he had met her here to receive the house keys and the thick operating manual for the computerized systems. She was surprised to find him with two champagne flutes and a chilled bottle of Dom Perignon. From the day they'd met, the doctor had been careful never to suggest that his interest in her went beyond her real-estate expertise; even with champagne in hand, he had struck a note of such erotic indifference that she didn't feel she, a married woman, was being romanced. Indeed, from the moment he'd met her and decided to have her, he had scattered hints, like breadcrumbs to a pigeon, that he was gay. Because he was so happy with his spectacular new house and because she wasn't displeased by the fat commission she'd earned, she saw no harm in celebrating with a glass of champagne—although hers was, of course, spiked.

Here in the wake of her death, conflicting emotions bedeviled Ahriman. He regretted the loss of Susan, all but swooned to the tug of a sweet sentimentality, but also felt wronged, betrayed. In spite of all the great good times they'd had together, she would still have ruined him if she'd had the chance.

At last he resolved his inner conflict, because he realized that she was just a girl like other girls, that she hadn't deserved all the time and attention he had lavished on her. To brood about her now would be to concede that she'd had a power over him no one else had ever exercised.

He was the collector, not her. He possessed things; they did not possess him.

"I'm glad you're dead," he said aloud in the dark living room. "I'm glad you're dead, you stupid girl. I hope the razor hurt."

After vocalizing his anger, he felt ever so much better. Oh, really, a thousand percent.

Although Cedric and Nella Hawthorne, the couple who managed the estate, were currently in residence, Ahriman was not concerned about being overheard. The Hawthornes were surely abed in their three-room apartment in the servants' wing. And regardless of what they might see or hear, he need not be concerned that they would ever remember anything that would endanger him.

"I hope it hurt," he repeated.

Then he took the elevator up to the next floor and followed the hallway to the master-bedroom suite.

He brushed his teeth, flossed meticulously, and dressed in black silk pajamas.

Nella had turned down the bed. White Pratesi sheets with black piping. Plenty of plump pillows.

As usual, on his nightstand was a Lalique bowl full of candy bars, two each of his six favorite brands. He wished he hadn't brushed his teeth.

Before turning in, he used the bedside Crestron touch-screen to access the automated-house program. With this control panel, he could operate lights throughout the residence, air-conditioning and heating room by room, the security system, landscape-surveillance cameras, pool and spa heaters, and numerous other systems and devices.

He entered his personal code to access a *vault* page that listed six wall safes of various sizes distributed throughout the residence. He touched *master bedroom* on the screen, and the image of a keypad replaced the list of locations.

When he keyed in a seven-digit number, a pneumatically driven section of granite on the face of the fireplace slid aside, revealing a small, embedded steel safe. Ahriman entered the combination on the keypad, and across the room, the lock released with an audible *click*.

He went to the fireplace, opened the twelve-inch-square steel door, and removed the contents from the safe box, which was lined with quilted padding. A one-quart jar.

He put the jar on a brushed-steel and zebrawood desk and sat down to study its contents.

After a few minutes, he could no longer resist the siren call of the candy bowl. He pondered the contents of the Lalique container and finally selected a Hershey's bar with almonds.

He would not brush his teeth again. Falling asleep with the taste of chocolate in his mouth was a sinful pleasure. Sometimes he was a bad boy.

Sitting at the desk again, Ahriman savored the candy, making it last, while he thoughtfully studied the jar. Although he didn't hurry through the snack, he had gained not a scintilla of new insight from his father's eyes by the time he finished the final crumbs of chocolate.

Hazel, they were, but with a milky film over the irises. The whites were no longer white, but pale yellow faintly marbled with pastel green. They were suspended in formaldehyde, in the vacuum-sealed jar, sometimes peering through the curved glass with a wistful expression and sometimes with what seemed to be unbearable sorrow.

Ahriman had been studying these eyes all his life, both when they had been seated in his father's skull and after they had been cut out. They held secrets that he wished to know, but they were, as ever, all but impossible to read.

42

Due to the lingering effects of three caplets of the sleep aid, Martie appeared to be unable to work herself into a state of panic, even after she was freed from the neckties, out of bed, and on her feet.

Her hands trembled almost nonstop, however, and she became alarmed when Dusty got too close to her. She still believed that she might suddenly claw out his eyes, chew off his nose, bite off his lips, and have a thoroughly unconventional breakfast.

Undressing to shower, she had an agreeably heavy-eyed, pouty look, which Dusty found appealing as he watched her from a distance that she deemed just barely safe. "Very erotic, smoldering. With that look, you could make a guy run barefoot across a tack-covered football field."

"I don't feel erotic," she said, her voice husky. She pouted without calculation but with powerful effect. "I feel like birdshit."

"Curious."

"Not me."

"What?"

Skinning out of her underwear, she said, "I don't want to go the way of the cat."

"No," he said, "I meant your choice of words. So you feel like birdshit—why in particular *bird*?"

She yawned. "Is that what I said?"

"Yeah."

"I don't know. Maybe because I feel like I've dropped a long way and splattered all over everything."

She didn't want to be alone to shower.

Dusty watched from the bathroom doorway while Martie spread the bath mat, opened the door of the shower stall, and adjusted the water. When she stepped into the stall, he moved into the room and sat on the closed lid of the toilet.

As Martie began to soap herself, Dusty said, "We've been married three years, but I feel like I'm at a peep show."

A bar of soap, a squeeze bottle of shampoo, and a tube of cream conditioner were objects so lacking in lethal potential that she was able to finish bathing without being seized by terror.

Dusty got the hair dryer out of a vanity drawer, plugged it in for her, and then retreated to the doorway once more.

Martie balked at using the hair dryer. "I'll just towel it a little and let it dry naturally."

"Then it'll just frizz up, and you'll hate the way it looks, and you'll bitch all day."

"I don't bitch."

"Well, you certainly don't whine."

"Damn right I don't."

"Complain?" he suggested.

"All right. I'll admit to that."

"You'll complain all day. Why don't you want to use the hair dryer? It's not dangerous."

"I don't know. It sort of looks like a gun."

"It's not a gun."

"I didn't claim any of this was *rational.*"

"I promise if you turn it up to maximum power and try to blow-dry me to death, I won't stand still for it."

"Bastard."

"You knew that when you married me."

"I'm sorry."

"For what?"

"Calling you a bastard."

He shrugged. "Hey, call me anything you want, as long as you don't kill me."

Gas flames weren't as blue as her eyes when anger brightened them. "That's not funny."

"I refuse to be afraid of you."

"You've got to be," she said plaintively.

"Nope."

"You stupid, stupid . . . man."

"Man. Ow. The ultimate insult. Listen, if you ever call me a man again . . . I don't know, it could mean we're through."

She glared at him, finally reached for the hair dryer, but then snatched her hand back. She tried again, recoiled again, and began to shake not with fear as much as with frustration and quiet anguish.

Dusty was afraid she might cry. Last night, the sight of her in tears had knotted his guts.

Approaching her, he said, "Let me do it."

She shrank from him. "Stay away."

He plucked a towel off the rack and offered it to her. "Do you agree this wouldn't be any homicidal maniac's weapon of choice?"

Her gaze actually traveled the length of the towel as though she were warily calculating its murderous potential.

"Grip it in both hands," he explained. "Pull it taut, hold it tight, concentrate and keep your grip on it. As long as your hands are occupied, you can't hurt me."

Accepting the towel, she looked skeptical.

"No, really," he said. "What could you do except snap my ass with it?"

"There'd be some satisfaction in that."

"But there's at least a fifty-percent chance I'd survive."

When she seemed hesitant, he said, "Besides, I've got the hair dryer. You try anything, I'll give you a case of chapped lips you won't forget."

"I feel like such a schlump."

"You're not."

From the doorway, Valet chuffed.

Dusty said, "The vote is two to one against schlumpdom."

"Let's get this over with," she said grimly.

"Face the sink and keep your back to me if you think I'll be safer that way."

She faced the sink, but she closed her eyes rather than look at herself in the mirror.

Though the bathroom wasn't cold, Martie's bare back was stippled with gooseflesh.

With a brush, Dusty repeatedly pulled her thick, black, glorious hair through the gush of hot air from the blow-dryer, shaping it as he had seen her shape it before.

Ever since they'd been together, Dusty enjoyed watching Martie groom herself. Whether she was shampooing her hair, painting her nails, applying her makeup, or massaging suntan lotion into her skin, she approached the task with an easy, almost lazy, meticulousness that was catlike and wonderfully graceful. A lioness, confident of her appearance but not vain.

Always, Martie had seemed strong and resilient, and Dusty had never worried about what might happen to her if fate dealt him an early death while he was climbing across some high roof. Now, he worried—and his worrying felt to him like an insult to her, as if he pitied her, which he didn't, couldn't. She was still too *Martie* to elicit pity. Yet now she appeared alarmingly vulnerable, neck so slender, shoulders so fragile, the vertebrae linked with such delicacy in the spinal cleft of her back, and Dusty feared for this dear woman to an extent that he must never allow her to perceive.

As the great philosopher Skeet once put it, *Love is hard.*

Something strange happened in the kitchen. In fact, virtually everything that happened in the kitchen was strange, but the last thing, just before they left the house, was the strangest of all.

First: Martie was rigid in one of the dinette chairs, hands trapped under her thighs, actually *sitting* on her hands, as though they would seize anything within reach and hurl it at Dusty if they were not restrained.

Because she was having blood drawn and tests conducted, she was required to fast from nine o'clock the previous night until the doctor was finished with her later this morning.

She was upset about lingering in the kitchen while Valet wolfed his morning kibble and while Dusty drank a glass of milk and ate a doughnut, though not because she resented their freedom to indulge. "I know what's in those drawers," she said with anxiety evident in her voice, meaning knives and other sharp utensils.

Dusty winked lecherously. "I know what's in your drawers, too."

"Damn it, you better start taking this more seriously."

"If I do, we might as well both kill ourselves now."

Though her frown deepened, he knew she recognized the wisdom of what he'd said.

"There you stand, drinking whole milk, eating a glazed doughnut with cream filling. Looks like you're already halfway to hara-kiri."

Finishing the milk, he said, "I figure the best way to live a *normal*—and probably long—life is to listen to everything the health Nazis say, then do exactly the opposite."

"What if tomorrow they say cheeseburgers and french fries are the healthiest diet you can eat?"

"Then it's tofu and alfalfa sprouts for me."

Washing out the glass, he turned his back to her, and she said, "Hey," sharply, and he faced her while he dried it, so she wouldn't have a chance to sneak up on him and beat him to death with a can of pork and beans.

They were not going to be able to take Valet on his morning constitutional. Martie refused to stay here alone while Dusty went out with the dog. And if she accompanied them, she would no doubt be terrified of pushing Dusty in front of a truck and feeding Valet into some gardener's portable woodchipper.

"There's a pretty funny aspect to all this," Dusty said.

"There's nothing funny about it," she grimly disagreed.

"We're both probably right."

He opened the back door and sent Valet out to spend the morning in the fenced backyard. The weather was cool but not chilly, and no rain was in the forecast. He put a full water dish on the porch and told the dog, "Poop where you want, and I'll pick it up later, but don't get the idea this is a new rule."

He closed the door, locked it, and looked toward the telephone, which was when the strange thing happened. He and Martie began to talk at once, over and through each other.

"Martie, I don't want you to take this the wrong way—"

"I have all the faith in the world in Dr. Closterman—"

"—but I think we really should consider—"

"—but it might take days for test results—"

"—getting a second opinion—"

"—and as much as I hate the idea—"

"—not from another medical doctor—"

"—I think I need to be evaluated—"

"—but from a therapist—"

"—by a psychiatrist—"

"—who treats anxiety disorders—"

"—with the right experience—"

"—someone like—"

"—I'm thinking maybe—"

"—Dr. Ahriman."

"—Dr. Ahriman."

They spoke the name in unison—and gaped at each other in the ensuing silence.

Then Martie said, "I guess we've been married too long."

"Much longer, and we'll start to look like each other."

"I'm not nuts, Dusty."

"I know you're not."

"But give him a call."

He went to the phone and obtained Ahriman's office number from the information operator. He left a request for an appointment on the doctor's voice mail and recited his cell-phone number.

43

At Skeet's apartment, the bedroom was as barren of decoration and as starkly furnished as any monk's cell.

Having backed into a corner to limit her options if a murderous impulse seized her, Martie stood with her arms crossed over her chest and her hands clamped tightly under her biceps. "Why didn't you tell me last night? Poor Skeet's back in rehab and you don't tell me till now?"

"You had enough on your mind," Dusty said as he searched under the neatly folded clothes in the bottom drawer of a dresser so plain it might have been crafted by a strict religious order that thought Shaker furniture was sinfully ornate.

"What're you looking for—his stash?"

"No. If there's any of that left, it'll take hours to find it. I'm looking for . . . well, I don't know what I'm looking for."

"We've got to be at Dr. Closterman's office in forty minutes."

"Plenty of time," Dusty said, elevating his search to a higher drawer.

"Did he show up at work stoned?"

"Yeah. He jumped off the Sorensons' roof."

"My God! How bad was he hurt?"

"Not at all."

"Not at *all*?"

"It's a long story," Dusty said, opening the top drawer

on the dresser. He wasn't going to tell her that he had gone off the roof with Skeet, not while she was in her current condition.

"What are you hiding from me?" she demanded.

"I'm not *hiding* anything."

"What are you *keeping* from me?"

"Martie, let's not play games with semantics, okay?"

"At times like this, it couldn't be clearer that you are the son of Trevor Penn Rhodes."

Closing the last dresser drawer, he said, "That was low. I'm not *keeping* anything from you."

"What are you protecting me from?"

"I guess what I'm hunting for," he said, instead of answering her question, "is evidence that Skeet's mixed up in some cult."

Because he'd already searched the single nightstand and under the bed, Dusty stepped into the adjoining bathroom, which was small, clean, and completely white. He opened the medicine cabinet and quickly sorted through the contents.

From the bedroom, in an anxious and accusatory tone, Martie said, "You don't know what I might be doing out here."

"Looking for an ax?"

"Bastard."

"We've been down that road."

"Yeah, but it's a long one."

When he came out of the bathroom, he saw that she was shaking and as pale as—though prettier than—something that lived under a rock. "You okay?"

"What do you mean—cult?"

Though she cringed when he approached her, he took her by the arm, drew her out of the corner, and led her into the living room. "Skeet said he jumped off the roof because an angel of death told him he should."

"That's just the drugs talking."

"Maybe. But you know how those cults operate—the brainwashing and all."

"What're you talking about?"

"Brainwashing."

In the living room, she backed into another corner and clamped her hands in her armpits again. "Brainwashing?"

"Rub-a-dub, cerebrum in a tub."

The living room contained only a sofa, an armchair, a coffee table, an end table, two lamps, and a set of shelves on which were stored both books and magazines. Dusty cocked his head to scan the titles on the spines of the books.

From her corner, Martie said, "What're you hiding from me?"

"There you go again."

"You wouldn't think he was mixed up in a cult—brainwashed, for God's sake—just because of what he said about some angel of death."

"There was an incident at the clinic."

"New Life?"

"Yeah."

"What incident?"

All the paperbacks on the shelves were fantasy novels. Tales of dragons, wizards, warlocks, and swashbuckling heroes in the land of long-ago or never-was. Not for the first time, Dusty was baffled by the kid's genre of choice; after all, Skeet pretty much lived in a fantasy, anyway, and wouldn't seem to need it for entertainment.

"What incident?" Martie repeated.

"Went into a trance."

"What do you mean, a trance?"

"You know, like a magician, one of those stage hypnotists, casts on you and then makes you cluck like a chicken."

"Skeet was clucking like a chicken?"

"No, it was more complicated than that."

As Dusty continued along the shelves, the titles began to make him terribly sad. He realized that perhaps his brother sought refuge in these make-believe kingdoms because they were all cleaner, better, more-ordered fantasies than the one in which the kid lived. In these books, spells worked, friends were always true and brave, good and evil were sharply defined, good always won—and no one became drug-dependent and screwed up his life.

"Quacking like a duck, gobbling like a turkey?" Martie asked from her corner exile.

"What?"

"How was it more complicated, what Skeet did at the clinic?"

Quickly sorting through a stack of magazines, finding nothing published by any cult more nefarious than the Time-Warner media group, Dusty said, "I'll tell you later. We don't have time for it now."

"You are exasperating."

"It's a gift," he said, leaving the magazines and books for a quick look through the small kitchen.

"Don't leave me alone here," she pleaded.

"Then come along."

"No way," she said, obviously thinking about knives and meat forks and potato mashers. "No way. That's a kitchen."

"I'm not going to ask you to cook."

The combination kitchen and dining area was open to the living room, all one big California floor plan, so Martie was in fact able to see him pulling open drawers and cabinet doors.

She was silent for half a minute, but when she spoke, her voice was shaky. "Dusty, I'm getting worse."

"To me, babe, you just keep getting better and better."

"I mean it. I'm serious. I'm on the edge here, and sliding fast."

Dusty wasn't finding any cult paraphernalia among the

pots and pans. No secret decoder rings. No pamphlets about Armageddon looming. No tracts about how to recognize the Antichrist if you run into him at the mall.

"What're you doing in there?" Martie demanded.

"Stabbing myself through the heart, so you won't have to."

"You bastard."

"Been there, done that," he said, returning to the living room.

"You're a cold man," she complained.

Her pale face squinched with anger.

"I'm ice," he agreed.

"You are. I mean it."

"Arctic."

"You make me so angry."

"You make me so happy," he countered.

Squinch became startled realization, and her eyes widened as she said, "You're my Martie."

"That doesn't sound like another insult."

"And I'm your Susan."

"Oh, this is no good. We'll have to change all our monogrammed towels."

"For a year, I've treated her like you're treating me. Jollying her along, always needling her out of her self-pity, trying to keep her spirits up."

"You've been a real bitch, huh?"

Martie laughed. Shaky, one tremble away from a sob, like those laughs in operas, when the tragic heroine pitches a soprano trill and lets it fall into a contralto quaver of despair. "I've been a bitch and a sarcastic wiseass, yeah, because I love her so much."

Smiling, Dusty held out his right hand toward her. "We've got to be going."

One step out of her corner, she stopped, unable to come farther. "Dusty, I don't want to be Susan."

"I know."

"I don't want to . . . fall that far down."

"You won't," he promised.

"I'm scared."

Rather than follow her customary preference for bright colors, Martie had gone to the dark side of her wardrobe. Black boots, black jeans, a black pullover, and a black leather jacket. She looked like a mourner at a biker's funeral. In this stark outfit, she should have appeared to be tough, as hard and as formidable as night itself. Instead, she seemed as ephemeral as a shadow fading and shrinking under a relentless sun.

"I'm scared," she repeated.

This was a time for truth, not for jollying, and Dusty said, "Yeah. Me, too."

Overcoming the fear of her imagined homicidal potential, she took his hand. Hers was cold, but touching was progress.

"I've *got* to phone Susan," she said. "She was expecting me to call last night."

"We'll phone her from the car."

Out of the apartment, along the common hall, down the stairs, across the small foyer where Skeet had penciled the name FARNER under CAULFIELD on his mailbox label, and out of the building, Dusty felt Martie's hand warming in his and dared to think he could save her.

A gardener, early to work, was bundling hedge trimmings into a burlap tarpaulin. A handsome young Hispanic with eyes as dark as mole sauce, he smiled and nodded.

Lying on the lawn, near him, were a small pair of hand clippers and a large pair of two-hand shears.

At the sight of the blades, Martie let out a strangled cry. She wrenched her hand free of Dusty's and ran, not toward those makeshift weapons but away from them, to the red Saturn that was parked at the curb.

"*Disputa?*" the gardener asked Dusty sympathetically, as if he himself had a regrettable amount of experience arguing with women.

"*Infinidad,*" Dusty replied as he hurried past, and he was all the way to the car before he realized he had meant to say *enfermedad*, meaning "illness," but had instead said "infinity."

The gardener stared after him, not frowning with puzzlement, but nodding solemnly, as though Dusty's wrong word choice were in fact an indisputable profundity.

Thus are reputations for wisdom raised on foundations flimsier than those of castles built on air.

By the time Dusty got behind the wheel of the car, Martie was in the passenger's seat, doubled over as far as the dashboard would allow, shuddering, groaning. Her thighs were pressed together, trapping her hands as though they itched with the desire to make mayhem.

When Dusty pulled his door shut, Martie said, "Is there anything sharp in the glove box?"

"I don't know."

"Is it locked?"

"I don't know."

"Lock it, for God's sake."

He locked it and then started the engine.

"Hurry," she pleaded.

"All right."

"But don't drive too fast."

"Okay."

"But *hurry.*"

"Which is it?" he asked, pulling away from the curb.

"If you drive too fast, maybe I might try to grab the wheel, try to pull the car off the road, roll it, or plow us head-on into a truck."

"Of course you won't."

"I might," she insisted. "I *will.* You don't want to see what's in my head, the pictures in my head."

The residual effect of three caplets of sleep-aid medication was fading from her by the second, while Dusty's heartburn from the cream-filled, glazed doughnut was steadily growing.

"Oh, God," she groaned. "God, please, please, don't let me see these things, don't make me see them."

Huddled forward in abject misery, apparently sickened by the violent images spurting unwanted through her mind, Martie gagged, and soon the gagging evolved into fierce spasms of retching that would have brought up her breakfast if she had eaten any.

The morning traffic on these surface streets was moderately heavy, and Dusty weaved from lane to lane, sometimes taking risks to wedge into a gap, ignoring the angry looks of other motorists and the occasional hard bark of a horn. Martie appeared to be on an emotional toboggan run, rocketing along slick ice, with a panic attack at the end of the chute. Dusty wanted to be as close to Dr. Closterman's office as possible if she hit the wall and ricocheted into a crack-up like the one he had witnessed the previous night.

Although dry heaves racked her with greater force than ever, she achieved no relief, not merely because her stomach was empty, but because she needed to disgorge the undisgorgeable vomitous images churning in her mind. Perhaps her mouth flooded with saliva, as is usual during bouts of nausea, because more than once she spat on the floorboards.

Between fits of retching, she gasped vehemently for breath, her throat surely parched and half raw from the sheer force of these inhalations. Shudders shook Martie, too, and with such violence that Dusty was shivered by a sympathetic cold revulsion, even though he could not imagine what ghastly visions plagued her.

He drove faster yet, weaving with greater aggression from lane to lane, taking bigger risks, to the accompaniment of more blaring horns and, now, the frequent squeal of brakes. He almost hoped that a policeman would pull him over. Considering Martie's condition, any cop was likely to forgo issuing a traffic citation and, instead, provide an emergency escort, with siren.

Worsening condition. For the moment, her convulsive retching passed, but she began to rock back and forth in her seat, groaning, thumping her forehead against the padded dashboard, softly at first, slow and easy, as though to distract herself from the hobgoblins that seethed through her mind, but then with greater force, faster, and faster still, no longer groaning but grunting like a football player slamming into a tackling dummy, faster, harder: "*Uh, uh, uh, uh, uuuhhh.*"

Dusty spoke to her, urged her to calm down, to hang on, to remember that he was here for her, that he trusted her, and that everything was going to be all right. He didn't know if she could hear him. Nothing he said appeared to comfort her.

He wanted desperately to reach out to her and gentle her with his touch, but he suspected that during this seizure, any contact would have the opposite effect of what he intended. His hand upon her shoulder might send her into even greater paroxysms of terror and revulsion.

Dr. Closterman's offices were in a medical high-rise adjacent to the hospital. Both buildings rose in the next block, the tallest structures in sight.

Regardless of the padding, she was certain to hurt herself if she kept knocking her head against the dashboard, but she would not relent. She didn't cry out in pain, only grunted with each impact, cursed, and quarreled with herself—"Stop it, stop it, stop it"—and seemed like nothing less than a woman possessed. More precisely, she was both the possessed and the exorcist, striving mightily to cast out her own demons.

At the medical complex, the surrounding parking lots were shaded by aisles of big carrotwood trees. He searched for and found a space close to the office high-rise, under a canopy of branches.

Even after he braked to a halt and put the car in park,

Dusty felt as though he were still moving. A morning breeze shivered leaf shadows across the windshield, while interleaved blades of sunshine fluttered against the curve of glass and seemed to tumble away to each side as if they were bright scraps of foliage spinning into his wake on a slipstream.

As Dusty switched off the engine, Martie stopped butting the dash. Her hands, until now trapped between her clamped thighs, broke free. She clasped her head as though trying to suppress the waves of pain from a migraine headache, pressing so hard on her skull that the skin over her knuckles tightened until it was as smooth and white as the bone beneath.

She was no longer grunting or cursing, no longer quarreling with herself. Worse, bending forward once more, she began to scream. Shrill shrieks punctuated by hard swallows of air, like a swimmer in trouble. Terror in her cries. But also outrage, disgust, shock. Screams that shuddered with revulsion, as those of a swimmer who had felt something strange sliding past beneath the water, something cold and slick and terrible.

"Martie, what? Talk to me. Martie, let me help."

Maybe her cries and the booming of her heart and the rush of blood in her ears didn't allow her to hear him, or maybe there was simply nothing he could do, therefore no reason to answer him. She was struggling against riptides of powerful emotion that seemed to be dragging her out into deep waters, toward a drowning abyss that might be madness.

Against his better judgment, Dusty touched her. She reacted as he had been afraid she would, shrinking from him, swatting his hand off her shoulder, jamming herself up against the passenger's door, still irrationally convinced that she was capable of blinding him or worse.

A young woman, crossing the parking lot with two small children, heard Martie's screams, came closer to the Saturn, frowning-peering, and locked eyes with Dusty, her gaze darkening as if she saw in him the evil of every tower sniper, schoolboy assassin, serial strangler, mad bomber, and head-collector who had made the news in her lifetime. She pulled her kids close to her and moved them more quickly toward the hospital, probably seeking a security guard.

Martie's frenzy passed more abruptly than it had arisen, not by slow degrees but nearly all at once. A final scream, resounding glass to glass to glass in this small space, gave way to quaking gasps, until soon the gasps were only deep shuddery breaths, and threaded through them was a disheartening wounded-animal mewl, as thin as a silken filament, fading in and out, sewing one ragged breath to the next.

Although Dusty had seen not one frame of the spook show that had stuttered through the sprockets of Martie's mind, the ordeal of observation, in itself, had left him weak. His mouth was dry. His heart raced. He raised his hands to watch them tremble, and then blotted his damp palms on his jeans.

The keys still dangled from the ignition. He plucked them out, muffled their jingle in his clenched hand, and stuffed them into one of his pockets before Martie could raise her bowed head and catch sight of them.

He was not concerned that she would grab the keys and stab at his face in a furious determination to blind him, as she claimed to have seen herself doing in a vision. He was no more afraid of her now than he had been before this latest episode.

In the immediate aftermath of her seizure, however, perhaps a glimpse of the keys would be enough to send her tumbling down the stairs of panic yet again.

Silent now except for her hard breathing, she sat up straighter and lowered her hands from her head.

"I can't take much more like that," she whispered.

"It's over."

"I'm afraid it isn't."

"For now, anyway."

Dappled with sunshine and leaf shadows, Martie's face appeared to flicker, gold and black, as if it were no more substantial than a face in a dream, likely to glimmer less with gold and darkle more with black, until at last it lost all composition and sparkled into extinction like the last few bright crackles of a Roman candle in a bottomless night sky.

Though intellectually he rejected the possibility that he was losing her, in his heart he knew that she was slipping away from him, captive of a force that he could not understand and against which he could offer no defense.

No. Dr. Ahriman could help her. Could, would, must.

Perhaps Dr. Closterman, with MRIs and EEGs and PET scans and all the abbreviations and acronyms of high-tech medicine, would identify her condition, isolate the cause, and provide the cure.

But if not Closterman, then surely Ahriman.

From out of a wilderness of wind-stirred leaf shadows, as blue as the two jewels in the sockets of a jungle-wrapped stone goddess, Martie's eyes met his. No illusions in her gaze. No superstitious surety that all would be well in this best of all possible worlds. Just a stark appreciation of her dilemma.

Somehow she overcame the dread of her lethal potential. She extended her left hand to him.

He held it gratefully.

"Poor Dusty," she said. "A druggie brother and a crazy wife."

"You're not crazy."

"I'm working at it."

"Whatever happens to you," he said, "won't happen just to you. It happens to both of us. We're in this together."

"I know."

"Two musketeers."

"Butch and Sundance."

"Mickey and Minnie."

He didn't smile. Neither did she. But with characteristic fortitude, Martie said, "Let's go see if Doc Closterman learned any damn thing at all in medical school."

44

Taking of the temperature, blood pressure, pulse rate, careful ophthalmoscopic examination of the left eye, then the right, a peek with auriscope at the secrets of the ears, much solemn listening with stethoscope at the chest and the back—*Breathe deep and hold, breathe out, breath deep and hold*—palpation of the abdomen, a quick test of the audito-oculogyric reflex, one gentle rap of a small hammer on a pretty kneecap to gauge patellar reflex: All the easy stuff led Dr. Closterman to conclude that Martie was an exceptionally healthy young woman, physiologically even younger than her twenty-eight years.

From the spare chair in the corner of the examination room, Dusty said, "She seems to get younger week by week."

To Martie, Closterman said, "Does he spread it on this heavy all the time?"

"I have to shovel out the house every morning." She smiled at Dusty. "I love it."

Closterman was in his late forties but, unlike Martie, looked—and no doubt tested—older than his age, and not solely because of his prematurely white hair. Double chins and dewlaps, generous jowls and a proud knob of a nose, eyes pink in the corners with a perpetual bloodshot sheen from too much time in salt air and wind and sun, and a tan that would leave any dermatologist hoarse from lecturing—all marked him as a dedicated gourmet, deep-sea fisherman, windsurfer, and probably connoisseur of beer. From his broad brow to his broader belly, he was a living example of the consequences of ignoring the sound advice that he unabashedly doled out to his patients.

Doc—his surfer handle—had a mind as sharp as a scalpel, the bedside manner of a favorite grandfather with a storybook in hand, and a dedication to his practice that would have shamed Hippocrates, yet Dusty preferred him over all other possible internists less for those fine qualities than for his very human, if medically unsound, indulgences. Doc was that rare expert without arrogance, free of dogma, able to view a problem from a fresh perspective rather than through the lenses of preconception that often blinded others who claimed high expertise, humbled by an awareness of his weaknesses and his limitations.

"Gloriously healthy," Closterman proclaimed as he entered notes in Martie's file. "Tough constitution. Like your dad."

Sitting on the edge of the examination table, in a paper gown and rolled red kneesocks, Martie did indeed appear to be as healthy as any aerobics instructor on one of those cable-television shows devoted to obsessive exercise with a host who believed that death was a personal choice rather than an inevitability.

Dusty could see the changes in Martie that Closterman, in spite of his sensitivity to his patients, couldn't perceive. A bleak shadow in her eyes that dimmed her usually bright gaze. A persistent grim set to her mouth and a defeatist slump to her shoulders.

Although Closterman agreed to refer Martie to the hospital next door for a series of diagnostic procedures, he clearly was thinking of it as just an elaborate annual checkup, not as an essential step in diagnosing the cause of a life-threatening condition. Doc had listened to a highly abbreviated account of her bizarre behavior during the past twenty-four hours, and though she'd not described her violent visions in detail, she'd recounted enough to make Dusty wish he had not eaten that greasy doughnut. Nevertheless, as the physician finished making notes in his patient's file, he launched into an explanation of the many sources of stress, the mental and physiological problems arising from stress, and the best techniques that one might use to deal with stress—as though Martie's problem resulted from overwork, too little leisure, a tendency to sweat the small stuff, and a lumpy mattress.

She interrupted Closterman to ask if he would please put away the reflex hammer.

Blinking, derailed from the tracks of his stress homily, which had been chugging along so nicely, he said, "Put it away?"

"It makes me nervous. I keep looking at it. I'm afraid of what I might do with it."

The polished-steel instrument was as small as a toy hammer and appeared to be of no use as a weapon.

"If I snatched it up and threw it at your face," Martie said, her words more disturbing for the fact that her voice was soft and reasonable, "it would stun you, maybe worse, and then I'd have time to grab something more lethal. Like the pen. Would you put the pen away, please?"

Dusty moved to the edge of his chair.

Here we go.

Dr. Closterman looked at the ballpoint that lay atop the closed patient file. "It's just a Paper Mate pen."

"I'll tell you what I could do with it, Doctor. A little sample of what goes through my mind, and I don't know where it comes from, this evil stuff, or how to stop it from coming." The blue paper gown made a crisp and ominous crinkling sound like a dry chrysalis within which something deadly was struggling to be born. Her voice remained soft, though now there was an edge to it. "I don't really care if it's a Montblanc or a Bic, because it's also a stiletto, a skewer, and I could snatch it off that folder and be at you before you knew what was happening, ram it into your eye, shove it halfway back into your skull, twist it around, twist it, twist, really screw with your brain, and either you'd fall down dead on the spot or spend the rest of your life with the mental capacity of a fucking potato." She was shaking. Her teeth chattered. She clasped both hands to her head, as she had done in the car, as though striving to repress the hideous images that bloomed unwanted in the midnight garden of her mind. "And whether you were dead or alive on the floor, there are all kinds of things I could do to you after the pen. You've got syringes in one of those drawers, needles—and there on that counter, a glass beaker full of tongue depressors. Break the glass, the shards are knives. I could carve your face—or slice it off in pieces and pin the pieces to the wall with hypodermic needles, make a collage from your face. I could do this. I can see . . . see it in my head *right now.*" She buried her face in her hands.

Closterman came to his feet on the word *potato*, rising like a dancer in spite of his size, and now Dusty rose, too.

"First thing," said the rattled physician, "is a prescription for Valium. How many of these episodes have there been?"

"A few," Dusty said. "I don't know. But this one wasn't bad."

Closterman's round face was better suited to a smile; his frown was unable to achieve sufficient gravity, buoyed as it was by his ball of a nose, rosy cheeks, and merry eyes. "Not bad? The others were worse? Then I wouldn't recommend these tests *without* Valium. Some of these procedures, like an MRI, they disturb patients."

"I'm disturbed going in," Martie said.

"We'll mellow you out, so it's not such an ordeal." Closterman stepped to the door, then hesitated with his hand on the knob. He glanced at Dusty. "Are you okay here?"

Dusty nodded. "These are only things she's afraid of doing—not anything she *could* do. Not her, not Martie."

"Like hell I couldn't," she said from behind a veil of fingers.

When Closterman had gone, Dusty moved the reflex hammer and the ballpoint beyond Martie's reach. "Feel better?"

Between her fingers, she had seen his act of consideration. "This is mortifying."

"Can I hold your hand?"

A hesitation. Then: "Okay."

When Closterman returned, having phoned in a prescription for Valium to their usual pharmacy, he had two individually packaged samples of the drug. He opened one sample and gave it to Martie with a paper cup full of water.

"Martie," said Closterman, "I truly believe the tests are going to rule out any intracranial mass—neoplastic, cystic, inflammatory, and gummatous. A lot of us, we get an unusual headache that takes a while to go away—we right away think, at least in the back of our mind, it must be a tumor. But brain tumors aren't that common."

"This isn't a headache," she reminded him.

"Exactly. And headaches are a prime symptom of brain tumors. As is a retinal condition called choked disk, which I didn't find when I examined your eyes. You mentioned vomiting and nausea. If you were vomiting *without* nausea, then we'd have a classic symptom. From what you told me, you don't actually have hallucinations—"

"No."

"Just these unpalatable thoughts, grotesque images in your head, but you don't mistake them for things really happening. What I see is anxiety of a high order. So when all is said and done, though we have a lot of physiological conditions to eliminate first . . . Well, I suspect I'll need to recommend a therapist."

"We already know one," Martie said.

"Oh? Who?"

"He's supposed to be one of the best," Dusty said.

"Maybe you've heard of him. A psychiatrist. Dr. Mark Ahriman."

Although Roy Closterman's round face couldn't produce the sharp angles of a suitably disapproving frown, it smoothed at once into a perfectly inscrutable expression that could be read no more easily than alien hieroglyphics from another galaxy. "Yes, Ahriman, he has a fine reputation. And his books, of course. Where did you get the recommendation? I imagine his patient list is full."

"He's been treating a friend of mine," Martie said.

"May I ask for what condition?"

"Agoraphobia."

"A terrible thing."

"It's changed her life."

"How's she doing?"

Martie said, "Dr. Ahriman thinks she's nearing a breakthrough."

"Good news," Closterman said.

The sun-leathered skin at the corners of his eyes crinkled, and his lips tweaked up to precisely the same degree at both sides of his mouth, but this was not the broad and winning smile of which he was capable. In fact, it was hardly a smile at all, just a variation of his inscrutable look, reminiscent of the smile on a statue of Buddha: benign but conveying more mystery than mirth.

Still tweaked and crinkled, he said, "But if you find that Dr. Ahriman isn't taking on new patients, I know a wonderful therapist, a compassionate and quite brilliant woman, who I'm sure would see you." He picked up Martie's file and the pen with which she could have put out his eye. "First, before there's any talk of therapy, let's get those tests done. They're expecting you at the hospital, and the various departments have promised to squeeze you into their schedules as if you were an emergency-room admission, no appointments needed. I'll have all the results by Friday, and then we can decide what's next. By the time you dress and get next door, that Valium will have kicked in. If you need another one before you can get the prescription filled, you've got the second sample. Any questions?"

Why don't you like Mark Ahriman? Dusty wondered.

He didn't ask the question. Considering his distrust of most academics and experts—two labels Ahriman no doubt wore with pride—and considering his respect for Dr. Closterman, Dusty found his reticence inexplicable. Nevertheless, the question remained glued between his tongue and the roof of his mouth.

Minutes later, as he and Martie were crossing the quadrangle from the office tower to the hospital, Dusty realized that his reluctance to pose the question, though strange, was less puzzling than his failure to inform Dr. Closterman that he had already phoned Ahriman's office to seek an appointment later this same day and was awaiting a callback.

Hard *skreaks* from overhead drew his attention. Thin gray clouds like bolts of dirty linen had been flung across the azure sky, and three fat black crows wheeled through the air, jinking now and then as if plucking fibers from that raveled, rotting mist to build nests in graveyards.

For some reasons clear and others not, Dusty thought of Poe, of a bad-news raven perched above a doorway. Although Martie, in a Valium lull, held his hand with none of her previous reluctance, Dusty thought also of Poe's lost maiden, Lenore, and he wondered if the *skreak* of the crow, translated into the tongue of the raven, might be "nevermore."

In the hematology lab, while Martie sat watching her blood slowly fill a series of tubes, she chatted with the technician, a young Vietnamese American, Kenny Phan, who had gotten the needle into her vein quickly and without a sting.

"I cause much less discomfort than a vampire," Kenny said with an infectious grin, "and usually have sweeter breath."

Dusty would have watched with normal interest had this been his blood being drawn, but he was squeamish at the sight of Martie's.

Sensitive to his discomfort, she asked that he use the moment to get Susan Jagger on his cell phone.

He placed the call and waited through twelve rings. When Susan didn't answer, he pressed *end* and asked Martie for the number.

"You know the number."

"Maybe I entered it wrong."

He keyed it in again, reciting it aloud, and when he pressed the final number, Martie said, "That's it."

This time he waited through sixteen rings before terminating the call. "She isn't there."

"But she must be there. She's never anywhere else—unless she's with me."

"Maybe she's in the shower."

"No answering machine?"

"No. I'll try later."

Mellowed by the Valium, Martie looked thoughtful, perhaps even concerned, but not worried.

Replacing a full tube of blood with the final empty vial, Kenny Phan said, "One more for my personal collection."

Martie laughed, this time without an underlying tremor of any darker emotion.

In spite of the circumstances, Dusty felt as though normal life might be within their grasp again, much easier to rediscover than he had imagined in the grimmer moments of the past fourteen hours.

As Kenny Phan was applying a small, purple Barney the Dinosaur adhesive bandage to the needle puncture, Dusty's cell phone rang. Jennifer, Dr. Ahriman's secretary, was calling to confirm that the psychiatrist would be able to rearrange his afternoon schedule to see them at one-thirty.

"That's a bit of luck," Martie said with evident relief when Dusty gave her the news.

"Yeah."

Dusty, too, was relieved—curiously so, considering that if Martie's problem was psychological, the prognosis for a quick and full recovery might be less reassuring than if the malady had an entirely physical cause. He had never met Dr. Mark Ahriman, and yet a warm sense of security, a comforting flame, had been lit in him by the call from the psychiatrist's secretary—which was also a curious and surprising reaction.

If the problem wasn't medical, Ahriman would know what to do. He would be able to uncover the roots of Martie's anxiety.

Dusty's reluctance to put his trust entirely in experts of any kind was borderline pathological, and he was the first to admit as much. He was somewhat dismayed with himself for being so eager to hope that Dr. Ahriman, with all his degrees and his best-selling books and his exalted reputation, would possess a nearly magical ability to set things right.

Evidently he was more like the average sucker than he had wanted to believe he could be. When everything he cared most about—Martie and their life together—was at risk, and when his own knowledge and common sense were inadequate to solve the problem, then in his abject fear, he turned to the experts not merely with a pragmatic degree of hope but also with something uncomfortably close to faith.

All right, okay. So what? If he could just have Martie back in charge of herself, as she had been, healthy and happy, he would humble himself before anyone, anytime, anywhere.

Still all in black but with purple Barney on her arm,

Martie left the hematology lab hand-in-hand with Dusty. An MRI scan was next.

The corridors smelled of floor wax, disinfectant, and a faint underlying scent of illness.

A nurse and an orderly approached, rolling a gurney on which lay a young woman no older than Martie. She was connected to an IV drip. Compresses had been applied to her face; they were spotted with fresh blood. One of her eyes was visible: open, gray-green, and glazed with shock.

Dusty looked away, feeling that he had violated this stranger's privacy, and he tightened his hold on Martie's hand, superstitiously certain that in this injured woman's glassy stare was more bad luck poised to jump, quick as a blink, from her to him.

Tweaked and crinkled, the inscrutable smile of Closterman rose Cheshire-like in Dusty's memory.

45

From dreamless sleep, the doctor woke late, refreshed and looking forward to the day.

In the fully equipped gym that was part of the master suite, he completed two full circuits on the weight-training machines and half an hour on a reclining, stationary bicycle.

This was the sum of his exercise regimen, three times a week, yet he was as fit as he had been twenty years ago, with a thirty-two-inch waist and a physique that women liked. He credited his genes and the fact that he had the good sense not to let stress accumulate.

Before showering, he used the telephone intercom to call the kitchen and ask Nella Hawthorne to prepare breakfast. Twenty minutes later, hair damp, smelling faintly of a spice-scented skin lotion, wearing a red silk robe, he returned to the bedroom and retrieved his breakfast from the electric dumbwaiter.

On the antique sterling-silver tray were a carafe of freshly squeezed orange juice kept cold in a small silver bucket full of ice, two chocolate croissants, a bowl of strawberries accompanied by supplies of brown sugar and heavy cream, an orange-almond muffin with a half cup of whipped butter on the side, a slice of coconut pound cake with lemon marmalade, and a generous serving of french-fried pecans sprinkled with sugar and cinnamon for nibbling between other treats.

Though forty-eight, the doctor boasted the metabolism of a ten-year-old boy on methamphetamines.

He ate at the brushed-steel and zebrawood desk where a few hours ago he had studied his father's disembodied eyes.

The jar of formaldehyde was still here. He had not returned it to the safe before retiring for the night.

Some mornings, he switched on the television to watch the news with his breakfast; however, none of the anchormen or anchorwomen, regardless of the channel, had eyes as intriguing as those of Josh Ahriman, dead now for twenty years.

The strawberries were as ripe and flavorful as any the doctor had ever eaten. The croissants were sublime.

Dad's gaze settled languishingly upon the morning feast.

A formidable prodigy, the doctor had completed all his education and opened his psychiatric practice while still in his twenties, but though learning had come easily to him, well-heeled patients had not, in spite of his Hollywood connections through his father. Although the film-business elite loudly proclaimed their egalitarianism, many harbored a prejudice against youth in psychiatry, and they were not ready to lie down on the couch of a twenty-something therapist. To be fair, the doctor had looked much younger than his age—still did—and could have passed for eighteen when he hung out his shingle. Nevertheless, in the movie biz, where the sight of someone wearing his heart on his sleeve was more commonly encountered than the name of even the most spectacularly successful fashion designer of the moment, Ahriman had been frustrated to find himself a victim of such hypocrisy.

His father had continued to provide generous support, but the doctor had been increasingly reluctant to accept his old man's largesse. How embarrassing it was to be dependent at twenty-eight, especially considering his considerable academic achievements. Besides, as open as Josh Ahriman's wallet had been, the allowance that he provided was not sufficient for the doctor to live in the style he desired or to finance research he wished to conduct.

Only child and sole heir, he killed his father with a massive dose of ultrashort-acting thiobarbital combined with paraldehyde, injected into a pair of delicious chocolate-covered marzipan petits fours, for which the old man had a weakness. Before torching the house to destroy the mutilated body, the doctor performed a partial dissection of Dad's face, searching for the source of his tears.

Josh Ahriman was a spectacularly successful writer, director, and producer—a genuine triple threat—whose work ranged from simple love stories to patriotic tales of courage under fire. Diverse as these films were, they had one thing in common: Audiences the world over were reduced to tears by them. Some critics—though by no means all—labeled them sentimental hogwash, but the paying public flocked to the theaters, and Dad picked up two Oscars—one for directing, one for writing—before his untimely death at fifty-one.

His movies were box-office gold because the sentiment in them was sincere. Although he had the requisite ruthlessness and duplicity to succeed big-time in Hollywood, Dad also possessed a sensitive soul and such a tender heart that he was one of the championship criers of his time. He wept at funerals even when the deceased was someone for whose death he had often and fervently prayed. He wept unashamedly at weddings, at anniversary celebrations, at divorce proceedings, at bar mitzvahs, at birthday parties, at political rallies, at cockfights, on Thanksgiving and Christmas and New Year's Eve and the Fourth of July and Labor Day—and most copiously, bitterly, on the anniversary of his mother's death, when he remembered it.

Here was a man who knew all the secrets of tears. How

to wring them from sweet grandmothers and labor racketeers alike. How to move beautiful women with them. How to use them to purge himself of grief, pain, disappointment, stress. Even his moments of joy were heightened and made more exquisite with the spice of tears.

Thanks to a superb medical education, the doctor knew exactly how tears were manufactured, stored, and dispensed by the human body. Nevertheless, he expected to learn something from the dissection of his father's lacrimal apparatus.

In this he was to be disappointed. After trimming away Dad's eyelids and then gently extracting his eyes, the doctor discovered each lacrimal gland where he expected it: in orbit, superior and lateral to the eyeball. The glands were of normal size, shape, and design. The superior and inferior lacrimal ducts serving each eye were likewise unremarkable. Each lacrimal sac—seated in a groove of lacrimal bone, behind the tarsal ligament and tricky to tease out intact—measured thirteen millimeters, which was the median size for an adult.

Because the lacrimal apparatus was tiny, composed of very soft tissue, and damaged in the doctor's limited autopsy, he had not been able to save any of it. He had only the eyeballs now, and in spite of his diligent preservation efforts—fixative, vacuum-packaging, regular maintenance—he could not entirely prevent their gradual deterioration.

Shortly after his father's death, Ahriman had carried the eyes with him to Santa Fe, New Mexico, where he believed that he would be better able to become his own man beyond the great director's shadow, in which he would always stand if he remained in Los Angeles. Out there on the high desert, he achieved his initial successes and discovered his abiding passion for games of control.

From Santa Fe to Scottsdale, Arizona, the eyes came with him, and most recently to Newport Beach. Here, little more than one hour south of Dad's old stomping grounds, the passage of time and his own numerous accomplishments had brought the doctor forever out of that patriarchal shadow, and he felt as if he had come home.

When Ahriman bumped the leg of the desk with his knee, the eyes rolled slowly in the formaldehyde and seemed to follow the progress of the last fried pecan as he conveyed it to his mouth.

He left the dirty dishes on the desk but returned the jar to the safe.

He dressed in a sartorial-cut, double-breasted, blue wool suit by Vestimenta, a custom-tailored white shirt with spread collar and French cuffs, and a figured silk tie with a plain but complimentary pocket square. From his father's flair for period dramas, he had learned the value of costume.

The morning was almost gone. He wanted to get to his office as much as two hours ahead of Dustin and Martie Rhodes, to review all his strategic moves to date and decide how best to proceed to the next level of the game.

In the elevator, descending to the garage, he thought fleetingly of Susan Jagger, but she was the past, and the face that most easily came to mind now was Martie's.

He could never wring tears from multitudes, as his father had done time and again. Delight could be found, however, in the drawing of tears from an audience of one. Considerable intelligence, skill, and craft were required. And a vision. No one form of entertainment was more legitimate than another.

As the elevator doors opened at the garage, the doctor wondered if Martie's lacrimal glands and sacs were plumper than Dad's.

46

Already scanned, rayed, scoped, graphed, and bled, Martie was required only to pee in a small plastic cup before she could leave the hospital with all tests completed and samples given. Thanks to the Valium, she was sufficiently calm to risk going into the bathroom alone, without the mortified and mortifying presence of Dusty, though he offered to be her "urine-sample sentinel."

She was still not herself. Her irrational anxiety had not been drenched by the drug, merely dampened; hot coals smoldered sullenly in the darker corners of her mind, capable of flaring again into an all-consuming fire.

As she washed her hands at the sink, she dared to look into the mirror. Mistake. Within the reflection of her eyes, she glimpsed the Other Martie, pent-up and full of rage, chafing at this chemical restraint.

As she finished washing her hands, she kept her eyes downcast.

By the time that she and Dusty were leaving the hospital, those embers of anxiety were glowing bright.

Only three hours had passed since she'd taken the first Valium, not an ideal spacing of doses. Nevertheless, Dusty tore open the sample package and gave her the second tablet, which she washed down at a drinking fountain in the lobby.

A greater number of people than earlier were going to and fro in the quadrangle. A quiet voice in Martie, as soft as a sinister spirit speaking at a seance, kept up a running commentary regarding the comparative vulnerability of the other pedestrians. Here was a man in a leg cast, walking with the aid of crutches, so easy to topple, defenseless when down, vulnerable to the toe of a boot in the throat. And here, now, rolling along with a smile, was a woman in a battery-powered wheelchair, left arm withered and slack in her lap, right hand operating the controls, as defenseless a target as might pass this way all day.

Martie lowered her attention to the pavement ahead of her and tried to block out all awareness of the people she passed, which might also silence the hateful inner voice that so terrified her. She held fast to Dusty's arm, relying on Valium and her husband to get her to the car.

As they reached the parking lot, the January breeze quickened and brought a slight chill out of the northwest. The big carrotwoods whispered conspiratorially. The busy flickers and flashes of sunshine and shadow off scores of automobile windshields were like semaphored warnings in a code she could not read.

They had time for lunch before the appointment with Dr. Ahriman. Even though the second Valium would soon be kicking in, Martie didn't trust herself to spend forty-five minutes in even the coziest café without making a scene, so Dusty went in search of a drive-through, fast-food restaurant.

He had driven little more than a mile before Martie asked him to pull over in front of a sprawling, three-story, garden-apartment complex. The development stood behind a lawn as green as a golf course, shaded by graceful California pepper trees, lacy melaleucas, and a few tall jacarandas with early purple flowers. Pale yellow stucco walls. Red tile roofs. It looked like a clean, safe, comfortable place.

"They had to rebuild half of it after the fire," Martie said. "Sixty apartments burned down."

"How long ago was that?"

"Fifteen years. And they replaced the roofs on the buildings that weren't destroyed, because it was the old cedar shingles that allowed the blaze to spread so fast."

"Doesn't look haunted, does it?"

"Ought to be. Nine died, three of them small children. Seems funny . . . how it looks so nice now, you know, like that night must've been just a dream."

"Would've been worse without your dad."

Although Dusty knew all the details, Martie wanted to talk about the fire. All she had of her father now were memories, and by talking about them, she kept them fresh. "It was already an inferno when the pumpers got here. They couldn't hope to knock it down fast. Smilin' Bob went in there four times, four times into the fiery smoky hellish heart of it, and each time he came out. He was the worse for it, but he always came out with people who wouldn't have survived otherwise, carrying some of them, leading others. One whole family of five, they were disoriented, blinded by smoke, trapped, encircled by fire, but out he came with them, all five safe. There were other heroes there, every man on every crew called to the scene, but none of them could keep at it the way he could, eating the smoke as though it was tasty, all but reveling in the heat like he would a sauna, just going at it and going at it—but that's how he always was. Always was. Sixteen people saved because of him, before he collapsed and they packed him out of here in an ambulance."

That night, rushing with her mother to the hospital, and then at Smilin' Bob's bedside, Martie had been in the grip of a fear she had thought would crush her. His face red with a first-degree burn. And streaked with black: particles of soot pounded so deep into his pores by the concussive force of an explosion that they could not be easily washed out. Eyes bloodshot, one swollen half-shut. Eyebrows and most of his hair singed away, and a mean second-degree burn on the back of his neck. Left hand and forearm cut by glass, stitched and bandaged. And his voice so scary—scratchy, raw, weak as it had never been before. Words wheezing out of him and with them the sour odor of smoke, the scent of smoke still on his breath, the stink of it coming out of his *lungs.* Martie, thirteen, had only that morning felt grown-up and had been impatient for the world to admit that she was an adult. But there in the hospital, with Smilin' Bob brought down so hard, she suddenly felt insignificant and vulnerable, as helpless as a four-year-old kid.

"He reached for my hand with his good one, the right, and he was so exhausted he could hardly hold on to me. And in that awful voice, that smoky voice, he says, 'Hey, Miss M.,' and I say, 'Hey.' He tried to smile, but his face hurt pretty bad, so it was a weird smile that didn't do anything to cheer me up. He says, 'I want you to promise me something,' and I just nod, because, God, I would promise to cut off my arm for him, anything, and he must know that. He wheezes and coughs a lot, but he says, 'When you go to school tomorrow, don't you brag about your dad did this, your dad did that. They'll be asking you, and they'll be repeating things said on the news about me, but don't you bask in it. Don't you bask. You tell 'em I'm here . . . eating ice cream, tormenting nurses, having a high old time, collecting as much sick pay as I can get before they figure out I'm goldbricking.' "

Dusty had not heard this part of the story before. "Why'd he make you promise that?"

"I asked why, too. He said all the other kids at school had fathers, and they all thought their fathers were heroes, or they badly wanted to think so. And most of them *were* heroes, according to Daddy, or would be if given a chance. But they were accountants and salesmen and mechanics and data processors, and they just weren't lucky enough to be in the right place at the right time, like my dad was lucky because of his job. He says, 'If some kid goes home and looks at his father with disappointment, because of you bragging on me, then you've done a dishonorable thing, Miss M. And I know you're not dishonorable. Not you, ever. You're a peach, Miss M. You're a perfect peach.'"

"Lucky," Dusty said wonderingly, and shook his head.

"He was something, huh?"

"Something."

The commendation her father received from the fire department for his bravery that night had not been his first and would not be his last. Before cancer did to him what flames could not, he had become the most-decorated fireman in the history of the state.

He insisted on receiving every commendation in private, without ceremony and without a press release. To his way of thinking, he was only doing what he was paid to do. Besides, all the risks and all the injuries were evidently insignificant compared to what he'd been through in the war.

"I don't know what happened to him in Vietnam," Martie said. "He never talked about it. When I was eleven, I found his medals in a box in the attic. He told me he'd won them because he'd been the fastest typist in the division commander's secretarial pool, and when that didn't wash, he said they used to have Bake-Offs a lot in Nam, and he made a fabulous bundt cake. But even at eleven, I knew they don't give you multiple Bronze Stars for bundt cakes. I don't know if he was as fine a man when he went to Nam as when he came out, but for some reason I think that maybe he was better for what he suffered, that it made him very humble, so gentle and so generous—so full of love for life, for people."

The willowy pepper trees and the melaleucas swayed in the breeze, and the jacarandas shimmered purple against graying sky.

"I miss him so damn much," she said.

"I know."

"And what I'm so afraid . . . about this crazy thing that's happening to me . . ."

"You'll beat it, Martie."

"No, I mean, I'm afraid that because of it . . . I'll do something to dishonor him."

"Not possible."

"You don't know," she said with a shudder.

"I *do* know. Not possible. You *are* your father's daughter."

Martie was surprised to be able to manage even a frail smile. Dusty blurred before her, and though she pressed her trembling lips tightly together, the taste of salt seeped in at the corner of her mouth.

They took lunch in the car, in the parking lot behind a drive-through restaurant.

"No tablecloth, no candle, no vase of flowers," Dusty said, enjoying a fish sandwich and french fries, "but you must admit we've got a lovely view of that Dumpster."

Although she had skipped breakfast, Martie ordered only a small vanilla milk shake, sipping it slowly. She didn't fancy having a full stomach of greasy food if she were stricken again by that devastating spook show of death images that had flashed through her mind in the car between Skeet's apartment and Dr. Closterman's office.

With the cell phone, she called Susan. She waited through twenty rings before she pressed *end*.

"Something's wrong," she said.

"Let's not jump to conclusions."

"Can't jump. All the spring's out of my legs," she said, which was true, thanks to the double Valium. Indeed, her worry was soft and fuzzy around the edges, but it was worry nonetheless.

"If we can't reach her after seeing Dr. Ahriman, we'll swing by her place, check up on her," Dusty promised.

Tormented by this bizarre affliction of her own, Martie hadn't found an opportunity to tell Dusty about Susan's incredible claim that she was being victimized by a night visitor who came and went at will, leaving her with no memory of his intrusion.

This wasn't the moment, either. She had achieved a precarious balance; she was concerned that recounting her emotional conversation with Susan would make her wobbly again. Besides, they were due at Dr. Ahriman's office in a few minutes, and she didn't have time to report the conversation to Dusty in appropriate detail. Later.

"Something's wrong," she repeated, but she said no more.

Odd, to be here in this stylish, black-and-honey-toned waiting room without Susan.

Crossing the threshold, setting foot on the black granite floor, Martie felt her burden of anxiety lift significantly. A new lightness in body and mind. A welcome hope in the heart.

This, too, struck her as odd, and quite different from the effect of the Valium. The drug covered her anxiety, repressed it, yet she was still aware of it squirming under the chemical blanket. In this place, however, she felt a measure of her apprehension float up and away from her, not merely repressed any longer, but dissipated.

Twice a week for the past year, without exception, Susan, too, had brightened noticeably upon reaching this office. The heavy hand of agoraphobia never lifted from her in other enclosed spaces beyond the walls of her own apartment, but past this threshold, she found surcease.

An instant after Jennifer, the secretary, looked up and

saw them enter from the corridor, the door to Dr. Ahriman's office opened, and the psychiatrist came out into the lounge to greet them.

He was tall and handsome. His posture, carriage, and impeccable attire reminded Martie of elegant leading men in movies of another era: William Powell, Cary Grant.

Martie didn't know how the doctor was able to project such a reassuring air of quiet authority and competence, but she didn't try to analyze it because the very sight of him, even more than stepping through the doorway into this room, put her at peace, and she was just grateful to feel a surge of hope.

47

Ominous, this darkness that came into the sea hours before twilight, as though some primal malevolence were rising from deep oceanic trenches and spreading to every shore.

The sky had completely shrouded itself in the gray clouds that it had been steadily knitting since morning, leaving no blue to give the water color by reflection, no sun to glitter off the teeth of the waves. Nevertheless, to Dusty, the lead-gray Pacific was far darker than it should have been at this hour, marbled with veins of black.

Somber, too, was the long coastline—the shadowed beaches, the slump of hills to the south, and the peopled plains to the west and north—seen from this fourteenth floor. Nature's green appeared to be thinly painted over a mold-gray base coat, and all the works of man were rubble unrealized, waiting for the thousand-year quake or thermonuclear war.

When he looked away from the view beyond the huge wall of glass, Dusty's peculiar uneasiness left him as completely and suddenly as if a switch had been thrown. The mahogany-paneled office, the bookshelves with neatly ordered tomes, the array of degrees from the nation's most prestigious universities, the warm multicolored light from three Tiffany-style lamps—genuine Tiffany?—and the tasteful furnishings exerted a calming influence. He had been surprised to feel relieved when he'd stepped with Martie into

Ahriman's waiting room; but here, his relief gave way to an almost Zen-like serenity.

His chair stood near the immense window, but Martie and Dr. Ahriman sat apart from him, in two armchairs that faced each other across a low table. With more self-possession than she'd shown since Dusty had encountered her in the garage the previous evening, Martie spoke of her panic attacks. The psychiatrist listened attentively and with an evident compassion that was comforting.

In fact, so comforted was Dusty that he found himself smiling.

This was a safe place. Dr. Ahriman was a great psychiatrist. Everything would be all right now that Martie was in Dr. Ahriman's care. Dr. Ahriman was deeply committed to his patients. Dr. Ahriman would make this trouble go away.

Then Dusty turned his attention to the view again, and the ocean appeared to be a vast slough, as though its waters were so thick with clouds of mud and tangles of seaweed that only low viscous waves were able to form. And in this peculiar light, the serried whitecaps were not white, but mottled-gray and chrome yellow.

On winter days, under overcast skies, the sea had often looked like this, and never before had he found it so disquieting. Indeed, in the past, he had seen a rare, stark beauty in such scenes.

A small voice of reason told him that he was projecting feelings onto this view that were not actually a response to it, feelings that had another source. The sea was just the sea, as it had always been, and the true cause of this uneasiness lay elsewhere.

That thought was puzzling, because there was nothing *in* this room to account for his disquiet. This was a safe place. Dr. Ahriman was a great psychiatrist. Everything would be all right now that Martie was in Dr. Ahriman's care. Dr. Ahriman was deeply committed—

"We must have additional dialogue," Dr. Ahriman said,

"further discovery, before I can make a diagnosis with full confidence. But I'll risk putting a name to what you've been experiencing, Martie."

Martie leaned forward slightly in her chair, and Dusty saw that she was anticipating the psychiatrist's preliminary diagnosis with a half smile, no apparent trepidation visible in her face.

"It's an intriguing and rare condition," said the psychiatrist. "Autophobia, fear of oneself. I've never encountered a case of it, but I'm familiar with the literature on the disorder. It manifests in astonishing ways—as you are now unfortunately well aware."

"Autophobia," Martie marveled, with more fascination and less angst than seemed appropriate, as though the psychiatrist had cured her simply by putting a name to the affliction.

Maybe the Valium accounted for it.

Even as Dusty wondered at Martie's response, he realized that he, too, was smiling and nodding.

Dr. Ahriman would make this trouble go away.

"Statistically speaking," Ahriman said, "it's incredible that your best friend *and* you would acquire profound phobic conditions. Phobias as powerfully affecting as yours and Susan's are not common, so I suspect there's a connection."

"Connection? How so, Doctor?" Dusty asked, and that small inner voice of reason couldn't resist remarking on his tone of voice, which was not unlike that of a twelve-year-old boy posing a question to Mr. Wizard, on the now-canceled children's television program that had once endeavored to find the fun in science.

Ahriman steepled his fingers under his chin, looked thoughtful, and said, "Martie, you've been bringing Susan here for a year now—"

"Since she and Eric separated."

"Yes. And you've been Susan's lifeline, doing her shopping, other errands. Because she's shown such little apparent progress, you've become ever more worried. As your worry grows, you begin to blame yourself for her failure to respond quickly to therapy."

Surprised, Martie said, "I do? Blame myself?"

"As much as I know about you, it appears to be in your nature to have a strong sense of responsibility for others. Perhaps even an excessive sense of responsibility."

Dusty said, "The Smilin' Bob gene."

"My father," Martie explained to Ahriman. "Robert Woodhouse."

"Ah. Well, what I think's happened is that you've been feeling as though you've somehow failed Susan, and this sense of failure has metastasized into guilt. From the guilt comes this autophobia. If you have failed your friend, whom you love so much, then . . . well, you begin telling yourself that you evidently aren't the good person you thought you were, possibly even a bad person, but certainly a bad friend, certainly that at least, and not to be trusted."

Dusty thought the explanation seemed too simple to be true—and yet it rang with a convincing note.

When Martie met his eyes, he saw that her reaction was much the same as his.

Could such a weird, complex affliction befall someone overnight, someone previously as stable as the Rocky Mountains?

"Only yesterday," Ahriman reminded Martie, "when you brought Susan for her appointment, you took me aside to tell me how worried you were about her."

"Well, yes."

"And do you recall what else you said?" When Martie hesitated, Ahriman reminded her: "You told me that you felt you had failed her."

"But I didn't mean—"

"You said it with conviction. With anguish. That you failed her."

Thinking back, she said, "I did, didn't I?"

Unsteepling his fingers, turning his hands palms up as though to say *There you have it,* Dr. Ahriman smiled. "If further dialogue tends to confirm this diagnosis, then there's good news."

"I need some good news," Martie said, though she'd not appeared distraught at any moment since entering the office.

"Finding the root of the phobia, the hidden cause, is often the most difficult phase of therapy. If your autophobia arises from this guilt about Susan, then we've leaped over a year of analysis. Better yet, what you have is less a genuine phobic condition than . . . well, call it sympathetic phobia."

"Like some husbands get sympathetic cramps and morning sickness when their wives are pregnant?" Martie suggested.

"Exactly," Ahriman affirmed. "And a sympathetic phobia, if that is what you have, is infinitely easier to cure than a deeper-rooted condition like Susan's. I all but guarantee you won't be coming to me for long before I'm done with you."

"How long?"

"One month. Perhaps three. You must understand, there's really no way to fix an exact date. So much depends on . . . you and me."

Dusty leaned back in his chair, further relieved. One month, even three, was not such a long time. Especially if she experienced steady improvement. They could endure this.

Dr. Ahriman was a great psychiatrist. Dr. Ahriman would make this trouble go away.

"I'm ready to begin," Martie announced. "Already this morning, I saw our internist—"

"And his opinion?" Ahriman wondered.

"He thinks we should take the necessary steps to rule out brain tumors, that sort of thing, but more likely than not it's a matter for therapy, not medicine."

"Sounds like a good, thorough physician."

"I've had some tests done at the hospital, everything he wanted me to have. But now . . . well, nothing's for sure, but I think this is where I'm going to get help."

"Then let's proceed!" Dr. Ahriman said brightly, with an almost boyish enthusiasm that Dusty found heartening because it seemed to be an expression of dedication to his work and confidence in his skills.

Dr. Ahriman would make this trouble go away.

"Mr. Rhodes," the psychiatrist said, "traditional therapy is, of course, a process requiring confidentiality for the patient if he—in this case, she—is to be forthcoming. So I'll have to ask you to adjourn to our outgoing waiting room for the rest of this session."

Dusty looked at Martie for guidance.

She smiled and nodded.

This was a safe place. She would be all right here.

"Of course, sure." Dusty rose from his chair.

Martie handed her leather jacket to him, which she had removed upon entering the office, and he put it over his arm with his coat.

"Right this way, Mr. Rhodes," Dr. Ahriman said, crossing the large office toward the door to the outgoing waiting room.

Scaled clouds, as greasy and sour-gray as rotting fish, seemed to be foul ejecta spewed out by the rolling Pacific, clotted on the heavens. The coaly veins in the water were varicose and more numerous than previously, and large sections of the sea were fearfully black to Dusty's eyes if to no other's.

His brief ripple of disquiet at once smoothed away as he turned from the enormous window and followed Dr. Ahriman.

The door between the mahogany-paneled office and the outgoing waiting room was surprisingly thick. As tightly fitted as a Mason-jar lid, it produced a soft pop and a sigh when opened, as though a vacuum seal were being broken.

Dusty supposed that a serious door was required to protect the doctor's patients from eavesdroppers. No doubt the core of it was composed of layers of soundproofing.

The honey-toned walls, black-granite floor, and furnishings in this second waiting room were like those in the larger, incoming lounge at the main entrance of the suite.

"Would you like Jennifer to bring you coffee, cola, ice water?" Ahriman asked Dusty.

"No, thank you. I'll be fine."

"Those," Ahriman said, indicating a fanned array of periodicals on a table, "are current." He smiled. "This is one doctor's office that isn't a graveyard for the magazines of prior decades."

"Very thoughtful."

Ahriman placed one hand reassuringly on Dusty's shoulder. "She is going to be fine, Mr. Rhodes."

"She's a fighter."

"Have faith."

"I do."

The psychiatrist returned to Martie.

The door fell shut with a muffled but impressive thud, and the latch automatically engaged. There was no handle on this side. The door could only be opened from the inner office.

48

Black hair, black attire. Blue eyes shine like Tiffany. Her light, too, a lamp.

The doctor polished that haiku in his mind, rather pleased with it, as he returned to his armchair and sat across the low table from Martie Rhodes.

Without a word, he studied her face, feature by feature and then as a whole, taking his time, curious to see if his protracted silence would make her uneasy.

Unperturbed, she waited, evidently confident that the doctor's mute inspection had a clinical purpose that would be explained to her when the time was right.

As with Susan Jagger, Dr. Ahriman had previously implanted in Martie and Dustin Rhodes the suggestion that they would feel deeply at ease in his office. Likewise, they were always to be reassured at the sight of him.

In their unconscious minds, he had embedded six thoughts, like little prayers, to which they were able to resort one sentence at a time or in a single long calming mantra, if any doubt or nervousness overcame them in his presence. *This is a safe place. Dr. Ahriman is a great psychiatrist. Everything will be all right now that I am*—or in Dustin's case, *Martie is—in Dr. Ahriman's care. Dr. Ahriman is deeply committed to his patients. Dr. Ahriman will make this trouble go away.* Even when they were fully conscious, these mini-meditations would reinforce their perception that Dr. Mark Ahriman was their sole salvation.

The doctor had found it richly amusing to watch them smiling and nodding, even as they must have wondered at their sudden shedding of anxiety. And what fun it was to have a man so gratefully entrust his wife to you when your intention was to debase, demean, humiliate, and ultimately destroy her.

After the unanticipated halftime occasioned by Susan's suicide, the game would now resume.

"Martie?" he said.

"Yes, Doctor?"

"Raymond Shaw."

Her demeanor changed at once. She stiffened and sat straighter in her chair. Her lovely half smile froze, faded, and she said, "I'm listening."

Having switched her on with that name, the doctor now loaded the elaborate program that was so succinctly coded in her personal haiku. "Blown from the west—"

"You are the west and the western wind," she said dutifully.

"—fallen leaves gather—"

"The leaves are your instructions."

"—in the east."

"I am the east," Martie said, and now all instructions that the doctor gave her would be gathered in like autumn leaves, to compost in the dark warm depths of her subconscious mind.

As Dusty hung Martie's black leather jacket on the coatrack, he felt the paperback in the right-hand pocket. It was the novel she had carried here when escorting Susan, not for the entire past year, but at least for four or five months.

Although she had claimed that it was an entertaining read, the book appeared to be as pristine as when it had first been stocked on a bookstore shelf. The spine was smooth, uncreased. When he riffled the pages, they were so crisp and fresh that this might have been the first time they had been parted from one another since being married at the bindery.

He remembered how Martie had spoken of this story in the vague language of a high-schooler faking a report on a book she'd never taken the time to crack. He was suddenly sure that Martie had read none of the novel, but he couldn't imagine why she would lie about anything this trivial.

Indeed, Dusty found it hard to get his mind around the thought that Martie would ever lie about any matter whatsoever, whether great or small. Uncommon respect for the truth was one of the touchstones by which she constantly tested her right to call herself Smilin' Bob Woodhouse's daughter.

After hanging up his own jacket, still holding the paperback, he looked at the magazines fanned on the table. They were of one ilk, dedicated either to shameless fawning over celebrities or to the supposedly witty skewering and hip analysis of the doings and sayings of celebrities, which in the end had essentially the same effect as shameless fawning.

Leaving the magazines untouched, he sat down with the book.

He was vaguely familiar with the title. In its time, this novel had been a best-seller. A famous film had been adapted from it. Dusty had neither read the book nor seen the movie.

The Manchurian Candidate by Richard Condon.

According to the copyright page, the first edition was published in 1959. An age ago. Another millennium.

Yet still in print. A good sign.

Chapter 1. Although a thriller, the book opened not on a dark stormy night, but in San Francisco, in sunshine. Dusty began to read.

The doctor asked Martie to sit on the couch, where he could sit beside her. Obediently, she moved from the armchair.

Wrapped up all in black. Odd color to wrap a toy—one not yet broken.

That haiku also resonated with him, and he ran it through his mind a few times with increasing pleasure. It wasn't as good as the Tiffany one, but far better than his recent efforts to capture Susan Jagger in verse.

Sitting on the couch close to Martie but not thigh to thigh, the doctor said, "Today, together, we enter a new phase."

In the solemn and hushed confines of her mind chapel, where the only votive candles were lit to the god Ahriman, Martie attended his every word with the quiet acceptance and the shining visionary stare of Joan of Arc listening to her Voice.

"From this day forward, you will discover that destruction and self-destruction are ever more appealing. Terrifying, yes. But even terror has a sweet appeal. Tell me if you have ever ridden a roller coaster, one of those that takes you on barrel rolls, loops at high speed."

"Yes."

"Tell me how you felt on that roller coaster."

"Afraid."

"But you felt something else."

"Exhilaration. Delight."

"There. Terror and pleasure are linked in us. We are a badly miswired species, Martie. Terror delights us, both the experience of terror and the dealing out of it to others. We are healthier if we admit to this miswiring and do not struggle to be better than our natures allow. You do understand what I'm saying."

Her eyes jiggled. REM. She said, "Yes."

"Regardless of what our Creator intended us to be, what we have become is what we *are*. Compassion, love, humility, honesty, loyalty, truthfulness—these are like those enormous plate-glass windows into which small birds crash repeatedly, stupidly. We bash ourselves to pieces against the glass of love, the glass of truth, foolishly struggling to go where we can never go, to be what we are not wired to be."

"Yes."

"Power and its primary consequences—death and sex. That's what drives us. Power over others is the thrill of thrills for us. We idolize politicians because they have so much power, and we worship celebrities because their lives appear to be more charged with power than our own. The strong among us seize power, and the weak have the thrill of sacrificing themselves to the power of the strong. Power. The power to kill, to maim, to hurt, to tell other people what to do, how to think, what to believe and what not to believe. The power to terrorize. Destruction is our talent, our destiny. And I am going to prepare you to wallow in destruction, Martie, and ultimately to destroy yourself—to know both the thrill of crushing and of being crushed."

Blue jiggle. Blue stillness.

Her hands in her lap, both palms up as though to receive. Lips parted to intake. Head cocked slightly to one side in the posture of an attentive student.

The doctor put one hand to her face, caressed her cheek. "Kiss my hand, Martie."

She pressed her lips to his fingers.

Lowering his hand, the doctor said, "I'm going to show you more photographs, Martie. Images that we will study together. They are similar to those we studied yesterday, when you were here with Susan. Like those photographs, these images are all repulsive, disgusting, horrifying. However, you will examine them calmly and with careful attention to detail. You will store them away in your memory, where they will apparently be forgotten—but each time your anxiety swells into a full-scale panic attack, these images will flood back into your mind. And then you *will not* see them as photographs in a book, neatly boxed, with white borders and captions underneath. Instead, they will be wall-to-wall images in your mind, more vivid and real to you than things you have actually experienced. Please tell me whether or not you understand, Martie."

"I understand."

"I am proud of you."

"Thank you."

Her blue eyes seeking. His wisdom gives her vision. Teacher and student.

Not bad technically, but false. He isn't primarily her teacher, and she isn't his student in any meaningful sense. Player and toy. Master and possession.

"Martie, when these images return to you during panic attacks, they will disgust and sicken you, fill you with nausea and even with despair . . . but they will *also* hold a strange fascination. You will find them repulsive but compelling. Although you might despair for the victims in these images, in a deep precinct of your mind, you will admire the killers who savaged them. A part of you will envy those killers their power, and you'll recognize this murderous aspect of yourself. You will fear this violent other Martie . . . and yet yearn to surrender control to her. You will see these images as *wishes*, as frenzies of violence that you yourself would indulge in if only you could be true to that other Martie, that cold savage self who is, in fact, your true human nature. That other Martie is the *real* you. The gentle woman you appear to be . . . she is nothing but a deception, a shadow you cast in the light of civilization, so you can pass for one of the weak and not alarm them. Over the next few sessions, I will show you how to become the Martie you are meant to be, how to shed this shadow existence and become truly *alive*, how to fulfill your potential, seize the power and the glory that are your destiny."

The doctor had brought two large and beautifully illustrated textbooks with him to the couch. These expensive volumes were used in criminology courses in many universities. Most police detectives and big-city medical examiners were familiar with them, but few in the general public knew of their existence.

The first was a definitive study of forensic pathology, which is the science of recognizing and interpreting diseases, injuries, and wounds in the human body. Forensic pathology was of interest to Dr. Ahriman, because he was a man of medicine and because he was determined never to leave evidence—in the organic ruins resulting from his games—that might result in his transferral from mansion to cell, padded or not.

GO TO JAIL, GO DIRECTLY TO JAIL was a card he intended never to accept. After all, unlike in Monopoly, this game included no GET OUT OF JAIL FREE cards.

The second textbook was a comprehensive study of the tactics, the procedures, and the forensic techniques of practical homicide investigation. The doctor had acquired it on the principle that good gamesmanship requires one to understand fully the strategies of opposing players.

Both volumes held galleries of Death's dark art. The forensic-pathology textbook featured more examples and a greater variety of soul-shriveling grisliness, but the volume on homicide investigation offered more shots of victims in situ, which had a charm not always to be found in photographs taken at the morgue, as any slaughterhouse is visually more arresting than any butcher-shop display. Guggenheims of blood, Louvres of violence, museums of human evil and misery bound with tables of contents and indexes for easy reference.

Docile, she waited. Lips parted. Eyes wide. A vessel ready to be filled.

"You're quite lovely," the doctor told her. "Martie, I must admit, blinded by Susan's light, I had too little appreciation for your beauty. Until now."

Seasoned by more suffering, she would be exquisitely erotic.

He began, then, with the homicide-investigation textbook. He opened to a page marked with a pink Post-it.

Holding the volume in front of Martie, Ahriman directed her attention to a photograph of a dead man lying supine on a hardwood floor. Naked, he was, and ravaged by thirty-six stab wounds. The doctor made sure that Martie noted, in particular, the imaginative use to which the killer had put the victim's genitals.

"And there, the railroad spike in the forehead," Ahriman said. "Steel, ten inches in length, with a one-inch-diameter nailhead, but you can't see much of the length. It pins him to the oak flooring. A crucifixion reference, no doubt—the nail through the hand and the crown of thorns combined in one efficient symbol. Absorb it, Martie. Every glorious detail."

She stared intensely, as instructed, gaze traveling wound to wound across the photograph.

"The victim was a priest," the doctor informed her. "The killer most likely found the oak flooring regrettable, but no manufacturer of home-improvement products has had the panache to market dogwood tongue and groove."

Blue jiggle. Blue stillness. A blink. The image captured now and stored away.

Ahriman turned the page.

As worried as he had been about Martie, Dusty had not expected to be able to concentrate on the novel. The peace of mind that had settled upon him when he entered Dr. Ahriman's office did not fade, however, and he found himself more easily captured by the story than he expected to be.

The Manchurian Candidate offered an entertaining plot

peopled with colorful characters, just as Martie had promised in her curious wooden tone and phrases. Considering the high quality of the novel, her failure to finish it—or even to read a significant portion of it—during the months she had carried it to Susan's sessions was more inexplicable than ever.

In Chapter 2, Dusty came to a paragraph that began with the name *Dr. Yen Lo.*

Shock triggered a reflex action that nearly sent the book flying out of his hands. He held on to it, but lost his place.

Flipping through the text in search of his page, he was sure that his eyes had tricked him. Some phrase containing four syllables similar to those in that Asian name must have made the connection for him, causing him to misread.

Dusty located the second chapter, the page, the paragraph, and there indisputably was the name in clear black type, spelled just as Skeet had spelled it over and over again on the pages of the notepad: *Dr. Yen Lo.* The type jittered up and down as his hands shook.

The name had caused the kid to drop instantly into that strange dissociative state, as though he were hypnotized, and now it gave Dusty a case of the whim-whams that left the nape of his neck more corrugated than corduroy. Even the singularly calming influence of the waiting-room decor could not raise any warmth along his spine, which was as cold as a thermometer in a meat locker.

Using one finger as a bookmark, he got to his feet and paced the small room, trying to work off sufficient nervous energy to be able to hold the book still enough to read.

Why was Skeet so tormented and so affected by a name that was nothing more than that of a character in a work of fiction?

Considering the kid's taste in literature, the groaning shelves of fantasy novels in his apartment, he probably hadn't even read this thriller. There was nary a dragon in it, neither elf nor wizard.

After several circuits of the room, beginning to understand the frustration of a zoo-kept panther, Dusty returned to his chair, even though he still felt as if all the fluid in his spine had collected, like chilled mercury, in the small of his back.

He continued reading. *Dr. Yen Lo . . .*

49

Sloppy work, this decapitation, obviously performed with the wrong cutting tool.

"The victim's eyes are a point of interest here, Martie. How wide they appear. The upper lids crimped back so far by shock that they almost look as though they were cut off. Such mystery in his gaze, such an otherworldly quality, as though in the moment of death, he had been granted a glimpse of what awaited him beyond."

She looked into the pitiable eyes in the photograph. Blinked. Blinked.

Paging to the next pink Post-it, the doctor said, "This one is of special importance, Martie. Study it well."

She lowered her head slightly toward the page.

"You and Dusty will eventually be required to mutilate a woman in a similar manner to this, and you will arrange the various body parts in a tableau as clever as this one. The victim here is a girl, just fourteen years old, but the two of you will be dealing with a somewhat older person."

The doctor's interest was so gripped by the photograph that he didn't see the first two tears until they had tracked most of the way down Martie's face. Looking up, catching sight of those twin pearls, he was astonished.

"Martie, you are supposed to be in that deepest of deep places in your mind, far down in the chapel. Tell me whether or not that is where you are."

"Yes. Here. The chapel."

With her personality this deeply repressed, she should not have been able to respond emotionally either to anything that she witnessed or to anything that was done to her. As with Susan, the doctor should have had to bring her out from the chapel and up a flight or two of stairs, figuratively speaking, to a higher level of consciousness, before she would be capable of any reaction as savory as this.

"Tell me what's wrong, Martie."

Her voice was barely louder than a breath: "Such pain."

"You're in pain?"

"Her."

"Tell me who."

As more tears welled and shimmered in her eyes, she pointed to the rearranged young girl in the photograph.

Puzzled, Ahriman said, "It's just a photograph."

"Of a real person," she murmured.

"She's been dead a long time."

"She was alive once."

Martie's lacrimal glands were evidently fine specimens. Her lacrimal sacs emptied into the lacrimal lakes, which reached flood stage, and two more droplets sluiced a little misery out of her eyes.

Ahriman was reminded of Susan's final tear, squeezed out in the last minute of her life. Dying, of course, must be a stressful experience, even when one perishes quietly in a state of extreme personality submersion. Martie was not dying. Yet, these tears.

"You didn't know this girl," the doctor persisted.

Barely a whisper: "No."

"She might have deserved this."

"No."

"She might have been a teenage prostitute."

Softly, bleakly: "Doesn't matter."

"Perhaps she was a murderer herself."

"She's me."

"What does that mean?" he asked.

"What does that mean?" she parroted.

"You say that she is you. Explain."

"It can't be explained."

"Then it's meaningless."

"It can only be known."

"It can only be known," he repeated scornfully.

"Yes."

"Is this a riddle, maybe a Zen koan or something?"

"Is it?" she asked.

"Girls," he said impatiently.

Martie said nothing.

The doctor closed the book, studied her profile for a moment, and then said, "Look at me."

She turned her head to face him.

"Be still," he said. "I want to taste."

Ahriman pressed his lips to each of her welling eyes. A little tongue work, too.

"Salty," he said, "but something else. A subtle something quite intriguing."

He required another sip. A spasm of REM caused her eye to quiver erotically against his tongue.

Sitting back from her again, Ahriman said, "Astringent but not bitter."

Girl's face shiny damp. All the sorrow of the world. Yet such bright beauty.

Daring to believe that those three lines were the beginning of yet another haiku worth committing to paper, the doctor tucked the verses away in his mind to be polished later.

As if the heat of Ahriman's lips had withered Martie's lacrimal apparatus, her eyes grew dry once more.

"You're going to be a lot more fun than I thought," Ahriman said. "You'll require considerable finesse, but the extra effort ought to be worthwhile. Like all the best toys, the art of your form—your mind and heart—at least equals the thrill of your function. Now I want you to be calm, perfectly calm, detached, observant, obedient."

"I understand."

He opened the textbook again.

With the doctor's patient guidance, dry-eyed this time, Martie studied the crime-scene photograph of the dismembered girl, whose parts had been creatively rearranged. He instructed her to imagine what it would be like to commit this atrocity herself, to glory in the reeking wet reality of what she saw here on the glossy page. To be certain Martie involved all five of her senses in this exercise, Ahriman employed his medical knowledge, his personal experience, and his well-conditioned imagination to assist her with many details of color, texture, and stench.

Then other pages. Other photographs. Fresh corpses but also bodies in various stages of decomposition.

Blink.

Blink.

Finally he returned the two heavy volumes to the bookshelves.

He had spent fifteen minutes too long with Martie, but he had taken considerable satisfaction in refining her appreciation for death. Sometimes the doctor thought he might have been a first-rate teacher, costumed in tweed suits, suspenders, bow ties; and he *knew* he would have enjoyed working with children.

He instructed Martie to lie on her back, on the couch, and close her eyes. "I'm going to bring Dusty in here now, but you will not hear a word of what either of us says. You will not open your eyes until I tell you to do so. You will go away now into a soundless, lightless place, into a deep sleep, from which you will awake back in the mind chapel only when I kiss your eyes and call you *princess*."

After waiting a minute, the doctor timed the pulse in Martie's left wrist. Slow, thick, steady. Fifty-two beats per minute.

Now on to Mr. Rhodes, housepainter, college dropout, closet intellectual, soon to be infamous from sea to shining sea, unwitting instrument of vengeance.

The novel was about brainwashing, which Dusty realized within a page or two of encountering Dr. Yen Lo.

This discovery startled him almost as much as seeing the name from Skeet's notepad. He didn't fumble the book this time, kept his place, but muttered, "Son of a bitch."

At the kid's apartment, Dusty had searched without success for evidence of cult membership. No tracts or pamphlets. No religious vestments or icons. Not one caged chicken clucking worriedly as it awaited sacrifice. Now, when Dusty hadn't even been *thinking* about Skeet's troubles, here came the mysterious Chinese physician, popping up from Condon's novel, revealing himself to be an expert in the science and art of *brainwashing*.

Dusty didn't believe in coincidence. Life was a tapestry with patterns to be discerned if you looked for them. This book didn't just *happen* to be the one Martie had been carrying around for months. It had been made available to them because it contained a clue to the truth of this insane situation. He would have given his left testicle—or, with more alacrity, all the money in their checking account—to know who had ensured *The Manchurian Candidate* would be here, now, when needed. Although Dusty believed in a universe intelligently designed, he had difficulty crediting God with working miraculously through a paperback thriller rather than a burning bush or the more traditional and flashier signs in the sky. Okay, so it wasn't God, wasn't coincidence, and therefore must be someone of flesh and bone.

Dusty heard himself speaking aloud, as though he were

imitating an owl, and he silenced himself with the realization that he knew too little to answer his question.

In Condon's novel, which was set during and after the Korean War, Dr. Yen Lo had brainwashed some American soldiers, turning one of them into a robotic killer who remained unaware of what had been done to him. Back home, acclaimed a hero, the soldier would lead a normal life—until, activated by a game of simple solitaire and then instructed, he became an obedient assassin.

But the Korean War had ended in 1953, and this thriller had been published in 1959, long before Dusty had been born. Neither the young soldier nor Dr. Yen Lo was real. There was no apparent reason why a connection should exist between this novel and Dusty, Martie, and Skeet with his haiku rules.

He could only read further, in search of revelation.

After he had shot through several more pages, Dusty heard the lever-action handle squeak against its escutcheon on the other side of the door to Ahriman's office, heard the click of the latch, and suddenly felt that he must let no one catch him reading this book. He was abruptly, inexplicably nervous, and when the door seal broke with the pop and sigh of a violated vacuum, he tossed the paperback aside with alarm, as though he were about to be caught reading vile pornography or, worse, one of the numerous pompous tomes pumped out by his father and stepfathers.

The book slid across the small end table beside his chair, off the edge, and hit the floor with a *plop* just as the heavy door opened and Dr. Ahriman appeared. Unaccountably flushed, Dusty was getting to his feet even as the paperback was still falling, and he coughed to cover the *plop*.

Flustered, he heard himself say, "Doctor, is Martie—Did it go—Will she—"

"Viola Narvilly," the doctor said.

"I'm listening."

50

After they went through the enabling litany of Dusty's personal haiku, Dr. Ahriman escorted him into the office and led him directly to the armchair in which Martie had been seated earlier. She slept upon the couch, and Dusty didn't glance at her.

Ahriman sat in the facing armchair and studied his subject for a minute. The man had a slightly detached attitude, but he responded immediately to the doctor's voice. His passive expression was nothing stranger than the looks one saw on the faces of motorists caught in the boredom of bumper-to-bumper, rush-hour traffic.

Dustin Rhodes was a relatively new acquisition in the Ahriman collection. He had been fully controlled by the doctor less than two months.

Martie herself, operating under the doctor's guidance, on three occasions had served to her husband the meticulously blended dose of drugs required to slip him into the twilight sleep that allowed him to be effectively programmed: Rohypnol; phencyclidine; Valium; and a substance known—although only to a few cognoscenti—as Santa Fe #46. Because Dusty always had dessert with dinner, the first dose had come in a slice of peanut butter pie; the second, two nights later, lent neither flavor nor odor to a bowl of crème brûlée with a crown of toasted coconut curls; the third, three nights after the second, would have been undetectable to a bloodhound, tucked away in an ice-cream sundae topped with fudge sauce, maraschino cherries, almonds, and chopped dates.

The man knew how to eat. As regarded culinary preferences, at least, the doctor felt a certain kinship with him.

The programming had been conducted in the Rhodeses' bedroom: Dusty on the bed, Martie sitting cross-legged and out of the way on the big sheepskin pillow in the corner, a floor lamp serving as an IV rack. All had gone well.

The dog wanted to be a problem but was too sweet and obedient to do more than growl and sulk. They shut him away in Martie's study with a bowl of water, a yellow Booda duck with a squeaking tummy, and a Nylabone.

Now, after a seizure of REM passed out of Dusty's eyes, Dr. Ahriman said, "This won't take long, but my instructions today are very important."

"Yes, sir."

"Martie will return here for an appointment on Friday, the day after tomorrow, and you will arrange your schedule to be able to bring her. Tell me if this is clear."

"Yes. Clear."

"Now. You surprised me yesterday—all your heroics at the Sorensons' house. That was not according to my plan. In the future, if you are present when your brother Skeet attempts suicide, you will not interfere. You may make some effort to talk him out of it, but you'll do nothing but talk, and in the end you will allow Skeet to destroy himself. Tell me if you understand."

"I understand."

"When he does destroy himself, you will be utterly devastated. And angry. Oh, enraged. You will give yourself completely to your emotions. You'll know at whom to direct your rage, because the name will be there in the suicide note. We'll discuss this further on Friday."

"Yes, sir."

Always one to find time for some fun, even when he had a busy schedule, the doctor glanced at Martie on the couch, and then turned his attention to Dusty. "Your wife is succulent, don't you think?"

"Do I?"

"Whether you do or not, I think she is a succulent piece."

Dusty's eyes were primarily gray, but with blue striations that made them unique. As a boy, Ahriman had been a marble collector, with many sacks of fine glass shooters, and he had owned three that had been similar to, but not as lustrous as, Dusty's eyes. Martie found her husband's eyes particularly beautiful, which was why the doctor had gotten such a kick out of implanting the suggestion that her autophobia would *really* begin to get a grip on her when she had a sudden vision of sticking a key into one of those beloved eyes.

"On this subject," Ahriman said, "no more curt answers. Let's have a genuine discussion of your wife's succulence."

Dusty's gaze was fixed not on Ahriman, but on a point in the air midway between them, as he said with no inflection whatsoever, as flatly as a machine might speak, "Succulent, I guess, meaning *juicy.*"

"Exactly," the doctor confirmed.

"Grapes are juicy. Strawberries. Oranges. Good pork chops are succulent," said Dusty. "But the word isn't . . . accurately descriptive of a person."

Smiling with delight, Ahriman said, "Oh, really—not accurately descriptive? Be careful, housepainter. Your genes are showing. What if I were a cannibal?"

Unable, in this state, to answer a question with anything but a request for further information, Dusty asked, "Are you a cannibal?"

"If I were a cannibal, I might be accurately descriptive when calling your tasty wife *succulent.* Enlighten me with your opinion of that, Mr. Dustin Penn Rhodes."

Dusty's emotionless tone of voice remained unchanged,

but now it seemed drily pedantic, much to the doctor's amusement. "From a cannibalistic point of view, the word works."

"I'm afraid that under all your blue-collar earthiness lurks a droning professor."

Dusty said nothing, but his eyes jiggled with REM.

"Well, though I'm no cannibal," said Ahriman, "I think your wife is succulent. From now on, in fact, I'll have a new pet name for her. She'll be my little *pork chop.*"

The doctor concluded the session with the usual instructions not to retain any conscious or any accessible subconscious memory of what had transpired between them. Then: "You will return to the outgoing waiting room, Dusty. Pick up the book that you were reading and sit where you were sitting before. Find the point in the text where you were interrupted. Then, in your mind, you'll leave the chapel where you are now. As you close the chapel door, all recollection of what happened from the moment I stepped out of my office, just after you heard the click of the latch, until you wake from your current state, will have been erased. Then, counting slowly to ten, you'll ascend the stairs from the chapel. When you reach ten, you will regain full consciousness—and continue reading."

"I understand."

"Have a good afternoon, Dusty."

"Thank you."

"You're welcome."

Dusty rose from his armchair and crossed the office, not once glancing at his wife upon the couch.

When the mister was gone, the doctor went to the missus and stood studying her. Succulent, indeed.

He dropped to one knee beside the couch, kissed each of her closed eyes, and said, "My pork chop."

This, of course, had no effect, but it gave the doctor a laugh.

Another kiss to each eye. "Princess."

She woke but was still in the mind chapel, not yet permitted full consciousness.

At Ahriman's instruction, she returned to the armchair in which she had been sitting earlier.

Settling into his chair, he said, "Martie, through the rest of the afternoon and early evening, you will feel somewhat more at peace than you have been during the past twenty-four hours. Your autophobia hasn't disappeared, but it has relented a bit. For a while, you'll be troubled only by a low-grade uneasiness, a sense of fragility, and brief spells of sharper fear at the rate of about one an hour, each only a minute or two in duration. But later, at about . . . oh, at about nine o'clock, you will experience your worst panic attack yet. It'll begin in the usual way, escalate as before—but suddenly through your mind will pass the dead and tortured people we studied together, all the stabbed and shot and mutilated bodies, the decomposing cadavers, and you'll become convinced, against all reason, that you personally are responsible for what happened to them, that your hands committed all this torture and murder. Your hands. Your hands. Tell me if you understand what I have said."

"My hands."

"I leave the details of your big moment to you. You've certainly got the raw materials for it."

"I understand."

Sizzling passion eyes. Simmer in broth of eros. My juicy pork chop.

Haiku with culinary metaphor. This was nothing the masters of Japanese verse were likely to endorse, but although the doctor respected the demandingly formal structures of haiku, he was enough of a free spirit to make his own rules from time to time.

Dusty was reading about Dr. Yen Lo and the team of dedicated Communist mind-control specialists who were screwing with the brains of the hapless American soldiers, when suddenly he exclaimed, "What the hell is *this*," referring to the paperback that he was holding in his hands.

He nearly pitched *The Manchurian Candidate* across the waiting room, but checked himself. Instead, he dropped it on the little table next to his chair, shaking his right hand as though the book had burnt him.

He sprang to his feet and stood looking down at the damn thing. He was no less shocked and spooked than he would have been if an evil sorcerer's curse had transformed the novel into a rattlesnake.

When he dared to look away from the book, he glanced at the door to Dr. Ahriman's office. Closed. It looked as though it had been closed since time immemorial. As formidable as a stone monolith.

The squeak of the lever-action handle, the click of the latch: He had clearly heard both those sounds. Embarrassment, alarm, shame, a sense of danger. Inexplicably, those feelings and more had crackled through him as quick as an electric arc snapping across a tiny gap in a circuit: *Don't be caught reading this!* Reflexively, he had tossed the book on the table, and because its shiny cover was slippery, it had sailed right off the granite top. The door had done its pop-sigh vacuum thing, and he had started to shoot to his feet as the book hit the floor with a *plop*, and then . . .

. . . and then the novel was back in his hand, and he was reading, sitting in his chair, as if the squeak-click-pop-sigh-plop moment of alarm had never happened. Maybe his entire life, from birth to death, was on a videotape up there in kingdom come, where one of the celestial editors had rewound it a few seconds, to the moment immediately before the sounds of the door had alarmed him, erasing all those events from his past but forgetting to erase his memory of them. Apparently, an apprentice editor with a lot to learn.

Magic. Dusty recalled the fantasy novels in Skeet's

apartment. Wizards, warlocks, necromancers, sorcerers, spellcasters. This was the kind of experience that made you believe in magic—or question your sanity.

He reached for the book on the table, where he had dropped it—for the second time?—and then he hesitated. He poked the book with one finger, but it didn't hiss or open an eye and wink at him.

He picked it up, turned it wonderingly in his hands, and then riffled the pages across his thumb.

That sound reminded him of a deck of cards being snap-shuffled, which reminded him, in turn, that the brainwashed American soldier in the novel, the one programmed to be an assassin, was activated when handed a pack of cards and asked *Why don't you pass the time by playing a little solitaire?* To be effective, the question had to be asked in exactly those words. The guy then played solitaire until he turned up the queen of diamonds, whereupon his subconscious mind became accessible to his controller, making him ready to receive his instructions.

Gazing thoughtfully at the paperback, Dusty let the edges of the pages fan across his thumb again.

He sat down, still thoughtful. Still thumbing the pages.

What he had here wasn't magic. What he had here was another bit of missing time, only a few seconds, shorter even than his moment on the phone in the kitchen, the previous day.

Shorter?

Was it really?

He consulted his wristwatch. Maybe not shorter. He couldn't be sure, because he hadn't checked the time since reading the first words of the novel. Maybe he had been zoned out for a few seconds or maybe for ten minutes, even longer.

Missing time.

What sense did this make?

None.

Energized by gut instinct, mind spinning along a trail of logic twistier than the human intestinal tract, he couldn't concentrate on Condon's novel right now. He crossed the room to the coatrack and tucked the book in his own jacket rather than in Martie's.

From another jacket pocket, he withdrew his phone.

Instead of activating the brainwashed, programmed person with a precisely worded question—*Why don't you pass the time by playing a little solitaire?*—why not activate him with a name? *Dr. Yen Lo.*

Instead of the deep subconscious becoming accessible to the controller upon the appearance of the queen of diamonds . . . why not access it by the recitation of a few lines of poetry? Haiku.

Pacing, Dusty entered Ned Motherwell's mobile number.

Ned answered on the fifth ring. He was still at the Sorensons' house. "Couldn't paint today, still damp from the rain, but we've done a lot of prep work. Hell, Fig and I have gotten more done today, just us, than we get done in two days with that hopeless little turd hanging around, smacked on one kind of dope or another."

"Skeet's doing fine," Dusty said. "Thanks for asking."

"I hope wherever you took him, they're kicking his skinny ass around the clock."

"Absolutely. I checked him into Our Lady of the Ass-Kickers Hospital."

"There ought to be such a place."

"I'm sure if Straight Edgers take over the church, there'll be one in every town. Listen, Ned, can you let Fig close up the job today while you do something for me?"

"Sure. *Fig* isn't a dope-sucking, self-destructive, walking scrotum. *Fig* is reliable."

"Has he seen Big Foot recently?"

"If he ever said he did, I'd believe him."

"Me, too," Dusty admitted.

He told Ned Motherwell what he needed to have done, and they agreed on when and where to meet.

After terminating the call, Dusty clipped the phone to his belt. He checked his watch. Almost three o'clock. He sat down again.

Two minutes later, hunched forward in his chair, forearms on his thighs, hands clasped between his knees, staring at the black granite floor, Dusty was thinking so hard that the wax should have been blown out of his ears with the velocity of bullets. When the lever-action handle squeaked and the latch clicked, he twitched but didn't explode to his feet.

Martie came out of the office first, smiling prettily, and Dusty rose to greet her, smiling less prettily, and Dr. Ahriman entered the waiting room behind her, smiling paternally, and maybe Dusty smiled a little more prettily when he saw the psychiatrist, because the man virtually radiated competence and compassion and confidence and all sorts of good stuff.

"Excellent session," Dr. Ahriman assured Dusty. "We're already making progress. I believe Martie is going to respond brilliantly to therapy, I really do."

"Thank God," Dusty said, getting Martie's jacket from the rack.

"Not to say there won't be difficult times ahead," the doctor cautioned. "Perhaps even worse panic attacks than any heretofore. This is, after all, a rare and challenging phobia. But whatever short-term setbacks there may be, I'm absolutely sure that in the long term there will be a complete cure."

"Long term?" Dusty asked, but not worriedly, because no one could be worried in the presence of the doctor's confident smile.

"Not more than a few months," Dr. Ahriman said, "perhaps much more quickly. These things have clocks of their own, and we can't set them. But there's every reason to be optimistic. I'm not even going to consider a medication component at this time, just therapy for a week or two, and then see where we are."

Dusty almost mentioned the prescription for Valium that Dr. Closterman had issued, but Martie spoke first.

Shrugging into her black leather jacket as Dusty held it for her, she said, "Honey, I feel pretty good. Really much, much better. I really do."

"Friday morning. Ten o'clock appointment," Dr. Ahriman reminded them.

"We'll be here," Dusty assured him.

Smiling, nodding, Ahriman said, "I'm certain you will."

When the doctor retreated to his inner office and closed the heavy door, a measure of warmth went out of the waiting room. A little chill came in from somewhere.

"He's really a great psychiatrist," Martie said.

Zipping up his jacket, Dusty said, "He's deeply committed to his patients," and though he was smiling and still felt good, some cranky part of him wondered how he knew Ahriman was committed to anything more than collecting his fees.

Opening the door to the fourteenth-floor corridor, Martie said, "He'll make this trouble go away. I feel good about him."

In the long corridor, heading toward the elevator, Dusty said, "Who uses the word *heretofore*?"

"What do you mean?"

"He used it. Dr. Ahriman. *Heretofore.*"

"Did he? Well, it's a word, isn't it?"

"But how often do you ever hear it? I mean outside a lawyer's office or a courtroom."

"What's your point?"

Frowning, Dusty said, "I don't know."

In the elevator alcove, when she pushed the call button, Martie said, "Heretofore, you have generally made sense, but not now."

"It's a pompous word."

"No, it's not."

"In everyday conversation it is," he insisted. "It's something my old man would say. Trevor Penn Rhodes. Or Skeet's old man. Or either of her other two elitist-bastard husbands."

"You're ranting, which you've seldom done heretofore. What's your point?"

He sighed. "I guess I don't have one."

On the way down to the ground floor, Dusty's stomach dropped out of him, as though they were in an express elevator to Hell.

Crossing the lobby, he seemed to be decompressing after a dive into a deep ocean trench, or adjusting to gravity after living in a space shuttle for a week. Coming out of a dream.

As they approached the doors, Martie took his arm, and he said, "I'm sorry, Martie. I'm just feeling . . . weird."

"That's okay. You were weird when I married you."

51

Unlike Dr. Ahriman's fourteenth-floor suite, the parking lot offered no view of the nearby Pacific. Dusty couldn't see whether the ocean was as ominously dark now as it had appeared to be from the psychiatrist's office.

The sky was sludge, but it didn't press down with full doomsday weight as before, and within the works of man, he could no longer see the future wreckage from pending cataclysms.

The breeze was promoting itself to a wind, busily sweeping dead leaves and a few small scraps of litter across the pavement.

In the car, Martie had a nervous edge to her, although it was only a fraction as sharp as it had been this morning. Still in a post-therapy glow, she rummaged through the glove box, found a roll of chocolate candies, and popped them into her mouth one at a time, chewing each with relish. Evidently she had no concern that she would have to give them back later, in a panic attack, if she found herself bent forward, retching uncontrollably.

Declining a chocolate when Martie offered it, Dusty withdrew the paperback from his jacket pocket and said, "Where did you get this?"

She glanced at the book and shrugged. "Picked it up somewhere."

"Did you buy it?"

"Bookstores don't give the things away, you know."

"Which bookstore?"

Frowning, she said, "What's this about?"

"I'll explain. But first I need to know. Which store? Barnes and Noble? Borders? Book Carnival, where you buy mysteries?"

Chewing chocolate, she studied the paperback for a long moment, and a bemused look came over her. "I don't know."

"Well, it's not as if you buy a hundred books a week from twenty different stores," he said impatiently.

"Yeah, okay, but I never claimed to have your memory. Don't *you* remember where I got it?"

"I must not have been with you."

Martie put down the roll of candies and took the paperback from him. She didn't open the book or even fan the pages with her thumb, as he might have expected, but she held it in both hands, staring at the title, held it very tightly, as though trying to squeeze out its origins as she might squeeze juice from an orange.

"I better go back to the hospital, get a test for early-onset Alzheimer's," she finally said, returning the book to Dusty and picking up the chocolates.

"Maybe it was a gift," he suggested.

"From whom?"

"That's what I'm asking."

"No. If it was a gift, I'd remember."

"When you examined the book just now, why didn't you open it?"

"Open it? There's nothing in it that'll tell me where I bought it." She held out the half-depleted roll of candy. "Here. You're a little irritable. Maybe you're hypoglycemic. Pump in some sugar."

"Pass. Martie, do you know what this novel is about?"

"Sure. It's a thriller."

"But a thriller about *what*?"

"Entertaining plot, colorful characters. I'm enjoying it."

"And what's it *about*?"

She stared at the paperback, chewing the candy more slowly. "Well, you know thrillers. Run, jump, chase, shoot, run some more."

In Dusty's hands, the book seemed to grow cold. Heavier. Its texture began to change, too: The colorful cover seemed slicker than before. As if it weren't just a book. More than a book. A talisman, too, that might at any moment work its witchery and send him plunging through a magical doorway into a dragon-infested alternate reality of the type Skeet liked to read about. Or maybe the talisman already had performed that trick, without him realizing that he'd stepped out of one world and into another. *Here* there be dragons.

"Martie, I don't think you've read a sentence of this book. Or even opened it."

Holding a chocolate between thumb and forefinger, poised to pop it into her mouth, she said, "I told you, it's a real thriller. The writing's good. The plot is entertaining, and the characters are colorful. I'm . . . enjoying . . . it."

Dusty saw that she recognized the singsong quality in her voice. Her mouth was open, but the chocolate morsel remained unpopped. Her eyes widened as if with surprise.

Holding the book up, back cover turned to her, he said, "It's about brainwashing, Martie. Even the sales copy makes that clear."

Her expression, better than any words she could have spoken, revealed that the subject of the novel was news to her.

"It takes place during and a few years after the Korean War," he told her.

The circlet of chocolate was beginning to get tacky between her fingers, so she slipped it into her mouth.

"It's about this guy," Dusty said, "this soldier, Raymond Shaw, who has—"

"I'm listening," she said.

Dusty's attention was on the book when Martie interrupted him, and when he looked up, he saw that a placid, detached expression had claimed her face. Her mouth hung open. He saw the chocolate lozenge on her tongue.

"Martie?"

"Yeah," she said thickly, not bothering to close her mouth, the candy quivering on her tongue.

Here was the episode with Skeet at New Life Clinic, repeating with Martie.

"Oh, shit," he said.

She blinked, closed her mouth, tongued the candy into her left cheek, and said, "What's wrong?"

She was back with him, no longer detached, eyes clear.

"Where did you go?" he asked.

"Me? When?"

"Here. Just now."

She cocked her head. "I really think you need a hit of sugar."

"Why did you say 'I'm listening'?"

"I didn't say it."

Dusty looked through the windshield and saw no obsidian castle with red-eyed fiends manning its saw-toothed battlements, no dragons devouring knights. Just the breeze-swept parking lot, the world as he knew it, though it was less knowable than it had once seemed.

"I was telling you about the book," he reminded her. "Do you remember the last thing I said about it?"

"Dusty, what on earth—"

"Humor me."

She sighed. "Well, you said it's about this guy, this soldier—"

"And?"

"And then you said, 'Oh, shit.' That's all."

He was getting creeped out just holding the book. He put it on the dashboard. "You don't remember the name of the soldier?"

"You didn't tell me."

"Yes, I did. And then . . . you were gone. Last night you told me you feel like you're missing bits of time. Well, you've got a few seconds missing right here."

She looked disbelieving. "I don't feel it."

"Raymond Shaw," he said.

"I'm listening."

Detached again. Eyes out of focus. But not as profoundly in a trance as Skeet had been.

Suppose the name activates the subject. Suppose the haiku then makes the subconscious accessible for instruction.

"Clear cascades," Dusty said, because it was the only haiku with which he was familiar.

Her eyes were glazed, but they didn't jiggle like Skeet's.

She hadn't responded to these lines last night, when she'd been falling asleep; and she wasn't going to respond to them now. Her trigger was *Raymond Shaw*, not *Dr. Yen Lo*, and her haiku was different from Skeet's.

Nevertheless, he said, "Into the waves scatter."

She blinked. "Scatter what?"

"You were gone again."

Regarding him dubiously, she said, "Then who kept my seat warm?"

"I'm serious. You were gone. Like Skeet but different. Just the name, just *Dr. Yen Lo*, and he got loosey-goosey, babbling about the rules, upset with me because I wasn't operating him correctly. But you're tighter, you just wait for the right thing to be said, and then if I don't have the verse to open you for instruction, you snap right out of it."

She looked at him as though he were addled.

"I'm not addled," he insisted.

"You're definitely *weirder* than when I married you. What's this stuff about Skeet?"

"Something bizarre happened at New Life yesterday. I haven't had a chance to tell you about it."

"Here's your chance."

He shook his head. "Later. Let's settle this first, prove to you what's happening. Do you have any candy in your mouth?"

"In my mouth?"

"Yeah. Did you finish that last piece you took, or is some of it still in your mouth?"

She slipped the half-dissolved chocolate morsel out of the pocket of her cheek, showed it to him on the tip of her tongue, and then tucked it away again. Holding the half-finished roll of candy toward him, she said, "But wouldn't you prefer an unused piece?"

Taking the roll from her, he said, "Swallow the candy."

"Sometimes I like to let it melt."

"You can let the next one melt," he said impatiently. "Come on, come on, swallow it."

"Definitely hypoglycemic."

"No, I'm irritable by nature," he said, peeling a chocolate from the roll. "Have you swallowed?"

She swallowed theatrically.

"No candy in your mouth?" he pressed. "It's gone? All of it?"

"Yeah, yeah. But what does this have to do with—"

"Raymond Shaw," Dusty said.

"I'm listening."

Eyes drifting out of focus, a subtle slackness pulling down on her face, mouth open expectantly, she waited for the haiku that he didn't know.

Instead of poetry, Dusty gave her candy, slipping the chocolate lozenge between her open lips, past her teeth, onto her tongue, which didn't even twitch when the treat touched it.

Even as Dusty leaned away from her, Martie blinked, started to finish the sentence that Dusty had interrupted with the name *Raymond Shaw*—and became aware of the candy in her mouth.

For her, this moment was equivalent to Dusty's finding the book in his hand again, magically, the *instant* after dropping it on the waiting-room floor. He had almost thrown the paperback across the room, in shock, before he'd checked himself. Martie wasn't able to check herself: She gasped with surprise, choked, coughed, and ejected the candy with immeasurably more force than a Pez dispenser, scoring a direct hit on his forehead.

"I thought you liked to let them melt," he said.

"It's melting."

As he wiped the candy off his forehead with a Kleenex, Dusty said, "You were gone for a few seconds."

"I was gone," she agreed, a tremor in her voice.

Her post-therapy glow was fading. She scrubbed nervously at her mouth with the back of her hand, pulled down the sun visor to examine her face in the small mirror, at once recoiled from her reflection, and flipped the visor up again. She shrank back in the seat.

"Skeet," she reminded him.

As succinctly as possible, Dusty told her about the plunge off the Sorensons' roof, the pages from the notepad in Skeet's kitchen, the episode at New Life, and his recent realization that he himself was experiencing at least brief periods of missing time. "Blackouts, fugues, whatever you want to call them."

"You, me, and Skeet," she said. She glanced at the paperback on the dashboard. "But . . . brainwashing?"

He was acutely aware of how outlandish his theory seemed, but the events of the past twenty-four hours lent it credibility, though without diminishing the absurdity factor. "Maybe, yeah. *Something's* happened to us. Something's . . . been done to us."

"Why us?"

He checked his wristwatch. "We better go. Have to meet Ned."

"What's Ned got to do with this?"

Starting the engine, Dusty said, "Nothing. I asked him to get some things for me."

As Dusty backed the car out of the parking slot, Martie said, "Back to the big question. Why us? Why is this happening to us?"

"Okay, I know what you're thinking. A housepainter, a video-game designer, and poor Skeet the feeb. Who would have anything to gain by messing with our minds, controlling us?"

Plucking the paperback off the dashboard, she said, "Why do they brainwash the guy in this story?"

"They turn him into an assassin who can never be traced back to the people who control him."

"You, me, and Skeet—assassins?"

"Until he shot John Kennedy, Lee Harvey Oswald was at least as big a nobody as we are."

"Gee, thanks."

"True. And Sirhan Sirhan. And John Hinckley."

Whether or not the sea would prove to be heavily marbled with black when eventually he saw it, Dusty was aware of a new downshift in his mood, now that the comforting ambience of the psychiatrist's office was far behind him. At the exit from the parking lot, when he came to the cashier's kiosk with its striped crossbar blocking the lane, the little building seemed to house a threat, as though it were a guard post at some remote, godforsaken border crossing high in the Balkans, where uniformed thugs with machine guns routinely robbed and sometimes murdered travelers. The cashier was a pleasant woman—thirtyish, pretty, somewhat chubby, with a butterfly barrette in her hair—but Dusty had the paranoid feeling that she was someone other than whom she appeared to be. When the crossbar rose and he drove out of the lot, half the cars passing in the street seemed likely to harbor surveillance teams assigned to track him.

52

On Newport Center Drive, the wind-shaken rows of towering palm trees tossed their fronds, as if warning Dusty off the route that he was driving.

Martie said, "Okay, if something like this was done to us—who did it?"

"In *The Manchurian Candidate*, it's the Soviets, the Chinese, and the North Koreans."

"The Soviet Union doesn't exist anymore," she noted. "Somehow, I can't see the three of us being the instruments of an elaborate conspiracy of Asian totalitarians."

"In the movies, it would probably be extraterrestrials."

"Great," she said sarcastically. "Let's call Fig Newton and tap into his vast store of knowledge on the subject."

"Or some giant corporation bent on turning us all into mindless, robotic consumers."

"I'm halfway there without their help," she said.

"A secret government agency, scheming politicians, Big Brother."

"That one's a little too real for comfort. But again—why us?"

"If it wasn't us, it would have to be somebody else."

"That's weak."

"I know," Dusty said, smoldering with more frustration than a monastery full of celibates.

From the shadowy regions of his mind, another answer teased him, glimmering dully but not bright enough for him to get a clear look at it. Indeed, every time he went into the shadows after it, the thought slipped away altogether.

He remembered the drawing of the forest that became a city when his preconceived perception of it changed. Here was another situation where he couldn't see the city for the trees.

He recalled, as well, the dream of the lightning and the heron. The inflation bulb of the sphygmomanometer had floated in midair, being compressed and released by an invisible hand. In that dream with him and Martie, there had been a third presence as transparent as a ghost.

That presence was their tormentor, whether an extraterrestrial or an agent of Big Brother, or someone else. Dusty suspected that if he were indeed operating according to some hypnotically implanted program, then his programmers had hobbled him with the suggestion that if he ever became suspicious, his suspicion would not fall on them but on a host of other suspects both probable and improbable, such as aliens and government agents. His enemy might cross his path at any moment but be as effectively invisible in real life as he was in the nightmare of the shrieking heron.

As Dusty turned right onto Pacific Coast Highway, Martie opened *The Manchurian Candidate* and scanned the first sentence in it, which contained the name that had triggered her mini-blackout. Dusty saw a chill shiver through her when she read it, but she didn't switch into that detached, anticipatory state.

Then she spoke it aloud, "Raymond Shaw," with no more serious effect than another brief shiver.

"Maybe it doesn't work on you properly when you read it or say it yourself," he suggested, "only when someone says it to you."

"Or maybe just by knowing the name, I've taken away its power over me."

"Raymond Shaw," he said.

"I'm listening."

When Martie returned to full consciousness after about ten seconds, Dusty said, "Welcome back. And so much for that theory."

Scowling at the book, she said, "We should take it home and burn it."

"No point doing that. There are clues in it. Secrets. Whoever put the book into your hands—and I tend to think you *didn't* just go out and buy it—whoever they are, they must be working the other side of the street from the people who programmed us. They want us to wise up to what's happening to us. And the book is a key. They gave you a key to unlock all this."

"Yeah? Why didn't they just walk up to me and say, 'Hey, lady, some people we know are screwing with your brain, planting autophobia in your head and lots more stuff you don't even know about yet, for reasons you couldn't even imagine, and we just don't like it much.' "

"Well, let's say it *is* some secret government agency, and inside the agency there's this small faction that's morally opposed to the project—"

"Opposed to Operation Brainwash Dusty, Skeet, and Martie."

"Yeah. But they can't come to us publicly."

"Why?" she persisted.

"Because they'd be killed. Or maybe it's just that they're afraid of being fired and losing their pensions."

"Morally opposed but not to the extent of losing their pensions. That part sounds creepily real. But the rest of it . . . So they slip me this book. Wink, wink, nudge, nudge. Then for some reason they seem to program me not to read it."

Dusty braked to a stop in a backup at a red traffic light. "A little lame, huh?"

"A lot lame."

They were on a bridge that spanned the channel between Newport Harbor and its back bay. Under the sun-less sky, the broad expanse of water was dark gray-green, though not black, with hatching drawn on it by the breeze above and the currents below, so that it looked scaly, like the hide of a fearsome slumbering reptile out of the Jurassic Period.

"But there's something that isn't lame," Martie said, "not in the least lame. Something that's happening to Susan."

A grimness in her voice drew Dusty's attention from the harbor. "What about Susan?"

"She's missing periods of time, too. Not little pieces, either. Big blocks of time. Whole nights."

The Valium veil in her eyes had been gradually lifting, that welcome but artificial calm giving way to anxiety once more. At Dr. Ahriman's office, the unnatural paleness left her, replaced by peachy color, but now shadows were gathering in the tender skin under her eyes, as though her face were darkening in sympathy with the slowly waning winter afternoon.

Beyond the farther end of the bridge, the red signal changed to green. The traffic began to move.

Martie told him about Susan's phantom rapist.

Dusty had been worried. He had been frightened. Now a feeling worse than worry or fear wrapped his heart.

Sometimes, when he woke in the abyss of night and lay listening to Martie's sweet soft breathing, a mortal dread—more terrible than simple fear—crept into him. After one too many glasses of wine at dinner, too much cream sauce, and perhaps a bitter clove of garlic, his mind was as sour as his stomach, and he contemplated the silence of the predawn world without his usual appreciation for the beauty of stillness, hearing no peace in it, hearing instead the threat of the void. In spite of the faith that was his rock through most of his life, a worm of doubt chewed at his heart on these hushed nights, and he wondered if all that he and Martie had together was this one life, and nothing beyond it but a darkness that allowed no memory and was empty even of loneliness. He didn't want until-death-do-you-part, didn't want anything short of forever, and when a despairing inner voice suggested that forever was a fraud, he always reached out in the night to touch Martie in her sleep. His intention was not to wake her, only to feel in her what she invariably contained and what was detectable to even his lightest touch: her given grace, her immortality and the promise of his own.

Now, as he listened to Martie recount Susan's story, Dusty was an apple to the worm of doubt again. Everything that was happening to all of them seemed unreal, meaningless, a glimpse into the chaos underlying life. He was overcome by a feeling that the end, when it arrived, would be only the end, not also a beginning, and he sensed that it was coming fast, too, a cruel and brutal death toward which they were hurtling blindly.

When Martie finished, Dusty handed his cell phone to her. "Try Susan again."

She placed the call. The number rang and rang. And rang.

"Let's go see if the retirees downstairs know where she's gone," Martie suggested. "It's not far."

"Ned will be waiting for us. As soon as I pick up what he's got for me, we'll go to Susan's. But for sure, it can't be Eric creeping around there at night."

"Because whoever is doing this to her, he's one of them behind what's happening to you, me, Skeet."

"Yeah. And Eric, hell, he's an investment adviser, a numbers cruncher, not a mind-control wizard."

Martie keyed Susan's number in again. She pressed the phone tightly to her ear. Her face was pinched by the strain of wishing fervently for an answer.

53

Ned Motherwell's pride was an '82 Chevy Camaro: unpainted but with a periodically reapplied coat of flat-gray primer, chopped, fitted with frenched headlights, stripped of brightwork except for a pair of fat chrome tailpipes. Parked in the southeast corner of the shopping-center lot where they had arranged to meet, it looked like a getaway car.

As Dusty parked two spaces away, Ned climbed out of the Camaro, and though it was by no definition a subcompact, there seemed to be a lot more of Ned than there was vehicle. He towered over the low, customized car as he closed the door. Although the day was cool and the afternoon fading, he wore only white khakis and a white T-shirt, as usual. If the Camaro ever broke down, he appeared to be capable of carrying it to the garage.

The trees along the periphery of the lot trembled in the wind, and little funnels of dust and litter spun across the pavement, but Ned appeared unaffected by—and even unaware of—the turbulence.

When Dusty lowered his window, Ned looked in past him, smiled, and said, "Hey, Martie."

"Hey, Ned."

"Sorry to hear you're not feeling well."

"I'll live, they say."

On the phone from Ahriman's waiting room, Dusty had said that Martie was ill and didn't feel well enough to go into a pharmacy or a bookstore, and that he didn't want to leave her alone in the car.

"It's hard enough working for this guy," Ned told Martie, "so I imagine how sick you must get living with him. No offense, boss."

"None taken."

Ned passed a small bag from the pharmacy through the window. It contained the prescription for Valium that Dr. Closterman had phoned in earlier. He also had a larger bag from the bookstore.

"If you'd asked me this morning what haiku is," Ned said, "I'd have told you it's some kind of martial art like tae kwon do. But it's all these chopped poems."

"Chopped?" Dusty asked, peering into the bag.

"Like my car," Ned said. "Cut down, streamlined. They're kind of cool. Bought one book for myself."

Dusty saw seven collections of haiku in the bag. "So many."

"They've got this long shelf full of the stuff," Ned said. "For such a little thing, haiku's big."

"I'll cut you a check for all this tomorrow."

"No hurry. Used my credit card. Won't come due for a while."

Dusty passed Martie's house key through the window to Ned. "Are you sure you've got time to take care of Valet?"

"I'm on for it. But I don't know dogs."

"Not much to know." Dusty told him where to find the kibble. "Give him two cups. Then he'll expect a walk, but just let him into the backyard again for ten minutes, and he'll do the right thing."

"Then he'll be okay in the house alone?"

"As long as he's got a full water dish and the TV remote, he'll be happy."

"My mom is a cat woman," Ned said. "Not *the* Catwoman, like in *Batman*, but she always has a kitty-cat."

Hearing big Ned say *kitty-cat* was akin to seeing an

NFL fullback break into ballet steps and execute a perfect entrechat.

"Once, a neighbor poisoned an orange tabby my mom really loved. Mrs. Jingles. That was the cat's name, not the neighbor's."

"What kind of person would poison a cat?" Dusty commiserated.

"He was running a crystal-meth lab out of the rental next door," Ned said. "Piece of human garbage. I broke both his legs, called 911, pretending I was him, said I fell down the stairs, needed help. They sent an ambulance, saw the meth lab, busted his operation."

"You broke the legs of a drug thug?" Martie said. "Isn't that risky?"

"Not really. Couple nights later, one of his pals takes a shot at me, but he's so whacked on speed he misses. I broke both his arms, put him in his car, pushed it over an embankment. Called 911, said I was him, cried for help. They found dirty money and drugs in the car trunk, fixed his arms, and put him away for ten years."

"All this for a cat?" Dusty wondered.

"Mrs. Jingles was a nice cat. Plus she was my mom's."

Martie said, "I feel Valet's in good hands."

Smiling, nodding, Ned said, "I wouldn't let anything bad happen to your puppy."

On the peninsula, on Balboa Boulevard, a few blocks from Susan's place, Martie was paging through a haiku collection when she gasped, dropped the book, and huddled forward in the seat, her body clenched as though in pain. "Pull over. Pull over now, hurry, pull over."

Not pain, fear. That she would seize the wheel. Swing the car into oncoming traffic. The by now familiar the-monster-lurks-in-me blues.

In summer, with the beach crowds, Dusty would probably have had to cruise through an hour-long panic attack to find a parking place. January allowed a quick move to the curb.

On the sidewalk, a few kids whistled past on in-line skates, looking for senior citizens to knock into nursing homes. Bicyclists pumped past on the left, on a quest for death by traffic.

No one showed any interest in Dusty and Martie. That might change if she started screaming again.

He considered how best to restrain her if she began to bash her head against the dashboard. There was no low-risk way to do it. In her panic, she would strenuously resist, try to wrench free, and he would inadvertently hurt her.

"I love you," he said helplessly.

Then he began to talk to her, just talk quietly, as she rocked in her seat, gasped for breath, and groaned like a woman coping with early labor pains, her panic struggling to be born. He didn't try to reason with her or coddle her with words, because she already knew how irrational this was. Instead, he talked about their first date.

It had been a fine disaster. He had raved about the restaurant, but in the six weeks since he'd last been there, the ownership had changed. The new chef evidently received his training at the Culinary Institute of Rural Iceland, because the food was cold and every dish had an undertaste of volcanic ash. The busboy spilled a glass of water on Dusty, and Dusty spilled a glass of water on Martie, and their waiter spilled a boat of cream sauce on himself. The fire in the kitchen, during dessert, was minor enough to be doused without the fire department, but major enough to require one busboy, one waiter, the maître d', and the sous-chef (a large Samoan gentleman) to battle it with four extinguishers—though perhaps they required such an ocean of suppressant foam because they got more of it on one another than on the flames. After leaving the restaurant, starving, over a desperate make-good dinner at a coffee shop, Dusty and Martie had laughed so hard that they were bonded forever.

Neither of them was laughing now, but the bond was stronger than ever. Whether it was Dusty's quiet talk, the lingering effects of Valium, or Dr. Ahriman's influence, Martie didn't descend into a full-fledged panic attack. Within two or three minutes, her fear diminished, and she sat up straight in her seat again.

"Better," she said. "But I still feel like shit."

"Birdshit," he reminded her.

"Yeah."

Although nearly an hour of daylight remained, more than half the passing cars, whether going up or down the peninsula, traveled behind headlights. The sludge moving slowly west to east across the sky was ushering in an early and protracted twilight.

Dusty switched on the lights and pulled into a gap in traffic.

"Thanks for that," Martie said.

"I didn't know what else to do."

"Next time, just talk again. Your voice. It grounds me."

He wondered how long it would be until he could hold her close, without her stiffening in fear, without that glitter of incipient panic in her eyes. How long, if ever?

The grumbling sea tried to shoulder its way out of the deeps and claim the continent, while the wind-coaxed beach spread sandy fingers across the promenade, stealing the pavement.

Three gulls clung to angled perches along the stair railing, sentinels on a sea watch, trying to decide whether to abandon the blustery shore for more-sheltered roosts inland.

As Martie and Dusty climbed the steep stairs to the third-floor landing, the birds took flight, one at a time, each of them surfing eastward on tumbling waves of air. Though gulls are never taciturn, not one of these let out a cry as it departed.

Martie knocked on the door, waited, and knocked again, but Susan didn't answer.

She used her key to unlock the two dead bolts. She opened the door and called Susan's name, twice, but received no response.

They scrubbed their shoes on the coarse mat and went inside, closing the door behind them and calling her name again, louder.

Gloom filled the kitchen, but lights were on in the dining room.

"Susan?" Martie repeated, but again she went unanswered.

The apartment was full of conversation, but all the voices were those of the wind talking to itself. Chattering against the cedar-shingled roof. Hooting and jubilant in the eaves. Whistling at any chink and whispering at every window.

Darkness in the living room, all the shades down, drapes drawn. Darkness in the hall, too, but light spilling out of the bedroom, where the door stood wide. A hard fluorescent glow in the bath, the door only half open.

Hesitant, calling for Susan again, Martie went into the bedroom.

Hand on the bathroom door, even before he began to push it open, Dusty knew. The fragrance of rose water unsuccessfully masked an odor that vast trellises of roses could not have defeated.

She was not Susan anymore. Facial swelling from bacterial gas, greening of the skin, eyes goggling from the pressure in the skull, purge fluid draining from nostrils and mouth, that grotesque lolling of the tongue that makes each of us a dog in death: Thanks to the accelerant factor of the hot water in which she had died, she was already reduced by nature's tiniest civilizations to the stuff of nightmares.

He saw the notepad on the vanity by the sink, the neat lines of handwriting, and suddenly his leaping heart was pumping as much terror as blood, not a terror of the poor dead woman in the tub, not a cheap horror-movie scare, but icy fear of what this meant for him and Martie and Skeet. He saw through this tableau at once, intuited the truth of it, and knew they were even more vulnerable than they had imagined, vulnerable to one another, vulnerable each to himself, in a way and to a degree that almost justified Martie's autophobia.

Before he had read more than a few words of the note, he heard Martie call his name, heard her coming out of the bedroom into the hall. He turned at once and moved forward, blocking her. "No."

As though she saw everything in his eyes that he had seen in the bathroom, she said, "Oh, God. Oh, tell me no, tell me not her."

She tried to push past him, but he held her and forced her back toward the living room. "You don't want a goodbye like this."

Something tore in her, which he had seen torn only once before, at the deathbed in the hospital, on the night her father had conceded victory to the cancer, rending her into limp rags of emotion, so that she could walk no more easily than a rag doll could walk, could stand no more erectly than the straw-stuffed rags of a scarecrow could ever stand without its props.

Half carried to the living-room sofa, Martie dropped there, in tears. She clawed a needlepoint pillow from an arrangement of them, and hugged it against her chest, hugged it fiercely, as though with the pillow she were trying to staunch her hemorrhaging heart.

While the wind pretended to mourn, Dusty called 911, though the emergency here had ended long hours ago.

54

With the blustery afternoon huffing at their backs, preceded by the fumes of wintergreen breath mints masking the reek of a garlic-rich lunch, two uniformed officers arrived first.

The mood in the apartment—set by Martie's quiet grieving, by Dusty's murmured sympathy, by the spirit voices of the haunting wind—had thus far allowed for the unreasonable thread of fragile hope that holds the heart together in the immediate aftermath of death. Dusty was aware of it in himself, in spite of what he'd seen: the crazy, desperate, so dimly burning, yet not quickly extinguished, pitiable desire to believe that an awful mistake has been made, that the deceased isn't deceased, but merely unconscious or in a coma, or sleeping, and that she will wake up and walk into the room and wonder what their glum faces signify. He had seen Susan's greenish pallor, the darkening of the flesh along her throat, her bloated face, the purge fluid; and yet a tiny irrational inner voice argued that maybe he had seen only shadows, tricks of light, which he'd misinterpreted. In Martie, who had not viewed the corpse, this faint mad hope must inevitably have had a stronger grip than in Dusty.

The cops put an end to hope merely by their presence. They were polite, soft-spoken, professional, but they were also big men, tall and solid, and by their size alone they imposed a hard reality that crowded out false hope. Their slanguage between themselves—"D.B." meaning *dead body,* "a probable 10-56" for *a case of apparent suicide*—pinned down the certainty of death with words, and the crackle of messages issuing from the transceiver clipped to one of their utility belts was the eerie voice of fate, unintelligible but unignorable.

Two additional uniformed officers arrived, followed closely by a pair of plainclothes detectives, and in the wake of the detectives were a man and a woman from the medical examiner's office. As the first two men had robbed the moment of hope, this larger group quite unintentionally stole from death its mystery and special dignity, by approaching it as an accountant approaches ledgers, with a workaday respect for routine and a seen-it-all detachment.

The cops had a lot of questions but fewer than Dusty expected, largely because the circumstances of the scene and the condition of the body provided nearly unimpeachable support for a determination of suicide. The declaration of the deceased, on four pages of the notepad, was explicit as to motivation yet contained enough emotion—and enough instances of the particular incoherence of despair—to appear authentic.

Martie identified the handwriting as Susan's. Comparisons with an unmailed letter from Susan to her mother and with samples from her address book all but eliminated any possibility of forgery. If the investigation raised any suspicion of homicide, a handwriting expert would provide an analysis.

Martie was also singularly qualified to confirm, as claimed in the suicide note, that Susan Jagger had been suffering from severe agoraphobia for sixteen months, that her career had been destroyed, that her marriage had fallen apart, and that she was enduring bouts of depression. Her protests that Susan was nevertheless far from suicidal sounded, even to Dusty, like nothing more than sad attempts to protect a good friend's reputation and to prevent Susan's memory from being tarnished.

Besides, Martie's emotional self-reproach, voiced not so much to the police or to Dusty as to herself, made it clear that she was convinced this was suicide. She blamed herself for not being here when Susan needed her, for not calling Susan the previous evening and, perhaps, interrupting her with the razor blade in hand.

Before the authorities arrived, Dusty and Martie had agreed not to mention Susan's story of a ghostly night visitor who left behind a very unghostly tablespoon or two of biological evidence. Martie thought this tale would only convince the police that Susan was unstable, even flaky, further damaging her reputation.

She also worried that broaching this sensitive subject would lead to questions requiring the revelation of her autophobia. She was loath to expose herself to their gimlet-eyed interrogation and cold psychologizing. She hadn't harmed Susan, but if she began to expound on her conviction that she had an exceptional potential for violence, the detectives would put a pin in their determination of suicide and would bulldog her for hours until they were certain that her fear of self was as irrational as it seemed to be. And if the stress of all this brought on another panic attack while they were present to witness it, the cops might even decide that she was a danger to herself and to others, committing her against her will to a psychiatric ward for seventy-two hours, which was within their authority.

"I couldn't tolerate being in a place like that," Martie had told Dusty before the first police arrived. "Locked up. Watched. I couldn't handle it."

"Won't happen," he had promised.

He shared her reasons for wanting to keep quiet about Susan's phantom rapist, but he had another reason, too, which he hadn't yet disclosed to her. He was convinced, as Martie only wished she were, that Susan had not killed herself, at least not with volition or with awareness of what she was doing. If he revealed this to the police, however, and even made a *failed* attempt to convince them that here was an extraordinary case involving faceless conspirators and wildly effective techniques of mind control, then he and Martie would be dead, one way or another, before the week was out.

And this was already Wednesday.

Since discovering Dr. Yen Lo in that novel, and especially since discovering the paperback magically returned to his shaky hands after it fell onto the waiting-room floor, Dusty had been burdened by a rapidly growing sense of danger. A clock was ticking. He couldn't see the clock, couldn't hear it, but he could feel the reverberation of each hard tick in his bones. Time was running out for him and for Martie. Indeed, with the weight of his fear now grown so great, he was concerned that the cops would detect his anxiety, misunderstand it, and grow suspicious.

Susan's mother, who lived in Arizona with a new husband, was notified by telephone, as was her father, who lived in Santa Barbara with a new wife. Both were on their way. After the case detective, Lieutenant Bizmet, had quizzed Martie as to the seriousness of the estrangement between Susan and her husband, he called Eric, too, got an answering machine, and left his name, rank, and number, but not any news.

Bizmet, a formidable bulk with buzz-cut blond hair and a stare as direct as a drill bit, was telling Dusty that they were no longer needed here, when Martie was hit by a spasm of autophobia.

Dusty recognized the signs of the seizure. The sudden alarm in her eyes. The pinched expression. Her face a whiter shade of pale.

She dropped to the sofa from which she had just risen, bent forward, hugging herself and rocking, as she had done in the car earlier, shuddering and gasping for breath.

This time, in the company of cops, he wasn't able to talk her down with reminiscences of their dating days. He could only stand by helplessly, praying that this would not escalate into an all-out panic attack.

To Dusty's surprise, Lieutenant Bizmet mistook Martie's autophobic misery for another seizure of grief. He stood looking down at her with evident dismay, awkwardly spoke a few consoling words, and cast a sympathetic expression at Dusty.

Some of the other cops glanced at Martie and then returned to their various tasks and conversations, their bloodhound instinct failing to catch the scent.

"Does she drink?" Bizmet asked Dusty.

"Does she what?" he replied, so tense that he was at first unable to puzzle out the meaning of the word *drink*, as though it were Swahili. "Oh, drink, yes, a little. Why?"

"Take her to a nice bar, pour a few into her, blur the edge off her nerves."

"Good advice," Dusty agreed.

"But not you," Bizmet amended with a scowl.

Heart leaping, Dusty said, "What?"

"A few drinks for her but just one for you if you're driving."

"Sure, of course. Never had a citation. Don't ever want one."

Martie rocked, shook, gasped, and had the presence of mind to throw in a few stifled sobs of grief. She shook off the seizure in a minute or two, as she'd done in the car on the way here.

With Bizmet's thanks and sympathies, after only one hour in the apartment, they were on their way into a day grown dark.

The afternoon's bluster had not faded with the early winter twilight. Its cool breath scented with Pacific brine and with the iodine in snarls of seaweed that lay withering on the nearby shore, the wind harried Dusty and Martie, huffing and squealing as though with accusations of cover-up and guilt.

In the chaotic rattle and click of clashing palm fronds, Dusty heard the half-masked, rhythmic ticking of a clock. He heard it, too, in their footsteps on the promenade, in the action of a three-foot-high decorative windmill that stood on the patio of one of the ocean-facing houses that they passed, and between each half of his two-part heartbeat. Time running out.

55

Davy Crockett was bravely defending the Alamo, but not solely with the support of his usual compatriots. This time Davy had the help of Eliot Ness and a considerable force of G-men.

One might expect that submachine guns, had they been available to the stalwart men at the Alamo, would have altered the historical outcome of that battle in 1836. After all, the Gatling gun, which was the first crude version of the machine gun, wouldn't be invented for another twenty-six years. Indeed, automatic rifles weren't in use at that time, and the most-advanced weapons in the hands of the combatants were muzzle-loaders.

Unfortunately for the defenders of the Alamo, this time they were under siege by both Mexican soldiers *and* a bunch of ruthless Prohibition-era gangsters with submachine guns of their own. The combination of Al Capone's vicious cunning and General Santa Anna's talent for military strategy might be more than Crockett and Ness could handle.

The doctor briefly considered complicating this epic battle by introducing spacemen and futuristic weapons from his Galaxy Command collection. He resisted this childish temptation, because experience had taught him that the greater number of anachronistic elements he combined on a board, the less satisfying the game. To be engrossing, a play session required him to control his flamboyant imagination and stick strictly to a scenario with one clever but believable concept. Frontiersmen, Mexican soldiers, G-men, gangsters, *and* spacemen would be just too silly.

Dressed comfortably in black ninja-style pajamas with a scarlet silk belt, barefoot, the doctor slowly circled the board, craftily analyzing the positions of the opposing armies. As he reconnoitered, he rattled a pair of dice in a casting cup.

His immense game board was actually an eight-foot-square table that stood in the center of the room. These sixty-four square feet of terrain could be redesigned for each new game, using his large collection of custom-crafted topographical elements.

The big room, thirty feet square, otherwise contained only an armchair and a small table to hold a telephone and snacks.

Currently, the only illumination came from the downlights in the ceiling directly over the game board. The rest of the room lay in shadows.

All four walls were lined with floor-to-ceiling display shelves on which were stored hundreds of plastic playsets in their original boxes. Most of the boxes were in mint or near-mint condition, and none could be rated less than excellent. Each set contained all its original complement of figures, buildings, and accessories.

Ahriman acquired only Marx playsets, those produced by Louis Marx during the 1950s, 1960s, and 1970s. The miniature figures in these sets were wonderfully detailed, beautifully produced, and sold for hundreds—even thousands—of dollars on the rare-toy market. In addition to the Alamo and Untouchables sets, his collection included Adventures of Robin Hood, American Patrol, Armored Attack, Ben Hur, Battleground, Captain Gallant of the Foreign Legion, Fort Apache, Roy Rogers Rodeo Ranch, Tom Corbett Space Academy, and scores of others, many in duplicate and triplicate, which allowed him to populate the tabletop with a large cast of characters.

This evening, the doctor was in an exceptionally fine mood. The game on the board before him promised to be tremendous fun. Better yet, his other and far bigger game, being played in the world beyond this room, was getting more interesting by the hour.

Mr. Rhodes was reading *The Manchurian Candidate.* Most likely, Dustin would lack the imagination and the intellect to absorb all the clues in that novel and wouldn't be able to build upon them enough to understand the web in which he was caught. His prospects of saving himself and his wife were still dismal, though better than they had been before he'd cracked open the book.

Only a hopeless narcissist, megalomaniac, or other psychotic would engage in any sport year after year, if he knew in advance that he would win every time. For the true—and well-balanced—gamesman, an element of doubt, at least a soupçon of suspense, was required to make the game worth playing. He must test his skills and challenge chance, not to be fair to the other players—fairness was for fools—but to keep himself sharp and to ensure amusement.

Always, the doctor salted his scenarios with traps for himself. Often, the traps were not triggered, but the *possibility* of disaster, when it loomed, was invigorating and kept him nimble. He loved this impish aspect of himself, and he indulged it.

He had, for instance, permitted Susan Jagger to be aware of the semen that he left in her. He could have instructed her to remain oblivious of this distasteful evidence, and she would have blocked it from her mind. By allowing her awareness and by suggesting that she direct her suspicion at her estranged husband, the doctor had established powerful character dynamics, the consequences of which he could not predict. Indeed, this had led to the near thing with the videotape, which was the *last* development that he could have imagined.

Among other traps in this game was *The Manchurian Candidate*. He had given the paperback to Martie, instructing her to forget from whom she had received it. He implanted the notion that during each of Susan's sessions, Martie was reading a little of the novel, though she was actually reading none at all, and he inadequately supported this suggestion by seeding in her a few sentences of an improbably general nature, which she could use to describe the story if Susan or anyone else asked her about it. If Martie's feeble, wooden description of the book had puzzled Susan, perhaps she might have delved into it, discovering connections to her real-life dilemma. Martie herself was not strictly forbidden from reading the novel, only discouraged from doing so, and eventually she might overcome that discouragement when Ahriman least expected. Instead, for whatever reason, Mr. Rhodes had gone fishing in this fiction.

Where does fiction end and reality begin? That is the essence of the game.

As the doctor circled the big table, wondering whether Crockett or Capone would be victorious, his black ninja pajamas rustled with silken sibilance. *Rattle-rattle*, the dice in the cup.

If asked, the interior designers would say that the theme was contemporary bistro, Italian modern. They wouldn't be lying, or necessarily disingenuous, but their answer would be beside the point. All this glossy dark wood and black marble, all these sleek polished surfaces, the vulviform amber-onyx sconces, the long back-bar mural of a Rousseau-like jungle with vegetation more lush than any in reality and with mysterious feline eyes peering from between rain-jeweled leaves—all this spoke to one theme and one theme only: sex.

Half the place was a restaurant, the other half a bar, connected by a massive archway flanked by mahogany columns on marble plinths. This early in the evening, with workers just getting out of offices, the bar was crowded with affluent young singles on the prowl more aggressively than any jungle cats, but the dining room wasn't yet busy.

The hostess seated Dusty and Martie in a booth with such high backs on its leather seats that it was virtually a private space, open on only one side to the room.

Martie was uneasy about being in such a public place, chancing utter mortification if she were stricken by an all-stops-pulled panic attack. She drew strength from the fact that her recent seizures, since leaving Dr. Ahriman's office, had been comparatively mild and of brief duration.

In spite of the risk of humiliation, she would rather eat here than in the shelter of her kitchen. She was reluctant to go home, where the untidied wreckage in the garage would remind her of her demented, manic determination to rid her house of potential weapons.

More daunting than the garage or other reminders of her loss of control, the answering machine waited in her study. On it, as sure as Halloween came in October, was a message from Susan, dating to the previous evening.

Duty and honor would not permit Martie to erase the tape without hearing it, nor was she able to allow herself to delegate that grim responsibility to Dusty. She owed Susan this personal attention.

Before she would be able to listen to that beloved voice and be prepared to bear the greater guilt that it would surely induce, she needed to polish up her courage. And wash down some fortitude.

As law-abiding citizens, they followed Lieutenant Bizmet's advice: a bottle of Heineken for Dusty, Sierra Nevada for Martie.

With her first chug of beer, she chased a Valium, in

spite of the warning on the pharmacy bottle, which cautioned about mixing benzodiazepines and alcohol.

Live hard, die young. Or die young anyway. Those seemed to be the choices facing them.

"If only I'd called her back last night," Martie said.

"You weren't in any condition to call her. You couldn't have helped her anyway."

"Maybe, if I'd heard it in her voice, I could have gotten help *for* her."

"It wouldn't have been in her voice. Not what you mean, not some worse note of depression, not suicidal despair."

"We'll never know," she said bleakly.

"I know, all right," Dusty insisted. "You wouldn't have heard suicidal despair because she didn't commit suicide."

Ness was already dead, an early casualty, a devastation to the defenders of the Alamo!

The noble lawman had been killed by a paper clip.

The doctor removed the little plastic cadaver from the board.

To determine which game piece in which army would open fire next, and to decide what weapon would be used, Ahriman employed a complex formula with calculations that derived from the roll of the dice and a blind draw from a deck of playing cards.

The only weapons were a paper clip fired from a rubber band and a marble shot with a snap of the thumb. Of course, these two simple devices could symbolize many dreadful deaths: by arrow, by gun, by cannonade, by bowie knife, by a hatchet in the face. . . .

Regrettably, it was not in the nature of plastic-toy figures to commit suicide, and it would be an unconscionable insult to America and its people to suggest that men like

Davy Crockett and Eliot Ness were even capable of considering self-destruction. These board games, therefore, lacked that intriguing dimension.

In the bigger game, where plastic was flesh and blood was real, another suicide would have to be engineered soon. Skeet had to go.

Initially, when the doctor had conceived this game, he believed that Holden "Skeet" Caulfield would be the star player, neck deep in the slaughter, come the final bloodbath. His face first on all the news programs. His screwy name immortalized in criminal legend, as infamous as Charles Manson.

Perhaps because his brain had been scorched with so many drugs since childhood, Skeet proved to be a poor subject for programming. His powers of concentration—even when in a hypnotic state!—were not good, and he had difficulty subconsciously retaining the rudimentary code lines of his psychological conditioning. Instead of the usual three programming sessions, the doctor had needed to devote six to Skeet, and subsequently the need had arisen for a few shorter—but unprecedented—repair sessions in which deteriorating aspects of his program were reinstalled.

Occasionally, Skeet even surrendered himself for control after hearing only *Dr. Yen Lo*, the activating name, and Ahriman didn't need to lead him through the haiku. The security risk posed by this easy access was intolerable.

Sooner rather than later, Skeet would have to take a paper clip, figuratively speaking. He should have died Tuesday morning. Later this evening, for sure.

The dice tumbled to a nine. The deck of cards gave up a queen of diamonds.

Swiftly calculating, Ahriman determined that the next shot would come from a figure positioned at the southwest corner of the Alamo roof: one of Eliot Ness' loyal subordinates. No doubt, the grieving G-man would be hot for vengeance. His weapon was a marble, which had greater lethal potential than a mere paper clip, and with the benefit of his high vantage point, he might be able to deliver extreme woe to the surrounding Mexican soldiers and to the gangland scumbags who would rue the day they agreed to do Al Capone's dirty work.

"She didn't commit suicide," Dusty repeated, speaking softly, leaning forward conspiratorially in the booth, even though the roar of voices from the bar prevented anyone from eavesdropping.

The certainty in his voice left Martie speechless. Slashed wrists. No indications of a struggle. A suicide note in Susan's handwriting. The determination of self-destruction was irrefutable.

Dusty held up his right hand, and with each point he made, he let a finger spring from his clenched fist. "One—yesterday at New Life, Skeet was activated by the name *Dr. Yen Lo* and then together we stumbled to the haiku that allowed me to access his subconscious for programming."

"Programming," she said doubtfully. "This is still so hard to believe."

"Programming is how I see it. He was waiting for instructions. *Missions*, he called them. Two—when I became frustrated with him and told him he should give me a break and just go to sleep, he went out instantly. He *obeyed* what seemed like an impossible order. I mean, how can you drop off to sleep in a blink, at will? Three—earlier yesterday, when he was going to jump off the roof, he said someone had *told* him to jump."

"Yeah, the angel of death."

"Granted, he was whacked on something. But that doesn't mean there wasn't some truth in what he said. Four—in *The Manchurian Candidate*, the brainwashed soldier is capable of committing murder on the direction of his controller, then forgetting every detail of what he's done, but, get this, he'll also follow instructions to kill himself if necessary."

"It's just a thriller."

"Yeah, I know. The writing's good. The plot is entertaining, and the characters are colorful. You're enjoying it."

Because she had no answer to that, Martie drank more beer.

General Santa Anna was dead, and history was being rewritten. Al Capone must now assume command of the combined forces of Mexico and the Chicago underworld.

The goody-two-shoes bunch defending the Alamo had better not start celebrating just yet. Santa Anna was a formidable strategist; but Capone had him beat for sheer ruthlessness.

Once, the real Capone, not this plastic figure, had tortured a snitch with a hand drill. He locked the guy's head in a machine-shop vice, and with henchmen holding the turncoat's arms and legs, old Al had personally cranked the drill handle, driving a diamond-tipped bit through the terrified man's forehead.

Once, the doctor had killed a woman with a drill, but it had been a Black & Decker power model.

Dusty said, "Condon's book is fiction, sure, but you get a sense that the psychological-control techniques described in it are based on sound research, that what he proposes as fiction was pretty much possible even at that time. And Martie, the book is set *almost fifty years in the past.* Before we had jet airliners."

"Before we went to the moon."

"Yeah. Before we had cell phones, microwave ovens, and fat-free potato chips with a diarrhea warning on the bag.

Just imagine what specialists in mind control might be able to do now, with unlimited resources and no conscience." He paused for Heineken. Then: "Five—Dr. Ahriman said it was *incredible* that both you and Susan should be stricken with such extreme phobias. He—"

"You know, he's probably right that mine is related to Susan's, that it comes from my sense of failure to help her, from my—"

Dusty shook his head and folded his fingers into a fist again. "Or your phobia and hers were implanted, programmed into you as part of an experiment or for some other reason that makes no damn sense."

"But Dr. Ahriman never even suggested—"

Impatiently, Dusty said, "He's a great psychiatrist, okay, and he's committed to his patients. But he's conditioned by education and experience to look for psychological cause and effect, for some *trauma* in your past that caused your condition. Maybe that's why Susan didn't seem to be making much progress, because there isn't any trauma to blame. And, Martie, if they can program you to fear yourself, to have all these violent visions, to do the things you did at the house yesterday . . . what else could they make you do?"

Maybe it was the beer. Maybe it was the Valium. Maybe it was even Dusty's logic. Whatever the reason, Martie found his argument increasingly compelling.

Her name was Viveca Scofield. She was a starlet slut, twenty-five years younger than the doctor's father, even three years younger than the doctor himself, who at that time was twenty-eight. While playing the second lead in the old man's latest film, she had used all her considerable wiles to set him up for marriage.

Even if the doctor hadn't yearned to escape his dad's shadow and make a name for himself, he would have had to deal with Viveca before she became Mrs. Josh Ahriman and either schemed to control the family fortune or squandered it.

As savvy as Dad was in the ways of Hollywood, as talented as he was at screwing associates and browbeating even the most vicious and psychotic studio bosses, he was also a widower of fifteen years and the champion crier of his time, as vulnerable in some ways as he was imperviously armored in others. Viveca would have married him, found a way to drive him to an early death, eaten his liver with chopped onions the night before the funeral, and then cast his son out of the mansion with nothing but a used Mercedes and a token monthly stipend.

In the interest of justice, therefore, the doctor was prepared to eliminate Viveca on the same night that he killed his father. He prepared a second syringe of the ultrashort-acting thiobarbital and paraldehyde, intending to inject it into something she might eat or directly into the starlet herself.

When the great director lay dead in the library, felled by the poisoned petits fours, but before surgery had been performed on his lacrimal apparatus, the doctor had gone in search of Viveca and had found her in his father's bed. A bobinga-wood crack pipe and other drug paraphernalia littered the nightstand, and a book of poetry was on the rumpled sheets beside her. The starlet was snoring like a bear that had gorged on late-season berries half fermented on the vine, spit bubbles swelling and popping on her lips.

She was as naked as nature had made her, and because nature had obviously been in a lascivious mood at the time, the young doctor got all sorts of hot ideas. A lot of money was at stake here, however, and money was power, and power was better than sex.

Earlier in the day, during a private moment, he and Viveca had gotten into an ugly little argument that ended when she coyly noted that she had never seen him well up with emotion the way his father did so routinely. "We're alike, you and me," she said. "Your father got his share of tears *and* yours, while I used up all of mine by the time I was eight. We're both bone-dry. Now, the problem for you, boy doctor, is that you've still got some little withered lump of a heart, but I don't have any heart at all. So if you try to turn your old man against me, I'll castrate you and have you singing show tunes, soprano, for my dinner entertainment every night."

The memory of this threat gave the doctor an idea better than sex.

He went to the far end of the three-acre estate, to the lavishly equipped tool room and woodworking shop housed in the building that also contained, upstairs, the apartments of the couple that managed the estate, Mr. and Mrs. Haufbrock, and the handyman-groundskeeper, Earl Ventnor. The Haufbrocks were away on a one-week vacation, and Earl was no doubt passed out after his nightly patriotic effort to ensure that the American brewing industry would not be driven into bankruptcy by competition from foreign beers.

Without the need to skulk, therefore, the doctor selected a Black & Decker power drill from the collection of tools. He had the presence of mind also to take a twenty-foot, orange extension cord.

In his father's bedroom once more, he plugged the extension cord into a wall outlet, plugged the drill into the extension cord, and thus equipped, climbed onto the bed with Viveca, straddling her but remaining on his knees. She was so doped that she snored through all his preparations, and he had to shout her name repeatedly to wake her. When she finally came around, blinking stupidly, she smiled up at him, as if she believed he was someone other than who he was, as if she thought the power drill was an elaborate new Swedish vibrator.

Thanks to the superb instruction provided by the Harvard Medical School, the doctor was able to position the half-inch steel bit with pinpoint accuracy. To the confused and smiling Viveca, he said, "If you don't have a heart, something else must be in there, and the best way to identify it is take a core sample."

The shriek of the powerful little Black & Decker motor brought her out of her drug stupor. By then, however, the drilling operation was under way and in fact nearly completed.

After taking time just to appreciate the loveliness of Viveca being dead, the doctor noticed the book of poetry that lay open on the sheets. A whorl of blood soiled both exposed pages, but in a pristine circle of white paper in the middle of the crimson stain were three lines of verse.

This phantasm
of falling petals vanishes into
moon and flowers . . .

He did not know then that the poem was a haiku, that it had been written by Okyo in 1890, that it was about the poet's own impending death, and that, like many haiku, it didn't translate into English with the ideal five-seven-five syllable pattern in which it was composed in the original Japanese.

What he *did* know was that this tiny poem moved him unexpectedly, profoundly, as he'd never been moved before. The verse expressed, as Ahriman himself could never express it, his heretofore half-repressed and formless sense of his mortality. Okyo's three lines brought him instantly and poignantly in touch with the terrible sad truth that he, too, was destined eventually to die. He, too, was a phantasm, as fragile as any flower, one day to drop like wilting petals.

As he knelt on the bed and held the book of haiku in both hands, reading those three lines over and over again, having forgotten the drill-pierced starlet whom he still straddled, the doctor felt his chest tighten and his throat thicken with emotion at the prospect of his eventual demise. How short life is! How unjust is death! How insignificant are we all! How cruel the universe.

So powerfully did these thoughts course through his mind, the doctor was sure he must be crying. Holding the book with only his left hand, he raised his right to his dry cheeks, then to his eyes, but he was tearless. He was convinced, however, that he'd been *close* to tears, and he knew now that he possessed the capacity to weep if ever he experienced anything sad enough to tap his salty well.

This realization pleased him because it meant that he had more in common with his father than he had supposed, and because it proved he wasn't like Viveca Scofield, as she had claimed. Perhaps *she* had no tears, but his were stored away and waiting.

She had also been wrong about not having a heart. She had one, all right. Of course, it was no longer beating.

The doctor climbed off Viveca, leaving her like an unfinished woodshop project, Black & Decker embedded, and for a long while he sat on the edge of the bed, poring through the book of haiku. Here, in this unlikely place and time, he discovered his artistic side.

When he could finally pry himself away from the book, he brought Dad's body upstairs, placed it on the bed, wiped the smears of dark chocolate off its mouth, dissected the great director's fine lacrimal apparatus, and collected the famous eyes. He tapped into Viveca for a few ounces of blood, gathered six pair of her thong-style panties from the dresser drawer—she was a live-in fiancée—and broke off one of her acrylic fingernails.

When he used a master key to let himself into Earl Ventnor's apartment, he found a crude replica of the Leaning Tower of Pisa constructed out of empty Budweiser cans on the living-room coffee table. The handyman, rather than leaning, lay in full collapse on the sofa, snoring almost as loudly as Viveca had been snoring, while Rock Hudson romanced Doris Day in an old movie on television.

Where does fiction end and reality begin? That is the essence of the game. Hudson romancing Day; Earl in a fit of drunken lust, raping the helpless starlet and committing a brutal double homicide—we believe what is easy to believe, whether fiction or fact.

The young doctor shook some of Viveca's blood on the pants and shirt of the sleeping handyman. He used the last of it to soak one pair of the thong panties. He carefully wrapped the broken-off fingernail in the blood-soaked underwear, then put all six pair of panties in the bottom drawer of Earl's bedroom dresser.

When Ahriman left the apartment, Earl was still sleeping deeply. The sirens would eventually wake him.

In the nearby gardening shed, where the lawn mowers were stored, the doctor found a five-gallon can of gasoline. He carried it into the main house and upstairs to his father's bedroom.

After bagging his own blood-spotted garments, quickly washing up, and changing into fresh clothes, he soaked the bodies in the gasoline, dropped the empty can on the bed, and lit the pyre.

The doctor had been staying the week at his father's vacation house in Palm Springs and had driven back to Bel Air this afternoon only to tend to these urgent family matters. With his work done, he returned to the desert.

In spite of the many lovely and valuable antiques that might burn if the fire department didn't respond quickly enough, Ahriman took with him only the bag full of his bloody clothes, the book of haiku, and his dad's eyes in a jar filled with a temporary fixative solution. Little more than an hour and a half later, in Palm Springs, he burned the incriminating clothes in the fireplace along with a few aromatic cedar splits and later mixed the ashes into the mulch in the little rose garden beyond the swimming pool. As risky as it was to keep the eyes and the slim volume of poetry, he was too sentimental to dispose of them.

He stayed up all night to watch a dusk-to-dawn marathon of old Bela Lugosi movies, ate an entire quart of Rocky-Road ice cream and a big bag of potato chips, swilled down all the root beer and cream soda he wanted, and caught a desert beetle in a big glass jar and tortured it with a match. His personal philosophy had been enriched immensely by Okyo's three lines of haiku, and he had taken the poet's teaching to heart: Life is short, we all die, so you better grab all the fun you can get.

Dinner was served with a second round of beers. Having had no breakfast and only a small vanilla milk shake for lunch, Martie was famished. Nevertheless, she felt as if having an appetite, so soon after finding Susan dead, was a betrayal of her friend. Life went on, and even as you grieved, you had a capacity for pleasure, too, as wrong as that might seem. Pleasure was possible in the midst of an abiding fear, as well, for she relished every bite of her jumbo prawns even as she listened to her husband reason his way toward an understanding of the doom hanging over them.

Fingers sprang from Dusty's fist once again: "Six—if Susan could be programmed to submit to repeated sexual abuse and have memories of those events scrubbed from her mind, if she could be instructed to submit to rape, then what *couldn't* she be made to do? Seven—she began to suspect what was happening, even though she had no proof, and maybe just that little suspicion was enough to alarm her controllers. Eight—she shared her suspicions with you, and they knew it, and they worried that she might share them with someone they didn't control, so that meant she had to be terminated."

"How would they know?"

"Maybe her phone was tapped. Maybe a lot of things.

But if they decided to terminate her and *instructed* her to commit suicide, and she obeyed because she was programmed, then that's not really suicide. Not morally, maybe not even legally. That's murder."

"But what can we do about it?"

Eating steak, he considered her question for a while. Then: "Hell if I know—yet. Because we can't prove anything."

"If they could just call her up and make her commit suicide, behind her locked doors . . . what do we do the next time our telephone rings?" Martie wondered.

They locked eyes, chewing the question, food forgotten. Finally he said, "We don't answer it."

"That's not a practical long-term solution."

"Frankly, Martie, if we don't figure this out real fast, I don't think we're going to be here long term."

She thought of Susan in the bathtub, even though she had never seen the body, and two hands strummed her heartstrings—the hot fingers of grief and the cold of fear. "No, not long," she agreed. "But just *how* do we figure it out? Where do we start?"

"Only one thing I can think of. Haiku."

"Haiku?"

"Gesundheit," he said, the dear thing, and opened the bookstore bag that he had brought into the restaurant. He sorted through the seven books that Ned had purchased, passed one across the table to Martie, and selected another for himself. "Judging by the jacket copy, these are some of the classic poets of the form. We'll try them first—and hope. There's probably so much contemporary stuff, we could be searching for weeks if we don't find it in the classics."

"What're we looking for?"

"A poem that gives you a shiver."

"Like when I was thirteen, reading Rod Stewart lyrics?"

"Good God, no. I'm going to try to forget I even heard

that. I mean the kind of shiver you got when you read that name in *The Manchurian Candidate.*"

She could speak the name without being affected by it the way she would be if she heard it spoken by someone else: "*Raymond Shaw.* There, I just shivered when I said it."

"Look for a haiku that does the same thing to you."

"And then what?"

Instead of answering, he divided his attention between his dinner and his book. In just a few minutes, he said, "Here! It doesn't chill my spine, but I sure am familiar with it. 'Clear cascades . . . into the waves scatter . . . blue pine needles.' "

"Skeet's haiku."

According to the book, the verse was written by Matsuo Bashō, who lived from 1644 to 1694.

Because haiku were so short, it was possible to speed through a great many of them in ten minutes, and Martie made the next big discovery before she was half finished with her scampi. "Got it. Written by Yosa Buson, a hundred years after your Bashō. 'Blown from the west . . . fallen leaves gather . . . in the east.' "

"That's yours?"

"Yeah."

"You're sure?"

"I'm still shivering."

Dusty took the book from her and read the lines to himself. The connection didn't escape him. "Fallen leaves."

"My repetitive dream," she said. Her scalp prickled as if she could even now hear the Leaf Man shambling toward her through the tropical forest.

So many dead: Sixteen hundred had perished in 1836, and hundreds more had been blown away on this January evening, at the whim of the dice and the playing cards. And still the battle raged so savagely.

While he played The Untouchables at the Alamo, the doctor worked out the details of Holden "Skeet" Caulfield's termination. Skeet must go before dawn, but one more death, in the midst of all this carnage, was of little import.

Snake eyes were rolled and the ace of spades was drawn on the same turn, which by the doctor's complex rules meant that the supreme commander of each army must turn traitor and flee to the other side. Now Colonel James Bowie, gravely ill with typhoid and pneumonia, was leading the Mexican Army, while Mr. Al Capone was fighting for the independence of the Texas Territory.

Skeet must not commit suicide on New Life property. Ahriman was a semi-silent partner in the clinic, with a substantial investment to protect. Although there was no need to worry that either Dustin or Martie would file a liability claim, some relative that the doctor *didn't* control, maybe a second cousin who had spent the last thirty years in a hut in Tibet and hadn't even *met* Skeet, would come riding in with a malpractice attorney and lodge a suit five minutes after the little dope fiend was stuck in the ground. Then an idiot jury—the only kind that seemed to be impaneled these days—would award the Tibetan cousin a billion dollars. No, Skeet would have to walk out of New Life, willfully, heedlessly, against the advice of his doctors—and then off himself elsewhere.

A marble, fired by one of the Alamo heroes, ricocheted around the landscape and took out an amazing nine Mexican soldiers and two of Capone's capos that hadn't defected to the Texans with him.

Saint Antonio of Valero, for whom the Franciscan priests had named the mission around which the great fortress of the Alamo was built, would have wept at this seemingly endless, grievous loss of life in the shadow of his church—except that he was dead and finished with weeping long before 1836. Most likely, he would have been dismayed, as well, to know that Al Capone was proving to be a better defender of this sacred ground than Davy Crockett.

The private nurse watching over Skeet on the evening shift was Jasmine Hernandez, she of the red sneakers and green laces, who was unfortunately professional and incorruptible. The doctor had neither the time nor the interest to put Nurse Hernandez through a complete schedule of programming just to be able to render her blind and deaf to the instructions he needed to give to Skeet. Therefore, he would have to wait until her shift ended. The nurse who came on at midnight was a lazy twit who'd happily park his butt in the employee lounge, watching the *Tonight* show and sucking on a Coke, while Ahriman had a powwow with Dustin's pathetic half brother.

He didn't want to chance instructing Skeet in suicide over the phone. The miserable junior Caulfield was such an iffy subject for programming that it was necessary to put him through the drill face-to-face.

Paper clip. *Ping.* Disaster. Colonel Bowie is down. Colonel Bowie is down! The Mexican Army is now leaderless. Capone gloats.

Lovely, the forest, deep and cool. The huge trees are crowded so close together that their smooth, red-brown, polished trunks blend into one encircling wall of wood. Martie somehow knows that they are mahogany trees, although she has never seen one before. She must be in a South American jungle, where mahoganies flourish, but she can't recall making the travel arrangements or packing her bags.

She hopes that she brought enough clothes, remembered the travel iron, and included a wide selection of antivenom, especially the last of those items, because even now a snake has sunk its fangs into her left arm. Fang, singular. The serpent appears to have only one fang, and the tooth is quite peculiar, as silvery and slen-

der as a needle. The snake has a thin, transparent body and hangs from a silver tree with no leaves and one branch, but you expect exotic reptiles and flora in the Amazon.

Evidently, the serpent isn't poisonous, because Martie isn't alarmed about it, and neither is Susan, who is also on this South American expedition. At the moment she is sitting in an armchair across the clearing, half turned away from Martie, visible only in profile, so still and quiet that she must be meditating or lost in thought.

Martie herself is lying on a cot, or perhaps even on something more substantial, like a sofa, which is button-tufted and has a warm leathery sheen. This must be a first-class wilderness tour if so much effort has been expended to bring along armchairs and sofas.

From time to time, magical and amusing things occur. A sandwich floats in the air—banana and peanut butter on thick slices of white bread, judging by the look of it—moves back and forth, up and down, and bites disappear from it, as though a ghost is here in the woods with her, a hungry ghost having lunch. A bottle of root beer floats in the air, too, tipping to invisible lips, to slake the thirst of the same ghost, and later a bottle of grape soda. She supposes this is to be expected, because, after all, South American writers created the literary style known as magical realism.

Another magical touch is the window in the woods, which is above and behind her, shedding light into the forest, which would otherwise be quite dark and forbidding. Everything considered, this is a fine spot for their camp.

Except for the leaves. Fallen leaves are scattered about the clearing, perhaps from the mahoganies, perhaps from other trees, and though they are only dead leaves, they make Martie uneasy. From time to time, they crunch, they crackle, though no one steps on them. Not even the slightest breeze weaves through the forest, but the restless leaves tremble singly and in small gatherings, shudder and scrape together, and creep along the floor of the campsite with sinister susurrant sounds, as if mere leaves could scheme and conspire.

Without warning, a hard wind blows out of the west. The window is west-facing, but it must be open, because the wind rushes through it and into the clearing, a great howling presence on which are borne more leaves, great seething masses, hissing and flapping like clouds of bats, some moist and supple, others dry and dead. The wind sweeps up the leaves on the floor, too, and the churning debris pumps around the perimeter of the clearing—red autumn leaves, moist green leaves, petals, stipules, whole bracts—pumps around like a carousel without horses but with strange beasts formed of leaves. Then as if drawn by the pipes of Pan, every leaf without exception flies to the center of the clearing and coalesces into the shape of a man, forming around the invisible presence that was always here, the sandwich-eating and soda-drinking ghost, giving it form, substance. The Leaf Man looms, huge and terrible: his bristling Halloween face, black holes where his eyes should be, the ragged maw.

Martie struggles to get up from the sofa, before he touches her, before it is too late, but she is too weak to rise, as if afflicted by a tropical fever, malaria. Or maybe the snake is poisonous after all, the venom finally producing an effect.

The wind has blown the leaves out of the west, and Martie is the east, and the leaves must enter her, because she is the east, and the Leaf Man places one massive bristly hand over her face. The substance of him is leaves, churning masses of leaves, some of them crisp and crimpled, others fresh and wet, still others slimy with fungus, with mold, and he pushes the leafy essence of himself into her mouth, and she bites off a piece of the beast, tries to spit it out, but more leaves are shoved into her mouth, and she must swallow, swallow or suffocate, because still more crushed and powdery leaves are forced up her nose, too, and now a moldy mass of leaves squeezes into each ear. She tries to scream for Susan's help, can't scream, can only gag, tries to cry out to Dusty, but Dusty didn't come here to South America or wherever this is, he's back there in California, there's no one to help, she is filling up with leaves, her belly full of leaves, her lungs clogged, her throat, choking on leaves, and now a frenzy of leaves whirling in her head, inside her skull, scraping across the surface of her brain, until she can't think clearly anymore, until her entire attention is focused on the sound of the leaves, the incessant scraping-rattling-ticking-clicking-crunching-crackling-hissing SOUND—

"And that's where I always wake up," Martie said.

She looked down at her last scampi, lying on what remained of a bed of pasta, and it less resembled seafood than it did a cocoon, one of those she'd encountered from time to time when she was a kid, climbing trees. In the upper branches of one spreading giant, in what seemed to be clean bowers of sunlight and emerald-green foliage and fresh air, she'd once come upon an infestation, dozens of fat cocoons firmly glued to leaves, which curved to half conceal them, as though the tree had been induced to help protect the parasites that fed on it. Only mildly repulsed, reminding herself that caterpillars, after all, can become butterflies, she studied these spun-silk sacs and saw that squirming life filled some of them. Deciding to free whatever golden or crimson winged wonder wriggled within, to release it into the world minutes or perhaps hours before it would otherwise be free, Martie delicately peeled back the layered fabric of the cocoon—and found not a butterfly, nor even a moth, but scores of baby spiders bursting from an egg case. Having made this discovery, she never again felt exalted merely to be in the airy tops of trees, or indeed to be in the upper reaches of any place; thereafter, she understood that for every creature living under a rock or crawling through the mud, there is another equally squirmy thing that flourishes in high realms, because although this is a wondrous world, it is fallen.

Appetite spoiled, she passed up the last scampi and resorted to her beer.

Pushing aside what remained of his dinner, Dusty said, "I wish you'd told me your nightmare in all this detail a lot sooner."

"It was just a dream. What would you have made of it, anyway?"

"Nothing," he admitted. "Not until after my dream last night. Then I'd have seen the connections right away. Though I'm not sure what they would've meant to me."

"What connections?"

"In your dream and mine, there's an . . . an invisible presence. And a theme of possession, of a dark and unwanted presence entering the heart, the mind. And the IV line, of course, which you didn't mention before."

"IV line?"

"In my dream it's clearly an IV line, dangling from the floor lamp in our bedroom. In your dream, it's a snake."

"But it *is* a snake."

He shook his head. "Not much in these dreams is what it appears to be. It's all symbol, metaphor. Because these aren't just dreams."

"They're memories," she guessed, and felt the truth of it as she spoke.

"Forbidden memories of our programming sessions," Dusty agreed. "Our . . . our handlers, I guess you'd call them, whoever they are—they erased all those memories, they must have, because they wouldn't want us to remember any of it."

"But the experience was still with us somewhere, deep down."

"And when it came back, it had to come distorted like this, all in symbols, because we were denied access to it any other way."

"It's like you can delete a document from your computer, and it disappears from the directory, and you can't access it anymore, but it's still on the hard disk virtually forever."

He told her about his dream of the heron, the lightning.

As Dusty finished, Martie felt that familiar mad fear suddenly squirming in her again, with frenzied energy like thousands of baby spiders bursting from egg cases along the length of her spine.

Lowering her head, she gazed down into her mug of beer, around which she had clamped both hands. Thrown, the mug could knock Dusty unconscious. Once broken against the tabletop, it could be used to carve his face.

Shaking, she prayed that the busboy wouldn't choose this moment to clear their plates.

The seizure passed in a minute or two.

Martie raised her head and looked out at the wedge of restaurant visible from their sheltered booth. More diners were seated than when she and Dusty had arrived, and more waiters were at work, but no one was staring at her, oddly or otherwise.

"You okay?" Dusty asked.

"That wasn't so bad."

"The Valium, the beer."

"Something," she agreed.

Tapping his watch, he said, "They're coming almost exactly an hour apart, but as long as they're this mild . . ."

A prickly premonition came to Martie: that these little recent seizures were merely previews of coming attractions, brief clips from the big show.

While they waited for their waiter to bring the check and then to bring their change, they pored through the haiku books once more.

Martie found the next one, too, and it was by Matsuo Basho, who had composed Skeet's haiku with blue pine needles.

Lightning gleams
and a night heron's shriek
travels into darkness.

Rather than recite it, she passed the book to Dusty. "This must be it. All three from classic sources."

She saw the chill quiver through him as he read the poem.

Change arrived with a final thank-you from the waiter, plus the traditional have-a-nice-day, though night had fallen two hours ago.

As Dusty calculated the gratuity and left it, he said, "We know the activating names come from Condon's novel, so it should be easy to find mine. Now we have our haiku. I want to know what happens when . . . we use them with each other. But this sure isn't the place to try that."

"Where?"

"Let's go home."

"Is home safe?"

"Is anywhere?" he asked.

56

Left alone most of the day, turned loose in the backyard rather than walked properly as any good dog deserved to be, given dinner by an intimidating giant whom he had met only twice before, Valet had every right to sulk, to be standoffish, and even to greet them with a disgruntled growl. Instead, he was all golden, grinning, wagging forgiveness, snuggling in for a cuddle, then bounding away in pure delight because the masters were home, seizing a plush yellow Booda duck and biting it to produce a cacophony of quacks.

They hadn't remembered to tell Ned Motherwell to switch lights on for Valet, but Ned did indeed mother well, leaving the kitchen brightly lit.

On the table, Ned had also left a note taped to a padded mailing envelope: *Dusty, found this propped against your front door.*

Martie tore the envelope, and the noise excited Valet, probably because it sounded like a bag of treats being opened. She withdrew a brightly jacketed hardback book "It's by Dr. Ahriman."

Puzzled, Dusty took the book from her, and Valet stretched his head up, flared his nostrils, sniffing.

This was Ahriman's current best-seller, a work of psychological nonfiction about learning to love yourself.

Neither Dusty nor Martie had read it, because they preferred to read fiction. Indeed, for Dusty, fiction was a much of a principle as it was a preference. In an age when distortions, deceptions, and outright lies were the primary currencies in much of society, he had often found more truth in one work of fiction than in slop pails full of learned analyses.

But this, of course, was a book by Dr. Ahriman, and was no doubt written with the same deep commitment that he brought to his private practice.

Looking at the jacket photo, Dusty said, "Wonder why he didn't mention mailing it."

"Wasn't mailed," Martie said, pointing to the lack of postage on the envelope. "Hand delivered—and not from Dr. Ahriman."

The label bore Dr. Roy Closterman's name and return address.

Tucked inside the book was a succinct note from the internist: *My receptionist passes your place on her way home, so I've asked her to drop this off. I thought you might find Dr. Ahriman's latest book of interest. Perhaps you've never read him.*

"Curious," Martie said.

"Yeah. He doesn't like Dr. Ahriman."

"Who doesn't?"

"Closterman."

"Of course he likes him," she protested.

"No. I sensed it. His expression, his tone of voice."

"But what's not to like? Dr. Ahriman's a great psychiatrist. He's so committed to his patients."

Quack, quack, quack went the plush toy duck.

"I know, yeah, and look how much better you are just after one session. He was *good* for you."

Bounding around the kitchen again, ears flopping, paws slapping the tile, duck in mouth, Valet raised more quacks than a feathered flock.

"Valet, settle," Martie commanded. Then: "Maybe Dr. Closterman . . . maybe it's professional jealousy."

Opening the book, leafing through it from the front,

Dusty said, "Jealousy? But Closterman's not a psychiatrist. He and Dr. Ahriman are in different fields."

Ever obedient, Valet stopped bounding around the kitchen, but he continued to savage the Booda until Dusty began to feel as though they had been zapped into a cartoon starring both famous ducks—Daffy and Donald.

Dusty was mildly irritated with Closterman for laying this unwanted gift on them. Considering the discreet and yet unmistakable dislike that the internist had shown for Dr. Ahriman, his intentions here were not likely to be either kind or charitable. The act seemed annoyingly petty.

Seven pages from the front of the psychiatrist's book, Dusty came across a brief epigraph prior to the first page of Chapter 1. It was a haiku.

This phantasm
of falling petals vanishes into
moon and flowers . . .
—Okyo, 1890

"What's wrong?" Martie asked.

Something like theremin music, out of a long-ago movie starring Boris Karloff, wailed and warbled through his mind.

"Dusty?"

"Odd little coincidence," he said, showing the haiku to her.

Reading the three lines, Martie cocked her head as if she, too, could hear music to which the poem had been set.

"Strange," she agreed.

Again, the dog made the duck talk.

Martie's pace slowed as she ascended the stairs.

Dusty knew she dreaded hearing Susan's voice on the answering machine. He had offered to listen alone and report back to her; but to her that would be moral cowardice.

In the upstairs study, Martie's large U-shaped desk provided all the work space that she needed to harry Hobbits out of Eriador and across the lands of Gondor and Rhovanion, into the evil kingdom of Mordor—assuming life ever gave her a chance to get back to the sanity of Tolkien's otherworld. Two complete computer workstations and a shared printer occupied less than a third of the territory.

Attached to the phone was an answering machine she'd used since graduating from college. In electronic-appliance years, it was not merely old but antique. According to the indicator window, the tape held five messages.

Martie stood well back from the desk, near the door, as though the distance would insulate her somewhat from the emotional impact of Susan's voice.

Here, too, was a sheepskin pillow for Valet, but he remained with his mistress, as though he knew she would need consolation.

Dusty pushed *messages.* The tape rewound, then played.

The first message was the one Dusty had left when he called her the previous evening from the parking lot at New Life.

"Scarlett, it's me. Rhett. Just calling to say I do *give a damn, after all. . . ."*

The second was a call from Susan, the one that must have come in just after Martie had fallen asleep the first time, from sheer exhaustion and a little Scotch, before she woke from a nightmare and raided the medicine cabinet for a sleep aid.

"It's me. What's wrong? You okay? You think I'm nuts? It's all right if you do. Call me."

Martie had retreated two steps, into the doorway, as if driven backward by the sound of her dead friend's voice. Her face was white, but the hands with which she covered it were whiter still.

Valet sat before her, gazing up, his ears perked, head cocked, hoping canine cuteness could counter grief.

The third message was also from Susan, received at 3:20 in the morning; it must have come in when Dusty was washing his hands in the bathroom and when Martie was "sleeping the perfect sleep of the innocent," as the television commercials for the patent medicine guaranteed.

"Martie, it's me. Martie, are you there?"

Susan paused on the tape, waiting for someone to pick up, and in the doorway Martie groaned. Remorsefully, bitterly, she said, "Yes," and the meaning was clear in that one word: Yes, I was here; yes, I might have been able to help; yes, I failed you.

"Listen, if you're there, for God's sake, pick up."

In the next pause, Martie lowered her hands from her face and stared with horror at the answering machine.

Dusty knew what she expected to hear next, for it was the same thing that he expected. Suicidal talk. A plea for support, for the counsel of a friend, for reassurance.

"It isn't Eric, Martie. It's Ahriman. It's Ahriman. *I've got the bastard on videotape. The* bastard*—after the good deal he got on his house. Martie, please, please call me. I need help."*

Dusty stopped the tape before the machine moved forward to the fourth message.

The house seemed to roll with a temblor, as though continental plates were colliding deep under the California coast, but this was strictly an earthquake of the mind.

Dusty looked at Martie.

Such eyes, her eyes. Shock waves had cracked even the hard grief that had made them a more intense blue than usual. Now, in her eyes was something that he'd never seen in anyone's eyes before, a quality he couldn't adequately name.

He heard himself say, "She must've been a little crazy there at the end. I mean, what sense does that make? What videotape? Dr. Ahriman is—"

"—a great psychiatrist. He's—"

"—deeply committed to—"

"—his patients."

That faint thereminlike music, eerie and tuneless, played in the concert hall inside Dusty's skull: not music, actually, but the psyche's equivalent of an acute ringing in the ears, tinnitus of the mind. It was caused by what hundred-dollar-an-hour psychologists call *cognitive dissonance:* simultaneously holding diametrically opposed convictions about the same subject. The subject in this instance was Mark Ahriman. Dusty was awash in cognitive dissonance because he believed Ahriman was a great psychiatrist and now also a rapist, believed Ahriman was a doctor deeply committed to the welfare of his patients and now also a murderer, compassionate therapist and cruel manipulator.

"It can't be true," he said.

"It can't," she agreed.

"But the haiku."

"The mahogany forest in my dream."

"His office is paneled in mahogany."

"And has a west-facing window," she said.

"It's crazy."

"Even if it could be him—why us?"

"I know why you," Dusty said darkly. "For the same reason as Susan. But why me?"

"Why Skeet?"

Of the last two messages on the tape, the first had come in at nine o'clock this morning, the second at four o'clock this afternoon, and both were from Martie's mother. The first was brief; Sabrina was just calling to chat.

The second message was longer, full of concern, because Martie worked at home and usually returned her mother's calls in an hour or two; the lack of a quick response gave Sabrina cause for apocalyptic speculations. Also unspoken in the rambling message—but clear to anyone familiar with Sabrina's skills of indirect expression—was the ardent hope that

(1) Martie was at an appointment with a divorce attorney, (2) Dusty had proved to be a drunk and was now being checked into a clinic to dry out, (3) Dusty had proved to be a philanderer and was now in the hospital recuperating from a beating—a severe beating—administered by another woman's husband, or (4) Dusty, the drunk, was drying out in a clinic after being beaten—severely—by another woman's husband, and Martie was at the divorce attorney's office.

Ordinarily, Dusty would have been annoyed in spite of himself, but this time, Sabrina's lack of faith in him seemed inconsequential.

He rewound the tape to Susan's key message. In every way, her words were harder to listen to the second time than they had been the first.

Susan dead, but now her voice.

Ahriman the healer, Ahriman the killer.

Cognitive dissonance.

The answering-machine tape was not the conclusive evidence they could have used, because Susan's message had not been sufficiently specific. She had not accused the psychiatrist of rape—or, indeed, of anything other than being a bastard.

Nevertheless, the tape was evidence of a sort, and they needed to preserve it.

While Dusty extracted the microcassette, grabbed a red felt-tip pen from the desk, and printed SUSAN on the label, Martie inserted a fresh tape into the answering machine. He put the marked cassette in the shallow center drawer in the desk.

Martie looked wounded.

Susan dead. And now Dr. Ahriman, who had seemed to be such a reliable pillar in an uncertain world, apparently had become a trapdoor.

57

From the kitchen, Dusty phoned Roy Closterman's office and got the physician's exchange that handled after-hours calls. He claimed that Martie was having an allergic reaction to medication prescribed by the doctor. "We've got an emergency situation here."

While his master and mistress sat at the kitchen table, waiting for a callback, Valet sprawled under the table, sighing to make it clear that they were wasting valuable time that could be better spent on tug-of-war or any game with a ball.

Dusty searched *The Manchurian Candidate* for a name that would give him a shiver like the one he'd gotten from the Bashō verse about the heron. In Dr. Ahriman's waiting room, he had read enough of the thriller to encounter most if not all of the leading characters, none of whose names made his skin crawl. Now, late in the book, scanning quickly, he found a walk-on character that did the trick: a second-rate opera singer, Viola Narvilly, which seemed to be a silly name for Ahriman—or whoever—to have chosen for such deadly purpose.

Now they read haiku to each other.

Dusty went first with the activating name. "Raymond Shaw."

"I'm listening," she said, detached, eyes glazed and yet alert.

"Blown from the west—"

"You are the west and the western wind."

Suddenly Dusty was reluctant to proceed through all three lines of verse, because he didn't know how to handle her if he succeeded in accessing her subconscious. Opened for instruction, she would surely be in a fragile state, vulnerable, and suggestions he made to her or questions he asked might have serious unintended consequences, cause unforeseeable psychological damage.

Besides, he didn't know how to bring her out of her trance, to full consciousness, except by telling her to sleep it off, as Skeet had done. And Skeet, at New Life, slept so deeply that calling his name, shaking him, even administering smelling salts failed to rouse him; he came around at his own pace. If Dusty's sense of time running out was perceptive rather than paranoid, they couldn't take a chance that Martie would tumble into a narcoleptic quasi-coma from which he could not make her stir.

When Dusty didn't proceed to the second line of the haiku, Martie blinked, and her rapt expression vanished as she returned to full awareness. "So?"

He told her. "But it would have worked. That's clear. Now you try me—through just the first line of my verse."

Unable to rely on memory, Martie resorted to the book of poetry.

He saw her open her mouth to speak—

—and then the retriever was pushing his burly head into Dusty's lap, seeking to comfort or be comforted.

A fraction of a second ago, Valet had been slumped in a furry pile at Dusty's feet.

No, not a fraction of one second. Ten or fifteen seconds had passed, maybe longer, a piece of time now lost to Dusty. Evidently, when Martie had used the activating name, *Viola Narvilly*, Dusty had responded—and the dog, sensing a wrongness in his master, had risen to investigate.

"That's spooky," Martie said, closing the poetry book,

grimacing as she pushed it aside, as though it were a satanic bible. "The way you looked . . . zoned out."

"I don't even have any memory of you saying the name."

"I said it, all right. And the first line of the poem, 'Lightning gleams.' And you said, 'You are the lightning.' "

The phone rang.

Getting up from the table, Dusty nearly knocked his chair over, and as he snatched the handset off the wall phone, he wondered if his *hello* would be answered by Dr. Closterman or by someone else saying *Viola Narvilly*. Enslavement was always a touch tone away.

Closterman.

Dusty apologized for lying in order to ensure a timely callback. "There's no allergic reaction, but there *is* an emergency, Doctor. This book you sent over . . ."

"*Learn to Love Yourself*," Closterman said.

"Yeah. Doctor, why did you send this to us?"

"I thought you ought to read it," Closterman replied without any inflection that could be interpreted as either a positive or negative judgment of the book or its author.

"Doctor . . ." Dusty hesitated, then plunged: "Oh, hell, there's no way to sneak up on it. I think maybe we have a problem with Dr. Ahriman. A big problem."

Even as he made the accusation, an inner voice argued with him. The psychiatrist, great and committed, had done nothing to earn this calumny, this disrespect. Dusty felt guilty, ungrateful, treacherous, irrational. And all those feelings scared him, because considering the circumstances, he had every reason to suspect the psychiatrist. The voice within, powerfully convincing, was not his voice, but that of an invisible presence, the same that pumped the inflation bulb of the sphygmomanometer in his dream, the same around which the fury of leaves formed in Martie's nightmare, and now this presence walked the halls of his mind, invisible but not silent, urging him to trust Dr. Ahriman, to let go of this absurd suspicion, to trust and have *faith*.

Into Dusty's silence, Closterman cast a question: "Martie's seen him already, hasn't she?"

"This afternoon. But we think now . . . it goes back farther than that. Back months and months, when she was taking her friend to see him. Doctor, you're going to think I'm crazy—"

"Not necessarily. But we shouldn't talk about this any further on the phone. Can you come here?"

"Where's here?"

"I live on Balboa Island." Closterman gave him directions.

"We'll be there soon. Can we bring a dog?"

"He can play with mine."

When Dusty hung up the phone and turned to Martie, she said, "Maybe this isn't the best thing to do."

She was listening to an inner voice of her own.

"Maybe," she said, "if we just call Dr. Ahriman and lay all this out for him . . . maybe he'll be able to explain everything."

The invisible walker of hallways in Dusty's mind argued for the same course of action, almost word for word, as Martie suggested it.

She rose suddenly to her feet. "Oh, God, what the hell am I saying?"

Dusty's face flushed, and he knew that if he looked in a mirror, he would see his cheeks ruddy. Shame burned in him, shame at his suspicion, at his failure to accord to Dr. Ahriman the well-earned trust and respect that the psychiatrist was due.

"Where we are here," Dusty said shakily, "is in the middle of a remake of *Invasion of the Body Snatchers.*"

Valet had come out from under the table. He stood with his tail held low, his shoulders slumped, his head half bowed, in tune with their mood.

"Why are we taking the dog with us?" Martie asked.

"Because I don't think we'll be coming back here for a while. I don't think we can risk it. Come on," he said, crossing the kitchen toward the hallway. "Let's throw some stuff in suitcases, clothes for a few days. And let's do it *fast.*"

Minutes later, before closing his suitcase, Dusty took the compact, customized .45 Colt out of the nightstand drawer. He hesitated, decided not to put the weapon beyond easy reach, closed the suitcase without adding to its contents, and pulled from the closet a leather jacket with deep pockets.

He wondered if the gun could really provide protection.

If Mark Ahriman walked into the bedroom this very minute, the treacherous voice inside Dusty might delay him long enough for the psychiatrist to smile and say *Viola Narvilly* before the trigger could be squeezed.

Then would I suck on the pistol as if it were a Popsicle, and blow my brains out as obediently as Susan slashed her wrists?

Out of the bedroom, down the narrow stairs, with the retriever in the lead, with Martie lugging one suitcase, with Dusty carrying another, pausing to snare the books in the kitchen, and then to the Saturn in the driveway, they moved with a quickening sense that they must outrace the spreading shadow of a descending doom.

58

A low, arched bridge connected Balboa Island, in Newport Harbor, to the mainland. Marine Avenue, lined with restaurants and shops, was nearly deserted. Eucalyptus leaves and blades torn from palm fronds spiraled in man-size whirlwinds along the street, as though Martie's dream of the mahogany woods were being re-created here.

Dr. Closterman didn't live on one of the interior streets, but along the waterfront. They parked near the end of Marine Avenue and, with Valet, walked out to the paved promenade that surrounded the island and that was separated from the harbor by a low seawall.

Before they found Closterman's house, one hour to the minute after her previous seizure, Martie was hit by a wave of autophobia. This was another endurable assault, as low-key as the previous three, but she couldn't walk under the influence of it, couldn't even stand.

They sat on the seawall, waiting for the attack to pass.

Valet was patient, neither cringing nor venturing forth to sniff out a potential friend when a man walked past with a dalmatian.

The tide was coming in. Wind chopped the usually calm harbor, slapping wavelets against the concrete seawall, and the reflected lights of the harborside houses wriggled across the rippled water.

Sailing yachts and motor vessels, moored at the private

docks, wallowed in their berths, groaning and creaking. Halyards and metal fittings clinked against steel masts.

When Martie's seizure passed quickly, she said, "I saw a dead priest with a railroad spike in his forehead. Briefly, thank God, not like earlier today when I couldn't clear my head of crap like that. But where does this stuff *come* from?"

"Someone put it there." Against the counsel of the insistent inner voice, Dusty said, "*Ahriman* put it there."

"But how?"

With her unanswered question blown out across the harbor, they set out again in search of Dr. Closterman.

None of the houses on the island was higher than three stories, and charming bungalows huddled next to huge showplaces. Closterman lived in a cozy-looking two-story with gables, decorative shutters, and window boxes filled with English primrose.

When he answered the door, the barefoot physician was wearing tan cotton pants, with his belly slung over the waistband, and a T-shirt advertising Hobie surfboards.

At his side was a black Labrador with big, inquisitive eyes.

"Charlotte," Dr. Closterman said by way of introduction.

Valet was usually shy around other dogs, but let off his leash, he immediately went nose-to-nose with Charlotte, tail wagging. They circled each other, sniffing, whereafter the Labrador raced across the foyer and up the stairs, and Valet bounded wildly after her.

"It's all right," Roy Closterman said. "They can't knock over anything that hasn't been knocked over before."

The physician offered to take their coats, but they held on to them because Dusty was carrying the Colt in one pocket.

In the kitchen, from a large pot of spaghetti sauce rose

the mouthwatering fragrance of cooking meatballs and sausages.

Closterman offered a drink to Dusty, coffee to Martie—"unless you've taken no more Valium"—and poured coffees at their request.

They sat at the highly polished pine table while the physician seeded and sliced several plump yellow peppers.

"I was going to feel you out a little bit," Closterman said, "before deciding how frank to be with you. But I've decided, what the hell, no reason to be coy. I admired your father immensely, Martie, and if you're anything like him, which I believe you are, then I know I can rely on your discretion."

"Thank you."

"Ahriman," Closterman said, "is a narcissistic asshole. That's not opinion. It's such a provable fact, they should be required by law to include it in the author's bio on his book jackets."

He glanced up from the peppers to see if he had shocked them—and smiled when he saw they were not recoiling. With his white hair, jowls, extra chins, dewlaps, and smile, he was a beardless Santa.

"Have you read any of his books?" he asked.

"No," Dusty said. "Just glanced at the one you sent."

"Worse than the usual pop-psych shit. *Learn to Love Yourself*. Mark Ahriman never had to learn to love Mark Ahriman. He's been infatuated with himself since birth. Read the book, you'll see."

"Do you think he's capable of *creating* personality disorders in his patients?" Martie asked.

"Capable? It wouldn't surprise me if half of what he cures are conditions he created in the first place."

The implications of that response were, to Dusty, breathtaking. "We think Martie's friend, the one we mentioned this morning—"

"The agoraphobic."

"Her name was Susan Jagger," Martie said. "I've known her since we were ten. She killed herself last night."

Martie shocked the physician as the physician had not succeeded in shocking them. He put down the knife and turned away from the yellow peppers, wiping his hands on a small towel. "Your friend."

"We found her body this afternoon," Dusty elaborated.

Closterman sat at the table and took one of Martie's hands in both of his. "And you thought she was getting better."

"That's what Dr. Ahriman told me yesterday."

Dusty said, "We have reason to think that Martie's autophobia—as we now know it's called—isn't naturally occurring."

"I went with Susan to his office twice a week for a year," she explained. "And I've begun to discover . . . odd memory lapses."

Sun-seared, windburnt, with permanent dashes of red in the corners, the doctor's eyes were nevertheless more kind than damaged. He turned Martie's hand over in his and studied her palm. "Here's everything important I can tell you about the slick sonofabitch."

He was interrupted when Charlotte raced into the kitchen with a ball in her mouth, Valet on her heels. The dogs slid on the tile floor and shot out of the room as pell-mell as they had entered.

Closterman said, "Toilet training aside, dogs can teach us more than we can teach them. Anyway, I do a little pro bono work. I'm no saint. Lots of doctors do more. My volunteer work involves abused children. I was battered as a child. Didn't scar me. I could waste time hating the guilty . . . or leave them to the law and to God, and use my energy to help the innocent. Anyway . . . remember the Ornwahl case?"

The Ornwahl family had operated a popular preschool in Laguna Beach for over twenty years. Every opening in their classrooms led to heated competition among parents of potential enrollees.

Two years ago, the mother of a five-year-old preschooler filed a complaint with the police, accusing members of the Ornwahl family of sexually abusing her daughter, and claiming that other children had been used in group sex and satanic rituals. In the hysteria that ensued, other parents of Ornwahl students interpreted every oddity in their kids' behavior as an alarming emotional reaction to abuse.

"I had no connections with the Ornwahls or with families whose children attended the school," Roy Closterman said, "so I was asked to perform pro bono examinations of the kids for Child Protective Services and the D.A.'s office. They were getting pro bono work from a psychiatrist, too. He was interviewing Ornwahl preschoolers to determine if they could give convincing accounts of abuse."

"Dr. Ahriman," Martie guessed.

Roy Closterman got up from the table, fetched the coffeepot, and refreshed their cups.

"We had a meeting to coordinate various aspects of the medical side of the Ornwahl investigation. I instantly disliked Ahriman."

A twinge of self-reproach caused Dusty to shift uneasily in his chair. That persistent inner voice shamed him for his disloyalty to the psychiatrist, for even *listening* to this negativity.

"And when he mentioned offhandedly that he was using hypnotic-regression therapy to help some kids revisit possible incidents of abuse," Closterman said, "all my alarm bells went off."

"Isn't hypnosis an accepted therapeutic technique?" Martie asked, perhaps echoing her own inner counselor.

"Less and less so. A therapist without finesse can easily, unwittingly implant false memories. Any hynotized subject is vulnerable. And if the therapist has an agenda and isn't ethical . . ."

"Do you think Ahriman had an agenda in the Ornwahl case?"

Instead of answering the question, Closterman said, "Children are highly susceptible to suggestion, even without hypnosis. Study after study has shown they'll 'remember' what they think a persuasive therapist wants them to remember. Interviewing them, you have to be very cautious to avoid leading their testimony. And any so-called repressed memories recovered from a child under hypnosis are virtually worthless."

"You raised this issue with Ahriman?" Martie asked.

Resuming his work with the yellow peppers, Closterman said, "I raised it—and he was a condescending, arrogant prick. But smooth. He's a good politician. Every concern I raised, he answered, and no one else in the investigation or the prosecution shared my concerns. Oh, the poor damn doomed Ornwahl family didn't like it, but this was one of those cases when mass hysteria subverts due process."

"Did your examinations of the children turn up any physical evidence of abuse?" Dusty asked.

"None. There's not always physiological evidence of rape with older children. But these were preschoolers, *small* children. If some of the things claimed to've been done to them actually *had* been done, I'd almost certainly have found tissue damage, scarring, and chronic infections. Ahriman was turning up all these stories of satanic sex and torture—but I couldn't find one scintilla of medical backup."

Five members of the Ornwahl family had been indicted, and the preschool had nearly been torn apart in the search for clues.

"Then," Closterman said, "I was approached by someone aware of my opinion of Ahriman . . . and told that before all this started, he'd been treating the sister of the woman who accused the Ornwahls."

"Shouldn't Ahriman have disclosed that connection?" Dusty asked.

"Absolutely. So I went to the D.A. The woman, it turns out, *was* the sister of the accuser, but Ahriman claimed he'd never been aware of their relationship."

"You didn't believe him?"

"No. But the D.A. did—and kept him on board. Because if they had admitted Ahriman was tainted, they couldn't have used any of his interviews with the kids. In fact, any stories the children told him would have to be treated as coerced or even *induced* memories. They wouldn't be worth spit in court. The prosecution's case depended on unwavering belief in Ahriman's integrity."

"I don't recall reading any of this in the papers," Martie said.

"I'm getting to that," Closterman promised.

His knife work at the cutting board grew less precise, more aggressive, as if he were not slicing just yellow peppers.

"My information was that Ahriman's patient was often brought to his office by the sister, by the woman who had accused the Ornwahls."

"Like I took Susan," Martie noted.

"If that were true, then there was no way he couldn't have met her at least once. But I didn't have proof, just hearsay. Unless you want to be sued for defamation of character, you don't go ranting in public about a man like Ahriman until you've got the evidence."

Earlier in the day, in his office, Closterman had tried a frown, which hadn't worked on his balloon-round features. Now anger overcame facial geometry, and a hard scowl fit where a frown had not.

"I didn't know how to get that proof. I'm no doctor

detective like on TV. But I thought . . . Well, let's see if there's anything in the bastard's past. It did seem odd that he'd made big moves twice in his career. After more than ten years in Santa Fe, he'd jumped to Scottsdale, Arizona. And after seven years there, he came here to Newport. Generally speaking, successful doctors don't throw over their practices and move to new cities on a whim."

Closterman finished cutting the peppers into strips. He rinsed the knife, dried it, and put it away.

"I asked around the medical community, to see if anyone might know someone who practices in Santa Fe. This cardiologist friend of mine had a friend from med school who settled in Santa Fe, and he made introductions. Turns out this doctor in Santa Fe actually knew Ahriman when he was out there . . . and didn't like him a damn bit more than I do. And then the kicker . . . there was a big sexual abuse case at a preschool out there, and Ahriman did the interviews of the children, like he did here. Questions were raised then, too, about his techniques."

Dusty's stomach had soured, and though he didn't think that the coffee had anything to do with it, he pushed his cup aside.

"One of the children, a five-year-old girl, committed suicide as the trial was starting," Roy Closterman said. "A *five-year-old.* Left a pathetic picture she'd drawn of a girl like her . . . kneeling before a naked man. The man was anatomically correct."

"Dear God," Martie said, pushing her chair back from the table. She started to get up, had nowhere to go, and sat down again.

Dusty wondered if the five-year-old girl's body would flicker through Martie's mind in grisly detail during her next panic attack.

"The case might as well have gone to jury right then, because the defendants were as good as cooked. The

Santa Fe prosecutor obtained convictions across the board."

The physician took a bottle of beer from the refrigerator and twisted off the cap.

"Bad things happen to good people when they're around Dr. Mark Ahriman, but he always comes out looking like a savior. Until the Pastore murders in Santa Fe. Mrs. Pastore, perfectly nice woman, never known to have a bad word for anyone or a moment of instability in her life, suddenly loads a revolver and decides to kill her family. Starts by blowing away her ten-year-old son."

This story fed Martie's fear of her own violent potential, and now she had somewhere to go. She rose from the table, went to the sink, turned on the water, pumped liquid soap from a dispenser, and vigorously washed her hands.

Although Martie hadn't said a word to Dr. Closterman, he didn't appear to find her actions either forward or peculiar.

"The boy was a patient of Ahriman's. He was a severe stutterer. There was some suspicion that Ahriman and the mother had been having an affair. And a witness placed Ahriman at the Pastore house the night of the murders. In fact, standing outside the house, watching the carnage through an open window."

"Watching?" Martie said, pulling paper towels off a wall-mounted roll. "Just . . . watching?"

"As if it were a sporting event," Roy Closterman said. "Like . . . he went there because he knew it was going to happen."

Dusty couldn't sit still, either. Getting to his feet, he said, "I've had two beers this evening, but if your offer still stands . . ."

"Help yourself," Roy Closterman said. "Talking about Dr. Mark Ahriman doesn't promote sobriety."

Tossing the paper towels in the trash can, Martie said, "So this witness saw him there—what came of that?"

"Nothing. The witness wasn't believed. And the rumored affair couldn't be proved. Besides, there was absolutely no doubt at all that Mrs. Pastore pulled the trigger. All the forensic evidence in the world. But the Pastores were well-liked, and a lot of people believed that Ahriman was in the background of the tragedy *somehow*."

Returning to the table with his beer, Dusty said, "So he didn't like the atmosphere in Santa Fe anymore, and he moved to Scottsdale."

"Where more bad things happened to more good people," Closterman said, stirring the meatballs and sausage in the pot of sauce. "I've got a file on all this. I'll give it to you before you leave."

"With all this ammunition," Dusty said, "you must've been able to get him off the Ornwahl case."

Roy Closterman returned to a seat at the table again, and so did Martie. The doctor said, "No."

Surprised, Dusty said, "But surely the other preschool case was enough, by itself, to—"

"I never used it."

The physician's deeply tanned face darkened further with anger, grew stormy and empurpled under the sun-browned surface.

Closterman cleared his throat and continued: "Someone discovered I was phoning around to people in Santa Fe and Scottsdale, asking about Ahriman. One evening, I came home from the office, and two men were here in the kitchen, sitting where the two of you are sitting. Dark suits, ties, well-groomed. But they were strangers—and when I turned around to get the hell out of the house, there was a third one behind me."

Of all the places Dusty had expected to follow Closterman, this wasn't on the list of itineraries. He didn't want to go here, because it seemed to be a highway to hopelessness for him and Martie.

If Dr. Ahriman was their enemy, he was enemy enough.

Only in the Bible could David win against Goliath. Only in the movies did the little guy have a chance against leviathan.

"Ahriman uses cheap muscle?" Martie asked, either because she hadn't quite leaped to the understanding that Dusty had reached—or because she didn't want to believe it.

"Nothing cheap about them. They've got good retirement plans, excellent medical coverage, full dental, and the use of a plain-Jane sedan during working hours. Anyway, they'd brought a videotape, and they played it for me on the TV in the den. On the tape was this young boy who's a patient of mine. His mom and dad are my patients, too, and close friends. Dear friends."

The physician had to stop. He was choking on rage and outrage. His hand was clamped so tight to his beer that it seemed the bottle would burst in his fist.

Then: "The boy is nine years old, a really good kid. Tears are streaming down his face in the videotape. He's telling someone off-camera about how he's been sexually molested, since the age of six, by his doctor. By me. I have never touched this boy in that way, never would, never could. But he's very convincing, emotional, and *graphic.* Anyone who knows him would know that he couldn't be acting, couldn't *sell* a lie like this. He's too naive to be this duplicitous. He believes all of it, every word of it. In his mind, it happened, these vile things I'm supposed to have done to him."

"The boy was a patient of Ahriman's," Dusty guessed.

"No. These three suits who have no damn right to be in my house, these well-tailored thugs, they tell me the boy's mother was Ahriman's patient. I didn't know. I've no idea what she was seeing him for."

"Through the mother," Martie said, "Ahriman got his hands on the boy."

"And worked him somehow, with hypnotic suggestion or something, implanting these false memories."

"It's more than hypnotic suggestion," Dusty said. "I don't know *what* it is, but it goes a lot deeper than that."

After resorting to his beer, Roy Closterman said, "The bastards told me . . . on the tape, the boy was in a trance. When fully conscious, he wouldn't be able to remember these false memories, these dreadful things he was saying about me. He would never dream about them or be troubled by them on a subconscious level, either. They would have no effect on his psychology, his life. But the false memories would still be buried in what they called his *sub*-subconscious, repressed, ready to gush out of him if he were ever *instructed* to remember them. They promised to give him that instruction if I tried to make trouble for Mark Ahriman in regard to the Ornwahl Preschool case or in any other matter. Then they left with the videotape."

The advocate for Ahriman, in the corridors of Dusty's mind, had wandered to far reaches, its voice fainter than before and no longer convincing.

Martie said, "You have any guesses who those three men were?"

"Doesn't matter much to me exactly which institution's name is printed on their paycheck," Roy Closterman said. "I know what they smelled like."

"Authority," Dusty said.

"Reeked of it," the physician confirmed.

Evidently, right now, Martie didn't fear her violent potential as much as she feared that of others, because she put her hand over Dusty's and gripped him tightly.

Panting and the pad of dog paws sounded in the hall. Valet and Charlotte returned to the kitchen, played out and grinning.

Behind them came footsteps, and a stocky, affable-looking man in a Hawaiian shirt and calf-length shorts entered the kitchen. He was carrying a manila envelope in his left hand.

"This is Brian," Roy Closterman said, and made introductions.

After they shook hands, Brian gave the envelope to Dusty. "Here's the Ahriman file that Roy put together."

"But you didn't get it from us," the physician cautioned. "And you don't need to bring it back."

"In fact," said Brian, "we don't want it back, ever."

"Brian," Roy Closterman said, "show them your ear."

Pushing his longish blond hair back from the left side of his head, Brian twisted, pulled, lifted, and detached his ear.

Martie gasped.

"Prosthetic," Roy Closterman explained. "When the three suits left that night, I went upstairs and found Brian unconscious. His ear was severed—and the wound sutured with professional expertise. They had put it down the garbage disposal, so it couldn't be sewn back on."

"Real sweethearts," Brian said, pretending to fan his face with his ear, exhibiting a macabre *je ne sais quoi* that made Dusty smile in spite of the circumstances.

"Brian and I have been together more than twenty-four years," the doctor said.

"More than twenty-*five*," Brian amended. "Roy, you're hopeless about anniversaries."

"They didn't need to hurt him," the physician said. "The video of the boy was enough, more than enough. They just did it to drive the point home."

"It worked with me," Brian said, reattaching his prosthetic ear.

"And," Roy Closterman said, "maybe now you can understand how the threat of the boy had extra punch. Because of me and Brian, our life together, some people would more easily credit accusations about child molestation. But I swear to God, if I ever felt *any* temptation along those lines, any yearnings for a child, I'd take a knife to my own throat."

"If I didn't slit it first," Brian said.

With Brian's entrance, Closterman's throttled rage had slowly subsided, and the stormy clotted coloration under his tan had faded. Now some of that darkness gathered in his face again. "I don't much love myself for backing down. The Ornwahl family was ruined, and all but certainly were innocent. If it was just me against Mark Ahriman, I'd have battled it out no matter what the cost. But these people who crawl out from under their rocks to protect him . . . I just don't understand that. And what I don't understand, I can't fight."

"Maybe we can't fight it, either," Dusty said.

"Maybe not," Closterman agreed. "And you'll notice I avoided asking you exactly what might've happened to your friend Susan and what your own problems with Ahriman are. Because, frankly, there's only so much I want to know. It's cowardly of me, I guess. I never thought of myself as a coward until this, until Ahriman, but I know now that I've got my breaking point."

Hugging him, Martie said, "We all do. And you're no coward, Doc. You're a dear, brave man."

"I tell him," Brian said, "but to me, he never listens."

Holding Martie very tightly for a moment, the physician said, "You're going to need all your father's heart and all his guts."

"She's got them," Dusty said.

This was the strangest moment of camaraderie that Dusty had ever known: the four of them so dissimilar in so many ways, and yet bonded as though they were the last human beings left on the planet after colonization by extraterrestrials.

"May we set two more places for dinner?" Brian wondered.

"Thanks," Dusty said, "but we've eaten. And we've got a lot to do before the night's out."

Martie clipped Valet to his leash, and the two dogs sniffed crotches in a last good-bye.

At the front door, Dusty said, "Dr. Closterman—"

"Roy, please."

"Thank you. Roy, I can't say that Martie and I would be in less of a mess right now if I had trusted my instincts and stopped calling myself paranoid, but we'd be maybe half a step ahead of where we are now."

"Paranoia," Brian said, "is the clearest sign of mental health in this new millennium."

Dusty said, "So . . . as paranoid as it sounds . . . I have a brother who's in drug rehab. It's his third time. The last two have been at the same facility. And last night, when I left him there, I had a disturbing reaction to the place, this paranoid feeling . . ."

"What's the facility?" Roy asked.

"New Life Clinic. Do you know it?"

"In Irvine. Yes. Ahriman is one of the owners."

Remembering the tall and imperial silhouette at Skeet's window, Dusty said, "Yeah. That would've surprised me yesterday . . . but not today."

After the warmth of the Closterman house, the January night seemed to have a colder, sharper edge. Skirling wind skimmed a foamy scruff off the surface of the harbor and flung it across the island promenade.

Valet pranced at the limit of his leash, and his masters hurried after him.

No moon. No stars. No certainty that dawn would come, and no eagerness to see what might arrive with it.

59

With no dimming of the lights or raising of the curtain to alert Martie that it was show time, with no previews of coming attractions to prepare her, dead priests with spiked heads and other mind movies of an apparently worse nature suddenly flickered across a screen in the multiplex cinema that occupied the most haunted neighborhood of her head. She cried out and jerked in her car seat, as if she'd felt a sleek theater rat, fat on spilled popcorn and Milk Duds, scampering across her feet.

Not a measured descent into panic this time, not a slow slide down a long chute of fear: Martie plunged in midsentence out of a conversation about Skeet and into a deep pit swarming with terrors. One gasp, two quick hard grunts, and then, already, the screaming. She tried to bend forward but was hampered by her safety harness. The entangling straps terrified her as much as her visions, perhaps because many of the monstrosities in her mind were restrained by chains, ropes, shackles, spikes through their heads, nails through their palms. She clawed with both hands at the nylon belts, but with no apparent recollection of the nature of the device that was hindering her, too desperately frightened to remember the buckle release.

They were traveling a wide avenue in light traffic, and Dusty angled across lanes to the curb. He stopped with a shriek of brakes on a carpet of dead evergreen needles, under an enormous stone pine at war with the wind.

When he tried to help Martie get out of the safety harness, she recoiled, thrashing more strenuously and even more ineffectively against the belts, while also swatting at him and trying to make him keep his distance. Nevertheless, he managed to find the release and disengage the buckle.

For a moment she fought the snaring straps, but then she slipped out of them and allowed them to retract. With this little freedom came no surcease, and her escalating panic drew squeals of sympathy from Valet in the backseat, until the fabric of her cries shredded into convulsive retching.

This time she had a full stomach, and when she bent forward in her misery, her dry heaves almost became wet. Choking down her gorge with a shudder of revulsion, she clawed at the door handle, trying to get out of the car.

Maybe she wanted to escape the car only to avoid soiling it if she brought up her dinner, but maybe once out, she would try to flee, not merely from the inescapable spook show in her head, but from Dusty and the possibility that she would turn on him in a fury. He couldn't allow her to leave, because in her panic she might dash into traffic and be run down.

Martie cracked open the door, and the militant wind at once attacked. Barrages of chilly air blasted through the gap, and her hair tossed like a flag.

"Raymond Shaw," Dusty said.

Because the wind's artillery keened across the edges of the door with a whistle like incoming mortar, boomed and boomed unrelentingly, and because her own fearful cries were loud, Martie didn't hear the name. She pushed the door open wider.

"*Raymond Shaw!*" Dusty shouted.

She was half turned away from him in her seat, and he couldn't hear her say *I'm listening*, but he knew she must have spoken those words, because she froze and fell silent, waiting for haiku.

Quickly reaching across her, he pulled the door shut.

In the comparative quiet, before Martie could blink and shake off this reverie and plunge back into her panic attack, Dusty put a hand under her chin, turned her face toward him, and said, "Blown from the west—"

"You are the west and the western wind."

"—fallen leaves gather—"

"The leaves are your instructions."

"—in the east."

"I am the east."

Fully accessed, waiting to be operated, Martie stared through Dusty, as though *he* were the invisible presence now, not Ahriman.

Shaken by Martie's placid, dull-eyed expression and the total obedience that it implied, Dusty turned away from her. His heart was pumping like a hard-driven piston, mind spinning like a flywheel.

She was unthinkably vulnerable now. If he gave her the wrong instruction, phrased it in such words that an entirely unintended second meaning could be derived from it, she might respond in ways he couldn't anticipate. The potential to do great psychological damage, inadvertently, seemed fearfully real.

When he had told Skeet to go to sleep, Dusty hadn't specified what length of time the nap should occupy. Skeet had been unwakable for more than an hour; however, there seemed to be no reason why he might not have slept for days, weeks, months, or for the rest of his life, kept alive by machines in the expectation of an awakening that would never occur.

Before Dusty gave even the simplest instruction to Martie, he needed to think it through carefully. The wording must be as unambiguous as possible.

In addition to being concerned about causing unintended harm, he was troubled by the degree of control he had over Martie, as she sat patiently awaiting his direction.

He loved this woman more than he loved life, but no one should be able to exercise absolute power over another human being, regardless of how pure his intentions might be. Anger was less poisonous to the soul than was greed, greed less toxic than envy, and envy only a fraction as corrupting as power.

Dead pine needles, like *I Ching* sticks, scattered across the windshield, forming continuously changing patterns, but if they were foretelling the future, Dusty wasn't able to read their predictions.

He gazed into his wife's eyes, which jiggled briefly, as Skeet's eyes had done. "Martie, I want you to listen carefully to me."

"I'm listening."

"I want you to tell me where you are now."

"In our car."

"Physically, yes. That's exactly where you are. But it seems to me that mentally you are somewhere else. I would like to know where that other place is."

"I'm in the mind chapel," she said.

Dusty had no idea what she meant by this, but he didn't have the time or presence of mind to explore her statement further just now. He was going to have to risk proceeding with nothing more than that term, *mind chapel.*

"When I hold my fingers in front of your face and snap them, you will fall into a deep and peaceful sleep. When I snap them a second time, you will wake from that sleep and you will also return from the mind chapel where you are now. You will be fully conscious again . . . and your panic attack will be over. Do you understand?"

"Do I understand?"

A fine sweat prickled along his hairline. He wiped his brow with one hand. "Tell me whether or not you understand."

"I understand."

He raised his right hand, thumb and middle finger pressed tightly together, but then he hesitated, restrained by doubt. "Repeat my instructions."

She repeated them word for word.

Doubt still hobbled him, but he couldn't sit here through the night, fingers poised to snap, hoping for confidence. He searched his deep troves of memory for all that he had learned about these control techniques from observing Skeet and from all the apparently correct deductions he had made based on so many little clues. He could find no fault with his plan—except that it was based more on ignorance than on understanding. In case he screwed up and put Martie in a coma forever, he left her with three whispered words to carry into that darkness and hold there with her—"I love you"—and then he snapped his fingers.

Martie slumped in her seat, instantly asleep, the back of her skull bouncing once against the headrest, and then her head tipped forward, chin to chest, raven wings of hair spreading to shield her face from him.

His lungs seemed to cinch shut like drawstring purses, so he had to make an effort to pay out his breath, and with the exhalation, he snapped his fingers again.

She sat up in her seat, awake, alert, that faraway gaze no longer in her eyes, and looked around in surprise. "What the hell?"

One instant she was gasping in blind panic, clawing-pushing her way out of the Saturn—and the next instant she was calm, and the car door was closed. The carnival of death that had pitched its tents inside her head, with all its spiked priests and decomposing corpses, was abruptly gone, as though blown away on the night wind.

She looked at him, and he saw that she understood. "You."

"I didn't think I had a choice. That was going to be one mean mother of an attack."

"I feel . . . clean."

From the back, Valet leaned forward between the front seats, rolling his eyes fearfully and seeking reassurance.

Petting the dog, Martie said, "Clean. Can it be over?"

"Not that easily," Dusty guessed. "Maybe with some thought and care . . . maybe we can undo what's been done to us. But first—"

"First," she said, buckling into her safety harness, "let's get Skeet out of that place."

60

The rat-stalking cat, as black as soot, moving as sinuously as smoke, looked up into the Saturn headlights, eyes flaring hot orange, and then vanished into burnt-out corners of the night.

Dusty parked next to a Dumpster, close to the building, leaving the alleyway unobstructed.

The dog watched them, nose pressed to a car window, his breath clouding one pane, as they walked quickly to the service entrance of New Life.

Although visiting hours had ended twenty minutes ago, they would most likely be permitted upstairs to see Skeet if they used the front door, especially if they announced that they had come to remove him from the clinic. That bold approach, however, would lead to a lot of discussion with the head shift nurse and with a physician if one were on duty, as well as to delays with paperwork.

Worse, Ahriman might have Skeet's file flagged with a directive requiring his notification if the patient or the patient's family requested a discharge. Dusty didn't want to risk a face-to-face encounter with the psychiatrist, at least not yet.

Fortunately, the service door was unlocked. Beyond lay a small, dimly lighted, empty receiving room with a drain in the center of the concrete floor. The astringent scent of pine disinfectant masked but didn't entirely conceal a sour odor, which was probably milk that had dripped from a punctured carton on delivery and then soaked into the porous concrete, but which smelled to Dusty like curdled blood or old puke, evidence of cruelty or crime. In this new millennium, when reality was so plastic, he could look at even this mundane space and imagine a secret abattoir where ritual sacrifices were practiced at the first midnight of each full moon.

He wasn't sufficiently paranoid to believe that every member of the clinic staff was a mind-controlled minion of Dr. Ahriman, but he and Martie proceeded stealthily, as if in enemy territory.

Beyond the first room was a long hallway leading to a junction with another hall, and farther to a pair of doors that probably opened to the lobby. Offices, storerooms, and perhaps the kitchen lay left and right off the corridor.

No one was in sight, but two people, speaking a language other than English, perhaps an Asian tongue, conversed in the distance. Their voices were ethereal, as if they didn't arise from one of the rooms ahead, but instead pierced a veil from a strange otherworld.

Immediately to the right, outside the receiving room, Martie indicated a door labeled STAIRS, and in the best tradition of premillennium reality, stairs actually lay beyond it.

Wearing a simple charcoal-gray suit, a white shirt with the collar unbuttoned, and a blue-and-yellow striped tie loosened at the neck, forgoing a pocket square, having allowed the wind to disarrange his thick hair and then having combed it distractedly with his fingers upon stepping into the lobby at New Life, Mark Ahriman was costumed and coiffed for the role of a dedicated doctor whose evenings were not his own when patients needed him.

At the security station sat Wally Clark, pudgy and dimpled and pink-cheeked and smiling, looking as though he were waiting to be buried in a sand pit lined with hot coals, and served at a luau.

"Dr. Ahriman," Wally inquired, as the doctor crossed the lobby with a black medical bag in hand, "no rest for the weary?"

"That should be 'No rest for the wicked,'" the doctor corrected.

Wally chuckled dutifully at this self-deprecatory witticism.

Smiling inwardly, imagining how quickly Wally would choke on that chuckle if presented with a certain jar containing two famous eyes, the doctor said, "But the rewards of healing far outweigh an occasional missed dinner."

Admiringly, Wally said, "Wouldn't it be nice if all doctors had your attitude, sir?"

"Oh, I'm sure most do," Ahriman said generously as he pushed the elevator call button. "But I'll agree, there's nothing worse than a man of medicine who doesn't care anymore, who's just going through the motions. If the joy of this job ever leaves me, Wally, I hope I have the good sense to move on to other work."

As the elevator doors slid open, Wally said, "Hope that day never comes. Your patients would miss you terribly, Doctor."

"Well, if that's so, then before I retire, I'll just have to kill them all."

Laughing, Wally said, "You tickle me, Dr. Ahriman."

"Guard the door against barbarians, Wally," he replied as he entered the elevator.

"You can count on me, sir."

On the way up to the second floor, the doctor wished that the night were not cool. In warmer weather, he could have entered with his suit coat slung over one shoulder and his shirtsleeves rolled up; the desired image would thus have been better conveyed with less need of supporting dialogue.

If he had chosen screen acting as a career, he was confident he would have become not merely famous but internationally renowned. Awards would have been showered on him. Initially, there would have been petty talk of nepotism, but his talent eventually would have silenced the naysayers.

Having grown up in Hollywood's highest circles and on studio lots, however, Ahriman could no longer see any romance in the movie industry, just as the son of any third-world dictator might grow up to be bored and impatient even with the spectacles in well-equipped torture chambers and with the pageantry of mass executions.

Besides, movie-star fame—and the loss of anonymity that went with it—allowed one to be sadistic only to film crews, to the high-priced call girls who serviced the kinkier members of the celluloid set, and to the young actresses dumb enough to allow themselves to be victimized. The doctor would never have been content with such easy pickings.

Ding. The elevator arrived at the second floor.

On the second floor, when Dusty and Martie cautiously ventured out of the back stairwell, their luck held. A hundred feet away, at the junction of the well-lighted main corridors, two women were at the nursing station, but neither happened to be looking toward the stairs. He led Martie to Skeet's nearby quarters without being seen.

The room was illuminated only by the television. A flurry of cops-and-robbers action on the screen caused pale forms of light to writhe like spirits up the walls.

Skeet was sitting in bed, propped like a pasha against pillows, drinking through a straw from a bottle of vanilla Yoo-hoo. When he saw his visitors, he blew bubbles in his beverage as though tooting a horn, and he greeted them with delight.

While Martie went to the bed to give Skeet a hug and a kiss on the cheek, Dusty said a cheery good-evening to Jasmine Hernandez, the suicide-watch nurse on duty, and he opened the small closet.

When Dusty turned from the closet, Skeet's suitcase in

hand, Nurse Hernandez had risen from the armchair and was consulting the luminous numbers on her wristwatch. "Visiting hours are over."

"Yes, that's right, but we're not visiting," Dusty said.

"This is an emergency," Martie said, as she coerced Skeet into putting down his Yoo-hoo and sitting on the edge of the bed.

"Illness in the family," Dusty added.

"Who's sick?" Skeet asked.

"Mom," Dusty told him.

"Whose mom?" Skeet asked, clearly unable to believe what he had heard.

Claudette ill? Claudette, who had given him Holden Caulfield for a father and then Dr. Derek "Lizard" Lampton for a stepfather? That woman with the beauty and the cool indifference of a goddess? That paramour of third-rate academics? That muse to novelists who found no meaning in the written word and to hack psychologists who despised the human race? Claudette, the hard-nosed existentialist with her pure contempt for all rules and laws, for all definitions of reality that did not begin with her? How could this unmovable and apparently immortal creature fall victim to anything in this world?

"Our mom," Dusty confirmed.

Skeet was already wearing socks, and Martie knelt beside the bed, jamming his feet into his sneakers.

"Martie," the kid said, "I'm still in my pajamas."

"No time to change here, honey. Your mom is really sick."

With a note of bright wonder in his voice, Skeet said, "Really? Claudette is really sick?"

Throwing Skeet's clothes into the suitcase as fast as he could pull them out of the dresser drawers, Dusty said, "It hit her so suddenly."

"What, a truck or something?" Skeet asked.

Jasmine Hernandez heard the note of almost-delight in

Skeet's voice, and she frowned. "*Chupaflor*, does this mean you're self-discharging?"

Looking down at his pajama bottoms, Skeet said, with complete sincerity, "No, I'm clean."

The doctor checked in at the station on the second floor to let the nurses know that neither he nor his patient in Room 246 were to be disturbed while in session.

"He called me, saying he intends to discharge himself in the morning, which would probably be the end of him. I've got to talk him out of it. He's still in deep addiction. When he hits the streets, he'll score heroin in an hour, and if I'm right about his psychopathology, he really wants to overdose and be done with it."

"And him," said Nurse Ganguss, "with everything to live for."

She was in her thirties, attractive, and usually a consummate professional. With this patient, however, she was more like a horny schoolgirl than an RN, always on the brink of a swoon from cerebral anemia, insufficient circulation to the brain, as a consequence of so much of her blood flooding into her loins and genitalia.

"And he's so sweet," Nurse Ganguss added.

The younger woman, Nurse Kyla Woosten, wasn't impressed by the patient in Room 246, but clearly she had an interest in Dr. Ahriman himself. Whenever the doctor had occasion to talk with her, Nurse Woosten performed the same repertoire of tricks with her tongue. Pretending to be unaware of what she was doing—but, in fact, with more calculation than a Cray supercomputer could accomplish in one full day of operation—she frequently licked her lips to moisten them: long, slow, sensuous licks. When considering a point that Ahriman made, the vixen sometimes stuck her tongue out, biting on the tip of it, as if to do so assisted thoughtful contemplation.

Yes, here came the tongue, questing into the right corner of her lips, perhaps seeking a sweet crumb lodged in that ripe and tender crease. Now her lips parted in surprise, tongue fluttering against the roof of her mouth. Again, the moistening of the lips.

Nurse Woosten was pretty, but the doctor wasn't interested in her. For one thing, he had a policy against brainwashing business employees. Although a mind-controlled workforce, throughout his various enterprises, would eliminate demands for increased wages and fringe benefits, the possible complications were not worth risking.

He might have made an exception of Nurse Woosten, because her tongue fascinated him. It was a perky, pink little thing. He would have liked to do something inventive with it. Regrettably, in a time when body piercing for cosmetic purposes was no longer shocking, when ears and eyebrows and nostrils and lips and navels and even tongues were regularly drilled and fitted with baubles, the doctor couldn't have done much to Woosten's tongue that, upon waking, she would have deemed horrifying or even objectionable.

Sometimes he found it frustrating to be a sadist in an age when self-mutilation was all the rage.

So, on to Room 246 and his star patient.

The doctor was the principal investor in New Life Clinic, but he didn't regularly treat patients here. Generally speaking, people with drug problems didn't interest him; they were so industriously wrecking their lives that any additional misery he could inflict on them would be merely filigree atop filigree.

Currently, his only patient at New Life was in 246. Of course, he also had a particular interest in Dustin Rhodes's brother, down the hall in 250, but he was not one of Skeet's official physicians; his consultation in that case was strictly off the record.

When he entered 246, which was a two-room suite with

full bath, he found the famous actor in the living room, standing on his head, palms flat on the floor, heels and buttocks against a wall, watching television upside down.

"Mark? What're you doing here at this hour?" the actor asked, holding his yoga position—or whatever it was.

"I was in the building for another patient. Thought I'd stop by and see how you're doing."

The doctor had lied to Nurses Ganguss and Woosten when he had said that the actor had phoned him, threatening to check out of the clinic in the morning. Ahriman's real purpose was to be here when the midnight shift arrived, so he could program Skeet after the too-diligent Nurse Hernandez went home. The actor was his cover. After a couple hours in 246, the few minutes that he spent with Skeet would seem like an incidental matter, and any staff who noticed the visit would not find it remarkable.

The actor said, "I spend about an hour a day in this position. Good for brain circulation. It'd be nice to have a second, smaller TV that I could turn upside down when I needed to."

Glancing at the sitcom on the screen, Ahriman said, "If that's the stuff you watch, it's probably better upside down."

"No one likes critics, Mark."

"Don Adriano de Armado."

"I'm listening," said the actor, quivering briefly but able to maintain his headstand.

For the name to activate this subject, the doctor had chosen a character from *Love's Labour's Lost* by William Shakespeare.

The upside-down actor, who collected twenty million dollars plus points for starring in a film, had accepted little education of any kind during his thirty-odd years, and had received no formal training in his profession. When he read a screenplay, he often didn't read anything except his own lines, and frogs were likely to fly before he ever read Shakespeare. Unless the legitimate theater was one day turned over to the management of chimps and baboons, there was no chance whatsoever that he would be cast in anything by the Bard of Avon, and so no danger that he would hear the name *Don Adriano de Armado* other than directly from the doctor himself.

Ahriman put the actor through his personal, enabling haiku.

As Martie finished tying the laces of Skeet's athletic shoes, Jasmine Hernandez said, "If you're checking him out of here, I'll need you to sign a release of liability."

"We're bringing him back tomorrow," Martie said, rising to her feet and encouraging Skeet to stand up from the edge of the bed.

"Yeah," Dusty said, still jamming clothes into the suitcase, "we just want to take him to see Mom, and then he'll be back."

"You'll still have to sign a release," Nurse Hernandez insisted.

"Dusty," Skeet warned, "you better never let Claudette hear you call her *Mom* instead of Claudette. She'll bust your ass for sure."

"He attempted suicide only yesterday," Nurse Hernandez reminded them. "The clinic can't take any responsibility for his discharge in this condition."

"We absolve the clinic. We take full responsibility," Martie assured her.

"Then I'll get the release form."

Martie stepped in front of the nurse, leaving Skeet to wobble on the uncertain support of his own two legs. "Why don't you help us get him ready? Then the four of us can go up to the nurses' station together and sign the release."

Eyes narrowing, Jasmine Hernandez said, "What's going on here?"

"We're in a hurry, that's all."

"Yeah? Then I'll get that release real quick," Nurse Hernandez replied, pushing past Martie. At the door, she pointed at Skeet, and ordered: "Don't you go anywhere until I come back, *chupaflor*."

"Sure, okay," Skeet promised. "But could you hurry? Claudette's really sick, and I don't want to miss anything."

The doctor instructed the actor to get off his head and then to sit on the sofa.

Ever the exhibitionist, the heartthrob was wearing only a pair of black bikini briefs. He was as fit as a sixteen-year-old, lean and well-muscled, in spite of his formidable list of self-destructive habits.

He crossed the room with the lithe grace of a ballet dancer. Indeed, although his personality was deeply repressed and although, in this state, he was hardly more self-aware than a turnip, he moved as if performing. Evidently, his conviction that he was at all times being watched and adored by admirers was not an attitude that he had acquired as fame had corrupted him; it was a conviction rooted in his very genes.

While the actor waited, Dr. Ahriman took off his suit coat and rolled up his shirtsleeves. He checked his reflection in a mirror above a sideboard. Perfect. His forearms were powerful, thatched with hair, manly without being Neanderthalian. When he left this room at midnight and strolled down the hall to Caulfield's room, he would sling his coat over his shoulder, the very picture of a weary, hard-working, deeply committed, and sexy man of medicine.

Ahriman drew a chair to the sofa and sat facing the actor. "Be calm."

"I am calm."

Jiggle, jiggle, the blue eyes that made Nurse Ganguss weak.

This prince of the box office had come to Ahriman the younger rather than to any other therapist because of the doctor's Hollywood pedigree. Ahriman the elder, Josh, had been dead of petits-fours poisoning when this lad had still been failing math, history, and assorted other courses in junior high school, so the two had never worked together. But the actor reasoned that if the great director had won two Oscars, then the son of the great director must be the best psychiatrist in the world. "Except, maybe, for Freud," he had told the doctor, "but he's way over there in Europe somewhere, and I can't be flying back and forth all the time for sessions."

After Robert Downey Jr. was finally sent to prison for a long stay, this hunk of marketable meat had worried that he, too, might be caught by "fascist drug-enforcement agents." While he was loath to change his lifestyle to please the forces of repression, he was even less enthusiastic about sharing a prison cell with a homicidal maniac who had a seventeen-inch neck and no gender preferences.

Although Ahriman regularly turned away patients with serious drug problems, he had taken on this one. The actor moved in elite social circles, where he could make rare mischief with a singularly high entertainment value for the doctor. Indeed, already, utilizing the actor, an extraordinary game was being prepared for play, one that would have profound national and international consequences.

"I have some important instructions for you," Ahriman said.

Someone rapped urgently on the door to the suite.

Martie was trying to get Skeet into a bathrobe, but he was resisting.

"Honey," she said, "it's chilly tonight. You can't go outside in just these thin pajamas."

"This robe sucks," Skeet protested. "They provided it here. It's not mine, Martie. It's all nubbly with fuzz balls, and I hate the stripes."

In his prime, before drugs wasted him, the kid had drawn women the way the scent of raw beef brought Valet running. In those days, he'd been a good dresser, the male bird in full plumage. Even now, in his ruin, Skeet's sartorial good taste occasionally resurfaced, although Martie didn't understand why it had to surface *now*.

Snapping shut the packed suitcase, Dusty said, "Let's go."

Improvising frantically, Martie tore the blanket off Skeet's bed and draped it over his shoulders. "How's this?"

"Sort of American Indian," he said, pulling the blanket around himself. "I like it."

She took Skeet by the arm and hustled him toward the door, where Dusty was waiting.

"Wait!" Skeet said, halting, turning. "The lottery tickets."

"What lottery tickets?"

"In the nightstand," Dusty said. "Tucked in the Bible."

"We can't leave without them," Skeet insisted.

In response to the rapping on the door, the doctor called out impatiently, "I am not to be disturbed here."

A hesitation, and then more rapping.

To the actor, Ahriman said quietly, "Go into the bedroom, lie down on the bed, and wait for me."

As though the direction he had just received was from a lover promising all the delights of the flesh, the actor rose from the sofa and glided out of the room. Each liquid step, each roll of the hips was sufficiently seductive to fill theater seats all over the world.

The rapping sounded a third time. "Dr. Ahriman? Dr. Ahriman?"

As he moved toward the door, the doctor decided that if this interruption was courtesy of Nurse Woosten, he would apply himself more diligently to the problem of what to do with her tongue.

Martie took the pair of lottery tickets out of the Bible and tried to give them to Skeet.

Clutching the blanket-cloak with his left hand, he waved away the tickets with his right. "No, no! If I touch them, they won't be worth anything, all the luck will go out of them."

As she thrust the tickets into one of her pockets, she heard someone farther down the hall calling for Dr. Ahriman.

When Ahriman opened the door to 246, he was even more dismayed to see Jasmine Hernandez than he would have been to see Nurse Woosten with pink tongue rampant.

Jasmine was an excellent RN, but she was too much like a few especially annoying girls the doctor had encountered in his boyhood and early adolescence, a breed of females that he referred to as The Knowers. They were the ones who mocked him with their eyes, with sly little looks and smug smiles that he caught in his peripheral vision as he turned away from them. The Knowers seemed to see through him, to understand him in ways he didn't wish to be understood. Worse, he had the curious feeling that they knew something hilarious about him, as well, something he himself didn't know, that he was a figure of fun to them due to qualities in himself he couldn't recognize.

Since the age of sixteen or seventeen, when his previous gangly cuteness had begun to mature into devastating good looks, the doctor had rarely been troubled by The Knowers, who for the most part seemed to have lost their ability to see into him. Jasmine Hernandez was one of that breed, however, and though she had not yet been able to x-ray him, there were times when he was sure that she was going to blink in surprise and peer more closely, her eyes filling with that special mockery and the corner of her mouth turning up in the faintest smirk.

"Doctor, I'm sorry to disturb you, but when I told Nurse Ganguss what's happening, and she said you were on the premises, I felt you ought to know."

She was so forceful that the doctor backed up a couple steps, and she took this as an invitation to enter the room, which was not what he had intended.

"A patient is self-discharging," Nurse Hernandez said, "and in my estimation, under peculiar circumstances."

Skeet said, "Could I have my Yoo-hoo?"

Martie looked at him as if he had gone a little mad. Of course, when she thought about it, there was ample evidence that *both* of them were in possession of less than half their marbles, so she tried to give him the benefit of the doubt. "Your *what*?"

"His soda," Dusty said from the doorway. "Grab it and let's get out of here!"

"Someone called Ahriman," Martie said. "He's here."

"I heard it, too," Dusty assured her. "Get the damn soda quick."

"Vanilla Yoo-hoo, or the chocolate for that matter," Skeet said, as Martie rounded the bed and snatched the bottle off the nightstand, "isn't a soda. It's not carbonated. It's more of a dessert beverage."

Shoving the bottle of Yoo-hoo into Skeet's right hand, Martie said, "Here's your dessert beverage, honey. Now *move* your ass, or I'll put a boot in it."

Initially, in his confusion, the doctor assumed that Nurse Ganguss had mentioned to Nurse Hernandez that the actor was going to check himself out of the hospital and that this was the self-discharging patient about whom she was so exercised.

Since the whole story about the actor was a lie to cover the doctor's true purpose in coming to the clinic this evening, he said, "Don't worry, Nurse Hernandez, he won't be leaving, after all."

"What? What're you talking about? They're trying to hustle him out of here right now."

Ahriman turned to look at the living room and the open door to the bedroom. He half expected to see several young women, perhaps members of a fan club, lowering the nearly naked and semicatatonic actor out of a window, with the intention of imprisoning him and making him their love slave.

No abductors. No movie star.

Turning to the nurse again, he said, "Who are you talking about?"

"*Chupaflor,*" she said. "The little hummingbird. Holden Caulfield."

Martie descended the stairs, supporting Skeet.

The kid was so pale and frail that in his pajamas and white blanket, he might have been a ghost haunting the back ways of New Life. A feeble ghost. He doddered down the stairs, weak-kneed, unsure of his balance, and with every step he took, the trailing blanket threatened to snare his feet and trip him.

Lugging the suitcase, Dusty followed Martie and Skeet, edging sideways down the steps, covering their backs by keeping a lookout for Ahriman above them in the stairwell. He had drawn the .45 Colt out of his jacket pocket.

Gunning down a prominent psychiatrist wouldn't ensure him a hallowed place in the Heroes Hall of Fame, alongside Smilin' Bob Woodhouse. Instead of being feted at testimonial dinners, he'd be standing in a prison chow line.

In spite of all they had learned about Dr. Ahriman and all they had deduced, the bitter truth was that they didn't have any proof that he was guilty of either any illegal or even unethical acts. The tape from the answering machine, with Susan's message, was the closest thing to admissible evidence that they possessed, but in it she accused the psychiatrist of nothing more than being a bastard. If Susan had somehow videotaped Ahriman, as claimed, that video was gone.

Skeet was taking the steps as a toddler would negotiate them. He lowered his right foot to the next tread, then put his left foot beside it, hesitated a moment to contemplate his subsequent move, and repeated the procedure.

They reached the landing, and still there was no pursuit from above. Dusty waited here, covering the upper flight of steps, while Martie and the kid continued toward the door below.

If Ahriman entered the stairwell at the second floor and saw them in flight, he would know they were on to him, a danger to him, and so Dusty would have to shoot him on sight. Because if Ahriman had time to say *Viola Narvilly* and then followed the name with the heron haiku, the psychiatrist would control the pistol even though it was still in Dusty's hand. Thereafter, anything might happen.

Alarmed but too experienced a performer to allow his concern to show, the doctor backed Nurse Hernandez out of 246 and into the hall as he assured her that Dustin and Martine Rhodes would make no rash decisions endangering Skeet's rehabilitation. "Mrs. Rhodes, in fact, recently became a patient of mine, and I know she has full confidence in the care we're giving her brother-in-law."

"They had some story about *chupaflor*'s mother being ill—"

"Well, that would be a shame."

"—but it sounded like so much refried beans, if you ask me. And considering the potential liability to the clinic—"

"Yes, yes, well, I'm sure I can straighten this out."

After firmly pulling shut the door to 246, Dr. Ahriman walked down the hall to Room 250, shadowed by Jasmine Hernandez. He refused to hurry because haste would indicate that in fact he considered this matter more important than he pretended it was.

He was glad that he'd taken the time to remove his coat and roll up his shirtsleeves. This working-Joe touch and his manly forearms supported the aura of confidence and competence he wished to project.

The only life in 250 was the false life on the television. The bed was disarranged, dresser drawers open and empty, a clinic-issued bathrobe rumpled on the floor, and the patient gone.

"Please go ask Nurse Ganguss if she saw them leave by the front stairs or elevator," the doctor instructed Jasmine Hernandez.

Because Nurse Hernandez wasn't programmed, because she was in possession of her free will and far too much of it, she started to argue: "But there can't have been enough time for them to—"

"Only one of us is needed to check the back stairs," the doctor interrupted. "Now please see Nurse Ganguss."

Scowling so fiercely that no one would have disputed her if she claimed to be a transsexual reincarnation of Pancho Villa, Jasmine Hernandez turned from him and stalked toward the nurses' station.

At the back stairs, Ahriman opened the door, stepped into the upper landing, listened, heard nothing, and leaped down the stairs two at a time, his heavy footfalls slapping off the concrete walls, echoing and re-echoing over one another, until by the time he came to the bottom of the second flight, he seemed to have left a wildly applauding audience behind him.

The ground-floor hallway was deserted.

He pushed through a door into the receiving room at the back of the building. Nobody here.

One more door, this opening to the alleyway.

As Ahriman stepped outside, the wind rattled the lid on one of the Dumpsters and seemed to *blow* a red Saturn past him.

Behind the wheel was Dustin Rhodes. He glanced at the doctor. Fright and too much knowledge were written across the housepainter's face.

The dope-withered, snot-nosed, useless little shit of a brother was in the backseat. He waved.

Taillights dwindling like those of a spaceship going to warp speed, the Saturn rocketed recklessly into the night.

The doctor hoped the car would slam into a Dumpster behind one of the buildings along the alleyway, hoped it would spin out of control and tumble and explode into flames. He hoped that Dusty and Martie and Skeet would be burned alive, their carcasses reduced to scorched bones and charred hunks of smoking meat, and then he hoped that out of the sky would come a great flock of big mutant crows that would settle into the blasted ruins of the Saturn and tear at the cooked flesh of the deceased, tear and tear and rip and rend, until not an edible scrap remained.

None of that happened.

The car traveled two blocks before turning left at a corner, onto a main street.

Long after the Saturn was out of sight, the doctor stood in the middle of the alleyway, staring into its wake.

The wind buffeted him. He welcomed its cold blasts, as though it might blow the confusion out of him and clear his head.

In the outgoing waiting room earlier in the day, Dusty had been reading *The Manchurian Candidate*, which the doctor had planted with Martie as a wild card that, if ever played, would add an acceptable measure of excitement to his game. Reading the thriller, Rhodes would experience little frissons of fear too piercing to be explained by the tale itself, especially when he found the name *Viola Narvilly*, and he would recognize odd connections to the events in his own life. The book would start him thinking, wondering.

Nevertheless, the possibility that the Condon novel alone would spur Dusty to make great leaps of logic, leading to his understanding of the doctor's true nature and real agenda, was so remote that there was a far greater likelihood of astronauts discovering a Kentucky Fried Chicken franchise on Mars, with Elvis chowing down in a corner booth. And he could see no—underscore that: *no*—chance whatsoever that the housepainter could have deduced all this *in one afternoon.*

Consequently, there must be other wild cards that the doctor himself had not stacked in the deck, that had been dealt by fate.

One of them would be Skeet. Skeet, with a brain so addled by drugs that he hadn't been entirely programmable.

Concerned about the apprentice painter's reliability, Ahriman had come here this evening expressly to establish a suicide scenario in Skeet's sub-subconscious and then send the wasted wretch toddling off to self-destruct before dawn. Now he would need a new strategy.

What other wild cards in addition to Skeet? Unquestionably, others had been played. However much Dusty and Martie knew—and their knowledge might not be quite as complete as it seemed—they had not put together a major portion of the puzzle with just the book and Skeet.

This unexpected development didn't appeal to Ahriman's sporting spirit. He enjoyed some risk in his games, but only manageable risk.

He was a gamester, not a gambler. He preferred the architecture of rules to the jungle of luck.

61

The trailer park huddled defensively in the high wind as though anticipating one of the tornadoes that always found such places and scattered them across blasted landscapes for the wicked delectation of television cameras. Fortunately, twisters were rare, weak, and short-lived in California. The residents of this park would not have to endure the practiced compassion of reporters torn between thrilling to a big story of destruction and admitting to what drams of human empathy had survived their years in service of the evening news.

The streets were laid out in a grid, one exactly like the next. The hundreds of mobile homes on concrete-block foundations were more alike than not.

Nevertheless, Dusty had no difficulty recognizing Foster "Fig" Newton's place when he saw it. This community was wired for cable television, and Fig's was the only trailer with a small satellite dish on its roof.

Actually, three satellite receivers were mounted on Fig's roof, silhouetted against the low night sky that was painted a sour yellow-black by the upwash of the suburban light pollution. Each dish was a different size from the others. One was aimed toward the southern heavens, one toward the northern; both were stationary. The third, mounted on a complex gimbal joint, tilted and swiveled ceaselessly, as if plucking tasty bits of elusive data from the ether in much the way that a nighthawk snatches flying insects out of the air.

In addition to the satellite dishes, exotic antennae prick

led from the roof: four- and five-foot spikes, each featuring a different number of stubby crossbars; a double helix of copper ribbons; an item resembling an inverted, denuded metal Christmas tree standing on its point, with all branch ends aimed toward the sky; and something else like a horned Viking helmet balanced on a six-foot pole.

Bristling with these data-gathering devices, the trailer might have been a spaceworthy extraterrestrial ship crudely disguised as a mobile home: the sort of thing that callers were always reporting on the talk-radio programs that Fig favored.

Dusty, Martie, Skeet, and Valet gathered on an eight-foot-square porch covered by an aluminum awning that might, after takeoff, deploy as a solar sail. Dusty knocked on the door when he couldn't find a bell push.

Clutching his blanket-cloak, which flapped and billowed in the wind, Skeet resembled a figure from a fantasy novel, following the trail of a fugitive sorcerer, exhausted by adventure, long harried by goblins. Raising his voice to compete with the wind, he said, "Are you really certain Claudette's not sick?"

"We're certain. She's not," Martie assured him.

Turning to Dusty, the kid said, "But you told me she was sick."

"It was a lie, something to get you out of the clinic."

Disappointed, Skeet said, "I truly thought she was sick."

"You wouldn't really want her to be ill," Martie said.

"Not dying, necessarily. Cramps and puking would be enough."

The porch light came on.

"And bad diarrhea," Skeet amended.

Dusty had a sense of being studied through the fish-eye lens in the door.

After a moment, the door opened. Standing on the threshold, Fig blinked behind his thick spectacles. His gray eyes were made huge by the magnifying lenses, brimming with the sorrow that never left them even when Fig laughed. "Hey."

"Fig," Dusty said, "I'm sorry to bother you at home, and this late, but I didn't know where else to go."

"Sure," Fig said, stepping back to let them in.

"Do you mind the dog?" Dusty asked.

"No."

Martie led Skeet up the steps. Valet and Dusty followed.

As Fig shut the door, Dusty said, "We've got big trouble, Fig. I might have gone to Ned, but he'd probably strangle Skeet sooner or later, so I—"

"Sit?" Fig asked, leading them to a dinette table.

As the three of them accepted the invitation, pulling chairs up to the table, and as the dog crawled under it, Martie said, "We might've gone to my mother, too, but she would just—"

"Juice?" Fig asked.

"Juice?" Dusty echoed.

"Orange, prune, or grape," Fig elaborated.

"Do you have any coffee?" Dusty asked.

"Nope."

"Orange," Dusty decided. "Thanks."

"Grape would be nice," Martie said.

"You have any vanilla Yoo-hoo?" Skeet asked.

"Nope."

"Grape."

Fig went to the refrigerator in the adjoining kitchen.

On the radio, as Fig poured the juice, people were talking about "active and inactive alien DNA grafted to the human genetic structure" and worrying about "whether the purpose of current Earth colonization by aliens is enslavement of the human race, elevation of the human race to a higher condition, or the simple harvesting of human organs to make sweetbreads for extraterrestrial dinner tables."

Martie raised her eyebrows as if to ask Dusty, *Is this going to work?*

Surveying the trailer, nodding, smiling, Skeet said, "I like this place. It's got a nice hum."

After Nurse Hernandez was sent home with a promise of a full night's pay for two hours less work than she had been contracted to provide, after Nurse Ganguss was repeatedly assured that there was nothing their movie-star patient required at the moment, and after Nurse Woosten found a few new excuses to display the gymnastic abilities of her sprightly pink tongue, Dr. Ahriman returned to his unfinished business in room 246.

The actor was in bed, where he'd been told to wait, lying atop the covers in his black bikini briefs. He stared at the ceiling with as much emotion as he had brought to any of the roles in his string of colossal hit pictures.

Sitting on the edge of the bed, the doctor said, "Tell me where you are now, not physically but mentally."

"I'm in the chapel."

"Good."

During a previous visit, Ahriman had instructed the actor never again to use heroin, cocaine, marijuana, or other illegal substances. Contrary to what the doctor had told Nurses Ganguss and Woosten, this man was now effectively cured of all drug addictions.

Neither compassion nor a sense of professional responsibility had motivated Dr. Ahriman to free the patient from these destructive habits. Simply, this man was more useful sober than stoned.

The movie star would soon be used in a dangerous game that would have enormous historical consequences; therefore, when the time came for him to be put into play, there must be no possibility that he'd be parked in a jail cell, awaiting bail for narcotics possession. He must remain free and ready for his appointment with destiny.

"You move in elite circles," said the doctor. "In particular, I'm thinking of an event you're scheduled to attend ten days from now, Saturday night of next week. Please describe the event to which I refer."

"It's a reception for the president," the actor said.

"The President of the United States."

"Yes."

In fact, the event was a major fund-raiser for the president's political party, to be held at the Bel Air estate of a director who had earned more money, garnered more Oscars, and risked contracting a sexually transmitted disease with more would-be actresses than had even the late Josh Ahriman, King of Tears. Two hundred of Hollywood's glitterati would pay twenty thousand dollars apiece for the privilege of fawning over this ultimate politico as they themselves were daily fawned over by everyone from famous talk-show hosts to riffraff in the streets. For their money, they would get, alternately throughout the evening, both an ego rush so tremendous it induced spontaneous orgasms and a deliciously perverse feeling that they were nothing more than servile pop-culture scum in the presence of greatness.

"Nothing whatsoever will deter you from attending this party for the president," the doctor instructed.

"Nothing."

"Illness, injury, earthquakes, nubile teenage fans of either sex—neither those distractions nor any others will prevent you from being on time for this event."

"I understand."

"I believe that the president is a particular fan of yours."

"Yes."

"On that evening, when you come face-to-face with the president, you'll use your charm and manipulative skills to put him instantly at ease. Then, induce him to lean especially close, as if you intend to impart an irresistible bit of gossip about one of the most beautiful actresses present.

When he is very close and most vulnerable, you will seize his head in both hands and bite off his nose."

"I understand."

The trailer was indeed humming, as Skeet had noted, but Martie found the hum more annoying than nice. In fact, an auditory tapestry of electronic buzzes and purrs and sighs and tiny tweets wove through the air, some constant in tone and volume, others intermittent, still others oscillating. All of these sounds were quite soft, whispery, never shrill, and the combined effect was not dissimilar to sitting in a meadow on a summer night, surrounded by cicadas and crickets and other insect troubadours as they sang of bug romance. Maybe that was why the hum made Martie itchy and gave her the feeling that things were crawling up her legs.

Two walls of the living room, of which this dining area was an open extension, were lined with floor-to-ceiling shelves holding computer monitors and ordinary televisions, most aglow and streaming with pictures, numerical data, flow charts, and abstract patterns of shifting forms and colors that made no sense to Martie. Also on these shelves was a large quantity of mysterious equipment featuring oscilloscopes, radar-display units, gauges, light-snake tracking graphs, and digital readouts in six different colors.

When everyone had been served juice, Fig Newton sat at the table, too. Behind him was a wall papered with star charts, Northern and Southern Hemisphere skyscapes. He looked like a hillbilly cousin of Captain James Kirk, skippering a bargain-basement version of the starship *Enterprise*.

The mascot of the space command, Valet, lapped water from a bowl the captain had provided for him. Judging by his happy attitude, the dog was not bothered by the trailer's hum.

Martie wondered if Fig's perpetually flushed face and

cherry-bright nose resulted from the radiation emitted by his collection of electronic gear, rather than from exposure to the sun during his day job as a housepainter.

"So?" Fig asked.

Dusty said, "Martie and I have to go to Santa Fe, and we need—"

"To be energized?"

"What?"

"It's an energy locus," Fig said solemnly.

"What is? Santa Fe? What kind of energy locus?"

"Mystic."

"Really? Well, no, we're just going to talk to some people who might be witnesses in . . . a criminal case. We need somewhere for Skeet to stay for a couple days, where no one would think to look for him. If you could—"

"Gonna jump?" Fig asked Skeet.

"Jump where?"

"Off my roof."

"No offense," Skeet said, "but it's not high enough."

"Shoot yourself?"

"No, nothing like that," Skeet promised.

"Okay," Fig said, sipping his prune juice.

This had been easier than Martie expected. She said, "We know it's an imposition, Fig, but could you make room for Valet, too?"

"The dog?"

"Yeah. He's really a sweetheart, doesn't bark, doesn't bite, and he's great company if—"

"He dump?"

"What?"

"In the house?" Fig asked.

"Oh, no, never."

"Okay."

Martie locked eyes with Dusty, and apparently his conscience was as guilty as hers, because he said, "Fig, I've got to be really straight with you. I think there's going to be someone looking for Skeet, maybe more than one someone. I don't believe they're likely to show up here, but if they do . . . they're dangerous."

"Drugs?" Fig asked.

"No. It has nothing to do with that. It's . . ."

When Dusty hesitated, struggling to capsulize their bizarre plight in words that wouldn't strain Fig's credulity to the breaking point, Martie took over: "Crazy as this might sound, we're caught up in some mind-control experiment, brainwashing, a conspiracy of some—"

"Aliens?" Fig asked.

"No, no. We—"

"Cross-dimensional beings?"

"No. This is—"

"Government?"

"Maybe," Martie said.

"American Psychological Association?"

Martie was speechless, and Dusty said, "Where'd you come up with that one?"

"Only five possible suspects," Fig said.

"Who's the fifth?"

Leaning over the table, his pink pie-round face as close to an expression of solemnity as it could ever get, limpid gray eyes flooded with the sorrow over the human condition that was always with him, Fig said, "Bill Gates."

"Good juice," Skeet said.

The naked actor. Frivolous man of movies. Fame and infamy.

Dreadful. If beautiful women did not easily inspire the doctor to reach the heights of poetic composition, this thespian with his surgically sculpted nose and collagen-enhanced lips was not likely to be the subject of immortal haiku.

Rising from the edge of the bed, staring down into the

placid face and the jiggling eyes, Ahriman said, "You will not chew the nose once you have bitten it off. You will at once spit it out in such a condition that it can be reattached by a team of first-rate surgeons. The intention here is *not* assassination and *not* permanent disfigurement. There are some people who wish to send the president a message—a warning, if you will—that he cannot ignore. You are simply the messenger. Tell me whether or not this is clear to you."

"It's clear."

"Repeat my instructions."

The actor repeated the instructions word for word, far more faithfully than he ever delivered the lines from one of his scripts.

"Although you will do no additional harm whatsoever to the president, all other attendees at this event will be fair game in your attempt to escape."

"I understand."

"The shock of the assault will give you a chance to slip out of arm's reach of Secret Service agents before they react."

"Yes."

"But they will be on your heels in an instant. After that, do what you must . . . though *you will not be taken alive.* You may want to think of yourself as Indiana Jones surrounded by Nazi thugs and their evil minions. Be inventive in creating mayhem, using ordinary objects as weapons, swashbuckling your way through the house until you're shot down."

This nice bit of work with the actor was a contract job, which the doctor was obligated to accept from time to time. This was the price he paid to be permitted to employ his control techniques for personal entertainment, with little or no fear of imprisonment in the event that any of his games went awry.

If this had been one of his private amusements, the scenario would not have been this simple. In spite of the lack of complexity, however, this little game had a high fun factor.

After programming the actor to have no accessible memory of what transpired between them here this evening, Ahriman led him into the living room of the suite.

Originally, the doctor had intended to spend at least an hour dictating semicoherent psychotic rants while the actor entered them into his personal, handwritten journal as if they were his own dark fantasies. They had done this during a few previous sessions, and almost two hundred pages of feverish paranoid terror, bitter hatred, and doomsday prophecies—virtually all related to the President of the United States—filled the first half of the journal. The actor would remember writing none of this and would open the journal only when instructed to do so by his psychiatrist; however, following the assault on the presidential nose, once the perp had been gunned down, the authorities would discover this heinous document buried under the collection of souvenir panties that the movie star had talked off the legions of women whom he had seduced.

Now, troubled by the Rhodeses' commando-style removal of Skeet from the clinic, Ahriman chose to skip dictation this time. The existing two hundred pages would be sufficiently convincing both to FBI agents and the nation's tabloid readers.

Taking direction well, the actor rolled back into a headstand against the living-room wall opposite the television, as nimble as an adolescent gymnast twenty years his junior.

"Begin counting," Ahriman said.

When the actor reached *ten*, he returned from the mind chapel to full consciousness. As far as he was aware, his psychiatrist had just now entered the room.

"Mark? What're you doing here at this hour?"

"I was in the building for another patient. What're *you* doing?"

"I spend about an hour a day in this position. Good for brain circulation."

"The results are obvious."

"They are, huh?" the movie star beamed, upside down.

Counseling himself to have patience, the doctor engaged in ten minutes of excruciatingly boring conversation regarding the huge box-office receipts pouring in from the actor's current megahit, giving the subject *something* to remember from this visit. When finally he left Room 246, he knew far more than he cared to know about typical attendance patterns at mall theaters in the greater Chicago area.

The famous actor. He bites democracy's nose. And the millions cheer.

Not great but much better. Work on that one.

With January wind blustering outside and fields of electronic crickets humming inside, Dusty activated Skeet with the name *Dr. Yen Lo.*

The kid sat up a little straighter at the table, his pale face becoming so expressionless that Dusty only now realized how subtly anguished it had been before. This observation sharpened the ever-present sorrow that he felt over the fact that his brother had been robbed, so young, of a full and purposeful life.

When they went through the haiku and Skeet's three responses, Fig Newton said, "Exactly," as if he knew about such psychological control mechanisms.

Minutes ago, in a hurried consultation in Fig's library—a small bedroom filled with books about UFOs, alien abductions, spontaneous human combustion, cross-dimensional beings, and the Bermuda Triangle—Dusty had outlined for Martie the effects he hoped to achieve with Skeet. What he proposed seemed fraught with risk to Skeet's already fragile psychological condition, and he worried that he would do more damage than good. To his surprise, Martie at once embraced his plan. He trusted her common sense more than he trusted the sun to rise in the east, so with her endorsement, he was prepared to take the awful responsibility for the consequences of his plan.

Now, with Skeet accessed and his eyes jiggling as they had jiggled at New Life Clinic, Dusty said, "Tell me if you can hear my voice, Skeet."

"I can hear your voice."

"Skeet . . . when I give you instructions, will you obey them?"

"Will I obey them?"

Reminding himself of everything he had learned in their previous session at the clinic, Dusty rephrased the question as a statement: "Skeet, you will obey all instructions that I give you. Confirm or deny that this is true."

"I confirm."

"I am Dr. Yen Lo, Skeet."

"Yes."

"And I am the clear cascades."

"Yes."

"In the past, I have given you many instructions."

"The blue pine needles," Skeet said.

"That's right. Now, Skeet, in a little while, I am going to snap my fingers. When that happens, you will fall into a restful sleep. Confirm or deny that you understand me so far."

"Confirm."

"And then I will snap my fingers a second time. On that second snap of my fingers, you will wake up, will become entirely conscious, but you will *also* forget forever all of my previous instructions to you. My control over you will come to an end. I—Dr. Yen Lo, the clear cascades—will never again be able to access you. Skeet, tell me whether or not you understand what I've said."

"I understand."

Dusty sought Martie's reassurance.

She nodded.

Not privy to their plan, Fig leaned forward over the table, rapt, his prune juice forgotten.

"Although you will forget all my previous instructions, Skeet, you will remember every word of what I am going to tell you now, and you will believe it, and you will act upon it for the rest of your life. Tell me whether you do or do not understand what I've just said."

"I do."

"Skeet, you will never again use illegal drugs. You will have no desire to use them. The only drugs you will use are those that may be prescribed for you by physicians in time of illness."

"I understand."

"Skeet, from this moment forward, you will understand that you are basically a good man, no more or less flawed than other people. The negative things your father has said about you over all these years, the judgments your mother has passed on you, the criticisms that Derek Lampton has leveled against you—none of those things will affect you, hurt you, or limit you ever again."

"I understand."

Across the table, tears shone in Martie's eyes.

Dusty had to pause and take a deep breath before continuing. "Skeet, you will look back into your childhood and find that time when you believed in the future, when you were full of dreams and hopes. You will believe in the future again. You will believe in yourself. You will have hope, Skeet, and you will never, never again lose hope."

"I understand."

Skeet staring into infinity. Fig riveted. Good Valet watching somberly. Martie blotting her eyes on the sleeve of her blouse.

Dusty put thumb to middle finger.

Hesitated. Thinking of all the things that might go wrong, and wondering about the unintended consequences of good intentions.

Snap.

Skeet's eyes slipped shut, and he slumped in his chair, sound asleep. His chin came to rest on his chest.

Overwhelmed by the responsibility that he'd just assumed, Dusty got up from the table, stood indecisively for a moment, and then went into the kitchen. At the sink, he twisted the COLD faucet, cupped his hands under the flow, and repeatedly splashed his face with water.

Martie came to him. "It'll be all right, baby."

The water might have concealed his tears, but he couldn't hide the emotion that wrenched his voice. "What if somehow I've screwed him up worse than he was?"

"You haven't," she said with conviction.

He shook his head. "You can't know. The mind is so delicate. One of the big things wrong with this world is . . . so many people want to screw with other people's minds, and they cause so much *damage.* So much damage. You can't know about this, neither of us can."

"I can know," she insisted gently, putting one hand to his damp face. "Because what you just did in there was done out of pure love, pure perfect love for your brother, and nothing bad can ever come of that."

"Yeah. And the road to Hell is paved with good intentions."

"So is the road to Heaven, don't you think?"

Shuddering, swallowing a hard lump in his throat, he put an even deeper fear into words: "I'm afraid of what might happen if it works . . . but even more afraid that it won't work. How crazy is that? What if I snap my fingers, and who wakes up is the old Skeet, still full of self-loathing, still confused, still the poor sweet feeb? This is his last chance, and I want so much to believe it's going to work, but what if I snap my fingers, and it turns out his last chance was no chance at all? What then, Martie?"

The strength in her voice lifted him, as always she lifted him: "Then at least you tried."

Dusty looked toward the dining area, at the back of Skeet's head, his hair rumpled and uncombed. The scrawny neck, the frail shoulders.

"Come on," Martie said softly. "Give him a new life."

Dusty turned off the running water.

He tore a few paper towels from a roll and blotted his face.

He wadded the towels and dropped them in the trash can.

He rubbed his hands together, as if he might be able to massage the tremors out of them.

Clickety-click, claws on linoleum: Inquisitive Valet padded into the kitchen. Dusty stroked the dog's golden head.

Finally he followed Martie back to the dinette table, and they sat once more with Fig and Skeet.

Thumb to middle finger again.

Come the magic now, good or bad, hope or despair, joy or misery, meaning or emptiness, life or death: *snap*.

Skeet opened his eyes, raised his head, sat up straighter in his chair, looked around at those assembled, and said, "Well, when do we start?"

He had no memory of the session.

"Typical," Fig pronounced, nodding his head vigorously.

"Skeet?" Dusty said.

The kid turned to him.

Taking a deep breath, then speaking the name as an exhalation, Dusty said, "Dr. Yen Lo."

Skeet cocked his head. "Huh?"

"Dr. Yen Lo."

Martie gave it a try: "Dr. Yen Lo."

And then Fig: "Dr. Yen Lo."

Skeet surveyed the expectant faces around him, including that of the dog, who had stood up with his forepaws on the table. "What is this, a riddle, a quiz or something?

Was this Lo some guy in history? I was never any good at history."

"Well," said Fig.

"Clear cascades," Dusty said.

Baffled, Skeet said, "Sounds like a dish-washing soap."

At least the first part of the plan had worked. Skeet was no longer programmed, no longer controllable.

Only the passage of time would prove, however, whether or not Dusty's second goal had also been achieved: Skeet's liberation from his tortured past.

Dusty pushed back his chair and rose to his feet. To Skeet, he said, "Get up."

"Huh?"

"Come on, bro, get up."

Letting the clinic blanket slip off his shoulders, the kid rose from the chair. He looked like a stick-and-straw scarecrow wearing a fat man's pajamas.

Dusty put his arms around his brother and held him very tight, very tight, and when at last he could speak, he said, "Before we go, I'll give you some money for vanilla Yoo-hoo, okay?"

62

The wheel of luck was turning. Two seats on United, out of John Wayne International Airport, to Santa Fe by way of Denver, were available on an early-morning flight. Using a credit card, Dusty secured the tickets from the phone in Fig Newton's kitchen.

"Gun?" Fig asked, a few minutes later, as Dusty and Martie were at the front door, preparing to leave brother and dog in his care.

"What about it?" Dusty asked.

"Need one?"

"No."

"Think you will," Fig disagreed.

"Please tell me you don't have an arsenal big enough to start a war," Martie said, clearly wondering if Foster Newton was something more troubling than a mere eccentric.

"Don't," Fig assured her.

"Anyway, I've got this," Dusty said, drawing the customized .45 Colt Commander from his jacket.

"Flying, aren't you?" Fig said.

"I'm not going to try to carry it on the plane. I'll pack it in one of our suitcases."

"Might get random scanned," Fig warned.

"Even if the baggage isn't carry-on?"

"Lately, yeah."

"Even on short-haul flights?"

"Even," Fig insisted.

"It's all these terrorist events recently. Everyone's nervous, and the FAA's issued some new crisis rules," Skeet explained.

Dusty and Martie regarded him with no less astonishment than they would have shown if he had suddenly opened a third eye in the center of his forehead. Subscribing to the philosophical contention that reality sucks, Skeet *never* read a newspaper, never tuned in to television or radio news.

Recognizing the source of their amazement, Skeet shrugged and said, "Well, anyway, that's what I overheard one dealer telling another."

"Dealer?" Martie asked. "Like in *drug dealer*?"

"Not blackjack. I don't gamble."

"Drug dealers sit around talking current events?"

"I think this impacted their courier business. They were ticked off about it."

To Fig, Dusty said, "So how random is random scanning? One bag in ten? One in five?"

"Maybe some flights, five percent."

"Well, then—"

"Maybe others, a hundred percent."

Looking at the pistol in his hand, Dusty said, "It's a legal gun—but I don't have a permit to carry."

"And crossing state lines," Fig warned.

"Even worse, huh?"

"Not better." Winking one owlish eye, he added: "But I have something."

Fig disappeared into back rooms of the trailer but returned only a minute later, carrying a box. From the box, he extracted a gleaming toy truck. With a swipe of one hand, he spun the wheels. "Vrooooom! Transport."

From black sky, black wind. Black, the windows of the house. Does wind live within?

On the back porch of the Rhodeses' miniature Victorian, which Ahriman found too precious for his taste, he hesitated at the door, listening to the maraca rhythms of the shaken trees in the night, and to the black-wind haiku in his mind, pleased with himself.

When he'd first come here to conduct programming sessions with Dusty, a couple months ago, he had acquired one of the Rhodeses' spare house keys, just as he had kept a key to Susan's apartment. Now he stepped inside and quietly closed the door behind him.

If the wind lived here, it wasn't home. This blackness was warm and still. No one else was in residence, either, not even the golden retriever.

Accustomed to a royal right of passage in the homes of those whom he ruled, he boldly switched on the kitchen lights.

He didn't know what he was looking for, but he was confident that he would recognize it when he saw it.

Almost at once, a discovery. A padded mailing envelope, torn open, discarded on the dinette table. His attention was snared by the return address on the label: Dr. Roy Closterman.

Because of Ahriman's spectacular success both in his practice and with his books, because he had inherited considerable wealth and was a figure of envy, because he did not suffer fools well, because he was more disposed to feel contempt rather than admiration for others in the healing community, whose self-congratulatory codes of ethics and dogmatic views he found suffocating, and for a number of other reasons, he made few friends but more than a few enemies among fellow physicians in every specialty. Consequently, he would have been surprised if the Rhodeses' internist had *not* been one of those harboring a negative opinion of him. That they were patients of the self-beatified Saint Closterman, therefore, was only marginally more troublesome than if they had consulted one of the other doctors to whom Ahriman disdainfully referred as pokers-and-prodders.

What concerned him was a handwritten message that lay with the torn envelope. The note was on Closterman's stationary, signed by him.

My receptionist passes your place on her way home, so I've asked her to drop this off. I thought you might find Dr. Ahriman's latest book of interest. Perhaps you've never read him.

Here was another wild card.

Dr. Ahriman folded the note and pocketed it.

The volume to which Closterman referred was not here. If it was truly the latest, then it must have been a hardcover copy of *Learn to Love Yourself.*

The doctor was pleased to know that even his enemies contributed to his book royalties.

Nevertheless, when this crisis had been resolved, Ahriman would have to turn his attention to Saint Closterman. Some balance could be restored to the boyfriend's head by clipping from it the remaining ear. From Closterman himself, perhaps the middle finger of the right hand could be removed, reducing his capacity to make vulgar gestures; a saint should not object to being relieved of a digit that had such obscene potential.

The fire truck—five inches wide, five inches high, and twelve inches long—was constructed of pressed metal. Nicely detailed, hand-painted, made in Holland by craftsmen with pride and flair, it would charm any child.

Sitting at the dining table, as his guests gathered around to watch, Fig used a tiny screwdriver with a quarter-inch head to remove eight brass screws, detaching the body of the truck from the base frame and wheels.

Inside the truck was a small felt bag of the type used to pack a pair of shoes in a suitcase to prevent rubbing.

"Gun," Fig said.

Dusty gave the .45 Colt to him.

Fig wrapped the compact pistol in the shoe bag so it wouldn't rattle, and he placed the bag inside the hollow body of the fire truck. If the weapon had been much larger, they would have needed a bigger truck.

"Spare magazine?" Fig asked.

"I don't have one," Dusty said.

"Should."

"Don't."

Fig reattached the body of the truck to the base, taped the little screwdriver to the underside, and handed it to Dusty. "Let 'em scan."

"Lay it on its side in a suitcase, and it makes a recognizable toy-truck silhouette on an X ray," Martie said admiringly.

"There you go," Fig said.

"They wouldn't make anyone open a bag to inspect anything like that."

"Nope."

"We could probably even take this in a carry-on," Dusty said.

"Better."

"Better?" Martie said. "Well, yeah, because sometimes airlines lose the luggage you don't carry."

Fig nodded. "Exactly."

"You ever use this yourself?" Skeet asked.

"Never," said Fig.

"Then why do you have it?"

"Just in case."

Turning the fire truck over in his hands, Dusty said, "You're a strange man, Foster Newton."

"Thanks," said Fig. "Kevlar body armor?"

"Huh?"

"Kevlar. Bulletproof."

"Bulletproof vests?" Dusty said.

"Got 'em?"

"No."

"Want 'em?"

"You have body armor?" Martie marveled.

"Sure."

Skeet said, "You ever needed it, Fig?"

"Not yet," said Fig.

Martie shook her head. "Next you'll be offering us an alien death-ray pistol."

"Don't have one," Fig said with evident disappointment.

"We'll skip the body armor," Dusty said. "They might notice how bulked up we look going through airport security."

"Might," Fig agreed, taking him seriously.

The doctor found nothing more to engage him downstairs. Though he had a lively interest in the arts and interior design, he didn't pause to admire even one painting, article of furniture, or *objet d'art.* The decor left him cold.

In the bedroom were signs of a hasty departure. Two dresser drawers weren't closed. A closet door stood open. A sweater lay discarded on the floor.

On a closer inspection of the closet, he saw two matched pieces of luggage stored overhead on a shelf. Beside those two was an empty space where two smaller bags might have been shelved.

Another bedroom and bath provided no clues, and then he came to Martie's office.

Busy blue-eyed girl. Busy making Hobbit games. Death waits in Mordor.

Across her large U-shaped work area were stacked books, maps of fantasy lands, sketches of characters, and other materials related to her project based on *The Lord of the Rings.* Ahriman took more time examining these items than was warranted, indulging his enthusiasm for anything to do with games.

As he pored through the computer-assisted designs for Hobbits and Orcs and other creatures, the doctor realized one reason why he was able to compose routinely better haiku about Martie than he'd been able to write when Susan and other women were his inspiration. He and Martie shared this gaming interest. She liked the power of being the game master, as did he. At least this one aspect of her mind resonated in sympathy with his.

He wondered if, in time, he might discover other attitudes and passions they shared. Once they were past the current regrettable ferment in their relationship, how ironic it would be to learn that they were fated to have a more complex future together than he had ever envisioned, distracted as he had been by Susan's exceptional beauty and by Martie's family connections.

The sweet sentimentalist in Ahriman delighted at the thought of falling in love or at least in something like it. Although his life was full and his habits long established, he would not be averse to the complication of romance.

Proceeding from desktop to desk drawers, he felt now less like a detective than like a naughty lover leafing through his darling's diary in search of the most guarded secrets of her heart.

In a bank of three drawers, he found nothing to interest either a detective or a lover. In the wide but shallow center drawer, however, among rulers and pencils and erasers and the like, he came upon a microcassette on which SUSAN had been printed in red letters.

He felt what a gifted Gypsy might feel when tipping a mess of tea leaves on a plate and glimpsing a particularly ominous fate in the soggy patterns: a chill that turned the pia mater of his spine into a membrane of ice.

He searched the remaining drawers for a tape recorder that would accept the microcassette. Martie didn't have one.

When he saw the answering machine on one corner of the desk, he realized what he held in his hand.

The aluminum awning, vibrating in the wind, had the guttural growl of a living beast, as though in the night something hungry waited for Dusty to open the trailer door.

"If the weather forecasts can be believed, the rest of the week is going to be a mess," he told Fig. "Don't even try to go out to the Sorenson job. Just look after Skeet and Valet for me."

"Till when?" Fig asked.

"I don't know. Depends on what we find out there. Probably be back the day after tomorrow, Friday. But maybe Saturday."

"We'll keep ourselves entertained," Fig promised.

"We'll play some cards," Skeet said.

"And monitor shortwave frequencies for alien code bursts," Fig said, in what was for him the equivalent of an oration.

"Listen to talk radio, I bet," Skeet predicted.

"Hey," Fig said to Skeet, "you want to blow up a courthouse?"

Martie said, "Whoa."

"Joke," said Fig, with an owlish wink.

"Bad one," she advised.

Outside, as Dusty and Martie descended the steps and crossed the small porch, the wind tore at them, and all the way to the car, large dead-brown magnolia leaves scuttled like rats at their feet.

Behind them, out of the open door of the trailer came a piercing and pathetic whine from Valet, as though canine precognition told him that he would never see them again.

The indicator window on the answering machine showed two waiting messages. Dr. Ahriman decided to listen to these before reviewing the cassette labeled SUSAN.

The first call was from Martie's mother. She sounded frantic to find out what was wrong, to learn why her previous calls had not been returned.

The second voice on the tape was that of a woman who identified herself as an airline ticket agent. *"Mr. Rhodes, I neglected to ask for the expiration date on your credit card. If you get this message, would you please call me back with the information?"* She provided an 800 number. *"But if I don't hear from you, your two tickets to Santa Fe will still be waiting for you in the morning."*

Dr. Ahriman marveled at their having focused so quickly on the central importance of his New Mexico days. Martie and Dusty seemed to be supernatural adversaries . . . until he realized that the Santa Fe connection must have been made for them by Saint Closterman.

Nevertheless, the doctor's slow and steady pulse, which even during the commission of murder was seldom elevated by more than ten beats per minute, accelerated upon the receipt of this news regarding the Rhodeses' travel plans.

With an athlete's intimate awareness of his body, ever sensitive to the maintenance of good health, the doctor sat down again, took several deep breaths, and then consulted his wristwatch to time his pulse. Usually, when he was seated, his rate ranged between sixty and sixty-two beats per minute, because he was in exceptional condition. Now, he counted seventy, a full eight-point elevation, and with no dead woman handy to credit for it.

In the car, as Dusty went in search of a hotel near the airport, Martie at last phoned her mother.

Sabrina was distraught and in full fluster. For minutes, she refused to believe that Martie was not injured or maimed, that she was not the victim of a traffic accident, a drive-by shooting, fire, lightning, a disgruntled postal employee, or that horrid flesh-eating bacteria that was in the news again.

As she listened to this rant, Martie was filled with a special tenderness that only her mother could evoke.

Sabrina loved her sole child with a crazy intensity that would have made Martie a hopeless neurotic by the age of eleven, if she had not been so determinedly independent almost from the day that she took her first steps. But this world harbored worse things than crazy love. Crazy hate. Oh, lots of that. And just plain crazy, in abundance.

Sabrina loved Smilin' Bob no less than she loved her daughter. The loss of him, when he was only fifty-three, had made her more protective of Martie than ever. The probability of her husband and her daughter both dying young, of separate causes, might be as low as the chances of the earth being destroyed by an asteroid impact before morning, but cold statistics and insurance-company actuarial tables offered no consolation to a wounded and wary heart.

Martie, therefore, wasn't going to say a word to her mother about mind control, haiku, the Leaf Man, the priest with the spike through his head, severed ears, or the trip to Santa Fe. Given this overload of weird news, Sabrina's anxiety would explode into hysteria.

She wasn't going to tell her mother about Susan Jagger, either, partly because she didn't trust herself to talk about the loss of her friend without breaking down, but also because Sabrina had loved Susan almost like a daughter. This was news that she had to deliver in person, holding her mother's hand, both to give emotional support and to receive it.

To explain her failure to return her mother's calls on a timely basis, Martie told her all about Skeet's attempted suicide and his voluntary commitment to New Life Clinic. Of course, these events had all occurred the previous morning, Tuesday, which didn't explain Martie's behavior on

Wednesday, but she fudged the story to make it sound as if Skeet had taken the plunge from the Sorensons' roof one day and entered the clinic the next, implying two days of turmoil.

Sabrina's reaction was only partly what Martie had expected—and surprisingly emotional. She didn't know Skeet all that well; and she had never expressed a desire to know him better. To Martie's mother, poor Skeet was no less dangerous than any machine-gun-toting member of Columbia's Medellin drug cartel, a violent and evil figure who wanted to pin down children on school playgrounds and forcibly inject heroin into their veins. Yet here, now, tears and sobs, worried questions about his injuries, his prospects, and more tears.

"This is what I've been afraid of, this is what eats at me all the time," Sabrina said. "I knew this was coming, it was bound to happen, and now here it is, and the next time it might not turn out so well. The next time Dusty might go off the roof, break his neck and be paralyzed for life, or die. And then what? I begged you not to marry a housepainter, to find a man with more ambition, someone who will have a nice office, who will sit at a desk, who won't fall off roofs all the time, won't even have a *chance* to fall off roofs."

"Mom—"

"I lived with this worry all my life, with your father. Your father and fire. Always fire and burning buildings and things blowing up and things maybe collapsing on him. *All my married life* I dreaded him going to work, panicked when I heard a fire siren, couldn't look at the news on TV because when they showed some breaking news story about a big fire, I'd think maybe he was there. And he *was* hurt, time and again. And maybe his cancer had something to do with breathing so much smoke at fires. All those *toxins* in the air at a big fire. And now you've got a husband with roofs like I had one with fires. Roofs and ladders, always falling, and you'll never know any peace."

This worried, heartfelt speech left Martie stunned and wordless.

On the other end of the line, Sabrina was crying.

Apparently sensing a mother-daughter moment of unusual import and assuming that it must have negative consequences for him, Dusty glanced away from the traffic ahead and whispered, "Now what?"

Finally Martie said, "Mom, you've never said a word about this before. You—"

"A fireman's wife doesn't talk about it, doesn't nag him about it or worry aloud," Sabrina said. "Never, not ever, my God, because if you talk about it, that's when it *happens.* A fireman's wife has to be strong, has to be positive, has to give him support, swallow her fear, and smile. But it's always in her heart, this dread, and now you go and marry a man who's on ladders all the time and running around roofs and falling off, when you could have found someone who worked at a desk and couldn't fall off worse than a *chair.*"

"The thing is, I love him, Mom."

"I know you do, dear," her mother sobbed. "It's just terrible."

"*This* is why you've been on my case about Dusty since forever?"

"I haven't been on your case, dear. I've been on your team."

"It felt like my case. Mom . . . can I infer from this you might actually sort of, kind of, at least a little bit *like* Dusty?"

Dusty was so startled to hear this question that his hands slipped on the steering wheel and the Saturn almost swerved out of its lane in traffic.

"He's a sweet boy," Sabrina said, as if Martie were still in junior high and dating adolescents. "He's very sweet and smart and polite, and I know why you love him. But he's going to fall off a roof and kill himself one day, and that's going to ruin your whole life. You'll never get over it. Your heart will die with him."

"Why didn't you just *say* this long ago, instead of all the sniping about everything he did?"

"I wasn't sniping, dear. I was trying to express my concern. I couldn't *talk* about him falling off a roof, not directly. Never, my God, when you talk about it, that's when it happens. And here we are, talking about it! Now he's going to fall off a roof, and it'll be my fault."

"Mom, that's irrational. It won't happen."

"It's *already* happened," Sabrina said. "And now it'll happen again. Firemen and fires. Painters and roofs."

Holding the phone between herself and Dusty, so that her mother could hear both of them, Martie said, "How many housepainters have you known, people who work for you, others in the trade who haven't?"

"Fifty? Sixty? I don't know. At least that."

"And how many have fallen off roofs?"

"Aside from me and Skeet?"

"Aside from you and Skeet."

"One that I know of. He broke a leg."

Putting the phone to her ear again, Martie said, "You hear that, Mom? One. Broke his leg."

"One *that he knows of*," Sabrina said. "One, and now he's next."

"He already fell off a roof. Chances of any one painter falling off a roof twice in his lifetime must be millions to one."

"His first fall didn't count," Sabrina said. "He was trying to save his brother. It wasn't an accident. The accident is still waiting to happen."

"Mom, I love you tons, but you're a little nuts."

"I know, dear. All those years of worrying. And you're going to end up a little nuts, too."

"We'll be busy the next couple days, Mom. Don't pass a kidney stone if I fail to return one of your calls right away, okay? We're not going to fall off any roofs."

"Let me talk to Dusty."

Martie passed the phone to him.

He looked wary, but he accepted it. "Hi, Sabrina. Yeah. Well, you know. Uh-huh. Sure. No, I won't. No, I won't. No, I promise I won't. That's true, isn't it? Huh? Oh, no, I never did take it seriously. Don't beat up on yourself. Well, I love you too, Sabrina. Huh? Sure. Mom. I love you, too, Mom."

He passed the phone back to Martie, and she pressed *end.*

They were both silent, and then Martie said, "Who would have thought—a mother-and-child reunion in the midst of all this crap."

Funny, how hope raises its lovely head when least expected, a flower in a wasteland.

Dusty said, "You lied to her, babe."

She knew he wasn't referring to her reconstruction of the time frame of Skeet's leap and hospitalization, nor to her leaving out the news about Susan and the rest of the mess they were in.

Nodding, she said, "Yeah, I told her we weren't going to fall off any roofs—and, hell, every one of us falls off a roof sooner or later."

"Unless we're going to be the first to live forever."

"If we are, then we'd better get a whole lot more serious about our retirement fund."

Martie was terrified of losing him. Like her mother, she could not bring herself to put the fear into words, lest what she dreaded would come to pass.

New Mexico was the state where the high plains met the Rockies, the roof of the American Southwest, and Santa Fe was a city built at a high altitude, nearly one and a half miles above sea level: a long way to fall.

On the answering-machine microcassette labeled SUSAN, only one of the five messages was important, but listening to it, the doctor felt his heartbeat accelerate once more.

Another wild card.

When he had reviewed the two messages from Martie's mother that followed Susan's bombshell, he erased the tape.

Once it was erased, he took the cassette out of the machine, dropped it on the floor, and stomped it underfoot until the plastic casing was well crushed.

From the ruins, he extracted the narrow magnetic tape and the two tiny hubs around which it was spooled. They didn't even fill the palm of his hand: so much danger compressed into such a small object.

Downstairs, in the living room, Ahriman opened the damper in the fireplace flue. He placed the tape and two plastic hubs atop one of the ceramic logs.

From his suit coat, he withdrew a slim Cartier cigarette lighter of elegant design and superb craftsmanship.

He had carried a lighter since he was eleven years old, first one that he had stolen from his father and then, later, this better model. The doctor didn't smoke, but there was always the possibility that he would want to set something on fire.

When he was thirteen, already in his first year of college, he had torched his mother. If he hadn't been carrying a lighter in his pocket when the need of one arose, his life might have changed much for the worse on that grim day thirty-five years ago.

Although his mother was *supposed* to be skiing—this was at their vacation house in Vail, during the Christmas holiday—she walked in on him while he was preparing a cat for live dissection. He had only just anesthetized the cat, using chloroform that he concocted from common household cleaning fluids, had used strapping tape to secure its paws to the plastic tarp that would serve as an autopsy table, had taped its mouth shut to muffle its cries when it woke, and had laid out the set of surgical tools he had acquired from the medical-supply company that offered a discount to premed students at the university. Then . . . hello, Mom. Often he didn't see her for months at a time, when she was on location with a film, or when she went on one of the gunless safaris she so enjoyed, but now suddenly she felt guilty about leaving him alone while she went skiing with her girl pals, and she decided they needed to spend an afternoon in some damn bonding activity or another. What lousy timing.

He could see that his mother knew at once what had happened to his cousin Heather's puppy at Thanksgiving, and perhaps she intuited the truth behind the disappearance of the four-year-old son of their estate manager a year previous. His mother was self-involved, the typical thirty-something actress who framed her magazine covers and decorated her bedroom with them, but she was not stupid.

As quick-thinking as always, young Ahriman plucked the stopper from the chloroform bottle and splashed her photogenic face with the contents. This gave him time to free the cat, put away the tarp and surgical kit, extinguish the pilot lights in the kitchen range, turn the gas on, set his mother ablaze while she still lay unconscious, grab the cat, and run for it.

The explosion rocked Vail and echoed like thunder through the snowy mountains, triggering a few avalanches too minor to have any entertainment value. The ten-room redwood chalet, shattered into kindling, burned furiously.

When firemen found young Ahriman sitting in the snow a hundred feet from the pyre, clutching the cat that he had saved from the blast, the boy was in such a state of shock that at first he could not speak and was even too dazed to cry. "I saved the cat," he told them eventually, in a stricken voice that haunted them for years after, "but I couldn't save my mom. I couldn't save my mom."

Later, they identified his mother's body with the help of dental records. The small mound of remains, once cremated, didn't even half fill the memorial jar. (He knew; he looked.) Her graveside service was attended by the royalty of Hollywood, and that noisy honor guard of celebrity funerals—press helicopters—circled overhead.

He had missed seeing new movies starring his mother, because she'd been smart about scripts and usually made only good pictures, but he had not missed his mother herself, as he knew she would not have much missed him, had their fates been reversed. She loved animals and was a staunch champion of all the causes related to them; children just didn't resonate with her as deeply as did anything with four feet. On the big screen, she could stir your heart, plunge it into despair or fill it with joy; this talent didn't extend to real life.

Two terrible fires, fifteen years apart, had made an orphan of the doctor (if you didn't know about the poisoned petits fours): the first a freak accident, for which the manufacturer of the gas range paid dearly, the second set by the drunken, lust-crazed, homicidal handyman, Earl Ventnor, who had finally died in prison two years ago, stabbed by another inmate during a brawl.

Now, as Ahriman thumbed the striker wheel on the old flint-style lighter and ignited the answering-machine tape in the fireplace, he meditated upon the fact that fire had played such a central role in both his life and Martie's, her father having been the most-decorated fireman in the history of the state. Here was yet another thing they shared.

Sad. After these latest developments, he would probably not be able to allow their relationship to evolve. He had so looked forward to the possibility that he and this lovely, game-loving woman might one day be something special to each other.

If he could locate her and her husband, he could activate them, take them down to their mind chapels, and find out what else they had learned about him, whom they might have told. More likely than not, the damage could be undone, the game resumed and played to its end.

He had their cell-phone number, but they knew he had

it, and they were unlikely to answer it in their current paranoid state of mind. And he could activate only one at a time by phone, thereby immediately alerting the one who was listening. Too risky.

Finding them was the trick. They were running, alert and wary, and they would stay well hidden until they boarded the flight to New Mexico in the morning.

Approaching them in the airport, at the boarding gate, was out of the question. Even if they didn't flee, he couldn't activate, quiz, and instruct them in public.

Once in New Mexico, they were as good as dead.

When the audiotape began to burn, issuing a noxious stink, the doctor switched on the fireplace gas. *Whoosh*, and in two minutes, nothing was left of the tape but a sticky residue on the topmost of the ceramic logs.

He was in a mood, the doctor, and sadness was not the greater component of his mood.

All the fun had gone out of this game. He had put so much effort into it, so much strategy, but now it would most likely not be played out above the beaches of Malibu, as he had planned.

He wanted to burn down this house.

Spite was not his sole motivation, nor was his distaste for the decor. Without spending the better part of a day searching the place inch by inch, he couldn't be sure that the microcassette with Susan's accusations was the only evidence against him that Martie and Dusty had accumulated. He didn't have a day to waste, and burning the house to the ground was the surest way to protect himself.

Granted, Susan's message on the tape was insufficient to convict him, not even damning enough to get him indicted. He was, however, a man who never made bargains with the god of chance.

Torching the house himself was far too risky. Once the fire was set, someone might see him leaving—and be able to identify him one day in court.

He shut off the fireplace gas.

Room by room, as he left the house, he extinguished the lights.

On the back porch, he slipped his spare key under the doormat, where the next visitor would be instructed to look for it.

Before morning, he would torch the house, but by proxy rather than with his own hands. He had a candidate, programmed and easily reached by phone, who would commit this bit of arson when told to do so, but who would never remember striking the match.

The night remained wind-rattled.

On the walk to his car, which was parked three blocks away, the doctor tried to compose a wind haiku, without success.

Driving past the Rhodeses' quaint Victorian, he imagined it in flames, and he searched his mind for a seventeen-syllable verse about fire, but the words eluded him.

Instead, he recalled the lines he had composed extemporaneously and so fluently when, on entering Martie's office, he had seen the work piled on her desk.

Busy blue-eyed girl. Busy making Hobbit games. Death waits in Mordor.

He edited the work, updating it to reflect recent developments: Busy blue-eyed girl. Busy playing detective. Death in Santa Fe.

63

Larger than San Quentin quarters, far different from the drab gray of prison decor, the colorful and overly patterned hotel room felt nonetheless like a cell. In the bath, the tub reminded Martie of Susan soaking in crimson water, though she had been spared the sight of her dead friend. All the windows were permanently sealed, and the pumped-in warm air, even with the thermostat dialed down to the lowest comfort zone, was suffocating. She felt isolated, hunted, all but cornered. Autophobia, which had been simmering at extremely low heat since nine o'clock, seemed about to be reborn as full-blown claustrophobia.

Action. Action, shaped by intelligence and a moral perspective, is the answer to most problems. So it is written on page 1 of the philosophy of Smilin' Bob.

They were taking action, too, although only time would reveal if there was enough intelligence shaping it.

First, they pored through Roy Closterman's file on Mark Ahriman, paying special attention to the information dealing with the Pastore murders and with the preschool case in New Mexico. From the Xeroxes of newspaper articles, they extracted names and made a list of those who had suffered and in whose suffering there might be both clues and damning testimony.

Finished with Closterman's file, Dusty used *Raymond Shaw* and the leaf haiku to access Martie and return her to her mind chapel—though first he made a solemn promise to leave her psyche utterly unaltered, all her faults intact, which she found both amusing and touching.

As with Skeet, he carefully instructed her to forget everything that Raymond Shaw had ever said to her, to forget all the images of death that Shaw had implanted in her mind, to be free of the control program that Shaw had installed in her, and to be forever free from the autophobia. On a conscious level, she heard nothing of what he said, and later remembered nothing that happened after he spoke the activating name until—

Snap, whereupon she woke and felt free and clean, as she had not felt in almost two days. Her old friend, hope, took up residence in her again. When tested, she did not respond to *Raymond Shaw* anymore.

In turn, Martie liberated Dusty after accessing him with *Viola Narvilly* and the heron haiku.

With a *snap*, he returned to her.

She was staring into his beautiful eyes when they cleared from the trance, and she understood the terrible sense of responsibility under which he had labored when accessing and instructing Skeet. How awesome and frightening it was to have had her husband so vulnerable before her, the innermost chambers of his mind presented to her for remodeling as she wished; how awesome, too, and humbling, to present her most fundamental self to him, to be so naked and helpless, with no defense except absolute trust.

When tested, he could not be accessed for control.

"Free," he said.

"Better yet," she said, "from now on, when I tell you to take out the garbage, you'll really hop to it."

His laughter was out of proportion to the joke.

As a declaration of independence, Martie flushed her Valium down the toilet.

Having been in high spirits when he'd left home earlier in the night, the doctor was driving his cherry-red Ferrari Testarossa, which was as low to the ground and as quick as a lizard, but it was too flashy to match his current mood. His Mercedes would also have been the wrong vehicle, too stately and ambassadorial for a guy in a down-and-dirty, throat-cutting frame of mind. One of his collection of street rods would have suited him better: in particular, the '63 black Buick Riviera with its chopped top, split grille, elliptical hood scoops, sectioned rear fenders, and other custom details, which looked like a demonic car that, in the movies, would drive itself on murderous missions, possessed and indestructible.

He stopped at a convenience store to make the call, because he didn't want to use either his cell phone or his phone at home.

This land of the brave new millennium was one giant confessional booth, with listening priests of the secular church monitoring every conversation from behind concealing electronic screens. The doctor swept his house, his offices, and his vehicles for listening devices once each month, doing the work himself, with equipment he purchased for cash, because he trusted no one among the private-security firms that offered such services. A phone, however, could be monitored by an off-site tap; therefore, incriminating calls must always be made from telephones not listed in his name.

The pay phone outside the convenience store was racked on the wall. The wind would foil a directional microphone if a surveillance team was stalking the doctor, though he was confident no one was tailing him. If this phone was a known contact for drug dealers, there might be a passive tap recording every conversation, in which case voice analysis could eventually be used to incriminate Ahriman in a court of law; but this was a minor and unavoidable risk.

Although the doctor's friends in high places could be

counted on to ensure him against a successful prosecution for virtually any crime, he was nonetheless cautious. Indeed, it was the possibility of being monitored by these *friends* that motivated him to conduct an electronic sweep of his house each month, and he was more concerned about keeping them ignorant of his private games than he was worried about the police. The doctor himself would have sold out a friend without hesitation if he benefited sufficiently from the sale, and he assumed that any friend would do the same to him.

He keyed in a number, fed coins to the phone, cupped his hand around the mouthpiece to keep out the shriek of the wind, and when he got an answer on the third ring, he said, "Ed Mavole," which was the name of a character in *The Manchurian Candidate*.

"I'm listening."

They proceeded through the lines of the enabling haiku, after which the doctor said, "Tell me whether or not you are alone."

"I'm alone."

"I want you to go to Dusty and Martie's house in Corona Del Mar." He checked his wristwatch. Nearly midnight. "I want you to go to their house at three o'clock in the morning, a little more than three hours from now. Tell me whether or not you understand."

"I understand."

"You will take with you five gallons of gasoline and a book of matches."

"Yes."

"Please be discreet. Take every precaution against being seen."

"Yes."

"You will enter by their back door. Under the doormat is a key that I have left for you."

"Thank you."

"You're welcome."

Convinced that his subject wouldn't have the technical knowledge necessary to commit a completely successful act of arson, wanting to be certain the house would be utterly destroyed, the doctor huddled against the pummeling wind and devoted five minutes to an explanation of how flammable liquids and highly combustible materials already on the premises could be best used to supplement the gasoline. Further, he enlightened his dutiful listener on the four crucial architectural details that could be used to serve an arsonist's purposes.

In spite of the danger in which they found themselves or perhaps because of it, in spite of their grief or because of it, Martie and Dusty made love. Their slow, easy coupling was as much affirmation as sex: an affirmation of life, of their love for each other, and of their faith in the future.

For sweet minutes, no fear troubled them, no demons of the mind or demons of the world, nor did the hotel room seem either small or stifling, as before. For the duration of these silken rhythms, there was no blurring of the line between fact and fiction, between reality and fantasy, because reality was reduced to their two bodies and the tenderness they shared.

At home, in his lacewood-paneled study, the doctor sat in his ergonomic ostrich-skin chair, touched one of the many buttons inset in an extractable writing slide, and watched as his computer rose out of the top of the desk. The lift mechanism purred softly.

He composed a message, warning of Martine and Dustin Rhodes's travel plans, providing detailed descriptions, and requesting, as a personal courtesy, that they be kept under surveillance from the moment they landed in New Mexico. If their investigation proved fruitless, they were to be allowed to return to California. If they obtained any information damaging to the doctor, he preferred to have them killed there in the Land of Enchantment, as the natives called it, to save him the trouble of disposing of them when they returned here to the Golden State. If termination in New Mexico was deemed necessary, then the couple should first be persuaded to reveal the whereabouts of Mr. Rhodes's brother, Skeet Caulfield.

As Ahriman reviewed his message to be sure it was clear, he was not optimistic that he'd ever again see either Dusty or Martie alive, and yet he was not entirely without hope. They had been astonishingly resourceful thus far, but he had to believe that a mere housepainter and a girl video-game designer would have their limits.

If they exhibited little talent for playing detectives, perhaps when they returned to California, Ahriman would be able to engineer a meeting with them. He could access them, interrogate them to learn what they knew about his true nature, and rehabilitate them, removing all memories that would either inhibit their continued obedience or diminish their programmed admiration for him.

If that could be done, the game would be salvaged.

He could have asked the operatives in New Mexico to abduct the couple and put them, one at a time, on the telephone with him, which would allow him to access, interrogate, and rehabilitate them long-distance. Unfortunately, this would make his friends privy to his private game, and he didn't want them to know anything about his strategies, motivations, and personal pleasures.

Currently, he and the fellowship of puppeteers in New Mexico had an ideal relationship, mutually beneficial. Twenty years ago, Dr. Ahriman had developed the effective formula of combined drugs that induced a programmable state of mind, and he had continually refined it ever since. He also had written the bible on programming techniques, from which others did not deviate to this day. A handful of men—and two women—could perform these miracles of control, but the doctor was without peer in the fellowship. He was the puppeteer of puppeteers, and when they had a particularly difficult or delicate job, they came to him. He never denied them, never charged them—but did receive reimbursement of all travel expenses, a generous per diem dining allowance when on the road, and a small but thoughtful gift of some personal item (lambskin driving gloves, lapis lazuli cuff links, a necktie hand-painted by the uncannily gifted children of a Tibetan orphanage for the mystic deaf) every Christmas.

Three or four times a year, at their request, he flew to Albany or to Little Rock, to Hialeah or to Des Moines, or to Falls Church, more often than not to places he would otherwise never have seen, costumed to pass unnoticed by the locals, traveling under such false names as Jim Shaitan, Bill Sammael, and Jack Apollyon. There, with a staff at his command, he conducted programming sessions—usually on one or two subjects—over three to five days, before winging home to the balmy shores of the Pacific. In compensation and as recognition of his unique status, Ahriman was the only member of the fellowship permitted by their overseers to apply his skills to private projects.

One of the other psychologists in the project—a young, goateed German American whose unfortunate surname was Fugger—had attempted to presume this fringe benefit for himself, but he had been caught. In front of the other programmers, as an object lesson, Fugger was dismembered and fed in pieces to a pit full of thrashing crocodiles.

Because Dr. Ahriman was not prohibited from private enterprises, he had not received an invitation and had learned of the disciplinary action only after the fact. He had lived his life in such a way that he had few regrets, but he sorely wished that he could have attended Fugger's going-out party.

Now, at the onyx-topped desk in his lacewood-paneled

study, the doctor added two lines to his message, to report that the actor had been fully programmed as requested and that the presidential nose was soon to receive wall-to-wall media coverage for at least a week, complete with learned analyses by the usual experts as well as by a few leading nasologists.

A team of aggressive investigators, turned loose by the White House and currently probing into the varied activities of certain overreaching bureaucrats in the Commerce Department, would no doubt be reined in within twenty-four hours of the reattachment of the chief executive's proboscis, and the government could get back to the business of the people.

Always a politician himself, the doctor added a few personal notes: a happy-birthday greeting to one of the other programmers; a query as to the health of the project director's oldest child, who had been ill with a particularly severe case of the flu; and hearty congratulations to Curly, in maintenance, whose girlfriend had accepted his proposal of marriage.

He sent the document to the institute in Santa Fe, via E-mail, using an unbreakable encryption program not available to the general public, one that had been designed for the exclusive use of the fellowship and its support staff.

What a day.

Such highs, such lows.

To lift his spirits and to reward himself for remaining so calm and focused in the face of adversity, the doctor went to the kitchen and constructed a large cherry ice-cream soda. He also gave himself a plate of Milano cookies by Pepperidge Farm, which had been one of his mother's favorites, too.

Banshees of wind shrieking down out of the sky, goblin cries of sirens cycling upward, trees caught between and tossing-roaring in torment, ragged scarves of orange sparks winding through the tresses of the palms and Indian laurels: This was Halloween in January or any day in Hell. Now more second-story windows exploded, shards of glass glittering with reflections of fire and plinking onto the front-porch roof like an unmelodious piano passage in a symphony of destruction.

Fire engines and emergency vehicles choked the narrow street, mars lights and spotlights revolving and blazing, departmental radios burning with dispatchers' voices that crackled like flames. Python colonies of hoses serpentined across the wet pavement, as if charmed forth by the rhythmic throbbing of the pumpers.

The Rhodes residence had been fully engulfed by the time the first engine company arrived, and because houses in this neighborhood stood so close together, the firemen's initial efforts were directed toward watering down neighbors' roofs and the surrounding trees to prevent the flames from spreading structure to structure. With that disaster narrowly averted, the deluge gun atop the largest pumper was brought to bear on the Victorian.

The house, with all its ornamental millwork, was bright in its wreaths of fire, but beneath the flames, the colorful San Francisco-style paint job was already scorched away, replaced by soot and char. The front wall buckled, shattering the last window. The main roof sagged. The porch roof collapsed. All the hoses were trained on the place at last, but the fire seemed to relish the water, sucking it down, unquenched.

When a large section of the main roof dropped out of sight into the fiery interior, a cry of dismay arose from a knot of neighbors gathered across the street. Sudden masses of dark smoke billowed forth and, stampeded by the wind, galloped westward like a herd of nightmare horses.

Martie was being carried through a raging fire, and the strong arms cradling her were those of her father, Smilin' Bob Woodhouse. He was dressed in working gear: helmet with unit and badge numbers on the frontpiece, turnout coat with reflective safety stripes, fireproof gloves. His fireboots crunched through smoldering rubble as he bore her purposefully toward safety.

"But, Daddy, you're dead," Martie said, and Smilin' Bob said, "Well, I'm dead and I'm not, Miss M., but since when does being dead mean I wouldn't be there for you?"

Flames encircled them, sometimes lambent and transparent, other times seeming to be as solid as stone, as though this were not merely a place being destroyed by fire, but a place constructed of fire, the Parthenon of the fire god himself, massive columns and lintels and archways of fire, mosaic floors of intricate flame patterns, vaulted ceilings of fire, room after room of eternal conflagrations, through which they passed in search of an exit that seemed not to exist.

Yet Martie felt safe in the cradle of her father's arms, holding on to him, with her left arm around his shoulders, certain he would carry her out of this place sooner or later—until, glancing behind them, she saw their pursuer. The Leaf Man followed, and though the very substance of him was ablaze, he wasn't diminished by the flames that fed on him. If anything, he appeared to grow both larger and stronger, because the fire wasn't his enemy; it was the source of his strength. As he drew closer to them, shedding sparkling leaves and veils of ashes, he reached out with both hands for Smilin' Bob and for the firefighter's daughter, clawing the hot air before her face. She began to shake and to sob with terror even in her father's arms, sobbing, sobbing. Closer, closer, the dark eyeholes and the hungry black maw, ragged-leaf lips and teeth of fire, closer, closer, and now she could hear the Leaf Man's autumn voice, as cold and prickly as a field of thistles under a full October moon: "I want to taste. I want to taste your tears—"

She was out of sleep in an instant and up from the bed, awake and alert, yet her face was as hot as if she were still surrounded by fire, and she could smell the faint scent of smoke.

They had left a light on in the bath and left the door ajar, so the claustrophobic hotel room would not be blind-dark. Martie could see well enough to know that the air was clear; there was no haze of smoke.

The faint but pungent smell was still with her, however, and she began to fear that the hotel was on fire, the scent—if not the smoke itself—seeping under the door from the hallway.

Dusty was asleep, and she was about to wake him, when she became aware of the man standing in the gloom. He was at the farthest remove from the pale wedge of bathroom light.

Martie couldn't see his face clearly, but there was no mistaking the shape of his fire helmet. Or the luminous safety stripes on his turnout coat.

A trick of shadows. Surely, surely. Yet . . . no. This wasn't mere illusion.

She was certain that she was wide-awake, as certain as she had ever been about anything in her life. And yet he stood there, only ten or twelve feet away, having carried her out of the nightmare of seething fire.

The dream world and the world in which this hotel room existed suddenly seemed equally valid, parts of the same reality, separated by a veil even thinner than the curtain of sleep. Here was truth, pure and piercing, as we are seldom given the chance to glimpse it, and Martie was breathless, transfixed by awareness.

She wanted to go to him but was restrained by a curious sense of propriety, by an innate understanding that his world was his and her world hers, that this temporary intersection of the two worlds was an ephemeral condition, a grace that she must not abuse.

In his shadows, the fireman—and also watchman—

appeared to nod approvingly at her restraint. She thought she saw the luminosity of teeth revealed in the crescent of a familiar and beloved smile.

She returned to bed, head propped on two pillows, and pulled the covers to her chin. Her face was no longer hot, and the scent of smoke was gone.

The nightstand clock showed 3:35 in the morning. She doubted that she would be able to sleep any more.

Wonderingly, she looked toward those special shadows, and still he was there.

She smiled and nodded and closed her eyes, and when in a little while she heard the distinctive squeak of his rubber fireboots and the rustle of his turnout coat, she didn't open her eyes. Nor did she open them when she felt the asbestos fireglove touch her head, nor when he smoothed her hair against the pillow.

Although Martie had expected to lie restless for the remainder of the night, a particularly peaceful sleep overcame her, until she stirred again more than an hour later, in the predawn stillness, just minutes before the wake-up call was due from the hotel operator.

She could no longer detect even the faintest trace of the scent of smoke, and no visitor stood watch in the satiny shadows. She was living in one world again, her world, so familiar, fearsome, and yet full of promise.

She couldn't prove to anyone else what had been real in the night and what had not, but to her own satisfaction, the truth was clear.

As the bedside phone rang with their wake-up call, she knew that she would never see Smilin' Bob again in this world, but she wondered how soon she would see him in his, whether in fifty years or sometime tomorrow.

64

High deserts seldom offer warmth in winter, and on Thursday morning at the Santa Fe Municipal Airport, the plane brought Martie and Dusty down into cold dry air, to a pale land as windless now as the surface of the moon.

They had carried both small pieces of luggage onto the flight, after the bag with the toy fire engine had passed inspection at the security gate in Orange County. With no need to visit the baggage carousel, they went directly to the car-rental agency.

Getting into the two-door Ford, Martie inhaled an orange grove's worth of citrus-scented air freshener. Yet the fragrance could not entirely mask the underlying noxiousness of stale cigarette smoke.

On Cerrillos Road, as Dusty drove into the city, Martie removed the brass screws from the bottom of the fire truck. She extracted the felt shoe bag from the truck, and the pistol from the shoe bag.

"You want to carry?" she asked Dusty.

"No, you go ahead."

Dusty had ordered the supertuned Springfield Armory Champion, a version of the Colt Commander produced by Springfield's custom shop, with numerous aftermarket parts. Featuring a beveled magazine well, a throated barrel, a lowered and flared ejection port, a Novak low-mount combat sight, a polished feed ramp, a polished extractor and ejector, and an A-1 style trigger tuned to a 4.5-pound pull, the seven-shot pistol was lightweight, compact, and easy to control.

Initially she had been opposed to owning the gun. After having fired two thousand rounds during a dozen visits to a shooting range, however, she'd proved to be somewhat more effective with the weapon than Dusty was, which surprised her more than it surprised him.

She slipped the pistol into her purse. This wasn't the ideal way to carry it, because making a quick and unhampered draw wasn't possible. Dusty had researched holsters, strictly for use on the shooting range, but he hadn't gotten around to selecting one yet.

Because she was wearing blue jeans, a navy-blue sweater, and a blue tweed jacket, Martie could have tucked the gun under her belt, either against her abdomen or in the small of her back, and concealed it with the sweater. In either case, the discomfort factor would be too high, so the purse was the only choice.

"We're now officially outlaws," she said, leaving the central compartment of the purse unzipped, for easier access.

"We were already outlaws the moment we boarded the plane."

"Yeah, well, now we're outlaws in New Mexico, too."

"How's it feel?"

"Didn't Billy Bonney come from Santa Fe?" she asked.

"Billy the Kid? I don't know."

"He came from New Mexico, anyway. How I feel is not a damn thing like Billy the Kid, let me tell you. Unless he walked around so scared that he worried about wetting his pants."

They stopped at a shopping center and purchased a tape recorder with a supply of minicassettes and batteries.

Using a directory chained in a public telephone booth, their breath pluming frostily over the pages, they went through the short list of names they had culled from the articles in Roy Closterman's file. Some were not listed, having either died or moved out of town—or perhaps the now grown-up girls had married and were living under new names. Still, they found addresses for a few people on the list.

In the car again, eating a lunch of chicken tacos from a fast-food joint, Dusty studied the city map provided by the rental agency, while Martie inserted batteries in the tape recorder and scanned the operating instructions. The recorder was the essence of simplicity and easy to use.

They weren't sure what testimony they would be able to gather, whether any of it would support the story that they themselves hoped to bring to the police in California, but they had nothing to lose by trying. Without the statements of others who'd suffered at the hands of Ahriman, to establish context, the complaints Martie and Dusty filed would have the grotesque quality of paranoid rants and would not be taken seriously, even with the tape of Susan's phone call.

Two advantages gave them heart. First, because of what Roy Closterman had uncovered, they knew there were people in Santa Fe who hated Ahriman, who suspected him of the worst offenses against his oaths as a medical doctor and therapist, and who were frustrated beyond endurance to see him escape prosecution and move out of state with his reputation intact and with his license to practice medicine unchallenged. Surely, these individuals were potential allies.

Second, because Ahriman wasn't aware that they knew of his past and because he wasn't likely to credit them with either the ambition or the intelligence to discover the roots of his earliest attempts at brainwashing, he wouldn't think to look for them in Santa Fe. Which meant that at least for a day or two, and perhaps longer, they could operate without attracting the frightening attention of the mystery men who had cut off Brian's ear.

Here in the land of Ahriman's past, flying below the

radar of the psychiatrist and his enigmatic associates, they might be able to gather enough information to make their story credible when at last they approached the authorities in California.

No. *Might* wasn't an acceptable word. *Might* was a loser's word. *Must* was the word she wanted, from the vocabulary of winners. They *must* gather enough information; and because they must, they would.

Action.

Leaving the shopping center, Martie drove while Dusty consulted the map and gave directions.

Over this high land, the sky was low and the color of New Mexico gypsum. Those slowly grinding clouds were icy, too, and according to the radio weather report, they were going to scrape some snow off one another before the day was out.

Only a few blocks from the Cathedral of Saint Francis of Assisi, the residence was surrounded by an adobe wall with a raised, stepped arch in which was set a spindled wooden gate.

Martie parked at the curb. She and Dusty went visiting with tape recorder and concealed pistol, bringing a little California style to mystic Santa Fe.

Beside the gate, a cascading *ristra* of red chiles spilled down the earthen wall under a copper lamp with coppery mica panes. This bright autumn decoration, long past its season, was frosty in parts but colorful and glossy where ice jacketed the chiles.

The gate was ajar, and beyond lay a brick forecourt. Agave and century plants bristled low, and tall piñons would have cast deep shadows had there been sun.

The single-story, pueblo-style house, by itself, validated the state's claim to be the Land of Enchantment. Solid and round-edged, all soft lines and earth tones. Deep door and window openings, with simple fenestration.

A porch extended the width of the structure, supported by time-smoothed fir-log columns and by carved corbels painted with blue star designs. In the ceiling, aspen *latillas* bridged the spaces between the large fir *vigas* that supported the roof.

Rosettes, conchas, and rope braids were carved into the arched front door. The hand-forged, hand-stamped iron coyote knocker hung from its hind legs. Its forelegs swung against a large iron *clavo* set in the door, and when Dusty knocked, the sound carried across the forecourt in the cold, still air.

The thirty-something woman who responded to the knock must have been only two generations out of Italy on one side of her family; but another branch of her tree unmistakably had Navajo grafted onto it. Lovely, with high cheekbones, eyes as black as raven feathers, hair even blacker than Martie's, she was a Southwest princess in a white blouse with bluebirds embroidered on the collar, a faded denim skirt, folded bobbysocks, and scuffed white sneakers.

Dusty introduced himself and Martie. "We're looking for Chase Glyson."

"I'm Zina Glyson," she said, "his wife. Maybe I can help."

Dusty hesitated, and Martie said, "We'd very much like to talk to him about Dr. Ahriman. Mark Ahriman."

No tension came into Mrs. Glyson's serene face, and her voice remained pleasant when she said, "You come here to my door, speaking the devil's name. Why should I talk to you?"

"He's not the devil," Martie said. "He's more a vampire, and we want to drive a stake straight through the bastard's heart."

Mrs. Glyson's direct and analytic stare was as penetrating as that of any elder sitting on a tribal council. After a moment, she stepped back and invited them off the cold porch, into the warm rooms beyond the thick adobe walls.

Ordinarily, the doctor did not carry a concealed weapon, but with all the unknowables of the Rhodes situation, he believed that prudence required him to be armed.

Martie and Dusty were no immediate danger to him out there in New Mexico. They would pose no threat when and if they returned, either, unless he wasn't able to get close enough to them to speak the names—*Shaw*, *Narvilly*—that activated their programs.

Skeet was another matter. His holey brain, drilled by drugs, didn't seem able to hold the essential details of a control program without periodic reloading. If the little dope fiend, for whatever reason, got it into his addled head to stalk Ahriman, he might not respond immediately to *Dr. Yen Lo* and might be able to use a knife or gun or whatever other weapon he was carrying.

The doctor's double-breasted, gray pinstripe suit by Ermenegildo Zegna was elegantly tailored; and strictly as a fashion issue, there ought to have been a federal law against spoiling the garment's lines by wearing a shoulder holster under it. Fortunately, ever the man of foresight, the doctor had commissioned a custom holster of supple leather, which carried his pistol so deep under the arm and so snugly against the body that even the master tailors in Italy would not have been able to detect the weapon.

Unsightly bulge was eliminated, as well, by the fact that the weapon was a compact automatic, the Taurus PT-111 Millennium fitted with a Pearce grip extension. Quite small, but powerful.

After his busy night, the doctor had slept late, which was possible because he didn't need to keep the usual Thursday-morning appointment with Susan Jagger now that she was so dead. With no commitments until after lunch, he enjoyed a visit to his favorite antique-toy store, where he purchased a mint-condition Gunsmoke Dodge City playset by Marx for only $3,250, and a die-cast Johnny Lightning Custom Ferrari for only $115.

A couple of other customers were browsing in the store, chatting with the owner, and Dr. Ahriman had great fun imagining what it would be like to surprise them by drawing his pistol and gutshooting them without provocation. He did not do this, of course, because he was pleased with his purchases and wanted the owner to feel comfortable with him when he returned to shop for other treasures in the future.

The kitchen was redolent of baking corn bread, and from a large pot on the stove rose the beefy aroma of beanless chili.

Zina phoned her husband at work. They owned a gallery on Canyon Road. When he heard why Martie and Dusty had sought him out, he came home in less than ten minutes.

While waiting for him, Zina set out red ceramic mugs of strong coffee mellowed with cinnamon, and pinwheel cookies topped with toasted pine nuts.

Chase, when he arrived, appeared to earn his living not in an art gallery but as a cowboy on the range: tall and lanky, tousled straw-yellow hair, a handsome face abraded by wind and sun. He was one of those men who, just by walking through any stable, would win the trust of horses, which would nicker softly at him and strain their necks across stall doors to nuzzle his hands.

His voice was quiet but intense as he sat down at the kitchen table with them. "What has Ahriman done to you and yours?"

Martie told him about Susan. The worsening agoraphobia, the suspected rapes. The sudden suicide.

"He made her do it somehow," Chase Glyson said. "I believe it. I absolutely do. You came all this way because of your friend?"

"Yes. My dearest friend." Martie saw no reason to tell more.

"Over nineteen years," Chase said, "since he ruined my family, and more than ten since he hauled his sick ass out of Santa Fe. For a while, I hoped he was dead. Then he got famous with his books."

"Do you mind if we tape what you tell us?" Dusty asked.

"No, don't mind at all. But what I've got to say . . . hell, I've said it all maybe a hundred times to the cops, to different district attorneys over the years, until I was bluer in the face than a blue coyote. No one listened to me. Well, the once when someone listened and thought I might be telling the truth, then some big-shot friends of Ahriman's paid him a visit, taught him some religion, so he'd know what he damn well was *supposed* to believe about my mom and dad."

While Martie and Dusty taped Chase Glyson, Zina perched on a stool before an easel near the adobe fireplace, drawing a pencil study of a humble tableau that she'd earlier set up on one corner of the distressed-pine table at which the rest of them sat. Five pieces of Indian pottery in unusual shapes, including a double-spouted wedding pitcher.

The essence of Chase's story was the same as in the clippings from Roy Closterman's file. Teresa and Carl Glyson had for years operated a successful preschool, the Little Jackrabbit School, until they and three employees were accused of molesting children of both sexes. As in the Ornwahl case in Laguna Beach years later, Ahriman conducted supposedly careful, psychiatrically valid exploratory conversations with the kids, sometimes using hypnotic regression—and found a pattern of stories supporting the original accusations.

"The whole thing was a lot of bushwa, Mr. Rhodes,"

said Chase Glyson. "My folks were the best people you'd want to meet."

Zina said, "Terri, that was Chase's mother, would have cut off her hand before she'd raise it to hurt a child."

"My daddy, too," said Chase. "Besides, he was hardly ever at the Little Jackrabbit. Only to do some repairs now and then, 'cause he was handy. The school was my mother's business. Daddy was half owner of a car dealership, and it kept him busy. Lots of people in town, they never believed a word of it."

"But there were those who did," Zina added darkly.

"Oh," said Chase, "there's always those who'll believe anything about anybody. You whisper in their ear that 'cause there was wine at the Last Supper, Jesus must've been a drunkard, and they'll gossip their souls into perdition, passing it along. Most people figured it couldn't be true, and with no physical evidence, it might never have resulted in convictions . . . until Valerie-Marie Padilla killed herself."

Martie said, "One of the students, that five-year-old girl."

"Yes, ma'am." Chase's face seemed to darken as if a cloud had passed between him and the ceiling lights. "She left that good-bye of hers, that colored-pencil drawing, that sad little scribble drawing that changed everything. Her and a man."

"Anatomically correct," Martie said.

"Worse, the man had a mustache . . . like my daddy. In the drawing, he's wearing a cowboy hat, white with a red band, and a black feather tucked in it. Which is the type of hat my daddy always wore."

With a violence that drew their attention, Zina Glyson tore off the top sheet from her drawing pad, balled it up, and threw it into the fireplace. "Chase's father was my godfather, my own father's best friend. I knew Carl from when I was a toddler. That man . . . he respected people, no matter who they were, no matter how little they had or what their faults. He respected children, too, and listened to them, and cared. Never once did he ever put his hand on me *that* way, and I know he didn't touch Valerie-Marie. If she killed herself, it's because of the hateful, evil stuff Ahriman put in her head, all the twisted sex and stories about sacrificing animals at the school and being forced to drink their blood. This child was *five*. What mess do you make of a little child's mind, what awful depression do you instigate when you ask her about stuff like that under hypnosis, when you *help* her remember what never happened?"

"Easy, Zee," her husband said softly. "It's all over long ago."

"Not for me, it isn't." She went to the ovens. "It won't be over until he's dead." She slipped her right hand into an oven mitt. "And then I won't believe his obituary." She drew a pan of finished corn bread from the oven. "I'll have to look at his corpse myself and stick a finger in its eye to see if he reacts."

If she was Italian, then she was Sicilian, and if she was part Indian, she was not a peaceful Navajo but an Apache. There was an unusual strength in her, a toughness, and if she'd had the chance to finish Ahriman herself without being caught, she probably would have acted on the opportunity.

Martie liked her a lot.

"I was seventeen at the time," Chase said, almost to himself. "God knows why they didn't accuse me, too. How did I escape? When they're burning witches, why not the whole family?"

Returning to something that Zina had said, Dusty raised a key question: "*If* she committed suicide? What did you mean by that?"

"Tell him, Chase," said Zina, moving from the corn bread to the pot of chili. "See if they think it sounds like something a little child would do to herself."

"Her mother was in the next room," Chase said. "She

heard the gunshot, ran, found Valerie-Marie seconds after it happened. No one else could've been there. The girl definitely killed herself with her father's pistol."

"She had to get the pistol out of a box in the closet," Zina said. "And a separate box of ammunition. And load the thing. A child who'd never handled a gun in her life."

"Even that isn't the hardest to believe," Chase said. "What's hardest is . . ." He hesitated. "This is awful stuff, Mrs. Rhodes."

"I'm getting used to it," Martie grimly assured him.

Chase said, "The way Valerie-Marie killed herself . . . the news quoted Ahriman as calling it 'an act of self-loathing, of gender denial, an attempt to destroy the sexual aspect of herself that had led to her being molested.' That little girl, you see, before she pulled the trigger, she undressed herself, and then she put the gun . . . inside. . . ."

Martie was on her feet before she realized that she intended to get out of her chair. "Dear God." She needed to move, to go somewhere, do something, but there was nowhere to go except—as she discovered when she got there—to Zina Glyson, around whom she put her arms as she would have put them around Susan at such a moment as this. "Were you dating Chase then?"

"Yes," Zina said.

"And stood by him. And married him."

"Thank God," Chase murmured.

"What it must have been like," Martie said, "after the suicide, to defend Carl to other women, and stand by his son."

Zina had accepted Martie's embrace as naturally as it had been given. The memory made this Southwest princess tremble after all these years, but both Sicilian and Apache women were loath to cry.

"No one accused Chase," she said, "but he was suspected. And me . . . people smiled, but they kept their children at a distance from me. For years."

Martie brought Zina back to the table, and the four of them sat together.

"Forget all that psychological blather about gender denial and destroying her sexual aspect," said Zina. "What Valerie-Marie did, no child would think to do. No child. That little girl did what she did because someone put it in her head to do it. Impossible as it seems, crazy as it sounds, Ahriman showed her how to load a gun, and Ahriman told her what to do to herself, and she went home and just *did* it, because she was . . . she was, I don't know, hypnotized or something."

"It doesn't sound impossible or crazy to us," Dusty assured her.

The town was torn apart by Valerie-Marie Padillo's death, and the possibility that other Little Jackrabbit kids might be suicidally depressed caused a sort of mass hysteria that Zina called the Plague Year. It was during this plague that a jury of seven women and five men returned unanimous guilty verdicts against all five defendants.

"You probably know," said Chase, "other inmates consider child molesters the lowest of the low. My daddy . . . he lasted just nineteen months before he was killed at his job in the prison kitchen. Four stab wounds, one through each kidney from behind, two through the gut from in front. Probably, two guys sandwiched him. No one would ever talk, so no one was ever charged."

"Is your mother still alive?" Dusty asked.

Chase shook his head. "The other three ladies from the school, nice people, all of them—they served four years each. My mom, she was released after five, and when they let her go, she had cancer."

"Officially, the cancer killed her, but what really killed her was shame," Zina said. "Terri was a good woman, a kind woman, and a *proud* woman. She'd done nothing, *nothing*, but she was eaten up by shame just dwelling on what people *thought* she'd done. She lived with us, but it wasn't long. The school had been closed, Carl lost his interest in the car dealership. Legal bills took everything. We were still scraping by ourselves, and we hardly had money to bury her. Thirteen years, she's dead. Might as well be yesterday to me."

"What's it like here for you, these days?" Dusty asked.

Zina and Chase exchanged a look, volumes written in one glance.

He said, "A lot better than it used to be. Some people still believe it all, but not many after the Pastore killings. And some of the Little Jackrabbit kids . . . they eventually recanted their stories."

"Not for ten years." Zina's eyes in that moment were blacker than anthracite and harder than iron.

Chase sighed. "Maybe it took ten years for those false memories to start falling apart. I don't know."

"In all that time," Martie wondered, "did you ever think of just picking up and leaving Santa Fe?"

"We love Santa Fe," Chase said, and his heart seemed to be in his declaration.

"It's the best place on earth," Zina agreed. "Besides, if we'd ever left, there are a few out there who would've said our leaving proved all of it was true, that we were crawling away in shame."

Chase nodded. "But just a few."

"If it was just one," Zina said, "I wouldn't have left and given him the satisfaction."

Zina's hands were on the table, and Chase covered both of them with one of his. "Mr. Rhodes, if you think it would help you, some of those Little Jackrabbit kids, the ones who recanted, I know they would talk to you. They've come to us. They've apologized. They aren't bad people. They were used. I think they'd like to help."

"If you could set it up," Dusty said, "we'll devote tomorrow to them. Today, while there's still light and before it snows, we want to go out to the Pastore ranch."

Chase pushed his chair back from the table and got to

his feet, seeming taller than he had been earlier. “You know the way?”

“We’ve got a map,” Dusty said.

“Well, I’ll lead you halfway,” Chase said. “Because halfway to the Pastore ranch, there’s something you should see. The Bellon-Tockland Institute.”

“What’s that?”

“Hard to say. Been there twenty-five years. It’s where you’ll find Mark Ahriman’s friends, if he has any.”

Without pulling on a jacket or sweater, Zina walked with them to the street.

The piñons in the forecourt were as still as trees in a diorama, sealed behind glass.

The squeak of the iron hinges on the spindled gate was the only sound in the winter day, as if every soul in the city had vanished, as if Santa Fe were a ghost ship on a sea of sand.

No traffic moved on the street. No cats roamed, no birds flew. A great weight of stillness pressed down on the world.

To Chase, whose Lincoln Navigator was parked in front of them, Dusty said, “Does that van across the street belong to a neighbor?”

Chase looked, shook his head. “I don’t think so. Maybe. Why?”

“No reason. Nice-looking van, is all.”

“Something’s coming down,” Zina said, gazing at the sky.

At first Martie thought she meant snow was falling, but there was no snow.

The sky was more white than gray. If the clouds were moving at all, their motion was internal, concealed behind the pale skin that they presented to the world below.

“Something bad.” Zina put her hand on Martie’s arm. “My Apache premonition. Warrior blood senses violence coming. You be careful, Martie Rhodes.”

"We will be."

"Wish you lived in Santa Fe."

"Wish you lived in California."

"World's too big, and all of us too small," Zina said, and again they hugged each other.

In the car, as Martie pulled into the street, following Chase's Navigator, she glanced at Dusty. "What about the van?"

Turned in his seat, peering through the rear window, he said, "Thought maybe I'd seen it earlier."

"Where?"

"At the shopping center where we bought the recorder."

"Is it coming?"

"No."

One right turn and three blocks later, she asked, "Yet?"

"No. Guess I was wrong."

65

In California, one time zone farther west than Santa Fe, Mark Ahriman ate lunch alone, at a table for two, in a stylish bistro in Laguna Beach. A dazzling Pacific vista lay to his left; a generally well-dressed and monied luncheon crowd was seated to his right.

Not all was perfect. Two tables away, a thirtyish gentleman—and this was stretching the word to its elastic limits—let out a bray of laughter from time to time, so harsh and protracted that all donkeys west of the Pecos must have pricked their ears at each outburst. A grandmotherly woman at the next table was wearing an absurd mustard-yellow cloche hat. Six younger women at the far end of the room were obnoxiously giggly. The waiter brought the wrong appetizer, and then didn't return with the correct dish for a tedious number of minutes.

Nevertheless, the doctor didn't shoot any of them. For a true gamesman like him, little pleasure was to be had in a simple shooting spree. Mindless blasting appealed to the deranged, to the hopelessly stupid, to waxed-off teenage boys with far too much self-esteem and no self-discipline, and to the fanatical political types who wanted to change the world by Tuesday. Besides, his mini-9mm pistol had a double-column magazine that held only ten rounds.

After finishing lunch with a slice of flourless dark-chocolate cake and saffron ice cream, the doctor paid his check and departed, granting absolution even to the woman in the absurd cloche hat.

Thursday afternoon was pleasantly cool, not chilly. The wind had blown itself to far Japan during the night. The sky was pregnant, but the rain that was supposed to break shortly after dawn had not yet been delivered.

While the valet brought the Mercedes, Dr. Ahriman examined his fingernails. He was so pleased by the quality of his manicure that he almost didn't pay attention to the surrounding scene, didn't look up from his hands—strong, manly, and yet with the gracefully tapered fingers of a concert pianist—almost didn't see the stranger lounging against a pickup parked across the street.

The truck was beige, well maintained but not new, the type of vehicle that would never be collectible even a thousand years from now and, therefore, one in which Ahriman had so little interest that he had no idea what make or model year it was. The bed of the truck was covered by a white camper shell, and the doctor shivered at the thought of a vacation thus spent.

The lounging man, although a stranger, was vaguely familiar. He was in his early forties, with reddish hair, a round red face, and thick eyeglasses. He was not staring directly at Ahriman, but there was something about his demeanor that screamed *surveillance*. He made a production of checking his wristwatch, and then looking impatiently toward a nearby store, as if waiting for someone, but his acting ability was far inferior even to that of the movie star currently preparing for his once-in-a-career role as a presidential nose nosher.

The antique-toy shop. Just a few hours ago. A half-hour drive and six towns away from here. That was where the doctor had seen the blushing man. When he'd amused himself by imagining the surprise that would sweep the shop staff if he gut-shot the other customers for no reason other than whimsy, *this* was one of two patrons who, in his mind's eye, had been targets.

In a county with a population of three million, it was difficult to believe that this second encounter in only a few hours was merely happenstance.

A beige pickup with a camper shell was not a vehicle one would ordinarily associate with either undercover police surveillance or a private detective.

When Ahriman took a closer look at it, however, he saw that the truck boasted two antennae in addition to the standard radio aerial. One was a whip antenna, attached to the cab, most likely in support of a police-band receiver. The other was an odd item bolted to the rear bumper: a six-foot-long, straight, silvery antenna with a spiked knob at the top, surrounded by a black coil.

Driving away from the restaurant, Dr. Ahriman was not surprised to see the pickup following him.

The blushing man's trailing technique was amateurish. He did not stay on the bumper of the Mercedes, and he allowed one or even two vehicles to intervene and screen him, as perhaps he had learned from watching idiotic detective shows on television, but he didn't have sufficient confidence to let Ahriman out of his sight for more than a second or two; he constantly drove close to the center line of the street or as near to the parked cars on the right as he dared get, shifting back and forth as the traffic in front of him briefly obscured his view of the Mercedes. Consequently, in the doctor's rearview and side mirrors, the pickup was the only anomaly in the traffic pattern, unprofessionally visible, its big antennae slashing at the air, weaving like a Dodgem car in a carnival ride.

These days, with advanced transponder technology and even with satellite tracking available to them, the pros could trail a suspect all day and night without actually being within a mile of him. This tracker in the pickup was such a loser that his only professional act was *not* decorating his antennae with Day-Glo Styrofoam balls.

The doctor was baffled—and intrigued.

He began switching streets with regularity, steadily moving into less-traveled residential neighborhoods, where there was no traffic to screen the pickup. As expected, the stalker compensated for the loss of cover merely by dropping farther back, nearly one block, as though confident that his quarry's mental capacity and radius of concern were equal to that of a myopic cow.

Without indicating his intention with a turn signal, the doctor abruptly hung a hard right, sped to the nearest house, shot into the driveway, shifted into reverse, backed into the street, and returned the way he had come—just in time to meet the pickup as it rounded the corner in lame-brained pursuit.

As he approached and passed the truck, Dr. Ahriman pretended to be looking for an address, as if utterly unaware of being tailed. Two quick leftward glances were sufficient to take a great deal of the mystery out of this game. At the corner, he actually stopped, got out of the Mercedes, and went to the street sign, where he stood peering up at the name and the block numbers, scratching his head and consulting an imaginary address on an imaginary piece of paper in his hand, as though someone had given him incorrect information.

When he returned to his car and drove away, he poked until he saw the beige pickup fall in behind him once more. He didn't want to lose them.

But for the shared browsing at the toy shop this morning, the driver was still a stranger to him; however, the driver was not alone in the truck. Boggling in surprise and then quickly turning his head away when he saw Ahriman's Mercedes, Skeet Caulfield had been riding in the passenger's seat.

While Dusty and Martie were digging into the doctor's past in New Mexico, Skeet was playing detective, too. This was undoubtedly his own half-baked idea, because his brother was too smart to have put him up to it.

The blushing man with the Mount Palomar spectacles was probably one of Skeet's dope-smoking, dope-swilling, dope-shooting buddies. Sherlock Holmes and Watson played by Cheech and Chong.

Regardless of what happened to Dusty and Martie in New Mexico, Skeet was the biggest loose end. Getting rid of the cheese-headed doper had been a priority for two days, since the doctor had sent him toddling away to jump off a roof.

Now, relieved of the need to locate Skeet, Dr. Ahriman must only drive considerately, keeping the boy in tow, until he had time to assess the situation and to settle upon the best strategy to take advantage of this fortuitous development. The game was on.

Martie followed Chase Glyson's Navigator into the parking lot of a roadhouse a few miles past the city line, where a giant dancing cowboy was depicted in mid sashay with a giant cowgirl, outlined in neon but unlit now, with a few hours remaining till the music and the drinking started. They parked facing away from the building, looking toward the highway.

Chase left his SUV and settled into the back of the rental Ford. "That, over there, is the Bellon-Tockland Institute."

The institute occupied approximately twenty acres in the middle of a much larger tract of undeveloped sage. It was surrounded by an eight-foot-high, stacked-stone wall.

The building looming beyond the wall had been inspired by Frank Lloyd Wright, in particular by his most famous house, Fallingwater. Except that this was

Fallingwater without the water, and it was overscaled in violation—perhaps even in contempt—of Wright's belief that every structure must be in harmony with the land on which it rested. This massive stone-and-stucco pile, two hundred thousand square feet if it was an inch, didn't hug the stark desert contours; it seemed to *explode* from them, more an act of violence than a work of architecture. This was what one of Wright's works might look like if reinterpreted by Albert Speer, Hitler's favorite architect.

"A bit Goth," Dusty said.

"What do they do in there?" Martie asked. "Plan the end of the world?"

Chase wasn't reassuring. "Probably, yeah. I've never been able to make sense of what they *say* they do, but maybe you're not as dense as me. Research, they say, research that leads to . . ." Now he quoted from something he must have read: " 'Applying the latest discoveries in psychology and psychopharmacology to design more equitable and stable structural models for government, business, culture, and for society as a whole, which will contribute to a clean environment, a more reliable system of justice, the fulfillment of human potential, and world peace—' "

"And, at long last, the end of that nasty old rock-'n'-roll," Dusty added scornfully.

"Brainwashing," Martie declared.

"Well," said Chase, "I guess I wouldn't argue with you on that—or on much of anything you chose to say. Might even have a crashed alien spaceship in there, for all I know."

"I'd rather it was aliens, even nasty ones with a taste for human livers," Dusty said. "That wouldn't scare me half as much as Big Brother."

"Oh, this isn't a government shop," Chase Glyson assured him. "At least there's not a visible connection."

"Then who are they?"

"The institute was originally capitalized by twenty-two major universities and six big-bucks private foundations from all over the country, and they're the ones who keep it running year after year, along with some large grants from major corporations."

"Universities?" Martie frowned. "That disappoints the raving paranoid in me. Big Professor isn't as spooky as Big Brother."

"You wouldn't feel that way if you'd spent more time with Lizard Lampton," Dusty said.

"Lizard Lampton?" Chase asked.

"Dr. Derek Lampton. My stepfather."

"Considering that they're working for world peace," Chase said, "it's a damn tightly guarded place."

Less than fifty yards to the north, cars entering the institute had to stop at a formidable-looking gate next to a guardhouse. Three uniformed men attended to each visitor as he came to the head of the line, and one of them even circled each vehicle with an angled mirror on a pole, to inspect the undercarriage.

"Looking for what?" Dusty wondered. "Stowaways, bombs?"

"Maybe both. Heavy electronic security, too, probably better than out at Los Alamos."

"Maybe that's not saying much," Dusty noted, "since the Chinese waltzed out of Los Alamos with all our nuclear secrets."

Martie said, "Judging by all this security, we don't need to worry about the Chinese making off with our *peace* secrets."

"Ahriman was deep into this place," Chase said. "He had his own practice in town, but this was his real work. And when strings had to be pulled to save his ass, after the Pastore killings, these were the people pulling them."

Martie didn't get it. "But if they aren't government types, how can they make cops and district attorneys and everyone else dance to their tune?"

"Lots of money, for one thing. And connections. Just

because they aren't government doesn't mean they don't have influence in all branches of the government . . . and the police, and the media. These guys are more connected than the Mafia but with a whole lot better image."

"Creating world peace instead of peddling dope, counterfeiting CDs, and loan-sharking."

"Exactly. And if you think about it, they've got a better setup than if they were government. No congressional oversight committees. No humbug politicians to answer to. Just some good guys, doing good stuff, for a good tomorrow, which makes it unlikely anyone would take a really close look at them. Hell, whatever they're doing in that place, I'm sure most of them *believe* they're good guys saving the world."

"But you don't."

"Because of what Ahriman did to my folks and because he was in so tight with this place. But most people around here, they don't think about the institute. It's not important to them. Or if they do think about it, they just have this sort of fuzzy-warm feeling."

"Who are Bellon and Tockland?" Martie asked.

"Kornell Bellon, Nathaniel Tockland. Two bigwigs in the world of psychology, professors once. The place was their idea. Bellon died a few years ago. Tockland's seventy-nine, retired, married to this knockout-looking, smart, funny lady—a rich heiress, too!—about fifty years younger. If you met the two of them, you'd never in this life figure out what she sees in him, because he's as humorless and dull and ugly as he is old."

Martie's eyes met Dusty's. "Haiku."

"Or something like."

Chase said, "Anyway, I thought you ought to see this. Because somehow, I don't know, but somehow it explains Ahriman. And it gives you a better idea what you're up against."

In spite of its Wrightian influence, the institute nevertheless looked as though it would be better suited to its environment if it were situated high in the Carpathians, just down the road from the castle of Baron von Frankenstein, wreathed ever in mists and struck with regularity by great bolts of lightning that sustained rather than damaged it.

Following a fine lunch, Dr. Ahriman had intended to swing by the Rhodeses' residence and have a look at what the fire had wrought. Now that Skeet and the reincarnation of Inspector Clouseau were on his tail, taking that scenic route seemed unwise.

Anyway, his day was not entirely given to leisure, and he did have a patient scheduled this afternoon. He drove directly, though sedately, to his offices in Fashion Island.

He pretended to be unaware of the pickup as it parked in the same lot, two rows back from his Mercedes.

His suite on the fourteenth floor was ocean-facing, but he went first to the offices of an ear-nose-and-throat specialist on the east side of the building. The waiting room featured windows that looked down on the parking lot.

The receptionist, busy with typing, never looked up as Ahriman went to the window, no doubt assuming he was just another patient who would have to wait with the rest of the runny-nosed, red-eyed, raspy-throated, forlorn bunch sitting in uncomfortable chairs and reading ancient, bacteria-infested magazines.

He spotted his Mercedes and quickly located the beige pickup with the white camper shell. The intrepid duo had gotten out of the truck. They were stretching their legs, rolling their shoulders, getting a breath of fresh air, obviously prepared to wait until their quarry reappeared.

Good.

Arriving at his suite, the doctor asked his secretary, Jennifer, if she had enjoyed her sandwich of tofu cheese and bean sprouts on rye crackers, which was her Thursday lunch.

When he was assured that it had been delicious—she was a health-food nut, no doubt born with less than half the usual number of taste buds—he spent a few minutes pretending to be interested in the nutritional imperative of taking huge regular supplements of ginko biloba, and then closeted himself in his office.

He phoned Cedric Hawthorne, his house manager, and requested that the least conspicuous car in his street-rod collection—a 1959 Chevrolet El Camino—be left in the parking lot of the building next door to the one in which the doctor had his offices. The keys were to be placed in a magnetic box under the right rear fender. Cedric's wife could follow in another car and return him to the house.

"Oh, and bring a ski mask," the doctor added. "Leave it under the driver's seat."

Cedric did not ask why a ski mask was wanted. It was not his job to pose questions. He was too well trained for that. Very well trained. "Yes, certainly, sir, one ski mask."

The doctor already had a handgun.

He had arrived at a strategy.

The game pieces were now all in place.

Soon, playtime.

66

The ranch house featured time-worn Mexican-paver floors and ceilings of exposed *vigas* separating inlays of aspen *latillas*. In the main rooms, aromatic fires—subtly scented by pine cones and by a few cedar splits—crackled in sensuously sculpted adobe fireplaces. Except for the upholstered armchairs and sofas, the tables and chairs and cabinets were mostly WPA-era pieces, reminiscent of Stickley furniture, and everywhere underfoot were fine Navajo rugs—except in the room where the deaths had occurred.

No fire burned here. All but one piece of the furniture had been removed and sold. The floor was bare.

Thin gray light pierced the curtainless window, and a chill radiated from the walls. Now and then, in her peripheral vision, Martie thought she saw the gray light bend around something, as if strangely deflected by the soundless passage of a nearly transparent figure, but when she looked directly, nothing was there; the light was hard and unbent. And yet, here, it was easy to believe in unseen presences.

In the center of the room stood a wooden chair with a spindle back, no padding on the flat seat. Perhaps it had been selected for the degree of discomfort that it ensured. Some monks believed that the ability to focus for meditation and prayer was diminished by comfort.

"I sit here a few times each week," said Bernardo

Pastore, "for ten or fifteen minutes usually . . . but sometimes for hours."

His voice was thick and slightly slurred. Words were marbles in his mouth, but he patiently polished them and got them out.

Dusty held the tape recorder with the built-in microphone turned toward the rancher, to be sure that his awkward speech was clearly captured.

The right half of Bernardo Pastore's rebuilt face was incapable of expression, the nerves irreparably damaged. His right jaw and part of his chin had been put back together with metal plates, wire, surgical screws, silicone parts, and bone grafts. The result was reasonably functional but not an aesthetic triumph.

"For the first year," Bernardo said, "I spent a lot of time in that chair just trying to understand how such a thing could be, how it could happen."

When he had hurried into this room in response to the gunfire that had killed his sleeping son, Bernardo had been hit by two rounds fired at close range by his wife, Fiona. The first had torn through his right shoulder, and the second had shattered his jaw.

"After a while there seemed to be no sense trying to understand. If it wasn't black magic, it was as good as. These days, I sit here just thinking about them, letting them know I love them, letting her know I don't blame her, that I know what she did was as big a mystery to her as it is to me. 'Cause I think that's true. It must be true."

His survival, surgeons claimed, was against all odds. The high-powered round that shattered his jaw had been miraculously deflected upward and back by the mandible, had traveled along the mastoid, and had exited his face above the zygomatic arch, without damaging the external carotid artery in the temple, which would have led to death long before medical assistance arrived.

"She loved Dion as much as I did, and all those accusations she made in her note, the things she said I'd done to her and Dion, they were untrue. And even if I'd done those things, and even if she had been suicidal, she wasn't the kind of woman to kill a child, her own child or any other."

Hit twice, Pastore had staggered to a tall chest of drawers near the window, which had been open to the summer night.

"And there he was, standing just outside, looking in at us, and the most godawful expression on his face. Grinning, he was, and his face all sweaty with excitement. His eyes shining."

"You're talking about Ahriman," Dusty clarified for the tape.

"Dr. Mark Ahriman," Pastore confirmed. "Standing there like he knew what was coming, like he had tickets to the killings, a front-row seat. He looked at me. What I saw in those eyes, I can't put into words. But if I've done more bad than good in my life, and if there's a place where we have to account for all we've done in this world, then I've no doubt I'll see eyes like that again." He was silent awhile, staring at the window that was now empty of everything but the austere light. "Then I fell."

Down, lying with the undamaged half of his face to the floor, vision swimming in and out, he had seen his wife kill herself and fall inches beyond his reach.

"Calm, so strangely calm. As if she didn't know what she was doing. No hesitation, no tears."

Bleeding, nauseous with pain, Bernardo Pastore had washed in and out of consciousness, minute by minute, but during each spell of awareness, he had dragged himself toward the telephone on the nightstand.

"I could hear coyotes outside, far away in the night at first, but then closer and closer. I didn't know if Ahriman was still at the window, but I suspected he was gone, and I was afraid that the coyotes, drawn by the scent of blood, might come through the window screen. They're shy creatures alone . . . but not in a pack."

He reached the phone, pulled it down onto the floor, and called for help, barely able to torture half-comprehensible words out of his swollen throat and shattered face.

"And then I waited, figuring I'd be dead before anyone got here. And that would have been all right. Maybe that would have been best. With Fiona and Dion gone, I didn't care much about living. Only two things made me want to hang on. Dr. Ahriman's involvement had to be uncovered, understood. I wanted justice. And second . . . though I was ready to die, I didn't want coyotes feeding on me and my family as if we were no different from chased-down rabbits."

Judging by how loud their cries became, the pack of coyotes had gathered under the window. Forepaws clawing at the sill. Snarling muzzles pressed against the screen.

As Pastore had grown weaker and his mind had become increasingly muddled, he had begun to believe that these were not coyotes seeking entrance, but creatures previously unknown to New Mexico, having come out of Elsewhere, through a door in the night itself. Brethren to Ahriman, with even stranger eyes than the doctor's. Pressing at the screen not because they were eager to feed on warm flesh, but drawn instead by a hunger for three fading souls.

The doctor's sole patient of the day was the thirty-two-year-old wife of a man who had made half a billion dollars in Internet-stock IPOs in just four years.

Although she was an attractive woman, he had not accepted her as a patient because of her looks. He had no sexual interest in her, because by the time she came to him, she was already as neurotic as a lab rat tortured for months by continuous changes in its maze and by randomly administered electric shocks. Ahriman was aroused only by women who came to him whole and healthy, with everything to lose.

The vast wealth of the patient was not a consideration, either. Because he had never experienced a shortage of wealth himself, the doctor harbored nothing but contempt for those who were motivated by money. The finest work was always done for the sheer pleasure of it.

The husband had harried the wife into Ahriman's care not so much because her condition concerned him as because he intended to run for the United States Senate. He believed that his political career would be jeopardized by a spouse given to eccentric outbursts bordering on lunacy, which was probably an unrealistic concern, considering that such outbursts had been for many years a staple of both politicians and their spouses, across the entire political spectrum, resulting in little negative consequences at the polls. Besides, the husband was as boring as a dead toad and unelectable in his own right.

The doctor had accepted her as a patient strictly because her condition interested him. This woman was steadily working herself into a unique phobia that might supply him with interesting material for future games. He was also likely to use her case in his next book, which would concern obsessions and phobias, and which he had tentatively titled *Fear Not for I Am with You*, though of course he would change her name to protect her privacy.

The would-be senator's wife had for some time been increasingly obsessed with an actor, Keanu Reeves. She assembled dozens of thick scrapbooks devoted to photographs of Keanu, articles about Keanu, and reviews of Keanu's films. No critic was half as familiar with this actor's filmography as she was, for in the comfort of her forty-seat home theater, on a full-size screen, she had watched each of his movies a minimum of twenty times and had once spent forty-eight hours watching *Speed* over and over, until she had at last passed out from a lack of sleep and a surfeit of Dennis Hopper. Not long ago she had purchased a two-hundred-thousand-dollar Cartier heart-shaped pendant, gold and diamonds, on the back of which she ordered engraved the words *I Krave Keanu.*

This lovefest had suddenly turned sour, for reasons the patient herself didn't understand. She began to suspect that Keanu had a dark side. That he had become aware of her interest in him and was not pleased. That he was hiring people to watch her. Then that he was watching her himself. When the telephone rang and the caller hung up without speaking, or when the caller said, *Sorry, wrong number,* she was convinced that it was Keanu. Once she had adored his face; now she became terrified of it. She destroyed all the scrapbooks and burned all the photographs of him in her bedroom, because she grew convinced that he could view her remotely through any picture of himself. Indeed, at the sight of his face, she was now stricken by a panic attack. She could no longer watch television, for fear of seeing an advertisement for his latest film. She dared not read most magazines, because she might turn a page and find Keanu watching her; even the sight of his name in print alarmed her, and her list of safe periodicals now included little more than *Foreign Policy Journal* and such medical publications as *Advancements in Kidney Dialysis.*

Dr. Ahriman knew that soon, as was the pattern in these cases, his patient would become convinced that Keanu Reeves was stalking her, following her everywhere she went, whereupon her phobia would be fully established. Thereafter, she would either stabilize and learn to live as restricted a life as Susan Jagger had lived under the influence of her agoraphobia, or she would descend into complete psychosis and perhaps require at least short-term care in a good institution.

Drug therapy offered hope to such patients, but the doctor did not intend to treat this one conventionally. Eventually, he would put her through three sessions of programming, not for the purpose of controlling her but simply to instruct her to be not afraid of Keanu. Thus, for his next book, he would have a great chapter about a miraculous cure, which he would attribute to his analytic skills and his therapeutic genius, concocting an elaborate story of therapy that he had, in fact, never performed.

He hadn't yet begun to brainwash her, because her phobia needed more time to ripen. She needed to suffer more in order that her cure would make a better story and to ensure that her gratitude, after she was made whole again, would be boundless. Properly played, she might even consent to appear on *Oprah* with him when his book was published.

Now, sitting in the armchair across the low table from her, he listened to her fevered speculations about the Machiavellian scheming of Mr. Reeves, not bothering to take notes because a hidden recorder was capturing her monologue and his occasional prodding question.

Impish as ever, the doctor suddenly thought how fun it would have been if the actor now waiting to assault the president's nose could have been Keanu himself. Imagine this patient's terror when learning of the news, which would absolutely convince her that hers would have been the savaged nose had not fate put the nation's chief executive in Keanu's path before her.

Ah, well. If there was a sense of humor behind the workings of the universe, it wasn't as acute as the doctor's.

"Doctor, you're not listening to me."

"But I am," he assured her.

"No, you were woolgathering, and I'm not paying these outrageous hourly rates so you can daydream," she said sharply.

Although just five short years ago, this woman and her boring husband had been barely able to afford fries with their Big Macs, they had become as imperious and demanding as if they had been born into vast wealth.

Indeed, her Keanu madness and her pan-faced husband's crazy need to seek validation at the ballot box resulted from the suddenness of their financial success, from a nagging guilt about having gained so much with so little effort, and from the unspoken fear that what had come so quickly could be quickly gone.

"You don't have a patient conflict here, do you?" she asked with sudden worry.

"Excuse me?"

"An unrevealed patient conflict? You don't *know* K-K-Keanu, do you, Doctor?"

"No, no. Of course not."

"Not to reveal a connection with *him* would be highly unethical. Highly. And how do I know you're not capable of unethical conduct? What do I really know about you at all?"

Rather than draw the Taurus PT-111 Millennium from his shoulder holster and teach this nouveau-riche ditz a lesson in manners, the doctor switched on his considerable charm and sweet-talked her into continuing with her delusional ramblings.

A wall clock revealed less than half an hour until he could send her out into the Keanu-haunted world. Then he would be able to deal with Skeet Caulfield and the blushing man.

In places, the glaze on the Mexican pavers had been worn away.

"Where I kept seeing bloodstains," Bernardo Pastore explained. "While I was in the hospital, friends cleaned out the room, got rid of the furniture, everything. When I came back, there were no stains . . . but I kept seeing them anyway. For a year, I scrubbed a little every day. It wasn't blood I was trying to get rid of. It was the grief. When I realized that, I finally stopped scrubbing."

During his first few days in the intensive-care unit, he had struggled to survive, only intermittently conscious; his injuries and his badly swollen face had prevented him from speaking even when he was alert. By the time he had accused

Ahriman, the psychiatrist had been able to establish a cover story, with witnesses.

Pastore stepped to the bedroom window and gazed out at the ranch. "I saw him right here. Right here, looking in. It wasn't anything I dreamed after I was shot, like they tried to say."

Moving to the rancher's side, keeping the tape recorder close to him, Dusty said, "And no one believed you?"

"A few. But only one that mattered. A cop. He started working on Ahriman's alibi, and maybe he was getting somewhere, because they cracked his knuckles hard. And shifted him to another case while they closed this one."

"You think he'd talk to us?" Dusty asked.

"Yeah. After all this time, I suspect he would. I'll call and tell him about you."

"If you could set it up for this evening, that would be good. I think Chase Glyson's going to keep us busy tomorrow with former students at Little Jackrabbit."

"None of what you're doing is going to matter," Pastore said, and he might have been staring into the past or the future rather than at the ranch as it was now. "Ahriman's untouchable somehow."

"We'll see."

Even in the gray light filtered through a skin of gray dust on the window, the thick keloid scars on the right side of Pastore's face were angry red.

As if sensing Martie's stare, the rancher glanced at her. "I'll give you nightmares, ma'am."

"Not me. I like your face, Mr. Pastore. There's honesty in it. Besides, once a person's met Mark Ahriman, there's nothing else could ever give her nightmares."

"That's right enough, isn't it?" Pastore said, turning his eyes once more to the waning afternoon.

Dusty switched off the recorder.

"They could remove most of these scars now,"

Bernardo Pastore said. "And they wanted me to have more surgeries on the jaw, too. They promised they could smooth out the line. But what do I care how I look anymore?"

Neither Dusty nor Martie knew what to say to that. The rancher was no older than forty-five, with many years ahead of him, but no one could make him want those coming years, no one but he himself.

Jennifer lived within two miles of the office. In good weather and in bad, she walked to and from work, because walking was as much a part of her health regimen as tofu cheese, bean sprouts, and ginko biloba.

The doctor asked her to do him the favor of driving his car to the Mercedes dealership and leaving it for an oil change and tire rotation. "They'll give you a lift home in their courtesy van."

"Oh, that's okay," she said, "I'll walk home from there."

"But that's probably nine miles."

"Really? Great!"

"What if it rains?"

"They've changed the forecast. Rain tomorrow, not today. But how will *you* get home?"

"I'm walking over to Barnes and Noble to browse, then meeting a friend for an early drink," he lied. "He'll take me home." He consulted his wristwatch. "Close up early . . . in say about fifteen minutes. That way, even with a nine-mile walk, you'll get home at the usual time. And take thirty dollars from petty cash, so you can stop at that place you like—Green Acres, is it?—for dinner if you want."

"You're the most considerate man," she said.

Fifteen minutes would be enough time for Ahriman to leave this building by the front entrance, where the boys in the beige pickup could not see him, proceed to the building next door, and then to the parking lot behind it, where his 1959 Chevrolet El Camino would be waiting for him.

The riding rings and the paddocks were deserted, all the quarter horses warmly stabled in advance of the coming storm.

When Martie paused beside the rental car, the adobe ranch house didn't appear quaint and romantic, as it had when she first arrived. As with so much of New Mexico's architecture, this place had been magical, as if sprung from the desert by an act of sorcery; but now the patinaed earthen walls looked no more romantic than mud, and the house seemed not to be rising up, but settling down, slumped, melting into the earth from which it had been born, soon to vanish as though it had never existed, along with the people who had once known love and joy within its walls.

"What are we dealing with, I wonder?" Dusty said as Martie drove away from the ranch house. "What is Ahriman . . . in addition to what he appears to be?"

"You're not talking just about his connections, the institute, who protects him and why."

"No." His voice had fallen, soft and solemn, as if he spoke now of sacred things. "Who is this guy, beyond the obvious and easy answers?"

"A sociopath. A narcissist, according to Closterman." But she knew these were not the words that he was looking for, either.

The private, graveled road leading from the ranch to the paved highway was more than a mile long, passing first across table-flat land and then down a series of hills. Under the bleak gypsum sky, in this last hour of winter light, the dark green sage appeared to be mottled with silver leafing. The tumbleweeds, in this breathless day, stood as untumbled as the strange rock formations that resembled the half-buried, knobby bones of prehistoric behemoths.

"If Ahriman came walking across the desert right now," Dusty said, "would rattlesnakes boil out of their dens by the thousands and follow him, as docile as kittens?"

"Don't go spooky on me, babe."

Yet Martie had no difficulty imagining Ahriman at Dion Pastore's bedroom window, in the aftermath of the gunfire, unperturbed by the arrival of the coyotes, standing among those predators as though he insisted upon and received a place of honor in the pack, pressing his face to the screen and into the thick smell of blood, while the prairie wolves growled low in their throats and, on both sides of him, scraped their teeth against the mesh.

Where the graveled road rounded the side of a hill and took a sharp turn downward, someone had left a spike strip, one of those tricks the police resorted to in high-speed urban chases when the target of the pursuit proved difficult to catch.

Martie saw it too late. She braked just as both front tires blew out.

The steering wheel ripped back and forth in her hands. She fought for control.

Rattling against the undercarriage, like a frenzied snake with a cracked spine, the spike strip whipped from front to back of the Ford, where it found more rubber with its fangs. The rear tires blew.

Four flats, sliding and shredding across loose gravel, down a runneled incline, allowed Martie less control than she might have had if the Ford were skating across ice. The car turned sideways to the road.

"Hang on!" she cried, though it hardly needed to be said.

Then the pothole.

The Ford jolted, canted, seemed to hesitate for a fraction of a second, and rolled.

Rolled twice, she thought, though it may have been three times, because counting was not her first concern, especially when they went over the edge of the road into a wide dry swale, tumbling and sliding twenty feet in a curiously lazy fall. The windshield burst and pieces of the car tore loose with shrieks and twangs before at last the Ford came to rest on its roof.

67

Faster than smelling salts, the pungent reek of gasoline brought Martie out of shock. She heard it gurgling, too, from some ruptured line.

"You all right?"

"Yeah," Dusty confirmed, struggling with his safety harness and cursing either because the buckle release wouldn't work or because he was too disoriented to locate it.

Hanging upside down in her harness, looking *up* at the steering wheel and, higher still, at her feet and the floorboards, Martie was a little disoriented, too. "They'll be coming."

"The gun," he said urgently.

The Colt was in her purse, but her purse was no longer on the seat, no longer wedged between her hip and the door.

Instinct told her to look toward the floor, but the floor was above her now. The purse couldn't have fallen upward.

With trembling fingers, she found the harness release, flailed out of the stubbornly entangling straps, and slid onto the ceiling.

Voices. Not close but drawing nearer.

She would have bet her house that the approaching men weren't paramedics rushing to the rescue.

Dusty clambered loose of his harness and eeled onto the ceiling. "Where is it?"

"I don't know." The words wheezed from her, because the stink of gasoline made breathing increasingly difficult.

The light inside the overturned car was dismal. Outside, the cloud-choked sky faded toward twilight. The broken-out windshield was clogged with tumbleweeds and other brush that filled the bottom of the swale, so hardly any light entered from that direction.

"There!" Dusty said.

Even as he spoke, she saw the purse, near the rear window, and she slithered on her belly across the ceiling.

The purse had been open, and several items had spilled from it. She swept a compact, a comb, a tube of lipstick, and other objects out of her way, and grabbed the bag, which was heavy with the weapon.

Small stones clattered down on the exposed undercarriage of the car, dislodged by men descending the slope from the graveled road.

Martie looked left and then right, at the side windows, which were low to the ground, expecting to see their feet first.

She tried to be quiet, listening for their footsteps, so she might have some advance warning of which side they would approach, but she was forced to gasp noisily for breath, because the air was thick with fumes. Dusty gasped, too, and the desperation in their wheezing was an even more frightening sound than the clatter of the falling stones.

Pitipat, pitipat—not the sound of her heart, because that was booming—*pitipat, pitipat,* and then a wetness dripping down the side of her face, which made her twitch and peer up toward the bottom of the car. Gasoline was drizzling through the floorboards.

Martie twisted her head, looked behind, and saw three or four other places where fuel was dripping down through the inverted Ford. The droplets caught what little light there was and glimmered like pearls as they fell.

Dusty's face. Eyes wide with the realization of their hopeless situation.

Stinging fumes pricked tears from Martie's eyes, and

just as her husband's face blurred, she saw him mouth the words *Don't shoot* more clearly than she heard him wheeze them.

If the muzzle flash didn't touch off an explosion—and it would—then the spark from a ricochet was sure to destroy them.

She wiped the back of her hand across her streaming eyes and glimpsed a pair of cowboy boots at the nearest window, and someone began wrenching on a stubborn, buckled door.

The grape-purple '59 Chevrolet El Camino was smartly customized: a dechromed, filled, and louvered hood; smoothed, one-piece bumpers; a sweet tubular grille; an air-activated hard tonneau roof; lowered on McGaughly's Classic Chevy dropped spindles.

Dr. Ahriman waited at the wheel, parked in the street within sight of the exit from the parking lot behind his office building.

Under the driver's seat was the ski mask. He had checked for it before starting the engine. Good, reliable Cedric.

The weight of the mini-9mm pistol in the holster under his left arm was not in the least uncomfortable. Indeed, it was a pleasant, warm little weight. Bang, bang, you're dead.

And here came Jennifer in the Mercedes, pausing at the tollbooth only to say hello to the clerk, because the car had a monthly sticker on its windshield. Then the striped barrier rose, and she proceeded to the stop sign at the street.

Behind her, the pickup braked to a hard stop at the booth, all its antennae quivering violently.

Jennifer turned left into the street.

Judging by the length of time they spent at the booth, the two dithering detectives had failed to have change in hand to ensure a quick exit. By the time they reached the street, the Mercedes was turning the corner at the far end of the block, and they nearly lost sight of it.

The doctor had been concerned that seeing only Jennifer and not their true quarry, Skeet and his sidekick would wait in the parking lot for him to reappear or until they died of thirst, whichever came first. Perhaps they were unprepared for the parking toll precisely because they had been debating the wisdom of tailing the car without their target in it. In the end, they had taken the bait, as the doctor had expected.

He didn't follow them. He knew where Jennifer was going, and he set out for the Mercedes dealership via a route of his own, making use of a shortcut or two.

The El Camino was smartly powered by a 9.5:1 small-block Chevy 350 engine. The doctor enjoyed scooting across Newport Beach with one eye out for traffic cops and a quick hand on the horn for those pedestrians who dared enter a crosswalk.

He parked across the street from the service entrance to the dealership and waited more than four minutes for the Mercedes and the pickup to appear. Jennifer drove directly into a service bay, while the truck parked farther along the street, a few spaces in front of the El Camino.

With the camper shell blocking their view through the rear cab window of the pickup, neither Skeet nor his partner in adventure was easily able to see who was parked behind them. They could have used their side mirrors to scope the street, but Ahriman suspected that because they saw themselves as the intrepid surveillance team, they didn't comprehend the possibility that they themselves could also be surveilled.

The compact, customized, slab-sided Colt slipped under Martie's belt and snugged into the small of her back more easily than she had expected.

She pulled her sweater over it and tugged her tweed

jacket into shape as the driver's door was wrenched open with a hard screech-pop of twisted metal.

A man ordered them out.

Desperately sucking fumes, her lungs aching for a clean breath, Martie belly-crawled across the car ceiling, through the door, and into the open air.

A man grabbed her left arm and jerked her to her feet, pulled her, stumbling, after him, and then shoved her aside. She staggered and fell, landing hard on the sandy soil and half in a snagging mass of sagebrush.

She didn't at once reach for the pistol, because she was still gasping uncontrollably and half blinded by a flood of tears. Her throat was hot and raw, her mouth full of an astringent taste. The lining of her nostrils felt scorched, and gasoline fumes writhed all the way into her sinuses, caustic in the hollows of her brow, where now a throbbing headache flared.

She heard Dusty being dragged from the rental car and knocked to the ground as she had been.

They both sat where they had fallen, sucking in great shuddering breaths, but choking on the too-sweet air and explosively exhaling before their lungs could get full benefit.

Martie's watering eyes blurred and distorted everything, but she saw two men, one watching over them with what appeared to be a gun in his hand, the other circling the overturned car. Big men. Dark clothes. No facial details yet.

Something fluttered against her face. Gnats. Clouds of gnats. But cold. Not gnats, snow. Snow had begun to fall.

She was breathing easier but not normally, her vision clearing as her eyes dried out, when she was grabbed by her hair and urged to her feet once more.

"Come on, come on," one of the strangers growled impatiently. "If you slow us down, I'll just blow your brains out and leave you here."

Martie took the threat seriously and started up the gentle slope of the swale along which the car had rolled.

When Jennifer appeared on the far side of the street, walking away from the Mercedes dealership, the sleuthhounds were flummoxed. They were prepared to trail her in their flivver, but neither frail Skeet nor his round-faced friend was in good enough condition to undertake a protracted foot pursuit.

Worse, Jennifer walked as if all the hounds of Hell and half a dozen aggressive insurance salesmen were after her. Head erect, shoulders back, bosom thrust forward, hips rolling, she strode into the cool afternoon like a woman intent on making the Nevada border before sundown.

She was wearing the same pantsuit she had worn at the office, but her feet were shod in Rockport's best walking shoes instead of in high heels. Everything she needed to carry was secure in a fanny pack, freeing her hands; she swung her arms rhythmically, as if she were an Olympic racewalker. Her hair was tied back; her ponytail bobbed cutely as she burned up the pavement, on her way to dinner.

The El Camino windows were lightly tinted, and Jennifer wasn't familiar with this car. When she passed, across the street, she didn't even glance in the doctor's direction.

She turned at the corner, still in sight, and started up a long but gentle incline.

Bounce, bounce, bounce: the ponytail. Her clenching butt muscles looked hard enough to crack walnuts.

Gesticulating at each other, the detectives pulled away from the curb, hung a sharp U-turn, drove past the El Camino without giving it a look, and proceeded to the corner, where they drew to the curb and stopped again.

A few hundred yards uphill, at the next intersection, Jennifer turned right. She headed west.

When she was nearly out of sight, the pickup pursued her.

After a decent interval, the doctor followed the pickup.

Once more, the funky truck pulled to a stop on the shoulder of the roadway about a hundred yards behind Jennifer.

The street ahead led uphill for perhaps a mile, and apparently the gumshoes intended to watch Jennifer until she reached the crest, then catch up to her, pull to the shoulder, and watch her some more as she strode onward.

Green Acres, culinary mecca to the alfalfa-sprouts set, was about four miles away, and Ahriman saw no reason to follow the pickup there in fits and starts. He drove past the truck, past Jennifer, and on to the restaurant.

The two amateur detectives greatly amused the doctor, Sherlock and Watson without wisdom or good costumes. Their sweet idiocy gave them a charm all their own. He almost wished that he didn't have to kill them, that he could keep them around like two pet monkeys, to enliven the occasional dull afternoon.

Of course, it had been a long time since he had directly taken a human life, rather than through an intermediary, and he was looking forward to getting his hands wet, so to speak.

Silver fleece, shorn from a woolly sky, drifted straight down through the windless twilight, and every clump of sage and every frozen tumbleweed was already knitting itself a white sweater.

By the time they reached the top of the slope, Martie's vision cleared, and her breathing was labored but not ragged. She was still spitting out saliva soured by gasoline fumes, but she wasn't choking anymore.

A midnight-blue BMW was stopped on the ranch road, doors open, engine running, clouds of vapor billowing from its exhaust pipe. The heavy winter tires were fitted with snow chains.

Martie glanced back into the swale, at the wrecked Ford, hoping that it would explode. In this still and open land, the sound might be heard even half a mile away at the ranch house; or looking out a window at an opportune moment, maybe Bernardo Pastore would spot the glow of fire just beyond the hill, a beacon.

False hopes, and she knew it.

Even in this dying light, Martie could see that both gunmen were carrying machine pistols with extended magazines. She didn't know much about such guns, just that they were point-and-spray weapons, deadly even in the hands of a lousy marksman, deadlier still when wielded by men who knew what they were doing.

These two appeared to have been created in a cloning lab, using a genetic formula labeled *presentable thugs.* Although good-looking, clean-cut, and almost cuddly in their Eddie Bauer winter togs, they were a formidable pair, with necks thick enough to foil any garroting wire thinner than a winch cable and with shoulders of such massive width that they ought to be able to carry horses out of a burning stable.

The one with blond hair opened the trunk of the BMW and ordered Dusty to get into it. "And don't do anything stupid, like trying to come out at me later with a lug wrench, because I'll blow you away before you can swing it."

Dusty glanced at Martie, but they both knew this wasn't a good time to pull the Colt. Not with the two machine pistols trained on them. Their advantage wasn't the concealed pistol; it was surprise, a pathetic advantage but an advantage nonetheless.

Angry at the delay, the blond moved fast and kicked Dusty's legs out from under him, tumbling him to the ground. He screamed, "*Get in the trunk!*"

Reluctant to leave Martie alone with them but with no rational choice except to obey, Dusty got to his feet and climbed into the trunk of the car.

Martie could see her husband in there, on his side, peering out, face bleak. This was the pose of victims on the covers of tabloids, related to stories about Mafia hits, and the only things missing from the composition were the fixed stare of death and the blood.

As if weaving shroud cloth, snow shuttled into the trunk, laying a white weft first on Dusty's eyebrows and lashes.

She had the sickening feeling she would never see him again.

The blond slammed the lid and twisted the key in the lock. He went around to the driver's side and got in behind the wheel.

The second man pushed Martie into the backseat and quickly slid in after her. He was directly behind the driver.

Both gunmen moved with the grace of athletes, and their faces were not like those of traditional hired muscle. Unscarred, fresh, with high brows, good cheekbones, patrician noses, and square chins, either was a man whom an heiress could bring home to Mummy and Daddy without having her allowance slashed and her dowry reduced to one teapot. They looked so much alike that their essential clone nature was disguised only by hair color—dark blond, coppery red—and by personal style.

The blond seemed to be the more volatile of the two. Still hot because of Dusty's hesitancy about getting into the trunk, he slammed the car into gear, spun the tires, causing gravel to clatter against the undercarriage, and he drove away from the Pastore ranch, toward the highway half a mile ahead.

The redhead smiled at Martie and raised his eyebrows, as though to say that sometimes his associate was a tribulation.

He held the machine pistol in one hand, pointed at the floor between his feet. He seemed unconcerned that Martie might offer effective resistance.

Indeed, she could never have taken the weapon away from him or landed a disabling blow. As quick and big as he was, he would crush her windpipe with a hard chop of his elbow or pound her face through the side window.

Now more than ever, she needed Smilin' Bob beside her, either in the flesh or in spirit. And with a fire ax.

She thought they were headed toward the highway to the south. In less than a quarter mile, however, they turned off the ranch road and traveled due east on a rutted track defined almost solely by the clear swath it carved through sagebrush, mesquite, and cactus.

If her memory of the map could be trusted—and judging by what she had seen of the landscape on the trip out from Santa Fe—nothing lay in this direction but wasteland.

Cascades of snow, a foaming Niagara of flakes, resisted the probing headlights, so a city might have waited ahead of them. She held out no hope for a metropolis, however, and expected instead a killing ground with unmarked graves.

"Where are we going?" she asked, because she thought they would expect her to be full of nervous questions.

"Lover's lane," said the driver, and his eyes in the rearview mirror met hers, looking for a thrill of fear.

"Who are you people?"

"Us? We're the future," the driver said.

Again, the man in the backseat smiled and raised his eyebrows, as if to mock his partner's dramatic flair.

The BMW wasn't moving as fast as it had been on the ranch road, though it was still going too fast for the terrain. Encountering a bad pothole, the car bounced hard; the muffler and the gas tank scraped on the down side of the bounce, and they were jolted again.

Because neither the redhead nor Martie was wearing a seat belt, they were lifted and rocked forward.

She seized the opportunity, reached behind herself, and slid her right hand up under her coat and sweater. She pulled the pistol from her belt while they were being pitched around.

As the car settled down, Martie held the gun at her side, on the seat, against her thigh, letting her unbuttoned jacket trail over it. Her body also blocked the redhead's view of the Colt.

The driver's pistol was probably on the seat at his side, within easy reach.

Beside Martie, the redhead was still gripping his gun in his right hand, between his knees, muzzle aimed at the floor.

Action. Action informed by intelligence and a moral perspective. She trusted her intelligence. Murder wasn't moral, of course, though killing in self-defense surely was.

But the time wasn't right.

Timing. Timing was equally important in ballet and gunplay.

She'd heard that somewhere. Unfortunately, in spite of her visits to the shooting range, having shot at nothing more than paper silhouettes of the human form, she knew nothing about *either* ballet or gunplay.

"You'll never get away with this," she said, letting them hear the genuine terror in her voice, because it would reinforce their conviction that she was helpless.

The driver was amused. To his partner, he said, with a mock tremor of doubt in his voice, "Zachary, you think we'll get away with this?"

"Yeah," said the redhead. He raised his eyebrows again and shrugged.

"Zachary," the driver said, "what do we call an operation like this?"

"A simple hump and dump," said Zachary.

"You hear that, girl? With the emphasis on *simple.* Nothing to it. A walk in the park. A piece of cake."

"You know, Kevin, for me," Zachary said, "the emphasis is on *hump.*"

Kevin laughed. "Girl, since you're the humpee and you

and your husband are the dumpees, it's naturally a big deal to you. But it's no big deal to us, is it, Zachary?"

"No."

"And it won't be to the cops, either. Tell her where she's going, Zachary."

"With me, to Orgasmo City."

"Man, you're delusional but fun. And after Orgasmo City?"

"You're going down an old Indian well," Zachary told Martie, "and God knows how deep into the aquifer under it."

"Been no Indians living there or using it for more than three hundred years," Kevin explained.

"Wouldn't want to contaminate anybody's drinking water," said Zachary. "Federal offense."

"Nobody'll ever find your bodies. Maybe after your car crash, you just wandered off into the desert, got disoriented and lost in the storm, and froze to death."

As the speed of the car dropped, eerie shapes appeared in the snow on both sides. They were low and undulant, pale formations reflecting the headlights, gliding past like ghost ships in a fog. Weathered ruins. Fragments of buildings, the stacked-stone and adobe walls of a long-abandoned settlement.

When Kevin braked to a stop and put the car in park, Martie turned toward Zachary and jammed the .45 Colt into his side so hard that his face clutched in pain.

His eyes revealed a man who was both fearless and pitiless, but not a stupid man. Without her saying a word, he dropped the machine pistol onto the floor between his feet.

"What?" Kevin asked, instinct serving him well.

As the driver sought Martie in the rearview mirror, she said, "Reach behind and put your hands on the headrest, you sonofabitch."

Kevin hesitated.

"Now," Martie screamed, "before I gut-shoot this moron and blow out the back of your head. Hands on the headrest where I can see them."

"We have a situation here," Zachary confirmed.

Kevin's right shoulder dropped slightly, as he started to reach for the machine pistol on the front seat.

"HANDS ON THE HEADREST *NOW,* YOU FUCKER!" she roared, and she was shocked to hear how totally psychotic she sounded, not like a woman merely playing at being tough, but like a genuine crazy person, and in fact she probably was crazy right now, totally psychotic with raw fear.

Sitting up straight again, Kevin reached behind himself with both hands and gripped the headrest.

With the Colt jammed into his gut, Zachary was going to behave, because she could pull the trigger faster than he could move.

"You got off that plane with nothing but carry-ons," Kevin said.

"Shut up. I'm thinking."

Martie didn't want to kill anyone, not even human garbage like this, not if it could be avoided. But how to avoid it? How could she get out of the car and get them out of the car, too, without giving them a chance to try anything?

Kevin wouldn't leave it alone. "Nothing but carry-ons, so where did you get a gun?"

Two of them to watch. All that movement getting out. Moments of imbalance, vulnerability.

"Where did you get the gun?" Kevin persisted.

"I pulled it out of your buddy's ass. *Now shut up!*"

Going out of the driver's side, she'd have to turn her back on one of them, at some point. No good.

So then ease backward out of the passenger's side. Make Zachary slide across the seat with her, keeping the gun in his belly, looking past him to Kevin in the front.

With the windshield wipers off, the snow began to spread a thin coverlet on the glass. The motion of the descending flakes made her dizzy.

Don't look outside.

She met Zachary's eyes.

He recognized her irresolution.

She almost looked away, realized that would be dangerous, and jammed the muzzle of the Colt even deeper into his gut, until he broke eye contact.

"Maybe it's not a real gun," Kevin said. "Maybe it's plastic."

"It's real," Zachary was quick to inform him.

Feeling her way backward, out of the car, would be tricky. Could hook her foot on the doorsill or hook up on the door itself. Could fall.

"You're just damn housepainters," Kevin said.

"I'm a video-game designer."

"What?"

"My husband's the housepainter."

And after she was out, when Zachary followed her, he would for a moment fill the open door, her gun in his belly, and Kevin would be blocked from her sight.

The only smart thing to do was shoot them while she had a clear advantage. Smilin' Bob hadn't told her what to do when intelligence and morality collided head-on.

"I don't think the lady knows what's next," Zachary told his partner.

"Maybe we got a stalemate here," Kevin said.

Action. If they thought she was incapable of ruthless action, then *they* would act.

Think. Think.

68

A winter scene frozen in a liquid-filled glass globe: the soft and rounded lines of ancient Indian ruins, silvered sage, a midnight-blue BMW, two men and one woman therein, another man unseen in the trunk—two dumpers and two dumpees—and nothing moving, everyone and everything as still as the empty universe before the Big Bang, except for the snow, a windless blizzard, which falls and falls as though a giant's hand just shook the globe, an arctic winter's worth of fine white snow.

"Zachary," Martie finally said, "without turning away from me, using your left hand, open your door. Kevin, you keep your hands on the headrest."

Zachary tried the door. "Locked."

"Unlock it," she said.

"Can't. It's the childproof master lock. He has to do it up front."

"Where's the lock release, Kevin?" Martie asked.

"On the console."

If she allowed him to operate the lock release, his hand would be within inches of the machine pistol that was no doubt lying on the passenger's seat.

"Keep your hands on the headrest, Kevin."

"What kind of video games you design?" Kevin asked, trying to distract her.

Ignoring him, Martie said, "You have a pocket knife, Zachary?"

"Pocket knife? No."

"Too bad. If you so much as twitch, you'll need a knife to dig two hollowpoints out of your intestines, because you'll never live long enough to get to a hospital where a real doctor could do it."

As she slid backward across the seat, to a point at which she would be midway between the front headrests, Martie kept the pistol trained on the redhead, although the weapon would have been more intimidating if she could have continued to press the muzzle hard into his abdomen.

"In case you're wondering," she said, "this piece isn't double-action. Single-action. No ten-pound pull. Four and a half pounds, crisp and easy, so the barrel won't wobble. Shots aren't going to go wide or wild."

She couldn't see well enough into the front while sitting in the back, so she eased forward, rising off the seat, legs bent in a half squat, feet splayed and braced, twisted toward Zachary but her right shoulder against the back of the front seat, with a cross-body grip on the pistol. Awkward. Stupidly, dangerously awkward, but she couldn't figure any other way to keep the weapon trained on Zachary and be able to watch Kevin's hand as he lowered it to the console.

She didn't dare reach into the front seat herself. She would be unbalanced, completely distracted from Zachary.

Two angry Orcs and one Hobbit locked in a car. What are the chances that all three get out alive? Poor.

Either the Hobbit wins and moves on to the next level of play, or the game ends.

To peer into the front seat, she'd have to turn her head away from Zachary, leaving him visible only in her peripheral vision. "One sound of movement, one glimpse out of the corner of my eye, and you're dead."

"If you were me, I'd already be dead," Zachary noted.

"Yeah, well, I'm not you, shithead. If you're smart, you'll sit tight and thank God you have a chance of coming out alive."

Heart beating so hard it felt like it was tearing loose. That was okay. More blood to the brain. Clearer thinking.

She turned her head and leaned to look into the front seat.

As she expected, Kevin's machine pistol was on the passenger's seat, within his easy reach. Big magazine. Thirty rounds.

"Okay, Kevin, carefully use your right hand to pop the lock release, with the emphasis on *carefully*, and then put it back on the headrest."

"Don't get nervous and waste me for nothing."

"I'm not nervous," she said, and the steadiness of her voice astonished her, because she was shaking inside if not out, shaking like a field mouse in the shadow of an owl's wings.

"Gonna just do what you say." Kevin slowly lowered his right hand from behind his head.

Martie glanced quickly at Zachary, who was keeping his hands high, beside his face, in order not to alarm her, even though she hadn't told him to do that—and she *should* have told him—and then she looked into the front seat once more.

As Kevin's hand seemed to float down toward the lock release, he said, "I like to play *Carmageddon*. You know that game?"

"I'd figure you for *Kingpin*," she said.

"Hey, that's some cool action, too."

"Easy now."

He pressed the rocker switch.

What happened next seemed to have been planned between the two men telepathically.

The locks released with an audible sound.

Instantly, Zachary threw open the back door and rolled out, and from the corner of Martie's eye, she saw him reaching down to scoop the machine pistol off the floor as he went.

Even as Martie squeezed off two shots at the departing redhead and sensed that at least one might have hit its mark, Kevin dropped sideways onto the front seat and grabbed his weapon.

Her second round still booming like cannon fire in the confines of the car, Martie went to the floor, out of Kevin's line of sight, pointed the Colt at the back of the front seat, and rapid-fired a horizontal spread of one-two-three-four rounds into the upholstery, not sure if the slugs would punch through all that padding and support structure.

Vulnerable from the front and above. Nothing preventing Kevin from returning fire *through* the seat, and him with thirty rounds to find her. If unhit, he might rise up, shoot down on her. Vulnerable, too, from the open door, from Zachary outside with the second machine pistol. Couldn't stay. *Move, move.* Even as she fired the fourth round into the seat, she scrambled for safety.

She dared not waste time backing up to open the door behind her, so she went out of the door that Zachary had opened, maybe straight into a hard barrage, with only one round remaining in her seven-round magazine.

No barrage. Zachary—*for me, the emphasis is on* hump—wasn't waiting for her. He was hit, down, though not dead. With at least one and possibly two bullets in his broad back, the rugged beast was struggling onto his hands and knees.

Martie spotted what he was crawling toward. His pistol. When he'd gone down, the piece had tumbled out of his hand. It lay about ten feet in front of him on the snow-dusted ground.

All survival mechanism now, Sunday school and civilization no match for the savage in her heart, she kicked him in the ribs, and he grunted in pain, tried to grab her, but then he fell forward onto his face.

Heart knocking, knocking so hard that her vision pulsed, dimming at the edges with each beat. Throat crimped tight with fear. Breath falling like chunks of ice into her lungs, then rattling noisily out of her. She skated past Zachary to the machine pistol. Snatched it off the ground, expecting to be lifted and pitched by the powerful impact of multiple rounds in the back.

Dusty locked in the trunk of the BMW. Desperately shouting her name. Pounding on the inside of the lid.

Amazed to be alive, she dropped the Colt. Spun with the new weapon in both hands, squinting into snowy murk, searching for a target, but Kevin hadn't been behind her. The driver's door was closed. She couldn't see him in the car.

Maybe he was dead on the front seat.

Maybe he wasn't.

Hardly any glow remained in the winter sky. Not the color of gypsum anymore. Ashes now, and pure soot in the east. The falling snow was much brighter than the fading realm above, as if these were flakes of light, the last bits of day shaken loose and cast out by an impatient night.

Pearlescent in the car's headlights, the snow—curtains behind curtains behind more curtains of snow—played tricks on the eye, and shadowy shapes seemed to steal through it where, in fact, no shadows moved at all.

In a genuflection to God-given instinct, Martie dropped onto one knee, making a smaller target of herself, surveying the gloom and the bright wedges thrown by the headlights, searching for any movement other than the relentless and utterly vertical descent of snow, snow, snow.

Zachary lay facedown, unmoving. Dead? Unconscious? Faking? Better keep one eye on him.

In the trunk of the car, Dusty was still calling her name, and now he was desperately trying to kick his way through into the backseat.

"Quiet!" she shouted. "I'm all right. Quiet. One down, maybe two. Quiet, so I can hear."

Dusty fell silent at once, but now in spite of the hoof-beat thunder of Martie's own galloping heart, she realized the car was idling. Clockwork engine. Heavy, damping muffler: just a soft, low *whump-whump-whump.*

Nevertheless, there was enough noise to mask any sounds Kevin might make if he was lying, wounded, in the car.

Wiping laces of snow off her eyelashes, she rose slightly from her crouch, squinting, and saw that the front door on the passenger's side of the BMW was open. She hadn't noticed it before. Whether wounded or not, Kevin was out of the car and on the move.

Arriving at Green Acres well ahead of the unsuspecting Jennifer and the two idiot nephews of Miss Jane Marple, Dr. Ahriman went into the restaurant to select a takeout snack to curb his appetite until dinner, which he would most likely have to postpone until late this evening, depending on events.

The corn-pone decor stunned his sensibilities, and he felt as though someone had rapped a shiny steel reflex hammer lightly against the exposed surface of the frontal lobe of his cerebrum. Oak-plank flooring. Country-plaid fabrics. Striped gingham curtains. Horrid stained-glass depictions of wheat sheaves, ears of corn, green beans, carrots, broccoli, and other examples of Mother Nature's vast bounty separated one booth from another. When he saw the waitresses wearing blue-denim, bib-style culottes and red-and-white-checkered shirts, with small straw hats barely larger than skullcaps, he nearly fled.

He stood by the cashier's station, reading the menu, which he found more gruesome than any set of autopsy photographs he had ever perused. He would have thought that a restaurant offering such grim fare must go bankrupt in a month, but even at this early hour, the place had business. Diners were stuffing their flushed faces with enormous green salads glistening with yogurt dressing, steaming bowls of meatless soup, egg-white omelets with stacks of dry cracked-wheat toast, veggie burgers as appetizing as peat moss, and gloppy masses of tofu-potato casserole.

Appalled, he wanted to ask the hostess why the restaurant didn't carry this insane theme one step further, to its logical fulfillment. Simply line the customers up at a trough or scatter their meals on the floor and allow them to graze barefoot at their leisure, baaing and mooing as they pleased.

Preferring to be ravaged by hunger rather than to eat anything on this menu, the doctor hopefully turned his attention to the big, individually wrapped cookies displayed near the cash register. A hand-lettered sign proudly proclaimed that they were HOMEMADE AND WHOLESOME. Rhubarb-apple crisps. No. Bean-nut butter macaroons. No. Sweet carrot gingersnaps. No. He was so excited by the very sight of the fourth and last variety that he had his wallet out of his pocket before he realized they were not chocolate-chip cookies but were made instead of carob morsels, goat's milk, and rye flour.

"We have this one other," the hostess said, sheepishly producing a basket of cellophane-wrapped cookies that had been hidden behind a display of dried fruit. "They don't sell very well. We're going to stop carrying them." She held the basket at arm's length, blushing as though she were pushing pornographic videos. "Chocolate-coconut bars."

"Real chocolate, real coconut?" he asked suspiciously.

"Yes, but I assure you—no butter, margarine, or hydrogenated vegetable shortening."

"Nevertheless, I'll take them all," he said.

"But there are nine here."

"Yes, fine, all nine," he said, scattering money on the counter in his haste to make the purchase. "And a bottle of apple juice if that's the best you've got."

The chocolate-coconut bars were three dollars apiece, but the hostess was so relieved to be shed of them that she let the doctor have all nine for eighteen dollars, and he returned to his El Camino more exuberant than he could have imagined being only moments ago.

Ahriman had positioned himself so that he enjoyed a clear view of both the entrance to the parking lot and the front door of Green Acres. He was settled behind the wheel, slumped in his seat, working on the second cookie, when Jennifer strode out of the rapidly fading afternoon.

Her stride was as quick and impressively long as it had been at the start of her trek, and her arms swung with undiminished vigor. Her ponytail bounced cheerily. Looking as though she had not raised the slightest sweat, she churned toward Green Acres, shiny-eyed and clearly eager to sit down to the finest of fodder and slops.

Creeping after Jennifer at an indiscreet distance, spewing blue exhaust fumes, as conspicuous as a spavined and flatulent fox on the trail of a rabbit, the aging pickup with camper shell entered the lot just as the ponytailed quarry opened the door to Green Acres and took her well-muscled haunches inside. They parked closer to the doctor than he would have preferred; but they would have been oblivious of him even if he had been sitting in a Rose Parade float, wearing a Carmen Miranda banana hat.

They waited a few minutes, apparently discussing their options, and then the blushing man got out of the truck, stretched, and went into Green Acres, leaving Skeet alone.

Perhaps they suspected that Jennifer had come here to meet the doctor himself, for a romantic tête-à-tête over bowls of bran mash and platters of steamed squash.

Ahriman considered walking over to the pickup, opening Skeet's door, and trying to access him with *Dr. Yen Lo.* If it worked, he might be able to bring Skeet back to the El Camino and drive away with him before the other man returned.

Skeet's program didn't always function properly, however, due to the unfortunate custard consistency of his drug-addled brain, and if the encounter *didn't* go smoothly, then the pie-faced partner might catch the doctor in the act.

He couldn't just walk over to the truck and shoot Skeet, either, because with twilight, multitudes of the terminally taste-challenged were driving into the restaurant lot. Witnesses were witnesses, after all, regardless of whether they were gourmets or gourmands.

The blushing man came out of the restaurant and returned to the pickup truck, and after only two minutes, both he and Skeet went into Green Acres. Evidently they were going to conduct surveillance of Jennifer while shoveling down some swill of their own.

The doctor's mood was ever rising, because he expected to have a clear shot at both men, in a suitably private setting, before the night was out, and then a dinner fit for a predator. He intended to use all ten shots in the magazine, whether he needed them or not, just for the fun of it.

The threatened rain had never fallen, and now the clouds were breaking apart in the twilight, revealing stars. This pleased the doctor, too. He liked stars. He'd once wanted to be an astronaut.

He was halfway through his third cookie when he saw something that threatened to spoil his wonderful mood. One row away and east in the parking lot stood a beautiful white Rolls-Royce with tinted windows, traditional hood ornament, and polished titanium hubcaps. He was shocked that anyone wealthy enough to own a Rolls and refined enough to choose to drive such a motorcar would come to Green Acres for dinner other than at gunpoint.

This truly was a dying culture. Rampant capitalism had spread wealth so widely that even root-chewing, grass-grazing vulgarians could drive in royal equipage to dine at the vegetarian equivalent of a Wienerschnitzel franchise.

The sight of this vehicle here, of all places, was enough to make the doctor want to consign his vintage Rolls-Royce

Silver Cloud to the nearest hydraulic automobile crusher. He looked away from the white beauty and vowed not to look again. To put the depressing sight out of his mind, he started the El Camino, popped a classic-radio tape of old Spike Jones programs into the cassette deck, and concentrated on his cookie.

On three sides, the ghost village. In centuries past, watch-fires and tallows burning, mica-lens lanterns holding back the night. Now, no resistance to the frigid dark. Populated by wraiths, perhaps all of them merely figures of snow, perhaps some spirits.

To the south, behind Martie, half seen in the murk, stood broken and weathered adobe walls, two stories in places, a few feet high in others, with deep-set window openings. Doorless doorways led to rooms more often than not roofless and filled with debris, inhabited in warm weather by tarantulas and scorpions.

In the east, better revealed by the car headlights but still resistant to full revelation, tall fractured chimneys of stone rose from round stone formations: perhaps ancient ovens or fireplaces.

North lay the low curving walls of a structure largely blocked from view by the BMW.

Surprisingly, looming throughout the crescent of ruins were tall cottonwoods. In addition to the deep well that Zachary had mentioned, there must be water near the surface, within reach of roots.

Kevin could be circling Martie, moving from one crumbling structure to the next, from tree to tree. She had to get out of the open, but she dreaded the thought of stalking him—and being stalked—through this strange and ancient place.

In a crouch, she hurried to the car and huddled against the rear tire on the driver's side.

The back door was open. Pale light from the ceiling fixture.

She dropped flat and risked a quick look under the car. Kevin wasn't there.

In the backwash of headlights, the thin mantle of snow on the far side of the BMW was aglow. From this ground-level perspective, the otherwise pristine whiteness appeared in one place to have been disturbed by someone heading away from the car.

Rising into a crouch again, she leaned into the light that came from within the BMW, and she examined the machine pistol to make sure that nothing about it would surprise her if and when she was forced to use it. The extended magazine scared her. From the high ammo capacity, she inferred that the pistol was fully automatic, not just semi, and she didn't have much confidence in her ability to control such a powerful weapon.

Her hands were cold, too. Fingers growing numb.

She closed the rear door and leaned with her back against it, studying Zachary. He remained motionless, facedown on the ground. If he was faking unconsciousness, waiting for her to lower her guard, he was supernaturally patient.

Before she could concentrate on Kevin, she had to know whether this man was still a threat.

After consideration, she approached him boldly rather than with caution, moving in fast and poking the muzzle of the machine pistol against the nape of his neck.

He didn't move.

She pulled back the collar of his quilted ski jacket and pressed her cold fingers against his throat, searching for a carotid-artery pulse. Nothing.

His head was turned to one side. She thumbed back his eyelid. Even in the poor light, his fixed stare was unmistakable.

Guilt sutured her heart and mind together, so that the

thought of what she had done caused stitches of pain to pull in her breast. She would never be the same person again, for she had taken a life. Although circumstances had given her no option but to kill or be killed, and though this man had chosen to serve evil and to serve it well, the gravity of Martie's action weighed on her nonetheless, and she felt diminished in more ways than she could count. Gone was a certain innocence that she would never be able to regain.

And yet, cohabiting with the guilt was a sense of gratification, a cold and keenly felt satisfaction that she had acquitted herself so well thus far, that her and Dusty's odds of survival had improved, and that she had shattered the gunmen's smug assumptions of superior power. A thrill of righteousness filled her, and she found it simultaneously heartening and terrifying.

To the car once more, to the front door on the driver's side, slowly rising until she could see through the window. The door open on the passenger's side. Kevin gone. Blood on the seat.

Crouching below the window again, she thought about what she had seen. At least one of the four rounds she had fired through the seat must have struck him. There hadn't been a lot of blood, but any at all meant that he was hurting and at a disadvantage.

The keys were in the car ignition. Switch off the engine, open the trunk, free Dusty? Then it would be two against one.

No. Kevin might be waiting for her to go after the keys, might have a clear line of sight on the interior of the car, through the open passenger's door. Even if she obtained the keys without being shot, she would be an easy target when she stood at the back of the car, fumbling at the lock and opening the trunk lid.

Although she loathed the idea, the safest thing seemed to be to retreat across this clearing into the ruins to the south. Use the cover of the crumbling structures and the cottonwoods to circle east, then north. Get around to the other side of the car, where Kevin had gone. If she made a wide enough loop, she might come in behind the northern position from which he was covering the BMW.

Of course, maybe he wasn't hunkered down and watching the car from a fixed position. He might be on the move, too, doing the same thing that she was doing, just in reverse. Using the long-abandoned village and the trees to travel east, then south. Circling in search of her.

If she had to stalk him through the adobe-and-cottonwood maze, while he, too, was on the prowl, her chances of being the one to come out alive were dismal. She no longer had the advantage of surprise. And though he was wounded, he was the pro, skilled at this, and she was the amateur. Luck didn't favor amateurs.

Luck didn't favor the hesitant, either. Action.

Action would be Kevin's motto, as well, drummed into him by whatever military or paramilitary specialists had trained him, and probably also by hard experience. She suddenly *knew* that he would be on the move, and that the last thing he might be expecting from a video-game designer and a housepainter's wife would be for her to follow him boldly, seeking him out by as direct a route as she could possibly take.

Maybe this was true. Maybe it wasn't. She convinced herself, nevertheless, that she should neither circle behind him nor lie in wait for him to appear, but aggressively pursue, tracking him by whatever spoor he had left in the fresh snow.

She didn't dare cross through the headlights. Might as well just shoot herself and save him the ammunition.

Instead, she retreated in a crouch along the side of the car, away from the headlights. Against the rear fender, she hesitated, but then she moved around to the back of the BMW.

The red taillights were far dimmer than the blaze of

headlamps, but the falling snowflakes turned to blood when they passed through the glow. The billowing exhaust was a sanguinary mist.

The plumes of vapor gave Martie cover but also blinded her, a crimson immersion, a fearful baptismal passage. Then she was out of the churning cloud, exposed and vulnerable on the north side of the car.

Action that seemed bold in the planning now seemed reckless in the execution. Staying low, but still a choice target, she angled at a run to the tracks leading from the open front door of the BMW.

Footsteps and drops of blood, half covered by the falling snow, revealed that Kevin had gone toward the round adobe structure, forty feet away.

She hadn't been able to see this building clearly from the other side of the car. Now that she had a better view, she found the place more rather than less mysterious. A six-foot-high wall curving away into the darkness. The suggestion of a low domed roof. Hard to judge the diameter of the structure from this one aspect, but surely thirty or forty feet. Stairs, flanked by decorative stepped walls, led to the roof, where the entrance appeared to be located, and the logical deduction was that most of the building lay underground.

Kiva.

The word came to her from a documentary that she had once seen. Kiva, a subterranean ceremonial chamber, the spiritual center of the village.

As Martie hurried farther from the car, the shadows grew deeper, and by the second, torrents of snow obscured the spoor. The trail remained clear enough, however, because the footprints deteriorated into broad shuffle marks, and the spots of blood were replaced by more liberal spatters.

Her heart a tom-tom, her eardrums vibrating with a sympathetic beat, she followed him to the steps, dreading the possibility that he had climbed to the roof, had then gone down into the kiva, and was waiting there in the smooth round darkness. At the steps, however, he had hesitated, losing more blood, and then he had continued along the curving wall.

Martie moved with her back against the adobe, sidling around the kiva into ever deeper darkness, beyond the last reflection of the BMW headlights, holding the machine pistol with both hands, finger tense upon the trigger. The deep pitchy shadows were relieved only by the faintly luminous cassock of snow spread across the ground and by the phosphorescent falling flakes.

Muffled by the intervening structure and by skeins of snow, the idling car engine faded until it was barely louder than an imagined sound, and something near to silence settled around her. She listened for her quarry, for the scrape of footsteps or ragged breathing, but she heard nothing.

Even in this gloom, she was able to follow Kevin, though hardly at all by the marks that his shuffling feet had left. Now only the blood was clear enough to lead her, a drizzle of blackness across the virgin snow, laid down in looping script, as though he were writing the same number over and over again, and she thanked God that there was so much of it.

Instantly, Martie cringed at having expressed gratitude for the blood of another human being, and yet she could not repress a flush of pride at her effectiveness. This pride, she warned herself, might yet earn her a few bullets of her own.

Inching, inching, inching sideways, she remembered now and then to glance back the way she'd come, in case he'd circled the building and stolen in behind her. While looking back, she knocked her left foot against an object on the ground, and turning her head, she saw a dark shape more geometric than the patterns of blood. The clatter had been distinctive.

She froze, afraid she'd been revealed by the noise, but she was frozen also by disbelief. Not daring to hope, she finally slid down along the kiva wall, squatting, to touch the thing she'd kicked.

The second machine pistol.

She would need both hands to control the weapon already in her possession. She pushed Kevin's dropped gun behind her, no longer worried that he might be creeping up from that direction.

Ten steps farther, she saw his large huddled form, his splayed legs dark against the snowy ground. He was slumped against the kiva wall, as though he had traveled all day on foot and was profoundly weary.

She stood just out of his reach, the machine pistol trained on him, waiting for her eyes to adapt even more fully to the unforgiving night. His head was tipped to his left. His arms hung at his sides.

As far as she could see, he produced no plume of breath.

On the other hand, there was insufficient light here to reflect upon the vapor. She couldn't see her own breath, either.

Finally Martie moved closer, crouched, and gingerly pressed her freezing fingers to his throat, as she had done with Zachary. If he was still alive, she couldn't walk away and leave him to die alone. She wasn't able to bring help in time to save him, and even if help could have been gotten, she didn't dare seek it under these circumstances, with possible charges of murder hanging over her. She could stand witness to his death, however, a vigil, because no one, even such a man as this, ought to die alone.

An arrhythmic pulse. A flush of hot breath across the back of her hand.

Like a spring-loaded trap, his hand flew up, seized her wrist.

She fell out of her squat, onto her back, squeezing the trigger. The pistol leaped with recoil in her hand, and bullets tore uselessly into the high branches of a nearby cottonwood.

Time out of whack, seconds as long as minutes, minutes as long as hours, here in the trunk of the BMW.

Martie had told Dusty to wait, to be quiet, because she needed to hear movement out there. One down, she had said. One down, and maybe two.

The *maybe* was the source of his terror. This little *maybe* was like the culturing medium in a petri dish, breeding fear rather than bacteria, and Dusty was already sick half to death with what it had bred.

From the moment they had put him in the trunk, he had blindly explored the space, especially along the bottom of the lid, searching for a latch release. He couldn't find one.

In a side well, a few tools. A combination lug wrench, jack handle, and pry bar. But even if the locked lid could be pried open, the leverage would have to be applied from outside, not from within.

The thought of her alone with them, and then the gunfire, and now the silence. Just the ticking of the engine, a low vibration in the floor of the trunk. Waiting, waiting, feverish with terror. Waiting, until finally the waiting was unendurable.

Lying on his side, he worked the blade end of the crowbar along the edges of the carpeted panel on the forward wall of the trunk, popped staples, bent the edges of the panel, got his fingers around it, and with considerable effort tore it out of the way, flattened it on the floor.

He put the crowbar aside, rolled onto his back, drew his knees toward his chest as far as the cramped space would allow, and jackhammered his feet into the forward wall of the trunk, which was formed by the backseat of the car. And again, again, and a fourth time, a fifth, gasping for breath, his heart booming—

—but not booming so loud that he failed to hear

another burst of gunfire, the hard ugly chatter of a fully automatic weapon, in the distance, *tat-tat-tat-tat-tat-tat.*

Maybe two down. Maybe not.

Martie didn't have a machine pistol. The creeps had them.

He held his breath, listening, but there was not immediately another burst of fire.

Again, he kicked, kicked, *kicked,* until he heard plastic or fiberboard crack, felt something shift. A ribbon-thin line of pale light in the blackness. Light from the passenger compartment. He swiveled around, pressing with his hands, putting his shoulder to it, heaving.

The dying man expended the last of his strength when he clutched Martie's wrist, perhaps not with the intention of harming her, but to get her keen attention. When she fell out of her squat and onto her back, squeezing off eight or ten rounds into the tree, Kevin's hand let go and dropped away from her.

As pieces of branches rattled down through the huge cottonwood, clicked off the kiva wall, and plopped in the snow, Martie scrambled backward and then onto her knees, gripping the machine pistol with both hands again. She trained the weapon on Kevin but didn't squeeze the trigger.

The last bits of cottonwood descended as Martie managed to stop gasping, and in the returning quiet, the man wheezed, "Who are you?"

She thought he must be delirious in these last moments of his life, his mind cloudy from the loss of so much blood.

"Better make your peace," she advised gently, because she could think of nothing else to say. This would have been the only valuable counsel anyone could have given even if this man had been a saint, and it was only more apt considering how far removed from saintliness he was.

When he summoned enough breath to speak again, the judgment of delirium seemed hasty. His voice as thready as any cloth that had been woven millennia ago: "Who are you, really?" She could barely see the faint shine of his eyes. "What were we . . . dealing with . . . in you?"

A chill passed through Martie, unrelated to the cold night or to the snow, for she was reminded of the similar questions that Dusty had asked about Dr. Ahriman, just before they rounded the turn in the ranch road and ran over the spike strip.

"Who . . . are you . . . really?" Kevin asked once more.

He choked and then gagged on a thickness rising in his throat. The crisp air became brittle with a coppery scent that steamed out of him with his last breath, and blood flooded from his mouth.

At his passing, there was not even an eddy in the snow, neither the briefest glimpse of the occluded moon nor the faintest stirring through the trees. In this regard, her death, when sooner or later it came, would be like his: the world indifferent, turning smoothly onward toward the fascination of another dawn.

As in a dream, Martie rose from the dead man and stood, chilled and half bewildered, unable to find an answer to his final question.

She followed in her footsteps and in his, returning by the route that had brought her to him. Once, she leaned against the kiva wall. And then went on.

Curving toward the light, through hard-falling snow that seemed eternal, Martie held the pistol ready in both hands, troubled by an almost superstitious sense that a dangerous creature still was afoot, but then she lowered the weapon when she realized that hers were the eyes through which this dangerous creature studied the night.

To the clearing, toward the idling car, the encircling

ruins. The world steadily dissolving and spinning away in the snowfall.

Dusty, having freed himself, was following a swiftly blurring trail of footprints and blood.

At the sight of him, Martie let the gun slip from her hands.

They met at the bottom of the kiva stairs and held each other.

He anchored her. The world could not dissolve or spin away with him in it, for he seemed eternal, as everlasting as mountains. Perhaps this was an illusion, too, as were the mountains, but she clung to it.

69

Long after twilight, hitching their pants up over full bellies, prying stubborn wads of mulch from their teeth with toothpicks, Skeet and his florid friend hurried out of Green Acres directly to their environmentally disastrous vehicle, which fired up with a wheeze of burnt oil that the doctor swore he could smell even inside his closed El Camino.

A minute later, Jennifer exited the restaurant, too, as glossy and robust as a young horse, revitalized by the feed bag. She did a few stretching exercises, working out the kinks in her rump, stifles, gaskins, hocks, and fetlocks. Then she set out for home, at an easy canter instead of a racewalk, her mane bobbing and her pretty head no doubt filled with dreamy thoughts of fresh straw bedding free of stable mice and a good crisp apple just before sleep.

As tireless as they were witless, the detectives gave pursuit, their task complicated by the filly's slower pace and the darkness.

Although even Skeet and his pal might soon realize that this woman had no rendezvous to keep with the doctor and that their true quarry had long ago given them the slip, Ahriman risked not following them. Once more, he skipped ahead, this time to the street in front of the apartment complex in which Jennifer lived. He parked beneath the spreading limbs of a coral tree large enough to serve as a guest house for the Swiss Family Robinson, protected here from the glow of nearby streetlamps.

In other circumstances, Martie and Dusty would have turned to the police, but this time they gave that option little consideration.

Remembering Bernardo Pastore's patched face and the frustration the rancher had met, at every turn, when trying to find justice for his murdered son and self-accused dead wife, Dusty shuddered at the prospect of bringing the police back here. Mere facts would probably not convince them that the Bellon-Tockland Institute, in its stirring quest for world peace, was in the habit of employing hit men.

What meaningful investigation had been conducted into five-year-old Valerie-Marie Padilla's supposed suicide? None. Who had been punished? No one.

Carl Glyson falsely accused, swiftly convicted, stabbed to death in prison. His wife, Terri, dead of shame, according to Zina. What justice for them?

And Susan Jagger. Dead by her own hand, yes, but her hand had not been under her control.

Convincing the police of all this, even the honest ones—which included the large majority—would be difficult if not impossible. And among them, the few corrupt would labor tirelessly to ensure the burial of the truth and the punishment of the innocent.

With a powerful six-battery flashlight that they found in the BMW, they searched the nearby ruins and quickly located the ancient well of which the two gunmen had spoken. This seemed to be a largely natural shaft in soft volcanic rock, widened by hand and fortified with masonry, surrounded by a low stone wall, but with no sheltering roof.

The big flashlight couldn't reveal the bottom of the well. Snow spiraled down, glowing like swarms of moths in the beam, disappearing into darkness, and a faint dank odor wafted upward.

Together, Dusty and Martie dragged Zachary's corpse

to the well, tipped it over the low wall, and listened to it ricochet from side to side of the irregular shaft. Bones cracked almost as loud as gunfire, and the dead man plummeted so long that Dusty wondered if the bottom would ever be struck.

When the body hit, it landed with neither a splash nor a thud, sending up instead a sound that had the character of both. Perhaps the water below was not as pure as it had been in ancient days, now thickened by centuries of sediment and perhaps by the grisly remains of others dumped here on previous nights.

Following the slap of impact, a wet and eerie churning arose, as though something that lived below were feeding or perhaps merely examining the dead man, striving to identify him by a braille-like reading of his face and body. More likely, the corpse had disturbed pockets of noxious gas trapped in the viscous soup, which now roiled, bubbled, burst.

For Dusty this was a little piece of Hell on earth, and for Martie, as well, judging by the ghastly look on her face. A precinct of Hell just outside Santa Fe. And the work before them was the work of the damned.

Bringing the second cadaver to the well taxed both him and her, though not solely because of the physical effort involved. The one named Kevin had spilled more blood than Zachary, seemingly most of his six or seven liters, and not all of it had yet frozen to his skin and clothes. He stank, too, apparently having been incontinent in his final throes. Heavy, sticky, as stubborn in death as in his dying, he was a difficult package to move.

Worse, however, was the sight of him, first in the questing beam of the flashlight, slumped against the kiva wall, and then as they half carried and half dragged him through the headlights. His beard of blood, his red-stained teeth and red mustache, his skin gray under a white freckling of snow. In his glazed eyes was fixed such a pure and piercing expression of terror that in the moment of his exit from this world, he must have glimpsed the face of Death himself, bending close to kiss—and then beyond the empty sockets of the Reaper's bony face, some unspeakable eternity.

The work of the damned, and still more to do.

Laboring in grim silence, neither of them dared to speak a word. If they were to speak of what they were doing, this essential work would become impossible. They would be forced to turn away from it in horror.

They dumped Kevin down the well, and when he hit bottom with an even more solid sound than his partner had raised, the impact was followed by more of that hideous churning. Dusty's imagination gave him the ghoulish spectacle of Zachary and Kevin being greeted below by their previous victims, nightmare figures in various stages of decomposition yet animated by vengeance.

Though much of New Mexico is parched on the surface, underlying the state is a reservoir so vast that only a tiny fraction of it has been explored. This secret sea is fed by subterranean rivers carrying water out of both the high plains of the central United States and the Rocky Mountains. The wonders of the Carlsbad Caverns were shaped by the ceaseless action of these waters flowing through fractures in soluble limestone; and there are doubtless undiscovered networks of caverns large enough to shelter cities. If ghost ships plied this secret sea, crewed by the restless dead, these two new recruits might pass eternity as rowers in an oar-propelled galley or as seamen tending the rotting sails of a moldering galleon driven by a phantom wind, under skies of stone, to unknown ports beneath Albuquerque, Portales, Alamogordo, and Las Cruces.

An ocean lay below, but no water could be found aboveground to wash the blood from their hands. They scooped up snow and scrubbed. And still more snow and still more scrubbing, until their freezing fingers ached, until their skin was red from the friction, and then until their skin was white from the cold, and yet more snow and more and harder scrubbing, harder, harder, striving not merely to cleanse but also to purify.

With a sudden sense of madness looming, Dusty looked up from his throbbing hands and saw Martie kneeling, bent forward, her face greasy with revulsion, her black hair mostly concealed under a lacy white mantilla. She was scouring her hands with hard-packed snow half turned to prickly ice, scrubbing so ferociously that she would soon begin to bleed.

He seized her wrists, gently forced her to drop the ice-crusted lumps of snow, and said, "Enough."

She nodded. In a voice shaky with horror and with gratitude, she said, "I'd scrub all night if I could scrub away the past hour."

"I know," he said. "I know."

In fifty minutes—or nearly two episodes of *The Phil Harris-Alice Faye Show,* if measured by the clock of classic radio—Jennifer cantered home, ready to be cooled down and blanketed.

Her shy pacers, Skeet and the blushing man, arrived close behind her. They actually drove into the apartment-complex parking lot and stopped to watch Jennifer disappear into her building.

From his dark post beneath the spreading coral tree, the doctor watched the watchers, and allowed himself to take some quiet pride in his all-but-inhuman patience. A good gamesman must know when to make his moves and when to wait, though waiting may sometimes put his very sanity to the test.

Evidently, Martie and Dusty had recklessly entrusted Skeet to the care of the blushing man. Patience, therefore, would be rewarded with two kills and the game prize.

By now he knew these two detectives well enough to predict with confidence that even they would be too bored and frustrated to resume their surveillance and would now at last admit to having screwed up. Besides, stuffed with rhubarb goulash and sweet-potato gumbo, these boys were feeling dull and sluggish, yearning for all the comforts of home: well-stained reclining chairs with pop-up footrests and the absolute dumbest sitcoms that the vasty, humming, puffing, cranking, thrumming, thermonuclear American entertainment industry knew how to provide.

Then, when they were comparatively isolated, feeling snug and secure, the doctor would strike. He only hoped that Martie and Dusty might live to identify the remains and to grieve.

To Dr. Ahriman's mild surprise, the man with the Mount Palomar eyeglasses got out of the pickup, went around to the back, and coaxed a dog out of the camper shell. This was a possible complication that would require an adjustment to his strategy.

The man led the dog to a grassy area in the apartment-complex landscaping. After much sniffing and several tentative starts, the canine completed his business.

Ahriman recognized the dog. Dusty and Martie's sweet-tempered and timid retriever. What was the name? Varney? Volley? Vomit? Valet.

No adjustment to his strategy would be necessary, after all. Oh, yes, a small change. He would have to save one bullet for the dog.

Valet was escorted back to the camper shell, and the blushing man returned to the cab of the pickup.

The doctor prepared for a leisurely pursuit, but the truck didn't move.

After a minute, Skeet appeared. Carrying a flashlight and an unidentifiable blue something, he searched the area where the dog had recently toileted.

Skeet located the prize. The blue something was a plastic bag. He made the collection, twisted the neck of the bag, tied a double knot, and delivered a deposit to the decorative redwood trash can that stood near the pickup.

Congratulations, Mr. and Mrs. Caulfield. Although your son is a shiftless, dope-smoking, coke-snorting, pill-popping, delusional, addle-brained fool with less common sense than a carp, he stands one rung up the ladder of social responsibility from those who don't scoop the poop.

The pickup drove out of the apartment parking lot, drove past the El Camino, and headed east.

Because the street was long and straight, with at least five blocks of visibility, and because the pickup was poking along, the doctor surrendered to an impish impulse. He bolted out of the El Camino, hurried to the redwood trash can, snatched up the blue bag, returned to his vehicle, and gave chase before the truck was out of sight.

During his background interrogatories with Skeet, which were part of the programming sessions, the doctor had learned about the prank once played on Holden Caulfield the Elder. When Skeet and Dusty's mother had tossed out Skeet's father in favor of Dr. Derek Lampton, the mad psychiatrist, the brothers had joyously collected dog droppings from all over the neighborhood and had mailed them anonymously to the great professor of literature.

Although Dr. Ahriman didn't yet know quite what he would do with Valet's product, he was certain that with some thought he would put it to amusing use. It would add a fragrant grace note of symbolic meaning to one of the many deaths soon to come.

He had put the blue bag on the floor in front of the passenger's seat. The knotted plastic was surprisingly effective: No hint of an unpleasant smell escaped it.

Now, confident that his skills of surveillance would render him all but invisible to Valet's toileting team, the doctor settled in behind the pickup. Into the adventure-filled night he went, with five of the nine chocolate-coconut cookies still to be eaten and all ten bullets as yet unused.

Physically exhausted, mentally numb, emotionally fragile, Martie got through the next hour by telling herself that the necessary tasks immediately ahead of them were just housekeeping. They were simply putting things in order, tidying. She disliked housekeeping, but she always felt better for having done it.

They dropped both machine pistols down the well.

Though it was unlikely that the bodies would be found, Martie wanted to dispose of the .45 Colt, too, because the slugs in both dead men could be matched to the pistol. Perhaps someone at the institute knew where their bad boys had intended to dump her and Dusty, and maybe they would look here for their own when Kevin and Zachary failed to report back. She wasn't taking any chances.

She couldn't drop the Colt down the well, lest it be found with the corpses and traced to Dusty. Between here and Santa Fe were miles of desolate land in which the pistol would stay lost forever.

Not a lot of blood was smeared across the front seat of the BMW, but it posed a problem. From the tool well in the trunk, Dusty retrieved two utility rags. He used one cloth and a handful of melted snow to clean the upholstery as much as possible.

Martie kept the second rag for later use.

On the floor in front of the passenger's seat, she discovered the tape recorder. Here, too, was her purse with what remained in it—including the minicassettes that they had used to record Chase Glyson and Bernardo Pastore.

Evidently, either Zachary or Kevin had made a quick search for the tapes while Martie had sat on the ground near the overturned car, gasping for breath and teary-eyed from the gasoline fumes. No doubt the cassettes would have been dropped down the well.

No wind had yet risen. Although the snow was not being driven in blinding sheets, visibility was poor, and they weren't confident of finding their way back from the haunted ruins to the ranch road.

The route was clear, however, because the flanking sagebrush and cactus defined the unpaved track. Less than two inches of snow had fallen, and none of it had drifted to block or obscure the path out. With winter tires and snow chains, the BMW was undaunted by the bad weather.

They returned along the ranch road to the spot where the rental Ford had hit the spike strip and rolled. Guided by the flashlight, on foot, they descended the gently sloping wall of the swale.

The overturned car was tipped forward, allowing the trunk to be opened just far enough for Dusty to extract the two suitcases. He and Martie each carried a bag up the slippery slope, abandoning Fig's toy truck and the few items from Martie's purse that were scattered inside the wreck; the interior of the car still reeked of gasoline, and neither of them wanted to tempt fate.

Later, before they reached the main highway, Dusty stopped the car, while Martie walked about fifty feet off the graveled road and found a place to bury the Colt. The sandy soil had not frozen. Digging was easy. She scooped with both hands, put the pistol in the hole, and covered it with eighteen inches of soil. She found a loose rock the size of a bag of sugar and placed it over the hole.

They were unarmed, defenseless now, and with more enemies than ever.

At this moment, she was too burnt out to care. Besides, she didn't want to fire a gun ever again. Maybe tomorrow or the day after, she would feel differently. Time might heal her. No, not heal. But time might harden her.

Housekeeping completed, Martie returned to the dead men's car, and Dusty drove into Santa Fe.

Cruising south on the Pacific Coast Highway, between Corona Del Mar and Laguna Beach. Not much traffic. The residents of the coast at dinner or cozy at home. Only tattered clouds remained, unraveling eastward.

Cold stars, moon of ice. And the silhouette of wings. Night bird seeking prey.

He wouldn't critique his compositions this evening. He'd grant himself a respite from his obsession with high artistic standards.

Tonight, after all, he was less artist than predator, although the two were not mutually exclusive.

The doctor felt as free as a night bird and young again, fresh from the nest.

He hadn't killed anyone since he presented poisoned petits fours to his father and made a lasting impression on Viveca's heart with a half-inch drill bit. For more than twenty years, he had contented himself with corrupting others, dealing death through their obedient hands.

Homicide by remote control was infinitely safer than direct action, of course. For a man who was a prominent member of his community with much to lose, it was necessary to develop a refined sensibility in these matters, to learn to take more pleasure from the power to control other human beings, from having the power to order them to murder, than from the act of murder itself. And the doctor took pride in the fact that his sensibilities were not merely refined or twice refined but distilled to an exquisite purity.

Nevertheless, in all honesty, he couldn't deny an occasional yearning for the old days. Ever the sentimentalist.

The prospect of getting right down into the wet nastiness of ultimate violence made him feel like a boy again.

This one night, then. This one indulgence. For old

times' sake. Then another twenty years of unwavering self-denial.

Ahead of him, without benefit of a turn signal, the pickup turned right, off the highway, onto an approach road that led down through a section of undeveloped shore property to a parking lot that served a public beach.

This turn of events surprised Ahriman. He drove onto the shoulder of the highway, stopped, and switched off his headlights.

The pickup had descended out of sight.

At this hour, especially on a cool January night, Skeet and the blushing man were most likely the only people visiting the beach. If Ahriman drove in immediately behind them, even this clueless pair would have to suspect a tail.

He would wait ten minutes. If they didn't return in that time, he'd have to follow them into the parking lot.

A lonely stretch of beach might be a fine place to whack them.

70

By daylight, Santa Fe had been enchanting. On this snowy night, every street along which they drove seemed sinister.

Martie had a far stronger awareness of altitude than previously. The air was too insipid to nourish her. She hunched around a weakness in her chest, a shriveling sensation, as though her lungs were half collapsed and wouldn't inflate in such thin atmosphere. A lightness in her body, an unpleasant buoyancy, gave her the queasy feeling that at these rarefied heights, gravity was diminished and her ties to the earth at risk.

All these sensations were subjective, and the truth was that she wanted out of Santa Fe neither because the air was really gruel-thin nor because she might slip the bonds of Earth. She wanted out because here she had discovered qualities within herself that she would have preferred never to recognize. The farther she traveled from Santa Fe, the more easily she might be able to make peace with these discoveries.

Besides, the risks of staying in the city even until they could catch the first flight out in the morning were too great. Perhaps Kevin and Zachary wouldn't be missed for many hours yet. More likely, they were expected to report to someone at the institute when they had completed their assignment, which they ought to have done by now. Soon, people might be looking for them, for their car—and then for Martie and Dusty.

"Albuquerque," Dusty suggested.

"How far?"

"About sixty miles."

"Can we make it in this weather?"

At last a commanding wind had risen, lashing the snowfall with discipline until it had become a snowstorm. Rigorously marshaled ghost-white armies blitzed across the high plains.

"Might be less snow as we lose some altitude."

"Albuquerque's bigger than Santa Fe?"

"Six or seven times bigger. Easier to hide until morning."

"They have an airport?" she asked.

"A big one."

"Then let's go."

The wipers brushed snow off the windshield and gradually swept away Santa Fe, as well.

Even as Dr. Ahriman waited along the side of the Coast Highway, a sudden onshore wind blew through the tall shore grass and buffeted the El Camino harder than did the slipstreams of passing cars and trucks. A good wind would help to cover the crack of gunshots and would at least distort them so that getting an accurate directional fix on the source would be difficult for anyone who happened to hear the reports.

Yet the doctor had doubts about the beach, too. What were these two geeks doing there at this time of night, in this cool weather?

What if they were two of those kooks who tested their stamina by swimming in very cold water? *Polar bears,* they called themselves. And what if they were polar bears who liked to *skinny-dip*?

The prospect of encountering Skeet and his pal sans clothing was enough to alter the doctor's relationship to the four cookies that he had eaten. One a walking skeleton, the other a Pillsbury Doughboy wanna-be.

He didn't believe they were gay, though he couldn't rule out the possibility, either. A little romantic assignation in a beach parking lot.

If he found them in their car, going at each other like two hairless monkeys, should he kill them as planned or give them a reprieve?

When the bodies were found, the police and media would assume that they had been killed because of their sexual orientation. That would be annoying. The doctor was not homophobic. He was not a bigot of any stripe. He chose his targets with a sense of fair play and a belief in equal opportunity.

Admittedly, he had brought suffering to more women than men. He was, however, in the process of redressing that imbalance within the hour—and especially by the time he finished playing out the game in which these two killings were but one inning.

After ten minutes, when the pickup didn't return, the doctor set aside his misgivings. In the interest of sport, he switched on the headlights and drove down to the parking lot.

The truck was indeed the only vehicle in sight.

Only moonlight brightened the lot, but Ahriman could see that no one was in the cab of the pickup.

If romance was in the picture, they might have adjourned to the camper shell. Then he remembered the dog. He grimaced with disgust. Surely not.

He parked two spaces from the truck and counseled himself to move quickly. The police might patrol lots like this, once or twice during the night, to discourage teenage drinkers from staging rowdy parties. If the patrolmen recorded license-plate numbers, Dr. Ahriman would have a problem come morning, when the bodies were discovered.

The trick was to hit them fast and get out before the cops or anyone else drove in from the highway.

He pulled the ski mask over his head, exited the El Camino, and locked the door. He might have saved a few precious seconds on his return if he'd left the vehicle unlocked; however, even here in this long stretch of the California Gold Coast, in Orange County where the crime rate was much lower than elsewhere, untrustworthy people were unfortunately still to be found.

The wind was lovely: cool but not chilling, turbulent but not so strong that it would hamper him, certain to damp and distort the gunfire. And the nearest house along the shore was a mile north.

Upon hearing the low thunder of the breaking surf, he realized that not only the wind would conspire with him. All of nature in this fallen world seemed allied with him, and he was overcome by a sweet sense of belonging.

Drawing the Taurus PT-111 Millennium from his shoulder holster, the doctor walked briskly to the pickup. He glanced through the cab window, just to be sure no one was inside.

At the back of the truck, he pressed one mask-covered ear to the door of the camper shell, listening for sounds of bestiality, and was relieved to hear nothing.

He stepped past the truck and, surveying the night, spotted an odd light down on the shore and perhaps fifty yards to the north. The moonlight revealed two men twenty feet back from the tide line, huddled at some task.

He wondered if they could be digging for clams. The doctor had no idea where clams were dug up, or when, because that was work, and he had little interest in the subject. Some were born to work, some to play, and he knew into which camp the stork had delivered him.

A set of concrete steps with a pipe railing led down a ten-foot-high embankment to the beach, but he preferred not to approach these men along the strand. In the moonlight, they would see him coming, and they might suspect that his intentions weren't good.

Instead, Ahriman headed north through soft sand and shore grass, staying well back from the edge of the embankment, so that his prey would not glance up and see him silhouetted against the sky.

His handmade Italian shoes were filling with sand. By the time this was finished, they would be too abraded to take a good shine.

Moonglow on the sand. Black shoes wear pale glowing scuffs. Should I blame the moon?

He wished he'd had an opportunity to change clothes. He still wore the suit in which he had started the day, and it was dreadfully rumpled. Appearance was an important part of strategy, and no game was what it ought to be if played in the wrong costume. Fortunately, the darkness and the moonlight would make him look better-pressed and more elegant than he actually was.

When he had mentally measured fifty yards, Ahriman approached the brink of the low bluff—and directly in front of him were Skeet and his buddy. They stood only fifteen feet from the foot of the embankment, facing away from him and toward the sea.

The golden retriever was with them. It, too, was facing the Pacific. The onshore flow, blowing toward Ahriman, ensured that the dog wouldn't catch his scent.

He watched them, trying to figure out what they were doing.

The Skeeter was holding a battery-powered signal light with a semaphore shutter and a quick-flick lens system that allowed him to change the color of the beam. Apparently, he was flashing a message to someone at sea.

In his right hand, the other man had what might have been a small directional microphone with a dish receiver and a pistol grip. In his left hand, he was holding a set of headphones, pressing one of the cups to his left ear, though he was unlikely to be able to pluck any conversations out of the blustering wind.

Mysterious.

Then Ahriman realized the men weren't aiming the signal light or the microphone at any ships at sea, but high into the night sky.

More mysterious.

Unable to understand what he might be walking into, the doctor almost decided to back off from his plan. He was too hot for action, however. Deciding to hesitate no longer, he quickly descended the crumbling embankment. The shifting sand was silent underfoot.

He could have shot them in the back. But ever since his fantasy in the antique-toy store earlier in the day, he had been itching to gut-shoot someone. Besides, blasting people in the back was no fun; you couldn't see their faces, their eyes.

He walked boldly around in front of the men, startling both of them. Pointing the Millennium at the blushing man, the doctor raised his voice to compete with the wind and the crashing surf. "What the hell are you doing here?"

"Aliens," the man answered.

"Making contact," said Skeet.

Assuming that they were high on a combination of drugs and that neither of them was likely to make any sense, Ahriman shot Skeet's pal twice in the gut. The man was flung backward, instantly dead or dying, dropping the microphone and the headset as he fell.

The doctor turned to the astonished Skeet and shot him twice in the gut, too, and Skeet dropped like a biology-lab skeleton clipped loose from its suspension rack.

Stars, moon, and gunshots. Two deaths here where life began. The sea and the surf.

Quickness counts. No time for poetry. Two more rounds in the chest for the downed Skeet—*wham, wham*—finishing him for sure.

"Your mother's a whore, your father's a fraud, your stepfather's got pig shit for brains," Ahriman gloated.

Swivel, aim. *Wham, wham.* Two more in the chest for Skeet's idiot buddy, just for good measure. Regrettably, the doctor knew nothing about this man's family, so he couldn't flavor the moment with any colorful insults.

The pungent stink of gunfire was satisfying, but unfortunately the inconstant moonlight wasn't the ideal illumination in which to enjoy the blood and the ravages of the shattered flesh.

Perhaps he could spare a minute with his penknife to take some mementos.

He felt so *young*. Rejuvenated. Death was definitely what life was all about.

Two shots left.

The mild-mannered retriever was whining, yelping, even daring to bark. The dog had backed off toward the surf and was not going to attack. Nevertheless, the doctor decided to save both the ninth and tenth rounds for Valet.

As the eighth shot was still ringing in his ears, he swung the gun toward the dog—and almost squeezed the trigger before realizing that Valet didn't appear to be barking at him but at something on the low bluff behind him.

When Ahriman turned, he saw a strange figure standing atop the embankment, gazing down at him. For an instant he had the crazy idea that this was one of the aliens with which Skeet and his pal had been trying to make contact.

Then he recognized the off-white St. John suit, luminous in the moonlight, and the blond hair, and the arrogant posture of the nouveau riche.

In the office, earlier in the day, in a spasm of paranoia, she had accused him of having a patient conflict, of possible unethical conduct. *You don't* know *K-K-Keanu, do you, Doctor?*

At the time, he thought he had charmed her out of her absurd suspicion, but evidently not.

The doctor, of all people, should have known better. This was one of his psychiatric specialties, and also the subject of his next best-selling book, *Fear Not for I Am with You.* Severe obsessives and severe phobics, of which she was *both,* were highly unpredictable and, in the worst cases, capable of extremely irrational behavior. She was trouble in six-hundred-dollar shoes.

In fact, she was holding those shoes, one in each hand, standing in her stocking feet. He felt stupid for having ruined his Italian wing tips.

He hadn't known what vehicle she drove, but now he did. A white Rolls-Royce.

While he'd been having so much fun following the deadhead dicks, this delusional woman had followed *him,* expecting to catch him in a conspiratorial meeting with Keanu Reeves. His shortsightedness mortified him.

All these startling realizations flew through the doctor's mind in perhaps two seconds. In the third, he raised the pistol and fired one of the rounds that he'd been saving for the dog.

Maybe he was foiled by the wind or the distance, or the angle, or the shock that shook him at the sight of her, but whatever the cause, he missed.

She ran. Away from the low bluff. Out of sight.

Regretting the necessity to leave without killing the dog and without harvesting souvenirs from the two men, the doctor raced after his Keanuphobic patient. He was eager to administer a complete and final cure for her condition.

Raced proved not to be an apt description of his pace once he reached the foot of the embankment. The sandy incline, carved by erosion, had no shore grass to bind it. Ascending it was trickier than his descent had been. The sand shifted treacherously under his feet. He sank in as deep as his ankles, and by the time he reached the top, he was almost reduced to crawling.

His suit was a mess.

The Keanuphobe was far ahead of Ahriman, as fleet as a gazelle, but at least she had no weapons except one high-heeled pump in each hand. If he could catch her, he would make good use of the one round left in the Millennium, and if somehow he missed even at point-blank range, he could rely on his greater size and strength to pummel her into submission and then choke the life out of her.

The problem was catching her. When she reached the hard surface of the parking lot, she picked up speed, while Dr. Ahriman was still slogging forward through sucking sand. The gap between them began to widen, and he regretted eating the third and fourth chocolate-coconut cookies.

The white Rolls-Royce was parked near the top of the approach road, facing toward the lot. She reached it and got in behind the wheel just as the doctor slapped shoe leather against blacktop.

The engine caught with a roar.

He was still at least sixty yards from her.

The dark headlights suddenly blazed.

Fifty yards.

She shifted into reverse. The tires barked against the pavement as she jammed her foot down on the accelerator.

The doctor stopped, raised the Millennium, gripped it in both hands, and assumed a perfect isosceles shooting stance: facing her squarely with head and torso, right leg quartering back for balance, left knee flexed slightly, no bend whatsoever at the waist. . . .

The distance was too great. The Rolls was receding. Then she was gone over the brow of the hill, reversing toward Pacific Coast Highway, out of sight. No point in taking the shot.

Time is of the essence, said Anonymous, possibly the most

quoted poet in history, and this was truer now for the doctor than ever it had been. *Backward, turn backward, O Time, in your flight,* wrote Elizabeth Akers Allen, and Ahriman fervently wished that he possessed a magical watch that could turn this trick, because Delmore Schwartz had never written a truer word than *Time is the fire in which we burn,* and the doctor dreaded burning, though the electric chair was not the instrument of capital punishment in the state of California. *Time, a maniac scattering dust,* wrote Tennyson, and the doctor feared his own dust being scattered, though he knew that he must calm himself and embrace the attitude of Edward Young, who had written *defy the tooth of time.* Sara Teasdale advised *Time is a kind friend,* but she hadn't known what the hell she was talking about, and *The bards sublime whose distant footsteps echo through the corridors of Time* wrote Henry Wadsworth Longfellow, which had absolutely no application to the current crisis, but the doctor was a genius, preposterously well educated, and distraught, so all these thoughts, and countless more, machine-gunned through his mind as he ran to the El Camino, started the engine, and drove out of the parking lot.

By the time Ahriman reached the Pacific Coast Highway, the Rolls-Royce was gone.

The rich ditz and her clam-dull husband lived in nearby Newport Coast, but she might not go directly home. Indeed, if her phobia had progressed to a more serious condition than he'd previously realized, to some form of paranoid psychosis, she might be reluctant to return home ever again, for fear that Keanu or one of his henchmen—such as her own pistol-packing psychiatrist—would be waiting there to do her harm.

Even if he'd thought she was headed home, Ahriman wouldn't have pursued her there. She and her husband were certain to have a lot of household staff, each one a potential witness, and considerable security.

Instead, the doctor tore off his ski mask and drove to his own house as fast as he dared.

71

On the way home, no more poetic observations about time tumbled out of Mark Ahriman's overturned memory chest, but during the first half of the ten-minute journey, he foamed at the mouth with vicious obscenities—all aimed at the Keanuphobe, as if she could hear—and with vivid oaths to humiliate, brutalize, mutilate, and dismember her in imaginative ways. This fit was adolescent and not worthy of him, which he realized, but he needed to vent.

During the second half of the trip, he pondered when or whether she would call the police to report the two murders. Paranoid, she might suspect that the nefarious Keanu controlled every police agency from the local cops to the Federal Bureau of Investigation, in which case she would keep silent or at least take time to mull and fret over whether to approach the authorities.

She might go away for a while, even flee the country and hide until she had puzzled out a strategy. With half a billion bucks to draw upon, she could go far and be difficult to find.

The thought of her possible vanishment alarmed him and an icy sweat oozed out of the nape of his neck. His friends in high places could easily help him conceal his links to any number of outrageous crimes committed by others who were under his control; but it was a very different thing, and a lot iffier, to expect them to protect him from the consequences of murders committed by his own hand, which was one reason he hadn't taken such risks in twenty years. The sweat from the nape of his neck was now trickling down his spine.

A man of sublime confidence, he had never felt anything remotely like this before. He realized that he had better quickly get a grip on himself.

He was the lord of memory, the father of lies, and he could meet any challenge. Okay, all right, a few things had gone wrong lately, but a little adversity now and then was a welcome spice.

By the time he drove into his labyrinthine underground garage, he was fully in control of himself once again.

He got out of the El Camino and looked with dismay at all the sand smeared on the upholstery and mashed into the carpeting.

Sand or soil of any kind was admissible evidence in a criminal trial. The scientific-investigation division of any competent police department would be able to compare the composition, grain size, and other aspects of this sand with a sample of sand taken from the scene of the murders—and make a match.

Leaving the keys in the ignition, Ahriman salvaged only two items from the El Camino. The knotted blue plastic bag of Valet's best work. The Green Acres sack half full of cookies. These he carefully set aside on the flamed-granite floor of the garage.

Quickly, the doctor pried off his ruined shoes, stripped off his socks and pants, and shrugged out of his suit coat, piling the garments on the floor. He put his wallet, the mini-9mm, and the shoulder holster aside with the two bags. The sand-crusted necktie and white shirt came off next and were added to the pile, although he salvaged the 24-karat tie chain.

Amazingly, considerable sand had even caked in his underwear. Consequently, he completely disrobed and committed his T-shirt and briefs to the heap of discards.

The doctor used his belt to cinch the garments together in a neat bundle. He placed it on the car seat.

An annoyance of sand, rather than a significant quantity, was stuck in his body hair. With his hands, he brushed himself off as best he could.

Naked except for his wristwatch, carrying the few items that he had salvaged, he entered the lowest floor of the house and took the elevator up to the third-floor master suite.

Using the Crestron touch panel, he opened the secret safe in the fireplace. He put the Taurus PT-111 Millennium in the small padded box with the jar containing his father's eyes, and after consideration, he added the blue bag.

This was only temporary storage for the incriminating handgun, until he had a day or two to decide how to dispose of it permanently. The poop he might need as early as the morning.

After donning a lime-green silk robe with black silk lapels and a black sash, Ahriman phoned downstairs to the house manager's apartment and asked Cedrick Hawthorne to come to the master-suite sitting room at once.

When Cedric arrived moments later, Ahriman accessed him with the name of a suspicious butler from an old Dorothy Sayers mystery novel and then took him through his enabling haiku.

The doctor had a policy against programming employees in his businesses, but in the interest of absolute privacy, he felt that it was vital to have such total control over the two key personnel on his household staff. He did not, of course, use his power to take undue advantage of them. They were paid well, provided with superb health-care and retirement plans and given adequate vacation—although he had implanted in each of them an iron restriction against exploiting their kitchen rights to poach upon supplies of his favorite nibbles.

Succinctly, he instructed Cedric to drive the El Camino to the nearest Goodwill collection station and deposit the undle of sand-filled clothes. From there, Cedric would top ff the fuel tank and cruise directly to Tijuana, Mexico, just cross the border from San Diego. In one of Tijuana's more langerous neighborhoods, if the valuable vehicle were not irst stolen out from under him, he would park it with the loors unlocked and the keys in the ignition to ensure its disppearance. He would walk to the nearest major hotel, rrange for a rental car, and drive back to Newport Beach vell before morning. (As it was not yet 8:00 P.M., the doctor stimated that Cedric should be able to return by 3:00 A.M.) n Orange County once more, he would turn the rental car n at the airport and hire a cab to bring him home. Thereupon, he would go to bed, sleep two hours, and wake ested, with no recollection of having gone anywhere.

Some of these arrangements would be tricky, considerng the late hour when he would arrive in Mexico, but with ive thousand dollars packed in a money belt—which hriman provided—he should be able to get done what was ecessary. And cash left less of a trail.

"I understand," Cedric said.

"I hope I see you alive again, Cedric."

"Thank you, sir."

After Cedric departed, the doctor phoned downstairs to Vella Hawthorne and asked her to come at once to the naster-suite sitting room from which her husband had just een dispatched on a Mexican adventure.

When Nella arrived, Ahriman accessed her with the ame of the scheming head housekeeper of Manderley, the nansion in Daphne du Maurier's *Rebecca.* He instructed her o sweep the garage clear of every trace of sand, to dig a leep hole in one of the backyard planting beds, and to bury he sweeper bag therein. When these tasks were completed, he was to forget that she had performed them.

"Then return to your quarters and await further nstructions," Ahriman directed.

"I understand."

With Cedric on his way to Mexico and with Nell busily occupied, the doctor went down one floor to hi lacewood-paneled office. His computer required only seve seconds to rise out of the desktop on its electric lift, but h tapped his fingers impatiently as he waited for it to lock int place and switch on.

Networked with his office computer, he was able t access his patient records and call up the Keanuphobe's tele phone number. She had given two: home and mobile.

Less than forty minutes had passed since her hasty exi from the beach parking lot.

Although he regretted having to call her from his hom phone, time was of the essence—as well as the fire in whic we burn—and he couldn't worry about leaving an evidenc trail. He tried the mobile number.

He recognized her voice when she answered on th fourth ring: "Hello?"

Apparently, as he suspected, she was in a state of para noid perplexion, driving around aimlessly as she tried t decide what to do about what she'd witnessed.

Oh, how he wished she were programmed.

This would be a delicate conversation. While instruct ing the Hawthornes and dealing with sundry other matter he'd been thinking furiously about how best to approac her. As far as he could see, there was but a single strateg that might work.

"Hello?" she repeated.

"You know who this is," he said.

She didn't reply, because she recognized his voice.

"Have you spoken to anyone about . . . the incident?"

"Not yet."

"Good."

"But I will. Don't you think I won't."

Remaining calm, the doctor asked: "Did you see *Th Matrix*?"

The question was unnecessary, as he already knew th

she had seen every Keanu Reeves film at least twenty times in the privacy of her forty-seat home theater.

"Of course, I saw it," she said. "How could you even ask the question if you were listening to me in the office? But you were probably woolgathering, as usual."

"It's not just a movie."

"Then what is it?"

"Reality," the doctor said, imbuing that single word with as much ominousness as his considerable acting talent made possible.

She was silent.

"As in the movie, this is not the beginning of a new millennium, as you think. It's actually the year 2300 . . . and humanity has been enslaved for centuries."

Although she said nothing, she was drawing shallower, faster breaths, a reliable physiological indicator of paranoid fantasizing.

"And, as in the movie," he continued, "this world you think is real—is *not* real. It's nothing but an illusion, a deception, a virtual reality, a stunningly detailed matrix created by an evil computer to keep you docile."

Her silence seemed thoughtful rather than hostile, and her soft rapid breathing continued to encourage the doctor.

"In truth, you and billions of other human beings, all but a few rebels, are kept in pods, fed intravenously, wired to the computer to provide it with your bioelectric power, and fed the fantasy of this matrix."

She said nothing.

He waited.

She outwaited him.

Finally he said, "Those two that you saw . . . on the beach tonight. They weren't men. They were machines, policing the matrix, just like in the movie."

"You must think I'm insane," she said.

"Precisely the opposite. We've identified you as one of those in the pods who have begun to question the validity of this virtual reality. A potential rebel. And we want to help se you free."

Though she said not a word, she was panting softly, lik a toy poodle or some other little rag mop of a dog contem plating a mental image of a biscuit treat.

If she was already a functional paranoid, as he sus pected, this scenario the doctor had laid out for her woul have enormous appeal. The world must suddenly seen less confusing to her. Previously she had sensed enemie on all sides, with numerous, often inexplicable, and fre quently conflicting motives, whereas now she had on enemy to focus upon: the giant, evil, world-dominatin computer and its drone machines. Her obsession wit Keanu—first based on love, then based on fear—had ofte baffled and distressed her, because it seemed so bizarre t vest so much importance in someone who was only a actor; but now she might come to understand that h wasn't *just* a movie star but also The One, the chosen wh would save humanity from machines, the hero of heroes and therefore worthy of her intense interest. As a para noid, she was convinced that reality as the mass of human ity accepted it was a sham, that the truth was stranger an more fearsome than the false reality that most peopl accepted, and now the doctor was confirming her suspi cions. He was offering paranoia with a logical format an a comforting sense of order, which ought to be irre sistible.

Finally she said, "Your implication seems to be tha K-K-Keanu is my friend, my ally. But I know now he's . . dangerous."

"You once loved him."

"Yes, well, then I saw the truth."

"No," the doctor assured her. "Your original feeling toward The One were perceptive. Your instinctive sens that he is special and worthy of adoration is true and righ Your subsequent fear of him was *implanted* in you by the ev computer, which wants to keep you productive in your battery pod."

Listening to himself, to the compassion and the *sincerity* in his voice, the doctor was beginning to feel like a raving lunatic.

She retreated into silence once more. But she didn't hang up.

Ahriman gave her all the time she needed to brood. He must not appear to be *selling* this concept to her.

While he waited, he thought about what he would like for dinner. About ordering a new Ermenegildo Zegna suit. About clever uses for the bag of poop. About the thrill of pulling the trigger. About Capone's surprising triumph at the Alamo.

"I'm going to need time to consider this," she said at last.

"Of course."

"Don't try to find me."

"Go anywhere you want in the virtual reality of the matrix," Ahriman said, "and in reality you're still suspended in the same battery pod."

After a moment of reflection, she said, "I suppose that's true."

Sensing that she was beginning to embrace the scenario he had put before her, the doctor took one daring step: "I have been given the authority to tell you that The One does not consider you to be just another potential rebel recruit."

A breathless silence was followed by more of the soft, shallow, rag-mop-dog panting, though this time the sound was different, with a subtle erotic quality.

Then she said, "Keanu has a personal interest in me?"

She hadn't stuttered on the actor's name.

Interpreting this as a sign of progress, the doctor carefully crafted his reply: "I've said everything on this subject that I'm authorized to say. By all means, take the night to think about what we've discussed. I'll make myself available in the office all day tomorrow, whenever you're ready to call me."

"*If* I call you," she said.

"If," he agreed.

She terminated the call.

"Rich bitch ditz nitwit," the doctor said, as he put down his phone. "And that's my *professional* diagnosis."

He was confident that she would call him and that he would be able to maneuver her into a face-to-face meeting. Then program her.

After a few rocky moments, the lord of memory was secure in his throne once more.

Before calling Nella Hawthorne to order dinner, Ahriman reviewed his E-mail and discovered two encrypted messages from the institute in New Mexico. He put them through decryption and then, after reading them, permanently burned each off his hard disk.

The first had come in this morning and was an acknowledgment of the communication that he'd sent the previous evening. Mr. and Mrs. Dustin Rhodes would be under continuous observation from the moment they stepped off the airplane at Santa Fe Municipal. Prior to their arrival, their rental car had been fitted with a transponder to allow electronic tracking. Curly, in maintenance, wanted Ahriman to know that he and his new fiancée had originally decided to start dating after discovering a mutual enthusiasm for *Learn to Love Yourself*.

The second message had come in only a few hours ago and was terse. Throughout the day, Mr. and Mrs. Rhodes had been aggressively questioning people involved in the Glyson and Pastore cases, and they had been receiving support from those they interviewed. Thus, they would be staying in the Santa Fe area forever or until the universe collapsed into a nugget of matter the size of a pea, whichever came first.

Ahriman was relieved that his colleagues could be

depended upon to protect his interests, but he was dismayed that his current game—one of the most important of his life—would now have to be canceled and reconceived. He needed at least Skeet or Dusty, or Martie—and preferably two of them—to make it possible to play out his elaborate strategy, and now they were all dead or dying.

He hadn't received confirmation of the executions in Santa Fe, but that would arrive soon, probably before he went to bed.

Well, he was still a player. As long as he remained a player, the outcome of any single contest was not of cataclysmic importance. As long as he was a player, there would always be another game, and by tomorrow he would have devised a new one.

Consoled, he phoned downstairs to Nella Hawthorne and ordered dinner: two chili dogs with chopped onions and cheddar cheese, a bag of potato chips, two bottles of root beer, and a slice of Black Forest cake.

When he returned upstairs to the master suite, he found that reliable Cedric had earlier gone to the car dealership and removed the morning purchases from the Mercedes; he had put them on the bedroom desk. The die-cast Johnny Lightning Custom Ferrari. The mint-condition Gunsmoke Dodge City playset by Marx.

He sat at the desk, opened the playset, and examined some of the small plastic figures. Lawmen and gunfighters. A dance-hall girl. The detail was superb, exciting to the imagination, as with virtually all of the late Louis Marx's products.

The doctor admired people who approached their work, regardless of its nature, with attention to detail, as he himself always did. An old folk saying passed through his always busy, always fertile mind: *The devil is in the details.* This tickled him perhaps more than it should have. He laughed and laughed.

Then he recalled a variation of the aphorism: *God is in*

the details. Although the doctor was a player, not a believer, this thought stopped his laughter. For the second time this evening, and only for the second time in his life, an icy sweat oozed out of the nape of his neck.

Frowning, he thought back through the long, surprise-filled day, searching his memory for a crucial detail that he might heretofore have misunderstood or overlooked. Like the white Rolls-Royce in the Green Acres parking lot, which he had grossly misunderstood.

Ahriman went into the bathroom and repeatedly washed his hands, using a lot of liquid soap and scrubbing at them with a soft-bristled brush meant for cleaning under fingernails. He worked the bristles vigorously from fingertips to wrists, both sides of each hand, with particular attention to the knuckle creases.

The Keanuphobe was not likely to call the police and report that the doctor had killed two men on the beach, and it was unlikely that anyone else had seen him in the vicinity of the murders. If the cops suddenly showed up, however, he couldn't afford to have any traces of gunpowder on his hands, which might show up in lab tests and prove that he had fired a weapon this evening.

He could think of no other detail that he needed to address.

After drying his hands, Ahriman returned to the desk in the bedroom, where he positioned Marshal Dillon and a badass gunslinger in a showdown.

"Bang, bang, bang," he said, and with a flick of his finger, he snapped the dead marshal so hard that the figure bounced off the wall twenty feet away.

Marshals and gunmen. Shootouts in the western sun. Vultures always eat.

He felt better.

Dinner arrived.

Life was good.

So was death when you dealt it.

From the higher desert to the high desert, descending more than two thousand feet from Santa Fe to Albuquerque, Dusty covered sixty miles in ninety minutes. The intensity of the storm diminished with the altitude, but snow was falling steadily in the lower city, too.

They found a suitable motel and checked in, paying cash because by morning someone might be trying to track them through the use of their credit cards.

After putting their suitcases in the room, they drove the BMW about a mile and left it on a side street where it wasn't likely to seem out of place or draw attention for days. Dusty had wanted to make this trip himself, while Martie remained in the warm motel room, but she refused to be separated from him.

Martie used the second utility cloth to wipe off the steering wheel, dashboard, door handles, and other surfaces that they might have touched.

Dusty didn't leave the keys in the car. If it were stolen and cracked up by kids on a joyride, the cops would contact the BMW's owners, and the institute would immediately shift their search to Albuquerque. He locked the car and dropped the keys through the grate on the nearest storm drain.

They walked back to the motel through the snow, hand in hand. The night was cold but not bitterly so, and the wind that had come to the higher desert was absent here.

The walk might have been fun, even romantic, on any night before this one. Now, Dusty associated snow with death, and he suspected that the two would be so closely linked in his mind for the rest of his life that he would prefer always to stay by the balmy California coast throughout the winter months.

At an all-night grocery, they purchased a loaf of white bread, a package of cheese, a jar of mustard, corn chips, and beer.

Moving along the aisles, making selections, engaged in what otherwise might have been a task that made him impatient, Dusty was so overcome with emotion, so thankful to be alive, so glad to have Martie at his side, that his legs grew weak, and gratitude almost drove him to his knees. He leaned against a shelf, pretending to read the label on a can of stew.

If others in the store saw him, they were probably fooled. Martie wasn't deceived. She stood with him, one hand on the back of his neck, pretending to read the label with him, and in a whisper she said, "I love you so much, babe."

Back in their room, he phoned an airline's 800 number, seeking the earliest possible flight. He found available seats and used a credit card solely to reserve them, asking the agent not to run the purchase. "I prefer to pay cash when I pick them up tomorrow."

They took very hot, long showers. The thin, miniature cakes of hotel soap had melted away by the time they finished.

Dusty discovered a skinned spot just behind his right ear. It was caked with blood. Perhaps he had taken a knock when the car rolled. He hadn't even felt it until now.

Sitting in bed, using a bath towel for a tablecloth, they made cheese sandwiches. They had kept the cans of beer cold in a snow-filled wastebasket.

The sandwiches and the chips tasted neither good nor bad. It was just something to eat. Fuel to keep them going. The beer was to help them sleep, if they could.

Neither of them had talked much on the trip from Santa Fe, and neither of them said much now. In the years to come, should they be lucky enough to have years left instead of mere hours or days, they probably wouldn't speak often or at length about what had happened in those Indian ruins. Life was too short to dwell on nightmares instead of dreams.

Too worn out to talk, they watched TV while they ate.

The television news was full of images of warplanes. Explosions in the night, somewhere half a world away.

On the advice of experts in international relations, the world's most powerful alliance of nations was once again trying to bring two military factions to the bargaining table by bombing the crap out of civilian infrastructure. Bridges, hospitals, electric-power plants, video-rental stores, waterworks, churches, sandwich shops. Judging by the news, no one across the spectrum of politics or media, or in fact anywhere in the higher reaches of the social order, questioned the morality of the operation. The debate among the experts centered, instead, on how many millions of pounds of bombs in what type of high-tech packages would have to be dropped to bring about a popular uprising against the targeted government, thereby avoiding a full-fledged war.

"To the people who were in that fucking sandwich shop," Martie said, "it's already a war."

Dusty turned off the TV.

After they'd eaten—and finished two beers each—they got under the covers and lay in the dark, holding hands.

The previous night, sex had been an affirmation of life. Now it would seem like blasphemy. Closeness was all they needed, anyway.

After a while, Martie asked, "Is there a way out of this?"

"I don't know," he said honestly.

"These people at the institute . . . whatever they're doing, they didn't really have any bone to pick with us before we came here. They went after us just to protect Ahriman."

"But now there's Zachary and Kevin."

"They'll probably take a practical view about that. I mean, for them, it's a cost of doing business. We don't have anything on them. We're no real threat to them."

"So?"

"So if Ahriman were dead . . . wouldn't they leave us alone?"

"Maybe."

Neither of them spoke for a while.

The night was so hushed that Dusty almost believed he could hear the snowflakes striking the ground outside.

"Could you kill him?" he finally asked.

She was a long time answering: "I don't know. Could you? Just . . . in cold blood? Walk up to him and pull the trigger?"

"Maybe."

She was silent for minutes, but he knew she wasn't drawing near to sleep.

"No," she said eventually. "I don't think I could. Kill him, I mean. Him or anyone. Not again."

"I know you wouldn't want to have to do it. But I think you could. And so could I."

To his surprise, he found himself telling her about the optical illusion that had fascinated him as a kid: the drawing of the forest that by a simple shift of perspective suddenly revealed a bustling metropolis.

"This applies?" she asked.

"Yeah. Because tonight *I* was that drawing. I always thought I knew exactly who I was. Then a simple shift of perspective, and I see a different me. Which one is real and which is fiction?"

"They're both the real you," she said. "And that's okay."

Hearing her say that it was okay actually *made* it okay in his mind. Although she didn't know it, and although he would never be able to quite put his feelings into words that she would understand, Martie was the only touchstone by which Dusty measured his value as a human being.

Later, when he was near sleep, she said, "There's got to be a way out. Just . . . shift perspective."

Maybe she was right. A way out. But he couldn't find it either in the waking world or in dreams.

72

In the blue morning, flying out of Albuquerque with neither a toy fire truck nor a handgun, stiff and sore from the previous day's exertions, Martie felt tired and old. While Dusty read *Learn to Love Yourself* to better understand their enemy, Martie pressed her forehead to the window and gazed down at the snow-dusted city as it rapidly disappeared below them. The whole world had grown so strange that she might as well have been flying out of Istanbul or another exotic capital.

Slightly less than seventy-two hours ago, she'd taken Valet for his morning walk, and her shadow had briefly frightened her. After the odd moment passed, she'd been amused. Her dearest friend had still been alive. She had not yet been to Santa Fe. Back then, she believed that life had a mysterious design, and she saw reassuring patterns in the events of her days. She still believed in the existence of design, though the patterns she saw now were different from those she'd seen before, different and troublingly more complex.

She had expected to suffer terrible nightmares—and not from two cans of beer and crummy cheese sandwiches. But her sleep hadn't been disturbed.

Smilin' Bob had not come to her in dreams, either, nor in those moments during the night when, awake, she had searched the shadows of the motel room for the distinctive shape of his helmet and the faintly luminescent stripes on his turnout coat.

Martie had badly wanted to see him in dreams or otherwise. She felt abandoned, as if she no longer deserved his guardianship.

With California coming and with all that waited there, she needed both the men in her life, Dusty and Smilin' Bob, if she were to have hope.

The doctor rarely saw patients other than on the first four days of the week. Only Martie and Dusty Rhodes were on his schedule this Friday, and they were not going to be able to keep their appointment.

"You better be careful," he told his reflection in the bathroom mirror. "Pretty soon, you're not going to have any practice at all if you keep killing off your patients."

Having sailed through the crises of the past two days with his tail unbobbed and both horns intact—a little metaphysical humor, there—he was in a splendid mood. Moreover, he had thought of a way to revive the game that had seemed hopelessly unplayable last night, and he had arrived at a lovely use for the fragrant contents of the blue bag.

He dressed in another fine Zegna suit: a black, sartorially cut number with the very latest lapel style and a two-button jacket. He cut such a dashing figure in the three-panel dressing mirror in his walk-in closet that he considered setting up the video camera to record how terrific he had looked on this historic day.

Unfortunately, time was of the essence, just as it had been the previous night. He had promised the Keanuphobe that he would be in the office all day, awaiting her decision as to whether or not she would join the rebellion against the malevolent computer. He must not disappoint the nouveau-riche nutcake.

For the second day in a row, he decided to carry a gun. The threat seemed to have been reduced, with so many potential enemies dead, but these were dangerous times.

Although the Taurus PT-111 Millennium was not registered—having been provided to him, as were all his weapons, by the good folks at the institute—he couldn't use it again. Now that it could be linked to the murders of two men, it was a hot piece; it would have to be broken down and disposed of with maximum discretion.

From his gun safe, concealed behind bookshelves in the master-suite sitting room, he selected a .380 Beretta model 85F, an elegant twenty-two-ounce pistol with an eight-round magazine. This, too, was an unregistered handgun with no traceable history.

He packed a compartmentalized, hand-tooled Mark Cross briefcase with the blue bag, the Green Acres bag, and the tape recorder that he used for dictation. While he waited for the Keanuphobe to call, he would do some game planning and compose a chapter of *Fear Not for I Am with You.*

In his study, he checked his E-mail and was surprised to find that he had still not received a confirmation of the double hit in New Mexico. Puzzled but not worried, he composed a short encrypted query and shot it off to the institute.

He drove his antique Rolls-Royce Silver Cloud.

The car inspired several haiku during the short trip to the office.

Blue day, Silver Cloud. Conveyance of kings, of queens. And blue bag of poop.

The doctor was in fine form, and his bubbly mood resulted in another playful verse only two blocks from his office:

Silver Cloud, blacktop. Blind man in crosswalk, cane taps. Compassion or fun?

He chose compassion and allowed the blind man to cross without incident. Besides, the Silver Cloud was pristine, and the doctor shuddered at the thought of the magnificent motorcar sustaining even minor body damage.

Coming fast down to California at a precipitous angle, Dusty suspected that he and Martie had a long descent ahead of them even after the wheels of the airliner were safely on the tarmac. Past this sunny day lay dark places yet unvisited.

Weaponless but armed with knowledge, he believed they had no choice but to confront Ahriman. He suffered under no illusions that the psychiatrist would confess or even explain himself. The best they could hope for was that Mark Ahriman would inadvertently reveal something that would give them a slight edge or at least deepen their understanding of him and of the institute in New Mexico.

"Besides, I don't think Ahriman has ever faced much in the way of adversity. He's had a smooth ride through life. Judging by what I've read of his stupid book, he's every bit the classic narcissist Dr. Closterman accused him of being."

"And damn smug," Martie added, because Dusty had read her some passages from *Learn to Love Yourself.*

"He's powerful, he's connected, he's smart, but at the core he might be soft. If we can rattle him, intimidate him, get in his face and shake him up, he probably won't come apart significantly, but he might do something stupid, reveal something he shouldn't. And right now, we need every tiny advantage we can get."

After they ransomed the Saturn from the airport parking garage, they drove to Fashion Island in Newport Beach, to the high-rise where Ahriman had his office. The Tower of Cirith Ungol, Martie called it, which was a place of evil in *The Lord of the Rings.*

On the elevator ride to the fourteenth floor, Dusty experienced a sinking sensation in his chest and stomach, as though the cab were descending rather than ascending. He almost decided not to get off the elevator, to ride it back downstairs again. Then . . . an idea.

The doctor was seated at his desk, taking a cookie break, when his computer—which was always running—issued a soft *bing*, and the screen filled with a security-camera view of the reception lounge, which happened every time someone entered from the public corridor. If he had been working on the computer, the camera shot would have appeared as a picture-in-picture, and he wouldn't have had such a clear view of Martie and Dusty Rhodes.

He checked his Rolex and saw that they were only six minutes late for their appointment.

Evidently, something had gone badly wrong in New Mexico.

Various security-system icons had appeared along the bottom of the screen. The doctor used his mouse to click on an image of a gun.

A highly refined metal detector indicated that both subjects were carrying small amounts of metal on their persons—coins, keys, and the like—but that neither of them was concealing a metal mass of sufficient size to be a firearm.

To another icon: a miniature skeleton. *Click*.

As the pair stood at the reception window, talking to Jennifer, they were aligned with roentgen tubes concealed between the louvers in an air-return grille in the wall to their left. Fluoroscopic images were relayed to Ahriman's screen.

They had good skeletons, these two. Solid bone structure, well-articulated joints, excellent posture. If they possessed the talent to match their physical gifts, they would be fine ballroom dancers.

As though floating in zero gravity, other objects were revealed by fluoroscopy, suspended around the well-poised bones. Coins, keys, buttons, metal zippers, but no knives in arm or leg sheaths, nothing lethal.

A jumble of small items in Martie's purse couldn't be easily identified. Among them might be a folded switchblade. Impossible to be sure.

The third icon was a drawing of a nose. As the doctor finished his cookie, he clicked the nose.

This activated a trace-scent analyzer that sampled air drawn from the reception lounge. The device, programmed to recognize the chemical profiles of thirty-two different explosive compounds, was sensitive enough to detect as few as three signature molecules per cubic centimeter of air. Negative. Neither of his visitors was carrying a bomb.

He had not really expected Dusty or Martie to have either the expertise with explosives or the sheer gumption to come calling with bombs strapped to their bodies. This extraordinary level of security had been installed because from time to time the doctor dealt with patients who were far less stable than these two.

Some might have looked at these elaborate precautions and called them indications of paranoia. To the doctor, however, this was simply paying attention to detail.

His dad had often counseled him on the importance of security. The great director's production offices were equipped with state-of-the-art (for that time) security to protect him from jilted starlets, volatile actors furious with the way he'd edited their performances, and any critic who might have discovered who had paid to have his mother's legs broken.

Now, confident that neither Dusty nor Martie could harm him faster than he could access them, Ahriman buzzed Jennifer and told her that he was ready for his appointment. Without rising from his desk, he triggered the electronic lock on the door to the reception lounge, and it swung slowly inward on powered hinges.

The doctor clicked an icon that showed a pair of headphones.

Martie and Dusty entered, appearing angry but more subdued than he expected. When he directed them to the two smaller chairs that faced his desk, they sat as instructed.

The door closed behind them.

"Doctor," Martie said, "we don't know what the hell's going on, but we know it's rotten, it stinks, it's sick, and we want answers."

Ahriman had been consulting his computer screen as she talked. Judging by the absence of the low-level electronic field associated with a voice-activated transmitter, she was not wired.

"A moment, please," he said, clicking a microphone icon.

"Listen," Dusty said angrily, "we're not going to just sit here while you—"

"Ssshhh," the doctor admonished, finger to his lips. "Only for a moment, please, absolute silence. Absolute."

They glanced at each other while Ahriman studied the report on the screen.

The doctor said, "Martie, there are highly sensitive microphones in this room that detect the precise, characteristic sound pattern of the rhythmically turning hubs in a cassette tape recorder. I see that you have left your purse open and are holding it tipped slightly toward me. Do you have such a device in your purse?"

Clearly shaken, she extracted the recorder.

"Put it on the desk, please."

She leaned forward from her chair and surrendered the recorder.

Ahriman switched it off and extracted the minicassette.

"You've got that tape," Martie said angrily. "All right, okay. But we've got a better one, you sonofabitch. We've got one of Susan Jagger—"

"Raymond Shaw," said the doctor.

"I'm listening," Martie responded, stiffening slightly in her chair as she was activated.

Immediately, as Dusty turned to frown at his wife, Ahriman said, "Viola Narvilly."

"I'm listening," Dusty replied, his attitude identical to that of his wife's.

Accessing the two simultaneously would be tricky but doable. If more than six seconds passed between exchanges in their enabling haiku, they would revert to full consciousness. Therefore, he would have to switch back and forth between them, like a juggler spinning plates on top of sticks.

To Martie, he said, "Blown from the west—"

"You are the west and the western wind."

To Dusty, he said, "Lightning gleams—"

"You are the lightning."

Now to Martie: "—fallen leaves gather—"

"The leaves are your instructions."

And back to Dusty: "—and a night heron's shriek—"

"The shrieks are your instructions."

Ahriman finished with Martie: "—in the east."

"I am the east."

Finally to Dusty: "—travels into darkness."

"I am the darkness."

Martie sat with her head tipped slightly forward, her eyes on her hands, which were clutching her purse.

Beautiful bowed head. If told to blow out her brains . . . obeys her master.

Admittedly, this was not first-rate haiku, but the doctor found the sentiment charming.

Still turned toward his wife, head half cocked in an attitude of puzzlement, Dusty appeared to be focused on her.

Of course, she was not actually interested in her purse, and her husband was not truly aware of her, because both of them were waiting for one thing: instructions.

Perfect.

Astonished and delighted, Ahriman leaned back in his chair and marveled at how abruptly his fortunes had improved. The game, which he'd been restructuring this morning, could now be played out with much of his original strategy. All his problems were solved.

Well, except for the Keanuphobe. But now with the universe seeming to be considerate of the doctor's every need, he expected that the issue of the hemi-billionaire bubblehead basket case would be resolved to his advantage before the day was out.

He was curious to know how this unlikely pair, the housepainter and the video-game designer, had survived New Mexico. Indeed, he had five hundred questions if he had one; he could have spent the entire day quizzing them about how they had puzzled out so much about him even with the few wild cards that had fallen in their favor.

As important as attention to detail was, however, one must also remember to keep one's eye on the prize. The prize in this case was the successful completion of the most important game of the doctor's career. Although originally he had intended to play with Martie for a while before using her and Dusty in Malibu, he was no longer willing to wait months, weeks, or even an extra hour for his final satisfaction.

Ultimately, in spite of their cleverness, Martie and Dusty were nothing but two plebs, two common little people desperately striving to rise above their social class, which is what all the plebs wanted even if they would never admit it, two earnest scrabblers with dreams far bigger than their ability to fulfill them. No doubt some of the details of their pathetic sleuthing would be amusing, but in the end, their escapades would be only slightly less witless than the doings of Detective Skeet and his nameless pal. They were interesting not for who they were but solely for how they could be controlled.

Before the Keanuphobe called or showed up to complicate matters, Ahriman needed to instruct Dusty and Martie, wind them up and send them off on the killing spree that would be the final inning of this game.

"Martie, Dusty, I am addressing both of you now. I will instruct you simultaneously to save time. Is this understood?"

"Is it understood?" Martie asked, even as Dusty asked, "Is it?"

"Tell me whether or not you understand what I've told you."

"I understand," they said simultaneously.

Leaning forward in his chair, savoring this moment, downright giddy with delight, not even regretting that now he would not have the chance to boff Martie a few times, the doctor said, "Later today you are going to take a drive out to Malibu—"

"Malibu . . ." Martie murmured.

"Yes, that's right. Malibu. You know the address. The two of you are going out to visit Dusty's mother, Claudette, and her husband—that greedy, grasping, self-aggrandizing little shit, Dr. Derek Lampton."

"I understand," Dusty said.

"Yes, I'm sure you do," Ahriman said, amused, "since you had to live under the same roof with the reeking little pisspot. Now, when you get to Malibu, if either Claudette or Dickhead Derek is out somewhere on an errand, you must wait until both are home."

The doctor realized that by heaping this ridicule on Lampton, he was indulging in adolescent name-calling. But, ah, what a sweet release it was.

With increasing excitement, he said, "You must wait, in fact, until their son is home, too, your venomous little half brother Derek junior—who is, by the way, as much of a suppurating pimple on the ass of humanity as his old man. Jackoff Junior will probably be there when you arrive, because he's home-schooled, as you know. Your syphilitic stepfather has his own ass-wipe theories about education, some of which I suppose he shoved down your throat, too, and Skeet's. Anyway, they must all be present before you act. You will disable all of them but not kill them immediately. You will mutilate and dismember them in the following order: Claudette first, then Junior, then Derek shit-for-brains Lampton himself. He must be last, so he can watch everything you do to Claudette and Junior. Wednesday, Martie, I showed you a photograph of a girl whose dismembered body had been rearranged by her killer in a particularly clever fashion, and I asked you to focus particularly on that tableau. Once you've cut her apart, you and Dusty are going to rearrange Claudette in the same fashion, with but one variation, involving her eyes—"

He halted, realizing that in his excitement he had gotten ahead of himself. He paused to take a deep breath and then a long swallow of black cherry soda.

"Excuse me. Sorry. I've got to back up a moment. Before you go to Malibu, you'll stop at a self-storage unit in Anaheim to pick up a satchel full of surgical instruments. And an autopsy saw with spare blades—including a few excellent cranial blades that'll open *any* skull, even one as dense as Derek's. I've also left a pair of Glock machine pistols and spare magazines . . ."

Involving her eyes.

Those three words from his instructions cycled back through the doctor's mind, and for a moment he didn't understand why.

Involving her eyes.

Abruptly he stood up from his chair, pushing it backward, out of his way. "Martie, look at me."

After a hesitation, the woman raised her bowed head and her downcast eyes.

Swiveling to the husband, Ahriman said, "Dusty, why have you been looking at Martie all this time?"

"Why have I been looking at Martie?" Dusty replied,

correctly answering a question with a question, as he was required to do in this deep programmed state.

"Dusty, look at me. Look directly at me."

Dusty turned his gaze from his wife to Ahriman.

Martie was staring down at her hands once more.

"Martie!" the doctor commanded.

Obediently, she met his eyes again.

Ahriman stared at Martie, studying her eyes, then turned to Dusty, turned from one to the other, one to the other, one to the other, until he said, more shakily than he would have liked, "No REM. No jiggle."

"No shit," Dusty said, getting to his feet.

Their attitude changed. Gone, the glazed expressions. Gone, the air of obedience.

Rapid eye movement couldn't be faked convincingly, so they hadn't tried.

Rising from her chair, Martie said, "What are you? What sort of disgusting, pathetic *thing* are you?"

The doctor did not like the tone of her voice, did not like it at all. The loathing. The contempt. People did not speak to him in this fashion. Such disrespect was intolerable.

He tried to reestablish control: "Raymond Shaw."

"Kiss my ass," she said.

Dusty began to circle the desk.

Sensing a potential for violence, the doctor drew the .380 Beretta from his shoulder holster.

The sight of the gun stopped them.

"You can't have been deprogrammed," Ahriman insisted. "You *can't* have been."

"Why?" Martie asked. "Because it's never happened before?"

"What do you have against Derek Lampton?" Dusty demanded.

People didn't demand things of the doctor. Not more than once, anyway. He wanted to shoot this stupid, stupid cheaply dressed, nobody, nothing *housepainter* right between the eyes, blow his face off, blow his brains out.

A shooting here, of course, would have unpleasant repercussions. Police with their endless questions. Reporters. Stains that might never come out of the Persian rug.

For a moment he suspected treachery at the institute: "Who reprogrammed you?"

"Martie did it for me," Dusty claimed.

"And Dusty freed me."

Ahriman shook his head. "You're lying. This isn't possible. You're both lying."

The doctor heard a note of panic in his voice and was ashamed. He reminded himself that he was Mark Ahriman, only son of the great director, greater in his own field than Dad had been in Hollywood, a puppeteer, not a puppet.

"We know a lot about you," Martie said.

"And we're going to find out more," Dusty promised. "Every ugly little detail."

Detail. That word again. Which last night had seemed to be an omen and not a good one.

Convinced they had been activated and accessed, he had told them too much. Now they had an advantage, and they might eventually find a way to use it effectively. Game point to the opposition.

"We're going to find out what you have against Derek Lampton," Dusty vowed. "And when we've figured out your motivation, that'll be another nail in your coffin."

"Please," the doctor said, wincing with pretended pain. "Don't torture me with clichés. If you're going to try to intimidate me, have the courtesy to go away for a while, acquire a better education, improve your vocabulary, and come back with some fresh metaphors."

That was better. He had slipped out of character for a moment. His was a demanding role, complex, intellectual, and richly nuanced. Of the actors who had won Oscars for starring in Dad's tearjerkers, none could have settled into this part as deeply and successfully as had the doctor. A rare departure from character was understandable, but once again he was the lord of memory.

Now, in response to their pathetic attempt at intimidation, he gave them a lesson in the real thing: "While you're embarked on this crusade to bring me to justice, you might need to move in with dear old Mom for a while. Your quaint little house burned to the ground Wednesday night."

The poor dumb children were bewildered for a moment, not sure if what he had said was true or if it was a lie, and if it was a lie, they couldn't puzzle out a purpose in the deceit.

"Your marvelous collection of thrift-shop furniture—all gone, I'm afraid. And the damning tape recording you mentioned earlier, the message from Susan—gone, too. The tragedy of fire. Insurance can never replace things with sentimental value, can it?"

They believed now. The stunned expression of the displaced, the dispossessed.

While they were emotionally reeling, the doctor hit them hard again. "The goggle-eyed idiot you left Skeet with. What's his name?"

They glanced at each other, and then Dusty said, "Fig."

The doctor frowned. "Fig?"

"Foster Newton."

"Ah. I see. Well, the Fig is dead. Shot four times in the gut and chest."

Rattled, Dusty asked, "Where's Skeet?"

"Dead, too. Also four shots in the gut and the chest. Skeet and the Fig. It was a nice two-for-one deal."

When Dusty started around the desk again, Ahriman aimed the Beretta point-blank at his face, and Martie seized her husband by the arm, halting him.

"Unfortunately," the doctor said, "I wasn't able to kill

your dog. That would have been a fine dramatic touch, leading to such a nice reveal just now. An *Old Yeller* moment. But life isn't as neatly structured as the movies."

The doctor was *back*. If he could have jumped into the air and high-fived himself, he would have done so.

Great emotions boiled in the plebs, because like all their kind, they were driven far less by intellect than by raw emotion, but the Beretta required them to control themselves, and second by second, they were forced to come to terms with the hard realization that the pistol was not the doctor's only weapon. If he was willing to confess to the killing of Skeet and the Fig, even here in the utter privacy of his sanctum sanctorum, then he must have no fear of being brought to trial for murder; he must be confident that he was untouchable. Reluctantly, bitterly, they were coming to the conclusion that no matter how vigorously they sought to defeat him, he would gun them down with his superior gamesmanship, with his superior intelligence, with his disregard for all rules other than his own, and with his exceptional talent for deception—which, in fact, made the handgun the *least* of his weapons.

After allowing them a moment for this truth to percolate down through their sadly porous gray matter, the doctor brought an end to the standoff. "I think you better go now. And I'll give you some advice to make this game a bit fairer."

"Game?" Martie said.

The contempt and revulsion in her voice couldn't touch Ahriman any longer.

"What do you people want?" Dusty asked, his voice thick with emotion. "The institute . . . *why*?"

"Oh," said the doctor, "surely you see that it's useful from time to time to remove someone who obstructs important public policy. Or to control someone who can advance it. And sometimes . . . a bombing by some right-wing fanatic, or next week by a left-wing fanatic, or a dramatic mass murder by a lone gunman, or a spectacular train wreck or a disastrous oil spill . . . these things can generate enormous media coverage, focus the national attention on a particular issue, and drive legislation that will ensure a more stable society, that will allow us to avoid the extremes of the political spectrum."

"People like *you* are going to save us from extremists?"

Ignoring her taunt, he said, "As for that advice I mentioned . . . From now on, don't sleep at the same time. Don't be apart. Cover each other's back. And remember that anyone on the street, anyone in a crowd, could belong to me."

He could see they were loath to leave. Their hearts were racing, their minds in a tumult of anger and grief and shock, and they wanted a resolution right now, right here, as their kind always did, because they had no appreciation for long-term strategy. They were unable to reconcile their desperate need for immediate emotional catharsis with the cold fact of their powerless position.

"Go," Ahriman said, gesturing to the door with the Beretta.

They went, because they had no other options.

Through the security-camera display on the computer screen, the doctor watched them cross the reception lounge and leave by the door to the public corridor.

Putting the Beretta on the desk rather than returning it to his shoulder holster, keeping it within easy reach, he sat down to brood over this latest development.

The doctor needed to know much more about how this pair of rubes discovered they were programmed and how they deprogrammed themselves. Their astounding self-liberation seemed to be less of an achievement than a flat-out miracle.

Unfortunately, he wasn't likely to learn anything further unless he could drug them again, rebuild their mind chapels, and reload the program, which meant taking them through the tedious three-session process that he had gone through with each of them before. They were too wary now, alert to the thin line between reality and fantasy in the modern world, and unlikely to give him that chance, no matter how clever he was.

He would have to live with this mystery.

Stopping them from doing further damage was more important than learning the truth of how they had rescued themselves.

He had no great respect for truth, anyway. Truth was a squishy thing, amorphous, changing shape before your eyes. Ahriman had spent his entire life shaping truth as easily as a potter shapes a wad of clay into a vase of any desired form.

Power trumped truth any day. He couldn't kill these people with the truth, but power properly applied could crush them and sweep them from the game board forever.

From his briefcase, he extracted the blue bag. He placed it in the center of his desk and stared at it for a minute or two.

The game could be played to its end within the next few hours. He knew where Martie and Dusty would go from here. All the principal figures would be in the same place, vulnerable to a strategist as nimble as the doctor.

We're going to find out what you have against Derek Lampton. And when we've figured out your motivation, that'll be another nail in your coffin.

What hopeless naïfs they were. After all that they had endured, they still believed in a world as ordered as any in a mystery novel. Clues, evidence, proof, and truth wouldn't avail them in this matter. This game was driven by more fundamental powers.

Hoping the Keanuphobe wouldn't call during his brief absence, the doctor holstered the .380 Beretta, took the elevator down to the ground floor, left the building, crossed Newport Center Drive to one of the restaurants in the nearby shopping-and-entertainment complex, and used a public telephone to place a call to the same number that he had used on Wednesday night, when he'd needed to arrange a fire.

The number was busy. He had to try it four times before at last it rang.

"Hello?"

"Ed Mavole," said the doctor.

"I'm listening."

After proceeding through the lines of the enabling haiku, the doctor said, "Tell me whether or not you're alone."

"I'm alone."

"Leave home. Take plenty of pocket change with you. Go directly to a pay phone where you'll have at least a little privacy. Fifteen minutes from now, call this number." He recited the direct line in his office, which didn't go through Jennifer. "Tell me whether or not you understand."

"I understand."

Ahriman conveyed the subject from the mind chapel up to full consciousness on the count of ten, whereupon he said, "Sorry, wrong number," and hung up.

Returning directly to his fourteenth-floor suite, the doctor was circumspect upon entering the reception lounge, lest the Keanuphobe be waiting there with a spike-heeled shoe in each hand.

Jennifer looked up from her desk, beyond the reception window, and waved perkily.

He waved but hurried to his office before she could launch into an enthusiastic harangue about the health benefits of eating five ounces of liquefied pine bark every day.

At his desk once more, he slipped the Beretta out of his holster and put it within easy reach.

He plucked a fresh bottle of black cherry soda from the office refrigerator and used it to wash down another cookie. He needed a blast of sugar.

He was in action again. He had gotten through a rock moment or two, but the crisis had only invigorated him

Ever the optimist, he knew that another spectacular win was only hours away, and he was excited.

Now and then, people asked the doctor how he managed to keep his youthful looks, his youthful figure, and such a high energy level day after day, through a busy life. His answer was always the same: What kept him young was his sense of *fun*.

When the phone rang, it was necessary to activate and access the subject once more: "Ed Mavole."

"I'm listening."

Following the haiku, Dr. Ahriman said, "You will go directly to a self-storage yard in Anaheim." He provided the address of the facility, the number of the unit that he had rented with false ID, and the combination of the lock on the door. "Among other things in the storage unit, you will find two Glock 18 machine pistols and several spare thirty-three-round magazines. Take one of the pistols and . . . four magazines ought to be enough."

Regrettably, with five rather than three people to subdue at the house in Malibu, and with only one person to subdue them instead of two, it would not be possible to take control of the residence quietly enough to be able, thereafter, to dismember all the victims and compose ironic tableaux according to the original game plan. So much gunfire would be required that police would arrive quickly and interrupt the work: Cops had a notoriously poor sense of both fun and irony.

Perhaps, however, there would be enough time to transform Derek Lampton Sr. into the object of ridicule that he deserved to be.

"Other than the pistol and the four magazines, the only items you'll take from the storage unit are an autopsy saw and a cranial blade. No, better take two blades, in case one snaps."

Attention to detail.

He described these tools to be sure no mistakes were

made, and then he gave directions to Derek Lampton's place in Malibu.

"Kill everyone you find at the house." He listed the people he expected to be present. "But if there are others—visiting neighbors, a meter reader, whoever—kill them, too. Enter forcefully, moving quickly from room to room, chasing them down if they flee, and waste no time. Then before the police arrive, you will remove the top of Dr. Derek Lampton's skull with the cranial saw." He described the technique by which this could be best accomplished. "Now tell me whether or not you understand."

"I understand."

"You will remove the brain and set it aside. Repeat, please."

"Remove the brain and set it aside."

The doctor gazed wistfully at the blue bag on his desk. There was no way, on a timely basis and beyond the eyes of witnesses, to rendezvous with this programmed killer and pass along Valet's useful product. "There is something you must put in the empty skull. If the Lamptons have a dog, you might find what you need, but if not, you'll have to produce it yourself." He gave his final instructions, including a suicide directive.

"I understand."

"I've given you very important work, and I'm convinced you will perform it impeccably."

"Thank you."

"You're welcome."

When he hung up the phone, Ahriman wished that he had been able to program the pustulant Lampton family themselves—the insufferable Derek, his slut of a wife, and their deranged son—and use *them* as puppets. Unfortunately, they were too aware of him and were sure to regard him with suspicion; he stood little or no chance of getting close enough to them to administer the requisite drugs and to conduct three long programming sessions.

Nevertheless, he was ebullient. Triumph was within reach.

Black cherry soda. Dead fool out in Malibu. Learn to love yourself.

Perfection. The doctor raised a toast to his poetic genius.

73

On Cape Cod or Martha's Vineyard, this house would have looked like the place that was central to the American Dream, the place you crossed over the river and went through the woods to reach on a cool Thanksgiving dawn, the place where Santa Claus seemed to be real even to adults on a snowy Christmas morning, the quintessential house for the idealized grandmother. Although a perfect house—and indeed a faultless grandmother—had never existed in real life, this nation of passionate sentimentalists believed this was the way grandmothers' houses universally *ought* to be. Slate roof with a widow's walk. Silvered cedar-shingle siding. Window frames and shutters glossy with white marine-finish paint. A deep porch with white wicker rocking chairs and a bench swing, and a manicured yard with foot-high white picket fences surrounding each lush flower bed. On Cape Cod or Martha's Vineyard, in a certain moment of the past, you might have found Norman Rockwell sitting at an easel in the front yard, painting two adorable children as they chased a goose with a red ribbon tied in a half-finished bow around its neck, while a happy dog frolicked in the background.

Here in Malibu, even in the middle of a coastal winter on a low bluff above the Pacific, with steps leading down to the beach, with palm trees aplenty, the house looked misplaced. Beautiful, graceful, well designed, and well constructed, but misplaced nonetheless. If anyone's grandmother lived herein, she would have had electric-blue fingernails, bleached-blond hair, lips sensuously recontoured with injections of collagen, and surgically enlarged breasts. The house was a shining fiction, harboring darker truths within, and the sight of it on this visit—only the fifth Dusty had paid since leaving almost twelve years ago, at the age of eighteen—affected him as it always had before, sending a chill through his heart rather than up his spine.

The house, of course, was not to blame. It was only a house.

Nevertheless, after he and Martie parked in the driveway, as they were ascending the front-porch steps, he said, "The Tower of Cirith Ungol."

He dared not think about their little house in Corona Del Mar. If it was really burned to the ground, as Ahriman had claimed, Dusty wasn't ready to deal with the emotional impact. A house is just a house, sure, and property is replaceable, but if you have lived well and loved in a house, if you have made good memories there, then you can't help but grieve over the loss of it.

He dared not think, either, about Skeet and Fig. If Ahriman was telling the truth, if he had killed them, both this world and Dusty's heart were darker places than they had been yesterday, and they were certain to remain darker for the rest of his life. The possible loss of his troubled but much-loved brother had left him half-numb, as he might have expected, but he was a little surprised at how profoundly disturbed he was, as well, by the thought of Fig's death; the quietly diligent painter had been peculiar indeed, but also kind and good-natured, and the hole he left in Dusty's life was the size and the shape of an odd but meaningful friendship.

His mother, Claudette, answered the bell, and as always Dusty was startled and disarmed by her beauty. At fifty-two, she could pass for thirty-five; and at thirty-five she'd had the power to rivet everyone in a crowded room merely by entering, a power that she no doubt would still have at eighty-five. His father, her second of four husbands, once said, "Since birth, Claudette has looked good enough to eat. Every day the world looks on her, and its mouth waters." This was so correct and so succinct that it was probably something Trevor, his father, had read somewhere rather than anything he had thought himself, and though it seemed at first crude, it was not, and it was true. Trevor hadn't been commenting on her sexuality. He had meant beauty as a thing apart from sexual desire, beauty as an ideal, beauty so striking that it spoke to the soul. Women and men, babies and centenarians alike, were drawn to Claudette, wanted to be near her, and deep in their eyes when they gazed at her was something like pure hope and something like rapture, but different and mysterious. The love so many brought to her was love unearned—and unreciprocated. Her eyes were similar to Dusty's, gray-blue, but with less blue than his; and in them he had never seen what any son longs to see in his mother's eyes, nor had he ever seen a reason to believe that she wanted or would accept the love that—more as a boy than now, but still now—he would have lavished on her.

"Sherwood," she said, offering neither a kiss nor a welcoming hand, "do all young people come unannounced these days?"

"Mother, you know my name's not Sherwood—"

"Sherwood Penn Rhodes. It's on your birth certificate."

"You know perfectly well that I had it legally changed—"

"Yes, when you were eighteen, rebellious, and even more foolish than you are now," she said.

"Dusty is what all my friends called me since I was a kid."

"Your friends were always the class losers, Sherwood. You've always associated with the wrong type, so routinely it almost seems willful. *Dustin* Rhodes. What were you thinking? How could we keep a straight face, introducing you to cultured people as Dusty Rhodes?"

"That's *exactly* what I was thinking."

"Hello, Claudette," Martie said, having been ignored thus far.

"Dear," Claudette said, "please use your good influence with the boy and insist he revert to a grown-up name."

Martie smiled. "I like Dusty—the name and the boy."

"Martine," Claudette said. "That's a real person's name, dear."

"I like people to call me Martie."

"I know, yes. How unfortunate. You're not setting a very good example for Sherwood."

"Dustin," Dusty insisted.

"Not in my house," Claudette demurred.

Always, upon arrival here, no matter how much time had passed since his previous visit, Dusty was greeted in this distant fashion, not routinely with a debate about his name, sometimes with lengthy comments on his blue-collar dress or his unstylish haircut, or with probing queries about whether he had yet pursued "real" work or was still painting houses. Once, she kept him on the porch, discussing the political crisis in China, for at least five minutes, though it had seemed like an hour. She always eventually invited him inside, but he was never sure that she would let him cross the threshold.

Skeet had once been enormously excited when he'd seen a movie about angels, with Nicholas Cage starring as one of the winged. The premise of the film was that guardian angels aren't permitted to know romantic love or other strong feelings; they must remain strictly intellectual beings in order to serve humanity without becoming too emotionally involved. To Skeet, this explained their mother, whose beauty even the angels might envy, but who could be cooler than a pitcher of unsweetened lemonade in midsummer.

Finally, having extracted whatever psychic toll she sought from these delays, Claudette stepped back, inviting them in without word or gesture. "One son shows up with a . . . guest at almost midnight, the other with a wife, and neither calls first. I know both took classes in manners and deportment, but apparently the money was wasted."

Dusty assumed that the other son was Junior, who was fifteen and lived here, but when he and Martie stepped past Claudette, Skeet bounded down the stairs to greet them. He appeared to be paler than when they had last seen him, thinner as well, with darker circles under his eyes, but he was alive.

When Dusty hugged him, Skeet said, "Ouch, ouch, ouch," and then said it again when he hugged Martie.

Astonished, Dusty said, "We thought you were—"

"We were told," Martie said, "that you were—"

Before either of them could finish the thought, Skeet hiked up his pullover and his undershirt, eliciting a wince of distaste from his mother, and displayed his bare torso. "Bullet wounds!" he announced with amazement and a curious pride.

Four wicked bruises with ugly dark centers and overlapping aureoles marked his wasted chest and stomach.

Relieved to see Skeet alive, joyous, but puzzled, Dusty said, "Bullet wounds?"

"Well," Skeet amended, "they would have been bullet wounds if me and Fig—"

"Fig and I," his mother corrected.

"Yeah, if Fig and I hadn't been wearing Kevlar vests."

Dusty felt the need to sit down. Martie was shaky, too. But they had come here with a sense of urgency, and it might be a mortal mistake to lose it now. "What were you doing in Kevlar vests?"

"Good thing you didn't want them for New Mexico," said Skeet. "Me and Fig—" A quick, guilty glance at his mother. "Fig and I figured we might as well make ourselves useful, so we decided to tail Dr. Ahriman."

"You *what*?"

"We followed him in Fig's truck—"

"Which I made them park in the garage," said Claudette. "I do not wish that vehicle to be seen in my driveway."

"It's a cool truck," Skeet said. "Anyway, we put on vests just to be safe, and we followed him, and somehow he turned the tables on us. We thought we lost him, and we were out on the beach, trying to make contact with one of the mother ships, and he just walked up and shot us both four times."

"Good God," Martie said.

Dusty was trembling, overcome by more emotions then he could name or sort out. Nevertheless, he noticed that Skeet's eyes were brighter and clearer than they had been since that celebratory day, over fifteen years ago, when the two of them had packaged a box of dog droppings and mailed it off to Holden Caulfield, the elder, after Claudette had thrown him out in favor of Derek.

"He was wearing a ski mask, so we couldn't positively identify him to the police. We didn't even go to the police. Didn't seem like we'd get anywhere with them. But we knew it was him, all right. He didn't fool us." Skeet was beaming, as if they had pulled one over on the psychiatrist. "He shoots Fig twice, then me four times, and it's like being slammed in the gut with a hammer, knocks all the breath out of me, and I'm almost unconscious, too, and I want to suck air, but I don't because even with the wind howling, he might hear me and know I'm not really dead. Fig's playing dead, too. So then before he turns back to Fig and shoots him two more times, the guy says to me, 'Your mother's a whore, and your father's a fraud, and your stepfather—he's got shit for brains.' "

Icily, Claudette said, "I've never even met this purveyor of pop-psych drivel."

"Then both me and Fig, Fig and I, we knew Ahriman went away in a hurry, but we laid there, 'cause we were scared. And for a while we *couldn't* move. Like we were stunned. You know? And then when we could move, we came here to find out why he thinks Mother's a whore."

"Have you been to a hospital?" Martie worried.

"Nah, I'm fine," Skeet said, finally lowering his sweater.

"You could have a cracked rib, internal injuries."

"I've made the same argument," Claudette said, "to no avail. You know what Holden's like, Sherwood. He's always had more enthusiasm than common sense."

"It's still a good idea to go to a hospital, be examined while the injuries are visible," Dusty advised Skeet. "That's admissible evidence if we're ever able to get this shithead into court."

"*Bastard*," Claudette admonished, "or *sonofabitch*. Either is adequate, Sherwood. Pointless vulgarities don't impress me. If you think *shithead* will shock me, better think again. But in this house we've never thought William Burroughs is literature, and we're not going to start thinking so now."

"I love your mother," Martie told Dusty.

Claudette's eyes narrowed almost imperceptibly.

"How was New Mexico?" Skeet asked.

"A land of enchantment," Dusty said.

At the end of the hall, the swinging door to the kitchen swung, and through it came Derek Lampton. He approached with his shoulders back, spine ramrod-straight, chest out, and although his bearing was military, he nevertheless seemed to slink toward them.

Skeet and Dusty had secretly called him Lizard virtually from the day he arrived, but Lampton was more accurately a mink of a man, compact and sleek and sinuous, hair as thick and shiny as fur, with the quick, black, watchful eyes of something that would raid a chicken coop the moment the farmer's back was turned. His hands, neither of which he offered to Dusty or Martie, featured slender fingers with wider than normal webbing and with slightly pointy nails, like clever paws. The mink is a member of the weasel family.

"Has someone died and are we having a reading of the will?" Lampton asked, which was his idea of humor and the closest thing to a greeting he would ever offer.

He looked Martie up and down, his attention lingering on the swell of her breasts against her sweater, as he always forthrightly examined attractive women. When at last he met her eyes, he bared his small, sharp, white-white teeth. This passed for his smile—and perhaps even for what he believed to be a *seductive* smile.

"Sherwood and Martine actually were in New Mexico," Claudette told her husband.

"Really?" Lampton said, raising his eyebrows.

"I told you," Skeet said.

"That's true," Lampton confirmed, addressing Dusty rather than Skeet. "He told us, but with such flamboyant detail, we assumed that it was less reality than just one of his dissociative fantasies."

"I don't have dissociative fantasies," Skeet objected, managing to put some iron in his voice, although he couldn't meet Lampton's eyes—and instead stared at the floor when he raised his objection.

"Now, Holden, don't be defensive," Lampton soothed. "I'm not judging you when I mention your dissociative fantasies, any more than I would be judging Dusty if I were to mention his pathological aversion to authority."

"I don't have a pathological aversion to authority," Dusty said, angry with himself for feeling the need to respond, striving to keep his voice calm, even friendly. "I have a legitimate aversion to the notion that a bunch of elitists should tell everyone else what to do and what to think. I have an aversion to self-appointed experts."

"Sherwood," said Claudette, "you don't advance your argument whatsoever when you use unintentional oxymorons like *self-appointed experts.*"

With a remarkably straight face and measured tone, Martie said, "Actually, Claudette, it wasn't an oxymoron. It was a metonymy in which he was substituting *self-appointed* for the more vulgar if more accurate *arrogant asshole* experts."

If he'd ever had the slightest doubt that he would love Martie forever, Dusty knew now that they would be bonded through eternity.

As if she had not heard her daughter-in-law, Claudette said to Skeet, "Derek is absolutely correct, Holden, as to both issues. He wasn't judging you. He's not that kind of person. And you do, of course, have dissociative fantasies. Until you acknowledge your condition, you're never going to heal."

Getting across the threshold, although difficult, was always less of a challenge than moving beyond the foyer.

"Holden has stopped taking his medications," Derek Lampton told Dusty, while his gaze slid down and lingered again on the shape of Martie's breasts.

"You had me on seven prescriptions," Skeet said. "By the time I took all of them in the morning, I didn't have room for breakfast."

"You will never be able to realize your potential," Claudette admonished, "until you acknowledge your condition and address it."

"I think he should have stopped taking his medications a long time ago," Dusty said.

Looking up from Martie's breasts, Lampton said, "Holden's recovery isn't facilitated when he's confused by uneducated advice."

"His father facilitated his recovery until he was nine, and you've facilitated it since." Dusty forced a smile and a light tone that he knew fooled no one. "And so far all I've seen is a lot of facilitating and no recovery."

Brightening, Skeet said, "Mother, did you know my father's name isn't really Holden Caulfield? It was Sam Farner before he had it legally changed."

Claudette's eyes pinched. "You're fantasizing again, Holden."

"No, it's true. I've got the proof at home. Maybe that's what Ahriman meant, after he shot me, when he called him a fraud."

Claudette pointed a finger at Dusty. "You encourage him to go off his medications, and this is where it leads." To Skeet, she said, "This Ahriman person called me a whore. Am I to assume, Holden, you think that word fits me as well as you think *fraud* fits your father?"

Dusty's head was filled with that ominous buzzing that usually didn't afflict him until he had been in this house for at least half an hour. Desperate to get back to the urgent issue, he said, "Derek, why would Mark Ahriman harbor such animosity toward you?"

"Because I've exposed him for what he is."

"And what is he?"

"A charlatan."

"And when did you expose him?"

"Every chance I get," Lampton said, his mink eyes gleaming with dark glee.

Moving to her husband's side, slipping an arm around his waist, giving him a playful hug, Claudette said, "When foolish men like this Mark Ahriman get stung by my Derek's wit, they don't forget it."

"How?" Martie pressed. "How did you expose him?"

"Analytical essays in two of the better journals," Lampton said, "putting his empty theories and his jejune prose under a spotlight."

"Why?"

"I was appalled by how many psychologists were beginning to take him seriously. The man's not an intellectual. He's the worst kind of poseur."

"And that's it?" Martie asked. "A couple of essays?"

Lampton's pointy teeth flashed. The corners of his eyes crinkled. Although this was an expression of mirth, he looked as though he had just spotted a mouse that he intended to snare and rip to bits. "Oh, lawdy, Miss Claudy, they don't understand what it means to be on the receiving end of a Lampton blitz, do they?"

"I think I do," Skeet said, but neither his mother nor his stepfather appeared to hear him.

As if Lampton had been witty or naughty, or both, Claudette let out a brief girlish giggle, as full of genuine humor as the rattle of a diamondback.

"Oh, lawdy, Miss Claudy," Lampton repeated, doing a jive wiggle and snapping his fingers, as if he thought he was making with the latest of street vernacular. "Essays in two journals. Some quite clever guerrilla warfare. And a parody of his style for 'Bookend,' the last page in *The New York Times Book Review*—"

"Wickedly funny," Claudette assured them.

"—plus I reviewed his latest for a major syndicate, and the review ended up in seventy-eight newspapers nationwide. I have all the clippings. Can you believe that dreadful book has been on the *Times* list for seventy-eight weeks?"

"You mean *Learn to Love Yourself*?" Martie asked.

"Pop-psych slush," Lampton declared. "It's probably done more damage to the American psyche than any book published in a decade."

"Seventy-eight weeks," Dusty said. "Is that a long time to be on the list?"

"For a book in this category, it's forever," said Lampton.

"How long was your last book on the list?"

Suddenly taking the high road, Lampton said, "I really don't count. Popular success isn't the issue. The quality of the work is the issue, how much impact it has on society, how many people it helps."

"Seems to me it was twelve or fourteen weeks," Dusty said.

"Oh, no, it was more than that," Lampton said.

"Fifteen, then."

Squirming with the need to have his accomplishment properly reported, but now in a trap of his own devising, Lampton looked at Claudette for help, and she said, "Twenty-two weeks it was on the list. Derek never cares about these things, but I do. I'm proud of him. Twenty-two weeks is a very good run, very good indeed for a work of substance."

"Well, there you have the problem, of course," Lampton lamented. "Pop-psych slush will always do better than solid work. It might not help anyone worth a damn, but it's easy to read."

"And the American public," Claudette said, "is as lazy and as poorly educated as it is in need of sound psychological counseling."

Looking at Martie, Dusty said, "We're talking about Derek's *Dare to Be Your Own Best Friend.*"

"I couldn't get through it," Skeet said.

"You're certainly bright enough to," Claudette told him. "But when you don't take your medication, your learning disability roars right back, and you can't read your name. 'Medicate to educate.' "

Glancing toward the living room, Dusty wondered what percentage of visitors ever made it farther than the foyer.

Skeet found a little more courage. "I don't have any trouble reading my fantasy novels, with or without medication."

"Your fantasy novels," said Lampton, "are part of the problem, Holden, not part of the cure."

"What about the guerrilla warfare?" Dusty asked.

Everyone regarded him with puzzlement.

"You said you used some clever guerrilla warfare against Mark Ahriman," Dusty reminded Lampton.

That coop-raiding, mouse-ripping smile again. "Come on, I'll show you!"

Lampton led them upstairs.

Valet was waiting in the second-floor hall, apparently because he had been too intimidated by the war zone in the foyer.

Martie and Dusty paused to cuddle him, to scratch under his chin, to rub behind his ears, and in return he lashed them with tongue and tail.

If he'd had a choice, Dusty would have preferred to sit on the floor and spend the rest of the day with Valet. Other than Skeet's hug—*Ouch, ouch, ouch!*—the dog's welcome was the only real and true moment Dusty had experienced since ringing the doorbell.

Lampton rapped on a door farther along the hall. Glancing back at Dusty and Martie, he said, "Come on, come on."

Claudette and Skeet went into a room on the opposite side of the hall: Lampton's study.

Although no one had spoken an invitation that Dusty could hear, Lampton opened the door on which he'd knocked, and when they caught up to him, they crossed the threshold after him.

This was Junior's bedroom. Dusty hadn't been here in about four years, since Derek Lampton Jr. was eleven. Back then, the decor had been sports-related. Posters of basketball and soccer stars.

Now all the walls and the ceiling were painted gloss black, and these surfaces soaked up the light, so the room seemed dark even with three hundred watts' worth of lamps aglow. The iron-pipe headboard of the bed was black, and the sheets and spread on it were black, too. The desk and chair were black, as were the bookshelves. The natural finish maple floor, so lovely through much of the rest of the house, had been painted black. The only color in the room was provided by the spines of the books on the black shelves, and by a pair of full-size flags stapled to the ceiling: the red field, white circle, and black swastika of the flag that Adolph Hitler had attempted to plant across the globe, and the hammer-and-sickle flag of the former Soviet Union. Four years ago, sports histories, sports biographies, books about archery, and science-fiction novels had crowded the shelves. Those had been replaced by books about Dachau, Auschwitz, Buchenwald, the Soviet gulags, the Ku Klux Klan, Jack the Ripper, several modern real-life serial killers, and a few mad bombers.

Junior himself was dressed in white sneakers, white socks, tan chinos, and a white shirt. He was lying on the bed, reading a book that featured a pile of decomposing human bodies on the dust jacket, and because of the high contrast between the boy and the black-satin bedclothes, he appeared to be levitating like a yogi.

"Hey, bro, how're you doing?" Dusty asked awkwardly. He never knew what to say to his half brother, as they were largely strangers. He had left home—fled—twelve years ago, when Junior was only three.

"Do I look dead yet?" Junior asked sullenly.

Actually, the boy appeared to be *magnificently* alive, too alive for this world, as though he were supercharged with a spectral energy pumped into him from a wall socket in the Beyond, so that he glowed. He hadn't been cursed with any of his father's slippery mink looks; Fate had decided to lavish his mother's genes on him, to bless him with a perfect form and perfect features, as had been given to none of her other children. If one day he ever decided to ascend to a stage, take a microphone in his hand, and sing, regardless of whether his voice was good or merely adequate, he would be bigger than Elvis and the Beatles and Ricky Martin combined, and both young women and young men would scream and weep and throw themselves at the stage, and a significant percentage of them would be pleased, if asked, to cut themselves and offer blood.

"What's this?" Dusty wondered, indicating the black room and the flags on the ceiling.

"What's it look like?" Junior asked.

"Post-Goth?"

"Goth sucks. It's for children."

"Looks like you're practicing for death," Martie said.

"Closer," Junior said.

"What's the point of that?"

Junior put his book aside. "What's the point of anything else?"

"Because we all die, you mean?"

"It's why we're here," Junior said. "To think about it. To watch it happen to other people. To prepare for it. And then to do it and be gone."

"What's this?" Dusty asked again, but this time he directed the question to his stepfather.

"Most adolescent boys, like Derek here, go through a period of intense fascination with death, and each of them thinks he has deeper thoughts about the subject than anyone before him has had," Lampton said, talking about his son as though Junior couldn't hear. When Dusty and Skeet had lived under his thumb, he'd done the same with them, talking about them as though they were interesting lab animal who didn't understand a word of what he was saying. "Se and death. They're *the* big issues in adolescence. Both boy and girls, but most especially boys, are obsessive about bot subjects. Periodically they go through phases that are borderline psychotic. It's a matter of hormonal imbalance, an the best thing to do is let them indulge the obsessio because nature will correct the imbalance soon enough."

"Well, gee, I don't remember being obsessed wit death," Martie said.

"You were," Lampton said, as though he'd known her

child, "but you sublimated it into other interests—Barbie lolls, makeup."

"Makeup is a sublimation of a death obsession?"

"How obvious can it be?" Lampton said with pedantic mugness. "The purpose of makeup is to defy the degradaions of time, and time is just a synonym for death."

"I'm still struggling with Barbie dolls," Dusty said.

"Think about it," Lampton urged. "What is a doll but n image of a corpse? Unmoving, unbreathing, stiff, lifeless. ittle girls playing with dolls are playing with corpses—and earning not to fear death excessively."

"I remember being obsessed with sex," Dusty admitted, but—"

"Sex is a lie," Junior said. "Sex is denial. People turn to ex to avoid facing the truth that life is about death. It's not bout creation. It's about dying."

Lampton smiled down on his son as though he might urst his shirt buttons with pride. "Derek here has chosen to nmerse himself in death for a while, in order to put the fear f it behind him much sooner than most people ever do. It's legitimate technique for self-forced maturation."

"I haven't put it behind me," Martie noted.

"You see?" Lampton said, as if she had made his point or him. "Last year, it was sex, as it always is with fourteenear-old boys. Next year—sex again, once he's done nmersing himself in this."

Dusty suspected that after a year of living in this black oom, obsessing on death, Junior might be the lead item on he evening news one night, and not because he had won a pelling bee.

To the boy, Lampton said, "Dusty and Martie are intersted in our guerrilla operation against Mark Ahriman."

"That creep," Junior said. "You want to whack him ome more?"

"Why don't we?" Lampton said, rubbing his hands ogether.

Junior rolled off the bed, onto his feet, stretched, an then headed out of the room. As he passed Martie, he said “Nice tits.”

Beaming after him, Lampton said, “You see? Already he's moving out of this phase of death obsession, eve though he doesn't entirely recognize it yet.”

In the past, Dusty and Martie had felt like kidnappin the boy, hiding out with him in some far place, and raisin him themselves, to give him a chance at a normal life. A glance at Martie confirmed that she, like Dusty, still felt lik hiding out, although perhaps *from* Junior rather than *wit* him anymore.

They followed the boy into Lampton's upstairs study where Skeet and Claudette were waiting with Foste Newton.

Fig was standing by the window, peering out at th front yard and the driveway.

“Hey, Fig,” Dusty said.

He turned. “Hey.”

“Are you okay?” Martie worried.

Fig rucked up his shirt to show them his chest and belly which were neither as pale nor as slim as Skeet's, and whic were darkened by a different but equally ugly pattern o bruises from the impact of four slugs that had been stoppe by Kevlar body armor.

“This is a very trying morning,” said Claudette, gri macing with distaste.

“I'm okay,” Fig assured her, missing the point.

“You saved our lives,” Martie told him.

“Fire truck?”

“Yes.”

“And he saved mine, too,” Skeet said.

Fig shook his head. “Kevlar.”

The boy was sitting at his father's desk, before th computer.

Lampton stood behind Junior, watching over his shoulder. "Here we go."

Dusty and Martie crowded close and saw that Junior was composing a scathing and well-written mini-review of *Learn to Love Yourself.*

"Where we're going with this," Lampton said, "is the reader's review page on the Amazon.com site. We've written and posted over a hundred and fifty denunciations of *Learn to Love Yourself,* using different names and E-mail addresses."

Appalled, Dusty flashed to the memory of the inhuman viciousness in Ahriman's face and eyes when they had confronted him in his office a short while ago. "*Whose* names and E-mail addresses?" he asked, wondering what vengeance the psychiatrist might have extracted from these unsuspecting and innocent people.

"Don't worry," Lampton said, "when we use real names, we choose brain-dead types who don't read much. They aren't likely to visit Amazon and see any of this."

"Anyway," Junior said, "most of the time we just make up names and E-mail addresses, which is even better."

"You can do that?" Martie wondered.

"The Net is liquid," Junior said.

Trying to puzzle out the full meaning of that statement, Dusty said, "It's difficult to separate fiction from reality."

"It's better than that. Fiction and reality don't matter. It's all the same, one river."

"Then how do you find the truth about anything?"

Junior shrugged. "Who cares? What matters isn't what's true . . . it's what works."

"I'm sure on Amazon's site, half the rave reviews of Ahriman's idiotic book were written by Ahriman himself," Lampton said. "I know some novelists who do more of this stuff than spend time writing. All we're trying to achieve here is to redress the imbalance."

"Did you post your own raves about *Dare to Be Your Own Best Friend*?" Martie asked.

"Me? No, no," Lampton assured her. "If the book is solid, the book takes care of itself."

Yeah, right. For hours, for days, those clever mink paws had no doubt pounded out self-praise at such a blistering pace that the keyboard had locked up repeatedly.

"After this," Junior promised, "we'll show you what we can do with various Ahriman-related sites on the Web."

"Derek is enormously clever with the computer," boasted Derek the Elder. "We go all over the Web after Ahriman, all over. No security wall, no program architecture is too much for him."

Turning away from the computer, Dusty said, "I think we've seen enough."

Gripping Dusty's right arm with both hands, Martie pulled him aside. Her expression, as ghastly as it was, could be no more horrified than his own face. She said, "When Susan was representing Ahriman's house, before it *was* Ahriman's house, she was the agent for the original owner, and she wanted me to see the place. Spectacular house, but very imposing, like a stage set for *Götterdämmerung*. Had to see it, she said. So I met her there. It was the day she first showed it to Ahriman, the day she met him. I arrived when she was finishing the tour with him. I met him that day, too. The three of us . . . talked a little."

"Oh, Jesus. Can you remember? . . ."

"I'm trying. But, I don't know. Maybe the subject of his book came up. Seventy-eight weeks on the best-seller list now. So back then it would have been fairly new. Eighteen months ago. And if I realized what kind of book it was . . . maybe I mentioned Derek."

Trying to pad the sharp points of the piercing conclusion toward which Martie was hurtling, Dusty said, "Miss M., stop right now. Stop what you're thinking. Ahriman would've gone after Susan anyway. As beautiful as she was, he had her in his sights before you came into the picture."

"Maybe."

"Definitely."

Lampton had turned away from the computer to listen. "You've actually met this pop-psych putz?"

Confronting Derek senior, fixing him with a glare that would have turned him to ice if there had been blood in his veins, Martie said, "We're all dead because of you."

Waiting to hear the punch line of what he assumed must be a joke, Lampton skinned his lips back from his nippy little teeth.

Martie said, "Dead because of your childish competitiveness."

Like a radiant Valkyrie flying to the assistance of her wounded warrior, Claudette came to Lampton's side. "There is nothing in the least childish about it. You don't understand the academic world, Martine. You don't understand intellectuals."

"Don't I?" Martie bristled.

Dusty heard so much loathing in *Don't I?* that he was glad Martie was no longer in possession of the .45 Colt.

"Competition among men like Derek," said Claudette, "isn't about egos or self-interest. It's about *ideas.* Ideas that shape society, the world, the future. For those ideas to be tested and tempered and readied for implementation, they have to survive challenges, debate of all types, in all arenas."

"Like Amazon.com reader reviews," Martie said scathingly.

Claudette was undaunted. "The battle of ideas is a very real war, not a childish competition, as you're trying to paint it."

Valet backed out of the room and stood watching from the hall.

Joining Dusty and Martie, though careful to stand

behind them, Skeet found the courage to say, "Martie's right."

"When you're off your medications," Lampton told him, "your judgment isn't good enough to make you a welcome ally, Holden."

"I welcome him," Dusty disagreed.

With her teeth into this issue, Claudette was more emotional than Dusty had ever seen her. "You think life is video games and movies and fashion and football and gardening, and whatever the hell else fills your days, but life is about *ideas*. People like Derek, people with ideas, shape the world. They shape government, religion, society, every tiniest aspect of our culture. Most people are drones by choice, spending their days in trivialities, absorbed with piffle, living their lives without ever realizing that Derek, people like Derek, have *made* this society and *rule* them by the power of ideas."

Here, in this ugly confrontation with Claudette, which for Dusty and surely for Skeet, as well, was rapidly growing into a showdown of mythic proportions, Martie was their paladin, lance raised and eye to eye with the dragon. Skeet had moved directly behind her, putting his hands on her shoulders, and Dusty was half tempted to move behind Skeet for additional protection.

"Daring to be your own best friend," Martie said, "and learning to love yourself—these are ideas that *shape*?"

"There's no comparison between my book and Ahriman's," Lampton objected, but after his wife's vigorous defense, he sounded as though he were pouting.

Moving half in front of Lampton, as if to physically defend her beleaguered man, but also to press her butt against him, Claudette insisted: "Derek writes vivid, solid psychologically profound work. Rigorously composed ideas. Ahriman spews out pop-psych vomit."

Dusty had never before seen his mother cast off her icy veil and reveal her sexual nature, and he hoped that he would *never* see anything like this again. What aroused her was not ideas themselves, but the idea that ideas were power. *Power* was her true aphrodisiac; not the naked power of generals and politicians and prize-fighters, or even the raw power of serial killers, but the power of those who shaped the minds of generals, politicians, ministers, teachers, lawyers, filmmakers. The power of manipulation. In her flared nostrils and glittering eyes, he saw now an eroticism as cold as that of the trapdoor spider and the whip-tailed skink.

"You still don't get it," Martie seethed. "In defense of *Dare to Be Your Own Best Friend*, you burned down our house. It might as well have been you, you directly. In defense of *Dare to Be Your Own Best Friend*, you shot Skeet and Fig. You think what they say happened last night is a dissociative fantasy, but it's real, Claudette. Those bruises are real, the bullets were real. Your stupid, stupid, stupid idea of what constitutes *debate*, your *idea* that harassment is the same as reasoned discussion—that's what influenced the finger that pulled the trigger. How's *that* for shaping society, huh? Maybe you're ready to die for Derek's vivid, solid, rigorously composed, psychologically profound narcissistic bullshit, *but I'm not*!"

From his post at the window, Fig said, "Lexus."

Claudette hadn't breathed fire yet, though she was full of it. "How easy it evidently is to make ignorant, specious arguments when you've never had a college course in logic. If Ahriman burns down houses and shoots people, then he's a maniac, a psychopath, and Derek is *right* to go after him any way he can. Indeed, if what you say is true, it's *courageous* to go after him."

Daring to be his own best friend, Lampton said, "I always sensed a sociopathic worldview in his writing. I always suspected there was risk in opposing him, but one takes risks if one cares."

"Oh, yes," Martie said, "let's call the Pentagon at once

and have them get a Medal of Honor ready for you. For valor on the field of academic battle, bravery at the computer keyboard with courageous use of false names and invalid E-mail addresses."

"You are not welcome in my house," said Claudette.

"Lexus in the driveway," Fig said.

"So what if there's a hundred fucking Lexuses in the driveway?" Claudette demanded, never taking her eyes off Martie. "Every idiot in this pretentious neighborhood has a Lexus or a Mercedes."

"Parking," said Fig.

Martie and Dusty joined Fig at the window.

The driver's door of the Lexus opened, and a tall, handsome, dark-haired man got out of the car. Eric Jagger.

"Oh, God," Martie said.

Through Susan, Ahriman had gotten at Martie. With or without the benefit of a college course in logic, Dusty was able to add this particular two-plus-two.

Eric reached back into the car to get something that he had left on the seat.

Through Susan, Ahriman had also gotten at Eric, programming him and instructing him to separate from his wife, thereby leaving Susan alone and more vulnerable, more accessible any time the psychiatrist was in the mood to have her. And now there was something else Ahriman wanted from Eric, something a little more strenuous than moving out of his wife's house.

"Hacksaw," Fig said.

"Autopsy saw," Dusty corrected.

"With cranial blades," Martie added.

"Gun," said Fig.

And here came Eric.

74

Death was as stylish as anyone now: gone, the black carriage drawn by black horses, traded in on a silver Lexus. Gone, the black robe with the melodramatic hood: instead, tasseled loafers, black slacks, a Jhane Barnes sweater.

The Kevlar body armor was in the pickup, and the pickup was in the garage, so Skeet and Fig were as unprotected as everyone else, and this time the gunman would be taking head shots, anyway.

"Gun?" Lampton said when Martie asked. "You mean here?"

"No, of course not, don't be ridiculous," Claudette said, as if spoiling for another argument even now, "we don't have a gun."

"Then too bad you don't have a really lethal *idea*," Martie said.

Dusty grabbed Lampton by the arm. "The back-porch roof. You can get onto it through Junior's room or the master bedroom."

Blinking in confusion, nose twitching as if trying to catch a scent that would explain the precise nature of the danger, the mink man said, "But why—"

"Hurry!" Dusty said. "All of you. Go, go. Onto the porch roof, down to the lawn, down to the beach, and hide out at one of the neighbors' houses."

Junior was the first through the study doorway, out and

gone in a sprint, apparently not in fact prepared to immerse himself in anything more than the *idea* of death.

Dusty followed the boy, pulling the wheeled office chair away from Lampton's desk and then pushing it ahead of him, racing down the hall to the top of the stairs, while the rest of them hurried off in the opposite direction.

No, not all of them. Here was Skeet, sweet but useless. "What can I do?"

"Damn it, kid, just get out!"

"Help me with this," Martie said.

She hadn't fled, either. She was at a six-foot-long Sheraton sideboard that stood along the wide hallway, opposite the head of the stairs. With a sweep of her arm, she cleared off a vase and an arrangement of silver candlesticks, which shattered and rattled to the floor. Evidently, she had figured out what Dusty intended to do with the office chair, but she was of the opinion that higher-caliber ammunition was needed.

Together, after moving the chair aside, the three of them dragged the sideboard away from the wall and stood it on one end at the head of the stairs.

"Now make him *go*," Dusty urged her. His voice was hoarse with terror, worse now than it had been when they had finished the slo-mo roll in the rental car outside Santa Fe, because at least then he'd had the comfort of knowing, as the gunmen descended the slope after them, that Martie had the Colt Commander, whereas now he had nothing but a damn sideboard.

Martie grabbed Skeet by the arm, and he tried to resist, but she was the stronger of the two.

Downstairs, a tattoo of automatic gunfire shattered the leaded glass in the front door, cracked off pieces of wood, too, and chopped into the walls of the foyer.

Dusty dropped onto the hall floor, behind the upended sideboard, looking past it down the long single flight of stairs.

The investment adviser slammed through the splintered door and stormed into the house as though a master's in business administration from Harvard now required courses in ass-kicking and heavy weaponry. He put the autopsy saw on the foyer table, gripped the machine pistol in both hands, and turned in a hundred-eighty-degree arc, spraying bullets into the downstairs rooms on three sides of him.

This was an extended magazine, probably thirty-three rounds, but it wasn't a magic well of cartridges, so at the end of Eric's arc, the gun ran dry.

Spare magazines were tucked under his belt. He fumbled with the pistol, trying to eject the spent magazine.

He couldn't be allowed to search the lower floor first, because when he went into the kitchen, he might see people dropping off the back-porch roof or fleeing across the backyard toward the beach.

Gunfire seemed to be still thundering through the house, but Dusty knew the inner workings of his ears were just vibrating in the aftermath, so he shouted, "Ben Marco!"

Eric looked up at the top of the stairs, but he didn't freeze or get that telltale glazed look. He continued fumbling with the pistol, which was clearly unfamiliar to him.

"Bobby Lembeck!" Dusty shouted.

The spent magazine clattered to the foyer floor.

In this case, maybe the activating name didn't come from *The Manchurian Candidate*. Maybe it came from *The Godfather* or *Rosemary's Baby*, or from *The House at Pooh Corner*, for all he knew, but he didn't have time to sample the last fifty years of popular fiction in search of the right character. "Johnny Iselin!"

After shoving another magazine into the machine pistol, Eric locked it in place with a hard whack from the palm of his hand.

"Wen Chang!"

Eric squeezed off a burst of eight or ten rounds, which tore through the solid cherry-wood top of the sideboard—

pock, pock, pock, too many *pocks* to count—cracked through the drawers, smashed out of the bottom, and thudded into the hallway wall behind Dusty, passing over his head and leaving a wake of splinters to rain over him. High-velocity rounds, jacketed in something way harder than he wanted to think about, and maybe with Teflon tips.

"Jocelyn Jordan!" Dusty shouted into the jarring silence that throbbed through his head following the skull-ringing peals of the gunshots. He had read a sizable piece of the novel, and he had skimmed the whole thing, looking for names, in particular for the one that would activate him. He remembered them all. His eidetic memory was the one gift with which he'd been born into this world, that and the common sense that had driven him to be a housepainter instead of a mover and shaker in the world of Big Ideas, but Condon's novel was chocked full of characters, major and minor—as minor as Viola Narvilly, who didn't even appear until past page 300—and he might not have time to run through the entire cast before Eric blew his head off. "Alan Melvin!"

Holding his fire, Eric climbed the steps.

Dusty could hear him coming.

Climbing fast, unfazed by the Sheraton-sideboard deadfall that loomed over him. Coming like a robot. Which was pretty much what he was, in fact: a living robot, a meat machine.

"Ellie Iselin!" Dusty shouted, and he was simultaneously half mad with fear and yet aware of what a ludicrous exit this would be, blown to kingdom come while shouting out names like a frantic quiz-show contestant trying to beat a countdown clock. "Nora Lemmon!"

Unmoved by *Nora Lemmon,* Eric kept coming, and Dusty scrambled up from the floor, shoved the sideboard, and dove to his left, away from the top of the stairs, behind a sheltering wall, as another burst of gunfire smacked into the toppling mass of fine eighteenth-century cherry wood.

Eric grunted and cursed, but it was impossible to tell from the thunderous descent of the sideboard whether he had been hurt or carried to the foyer below. The stairs were wider than the upended antique, and he might have been able to dodge it.

Standing with his back to the hallway wall, next to the stairs, Dusty didn't relish poking his head around the corner to have a look. In addition to never having attended a college class in logic, he'd never taken a class in magic, either, and he didn't know how to catch bullets in his teeth.

And, dear God, even as the thudding-crashing-cracking-banging still rose from the staircase, here came Martie—who was supposed to be gone with the rest of them—pushing a wheeled, three-drawer filing cabinet along the hallway, having commandeered it from Lampton's office.

Dusty glowered at her. What the hell was she thinking, anyway? That Eric would run out of bullets before they ran out of furniture?

Seizing the filing cabinet, pushing Martie away, using the four-foot-high stack of metal drawers as cover, Dusty moved to the head of the stairs again.

Eric had tumbled into the foyer with the sideboard. His left leg was pinned under it. He was still holding the machine pistol, and he fired toward the top of the stairs.

Ducking, Dusty heard the shots go wild. They slammed hard into the ceiling, and a few rounds twanged through ducts and pipes behind the plaster. Not even one ricocheted off the filing cabinet.

His heart was rattling in his chest as if several rounds were ricocheting from wall to wall of its chambers.

When he cautiously peered down into the foyer again, he saw that Eric had pulled his leg out from under the sideboard and was getting to his feet. Relentless as a robot, operating on programmed instructions rather than reason or emotion, the guy was nonetheless pissed.

"Eugenie Rose Cheyney!"

Not even limping, cursing fluently, Eric started toward the stairs. The filing cabinet wasn't half as massive as the sideboard. He would be able to dodge it, pumping out rounds as he came.

"Ed Mavole!"

"I'm listening."

Eric stopped at the foot of the stairs. The murderous glare melted off his face, and what replaced it was not the flat, grimly determined expression with which he had entered the house, but the glazed and slightly quizzical look that signified *activation*.

Ed Mavole was the name, all right, but Dusty was still lacking a haiku. According to Ned Motherwell, umpteen feet of shelves in the bookstore were devoted to haiku, so even if all the volumes Ned had bought were now near at hand—which they weren't—the accessing lines might not be in them.

Down in the foyer, Eric twitched, blinked, and reacquainted himself with his murderous intentions.

"Ed Mavole," Dusty said again, and once more Eric froze and said, "I'm listening."

This wouldn't be fun, but it ought to be doable. Keep using the magic name, snap Eric back into an activated state every time he came out of it, go straight down the stairs at him, snatch the gun from his hand, knock him ass over teakettle, clip him alongside the head with the butt of the gun, just hard enough to knock him unconscious without leaving him comatose for life, and then tie him up with whatever was at hand. Maybe when he regained consciousness, he would no longer be a robotic killer. Otherwise, they could keep him under restraint, buy all umpteen shelf feet of haiku, brew ten gallons of strong coffee, and read every verse to him until they got a response.

As Dusty rolled the filing cabinet aside, Martie said,

"Oh, God, please, babe, don't chance it," and Eric twitched back to his killing glare.

"Ed Mavole."

"I'm listening."

Dusty descended the stairs fast. Eric was looking straight at him but didn't seem to be able to work out the physics of what was about to happen. Before Dusty was a third of the way down, taking no chances, he shouted, "Ed Mavole," and Eric Jagger replied, "I'm listening," and then he was two-thirds of the way down, and he said, "Ed Mavole," and as he reached Eric, the answer came in that same mellow voice, "I'm listening." Looking straight into the muzzle, which seemed as big as any tunnel that he might drive through, Dusty closed one hand around the barrel, pushed it aside and out of his face, wrenched the gun from Eric's slack hands, and at the same time drove his shoulder into the dazed man, knocking him to the floor.

Dusty fell, too, and rolled across broken glass and chunks of wood from the bullet-riddled front door, afraid he might accidentally discharge the pistol. He tumbled into the half-moon table that stood against the foyer wall, rapping his forehead hard against the sturdy stretcher bar that connected its three legs, but he didn't shoot himself in the thigh, the groin, or anywhere else.

When Dusty staggered to his feet, he saw that Eric had already gotten off the floor. The guy looked confused but nonetheless angry and still in a programmed-killer mode.

From the stairs, which she was rapidly descending, Martie said, "Ed Mavole," even before Dusty could say it, and suddenly this seemed to be the lamest video game Martie had ever concocted: *Housepainter Versus Investment Adviser,* one armed with an automatic weapon and the other with furniture and magic names.

It might have been funny, this thought at this moment, if he'd not looked past Martie to the top of the stairs, where

Junior stood with a crossbow, cranked to full tension and loaded.

"No!" Dusty shouted.

Shusssh.

A crossbow quarrel, shorter and thicker than an ordinary arrow, is far more difficult to see in flight than is an arrow let off by a standard bow, so much faster does it move. Magic, the way this one appeared to pop *from* Eric Jagger's chest, as if out of his heart like a rabbit out of a hat: All but two inches of its notchless butt protruded in a small carnation of blood.

Eric dropped to his knees. The homicidal glare cleared from his eyes, and he looked around in bewilderment at the foyer, which apparently was altogether new to him. Then he blinked up at Dusty and seemed astonished as he fell forward, dead.

When Martie tried to stop Dusty from going upstairs, he shook her off, and he climbed two steps at a time, his forehead throbbing where he'd rapped it against the stretcher bar, his vision swimming, but not from the blow on the head, swimming because his body was flooded with whatever brain chemicals induce and sustain rage, his heart pumping as much pure *fury* as blood, the angelic-looking boy seen now through a dark lens and a red tint, as though Dusty's eyes were streaming tears of blood.

Junior tried to use the crossbow like a shield, to block the assault. Dusty grabbed the stock at midpoint, the revolving nut of the lock plate digging into the palm of his hand. He wrenched the bow out of the boy's grasp, threw it on the floor, and kept moving. He drove the boy across the hall, into the space where the sideboard had stood, shoving him against the wall so hard that his head bounced off the plaster with a *thock* like a tennis ball off a racket.

"You sick, rotten little shit."

"He had a gun!"

"I'd already taken it away from him," Dusty screamed,

spraying the boy with spittle, but Junior insisted, "I didn't see!" And they repeated the same useless things to each other, twice, three times, until Dusty accused him with such violence that his damning words boomed along the hall: "You saw, you knew, you did it *anyway*!"

Then came Claudette, pushing between them, forcing them apart, her back to Junior, confronting Dusty, eyes harder than before, the unyielding gray of flint and flashing as if with sparks. For the first time in her life, her face didn't astonish with its beauty: instead, such a hideous ferocity. "You leave him alone, leave him alone, you get away from him!"

"He killed Eric."

"*He saved us!* We'd all be dead, but he *saved* us!" Claudette was shrill, as never before, her lips pale and her skin gray, like some stone goddess come alive and raging, a termagant who, by sheer power of will, would alter this bitter reality to suit her, as only gods and goddesses could do. "He had the *guts*, and he had the *brains* to act, to *save* us!"

Lampton appeared, too, pouring out thick streams of soothing words, gouts of platitudes, slathers of anger-management jargon, no less containable than the oil spill from a floundering supertanker. Talking, talking, talking, even as his wife pressed her ceaseless strident defense of Junior, both of them chattering at once: Their words were like paint rollers, laying down obscuring swaths of new color over stains.

At the same time, Lampton was trying to get the machine pistol out of Dusty's right hand, which at first Dusty didn't even realize he was still holding. When he understood what Lampton wanted, he let go of the weapon.

"Better call the police," Lampton said, though surely neighbors had already done so, and he hurried away.

Skeet warily approached, staying well clear of his mother but nonetheless coming around to Dusty's side of the standoff, and Fig stood farther back down the hall, watching them as though he had, at last, made contact with the aliens he had so long desired to meet.

None of them had fled the house as Dusty had urged them to do—or if they had gotten as far as the roof of the back porch, they had returned. At least Lampton and Claudette must have known that Junior was loading his crossbow with the intention of joining the battle, and apparently neither of them had tried to stop him. Or perhaps they had been afraid to try. Any parents with common sense or a genuine love of their child would have taken the crossbow away from him and *dragged* him out of this house if necessary. Or maybe the *idea* of a boy with a primitive weapon defeating a man with a machine pistol—a twisted incarnation of Rousseau's concept of the noble savage, which set so many hearts aflutter in the academic literary community—had been too delicious to resist. Dusty could no longer pretend to understand the odd thought processes of these people, and he was weary of trying.

"He killed a man," Dusty reminded his mother, because for him no amount of shrill argument could change this fundamental truth.

"A lunatic, a maniac, a demented man with a gun," Claudette insisted.

"I'd taken the gun away from him."

"That's what you say."

"That's the *truth*. I could have handled him."

"You can't handle anything. You drop out of school, you drop out of life, you paint houses for a living."

"If customer satisfaction were the issue," he said, knowing he shouldn't say it, unable to restrain himself, "I'd be on the cover of *Time*, and Derek would be in prison, paying for all the patients' lives he's fucked up."

"You ungrateful bastard."

Distraught, on the verge of tears, Skeet pleaded, "Don't start this. Don't start. It'll never stop if you start now."

Dusty recognized the truth of what Skeet said. After all

these years of keeping his head down, all these years of enduring and being dutiful but distant, so much hurt remained unsalved, so many offenses had never been responded to, that the temptation now would be to redress all wrongs in one terrible venting. He wanted to avoid that dreadful plunge, but he and his mother seemed to be in a barrel on the roaring brink of Niagara, with nowhere to go but down.

"I know what I saw," Claudette insisted. "And you're not going to change my mind about that, not you of all people, not you, *Dusty.*"

He couldn't let it go and still be sure of who he was: "You weren't *here.* You weren't in a position to see anything."

Martie had joined them. Taking hold of Dusty's hand, gripping it tightly, she said, "Claudette, only two people saw what happened. Me and Dusty."

"I *saw,*" Claudette declared angrily. "No one can tell me what I saw or didn't see. Who do you think you are? I'm not a doddering old senile bitch who can be told what to think, what she saw!"

Behind his mother, Junior smiled. He met Dusty's eyes and was so lacking in shame that he didn't look away.

"What's *wrong* with you?" Claudette demanded of Dusty. "What's wrong with you that you'd rather see your brother's life ruined over something as meaningless as this?"

"Murder is meaningless to you?"

Claudette slapped Dusty, slapped him hard, grabbed handfuls of his shirt, tried to push him back, and as she shook him, words shook from her, too, one at a time: "You. Won't. Do. This. Vicious. Thing. To. Me."

"I don't want to ruin his life, Mother. That's the last thing I want. He needs help. Can't you see that? He needs help, and somebody better get it for him."

"Don't you judge him, *Dusty.*" Such venom in the emphasis that she gave to his name, such bitterness. "One year of college doesn't make you a master of psychology, you know. It doesn't make you any damn thing at all, except a loser."

Crying now, Skeet said, "Mother, please—"

"Shut up," Claudette said, rounding on her younger son. "You just shut up, Holden. You didn't see anything, and you better not pretend you did. No one will believe you, anyway, the mess you are."

As Martie pulled Skeet aside, out of the fray, Dusty looked past Claudette, to Junior, who was smirking as he watched Skeet.

Dusty almost heard the click as a switch was thrown and insight brightened a previously dark space in his mind. The Japanese called this a *satori*, a moment of sudden enlightenment: an odd word learned in one year of college.

Satori. Here was Junior, as fair of face as his mother, blessed with her physical grace, as well. And bright. No denying how very bright he was. At her age, he would be her last child, and the only one with the prospect to fulfill her expectations. Here was her last chance to be not merely a woman of ideas, to be not merely the bride to a man of ideas, but to be the mother of a man of ideas. Indeed, in her mind, though not in reality, here was her last chance to be associated with ideas that might move the world, because her first three husbands had proved to be men whose big ideas had no solidity and had popped at the first prick. Even Derek, with all his success, was a *chupaflor*, not an eagle, and Claudette knew it. Dusty was, in her mind, too pigheaded to fulfill his potential, and Skeet was too fragile. And Dominique, her first child, was long and safely dead. Dusty had never known his half sister, had seen one photo of her, perhaps the only ever taken: her sweet, small, gentle face. Junior was the only hope that remained for Claudette, and she was determined to believe that his mind and his heart were as fair as his face.

While she was still browbeating Skeet, Dusty heard himself say, "Mother, how did Dominique die?"

The question, dangerous in this context, silenced Claudette as nothing else except perhaps another gunshot would have done.

He met her eyes and didn't turn to stone, as she intended, and shame—rather than a lack of it—kept him from looking away. Shame that he had known the truth, intuitively at first and then through the application of logic and reflection, had known the truth since boyhood and yet had denied it to himself and had never spoken. Shame that he allowed her and Skeet's pompous father and then Derek Lampton to grind Skeet down, when ferreting out the truth about Dominique might have disarmed them and given Skeet a better life.

"You must have been heartbroken," Dusty said, "when your first child was born with Down's syndrome. Such high hopes, and such sad reality."

"What are you doing?" Her voice was softer now but even more highly charged with anger.

The hallway seemed to grow narrower, and the ceiling seemed to descend slowly, as if this were one of those deadly room-size traps in corny old adventure movies, and as if all of them were in danger of being crushed alive.

"And then another tragedy. Crib death. Sudden infant death syndrome. How difficult to endure it . . . the whispers, the medical inquiry, waiting for a final determination of the cause of death."

Martie drew a sharp breath with the realization of where this was going, and she said, "Dusty," meaning *Maybe you shouldn't do this.*

He had never spoken up when it might have helped Skeet, however, and now he was determined to do what he could to force her to get treatment for Junior while there might still be time. "One of my clearest early memories,

Mother, is a day when I was five, going on six . . . a couple weeks after Skeet was brought home from the hospital. You were born prematurely, Skeet. Did you know that?"

"I guess," Skeet said shakily.

"They didn't think you'd survive, but you did. And when they brought you home, they thought you were likely to have suffered some brain damage that would show up sooner or later. But that, of course, proved not to be the case."

"My learning disability," Skeet reminded him.

"Maybe that," Dusty agreed. "Assuming you ever really had one."

Claudette regarded Dusty as though he were a snake: wanting to stomp him before he coiled and struck, but afraid to make any move against him and thereby precipitate what she feared most.

He said, "That day when I was five, going on six, you were in a mood, Mother. Such a strange mood that even a little boy couldn't help but sense that something terrible was going to happen. You got out the photograph of Dominique."

She raised one fist as if to hit him again, but it hung in the air, the blow not struck.

In some respects, this was the hardest thing that Dusty had ever done, and yet in other ways it was so easy that it frightened him, easy in the same sense that jumping off a roof is easy if there are no consequences to the fall. But there would be consequences here. "It was the first time I'd ever seen that photograph, ever known I'd had a sister. You carried it with you around the house that day. You couldn't stop looking at it. And it was late in the afternoon when I found the photo lying in the hallway outside the nursery."

Claudette lowered her fist and turned away from Dusty.

His hand seemed to belong to another, bolder man as he watched it reach out and take her by the arm, halting her and forcing her to face him.

Junior stepped forward protectively.

"Better pick up your crossbow and load it," Dusty warned the boy. "Because you can't handle me without it."

Although the violence in his eyes was more fierce even than the hard rage in his mother's, Junior backed off.

"When I came into the nursery," Dusty said, "you didn't hear me. Skeet was in the crib. You were standing over him with a pillow in your hands. You stood over him for the longest time. And then you lowered the pillow toward his face. Slowly. And that's when I said something. I don't remember what. But you knew I was there, and you . . . stopped. At the time, I didn't know what had almost happened. But later . . . years later, I did understand, but wouldn't face it."

"Oh, Jesus," Skeet said, his voice as weak as that of a child. "Oh, dear sweet Jesus."

Although Dusty had faith in the power of truth, he didn't know for sure that this revelation would help Skeet more than harm him. He was so torn by the thought of the wreckage he might be causing that when a quiver of nausea passed briefly through him, he assumed he would throw up blood if he threw up anything at all.

Claudette's teeth were so tightly clenched that the muscles twitched in her jaws.

"A couple minutes ago, Mother, I asked if murder was meaningless to you, and the question didn't even give you pause. Which is odd, because *that* is a big idea. Worth discussion if ever anything was."

"Are you done?"

"Not quite. After all these years of putting up with this crap, I've earned the right to finish what I have to say. I know your worst secrets, Mother, all the worst. I've suffered for them, we all have, and we're going to suffer more—"

Clawing at his hand, drawing two thin tracks of blood with her fingernails, wrenching loose of him, she said, "If Dominique hadn't been a Down's baby, and if I hadn't spared her that half life she would've led, and if she were alive here and now, wouldn't that be worse? Wouldn't *that* be infinitely worse?"

The sense she made diminished as the volume of her voice rose, and Dusty had no idea what she meant.

Junior moved closer to his mother's side. They stood hand in hand, drawing a strange strength from each other.

Pointing toward the dead man sprawled in the foyer below, a gesture that seemed to have no connection to her words, she said, "Down's was at least an obvious condition. What if she'd seemed normal but then . . . all grown up, what if she'd been just like her father?"

Dominique's father, Claudette's first husband, had been more than twenty years her senior, a psychologist named Lief Reissler, a cold fish with pale eyes and a pencil mustache, who had thankfully played no role in either Dusty's or Skeet's life. A cold fish, yes, but not the monster that her question implied he was.

Before Dusty could express his bafflement, Claudette clarified. After three days of shocks that he'd thought had forever inoculated him against surprise, she rocked him with eight words: "What if she'd been just like Mark Ahriman?" The rest was superfluous: "You say he burns down houses, he shoots people, he's a sociopath, and this crazy man who's dead downstairs is somehow associated with him. So would you want his child for your half sister?"

She raised Junior's hand and kissed it, as though to say that she was especially glad that she had spared him the problem of this difficult sister.

When Dusty had claimed to know her worst secrets, all the worst, she assumed he'd been referring to more than the fact that the sudden infant death syndrome that claimed Dominique had truly been ruthless suffocation.

Now, because of his reaction and Martie's, Claudette realized this revelation need never have been made, but instead of retreating into silence, she tried to explain.

"Lief was infertile. We were never going to be able to have children. I was twenty-one, and Lief was forty-four, and he could have been the perfect father, with his tremendous knowledge, all his insights, his theories of emotional development. Lief had a brilliant child-rearing philosophy."

Yes, they all had their child-rearing philosophies, their deep insights, and their abiding interest in social engineering. Medicate to educate, and all that.

"Mark Ahriman was just seventeen, but he'd started college soon after his thirteenth birthday, and he'd already earned a doctorate by the time I met him. He was a prodigy's prodigy, and everyone at the university was in awe of him. A genius almost beyond measure. He was no one's idea of a perfect father. He was a snooty Hollywood brat. But the *genes*."

"Did he know the child was his?"

"Yes. Why not? None of us was that conventional."

The buzzing in Dusty's head, which was the accompanying theme music for any visit to this house, had settled into a more ominous tone than usual. "When Dominique was born with Down's . . . how did you handle that, Mother?"

She stared at the blood on his hand, which she had drawn with her fingernails, and when she raised her eyes to meet his, she said only, "You know how I handled it."

Once more, she lifted Junior's hand to her lips and kissed his knuckles, this time as if to say that all her problems with damaged children had been worth enduring now that she had been given him.

Dusty said, "I meant, not how did you handle Dominique. How did you handle the news of her condition? If I know you, Ahriman got his ear bent almost off. I'll bet you dished out more humiliation to him than a snotty Hollywood brat is used to."

"Nothing like *that* has ever showed up in my family," she said, confirming that Ahriman must have been the target of her full fury.

Martie could contain herself no longer. "So thirty-two years ago, you humiliate him, you kill his child—"

"He was glad when he heard she was dead."

"I'm sure he was, knowing him like I do now. But just the same, you humiliate him back then. And all these years later, the man who gave you Junior, this golden boy—"

Junior actually smiled, as if Martie were coming on to him.

"—the man who gives you this boy that Ahriman couldn't give you, your *husband*, goes out of his way to mock Ahriman, to belittle him, to tear him apart in every public forum he can find, and even sabotages him with this petty crap on Amazon.com. And you didn't put a stop to it?"

Claudette's anger flared anew at Martie's accusation of bad judgment. "I *encouraged* it. And why not. Mark Ahriman can't make a book any better than he can make a baby. Why should he have more success than Derek? Why should he have anything at all?"

"You foolish woman." Martie evidently chose this insult because she knew that it would sting Claudette worse than any other. "You foolish, ignorant woman."

Skeet, alarmed by Martie's directness, afraid for her, tried to draw her back.

Instead, Martie grasped his hand and held it tightly, just as Claudette held Junior's. But she wasn't taking strength from Skeet; she was giving it. "Stay cool, honey." Pressing the attack, she said, "Claudette, you don't have a clue what Ahriman is capable of doing. You don't understand jack about him—his viciousness, his relentlessness."

"I understand—"

"Like hell you do! You opened the door to him and let him into all our lives, not just your own. He wouldn't have looked twice at me if I hadn't had a connection to you. If not for you, none of this would have happened to me, and I wouldn't have had to do"—she looked miserably at Dusty and he knew she was thinking of two dead men in New Mexico—"the things I've had to do."

Claudette could be cowed neither by the virulence of an argument nor by the facts of it. "You make it sound as if it's all about you. Like they say, shit happens. I'm sure you've heard that kind of talk in your circles before. Shit happens, *Martie.* It happens to all of us. It's my house that was shot apart, in case you hadn't noticed."

"Get used to it," Martie countered. "Because Ahriman won't stop with this. He's going to send someone else, and someone else, and then ten more someone elses, people who're strangers and people we've known and trusted all our lives, blindsiding us time after time, and he's going to keep sending them until we're all dead."

"You aren't even making any damn sense," Claudette fumed.

"Enough! Shut up, shut up, all of you!" Derek stood downstairs in the foyer, near Eric's body, shouting up at them. "Neighbors must not be home, 'cause no one called the police till I just did. Before they get here, I'm *telling* you how it's going to be. This is my house, and I'm telling you. I wiped the gun off. I put it back in his hand. Dusty, Martie, if you want to go against us, you do what you have to do, but then it's warfare between us, and I'll smear the two of you any way I can. You said your house burned down? I'll tell them you gamble, you have debts, and you burned it down for the insurance."

Staggered by this grotesque threat and yet not surprised, Dusty said, "Derek, for God's sake, what good would that do any of us now?"

"It'll muddy the waters," Lampton said. "Confuse the cops. This guy was your friend's husband, Martie? So I'll tell the cops he came here to kill Dusty because Dusty was screwing with Susan."

"You stupid bastard," Martie said, "Susan's dead. She—"

Claudette embraced the conspiracy: "Then I'll say Eric confessed to killing Susan before he started shooting up this place, killed her because she was screwing Dusty. I'm warning you two, we'll muddy these waters until they can't even *see* my boy, let alone accuse him of murder, when all he did was save our lives."

Dusty couldn't recall having stepped through a looking glass or being sucked into a tornado full of dark magic, but here he was in a world where everything was upside down and backward, where lies were celebrated as truths, where truth was unwelcome and unrecognized.

"Come on, Claudette," Lampton urged, motioning her downstairs. "Come on, Derek. The kitchen. Quick. We've got to talk before the police get here. Our stories have to match."

The boy smirked at Dusty as he trailed his mother, still holding her hand, to the stairs and then down.

Dusty wheeled away from them and back down the hall to Fig, who had stood motionless through the storm.

"Wow," Fig said.

"You understand Skeet better now?"

"Oh, yeah."

"Where's Valet?" Dusty asked, because the dog was a link to reality, his own Toto, reminding him of a world where wicked witches were not real.

"Bed," Fig advised, pointing toward the open door of the master-bedroom suite.

The Sheraton bed stood high enough off the floor for Valet to have squeezed under it. He was betrayed by his tail, which trailed beyond the bedspread.

Dusty went around to the farther side of the bed, got down on the floor, lifted the spread, and said, "Got room in there for me?"

Valet whined as if inviting him under for a cuddle.

"They'd find us anyway," Dusty assured him. "Come out of there, fella. Come here and let me rub your tummy."

With coaxing, Valet crawled into the open, although he was too spooked to expose his belly even to those he trusted most.

Martie joined Dusty, sitting on the floor with the dog between them. "I'm reconsidering the whole idea of ever having a family. I think maybe this here is as good as it gets—you, me, and Valet."

The dog seemed to agree.

Martie said, "Driving here, I didn't think this mess could get any worse, and now look where we are. Neck deep and sinking. I'm numb, you know? I know what happened to Eric, but I don't feel it yet."

"Yeah. I'm beyond numb."

"What are you going to do?"

Dusty shook his head. "I don't know. What's the use, though? I mean, the kid's going to be a hero, right? No matter what I say. Or you. I can see it clear as I've ever seen anything. The truth won't play well enough to be believed."

"And what about Ahriman?"

"I'm scared, Martie."

"Me too."

"Who's going to believe us? It would have been hard enough to get anyone to listen to us before . . . this. But now, with the Lizard and Claudette willing to make up wild stories about us just to *muddy the waters* . . . If we start talking about brainwashing and programmed suicide, programmed killers . . . that'll only make their lies about us ring more true."

"And if someone did burn down our house—Ahriman or someone he sent—it'll be obvious arson. What's our alibi?"

Dusty blinked in surprise. "We were in New Mexico."

"Doing what?"

He opened his mouth to speak—but closed it without a word.

"If we mention New Mexico, we're going to get into

the Ahriman stuff. And yeah, there's some substantiation of it—all the things that happened to people out there a long time ago. But how do we get into all that and not risk . . . Zachary and Kevin?"

They stroked the dog in silence for a moment, and finally Dusty said, "I could kill him. I mean, last night, you asked me could I do it, and I said I didn't know. But now I know."

"I could do it, too," she said.

"Kill him, and then it stops."

"Assuming the institute doesn't come after us."

"You heard Ahriman in the office this morning. This wasn't any part of that. This was personal. And now we know just how personal."

"You kill him," she said, "and you'll spend the rest of your life in prison."

"Maybe."

"Definitely. Because no judge will allow a cockamamie defense like, 'I killed him because he was a brainwashing fiend.' "

"Then they'll put me away for ten years in an asylum. That's better, anyway."

"Not unless they put the two of us in the same asylum."

Valet raised his head and looked at them as if to say *three.*

Someone was running in the upstairs hall, and it proved to be Fig Newton when he burst into the room, his glasses askew and his face more red than usual. "Skeet."

"What about him?" Martie asked, thrusting to her feet.

"Gone."

"Where?"

"Ahriman."

"*What?*"

"Gun."

Dusty was on his feet, too. "Damn it, Fig, enough telegraphy already. Talk!"

Nodding, Fig stretched himself: "Took the gun off the dead man. And one of the full magazines. Took the Lexus. Said none of you was safe until he did it."

To Dusty, Martie said, "Tell the cops, let them stop him?"

"Tell them he's on his way to shoot a prominent citizen, armed with a machine pistol? In a stolen car? Skeet's as good as dead if we do that."

"Then we have to get there ahead of him," she said. "Fig, you watch out for Valet. There're people around here might kill him just for the fun of it."

"Don't feel too safe myself," Fig said.

"Do the others know where Skeet's gone?"

"No. Don't yet know he's gone at all."

"You tell them he popped pills earlier today and now suddenly got funny. Took the gun and said he was going up to Santa Barbara, settle with some people for selling him bad dope."

"Doesn't sound like Skeet. Too macho."

"Lampton will love it. Helps muddy the waters."

"What happens when I lie to cops?"

"You don't say a word to the cops. You're good at that. You just tell Lampton, and *he'll* do the rest. And tell him we went after Skeet. To Santa Barbara."

By the time Dusty and Martie reached the foyer, clambered around the body and the overturned sideboard, and reached the front porch, with Lampton and Claudette shouting behind them, Dusty could hear sirens in the distance.

They cleared the driveway, turned south on the highway, and went more than a mile before they saw the first black-and-white racing north toward the Lampton house.

Neck deep and sinking.

75

In his fourteenth-floor office, the doctor worked on his current book, polishing an amusing anecdote about a phobic patient whose fear of food had caused her to drop from one hundred forty pounds to just eighty-six, where she'd hovered near death for many days before he discovered the key to her condition and cured her with no time to spare. Her entire story wasn't amusing, of course, but rather dark and dramatic, just the right stuff to ensure him a long segment on *Dateline*, with the grateful patient, when the time came to promote; however, here and there in the gloom were bright moments of humor and even one knee-slapping hilarity.

He wasn't able to concentrate on his work as intensely as usual, because his mind kept straying to Malibu. After calculating the time Eric would need to visit the self-storage yard and drive all the way to the Lamptons' house, he decided that the first shot would be fired at approximately a quarter to one, perhaps as late as one o'clock.

He was also distracted, although not much, by thoughts of the Keanuphobe, who had not yet phoned. He wasn't concerned. She would call soon. Few people were more reliable than obsessives and phobics.

The .380 Beretta lay on the near-right corner of his desktop, within easy reach.

He did not expect that the Keanuphobe would rappel down from the roof and crash through his aerie window, carrying a submachine gun and lobbing grenades, but he didn't underestimate her, either. Over the years, the toughest women he'd ever encountered were attired in stylish but conservative St. John knit suits and Ferragamo shoes. Many of them had been the wives of long-married, older studio heads and power agents; they looked as Brahmin as any Boston dowager whose family tree had roots deep under Plymouth Rock, were refined and aristocratic—but nevertheless would eat your heart for lunch, with your kidneys in a mousse on the side, accompanied by a glass of fine Merlot.

Able to order in from a deli that believed in the righteousness of mayonnaise, butter solids, and animal fat in all forms, the doctor was content to have lunch at his desk. He ate with the blue bag near his plate, its neck crimped and angled jauntily. He wasn't offended by the knowledge of its contents, because it was a cheerful reminder of the condition in which Derek Lampton's body would be found by the police.

By one-fifteen, lunch finished, he had cleared his desk of deli plates and wrappings, but he had not resumed composing the bulimia anecdote for his book. On his Corinthian-leather blotter with faux-ivory inlays, the blue bag stood alone.

Regrettably, he could not enjoy Lampton's humiliation firsthand, and unless one of the sleazier tabloids did its job well, he wasn't likely to see even one satisfying picture. Photographs of uncapped skulls stuffed full of ordure were not rushed into print by *The New York Times* or even by *USA Today*.

Fortunately, the doctor had a good imagination. With the blue bag before him for inspiration, he had no trouble painting the most vivid and entertaining mind pictures.

By one-thirty, he assumed Eric Jagger had completed the shooting and was busy—perhaps nearly finished—with the amateur craniotomy. When he closed his eyes, the doctor could hear the rhythmic rasp of the cranial blade.

Considering the density of bone mass in Lampton's skull, sending a spare blade had been a wise decision. In the event that the Lamptons didn't have a dog, he hoped Eric's dietary regimen included a high-fiber cereal every morning.

His greatest regret was that he had not been able to play out his original game plan, in which Dusty, Skeet, and Martie would have tortured and killed Claudette and the two Dereks. Before committing suicide, Dusty, Skeet, and Martie would have written a long statement accusing the elder Derek and his wife of horrendous physical abuse of Skeet and Dusty when they were children, and of repeated Rohypnol-facilitated rapes of Martie and of Susan Jagger, whom Ahriman might even have chosen to include as part of the killing team if she hadn't gotten clever with a video camera. The death toll would have been seven, plus housekeepers and visiting neighbors, if any, which was by Ahriman's calculations the minimum magnitude of slaughter necessary to attract the attention of the national media—although with Derek's reputation as a pop-psych guru, seven deaths would receive as much coverage as a bomb blast that killed two hundred but that produced no celebrity among the casualties.

Well, although the game had been played with less grace than he would have preferred, he took satisfaction in winning. With no way to take possession of Derek Lampton's brain, perhaps he would have the blue bag vacuum-sealed in Lucite as a symbolic trophy.

Although Skeet's thought processes had grown clearer an more efficient during the past two drug-free days, he stil didn't have the mental acuity needed to manage a nuclea power plant or even to be trusted to sweep the floors of one Fortunately, he was aware of this, and he intended to thin carefully through each step of his attack on Dr. Ahrima during his drive from Malibu to Newport Beach.

He was also an emotional mess, frequently breaking into tears, even sobbing. Operating a motor vehicle with badly blurred vision was particularly dangerous along the Pacific Coast Highway during the rainy season, because sudden massive mudslides and dislodged boulders the size of semitrucks tumbling onto the roadway required drivers to have the reflexes of a wired cat. Worse, the early-afternoon traffic on the freeway was southbound at eighty miles per hour, in spite of a legal limit of sixty-five, and uncontrollable sobbing at that speed could have cataclysmic consequences.

His chest and belly were sore from the impact of four Kevlar-arrested bullets. Painful cramps twisted his stomach, unrelated to the bruising, born of stress and fear. He had a migraine, which he always had after seeing his mother, whether or not anyone was shot with a crossbow during the visit.

His heartache, however, was worse than any of the physical pains that he suffered. Dusty and Martie's house was gone, and he felt as if his own house had been burned to the ground. They were the best people in the world, Martie and Dusty, the best. They didn't deserve such trouble. Their terrific little house gone in flames, Susan dead, Eric dead, living in fear.

More heartache assailed him when he thought of himself as a baby, his mother standing over him with a pillow in her hands, his own beautiful mother. When Dusty called her on it, she didn't even deny that she'd been going to kill him. He knew he was a total screwup as an adult, had been a screwup as a kid, but now it seemed to him that he must have been such an obvious screwup-waiting-to-happen even as an *infant* that his own mother had felt justified in smothering him while he slept in his crib.

He didn't *want* to be such a screwup. He wanted to do the right thing, and he wanted to do well, to have his brother, Dusty, be proud of him, but he always lost his way without realizing he was losing it. He also realized he caused Dusty a lot of heartache, too, which made him feel worse.

With chest pain, belly pain, serial stomach cramps, migraine, heartache, blurred vision, and eighty-mile-per-hour traffic to keep him distracted, worried as well because his driver's license had been revoked years ago, he arrived in Newport Beach, in the parking lot behind Ahriman's office building, shortly before three o'clock in the afternoon, without having carefully thought out *any* step of his attack on Dr. Ahriman.

"I'm a total screwup," he said.

Screwup that he was, the chances that he would make it across the parking lot, up to the fourteenth floor, into Ahriman's office, and successfully execute the bastard were too small to be calculated. Like trying to weigh the hair on a flea's ass.

He *did* have one thing going for him. If he defied all the odds and managed to shoot the psychiatrist, he would probably not go to prison for the rest of his life, as Dusty or Martie surely would if either of them pulled the trigger. Considering his colorful record of rehab, a foot-tall stack of unflattering psychiatric evaluations, and his history of pathological meekness rather than violence, Skeet would probably end up in a mental institution, with a hope of being released one day, supposing that there was anything left of him after another fifteen years of massive drug therapy.

The pistol had a long magazine, but he was still able to tuck it under his belt and cover it with his sweater. Fortunately, the sweater was meant to be baggy; it was even baggier than intended, because he had bought it years ago, and after his continued weight loss, it was now two sizes too large.

He got out of the Lexus, remembering to take the keys with him. If he left them in the ignition, someone might steal the car, perhaps making him an accessory to grand theft auto. When his name was all over the newspapers and people were looking at him being arrested on TV, he didn't want them thinking that he was the type of person to be involved in car theft. He'd never stolen a penny in his life.

The sky was blue. The day was mild. There was no wind, and he was grateful for the calm, because he felt as if a stiff breeze might have blown him away.

He walked back and forth in front of the car, staring down at his sweater, cocking his head to one side and then the other, trying to detect the outline of the pistol from various angles. The weapon was completely concealed.

Hot tears welled again, just as he was ready to march into the building and do the deed, and so he walked back and forth, blotting his eyes on the sleeves of his sweater. A security guard was likely to be posted in the lobby. Skeet realized that a gaunt, gray-faced man in clothes two sizes too large for him, sobbing his eyes out, was likely to arouse suspicion.

One row in front of where Skeet had parked the Lexus and a few spaces to the north, a woman got out of a white Rolls-Royce and stood beside it, staring openly at him. His eyes were now dry enough to allow him to see that she was a nice-looking blond lady, very neat, in a pink knit suit, obviously a successful person and good citizen. She didn't appear to be the rude type who would stand and stare at a perfect stranger, so he figured he must look as suspicious as if he were wearing bandoliers of ammunition and openly carrying an assault rifle.

If this lady in the pink suit found him alarming, the security guard would probably spray him with Mace, shock him with a Taser, and club him to the floor the moment he walked through the door into the lobby. He was going to screw up again.

He couldn't bear the thought of failing Dusty and Martie, the only people who had ever loved him, really loved him, in his entire life. If he couldn't do this for them, he might as well pull the gun out from under his sweater and shoot himself in the head right now.

He was no more capable of suicide than he was capable of theft. Well, except for jumping off the Sorensons' roof on

Tuesday. From what he understood, however, that might not have been his own idea.

Under the scrutiny of the lady in pink, pretending not to notice her, trying to appear far too happy and too pleased with life to be a crazed gunman, whistling "What a Wonderful World," because it was the first thing that came to his mind, he crossed the parking lot to the office building and went inside, never looking back.

The doctor was not accustomed to having his schedule imposed by others, and he grew increasingly annoyed with the Keanuphobe for not calling sooner rather than later. He had no doubt she would respond to the evil-computer fantasy he had provided to her; her obsession allowed no other course of action. Apparently, however, the twit was without a shred of courtesy, without appreciation for the value of other people's time: the typical nouveau-riche clod.

Unable to concentrate on writing but unable to leave his office and go play, he contented himself with making haiku out of the humble material before him.

My little blue bag. My Beretta, seven rounds. Should I shoot the shit?

That was ghastly. Seventeen syllables, yes, and technically adequate in every regard. Nonetheless, he had never seen a better example of why technical adequacy was not the explanation for William Shakespeare's immortality.

My gun, seven shots. My little Keanuphobe. Kill, kill, kill, kill, kill.

Equally ghastly but more satisfying.

The security guard, twice Skeet's size and wearing clothes that fit him, sat behind the counter at the information station. He was reading a book, and he never glanced up.

Skeet checked the directory to locate Ahriman's office, went to the elevators, pressed the call button, and stared straight ahead at the doors. He figured that the guard, a highly trained professional, would immediately sense anyone staring worriedly at him.

One of the elevators arrived swiftly. Three birdlike elderly women and three tall handsome Sikhs in turbans exited the cab; the two groups headed in different directions.

Already stressed out and fearful, Skeet was rattled by the sight of the old ladies and the Sikhs. As he had learned from Fig during the previous thirty-six hours, the numbers three and six were somehow key to understanding why extraterrestrials were secretly on Earth, and here was three twice and six once. Not a good omen.

Two people followed Skeet onto the elevator. A United Parcel Service deliveryman wheeled in a hand truck on which were stacked three boxes. Behind him came the woman in the pink suit.

Skeet had pushed the button for the fourteenth floor. The UPS man tapped the button for the ninth floor. The lady in pink didn't press anything.

Entering the building, Dusty at once spotted Skeet getting into an elevator at the farther end of the lobby. Martie saw him, too.

He wanted to shout at his brother, but a guard sat nearby, and the last thing they needed was to attract the attention of building security.

They hurried without running. The cab doors slid shut before they were halfway across the lobby.

None of the other three elevators was at the ground floor. Two were ascending, two descending. Of the two headed down, the nearest was at the fifth floor.

"Stairs?" Martie asked.

"Fourteen floors. No." He pointed to the indicator board, as the elevator on the fifth floor moved down to the fourth. "This'll be faster."

The deliveryman got off at the ninth floor, and when the doors slid shut, the lady in pink pushed the *stop* button.

"You're not dead," she said.

"Excuse me?"

"You were shot four times in the chest last night on the beach, but here you are."

Skeet was amazed. "You were there?"

"As I'm sure you know."

"No, really, I didn't see you there."

"Why aren't you dead?"

"Kevlar."

"Not likely."

"It's true. We were tailing a dangerous man," he said, figuring he sounded totally lame, like he was trying to impress her, which in fact he was. She was a pretty lady, and Skeet felt a certain stirring in his loins that he had not felt in a long time.

"Or was the whole thing fake? A setup for my benefit?"

"No setup. My chest and belly are sore as hell."

"When you die in the matrix," she said, "you die for real."

"Hey, did you like that movie, too?"

"You die for real . . . unless you're a machine."

She was beginning to seem a little spooky to Skeet, and his intuition was confirmed when she drew a pistol from the white handbag that hung on straps from her left shoulder. It was fitted with what in the movies they called a silencer, but which he knew was more accurately called a sound suppressor.

"What're you carrying under your sweater?" she demanded.

"Me? This sweater? Nothing."

"Bullshit. Lift your sweater *very* slowly."

"Oh, man," he said with grave disappointment, because here he was screwing up again. "You're professional security, aren't you?"

"Are you with Keanu or against him?"

Skeet was certain that he hadn't taken any drugs in the past three days, but this sure had the feel of episodes that had followed some of his more memorable chemical cocktails. "Well, I'm with him when he's doing cool sci-fi stuff, you know, but I'm against him when he's making crap like *A Walk in the Clouds.*"

"Why are they stopped so long on the ninth floor?" Dusty asked, frowning at the indicator board above the elevator that Skeet had boarded.

"Stairs?" Martie suggested again.

After lingering at the third floor, the elevator for which they were waiting suddenly moved to the second. "We might get past him this way."

The machine pistol that she took from Skeet would not fit easily in her handbag. The butt of the extended magazine stuck out, but she didn't seem to care.

Still covering him with her own pistol, she took the elevator off *stop* and pressed the button for the fourteenth floor. The cab started up at once.

"Aren't sound suppressors illegal?" Skeet asked.

"Yes, of course."

"But you can get one because you're professional security?"

"Good God, no. I'm worth five hundred million dollars, and I can get anything I want."

He couldn't know if what she said was true or not. He didn't suppose it mattered.

Although the woman was quite pretty, Skeet began to recognize something in her green eyes or in her attitude, or both, that scared him. They were passing the thirteenth floor, appropriately, when he realized why she put ice in his spine: She possessed an indefinable but undeniable quality that reminded him of his mother.

At that moment, as they arrived at the fourteenth floor, Skeet knew that he was a dead man walking.

When the elevator doors slid open, Martie immediately stepped inside and pressed *14*.

Dusty followed, blocked two other men who tried to enter after them, and said, "Sorry, emergency. We're expressing to fourteen."

Martie had pressed *close door* immediately after pressing the floor number. She held her thumb on it.

One of the men blinked in surprise, and one of them started to object, but the doors closed before an argument could begin.

As they came out of the elevator alcove into the fourteenth-floor corridor, Skeet said, "Where are we going?"

"Don't be so stupidly disingenuous. It's annoying. You know perfectly well where we're going. Now move."

She seemed to want him to go to the left, so he did, not just because she had a gun, but because all his life he had gone where people told him to go. She followed him, jamming the muzzle of the sound suppressor into his back.

The long, carpeted corridor was quiet. The acoustic ceiling soaked up their voices. No sounds came from beyond the hallway walls. They might have been the last two people on the planet.

"What if I stop right here?" Skeet asked.

"Then I shoot you right here," she assured him.

Skeet kept moving.

As he passed the doors to office suites on both sides of the hall, he read the names on the etched-brass wall plates beside them. Mostly, they were doctors, specialists of one kind or another—though two were attorneys. This was convenient, he decided. If he somehow survived the next few minutes, he would no doubt need a few good doctors and one attorney.

They arrived at a door where the name on the brass plate was DR. MARK AHRIMAN. Under the psychiatrist's name, in smaller letters, Skeet read, A CALIFORNIA CORPORATION.

"Here?" he asked.

"Yes," she said.

As Skeet pushed the door inward, the lady in pink shot him in the back. If the silenced pistol made any noise at all, he didn't hear it, because the pain was so instantaneous and terrible that he wouldn't have heard a marching band going past. He was focused entirely, intensely on the pain, and he was amazed that being shot could hurt *so* much worse when you weren't wearing Kevlar. Even as the woman blew a hole in him, she shoved him hard through the door and into Dr. Ahriman's reception lounge.

Bing!

Ahriman's computer announced an arrival, and the screen filled with a security-camera view of the reception lounge.

With more amazement than he had experienced in years, the doctor swiveled away from his contemplation of the blue bag and saw Skeet stagger into the lounge, the door to the corridor slowly falling shut behind him.

A large blot of blood stained the front of his yellow sweater, which certainly ought to have been the case after he had taken four rounds in the chest and gut at close range. Although this might have been the same sweater Skeet had been wearing yesterday, the camera angle wasn't clear enough to allow Ahriman to see whether there were four bullet holes in the bloodstained fabric. Skeet clawed at the air as if for support, stumbled, and collapsed facedown on the floor.

The doctor had heard stories of dogs, accidentally separated from their masters when far from home, crossing hundreds and even thousands of miles of inhospitable terrain, through rain and snow and sleet and blazing sun, often with cut feet and worse injuries, and showing up weeks later on the very doorstep where they belonged, to the astonishment and tearful joy of their families. He had *never* heard even one story about a gut-shot man getting up from a beach, walking approximately six to eight miles over—he checked his watch—eighteen hours, through a densely populated area, ascending fourteen floors in an elevator, and staggering into the office of the man who had shot him, to point a finger of accusation, so he was convinced that there was more to this development than met the eye.

With his mouse, the doctor clicked on the security icon shaped like a gun. The metal detector indicated that Skeet was not carrying a firearm.

Lying flat on the floor, the would-be detective was not aligned with the roentgen tubes, so fluoroscopy wasn't possible.

Jennifer came out from behind the receptionist's window and stood over the fallen Skeet. She appeared to be screaming—although whether because the condition of this wounded man horrified her or because the sight of blood offended her vegetarian sensibilities, Ahriman couldn't be sure.

The doctor activated the audio. Yes, she was screaming though not loudly, hardly more than wheezing, as though she couldn't draw a breath deep enough to let go with a rea window-rattler.

As Jennifer dropped to one knee beside Skeet to check for vital signs, Ahriman clicked on the nose icon, activating the trace-scent analyzer. Any sane person's credulity would be stretched past the breaking point by the notion that this man, with four bullet wounds, had paused in his eighteen-hour trek to acquire explosives and build a bomb, which was now strapped to his chest. Nevertheless, reminding himself that attention to detail was important, the doctor waited for the system to report. Negative: no explosives.

Jennifer rose from the body and hurried out of camera range.

She no doubt intended to call the police and paramedics.

He buzzed her through the in-phone intercom. "Jennifer?"

"Doctor, oh, God, there's—"

"Yes, I know. A man's been shot. Do *not* call the police or the paramedics, Jennifer. I will do that. Do you understand?"

"But he's bleeding badly. He's—"

"Calm down, Jennifer. Call no one. I'm handling this."

Less than a minute had passed since Skeet had staggered into the reception lounge. The doctor calculated that he had one more minute, at most two, before his delay in calling paramedics would alarm Jennifer into action.

What worried him and what he needed an answer to was this: If one man with four serious bullet wounds could show up eighteen hours later, why not two?

As highly imaginative as he was, the doctor was not able to conjure in his mind a credible picture of the wounded Skeet and his wounded pal staggering up the coast, their arms around each other's shoulders, providing mutual support, like a pair of drunken pirates heading shipward after a long night of revelry ashore. Yet if one had shown up, there might be two, and the second could be lurking somewhere with bad intentions.

The worst delay was at the sixth floor. The elevator stopped and the doors opened, even though Martie kept pressing the *close door* button.

A stout, determined woman with iron-gray curls and the face of a longshoreman in drag insisted on boarding, though Dusty blocked her and claimed emergency privilege.

"*What* emergency?" She inserted a foot into the cab, triggering the safety mechanism and preventing the door from closing, regardless of how hard Martie leaned on the button. "I don't see any emergency."

"Heart attack. Fourteenth floor."

"You're not doctors," she said suspiciously.

"It's our day off."

"Doctors don't dress like you even on their day off. Anyway, I'm going all the way to fifteen."

"Then get in, get in," Dusty relented.

When she was safely inside, when the doors closed, the woman pressed the button for the twelfth floor and glared triumphantly.

Dusty was furious. "I love my brother, lady, and if anything happens to him now, I'll track you down and gut you like a fish."

She looked him up and down with undisguised contempt and said, *"You?"*

The doctor plucked the .380 Beretta off the desk and headed toward the door, but stopped when he remembered the blue bag. It still stood in the center of his desk blotter.

Whatever might happen next, eventually the police were going to arrive. If Skeet wasn't already dead, Ahriman intended to finish him before the authorities got here. Wit a corpse lying in a pool of blood in the reception lounge, the cops were certain to have a lot of questions.

They would at the least take a casual look around the premises. If their suspicions were in any way aroused, they would station a man in the office while they got a warrant for a thorough search.

They were not permitted by law to inspect his patient files, so he was not concerned about anything they might find—except for his Beretta and the blue bag.

The pistol was unregistered, and while he would never go to jail for possessing it, he didn't want to give them any reason whatsoever to wonder about him. Wondering, they might keep an eye on him in the days ahead, seriously cramping his style.

The bag of dog poop wasn't incriminating, but it was . . . peculiar. Definitely peculiar. Finding it on his desk, they would surely ask why he had brought it to the office. As clever as he was, the doctor could not think of a single answer, on such short notice, that made sense. Again, they would wonder about him.

He returned quickly to the desk, pulled open a deep drawer, and dropped the bag into it. Then he realized that if they went so far as to obtain a search warrant, they would find the bag in the drawer—where it would seem no less strange than if found in plain sight. Indeed, wherever he put the bag in the office, even in the waste can, it would seem weird to them when they found it.

All of these considerations flashed through the doctor's mind in mere seconds, since he was every bit as sharp as in the days when he'd been a child prodigy, but still he reminded himself that time was a maniac scattering dust. Hurry, hurry.

His intention was to get rid of the Beretta and the shoulder holster before the police arrived, so he might as well ditch the blue bag with the pistol. Which meant he had to take it with him now.

For several reasons, not the least being his sense of personal style, he didn't want Jennifer to see him carrying the bag. Besides, it would hamper him if he were forced to deal with Skeet's pal. What had Dusty called him? The Fig. Yes. The blue bag would hamper him if the Fig were lurking out there somewhere and had to be dealt with.

Hurry, hurry.

He started to slip the bag into an inside pocket of his coat, but the thought of it bursting and ruining this fine Zegna suit was too dreadful to bear. Instead, he carefully tucked it into his empty shoulder holster.

Pleased with his quick thinking, and sure that he had forgotten no detail that might destroy him, Ahriman went out to the reception lounge, holding the Beretta at his side, concealing it from Jennifer.

She was standing in the open door to the back work area, eyes wide, trembling. "He's bleeding, Doctor, he's bleeding."

Any fool could see that Skeet was bleeding. Indeed, he could not have been losing blood at this rate for eighteen hours and still have made his way here.

The doctor dropped to one knee beside Skeet. Keeping both eyes on the door to the corridor, he felt for a pulse. The little dope fiend was still alive, but his pulse was not good. He would be easy to finish off.

First, the Fig. Or whoever else was out there.

The doctor went to the door, put an ear to it, listened.

Nothing.

Gingerly, he opened the door and peered into the corridor.

No one.

He stepped across the threshold, holding the door open, and looked left and right. No one was in sight for the entire length of the hall.

Clearly, Skeet had not been shot here, because gunfir would surely have attracted some attention. No one ha even stirred from the office of the child psychologist across the hall—Dr. Moshlien, that insufferable boor and hopeless bonehead whose theories on the causes of youth violence were as improbable as his neckties.

The mystery of how Skeet had gotten here might remain a mystery, which would leave the doctor sleepless more than one night. The important thing now, however, was to clean up.

He would step back into the lounge and instruct Jennifer to call the police and the paramedics, after all. While she was occupied on the phone, he would stoop beside Skeet, ostensibly to assist as best he could, but actually to cover the man's mouth and pinch his nose shut for about a minute and a half, which should be long enough to finish him, considering his desperate condition.

Then, quickly back into the hallway, directly to a nearby maintenance closet that could be opened with his suite key. There, tuck the gun, the holster, and the blue bag deep behind rest-room supplies. Later, retrieve them after the police were gone.

Defy the tooth of time.

Hurry, hurry.

As he turned away from the corridor, intending to return to his office, he realized that no bloodstains marred the hallway carpet, which should have been liberally spattered if Skeet had traveled over it, gushing as he was now gushing in the reception lounge. Even as his lightning-quick gamesman's mind was arriving at the significance of this odd detail, the doctor heard Moshlien's door open behind him, and he cringed in expectation of the usual *Say, Ahriman, do you have a moment?* and the torrent of idiocies that would follow it.

The words never came, but bullets did. The doctor didn't hear a single shot, but he felt them, all right, at least three, slamming into him from the small of his back in a diagonal line to his right shoulder.

With less grace than he would have liked, he staggered into the reception lounge. Fell half on top of Skeet. Rolled off the little dope fiend in revulsion. Rolled onto his back, and looked up at the doorway.

The Keanuphobe stood on the threshold, bracing the door open with her body, holding a silenced pistol with both hands. "You're one of the machines," she said. "That's why you weren't really paying attention during our sessions. Machines don't care about real people like me."

Ahriman recognized in her eyes a fearsome quality that he had overlooked before: She was one of The Knowers, those girls who could see right through his disguises and deceptions, who mocked him with their eyes, with smug smiles and sly looks behind his back, who knew something hilarious about him that he himself did not know. Since he was fifteen, when he'd grown into his fine face, The Knowers had not been able to penetrate his facade, and so he had ceased to fear them. Now *this.*

He tried to raise the Beretta and return fire, but he discovered that he was paralyzed.

She pointed the pistol at his face.

She was reality and she was fantasy, truth and lie, an object of mirth, yet deadly serious, all things to all people and a mystery to herself, the quintessential person for her times. She was a nouveau-riche ditz with a husband as dull as a spoon, but she was also Diana, the goddess of the moon and the hunt, on whose bronze spear Minette Luckland had impaled herself in that Palladian mansion in Scottsdale, after first killing her father with a handgun and her mothe with a hammer.

How fun *that* had been, but how lacking in fun this was

My rich Diana. Fly me to the moon with you. Danc among the stars.

Treacle. Romantic hogwash. Derivative. Unworthy.

My rich Diana. I hate you, hate you, hate you. Hat you, hate you, hate.

"Do it," he said.

The goddess emptied the magazine into his face, and the doctor's phantasm of falling petals vanished into moon and flowers. And fire.

As she and Dusty came out of the elevator alcove, Martie saw a woman standing half in the doorway to Ahriman's reception lounge, near the end of the corridor. The pink Chanel suit marked her as the same woman who had followed Skeet into the elevator, downstairs in the lobby. She moved all the way into the office, out of sight.

Running along the hall, with Dusty close behind, Martie thought of enchanted New Mexico—and two dead men at the bottom of an ancient well. The purity of falling snow—and all the blood it covered. She thought of Claudette's face—and Claudette's heart. The beauty of haiku—and the hideous use to which it had been put. The glory of high green branches—and spiders squirming out of egg cases inside curled leaves. Things visible and invisible. Things revealed and hidden. This flash of cheerful pink, baby-pink, cherry-blossom pink, but a sense of darkness in the flash, poison in the pink.

All her dread expectations became dread realities in gruesome detail when she pushed through the door into Mark Ahriman's reception lounge and was received by bodies sprawled in blood.

The doctor lay faceup, but without a face: thin noxious smoke rising from scorched hair, terrible craters in the flesh, cheekbones imploded, red pools where eyes had once been—and beyond one torn and gaping cheek, half a grin.

Facedown, Skeet was the less dramatic figure of the two, and yet more real. His own red lake surrounded him, and he was so frail that he seemed to float in the crimson as though he were but a tangle of rags.

Martie was rocked harder by the sight of Skeet than she

would have expected to be. Skeet the feeb, perpetual boy, so earnest but so weak, self-destructive, always seeking to do to himself what his mother had failed to do with a pillow. Martie loved him, but only now did she realize how much she loved him—and only now was she able to understand why. For all his faults, Skeet was a gentle soul, and like his precious brother, his heart was kind; in a world where kind hearts were more rare than diamonds, he was a treasure flawed but a treasure nonetheless. She could not bear to stoop to him, touch him, and find that he was also a treasure broken beyond repair.

Heedless of the blood, Dusty dropped to his knees and put his hands on his brother's face, touched Skeet's closed eyes, felt the side of his neck, and in a voice torn as Martie had never heard it torn, he cried, "Oh, Jesus, an ambulance! Hurry, someone!"

Jennifer appeared at the open door to her work area. "I called. They're coming. They're on their way."

The woman in pink stood at the reception window, on the ledge of which she had placed two guns, including the machine pistol that Skeet had taken off Eric's body. "Jennifer, don't you think it would be a good idea if you put these out of the way someplace until the police arrive? Have you called the police?"

"Yes. They're coming, too."

Warily, Jennifer went around to the inside of the window, took possession of the guns, and put them aside on her desk.

Maybe it was because Skeet was dying, maybe it was the horror of Ahriman's ghastly face and the blood everywhere, but whatever the reason, Martie couldn't think clearly enough to make sense of what had happened here. Had Skeet shot Ahriman? Had Ahriman shot Skeet? Who had shot first and how often? The positions of the bodies didn't support any scenario that she could imagine. And the eerie calm of the woman in pink, as though she were accustomed to witnessing gun battles daily, seemed to argue that she had played some mysterious role.

The woman stepped to the least spattered corner of the lounge, withdrew a cell phone from her purse, and placed a call.

Still far away but drawing nearer, distorted by distance and topography, the shrillness of sirens sounded fearsome and curiously prehistoric, organic rather than mechanical, a pterodactyl shriek.

Jennifer hurried to the entrance door, opened it, and placed a small rubber wedge to prevent it from closing.

To Martie, she said, "Help me move these chairs out to the end of the hall, so the paramedics will have room to work when they get here."

Martie was glad to have something to do. She felt that she was standing on a crumbling brink. Helping Jennifer, she was able to step back from the abyss.

Holding the phone away from her mouth, the woman in pink paid a compliment to Jennifer: "You're quite impressive, young lady."

The receptionist cast an odd look at her. "Uh, thanks."

By the time the last chair and small table had been transferred to the nearer end of the corridor, multiple sirens had grown louder and then, one by one, had cycled into silence. Help must be in the elevators.

Speaking into her cell phone, the woman in pink said, "Will you stop babbling, Kenneth? For an expensive attorney, you're something of a ninny. I'll need the finest criminal-defense attorney, and I'll need him immediately. Now get a grip on yourself and *do* it."

When she terminated the call, the woman smiled at Martie.

Then she took a card from her purse and held it out to Jennifer. "You'll be needing a job, I suppose. I could use a young woman as competent as you, if you're interested."

Jennifer hesitated, but then she took the card.

On his knees in blood, repeatedly smoothing Skeet's hair back from his pale face, her special husband was talking softly to his brother, though there was no indication that the kid could hear him. Dusty spoke about the old days, about things they had done as boys, pranks they had played, discoveries they had made together, escapes they had planned, dreams they had shared.

Martie heard men running in the hall, the heavy booted feet of fire-department paramedics, and she had the crazy wonderful feeling, just for a moment, that when they burst through the open doorway, one of them would be Smilin' Bob.

76

Out of chaos, more chaos for a while. Too many strangers' faces and too many voices talking at once, paramedics and police, quickly but noisily negotiating jurisdictional boundaries between the living and the dead. If confusion had been loaves of bread and if suspicion had been fishes, no miracles would have been required to provide a banquet for multitudes.

Martie's confusion was only fed by the startling news that the woman in the pink Chanel suit had shot both Skeet and Ahriman. She admitted to the shooting, requested to be arrested, and would provide no further details, though she complained about the lingering stink from the doctor's burnt hair.

Skeet on a gurney, lifeless to the layman's eye, was attended by four beefy paramedics in white, their uniforms strangely radiant under the fluorescent corridor lights, as if they were linebackers who had gone to Heaven and now returned here dressed in this modern version of angels' robes. One sprinting ahead to block the elevator, one pulling, one pushing, one holding an IV bottle high and running alongside the gurney, they swept Skeet away, swiftly and smoothly, and to Martie it seemed that neither the wheels nor their feet were actually touching the floor, as though they were *flying* down the long corridor, not conveying a wounded man to a hospital, but escorting an immortal soul on a far longer journey.

Having been cleared by Jennifer—and by the pink lady's succinct confession—Dusty was given permission by the police to accompany his brother. He gripped Martie by the shoulders and pulled her close, held her fiercely for a moment, kissed her, and then ran after the gurney.

She watched him until he turned the corner into the elevator alcove, out of sight, and then she saw that his hands had left faint bloody impressions on her sweater. Shaking uncontrollably, Martie crossed her arms over her breasts, placing her hands on the terrible red marks, as though by touching those vague prints, she would be with Dusty and Skeet in spirit, allowing her to draw strength from them and they from her.

Martie was detained at the scene. Because the police in Malibu had, too late, contacted the police in Newport, the link between this shooting and Eric Jagger's death by crossbow was established, marking both Martie and Dusty as material witnesses in one case and perhaps in both. An officer was en route to the hospital, to question Dusty in the waiting room, but the police preferred to conduct the initial interrogation of at least one of them here rather than elsewhere, now rather than later.

Police photographer, SID technicians, representatives from the coroner's office, detectives, all bitching about the contamination of the crime scene, methodically gathered evidence, in spite of the pink lady's confession, because she might, of course, retract it later or claim police intimidation.

Jennifer was questioned at her desk, but Martie was asked to sit with two detectives, both soft-spoken and polite, in Ahriman's inner office. One of them perched beside her on the sofa, the other in a facing armchair.

Odd, to be once more in this mahogany forest of her nightmares, where the Leaf Man ruled. She felt his presence still, though he was dead. She crossed her arms, left hand on her right shoulder, right hand on her left, fingers spread across the red images of Dusty's fingers.

The detectives saw, and asked if she wanted to wash her hands. They didn't understand. She only shook her head.

Then, as the wind in her haiku had blown fallen leaves out of the west, the story blew out of her in one long gush. She held back no details, however fantastic or improbable—except that while she told them of the Glysons in Santa Fe, and of Bernardo Pastore and his lost family, she didn't mention the encounter with Kevin and Zachary in a snowy twilight.

She expected disbelief, and disbelief she received in squint-eyed and open-mouthed abundance, although even in the early hours of the aftermath, things happened to lend her at least a small measure of credibility.

Hearing news of the shooting on one of the first radio reports, Roy Closterman had come to the scene from his office, which was only a few miles away. She learned that he was in the corridor, talking to police, when one of her questioners was called away and, on his return, was shaken enough to reveal that Closterman was providing corroboration.

And then there was the matter of the unfired Beretta clutched in Ahriman's dead hand. A quick computer check of handgun registrations revealed no record of the psychiatrist ever having purchased this gun or any other. Likewise, he had never been granted a license to carry a concealed weapon in Orange County. His image as an upstanding and law-abiding citizen sustained some damage from these discoveries.

Perhaps what finally convinced the cops that this was a case involving unprecedented weirdness, even in the annals of southern California crime, was the discovery of a bag of feces in the doctor's finely tooled custom shoulder holster. Sherlock Holmes himself would have been hard-pressed to logically deduce an explanation for this startling find. An assumption of major kinkiness was made at once: The blue bag was bagged, tagged, and sent to the lab, with police officers wagering among themselves as to the sex and species of the mystery person or creature who had produced the sample.

Martie didn't think she was fit to drive, but once in the car, she drove as well as ever, directly to the hospital. She didn't wash her hands until she had found Dusty in the ICU waiting room and knew that Skeet had survived three hours of surgery. He was in critical condition, unconscious, but hanging on.

Even then, in the women's lavatory, Martie panicked and almost stopped scrubbing off the blood, for fear that this link to Skeet, once washed away, would leave him unable to draw needed strength from her, spirit to spirit. She surprised herself with this superstitious hysteria. Having survived an encounter with the devil, however, maybe she had reason to be superstitious. She finished washing her hands, reminding herself that the devil was dead.

Shortly after eleven o'clock, more than seven hours after he was admitted to the hospital, Skeet regained consciousness, coherent but weak. They were allowed to visit with him, but only for two or three minutes. That was long enough to say what needed to be said, which in the ICU is always the same simple thing that family members come there to say to every patient, the same and simple thing that matters more than all the words of all the doctors: *I love you.*

They stayed that night with Martie's mother, who set out home-baked bread and homemade vegetable soup for them, and by the time they returned to the hospital Saturday morning, Skeet's condition was upgraded from critical to serious.

How big the story would eventually become in the national news was foreshadowed by the fact that two TV crews and three print journalists were already camped out at the hospital, waiting for Martie and Dusty to appear.

Armed with a warrant, the police required three days to conduct a thorough search of Mark Ahriman's vast house. Initially, nothing stranger turned up than the psychiatrist's enormous collection of toys, and halfway through the first day, the investigation seemed as though it might founder.

The sprawling mansion featured an elaborate automated-house system. Police officers with specialized computer knowledge cracked the privacy code, which previously ensured that only Ahriman enjoyed full access to every aspect of the system; soon they discovered the existence of six hidden safes of various sizes.

Once combinations were decoded, the first safe—in the lacewood study—proved to contain only financial records.

The second, in the sitting room of the master suite, was larger and held five handguns, two fully automatic machine pistols, and an Uzi carbine. None were registered to Mark Ahriman, and none could be traced to any licensed gun dealer.

The third safe was a small box cleverly concealed in the master-bedroom fireplace. Therein, police discovered yet another handgun, a ten-shot Taurus PT-111 Millennium with an empty magazine, which appeared to have been fired recently.

Of greater interest both to criminologists and to film buffs was the second item in this box: a vacuum-sealed jar containing two human eyes in a chemical fixative. A gummed label on the lid bore a neatly hand-printed haiku.

Father's eyes, my jar.
Hollywood's great king of tears.
I prefer to laugh.

The media squall became a media storm.

Dusty and Martie could no longer stay at Sabrina's

house, which was for days thereafter under siege by newsmen.

On the third day, the police found a trove of videotapes stored in a vault that was not included in the list of safes known to the house computer. A contractor had come forward to report that he had bootlegged this bit of construction for Dr. Ahriman subsequent to the psychiatrist's purchase of the house. The tapes were the doctor's prized mementos, the record of his most dangerous games, including the candid video of Susan and her tormentor, shot from the potted ming tree in her bedroom.

The media storm became a media hurricane.

Ned Motherwell ran the business, while Martie and Dusty lived for a while with a series of friends, staying one step ahead of the microphones and cameras.

The only story that displaced the Ahriman extravaganza from the top of the nightly news was the insane attack on the President of the United States at a Bel Air fund-raiser, and the subsequent shooting to death of the megastar assailant by those outraged Secret Service agents who weren't otherwise occupied with recovering and preserving the nose. Within twenty-four hours, when the discovery was made that the megastar had known Mark Ahriman and had in fact recently been a patient at a drug-rehab clinic partly owned by Ahriman, the media hurricane became the storm of the century.

Eventually, the storm blew itself out, because it is in the character of these strange times that any outrage, regardless of its unprecedented dimensions and horror, is inevitably followed by another outrage more novel and more shocking still.

By late spring, Skeet was finished with physical rehabilitation and fleshed out as he had not been in years. The lady in pink, at her instigation and without threat of suit, settled upon Skeet the sum of one and three-quarter-million dollars, after taxes, and with his health restored, he decided to take a few months off from housepainting to travel and consider his options.

Together, Skeet and Fig Newton had planned an itinerary that would take them first to Roswell, New Mexico, and thereafter to other points of interest on the UFO trail. Now that Skeet's driving privileges had been restored, he and Fig would be able to spell each other at the wheel of Skeet's new motor home.

Because the pink lady contended that she had been brainwashed by Mark Ahriman and subjected to sexual depravities, she resorted to a plea of self-defense. Skeet, she claimed, had unfortunately gotten in the way of her first shot. After furious debate and tumult in the district attorney's office, she was charged with manslaughter and released on bail. By summer, the smart money was betting that she would never stand trial. If indeed she were hauled into court, what jury of her peers would ever find her guilty after her moving appearance on the talk show of all talk shows, at the end of which Oprah had embraced her and said, "You are an inspiration, girl," while an entire audience had wept uncontrollably.

Derek Lampton, the younger, was a hero for a week and appeared on the national news, giving archery demonstrations. When asked what he wanted to be when he grew up, Junior said, "An astronaut," which seemed not in the least childish, for he was a straight 4.0 student with a flair for the sciences and already a student pilot.

By midsummer, the Bellon-Tockland Institute in Santa Fe had been cleared of any involvement with Mark Ahriman's bizarre experiments in mind control. The belief that he had worked at the institute or had been associated with it in any way was disproved beyond contention. "He was a sociopath," noted the institute's director, "and a pathetic narcissist, a pop-psych lightweight who wanted to legitimize himself by claiming to be involved with this prestigious institution and its great work for world peace." Although the nature of the institute's research was described in various ways by the media, no reportage from that in *The New York Times* to that in the *National Enquirer* could make it comprehensible.

Martie canceled her contract to design a new video game based on *The Lord of the Rings.* She still loved Tolkien, but she felt the need to do something real. Dusty offered her a job painting houses, and she took him up on it for a while. The work was real enough to leave a delicious ache in her muscles, and it gave her time to think.

The surgery on the president's nose was successful.

Ned Motherwell sold three haiku to a literary magazine.

The two lottery tickets were losers.

From time to time during the summer, Martie and Dusty visited three cemeteries, where Valet loved to explore among the stones. In the first, they brought flowers to Smilin' Bob. In the second, they brought flowers to Susan and Eric Jagger. In the third, they brought flowers to Dominique, the half sister whom Dusty had never known.

Claudette claimed to have lost the only picture ever taken of her infant daughter. Perhaps that was true. Or perhaps she didn't want Dusty to have it.

Each time that Dusty described Dominique's sweet, gentle face as he recalled it from that photograph, Martie wondered if that baby, allowed to live, might have redeemed Claudette. By providing care and protection for one so innocent, perhaps Claudette would have found herself transformed, taught the meaning of compassion and humility. Though it was difficult to imagine that a Down's child conceived by the unholy union of Ahriman and Dusty's mother, could be a blessing in disguise, the universe was full of even stranger patterns that seemed, when considered in detail, to have meaning.

In late July, in its one hundredth week on *The New York Times* nonfiction best-seller list, *Learn to Love Yourself* was still riding high at the number five position.

In early August, Skeet and Fig called from Oregon, where they had taken a photograph of Big Foot, which they were sending along by express mail.

The photo was blurry but intriguing.

By late summer, Martie decided to keep the inheritance that had been granted to her by Susan Jagger's will. After liquidation of the assets, including the sale of the house on Balboa Peninsula, the sum was substantial. Initially, she had not wanted a penny; it felt like blood money. Then she realized that she could use it to realize the dream that she had cherished as a child, wind back the clock and take the road in life from which she had turned away for all the wrong reasons. Susan would never have the chance to wind back the clock and be the violinist that she had dreamed of being when she was a girl, so it seemed real and true to Martie that from this gift born of death should come a life set right.

Because Martie was a diligent student, not too many years passed before they celebrated her graduation from veterinary school and the near-simultaneous opening of her animal hospital and rescue shelter for abused cats and dogs. Not much was left of the inheritance, but not much was needed. With luck, her veterinary practice would pay for the rescue operation, with enough left over to bring as much home as Dusty cleared from painting houses.

The party was held at their home in Corona Del Mar, which had been rebuilt years ago on the ashes of the old. The new place was identical in every detail to the lost house, including the paint job that Sabrina, though mellow these days, still found "clownlike."

From Dusty's family, only Skeet was invited. He came with his wife, Jasmine, and their three-year-old boy, Foster, whom everyone called Chupaflor.

Fig and his wife, Primrose, who was Jasmine's older sister, brought lots of copies of the latest brochure from the enterprise that Fig and Skeet had launched together. Strange Phenomena Tours was prospering. If you wanted to follow Big Foot's trail, see the actual sites of the most famous alien abductions in the continental United States, stay in a series of haunted houses, or track Elvis in his peripatetic wanderings across this great country since his supposed death, Strange Phenomena Tours was the only travel agency with the packages that would satisfy your curiosity.

Ned Motherwell came with his girlfriend, Spike, bringing signed copies of his latest book of haiku. As he said, there wasn't a lot of money in poetry, certainly not enough to be able to stop painting houses for a living, but there was satisfaction in it. Besides, in his daily work, he found his inspiration: The new book was titled *Ladders and Brushes.*

Luanne Farner, Skeet's newfound grandmother, whom he had met while on the road with Fig a few years before, traveled all the way from Cascade, Colorado, bringing homemade banana-nut bread. She was a delightful lady, but the best thing was that no one could identify anything about her that was remotely similar to her son, Sam Farner, née Holden Caulfield, the elder.

Roy Closterman and Brian came with their black lab, Charlotte, and there were other dogs aplenty. Three Dog Bakery treats were provided for the four-legged set, and Valet was a generous host, even with the carob biscuits.

Chase and Zina Glyson flew in from Santa Fe, bringing a ristra of red chiles and other Southwest treasures. The ruined reputations of Chase's mother and father had been restored, and by now not one former student of the Little Jackrabbit School still clung to false memories of abuse.

Late that night, when the guests were gone, the three

members of the Rhodes family, with their eight legs and one tail, snuggled in the king-size bed. In recognition of his advanced age, Valet had at last been granted limited furniture privileges, bed being within the limits.

Martie was lying on her back, and Valet was draped across her feet, and she could feel the noble throb of his great heart against her ankles. Dusty lay on his side, close to her, and she was aware of the slow, steady rhythm of his heart, as well.

He kissed her shoulder, and in the silken warm darkness, she said, "If only this could last forever."

"It will," he said.

"I've got everything I could ever have hoped for, minus one dear friend and a father. But you know what?"

"What?"

"I love my life not because it's a dream, but because it's so *real*. All our friends, what we do, where we are . . . all so real. Am I making any sense?"

"Plenty," he assured her.

That night she dreamed of Smilin' Bob. He was wearing his black turnout coat with the two reflective stripes, but he was not striding through fire. They were walking together in a hillside meadow, under a blue summer sky. He said he was proud of her, and she apologized for not being so very brave as he had been. He insisted that she was brave in all the ways that counted, and that nothing could please him more than the knowledge that for years to come, her good strong hands would bring comfort and healing to the most innocent of this world.

When she woke from this dream in the middle of the night, the presence that she felt, in the darkness, was just as real as Valet snoring, just as real as Dusty at her side.

About the Author

DEAN KOONTZ, the author of many #1 New York Times bestsellers, lives in Southern California with his wife, Gerda, their golden retriever, Elsa, and the enduring spirits of their goldens, Trixie and Anna.

deankoontz.com
Facebook.com/DeanKoontzOfficial
@deankoontz

Correspondence for the author should be addressed to:

Dean Koontz
P.O. Box 9529
Newport Beach, California 92658

Don't miss any of the adventures of Odd Thomas, America's favorite hero.

"The nice young fry cook with the occult powers is Koontz's most likable creation."

—The New York Times